S H O R T
STORIES

Edited by
Henry I. Christ
Jerome Shostak

AMSCO

Amsco School Publications, Inc.
315 Hudson Street / New York, NY 10013

Henry I. Christ has had a long and distinguished career as writer, editor, teacher, and supervisor. A specialist in language, literature, and composition, he has written more than a hundred textbooks, many of which are published by Amsco. For nearly ten years, he was the editor of the magazine *High Points*. He has been active in professional organizations and has held office at the local, state, and national levels. A frequent speaker at conventions and workshops, he has also lectured on educational television and frequently participated in curriculum development and evaluation.

Marie E. Christ has worked with Henry I. Christ throughout his career. She played a major role in the development and preparation of this book.

Jerome Shostak has experienced the many and various facets of teaching language arts: he has taught in every grade from the primary through the intermediate and senior levels; his students ranged from the gifted in electives to the reluctant in remedial courses. He has been faculty adviser to the school newspaper, literary magazine, and senior yearbook staffs. He has chaired a department and been an active participant in local and national organizations. He has written several series of workbooks in language skills and in preparation for high school and college entrance. In addition to the present group of collections of short stories, he has edited contemporary novels for classroom use.

Illustrations by Joe Forté

When ordering this book, please specify:
either R 472 P or SHORT STORIES, PAPERBACK

ISBN 0-87720-775-5

Printed in the United States of America

CONTENTS

To the Student

"Tell me a story!"

Very young children soon learn how fascinating a good story can be. That love of storytelling lasts a lifetime. Like people of all ages you undoubtedly like a good yarn well told. You are about to satisfy that appetite and have fun with stories you'll enjoy.

All the stories in this book have been chosen because they are, first and foremost, good stories. They'll hold your interest. After you have begun each story, you'll be keenly interested in how it ends. "What happens next?" is one of the most important questions posed in this collection.

The stories are all quite different. They provide a variety of settings, from the turmoil of the inner city to the lonely reaches of the desert. They can be classified as mysteries, detective stories, tales of fantasy, science fiction, exhibitions of courage, human-interest stories, tales of the unexpected. They provide humor, character study, suspense, and a compassionate understanding of many types of people. The suspense is sometimes the suspense of a deserted waxwork museum at night, but there is also a more subtle kind of suspense: wonderment at the complexities of human motivation.

The stories show human beings face to face with challenges of many kinds. Familiar characters of your age group face problems like those you face. Then there are unusual characters who will stimulate your imagination and amazement at the diversity of humankind.

The stories have been grouped by themes that suggest relationships among all the stories in each group. Keeping the theme in mind will deepen your understanding of each story and increase your enjoyment of each unit.

There's excitement ahead. Let's read!

1

1

Detective Stories

The next time you go to the library, ask the librarian where the mystery shelf is. There you will find a special selection of mystery and detective stories selected by your librarian. You will notice that most of these books are well-worn. Even more than most books of fiction, they show the effects of much handling. Why are these books so popular?

"Tell me a story." Everyone loves a good tale where interesting things happen. Detective stories are, first and foremost, good stories. They have interesting plots that encourage readers to wonder, "What happens next?" They have colorful characters like Sherlock Holmes and Father Brown, but above all else they have exciting plots. The detectives help spin the plots. In the following stories, four great detectives solve four puzzling crimes.

Each great detective has a characteristic method of working. One arrives at a solution by shrewd character study; another depends on pure reason; still another makes inspired guesses from clever observation and analyses of appearances.

In the four samples you'll find some of the devices that detective story writers use to puzzle and entertain you. You'll be confronted by a murder committed in a locked room, with windows and doors bolted on the inside. You'll be puzzled by a mysterious invisible man who comes and goes before the eyes of four witnesses. You'll be amazed by the cleverness of the culprits and by the brilliance of the detectives as they work out their solutions.

An important ingredient in a good detective story is the fairness of the writer. All clues should be presented before the solution is reached. At a certain point in the story, you should be able to say, "Aha, that's the way it was done! Mr. X is the murderer!" Each of the following four stories is interrupted at that key moment. You will be given the opportunity to be a detective.

If you don't succeed, don't worry. Authors cleverly conceal their clues. You can always comfort yourself with the thought that there is, after all, only one Sherlock Holmes.

The Invisible Man

G. K. Chesterton

◆ "I heard James Welkin laugh as plainly as I hear you speak," said the girl steadily. "There was nobody there, for I stood just outside the shop at the corner, and could see down both streets at once."

In Edgar Allan Poe's famous story "The Purloined Letter," an important letter is stolen from a "certain royal personage" in France. The police know who the thief is and where the letter should be, but they cannot find it. They thoroughly search the thief's rooms, but without success. The great detective, Auguste Dupin, finds the letter. It has been visible . . . but invisible.

A letter can vanish, but a man is something else again. How can a man be visible . . . but invisible? In G. K. Chesterton's story "The Invisible Man," four men are detailed to guard a building. Inside the building is a man whose life has been threatened by a hated rival. The detective arrives on the scene and notices footprints in the snow leading up to the building. Obviously, someone had walked right past the guards. Inspection of the building proves that the threatened man has been murdered—and that the corpse also is "invisible." At any rate, it has vanished. But all four guards swear that no one had entered or left the premises. All four men are alert, honest observers; yet they failed to see the maker of the footprints.

Father Brown is one of the most unusual of detectives, for he solves his cases without a test tube or microscope. His method is shrewd observation and good common sense. He has an uncanny ability to look into the hearts of victims and criminals alike. He accepts contradictions. He understands paradox—how something can somehow be true and untrue at the same time. For example, in "The Invisible Man" the murderer is both obvious and invisible at the same time. Let Father Brown show you how a man can be a flesh-and-blood, ordinary individual and yet be an "invisible man."

THE INVISIBLE MAN

In the cool blue twilight of two steep streets in Camden Town, the shop at the corner, a confectioner's, glowed like the butt of a cigar. One should rather say, perhaps, like the butt of a firework, for the light was of many colors and some complexity, broken up by many mirrors and dancing on many gilt and gaily colored cakes and sweetmeats. Against this one fiery glass were glued the noses of many guttersnipes, for the chocolates were all wrapped in those red and gold and green metallic colors which are almost better than chocolate itself; and the huge white wedding cake in the window was somehow at once remote and satisfying, just as if the whole North Pole were good to eat. Such rainbow provocations could naturally collect the youth of the neighborhood up to the ages of ten or twelve. But this corner was also attractive to youth at a later stage; and a young man, not less than twenty-four, was staring into the same shop window. To him, also, the shop was of fiery charm, but this attraction was not wholly to be explained by chocolates; which, however, he was far from despising.

He was a tall, burly, red-haired young man, with a resolute face but a listless manner. He carried under his arm a flat, gray portfolio of black-and-white sketches, which he had sold with more or less success to publishers ever since his uncle (who was an admiral) had disinherited him for Socialism, because of a lecture which he had delivered against that economic theory. His name was John Turnbull Angus.

Entering at last, he walked through the confectioner's shop to the back room, which was a sort of pastry-cook restaurant, merely raising his hat to the young lady who was serving there. She was a dark, elegant, alert girl in black, with a high color and very quick,

5

dark eyes; and after the ordinary interval she followed him into the inner room to take his order.

His order was evidently a usual one. "I want, please," he said with precision, "one halfpenny bun and a small cup of black coffee." An instant before the girl could turn away he added, "Also, I want you to marry me."

The young lady of the shop stiffened suddenly and said, "Those are jokes I don't allow."

The red-haired young man lifted gray eyes of an unexpected gravity.

"Really and truly," he said, "it's as serious—as serious as the halfpenny bun. It is expensive, like the bun; one pays for it. It is indigestible, like the bun. It hurts."

The dark young lady had never taken her dark eyes off him, but seemed to be studying him with almost tragic exactitude. At the end of her scrutiny she had something like the shadow of a smile, and she sat down in a chair.

"Don't you think," observed Angus, absently, "that it's rather cruel to eat these halfpenny buns? They might grow up into penny buns. I shall give up these brutal sports when we are married."

The dark young lady rose from her chair and walked to the window, evidently in a state of strong but not unsympathetic cogitation. When at last she swung round again with an air of resolution, she was bewildered to observe that the young man was carefully laying out on the table various objects from the shop window. They included a pyramid of highly colored sweets, several plates of sandwiches, and the two decanters containing that mysterious port and sherry which are peculiar to pastry cooks. In the middle of this neat arrangement he had carefully let down the enormous load of white sugared cake which had been the huge ornament of the window.

"What on earth are you doing?" she asked.

"Duty, my dear Laura," he began.

"Oh, for the Lord's sake, stop a minute," she cried, "and don't talk to me in that way. I mean, what is all that?"

"A ceremonial meal, Miss Hope."

"And what is *that?*" she asked impatiently, pointing to the mountain of sugar.

"The wedding cake, Mrs. Angus," he said.

The girl marched to that article, removed it with some clatter, and put it back in the shop window; she then returned, and, putting her elegant elbows on the table, regarded the young man not unfavorably but with considerable exasperation.

"You don't give me any time to think," she said.

"I'm not such a fool," he answered; "that's my Christian humility."

She was still looking at him; but she had grown considerably graver behind the smile.

"Mr. Angus," she said steadily, "before there is a minute more of this nonsense I must tell you something about myself as shortly as I can."

"Delighted," replied Angus gravely. "You might tell me something about myself, too, while you are about it."

"Oh, do hold your tongue and listen," she said. "It's nothing that I'm ashamed of, and it isn't even anything that I'm specially sorry about. But what would you say if there were something that is no business of mine and yet is my nightmare?"

"In that case," said the man seriously, "I should suggest that you bring back the cake."

"Well, you must listen to the story first," said Laura, persistently. "To begin with, I must tell you that my father owned the inn called the 'Red Fish' at Ludbury, and I used to serve people in the bar."

"I have often wondered," he said, "why there was a kind of a Christian air about this one confectioner's shop."

"Ludbury is a sleepy, grassy little hole in the Eastern Counties, and the only kind of people who ever came to the 'Red Fish' were occasional commercial travelers, and for the rest, the most awful people you can see, only you've never seen them. I mean little, loungy men, who had just enough to live on and had nothing to do but lean about in barrooms and bet on horses, in bad clothes that were just too good for them. Even these wretched young rotters were not very common at our house; but there were two of them that were a lot too common—common in every sort of way. They both lived on money of their own, and were wearisomely idle and overdressed. But yet I was a bit sorry for them, because I half believe they slunk into our little empty bar because each of them had a slight deformity; the sort of thing that some yokels laugh at. It wasn't exactly a deformity either; it was more an oddity. One of them was a surprisingly small man, something like a dwarf, or at least like a jockey. He was not at all jockeyish to look at, though;

he had a round black head and a well-trimmed black beard, bright eyes like a bird's; he jingled money in his pockets; he jangled a great gold watch chain; and he never turned up except dressed just too much like a gentleman to be one. He was no fool though, though a futile idler; he was curiously clever at all kinds of things that couldn't be the slightest use; a sort of impromptu conjuring; making fifteen matches set fire to each other like a regular firework; or cutting a banana or some such thing into a dancing doll. His name was Isidore Smythe; and I can see him still, with his little dark face, just coming up to the counter, making a jumping kangaroo out of five cigars.

"The other fellow was more silent and more ordinary; but somehow he alarmed me much more than poor little Smythe. He was very tall and slight, and light-haired; his nose had a high bridge, and he might almost have been handsome in a spectral sort of way; but he had one of the most appalling squints I have ever seen or heard of. When he looked straight at you, you didn't know where you were yourself, let alone what he was looking at. I fancy this sort of disfigurement embittered the poor chap a little; for while Smythe was ready to show off his monkey tricks anywhere, James Welkin (that was the squinting man's name) never did anything except soak in our bar parlor, and go for great walks by himself in the flat, gray country all around. All the same, I think Smythe, too, was a little sensitive about being so small, though he carried it off more smartly. And so it was that I was really puzzled, as well as startled, and very sorry, when they both offered to marry me in the same week.

"Well, I did what I've since thought was perhaps a silly thing. But, after all, these freaks were my friends in a way; and I had a horror of their thinking I refused them for the real reason, which was that they were so impossibly ugly. So I made up some gas of another sort, about never meaning to marry anyone who hadn't carved his way in the world. I said it was a point of principle with me not to live on money that was just inherited like theirs. Two days after I had talked in this well-meaning sort of way, the whole trouble began. The first thing I heard was that both of them had gone off to seek their fortunes, as if they were in some silly fairy tale.

"Well, I've never seen either of them from that day to this. But

I've had two letters from the little man called Smythe, and really they were rather exciting."

"Ever heard of the other man?" asked Angus.

"No, he never wrote," said the girl, after an instant's hesitation. "Smythe's first letter was simply to say that he had started out walking with Welkin to London; but Welkin was such a good walker that the little man dropped out of it, and took a rest by the roadside. He happened to be picked up by some traveling show, and, partly because he was nearly a dwarf, and partly because he was really a clever little wretch, he got on quite well in the show business, and was soon sent up to the Aquarium, to do some tricks that I forget. That was his first letter. His second was much more of a startler, and I only got it last week."

The man called Angus emptied his coffee cup and regarded her with mild and patient eyes. Her own mouth took a slight twist of laughter as she resumed, "I suppose you've seen on the hoardings all about this 'Smythe's Silent Service'? Or you must be the only person that hasn't. Oh, I don't know much about it, it's some clockwork invention for doing all the housework by machinery. You know the sort of thing: 'Press a Button—A Butler Who Never Drinks.' 'Turn a Handle—Ten Housemaids Who Never Flirt.' You must have seen the advertisements. Well, whatever these machines are, they are making pots of money; and they are making it all for that little imp whom I knew down in Ludbury. I can't help feeling pleased the poor little chap has fallen on his feet; but the plain fact is, I'm in terror of his turning up any minute and telling me he's carved his way in the world—as he certainly has."

"And the other man?" repeated Angus with a sort of obstinate quietude.

Laura Hope got to her feet suddenly. "My friend," she said, "I think you are a witch. Yes, you are quite right. I have not seen a line of the other man's writing; and I have no more notion than the dead of what or where he is. But it is of him that I am frightened. It is he who is all about my path. It is he who has half driven me mad. Indeed, I think he has driven me mad; for I have felt him where he could not have been, and I have heard his voice when he could not have spoken."

"Well, my dear," said the young man, cheerfully, "if he were Satan himself, he is done for now you have told somebody. One goes mad all alone, old girl. But when was it you fancied you felt and heard our squinting friend?"

"I heard James Welkin laugh as plainly as I hear you speak," said the girl, steadily. "There was nobody there, for I stood just outside the shop at the corner, and could see down both streets at once. I had forgotten how he laughed, though his laugh was as odd as his squint. I had not thought of him for nearly a year. But it's a solemn truth that a few seconds later the first letter came from his rival."

"Did you ever make the specter speak or squeak, or anything?" asked Angus, with some interest.

Laura suddenly shuddered, and then said, with an unshaken voice, "Yes. Just when I had finished reading the second letter from Isidore Smythe announcing his success, just then, I heard Welkin say, 'He shan't have you, though.' It was quite plain, as if he were in the room. It is awful, I think I must be mad."

"If you really were mad," said the young man, "you would think you must be sane. But certainly there seems to me to be something a little rum about this unseen gentleman. Two heads are better than one—I spare you allusions to any other faculties—and really, if you would allow me, as a sturdy, practical man, to bring back the wedding cake out of the window—"

Even as he spoke, there was a sort of steely shriek in the street outside, and a small motor, driven at devilish speed, shot up to the door of the shop and stuck there. In the same flash of time a small man in a shiny top hat stood stamping in the outer room.

Angus, who had hitherto maintained hilarious ease from motives of mental hygiene, revealed the strain of his soul by striding abruptly out of the inner room and confronting the newcomer. A glance at him was quite sufficient to confirm the savage guesswork of a man in love. This very dapper but dwarfish figure, with the spike of black beard carried insolently forward, the clever unrestful eyes, the neat but very nervous fingers, could be none other than the man just described to him: Isidore Smythe, who made dolls out of banana skins and matchboxes; Isidore Smythe, who made millions out of undrinking butlers and unflirting housemaids of metal. For a moment the two men, instinctively understanding each other's air of possession, looked at each other with that curious cold generosity which is the soul of rivalry.

Mr. Smythe, however, made no allusion to the ultimate ground of their antagonism, but said simply and explosively, "Has Miss Hope seen that thing on the window?"

"On the window?" repeated the staring Angus.

"There's no time to explain other things," said the small millionaire shortly. "There's some tomfoolery going on here that has to be investigated."

He pointed his polished walking stick at the window, recently depleted by the bridal preparations of Mr. Angus; and that gentleman was astonished to see along the front of the glass a long strip of paper pasted, which had certainly not been on the window when he looked through it some time before. Following the energetic Smythe outside into the street, he found that some yard and a half of stamp paper had been carefully gummed along the glass outside, and on this was written in straggly characters, "If you marry Smythe, he will die."

"Laura," said Angus, putting his big red head into the shop, "you're not mad."

"It's the writing of that fellow Welkin," said Smythe gruffly. "I haven't seen him for years, but he's always bothering me. Five times in the last fortnight he's had threatening letters left at my flat, and I can't even find out who leaves them, let alone if it is Welkin himself. The porter of the flats swears that no suspicious characters have been seen, and here he has pasted up a sort of dado on a public shop window, while the people in the shop—"

"Quite so," said Angus modestly, "while the people in the shop were having tea. Well, sir, I can assure you I appreciate your common sense in dealing so directly with the matter. We can talk about other things afterwards. The fellow cannot be very far off yet, for I swear there was no paper there when I went last to the window, ten or fifteen minutes ago. On the other hand, he's too far off to be chased, as we don't even know the direction. If you'll take my advice, Mr. Smythe, you'll put this at once in the hands of some energetic inquiry man, private rather than public. I know an extremely clever fellow, who has set up in business five minutes from here in your car. His name's Flambeau, and though his youth was a bit stormy, he's a strictly honest man now, and his brains are worth money. He lives in Lucknow Mansions, Hampstead."

"That is odd," said the little man, arching his black eyebrows. "I live, myself, in Himylaya Mansions, round the corner. Perhaps you might care to come with me; I can go to my rooms and sort out these queer Welkin documents, while you run round and get your friend the detective."

"You are very good," said Angus politely. "Well, the sooner we act the better."

Both men, with a queer kind of impromptu fairness, took the same sort of formal farewell of the lady, and both jumped into the brisk little car. As Smythe took the handles and they turned the great corner of the street, Angus was amused to see a gigantesque poster of "Smythe's Silent Service," with a picture of a huge headless iron doll, carrying a saucepan with the legend, "A Cook Who Is Never Cross."

"I use them in my own flat," said the little black-bearded man, laughing, "partly for advertisements, and partly for real convenience. Honestly, and all above board, those big clockwork dolls of mine do bring your coals or claret or a timetable quicker than any live servants I've ever known, if you know which knob to press. But I'll never deny, between ourselves, that such servants have their disadvantages, too."

"Indeed?" said Angus; "is there something they can't do?"

"Yes," replied Smythe coolly; "they can't tell me who left those threatening letters at my flat."

The man's motor was small and swift like himself; in fact, like his domestic service, it was of his own invention. If he was an advertising quack, he was one who believed in his own wares. The sense of something tiny and flying was accentuated as they swept up long white curves of road in the dead but open daylight of evening. Soon the white curves came sharper and dizzier; they were upon ascending spirals, as they say in the modern religions. For, indeed, they were cresting a corner of London which is almost as precipitous as Edinburgh, if not quite so picturesque. Terrace rose above terrace, and the special tower of flats they sought rose above them all to almost Egyptian height, gilt by the level sunset. The change, as they turned the corner and entered the crescent known as Himylaya Mansions, was as abrupt as the opening of a window; for they found that pile of flats sitting above London as above a green sea of slate. Opposite to the mansions, on the other side of the gravel crescent, was a bushy enclosure more like a steep hedge or dike than a garden, and some way below that ran a strip of artificial water, a sort of canal, like the moat of that embowered fortress. As the car swept round the crescent it passed, at one corner, the stray stall of a man selling chestnuts; and right away at the other end of the curve, Angus could see a dim blue policeman walking slowly. These were the only human shapes in that high suburban solitude; but he had an irrational sense that they expressed the speechless poetry of London. He felt as if they were figures in a story.

The little car shot up to the right house like a bullet, and shot out its owner like a bombshell. He was immediately inquiring of a tall commissionaire in shining braid, and a short porter in shirt sleeves, whether anybody or anything had been seeking his apartments. He was assured that nobody and nothing had passed these officials since his last inquiries; whereupon he and the slightly bewildered Angus were shot up in the lift like a rocket, till they reached the top floor.

"Just come in for a minute," said the breathless Smythe. "I want to show you those Welkin letters. Then you might run round the corner and fetch your friend." He pressed a button concealed in the wall, and the door opened of itself.

It opened on a long, commodious anteroom, of which the only arresting features, ordinarily speaking, were the rows of tall half-human mechanical figures that stood up on both sides like tailors' dummies. Like tailors' dummies they were headless; and like tailors' dummies they had a handsome unnecessary humpiness in the shoulders, and a pigeon-breasted protuberance of chest; but barring this, they were not much more like a human figure than any automatic machine at a station that is about the human height. They had two great hooks like arms, for carrying trays; and they were painted pea green, or vermilion, or black for convenience of distinction; in every other way they were only automatic machines and nobody would have looked twice at them. On this occasion, at least, nobody did. For between the two rows of these domestic dummies lay something more interesting than most of the mechanics of the world. It was a white, tattered scrap of paper scrawled with red ink; and the agile inventor had snatched it up almost as soon as the door flew open. He handed it to Angus without a word. The red ink on it actually was not dry, and the message ran, "If you have been to see her today, I shall kill you."

There was a short silence, and then Isidore Smythe said quietly, "Would you like a little whiskey? I rather feel as if I should."

"Thank you; I should like a little Flambeau," said Angus,

gloomily. "This business seems to me to be getting rather grave. I'm going round at once to fetch him."

"Right you are," said the other, with admirable cheerfulness. "Bring him round here as quick as you can."

But as Angus closed the front door behind him he saw Smythe push back a button, and one of the clockwork images glided from its place and slid along a groove in the floor carrying a tray with syphon and decanter. There did seem something a trifle weird about leaving the little man alone among those dead servants, who were coming to life as the door closed.

Six steps down from Smythe's landing the man in shirt sleeves was doing something with a pail. Angus stopped to extract a promise, fortified with a prospective bribe, that he would remain in that place until the return with the detective, and would keep count of any kind of stranger coming up those stairs. Dashing down to the front hall, he then laid similar charges of vigilance on the commissionaire at the front door, from whom he learned the simplifying circumstances that there was no back door. Not content with this, he captured the floating policeman and induced him to stand opposite the entrance and watch it; and finally paused an instant for a pennyworth of chestnuts, and an inquiry as to the probable length of the merchant's stay in the neighborhood.

The chestnut seller, turning up the collar of his coat, told him he should probably be moving shortly, as he thought it was going to snow. Indeed, the evening was growing gray and bitter, but Angus, with all his eloquence, proceeded to nail the chestnut man to his post.

"Keep yourself warm on your own chestnuts," he said earnestly. "Eat up your whole stock; I'll make it worth your while. I'll give you a sovereign if you'll wait here till I come back, and then tell me whether any man, woman, or child has gone into that house where the commissionaire is standing."

He then walked away smartly, with a last look at the besieged tower.

"I've made a ring round that room, anyhow," he said. "They can't all four of them be Mr. Welkin's accomplices."

Lucknow Mansions were, so to speak, on a lower platform of that hill of houses, of which Himylaya Mansions might be called the peak. Mr. Flambeau's semiofficial flat was on the ground floor, and presented in every way a marked contrast to the American machinery and cold hotel-like luxury of the flat of the Silent Service. Flambeau, who was a friend of Angus, received him in a rococo artistic den behind his office, of which the ornaments were sabers, harquebuses, Eastern curiosities, flasks of Italian wine, savage cooking pots, a plumy Persian cat, and a small dusty-looking Roman Catholic priest, who looked particularly out of place.

"This is my friend Father Brown," said Flambeau. "I've often wanted you to meet him. Splendid weather, this; a little cold for Southerners like me."

"Yes, I think it will keep clear," said Angus, sitting down on a violet-striped Eastern ottoman.

"No," said the priest quietly, "it has begun to snow."

And, indeed, as he spoke, the first few flakes, foreseen by the man of chestnuts, began to drift across the darkening windowpane.

"Well," said Angus heavily. "I'm afraid I've come on business, and rather jumpy business at that. The fact is, Flambeau, within a stone's throw of your house is a fellow who badly wants your help; he's perpetually being haunted and threatened by an invisible enemy—a scoundrel whom nobody has ever seen." As Angus proceeded to tell the whole tale of Smythe and Welkin, beginning with Laura's story, and going on with his own, the supernatural laugh at the corner of two empty streets, the strange, distinct words spoken in an empty room, Flambeau grew more and more vividly concerned, and the little priest seemed to be left out of it, like a piece of furniture. When it came to the scribbled stamp paper pasted on the window, Flambeau rose, seeming to fill the room with his huge shoulders.

"If you don't mind," he said, "I think you had better tell me the rest on the nearest road to this man's house. It strikes me, somehow, that there is no time to be lost."

"Delighted," said Angus, rising also, "though he's safe enough for the present, for I've set four men to watch the only hole to his burrow."

They turned out in the street, the small priest trundling after them with the docility of a small dog. He merely said, in a cheerful way, like one making conversation, "How quick the snow gets thick on the ground."

As they threaded the steep side streets already powdered with silver, Angus finished his story; and by the time they reached the crescent with the towering flats, he had leisure to turn his attention to the four sentinels. The chestnut seller, both before and after receiving a sovereign, swore stubbornly that he had watched the door and seen no visitor enter. The policeman was even more emphatic. He said he had had experience of crooks of all kinds, in top hats and in rags; he wasn't so green as to expect suspicious characters to look suspicious; he looked out for anybody, and, so help him, there had been nobody. And when all three men gathered round the gilded commissionaire, who still stood smiling astride of the porch, the verdict was more final still.

"I've got a right to ask any man, duke or dustman, what he wants in these flats," said the genial and gold-laced giant, "and I'll swear there's been nobody to ask since this gentleman went away."

The unimportant Father Brown, who stood back, looking modestly at the pavement, here ventured to say meekly, "Has nobody been up and down stairs, then, since the snow began to fall? It began while we were all round at Flambeau's."

"Nobody's been in here, sir, you can take it from me," said the official, with beaming authority.

"Then I wonder what that is?" said the priest, and stared at the ground blankly like a fish.

The others all looked down also; and Flambeau used a fierce exclamation and a French gesture. For it was unquestionably true that down the middle of the entrance guarded by the man in gold lace, actually between the arrogant, stretched legs of that colossus, ran a stringy pattern of gray footprints stamped upon the white snow.

"God!" cried Angus involuntarily, "the Invisible Man!"

Without another word he turned and dashed up the stairs, with Flambeau following; but Father Brown still stood looking about him in the snow-clad street as if he had lost interest in his query.

Flambeau was plainly in a mood to break down the door with his big shoulders; but the Scotchman, with more reason, if less intuition, fumbled about on the frame of the door till he found the invisible button; and the door swung slowly open.

It showed substantially the same serried interior; the hall had grown darker, though it was still struck here and there with the last crimson shafts of sunset, and one or two of the headless machines had been moved from their places for this or that purpose, and stood here and there about the twilit place. The green and red of their coats were all darkened in the dusk; and their likeness to human shapes slightly increased by their very shapelessness. But in the middle of them all, exactly where the paper with the red ink had lain, there lay something that looked like red ink spilt out of its bottle. But it was not red ink.

With a French combination of reason and violence Flambeau simply said "Murder!" and, plunging into the flat, had explored every corner and cupboard of it in five minutes. But if he expected to find a corpse he found none. Isidore Smythe was not in the place, either dead or alive. After the most tearing search the two men met each other in the outer hall, with streaming faces and staring eyes. "My friend," said Flambeau, talking French in his excitement, "not only is your murderer invisible, but he makes invisible also the murdered man."

Angus looked round at the dim room full of dummies, and in some Celtic corner of his Scotch soul a shudder started. One of the life-size dolls stood immediately overshadowing the blood stain, summoned, perhaps, by the slain man an instant before he fell. One of the high-shouldered hooks that served the thing for arms was a little lifted, and Angus had suddenly the horrid fancy that poor Smythe's own iron child had struck him down. Matter had rebelled, and these machines had killed their master. But even so, what had they done with him?

"Eaten him?" said the nightmare at his ear; and he sickened for an instant at the idea of rent, human remains absorbed and crushed into all that acephalous clockwork.

He recovered his mental health by an emphatic effort, and said to Flambeau, "Well, there it is. The poor fellow has evaporated like a cloud and left a red streak on the floor. The tale does not belong to this world."

"There is only one thing to be done," said Flambeau, "whether it belongs to this world or the other. I must go down and talk to my friend."

They descended, passing the man with the pail, who again asseverated that he had let no intruder pass, down to the commissionaire and the hovering chestnut man, who rigidly reasserted their own watchfulness. But when Angus looked round for his fourth confirmation he could not see it, and called out with some nervousness, "Where is the policeman?"

"I beg your pardon," said Father Brown; "that is my fault. I just sent him down the road to investigate something—that I just thought worth investigating."

"Well, we want him back pretty soon," said Angus abruptly, "for the wretched man upstairs has not only been murdered, but wiped out."

"How?" asked the priest.

"Father," said Flambeau, after a pause, "upon my soul I believe it is more in your department than mine. No friend or foe has entered the house, but Smythe is gone, as if stolen by the fairies. If that is not supernatural, I—"

As he spoke they were all checked by an unusual sight; the big blue policeman came round the corner of the crescent, running. He came straight up to Brown.

"You're right, sir," he panted, "they've just found poor Mr. Smythe's body in the canal down below."

Angus put his hand wildly to his head. "Did he run down and drown himself?" he asked.

"He never came down, I'll swear," said the constable, "and he wasn't drowned either, for he died of a great stab over the heart."

"And yet you saw no one enter?" said Flambeau in a grave voice.

"Let us walk down the road a little," said the priest.

As they reached the other end of the crescent he observed abruptly, "Stupid of me! I forgot to ask the policeman something. I wonder if they found a light brown sack."

"Why a light brown sack?" asked Angus, astonished.

"Because if it was any other colored sack, the case must begin over again," said Father Brown; "but if it was a light brown sack, why, the case is finished."

"I am pleased to hear it," said Angus with hearty irony. "It hasn't begun, so far as I am concerned."

"You must tell us all about it," said Flambeau with a strange heavy simplicity, like a child.

[*All clues have been given. To refresh your memory, they are listed below. Can you guess how the murder was committed and the body removed under the watchful eyes of four men?*

    1. *the character of the murderer*
    2. *his "invisibility" even on a clear street*

3. *the footprints in the snow*
4. *the testimony of four alert individuals*
5. *the body in the canal*
6. *the light brown sack*

After you have made a guess, read on to check the accuracy of your deductions as compared with the insight of Father Brown.]

Unconsciously they were walking with quickening steps down the long sweep of road on the other side of the high crescent, Father Brown leading briskly, though in silence. At last he said with an almost touching vagueness, "Well, I'm afraid you'll think it so prosy. We always begin at the abstract end of things, and you can't begin this story anywhere else.

"Have you ever noticed this—that people never answer what you say? They answer what you mean—or what they think you mean. Suppose one lady says to another in a country house, 'Is anybody staying with you?' the lady doesn't answer 'Yes; the butler, the three footmen, the parlormaid, and so on,' though the parlormaid may be in the room, or the butler behind her chair. She says 'There is *nobody* staying with us,' meaning nobody of the sort you mean. But suppose a doctor inquiring into an epidemic asks, 'Who is staying in the house?' then the lady will remember the butler, the parlormaid, and the rest. All language is used like that; you never get a question answered literally, even when you get it answered truly. When those four quite honest men said that no man had gone into the Mansions, they did not really mean that *no man* had gone into them. They meant no man whom they could suspect of being your man. A man did go into the house, and did come out of it, but they never noticed him."

"An invisible man?" inquired Angus, raising his red eyebrows.

"A mentally invisible man," said Father Brown.

A minute or two after he resumed in the same unassuming voice, like a man thinking his way. "Of course you can't think of such a man, until you do think of him. That's where his cleverness comes in. But I came to think of him through two or three little things in the tale Mr. Angus told us. First, there was the fact that this Welkin went for long walks. And then there was the vast lot of stamp paper on the window. And then, most of all, there were the two things the young lady said—things that couldn't be true. Don't get annoyed," he added hastily, noting a sudden movement of the Scotchman's head; "she thought they were true. A person *can't* be quite alone in a street a second before she receives a letter. She can't be quite alone in a street when she starts reading a letter just received. There must be somebody pretty near her; he must be mentally invisible."

"Why must there be somebody near her?" asked Angus.

"Because," said Father Brown, "barring carrier pigeons, somebody must have brought her the letter."

"Do you really mean to say," asked Flambeau, with energy, "that Welkin carried his rival's letters to his lady?"

"Yes," said the priest. "Welkin carried his rival's letters to his lady. You see, he had to."

"Oh, I can't stand much more of this," exploded Flambeau. "Who is this fellow? What does he look like? What is the usual getup of a mentally invisible man?"

"He is dressed rather handsomely in red, blue and gold," replied the priest promptly with precision, "and in this striking, and even showy, costume he entered Himylaya Mansions under eight human eyes; he killed Smythe in cold blood, and came down into the street again carrying the dead body in his arms—"

"Reverend sir," cried Angus, standing still, "are you raving mad, or am I?"

"You are not mad," said Brown, "only a little unobservant. You have not noticed such a man as this, for example."

He took three quick strides forward, and put his hand on the shoulder of an ordinary passing postman who had bustled by them unnoticed under the shade of the trees.

"Nobody ever notices postmen somehow," he said thoughtfully; "yet they have passions like other men, and even carry large bags where a small corpse can be stowed quite easily."

The postman, instead of turning naturally, had ducked and tumbled against the garden fence. He was a lean fair-bearded man of very ordinary appearance, but as he turned an alarmed face over his shoulder, all three men were fixed with an almost fiendish squint.

Flambeau went back to his sabers, purple rugs and Persian cat, having many things to attend to. John Turnbull Angus went back to the lady at the shop, with whom that imprudent young man contrives to be extremely comfortable. But Father Brown walked those snow-covered hills under the stars for many hours with a murderer, and what they said to each other will never be known.

Understanding the Story

Main Idea

1. Which of the following bits of dialog best expresses the main idea of the story?
   (a) "Have you ever noticed this—that people never answer what you say? They answer what you mean—or what they think you mean."
   (b) "If you don't mind, I think you had better tell me the rest on the nearest road to this man's house. It strikes me, somehow, that there is no time to be lost."
   (c) "I'll give you a sovereign if you'll wait here till I come back, and then tell me whether any man, woman, or child has gone into that house where the commissionaire is standing."
   (d) "I want, please, one halfpenny bun and a small cup of black coffee. Also, I want you to marry me."

Details

2. Welkin had a   (a) huge appetite   (b) squint   (c) hatred of Laura   (d) desire to remain a bachelor.

3. Laura's first two suitors were   (a) Welkin and Angus   (b) Angus and Smythe   (c) Flambeau and Welkin   (d) Welkin and Smythe.

4. Laura thought she heard laughter from   (a) Flambeau   (b) Angus   (c) Welkin   (d) Father Brown.

5. Mechanical servants made the fortune of   (a) Angus   (b) Smythe   (c) Welkin   (d) Father Brown.

Inferences

6. Laura's attitude toward Angus was one of   (a) indifference
    (b) fear   (c) hatred   (d) affection.

7. A good word to apply to Welkin would be   (a) *pleasant*
    (b) *threatening*   (c) *loving*   (d) *stupid*.

8. At first Father Brown's attitude seemed   (a) frantic
    (b) uninterested   (c) bitter   (d) irritable.

9. The most surprising element in the search of Smythe's flat was
    (a) the mechanical servants   (b) Smythe's lack of neatness
    (c) the absence of a body   (d) the love letters to Laura.

10. The murderer's motive was   (a) jealousy   (b) greed
    (c) terror   (d) curiosity.

Order of Events

11. Arrange the items in the order in which they occurred. Use
    letters only.
    A. Angus puts four men to watch the building.
    B. Laura tells of hearing Welkin's voice without seeing
       Welkin.
    C. Angus asks Laura to marry him.
    D. Father Brown points out the footprints in the snow.
    E. Smythe asks Angus to help him.

Outcomes

12. If the observers had recognized the postman as a "man,"
    (a) they might have had their mail earlier   (b) the murder
    might have been prevented   (c) Flambeau might have scolded
    Father Brown   (d) Smythe might have murdered Welkin.

Cause and Effect

13. Laura would have accepted Angus's proposal with more en-
    thusiasm if   (a) he had been a neater dresser   (b) he had
    been as good a detective as Flambeau   (c) she hadn't seemed
    to make a promise to Smythe and Welkin   (d) he had been
    able to buy the confectioner's shop.

Fact or Opinion

Tell whether each of the following is a fact or an opinion.

14. Smythe owned a business that provided household robots.

15. Welkin was a much cleverer person than Smythe.

Words in Context

1. Such rainbow *provocations* could naturally collect the youth of the neighborhood up to the ages of ten or twelve.
   Provocations (page 5) are sources of (a) stimulation (b) regret (c) laziness (d) satisfaction.

2. He was a tall, burly, red-haired young man, with a *resolute* face but a listless manner.
   Resolute (5) means (a) ugly (b) lively (c) determined (d) funny.

3. The red-haired young man lifted gray eyes of an unexpected *gravity.*
   Gravity (6) means (a) darkness (b) brilliance (c) dullness (d) seriousness.

4. At the end of her *scrutiny* she had something like the shadow of a smile, and she sat down in a chair.
   Scrutiny (6) means (a) storytelling (b) inspection (c) patience (d) discovery.

5. The dark young lady rose from her chair and walked to the window, evidently in a state of strong but not unsympathetic *cogitation.*
   Cogitation (6) means (a) deep thought (b) casual annoyance (c) mild regret (d) fatigue.

6. She returned and regarded the young man not unfavorably but with considerable *exasperation.*
   Exasperation (7) means (a) indifference (b) ecstasy (c) irritation (d) gentleness.

7. He was curiously clever at all kinds of things that couldn't be the slightest use; a sort of *impromptu* conjuring.
   Impromptu (8) means (a) silly (b) deceptive (c) perplexing (d) unrehearsed.

8. He was very tall and slight, and light-haired; his nose had a high bridge, and he might almost have been handsome in a *spectral* sort of way.
   Spectral (8) means (a) shown (b) innocent (c) ghostlike (d) mottled.

9. Two heads are better than one—I spare you *allusions* to any other faculties.
   Allusions (10) means (a) indirect references (b) incorrect opinions (c) harmful substances (d) angry replies.

10. He pointed his polished walking stick at the window, recently *depleted* by the bridal preparations of Mr. Angus.
    Depleted   (11)   means   (a) disfigured   (b) emptied
    (c) decorated   (d) overlooked.

11. On this was written in *straggly* characters, "If you marry Smythe, he will die."
    Straggly   (11)   means   (a) dark   (b) impressive
    (c) rambling   (d) rigid.

12. The sense of something tiny and flying was *accentuated* as they swept up along white curves of road in the dead but open daylight of evening.
    Accentuated   (12)   means   (a) eliminated   (b) muted
    (c) reversed   (d) emphasized.

13. They were cresting a corner of London which is almost as *precipitous* as Edinburgh, if not quite so picturesque.
    Precipitous (12) means   (a) colorful   (b) dreary   (c) steep
    (d) slumlike.

14. It opened on a long, *commodious* anteroom, of which the only arresting features, ordinarily speaking, were the rows of tall half-human mechanical figures that stood up on both sides like tailors' dummies.
    Commodious   (13)   means   (a) pleasant   (b) roomy
    (c) neat   (d) overly decorated.

15. Like tailors' dummies they had a pigeon-breasted *protuberance* of chest.
    Protuberance   (13)   means   (a) bulge   (b) narrowness
    (c) decorativeness   (d) lack.

16. Angus stopped to extract a promise, fortified with a *prospective* bribe, that he would remain in that place until the return with the detective.
    Prospective (14) means   (a) expected   (b) reluctant   (c) ill-advised   (d) misleading.

17. They turned out in the street, the small priest trundling after them with the *docility* of a small dog.
    Docility   (15)   means   (a) nervousness   (b) ferocity
    (c) manner   (d) meekness.

18. They descended, passing the man with the pail, who again *asseverated* that he had let no intruder pass.
    Asseverated (17) means   (a) loudly denied   (b) wept bitterly
    (c) declared positively   (d) mentioned quietly.

19. John Turnbull Angus went back to the lady at the shop, with whom that *imprudent* man *contrives* to be extremely comfortable.

    Imprudent (20) means lacking   (a) money   (b) caution   (c) affection   (d) ability.

20. *Contrives* (20) means   (a) hopes   (b) lives   (c) manages   (d) argues.

Thinking About the Story

1. Why is the character of John Turnbull Angus introduced into the story? How does he play an important role in the outcome?

2. How does the personality of Father Brown differ from that of Angus? Flambeau? Does this difference make his personality stronger? Explain.

3. The footprints in the snow clearly indicate this story does NOT have a supernatural element. Do you think the author played fair in presenting the clues? Are the mechanical dolls included so that they might mislead the reader?

4. Mention other "invisible men and women." For example, in a house with servants, the wealthy owners soon forget that the servants are present and often talk with great freedom and lack of restraint. The "invisibility," however, holds only for certain places. Where would the postman lose his invisibility?

5. Life is filled with contradictions. Our language reflects them: *friendly enemies, love-hate relationship, poor little rich boy, lovable scoundrel.* A more extended contradiction is called *paradox.* The "invisible man" is a paradox. How can a man in plain sight be invisible? Father Brown stories abound in paradox, as do many other detective stories, with their "impossible crimes," their "locked rooms," their "mysteriously vanishing murder weapons." Some television programs abound in mystification and paradox.

    Tell about a book or short story you've read or a television play you've seen in which paradox plays a role.

The Adventure of the Speckled Band

Arthur Conan Doyle

♦ "It is not cold which makes me shiver," said the woman, in a low voice. "It is fear, Mr. Holmes. It is terror."

An impossible crime! Murder in a locked room, thoroughly barred on the inside! A mysterious whistle in the night . . . a wisp of cigar smoke . . . a dummy bellpull . . . a saucer of milk . . . the dying words "The speckled band" . . . these are a few of the clues in this powerful story of a puzzling murder case marked by suspense, terror, and a shocking climax.

Many critics consider this story one of the half dozen best detective stories ever written. It is a classic story of its kind. The author provides clue after clue and invites you to match wits with Sherlock Holmes. Indeed, we'll stop the story at page 46, summarize the clues, and then urge you to tell how you think a second murder was about to be committed.

In this story, the author, Arthur Conan Doyle, is at his best. It suggests why Holmes is probably the most popular detective in all fiction. Here we see Holmes the powerful antagonist, the logical reasoner, the true friend, the dramatic entertainer. We understand why so many people thought of Holmes as a real person. (Many still do!) At one point Doyle tired of Holmes and decided to kill him off. In a story called "The Final Problem," Holmes apparently falls to his death in a raging waterfall. The readers were shocked and dismayed. They rebelled. "Bring Holmes back!" they insisted. Doyle at last relented. In "The Adventure of the Empty House," Doyle's readers learned that Holmes had not fallen into the waterfall after all.

Sherlock Holmes, it seems, is immortal. Are you ready to match your wits against so great a detective? Look sharp.

THE ADVENTURE OF THE SPECKLED BAND

In glancing over my notes of the seventy-odd cases in which I have during the last eight years studied the methods of my friend Sherlock Holmes, I find many tragic, some comic, a large number merely strange, but none commonplace; for, working as he did rather for the love of his art than for the acquirement of wealth, he refused to associate himself with any investigation which did not tend toward the unusual, and even the fantastic. Of all these varied cases, however, I cannot recall any which presented more singular features than that which was associated with the well-known Surrey family of the Roylotts of Stoke Moran. The events in question occurred in the early days of my association with Holmes, when we were sharing rooms as bachelors in Baker Street. It is possible that I might have placed them upon record before, but a promise of secrecy was made at the time, from which I have only been freed during the last month by the untimely death of the lady to whom the pledge was given. It is perhaps as well that the facts should now come to light, for I have reasons to know that there are widespread rumors as to the death of Dr. Grimesby Roylott which tend to make the matter even more terrible than the truth.

It was early in April in the year '83 that I woke one morning to find Sherlock Holmes standing, fully dressed, by the side of my bed. He was a late riser as a rule, and as the clock on the mantelpiece showed me that it was only a quarter past seven, I blinked up at him in some surprise, and perhaps just a little resentment, for I was myself regular in my habits.

"Very sorry to wake you up, Watson," said he, "but it's the

common lot this morning. Mrs. Hudson has been stirred up, she retorted upon me, and I on you."

"What is it, then—a fire?"

"No; a client. It seems that a young lady has arrived in a considerable state of excitement, who insists upon seeing me. She is waiting now in the sitting room. Now, when young ladies wander about the metropolis at this hour of the morning, and knock sleepy people up out of their beds, I presume that it is something very pressing which they have to communicate. Should it prove to be an interesting case, you would, I am sure, wish to follow it from the outset. I thought, at any rate, that I should call you and give you the chance."

"My dear fellow, I would not miss it for anything."

I had no keener pleasure than in following Holmes in his professional investigations, and in admiring the rapid deductions, as swift as intuitions, and yet always founded on a logical basis, with which he unraveled the problems which were submitted to him. I rapidly threw on my clothes, and was ready in a few minutes to accompany my friend down to the sitting room. A lady dressed in black and heavily veiled, who had been sitting in the window, rose as we entered.

"Good morning madam," said Holmes, cheerily. "My name is Sherlock Holmes. This is my intimate friend and associate, Dr. Watson, before whom you can speak as freely as before myself. Ha! I am glad to see that Mrs. Hudson has had the good sense to light the fire. Pray draw up to it, and I shall order you a cup of hot coffee, for I observe that you are shivering."

"It is not cold which makes me shiver," said the woman, in a low voice, changing her seat as requested.

"What, then?"

"It is fear, Mr. Holmes. It is terror." She raised her veil as she spoke, and we could see that she was indeed in a pitiable state of agitation, her face all drawn and gray, with restless, frightened eyes, like those of some hunted animal. Her features and figure were those of a woman of thirty, but her hair was shot with premature gray, and her expression was weary and haggard. Sherlock Holmes ran her over with one of his quick, all-comprehensive glances.

"You must not fear," said he, soothingly, bending forward and patting her forearm. "We shall soon set matters right, I have no doubt. You have come in by train this morning, I see."

"You know me, then?"

"No, but I observe the second half of a return ticket in the palm of your left glove. You must have started early, and yet you had a good drive in a dogcart, along heavy roads, before you reached the station."

The lady gave a violent start, and stared in bewilderment at my companion.

"There is no mystery, my dear madam," said he, smiling. "The left arm of your jacket is spattered with mud in no less than seven places. The marks are perfectly fresh. There is no vehicle save a dogcart which throws up mud in that way, and then only when you sit on the left-hand side of the driver."

"Whatever your reasons may be, you are perfectly correct," said she. "I started from home before six, reached Leatherhead at twenty past, and came in by the first train to Waterloo. Sir, I can stand this strain no longer; I shall go mad if it continues. I have no one to turn to—none, save only one, who cares for me, and he, poor fellow, can be of little aid. I have heard of you, Mr. Holmes; I have heard of you from Mrs. Farintosh, whom you helped in the hour of her sore need. It was from her that I had your address. Oh, sir, do you not think that you could help me, too, and at least throw a little light through the dense darkness which surrounds me? At present it is out of my power to reward you for your services, but in a month or six weeks I shall be married, with the control of my own income, and then at least you shall not find me ungrateful."

Holmes turned to his desk, and unlocking it, drew out a small casebook, which he consulted.

"Farintosh," said he. "Ah yes, I recall the case; it was concerned with an opal tiara. I think it was before your time, Watson. I can only say, madam, that I shall be happy to devote the same care to your case as I did to that of your friend. As to reward, my profession is its own reward; but you are at liberty to defray whatever expenses I may be put to, at the time which suits you best. And now I beg that you will lay before us everything that may help us in forming an opinion upon the matter."

"Alas!" replied our visitor, "the very horror of my situation lies in the fact that my fears are so vague, and my suspicions depend so entirely upon small points, which might seem trivial to another, that even he to whom of all others I have a right to look for help and advice looks upon all that I tell him about it as the fancies of a nervous woman. He does not say so, but I can read it from his sooth-ing answers and averted eyes. But I have heard, Mr. Holmes, that you can see deeply into the manifold wickedness of the human heart. You may advise me how to walk amid the dangers which encompass me."

"I am all attention, madam."

"My name is Helen Stoner, and I am living with my stepfather, who is the last survivor of one of the oldest Saxon families in En-gland, the Roylotts of Stoke Moran, on the western border of Sur-rey."

Holmes nodded his head. "The name is familiar to me," said he.

"The family was at one time amongst the richest in England, and the estates extended over the borders into Berkshire in the north and Hampshire in the west. In the last century, however, four successive heirs were of a dissolute and wasteful disposition, and the family ruin was eventually completed by a gambler in the days of the Regency. Nothing was left save a few acres of ground, and the two-hundred-year-old house, which is itself crushed under a heavy mortgage. The last squire dragged out his existence there, living the horrible life of an aristocratic pauper; but his only son, my stepfather, seeing that he must adapt himself to the new con-ditions, obtained an advance from a relative, which enabled him to take a medical degree, and went out to Calcutta, where, by his pro-fessional skill and his force of character, he established a large practice. In a fit of anger, however, caused by some robberies which had been perpetrated in the house, he beat his native butler to death, and narrowly escaped a capital sentence. As it was, he suffered a long term of imprisonment, and afterward returned to England a morose and disappointed man.

"When Dr. Roylott was in India he married my mother, Mrs. Stoner, the young widow of Major-General Stoner, of the Bengal Artillery. My sister Julia and I were twins, and we were only two years old at the time of my mother's remarriage. She had a consid-erable sum of money—not less than £ 1000 a year—and this she bequeathed to Dr. Roylott entirely while we resided with him, with a provision that a certain annual sum should be allowed to each of us in the event of our marriage. Shortly after our return to England my mother died—she was killed eight years ago in a railway acci-dent near Crewe. Dr. Roylott then abandoned his attempts to establish himself in practice in London, and took us to live with him in the old ancestral house at Stoke Moran. The money which my mother had left was enough for all our wants, and there seemed to be no obstacle to our happiness.

"But a terrible change came over our stepfather about this time. Instead of making friends and exchanging visits with our neighbors, who had at first been overjoyed to see a Roylott of Stoke Moran back in the old family seat, he shut himself up in his house, and seldom came out save to indulge in ferocious quarrels with whoever might cross his path. Violence of temper approaching to mania has been hereditary in the men of the family, and in my stepfather's case it had, I believe, been intensified by his long residence in the tropics. A series of disgraceful brawls took place, two of which ended in the police court, until at last he became the terror of the village, and the folks would fly at his approach, for he is a man of immense strength, and absolutely uncontrollable in his anger.

"Last week he hurled the local blacksmith over a parapet into a stream, and it was only by paying over all the money which I could gather together that I was able to avert another public exposure. He had no friends at all save the wandering gypsies, and he would give these vagabonds leave to encamp upon the few acres of bramble-covered land which represent the family estate, and would accept in return the hospitality of their tents, wandering away with them sometimes for weeks on end. He has a passion also for Indian animals, which are sent over to him by a correspondent, and he has at this moment a cheetah and a baboon, which wander freely over his grounds, and are feared by the villagers almost as much as their master.

"You can imagine from what I say that my poor sister Julia and I had no great pleasure in our lives. No servant would stay with us, and for a long time we did all the work of the house. She was but thirty at the time of her death, and yet her hair had already begun to whiten, even as mine has."

"Your sister is dead, then?"

"She died just two years ago, and it is of her death that I wish to speak to you. You can understand that, living the life which I have described, we were little likely to see anyone of our own age and position. We had, however, an aunt, my mother's maiden sister, Miss Honoria Westphail, who lives near Harrow, and we were occasionally allowed to pay short visits at this lady's house. Julia went there at Christmas two years ago, and met there a half-pay major of marines, to whom she became engaged. My stepfather learned of the engagement when my sister returned, and offered no objection to the marriage; but within a fortnight of the day which had been fixed for the wedding, the terrible event occurred which has deprived me of my only companion."

Sherlock Holmes had been leaning back in his chair with his eyes closed and his head sunk in a cushion, but he half opened his lids now and glanced across at his visitor.

"Pray be precise as to details," said he.

"It is easy for me to be so, for every event of that dreadful time is seared into my memory. The manor house is, as I have already said, very old, and only one wing is now inhabited. The bedrooms in this wing are on the ground floor, the sitting rooms being in the central block of the buildings. Of these bedrooms the first is Dr. Roylott's, the second my sister's, and the third my own. There is no communication between them, but they all open out into the same corridor. Do I make myself plain?"

"Perfectly so."

"The windows of the three rooms open out upon the lawn. That fatal night Dr. Roylott had gone to his room early, though we knew that he had not retired to rest, for my sister was troubled by the smell of the strong Indian cigars which it was his custom to smoke. She left her room, therefore, and came into mine, where she sat for some time, chatting about her approaching wedding. At eleven o'clock, she rose to leave me, but she paused at the door and looked back.

" 'Tell me, Helen,' said she, 'have you ever heard anyone whistle in the dead of the night?'

" 'Never,' said I.

" 'I suppose that you could not possibly whistle, yourself, in your sleep?'

" 'Certainly not. But why?'

" 'Because during the last few nights I have always, about three in the morning, heard a low, clear whistle. I am a light sleeper, and it has awakened me. I cannot tell where it came from—perhaps from the next room, perhaps from the lawn. I thought that I would just ask you whether you had heard it.'

" 'No, I have not. It must be those wretched gypsies in the plantation.'

" 'Very likely. And yet if it were on the lawn, I wonder that you did not hear it also.'

" 'Ah, but I sleep more heavily than you.'

" 'Well, it is of no great consequence, at any rate.' She smiled back at me, closed my door, and a few moments later I heard her key turn in the lock."

"Indeed," said Holmes. "Was it your custom always to lock yourself in at night?"

"Always."

"And why?"

"I think that I mentioned to you that the doctor kept a cheetah and a baboon. We had no feeling of security unless our doors were locked."

"Quite so. Pray proceed with your statement."

"I could not sleep that night. A vague feeling of impending misfortune impressed me. My sister and I, you will recollect, were twins, and you know how subtle are the links which bind two souls which are so closely allied. It was a wild night. The wind was howling outside, and the rain was beating and splashing against the windows. Suddenly, amid all the hubbub of the gale, there burst forth the wild scream of a terrified woman. I knew that it was my sister's voice. I sprang from my bed, wrapped a shawl round me, and rushed into the corridor. As I opened my door I seemed to hear a low whistle, such as my sister described, and a few moments later a clanging sound, as if a mass of metal had fallen. As I ran down the passage my sister's door was unlocked, and revolved slowly upon its hinges. I stared at it horror-stricken, not knowing what was about to issue from it. By the light of the corridor lamp I saw my sister appear at the opening, her face blanched with terror, her hands groping for help, her whole figure swaying to and fro like that of a drunkard. I ran to her and threw my arms round her, but at that moment her knees seemed to give way and she fell to the ground. She writhed as one who is in terrible pain, and her limbs were dreadfully convulsed. At first I thought that she had not recognized me, but as I bent over her she suddenly shrieked out, in a voice which I shall never forget: 'Oh, my God! Helen! It was the band! The speckled band!' There was something else which she would fain have said, and she stabbed with her finger into the air in the direction of the doctor's room, but a fresh convulsion seized her and choked her words. I rushed out, calling loudly for my stepfather, and I met him hastening from his room in his dressing gown. When he reached my sister's side she was unconscious, and though he poured brandy down her throat and sent for medical aid from the village, all efforts were in vain, for she slowly sank and died without having recovered her consciousness. Such was the dreadful end of my beloved sister."

"One moment," said Holmes; "are you sure about this whistle and metallic sound? Could you swear to it?"

"That was what the county coroner asked me at the inquiry. It is my strong impression that I heard it, and yet, among the crash of the gale and the creaking of an old house, I may possibly have been deceived."

"Was your sister dressed?"

"No, she was in her nightdress. In her right hand was found the charred stump of a match, and in her left a matchbox."

"Showing that she had struck a light and looked about her when the alarm took place. That is important. And what conclusions did the coroner come to?"

"He investigated the case with great care, for Dr. Roylott's conduct had long been notorious in the county, but he was unable to find any satisfactory cause of death. My evidence showed that the door had been fastened upon the inner side, and the windows were blocked by old-fashioned shutters with broad iron bars, which were secured every night. The walls were carefully sounded, and were shown to be quite solid all round, and the flooring was also thoroughly examined, with the same result. The chimney is wide, but is barred up by four large staples. It is certain, therefore, that my sister was quite alone when she met her end. Besides, there were no marks of any violence upon her."

"What about poison?"

"The doctors examined her for it, but without any success."

"What do you think that this unfortunate lady died of, then?"

"It is my belief that she died of pure fear and nervous shock, though what it was that frightened her I cannot imagine."

"Were there gypsies in the plantation at the time?"

"Yes, there are nearly always some there."

"Ah, and what did you gather from this allusion to a band—a speckled band?"

"Sometimes I have thought that it was merely the wild talk of delirium, sometimes that it may have referred to some band of people, perhaps to these very gypsies in the plantation. I do not know whether the spotted handkerchief which so many of them wear over their heads might have suggested the strange adjective which she used."

Holmes shook his head like a man who is far from being satisfied.

"These are very deep waters," said he; "pray go on with your narrative."

"Two years have passed since then, and my life has been until lately lonelier than ever. A month ago, however, a dear friend, whom I have known for many years, has done me the honor to ask my hand in marriage. His name is Armitage—Percy Armitage—the second son of Mr. Armitage, of Crane Water, near Reading. My stepfather has offered no opposition to the match, and we are to be married in the course of the spring. Two days ago some repairs were started in the west wing of the building, and my bedroom wall has been pierced, so that I have had to move into the chamber in which my sister died, and to sleep in the very bed in which she slept. Imagine, then, my thrill of terror when last night, as I lay awake, thinking over her terrible fate, I suddenly heard in the silence of the night the low whistle which had been the herald of her own death. I sprang up and lit the lamp, but nothing was to be seen in the room. I was too shaken to go to bed again, however, so I dressed, and as soon as it was daylight I slipped down, got a dogcart at the 'Crown Inn,' which is opposite, and drove to Leatherhead, from whence I have come on this morning with the one object of seeing you and asking your advice."

"You have done wisely," said my friend. "But have you told me all?"

"Yes, all."

"Miss Roylott, you have not. You are screening your stepfather."

"Why, what do you mean?"

For answer Holmes pushed back the frill of black lace which fringed the hand that lay upon our visitor's knee. Five little livid spots, the marks of four fingers and a thumb, were printed upon the white wrist.

"You have been cruelly used," said Holmes.

The lady colored deeply and covered over her injured wrist. "He is a hard man," she said, "and perhaps he hardly knows his own strength."

There was a long silence, during which Holmes leaned his chin upon his hands and stared into the crackling fire.

"This is a very deep business," he said, at last. "There are a thousand details which I should desire to know before I decide upon our course of action. Yet we have not a moment to lose. If we were to come to Stoke Moran today, would it be possible for us to see over these rooms without the knowledge of your stepfather?"

"As it happens, he spoke of coming into town today upon some most important business. It is probable that he will be away all day, and that there would be nothing to disturb you. We have a house-keeper now, but she is old and foolish, and I could easily get her out of the way."

"Excellent. You are not averse to this trip, Watson?"

"By no means."

"Then we shall both come. What are you going to do yourself?"

"I have one or two things which I would wish to do now that I am in town. But I shall return by the twelve o'clock train, so as to be there in time for your coming."

"And you may expect us early in the afternoon. I have myself some small business matters to attend to. Will you not wait and breakfast?"

"No, I must go. My heart is lightened already since I have con-fided my trouble to you. I shall look forward to seeing you again this afternoon." She dropped her thick black veil over her face and glided from the room.

"And what do you think of it all, Watson?" asked Sherlock Holmes, leaning back in his chair.

"It seems to me to be a most dark and sinister business."

"Dark enough and sinister enough."

"Yet if the lady is correct in saying that the flooring and walls are sound, and that the door, window, and chimney are impassable, then her sister must have been undoubtedly alone when she met her mysterious end."

"What becomes, then, of these nocturnal whistles, and what of the very peculiar words of the dying woman?"

"I cannot think."

"When you combine the ideas of whistles at night, the presence of a band of gypsies who are on intimate terms with this old doctor, the fact that we have every reason to believe that the doctor has an interest in preventing his stepdaughter's marriage, the dying allusion to a band, and, finally, the fact that Miss Helen Stoner heard a metallic clang, which might have been caused by one of those metal bars which secured the shutters falling back into its place, I think that there is good ground to think that the mystery may be cleared along those lines."

"But what, then, did the gypsies do?"

"I cannot imagine."

"I see many objections to any such theory."

"And so do I. It is precisely for that reason that we are going to Stoke Moran this day. I want to see whether the objections are fatal, or if they may be explained away. But what in the name of the devil!"

The outburst had been drawn from my companion by the fact that our door had been suddenly dashed open, and that a huge man had framed himself in the aperture. His costume was a peculiar mixture of the professional and of the agricultural, having a black top hat, a long frock coat, and a pair of high gaiters, with a hunting crop swinging in his hand. So tall was he that his hat actually brushed the crossbar of the doorway, and his breadth seemed to span it across from side to side. A large face, seared with a thousand wrinkles, burned yellow with the sun, and marked with every evil passion, was turned from one to the other of us, while his deepset, bile-shot eyes and his high, thin, fleshless nose gave him somewhat the resemblance to a fierce old bird of prey.

"Which of you is Holmes?" asked this apparition.

"My name, sir; but you have the advantage of me," said my companion, quietly.

"I am Dr. Grimesby Roylott, of Stoke Moran."

"Indeed, doctor," said Holmes, blandly. "Pray take a seat."

"I will do nothing of the kind. My stepdaughter has been here. I have traced her. What has she been saying to you?"

"It is a little cold for the time of the year," said Holmes.

"What has she been saying to you?" screamed the old man, furiously.

"But I have heard that the crocuses promise well," continued my companion, imperturbably.

"Ha! You put me off, do you?" said our new visitor, taking a step forward and shaking his hunting crop. "I know you, you scoundrel! I have heard of you before. You are Holmes, the meddler."

My friend smiled.

"Holmes, the busybody!"

His smile broadened.

"Holmes, the Scotland Yard Jack-in-office!"

Holmes chuckled heartily. "Your conversation is most entertaining," said he. "When you go out close the door, for there is a decided draft."

"I will go when I have said my say. Don't you dare to meddle with my affairs. I know that Miss Stoner has been here. I traced her! I am a dangerous man to fall foul of! See here." He stepped swiftly forward, seized the poker, and bent it into a curve with his huge brown hands.

"See that you keep yourself out of my grip," he snarled; and hurling the twisted poker into the fireplace, he strode out of the room.

"He seems a very amiable person," said Holmes, laughing. "I am not quite so bulky, but if he had remained I might have shown him that my grip was not much more feeble than his own." As he spoke he picked up the steel poker, and with a sudden effort straightened it out again.

"Fancy his having the insolence to confound me with the official detective force! This incident gives zest to our investigation, however, and I only trust that our little friend will not suffer from her imprudence in allowing this brute to trace her. And now, Watson, we shall order breakfast, and afterward I shall walk down to Doctors' Commons, where I hope to get some data which may help us in this matter."

It was nearly one o'clock when Sherlock Holmes returned from his excursion. He held in his hand a sheet of blue paper, scrawled over with notes and figures.

"I have seen the will of the deceased wife," said he. "To determine its exact meaning I have been obliged to work out the present prices of the investments with which it is concerned. The total income, which at the time of the wife's death was little short of £1100, is now, through the fall in agricultural prices, not more than £750. Each daughter can claim an income of £250, in case of marriage. It is evident, therefore, that if both girls had married, this beauty would have had a mere pittance, while even one of them would cripple him to a very serious extent. My morning's work has not been wasted, since it has proved that he has the very strongest motives for standing in the way of anything of the sort. And now, Watson, this is too serious for dawdling, especially as the old man is aware that we are interesting ourselves in his affairs; so if you are ready, we shall call a cab and drive to Waterloo. I should be very much obliged if you would slip your revolver into your pocket. An Eley's No. 2 is an excellent argument with gentlemen who can twist steel pokers into knots. That and a toothbrush are, I think, all that we need."

At Waterloo we were fortunate in catching a train for Leatherhead, where we hired a trap at the station inn, and drove for four or five miles through the lovely Surrey lanes. It was a perfect day, with a bright sun and a few fleecy clouds in the heavens. The trees and wayside hedges were just throwing out their first green shoots, and the air was full of the pleasant smell of the moist earth. To me at least there was a strange contrast between the sweet promise of spring and this sinister quest upon which we were engaged. My companion sat in front of the trap, his arms folded, his hat pulled down over his eyes, and his chin sunk upon his breast, buried in the deepest thought. Suddenly, however, he started, tapped me on the shoulder, and pointed over the meadows.

"Look there!" said he.

A heavily timbered park stretched up in a gentle slope, thickening into a grove at the highest point. From amid the branches there jutted out the gray gables and high rooftree of a very old mansion.

"Stoke Moran?" said he.

"Yes, sir, that be the house of Dr. Grimesby Roylott," remarked the driver.

"There is some building going on there," said Holmes; "that is where we are going."

"There's the village," said the driver, pointing to a cluster of roofs some distance to the left; "but if you want to get to the house, you'll find it shorter to get over this stile, and so by the footpath over the fields. There it is, where the lady is walking."

"And the lady, I fancy, is Miss Stoner," observed Holmes, shading his eyes. "Yes, I think we had better do as you suggest."

We got off, paid our fare, and the trap rattled back on its way to Leatherhead.

"I thought it as well," said Holmes, as we climbed the stile, "that this fellow should think we had come here as architects or on some definite business. It may stop his gossip. Good afternoon, Miss Stoner. You see that we have been as good as our word."

Our client of the morning had hurried forward to meet us with a face which spoke her joy. "I have been waiting so eagerly for you!" she cried, shaking hands with us warmly. "All has turned out splendidly. Dr. Roylott has gone to town, and it is unlikely that he will be back before evening."

"We have had the pleasure of making the doctor's acquaintance," said Holmes, and in a few words he sketched out what had occurred. Miss Stoner turned white to the lips as she listened.

"Good heavens!" she cried. "He has followed me, then."

"So it appears."

"He is so cunning that I never know when I am safe from him. What will he say when he returns?"

"He must guard himself, for he may find that there is someone more cunning than himself upon his track. You must lock yourself up from him tonight. If he is violent, we shall take you away to your aunt's at Harrow. Now, we must make the best use of our time, so kindly take us at once to the rooms which we are to examine."

The building was of gray, lichen-blotched stone, with a high central portion, and two curving wings, like the claws of a crab, thrown out on each side. In one of these wings the windows were broken, and blocked with wooden boards, while the roof was partly caved in, a picture of ruin. The central portion was in little better repair, but the right-hand block was comparatively modern, and the blinds in the windows, with the blue smoke curling up from the chimneys, showed that this was where the family resided. Some scaffolding had been erected against the end wall, and the stonework had been broken into, but there were no signs of any workmen at the moment of our visit. Holmes walked slowly up and down the ill-trimmed lawn, and examined with deep attention the outsides of the windows.

"This, I take it, belongs to the room in which you used to sleep, the center one to your sister's, and the one next to the main building to Dr. Roylott's chamber?"

"Exactly so. But I am now sleeping in the middle one."

"Pending the alterations, as I understand. By the way, there does not seem to be any very pressing need for repairs at that end wall."

"There were none. I believe that it was an excuse to move me from my room."

"Ah! that is suggestive. Now, on the other side of this narrow wing runs the corridor from which these three rooms open. There are windows in it, of course?"

"Yes, but very small ones. Too narrow for anyone to pass through."

"As you both locked your doors at night, your rooms were unapproachable from that side. Now, would you have the kindness to go into your room and bar your shutters."

Miss Stoner did so, and Holmes, after a careful examination through the open window, endeavored in every way to force the shutter open, but without success. There was no slit through which a knife could be passed to raise the bar. Then with his lens he tested the hinges, but they were of solid iron, built firmly into the massive masonry. "Hum!" said he, scratching his chin in some perplexity; "my theory certainly presents some difficulties. No one could pass these shutters if they were bolted. Well, we shall see if the inside throws any light upon the matter."

A small side door led into the whitewashed corridor from which the three bedrooms opened. Holmes refused to examine the third chamber, so we passed at once to the second, that in which Miss Stoner was now sleeping, and in which her sister had met with her fate. It was a homely little room, with a low ceiling and a gaping fireplace, after the fashion of old country houses. A brown chest of drawers stood in one corner, a narrow white-counterpaned bed in another, and a dressing table on the left-hand side of the window. These articles, with two small wickerwork chairs, made up all the furniture in the room, save for a square of Wilton carpet in the center. The boards round and the paneling of the walls were of brown, worm-eaten oak, so old and discolored that it may have dated from the original building of the house. Holmes drew one of the chairs into a corner and sat silent, while his eyes traveled round and round and up and down, taking in every detail of the apartment.

"Where does that bell communicate with? " he asked, at last, pointing to a thick bell rope which hung down beside the bed, the tassel actually lying upon the pillow.

"It goes to the housekeeper's room."

"It looks newer than the other things."

"Yes, it was only put there a couple of years ago."

"Your sister asked for it, I suppose?"

"No, I never heard of her using it. We used always to get what we wanted for ourselves."

"Indeed, it seemed unnecessary to put so nice a bellpull there. You will excuse me for a few minutes while I satisfy myself as to this floor." He threw himself down upon his face with his lens in his hand, and crawled swiftly backward and forward, examining minutely the cracks between the boards. Then he did the same with the woodwork with which the chamber was paneled. Finally he walked over to the bed, and spent some time in staring at it, and in running his eye up and down the wall. Finally he took the bell rope in his hand and gave it a brisk tug.

"Why, it's a dummy," said he.

"Won't it ring?"

"No, it is not even attached to a wire. This is very interesting. You can see now that it is fastened to a hook just above where the little opening for the ventilator is."

"How very absurd! I never noticed that before."

"Very strange!" muttered Holmes, pulling at the rope. "There are one or two very singular points about this room. For example, what a fool a builder must be to open a ventilator into another room, when, with the same trouble, he might have communicated with the outside air!"

"That is also quite modern," said the lady.

"Done about the same time as the bell rope?" remarked Holmes.

"Yes, there were several little changes carried out about that time."

"They seem to have been of a most interesting character—

dummy bell ropes, and ventilators which do not ventilate. With your permission, Miss Stoner, we shall now carry our researches into the inner apartment."

Dr. Grimesby Roylott's chamber was larger than that of his stepdaughter, but was as plainly furnished. A camp bed, a small wooden shelf full of books, mostly of a technical character, an armchair beside the bed, a plain wooden chair against the wall, a round table, and a large iron safe were the principal things which met the eye. Holmes walked slowly round and examined each and all of them with the keenest interest.

"What's in here?" he asked, tapping the safe.

"My stepfather's business papers."

"Oh! you have seen inside, then?"

"Only once, some years ago. I remember that it was full of papers."

"There isn't a cat in it, for example?"

"No. What a strange idea!"

"Well, look at this!" He took up a small saucer of milk which stood on the top of it.

"No; we don't keep a cat. But there is a cheetah and a baboon."

"Ah, yes, of course! Well, a cheetah is just a big cat, and yet a saucer of milk does not go very far in satisfying its wants, I dare say. There is one point which I should wish to determine." He squatted down in front of the wooden chair, and examined the seat of it with the greatest attention.

"Thank you. That is quite settled," said he, rising and putting his lens in his pocket. "Hello! Here is something interesting!"

The object which had caught his eye was a small dog leash hung on one corner of the bed. The leash, however, was curled upon itself, and tied so as to make a loop of whipcord.

"What do you make of that, Watson?"

"It's a common enough leash. But I don't know why it should be tied."

"That is not quite so common, is it? Ah, me! It's a wicked world, and when a clever man turns his brains to crime it is the worst of all. I think that I have seen enough now, Miss Stoner, and with your permission we shall walk out upon the lawn."

I had never seen my friend's face so grim or his brow so dark as it was when we turned from the scene of this investigation. We had walked several times up and down the lawn, neither Miss

Stoner nor myself liking to break in upon his thoughts before he roused himself from his reverie.

"It is very essential, Miss Stoner," said he, "that you should absolutely follow my advice in every respect."

"I shall most certainly do so."

"The matter is too serious for any hesitation. Your life may depend upon your compliance."

"I assure you that I am in your hands."

"In the first place, both my friend and I must spend the night in your room."

Both Miss Stoner and I gazed at him in astonishment.

"Yes, it must be so. Let me explain. I believe that that is the village inn over there?"

"Yes, that is the 'Crown.' "

"Very good. Your windows would be visible from there?"

"Certainly."

"You must confine yourself to your room, on pretence of a headache, when your stepfather comes back. Then when you hear him retire for the night, you must open the shutters of your window, undo the hasp, put your lamp there as a signal to us, and then withdraw quietly with everything which you are likely to want into the room which you used to occupy. I have no doubt, that, in spite of the repairs, you could manage there for one night."

"Oh yes, easily."

"The rest you will leave in our hands."

"But what will you do?"

"We shall spend the night in your room, and we shall investigate the cause of this noise which has disturbed you."

"I believe, Mr. Holmes, that you have already made up your mind," said Miss Stoner, laying her hand upon my companion's sleeve.

"Perhaps I have."

"Then, for pity's sake, tell me what was the cause of my sister's death."

"I should prefer to have clearer proofs before I speak."

"You can at least tell me whether my own thought is correct, and if she died from some sudden fright."

"No, I do not think so. I think that there was probably some more tangible cause. And now, Miss Stoner, we must leave you, for if Dr. Roylott returned and saw us, our journey would be in vain.

Good-bye, and be brave, for if you will do what I have told you, you may rest assured that we shall soon drive away the dangers that threaten you."

Sherlock Holmes and I had no difficulty in engaging a bedroom and sitting room at the "Crown Inn." They were on the upper floor, and from our window we could command a view of the avenue gate, and of the inhabited wing of Stoke Moran manor house. At dusk we saw Dr. Grimesby Roylott drive past, his huge form looming up beside the little figure of the lad who drove him. The boy had some slight difficulty in undoing the heavy iron gates, and we heard the hoarse roar of the doctor's voice, and saw the fury with which he shook his clinched fists at him. The trap drove on, and a few minutes later we saw a sudden light spring up among the trees as the lamp was lit in one of the sitting rooms.

"Do you know, Watson," said Holmes, as we sat together in the gathering darkness, "I have really some scruples as to taking you tonight. There is a distinct element of danger."

"Can I be of assistance?"

"Your presence might be invaluable."

"Then I shall certainly come."

"It is very kind of you."

"You speak of danger. You have evidently seen more in these rooms than was visible to me."

"No, but I fancy that I may have deduced a little more. I imagine that you saw all that I did."

"I saw nothing remarkable save the bell rope, and what purpose that could answer I confess is more than I can imagine."

"You saw the ventilator, too?"

"Yes, but I do not think that it is such a very unusual thing to have a small opening between two rooms. It was so small that a rat could hardly pass through."

"I knew that we should find a ventilator before ever we came to Stoke Moran."

"My dear Holmes!"

"Oh yes, I did. You remember in her statement she said that her sister could smell Dr. Roylott's cigar. Now, of course, that suggested at once that there must be a communication between the two rooms. It could only be a small one, or it would have been remarked upon at the coroner's inquiry. I deduced a ventilator."

"But what harm can there be in that?"

"Well, there is at least a curious coincidence of dates. A ventilator is made, a cord is hung, and a lady who sleeps in the bed dies. Does not that strike you?"

"I cannot as yet see any connection."

"Did you observe anything very peculiar about that bed?"

"No."

"It was clamped to the floor. Did you ever see a bed fastened like that before?"

"I cannot say that I have."

"The lady could not move her bed. It must always be in the same relative position to the ventilator and to the rope—for so we may call it, since it was clearly never meant for a bellpull."

"Holmes," I cried, "I seem to see dimly what you are hinting at! We are only just in time to prevent some subtle and horrible crime."

"Subtle enough and horrible enough. When a doctor does go wrong, he is the first of criminals. He has nerve and he has knowledge. Palmer and Pritchard were among the heads of their profession. This man strikes even deeper; but I think, Watson, that we shall be able to strike deeper still. But we shall have horrors enough before the night is over; for goodness' sake let us have a quiet pipe, and turn our minds for a few hours to something more cheerful."

[*All the clues have now been given. Here is a list to refresh your memory. Can you guess how the murder was done?*

the Indian pets	*the mysterious repairs*
the character of the doctor	*the locked room*
the sister's engagement	*the dummy bell rope*
the smell of cigar smoke	*the ventilator*
the whistle	*the saucer of milk*
the metallic clang	*the safe*
the dying words	*the whipcord*
Miss Stoner's engagement	*the fastened bed*

After you have made a guess, read on to check the accuracy of your deductions as compared with those of Holmes.]

About nine o'clock the light among the trees was extinguished, and all was dark in the direction of the manor house. Two hours passed slowly away, and then, suddenly, just at the stroke of eleven, a single bright light shone out in front of us.

"That is our signal," said Holmes, springing to his feet; "it comes from the middle window."

As we passed out he exchanged a few words with the landlord, explaining that we were going on a late visit to an acquaintance, and that it was possible that we might spend the night there. A moment later we were out on the dark road, a chill wind blowing in our faces, and one yellow light twinkling in front of us through the gloom to guide us on our somber errand.

There was little difficulty in entering the grounds, for unrepaired breaches gaped in the old park wall. Making our way among the trees, we reached the lawn, crossed it, and were about to enter through the window, when out from a clump of laurel bushes there darted what seemed to be a hideous and distorted child, who threw itself upon the grass with writhing limbs, and then ran swiftly across the lawn into the darkness.

"My God!" I whispered; "did you see it?"

Holmes was for the moment as startled as I. His hand closed like a vise upon my wrist in his agitation. Then he broke into a low laugh, and put his lips to my ear.

"It is a nice household," he murmured. "That is the baboon."

I had forgotten the strange pets which the doctor affected. There was a cheetah, too; perhaps we might find it upon our shoulders at any moment. I confess that I felt easier in my mind when, after following Holmes's example and slipping off my shoes, I found myself inside the bedroom. My companion noiselessly closed the shutters, moved the lamp onto the table, and cast his eyes round the room. All was as we had seen it in the daytime. Then creeping up to me and making a trumpet of his hand, he whispered into my ear again so gently that it was all that I could do to distinguish the words:

"The least sound would be fatal to our plans."

I nodded to show that I had heard.

"We must sit without light. He would see it through the ventilator."

I nodded again.

"Do not go asleep; your very life may depend upon it. Have your pistol ready in case we should need it. I will sit on the side of the bed, and you in that chair."

I took out my revolver and laid it on the corner of the table.

Holmes had brought up a long, thin cane, and this he placed upon the bed beside him. By it he laid the box of matches and the stump of a candle. Then he turned down the lamp, and we were left in darkness.

How shall I ever forget that dreadful vigil? I could not hear a sound, not even the drawing of a breath, and yet I knew that my companion sat open-eyed, within a few feet of me, in the same state of nervous tension in which I was myself. The shutters cut off the least ray of light, and we waited in absolute darkness. From outside came the occasional cry of a night bird, and once at our very window a long-drawn, catlike whine, which told us that the cheetah was indeed at liberty. Far away we could hear the deep tones of the parish clock, which boomed out every quarter of an hour. How long they seemed, those quarters! Twelve struck, and one and two and three, and still we sat waiting silently for whatever might befall.

Suddenly there was the momentary gleam of a light up in the direction of the ventilator, which vanished immediately, but was succeeded by a strong smell of burning oil and heated metal. Someone in the next room had lit a dark lantern. I heard a gentle sound of movement, and then all was silent once more, though the smell grew stronger. For half an hour I sat with straining ears. Then suddenly another sound became audible—a very gentle, soothing sound, like that of a small jet of steam escaping continually from a kettle. The instant that we heard it, Holmes sprang from the bed, struck a match, and lashed furiously with his cane at the bellpull.

"You see it, Watson?" he yelled. "You see it?"

But I saw nothing. At the moment when Holmes struck the light I heard a low, clear whistle, but the sudden glare flashing into my weary eyes made it impossible for me to tell what it was at which my friend lashed so savagely. I could, however, see that his face was deadly pale, and filled with horror and loathing.

He had ceased to strike, and was gazing up at the ventilator, when suddenly there broke from the silence of the night the most horrible cry to which I have ever listened. It swelled up louder and louder, a hoarse yell of pain and fear and anger all mingled in the one dreadful shriek. They say that away down in the village, and even in the distant parsonage, that cry raised the sleepers from their beds. It struck cold to our hearts, and I stood gazing at Holmes, and he at me, until the last echoes of it had died away into the silence from which it rose.

"What can it mean?" I gasped.

"It means that it is all over," Holmes answered. "And perhaps, after all, it is for the best. Take your pistol, and we will enter Dr. Roylott's room."

With a grave face he lit the lamp and led the way down the corridor. Twice he struck at the chamber door without any reply from within. Then he turned the handle and entered, I at his heels, with the cocked pistol in my hand.

It was a singular sight which met our eyes. On the table stood a dark lantern with the shutter half open, throwing a brilliant beam of light upon the iron safe, the door of which was ajar. Beside this table, on the wooden chair, sat Dr. Grimesby Roylott, clad in a long gray dressing gown, his bare ankles protruding beneath, and his feet thrust into red heelless Turkish slippers. Across his lap lay the short stock with the long leash which we had noticed during the day. His chin was cocked upward and his eyes were fixed in a dreadful, rigid stare at the corner of the ceiling. Round his brow he had a peculiar yellow band, with brownish speckles, which seemed to be bound tightly round his head. As we entered he made neither sound nor motion.

"The band! the speckled band!" whispered Holmes.

I took a step forward. In an instant his strange headgear began to move, and there reared itself from among his hair the squat diamond-shaped head and puffed neck of a loathsome serpent.

"It is a swamp adder!" cried Holmes; "the deadliest snake in India. He has died within ten seconds of being bitten. Violence does, in truth, recoil upon the violent, and the schemer falls into the pit which he digs for another. Let us thrust this creature back into its den, and we can then remove Miss Stoner to some place of shelter, and let the county police know what has happened."

As he spoke he drew the dog whip swiftly from the dead man's lap, and throwing the noose round the reptile's neck, he drew it from its horrid perch, and carrying it at arm's length, threw it into the iron safe, which he closed upon it.

Such are the true facts of the death of Dr. Grimesby Roylott, of Stoke Moran. It is not necessary that I should prolong a narrative which has already run to too great a length, by telling how we broke the sad news to the terrified girl, how we conveyed her by the morning train to the care of her good aunt at Harrow, of how the slow process of official inquiry came to the conclusion that the doctor met his fate while indiscreetly playing with a dangerous pet. The little which I had yet to learn of the case was told me by Sherlock Holmes as we traveled back next day.

"I had," said he, "come to an entirely erroneous conclusion, which shows, my dear Watson, how dangerous it always is to reason from insufficient data. The presence of the gypsies, and the use of the word 'band,' which was used by the poor girl, no doubt to explain the appearance which she had caught a hurried glimpse of by the light of her match, were sufficient to put me upon an entirely wrong scent. I can only claim the merit that I instantly reconsidered my position when, however, it became clear to me that whatever danger threatened an occupant of the room could not come either from the window or the door. My attention was speedily drawn, as I have already remarked to you, to this ventilator, and to the bell rope which hung down to the bed. The discovery that this was a dummy, and that the bed was clamped to the floor, instantly gave rise to the suspicion that the rope was there as bridge for something passing through the hole and coming to the bed. The idea of a snake instantly occurred to me, and when I coupled it with my knowledge that the doctor was furnished with a supply of creatures from India, I felt that I was probably on the right track. The idea of using a form of poison which could not possibly be discovered by any chemical test was just such a one as would occur to a clever and ruthless man who had had an Eastern training. The rapidity with which such a poison would take effect would also, from his point of view, be an advantage. It would be a sharp-eyed coroner, indeed, who could distinguish the two little dark punctures which would show where the poison fangs had done their work. Then I thought of the whistle. Of course he must recall the snake before the morning light revealed it to the victim. He had trained it, probably by the use of the milk which we saw, to return to him when summoned. He would put it through this ventilator at the hour that he thought best, with the certainty that it would crawl down the rope and land on the bed. It might or might not bite the occupant, perhaps she might escape every night for a week, but sooner or later she must fall a victim.

"I had come to these conclusions before ever I had entered his room. An inspection of his chair showed me that he had been in the habit of standing on it, which of course would be necessary in order that he should reach the ventilator. The sight of the safe, the saucer of milk, and the loop of whipcord were enough to finally dispel any doubts which may have remained. The metallic clang heard by Miss Stoner was obviously caused by her stepfather hastily closing the door of his safe upon its terrible occupant. Having once made up my mind, you know the steps which I took in order to put the matter to the proof. I heard the creature hiss, as I have no doubt that you did also, and I instantly lit the light and attacked it."

"With the result of driving it through the ventilator."

"And also with the result of causing it to turn upon its master at the other side. Some of the blows of my cane came home, and aroused its snakish temper, so that it flew upon the first person it saw. In this way I am no doubt indirectly responsible for Dr. Grimesby Roylott's death, and I cannot say that it is likely to weigh very heavily upon my conscience."

Understanding the Story ───────────

Main Idea

1. To solve the mystery of the speckled band, Sherlock Holmes had to rely heavily on observation and   (a) luck (b) sentiment   (c) reasoning   (d) strength.

Details

2. A low, clear whistle was used to signal   (a) the gypsies (b) the adder   (c) the cheetah   (d) the baboon.

3. Helen's wrist had been injured by   (a) an animal (b) Holmes himself   (c) her stepfather   (d) a fall.

4. Holmes was called a busybody by   (a) Watson   (b) Mrs. Hudson   (c) Miss Stoner   (d) Dr. Roylott.

5. The odd fact about the ventilator was that   (a) it was too high
    (b) it seemed unduly large   (c) it didn't ventilate   (d) it was
    made of a strange metal.

Inferences

6. In first speaking to Helen Stoner, Sherlock Holmes quickly
    showed that   he   was   (a) indifferent   (b) observant
    (c) unfriendly   (d) humorous.

7. In his dealings with the townspeople, Dr. Roylott was
    (a) cruel   and   quarrelsome   (b) calm   and   concerned
    (c) friendly but sometimes cross   (d) creative and ingenious.

8. When Dr. Roylott heard of Helen Stoner's approaching mar-
    riage, he was   (a) happy and relieved   (b) eager to be best
    man   (c) outspokenly opposed   (d) inwardly furious.

9. The purpose of Dr. Roylott's visit to Holmes's office was to
    (a) welcome Holmes to Stoke Moran   (b) meet Dr. Watson
    (c) threaten Sherlock Holmes   (d) attend a convention.

10. In   a   word,   the   motive   for   the   sister's   murder   was
    (a) jealousy   (b) money   (c) anger   (d) power.

Order of Events

11. Arrange the items in the order in which they occurred. Use
    letters only.
    A. Dr. Roylott marries Helen's mother.
    B. Helen's sister dies mysteriously.
    C. Helen's mother dies in a railway accident.
    D. Helen visits Sherlock Holmes's office.
    E. Helen's sister becomes engaged.
    F. Dr. Roylott visits Sherlock Holmes's office.
    G. Helen becomes engaged.

Outcomes

12. If Holmes had come openly to Stoke Moran, he   (a) would
    not have been admitted   (b) would have prevented the mur-
    der more effectively   (c) would have had no need of Dr. Wat-
    son   (d) would have made Miss Stoner happy.

Cause and Effect

13. If Helen's sister had not become engaged, the sister
    (a) would have visited her aunt   (b) would have disagreed
    violently with Dr. Roylott   (c) would not have been mur-
    dered   (d) would have moved into her sister's room.

Fact or Opinion

Tell whether each of the following is a fact or an opinion.

14. Despite her fears, Helen Stoner was unusually courageous.

15. Dr. Roylott had spent many years in India.

Words in Context

1. Of all these varied cases, however, I cannot recall any which presented more *singular* features than that which was associated with the well-known Surrey family of the Roylotts of Stoke Moran.
   Singular (27) means (a) dramatic (b) unusual (c) low-key (d) violent.

2. Her hair was shot with premature gray, and her expression was weary and *haggard*.
   Haggard (28) means (a) cheerful (b) animated (c) vicious (d) gaunt.

3. "You are at liberty to *defray* whatever expenses I may be put to, at the time which suits you best."
   Defray (29) means (a) overlook (b) pay (c) increase (d) report.

4. "My suspicions depend so entirely upon small points, which might seem *trivial* to another."
   Trivial (29) means (a) unimportant (b) exciting (c) unpopular (d) surprising.

5. "In the last century, however, four successive heirs were of a *dissolute* and wasteful disposition."
   Dissolute (30) means (a) enlightened (b) immoral (c) personable (d) mild.

6. "In a fit of anger, however, caused by some robberies which had been *perpetrated* in the house, he beat his native butler to death."
   Perpetrated (30) means (a) cleverly planned (b) observed (c) committed (d) prevented.

7. "He suffered a long term of imprisonment, and afterward returned to England a *morose* and disappointed man."
   Morose (30) means (a) optimistic (b) realistic (c) distinguished (d) sullen.

8. "A vague feeling of *impending* misfortune impressed me."
    Impending (33) means   (a) menacing   (b) unexpected
    (c) expected   (d) annoying.

9. "By the light of the corridor lamp I saw my sister appear at
    the opening, her face *blanched* with terror."
    Blanched (33) means   (a) slightly upset   (b) made pale
    (c) smoothed   (d) muddled.

10. "She *writhed* as one who is in terrible pain, and her limbs were
    dreadfully convulsed."
    Writhed   (33)   means   (a) screamed   (b) danced
    (c) twisted   (d) stiffened.

11. "Dr. Roylott's conduct had long been *notorious* in the county."
    Notorious (34) means   (a) unfavorably famous   (b) mildly
    irritating   (c) outstandingly brilliant   (d) persistently cu-
    rious.

12. "Ah, and what did you gather from this *allusion* to a band—a
    speckled band?"
    Allusion (35)   means   (a) conversion   (b) reference
    (c) challenge   (d) presentation.

13. "You are not *averse* to this trip, Watson?"
    Averse (36) means   (a) warmly disposed   (b) mildly prone
    (c) indifferent   (d) unfavorably inclined.

14. "What becomes, then, of these *nocturnal* whistles, and what of
    the very peculiar words of the dying woman?"
    Nocturnal (37) means   (a) by day   (b) at night   (c) panicky
    (d) unexpected.

15. Our door had been suddenly dashed open, and a huge man had
    framed himself in the *aperture*.
    Aperture (37) means   (a) window   (b) scene   (c) outer
    room   (d) opening.

16. "But I have heard that the crocuses promise well," continued
    my companion, *imperturbably*.
    Imperturbably (38) means   (a) hesitantly   (b) angrily
    (c) coolly   (d) dramatically.

17. "He seems a very *amiable* person," said Holmes, laughing.
    Amiable   (38)   means   (a) curious   (b) agreeable
    (c) comical   (d) unpredictable.

18. We had walked several times up and down the lawn, neither Miss Stoner nor myself liking to break in upon his thoughts before he roused himself from his *reverie.*
    Reverie (44) means   (a) anger   (b) daydream   (c) laziness (d) chair.

19. How shall I ever forget that dreadful *vigil?*
    Vigil (48) means   (a) watch   (b) chill   (c) incident (d) exercise.

20. "The sight of the safe, the saucer of milk, and the loop of whip-cord were enough to finally *dispel* any doubts which may have remained."
    Dispel (51) means   (a) confirm   (b) banish   (c) enlarge (d) conceal.

Thinking About the Story

1. Turn to page 46. How does each of the clues play a part in the solution of the mystery? Consider each clue in turn.

2. Sometimes a detective-story writer will provide misleading clues, called "red herrings." Are any such clues provided in this story? (For example, could the "speckled band" be a band of gypsies?) Identify any of this type and explain why you think it was put in to mislead the reader. Does the author play fair, allowing each reader a fair chance to solve the mystery? Explain.

3. List five adjectives that could be applied to Dr. Roylott—for example, *menacing.* How does the author show skill in describing the character of Dr. Roylott? (Hint: think of what he does.)

4. How would you describe Stoke Moran? Is Doyle's description vivid? Explain.

5. Once the mystery is solved, the story ends quickly. Is this a sound literary device? Why or why not?

6. Did the title arouse your curiosity? In each of the following pairs of titles, choose the one that seems superior. Tell why.
   1. The Red-headed League   An Exciting Adventure
   2. A Jewel of a Story   The Adventure of the Blue Carbuncle
   3. The Man with the Twisted Lip   An Unusual Character
   4. An Unbelievable Story   The Adventure of the Engineer's Thumb
   5. Was It a Ghost?   The Hound of the Baskervilles

The Tragedy at Marsdon Manor

Agatha Christie

♦ The man I had seen on the bed upstairs stood
there, facing us, gleaming with a faint ghostly
light. There was blood on his lips, and he held his
right hand out, pointing. Suddenly a brilliant light
seemed to proceed from it. It passed over Poirot
and me, and fell on Mrs. Maltravers. I saw her white
terrified face, and something else!

Agatha Christie may be the most successful mystery writer of
all time. In popularity and frequency of reprinting, her books are
probably second only to the Bible. Her name is famous around
the world, in many languages, including Russian.

Agatha Christie created many sleuths, including Miss Marple,
Harley Quin, and Tuppence and Tommy. Her most famous detective, however, fit to rank with Sherlock Holmes and Father Brown
as household words, is the Belgian detective Hercule Poirot.

"The Tragedy at Marsdon Manor" is a typical Poirot story. In
it the detective demonstrates his method, his use of the "little
gray cells" as he often called the logical powers of his brain. What
looks like an obvious death by natural causes begins to look suspiciously like suicide. But Poirot is never satisfied with obvious
explanations. He looks beyond. Like Sherlock Holmes, he observes carefully and picks up elements that somehow don't fit the
accepted pattern. Like Father Brown, he is aware of dark places
in the human heart.

In this story you will find Poirot playing the amateur psychologist with a free-association test as a guide. You will meet
several intriguing characters, at least one of whom is not what he
or she appears. You will watch a theatrical Poirot, trying any device to arrive at the truth. You will see how a rifle used to shoot
birds (rooks) plays a role in the story.

THE TRAGEDY AT MARSDON MANOR

I had been called away from town for a few days, and on my return found Poirot in the act of strapping up his small valise.

"*A la bonne heure*, Hastings. I feared you would not have returned in time to accompany me."

"You are called away on a case, then?"

"Yes, though I am bound to admit that, on the face of it, the affair does not seem promising. The Northern Union Insurance Company have asked me to investigate the death of a Mr. Maltravers who a few weeks ago insured his life with them for the large sum of fifty thousand pounds."

"Yes?" I said, much interested.

"There was, of course, the usual suicide clause in the policy. In the event of his committing suicide within a year the premiums would be forfeited. Mr. Maltravers was duly examined by the Company's own doctor, and although he was a man slightly past the prime of life was passed as being in quite sound health. However, on Wednesday last—the day before yesterday—the body of Mr. Maltravers was found in the grounds of his house in Essex, Marsdon Manor, and the cause of his death is described as some kind of internal hemorrhage. That in itself would be nothing remarkable, but sinister rumors as to Mr. Maltravers' financial position have been in the air of late, and the Northern Union have ascertained beyond any possible doubt that the deceased gentleman stood upon the verge of bankruptcy. Now that alters matters considerably. Maltravers had a beautiful young wife, and it is suggested that he got together all the ready money he could for the purpose of paying the premiums on a life insurance for his wife's benefit, and then committed suicide. Such a thing is not uncommon. In any case, my friend Alfred Wright, who is a director of the Northern Union, has asked me to investigate the facts of the case, but, as I told him, I am not very hopeful of success. If the cause of the death had been heart failure, I should have been more sanguine. Heart failure may always be translated as the inability of the local G. P. to discover what his patient really did die of, but a hemorrhage seems fairly definite. Still, we can but make some necessary inquiries. Five minutes to pack your bag, Hastings, and we will take a taxi to Liverpool Street."

About an hour later, we alighted from a Great Eastern train at the little station of Marsdon Leigh. Inquiries at the station yielded the information that Marsdon Manor was about a mile distant. Poirot decided to walk, and we betook ourselves along the main street.

"What is our plan of campaign?" I asked.

"First I will call upon the doctor. I have ascertained that there is only one doctor in Marsdon Leigh, Dr. Ralph Bernard. Ah, here we are at his house."

The house in question was a kind of superior cottage, standing back a little from the road. A brass plate on the gate bore the doctor's name. We passed up the path and rang the bell.

We proved to be fortunate in our call. It was the doctor's consulting hour, and for the moment there were no patients waiting for him. Dr. Bernard was an elderly man, high-shouldered and stooping, with a pleasant vagueness of manner.

Poirot introduced himself and explained the purpose of our visit, adding that insurance companies were bound to investigate fully in a case of this kind.

"Of course, of course," said Dr. Bernard vaguely. "I suppose, as he was such a rich man, his life was insured for a big sum?"

"You consider him a rich man, doctor?"

The doctor looked rather surprised.

"Was he not? He kept two cars, you know, and Marsdon Manor is a pretty big place to keep up, although I believe he bought it very cheap."

"I understand that he had had considerable losses of late," said Poirot, watching the doctor narrowly.

The latter, however, merely shook his head sadly.

"Is that so? Indeed. It is fortunate for his wife, then, that there is this life insurance. A very beautiful and charming young creature, but terribly unstrung by this sad catastrophe. A mass of nerves, poor thing. I have tried to spare her all I can, but of course the shock was bound to be considerable."

"You have been attending Mr. Maltravers recently?"

"My dear sir, I never attended him."

"What?"

"I understand Mr. Maltravers was a Christian Scientist—or something of that kind."

"But you examined the body?"

"Certainly. I was fetched by one of the under-gardeners."

"And the cause of death was clear?"

"Absolutely. There was blood on the lips, but most of the bleeding must have been internal."

"Was he still lying where he had been found?"

"Yes, the body had not been touched. He was lying on the edge of a small plantation. He had evidently been out shooting rooks, a small rook rifle lay beside him. The hemorrhage must have occurred quite suddenly. Gastric ulcer, without a doubt."

"No question of his having been shot, eh?"

"My dear sir!"

"I demand pardon," said Poirot humbly. "But, if my memory is not at fault, in the case of a recent murder, the doctor first gave a verdict of heart failure—altering it when the local constable pointed out that there was a bullet wound through the head!"

"You will not find any bullet wounds on the body of Mr. Maltravers," said Dr. Bernard dryly. "Now, gentlemen, if there is nothing further—"

We took the hint.

"Good morning, and many thanks to you, doctor, for so kindly answering our questions. By the way, you saw no need for an autopsy?"

"Certainly not." The doctor became quite apoplectic. "The cause of death was clear, and in my profession we see no need to distress unduly the relatives of a dead patient."

And, turning, the doctor slammed the door sharply in our faces.

"And what do you think of Dr. Bernard, Hastings?" inquired Poirot, as we proceeded on our way to the Manor.

"Rather an old ass."

"Exactly. Your judgments of character are always profound, my friend."

I glanced at him uneasily, but he seemed perfectly serious. A twinkle, however, came into his eye, and he added slyly:

"That is to say, when there is no question of a beautiful woman!"

I looked at him coldly.

On our arrival at the manor house, the door was opened to us by a middle-aged parlormaid. Poirot handed her his card, and a letter from the insurance company for Mrs. Maltravers. She showed us into a small morning room, and retired to tell her mistress. About ten minutes elapsed, and then the door opened, and a slender figure in widow's weeds stood upon the threshold.

"Monsieur Poirot?" she faltered.

"Madame!" Poirot sprang gallantly to his feet and hastened towards her. "I cannot tell you how I regret to derange you in this way. But what will you? *Les affaires*—they know no mercy."

Mrs. Maltravers permitted him to lead her to a chair. Her eyes were red with weeping, but the temporary disfigurement could not conceal her extraordinary beauty. She was about twenty-seven or -eight, and very fair, with large blue eyes and a pretty pouting mouth.

"It is something about my husband's insurance, is it? But must I be bothered *now*—so soon?"

"Courage, my dear madame. Courage! You see, your late husband insured his life for rather a large sum, and in such a case the company always has to satisfy itself as to a few details. They have empowered me to act for them. You can rest assured that I will do all in my power to render the matter not too unpleasant for you. Will you recount to me briefly the sad events of Wednesday?"

"I was changing for tea when my maid came up—one of the gardeners had just run to the house. He had found—"

Her voice trailed away. Poirot pressed her hand sympathetically.

"I comprehend. Enough! You had seen your husband earlier in the afternoon?"

"Not since lunch. I had walked down to the village for some stamps, and I believe he was out pottering round the grounds."

"Shooting rooks, eh?"

"Yes, he usually took his little rook rifle with him, and I heard one or two shots in the distance."

"Where is this little rook rifle now?"

"In the hall, I think."

She led the way out of the room and found and handed the little weapon to Poirot, who examined it cursorily.

"Two shots fired, I see," he observed, as he handed it back. "And now, madame, if I might see—"

He paused delicately.

"The servant shall take you," she murmured, averting her head.

The parlormaid, summoned, led Poirot upstairs. I remained with the lovely and unfortunate woman. It was hard to know whether to speak or remain silent. I essayed one or two general reflections to which she responded absently, and in a very few minutes Poirot rejoined us.

"I thank you for all your courtesy, madame. I do not think you need be troubled any further with this matter. By the way, do you know anything of your husband's financial position?"

She shook her head.

"Nothing whatever. I am very stupid over business things."

"I see. Then you can give us no clue as to why he suddenly decided to insure his life? He had not done so previously, I understand."

"Well, we had only been married a little over a year. But, as to why he insured his life, it was because he had absolutely made up his mind that he would not live long. He had a strong premonition of his own death. I gather that he had had one hemorrhage already, and that he knew that another one would prove fatal. I tried to dispel these gloomy fears of his, but without avail. Alas, he was only too right!"

Tears in her eyes, she bade us a dignified farewell. Poirot made a characteristic gesture as we walked down the drive together.

"*Eh bien,* that is that! Back to London, my friend, there appears to be no mouse in this mousehole. And yet—"

"Yet what?"

"A slight discrepancy, that is all! You noticed it? You did not? Still, life is full of discrepancies, and assuredly the man cannot have taken his own life—there is no poison that would fill his mouth with blood. No, no, I must resign myself to the fact that all here is clear and aboveboard—but who is this?"

A tall young man was striding up the drive towards us. He passed us without making any sign, but I noted that he was not ill-looking, with a lean, deeply bronzed face that spoke of life in a tropic clime. A gardener who was sweeping up leaves had paused for a minute in his task, and Poirot ran quickly up to him.

"Tell me, I pray you, who is that gentleman? Do you know him?"

"I don't remember his name, sir, though I did hear it. He was staying down here last week for a night. Tuesday, it was."

"Quick, *mon ami*, let us follow him."

We hastened up the drive after the retreating figure. A glimpse of a black-robed figure on the terrace at the side of the house, and our quarry swerved and we after him, so that we were witnesses of the meeting.

Mrs. Maltravers almost staggered where she stood, and her face blanched noticeably.

"You," she gasped. "I thought you were on the sea—on your way to East Africa?"

"I got some news from my lawyers that detained me," explained the young man. "My old uncle in Scotland died unexpectedly and left me some money. Under the circumstances I thought it better to cancel my passage. Then I saw this bad news in the paper and I came down to see if there was anything I could do. You'll want someone to look after things for you a bit perhaps."

At that moment they became aware of our presence. Poirot stepped forward, and with many apologies explained that he had left his stick in the hall. Rather reluctantly, it seemed to me, Mrs. Maltravers made the necessary introduction.

"Monsieur Poirot, Captain Black."

A few minutes' chat ensued, in the course of which Poirot elicited the fact that Captain Black was putting up at the Anchor Inn. The missing stick not having been discovered (which was not surprising), Poirot uttered more apologies and we withdrew.

We returned to the village at a great pace, and Poirot made a beeline for the Anchor Inn.

"Here we establish ourselves until our friend the Captain returns," he explained. "You notice that I emphasized the point that we were returning to London by the first train? Possibly you thought I meant it. But no—you observed Mrs. Maltravers' face when she caught sight of this young Black? She was clearly taken aback, and he—*eh bien*, he was very devoted, did you not think so? And he was here on Tuesday night—the day before Mr. Maltravers died. We must investigate the doings of Captain Black, Hastings."

In about half an hour we espied our quarry approaching the inn. Poirot went out and accosted him and presently brought him up to the room we had engaged.

"I have been telling Captain Black of the mission which brings us here," he explained. "You can understand, *monsieur le capitaine*, that I am anxious to arrive at Mr. Maltravers' state of mind immediately before his death, and that at the same time I do not wish to distress Mrs. Maltravers unduly by asking her painful questions. Now, you were here just before the occurrence, and can give us equally valuable information."

"I'll do anything I can to help you, I'm sure," replied the young soldier; "but I'm afraid I didn't notice anything out of the ordinary. You see, although Maltravers was an old friend of my people's, I didn't know him very well myself."

"You came down—when?"

"Tuesday afternoon. I went up to town early Wednesday morning, as my boat sailed from Tilbury about twelve o'clock. But some news I got made me alter my plans, as I dare say you heard me explain to Mrs. Maltravers."

"You were returning to East Africa, I understand?"

"Yes. I've been out there ever since the War—a great country."

"Exactly. Now what was the talk about at dinner on Tuesday night?"

"Oh, I don't know. The usual odd topics. Maltravers asked after my people, and then we discussed the question of German reparations, and then Mrs. Maltravers asked a lot of questions about East Africa, and I told them one or two yarns, that's about all, I think."

"Thank you."

Poirot was silent for a moment, then he said gently: "With your permission, I should like to try a little experiment. You have told us all that your conscious self knows, I want now to question your subconscious self."

"Psychoanalysis, what?" said Black, with visible alarm.

"Oh, no," said Poirot reassuringly. "You see, it is like this, I give you a word, you answer with another, and so on. Any word, the first one you think of. Shall we begin?"

"All right," said Black slowly, but he looked uneasy.

"Note down the words, please, Hastings," said Poirot. Then he took from his pocket his big turnip-faced watch and laid it on the table beside him. "We will commence. Day."

There was a moment's pause, and then Black replied:

"Night."

As Poirot proceeded, his answers came quicker.

"Name," said Poirot.

"Place."

"Bernard."

"Shaw."

"Tuesday."

"Dinner."

"Journey."

"Ship."

"Country."

"Uganda."

"Story."

"Lions."

"Rook Rifle."

"Farm."

"Shot."

"Suicide."

"Elephant."

"Tusks."

"Money."

"Lawyers."

"Thank you, Captain Black. Perhaps you could spare me a few minutes in about half an hour's time?"

"Certainly." The young soldier looked at him curiously and wiped his brow as he got up.

"And now, Hastings," said Poirot, smiling at me as the door closed behind him. "You see it all, do you not?"

"I don't know what you mean."

"Does that list of words tell you nothing?"

I scrutinized it, but was forced to shake my head.

"I will assist you. To begin with, Black answered well within the normal time limit, with no pauses, so we can take it that he himself has no guilty knowledge to conceal. 'Day' to 'Night' and 'Place' to 'Name' are normal associations. I began work with 'Bernard' which might have suggested the local doctor had he come across him at all. Evidently he had not. After our recent conversation, he gave 'Dinner' to my 'Tuesday,' but 'Journey' and 'Country' were answered by 'Ship' and 'Uganda,' showing clearly that it was his journey abroad that was important to him and not the one which brought him down here. 'Story' recalls to him one of the 'Lion' stories he told at dinner. I proceed to 'Rook Rifle' and he answered with the totally unexpected word 'Farm.' When I say 'Shot,' he answers at once 'Suicide.' The association seems clear. A man he knows committed suicide with a rook rifle on a farm somewhere. Remember, too, that his mind is still on the stories he told at dinner, and I think you will agree that I shall not be far from the truth if I recall Captain Black and ask him to repeat the particular suicide story which he told at the dinner table on Tuesday evening.''

Black was straightforward enough over the matter.

"Yes, I did tell them that story now that I come to think of it. Chap shot himself on a farm out there. Did it with a rook rifle through the roof of the mouth, bullet lodged in the brain. Doctors were no end puzzled over it—there was nothing to show except a little blood on the lips. But what—''

"What has it got to do with Mr. Maltravers? You did not know, I see, that he was found with a rook rifle by his side.''

"You mean my story suggested to him—oh, but that is awful!''

"Do not distress yourself—it would have been one way or another. Well, I must get on the telephone to London.''

Poirot had a lengthy conversation over the wire, and came back thoughtful. He went off by himself in the afternoon, and it was not till seven o'clock that he announced that he could put it off no longer, but must break the news to the young widow. My sympathy had already gone out to her unreservedly. To be left penniless, and with the knowledge that her husband had killed himself to assure her future was a hard burden for any woman to bear. I cherished a secret hope, however, that young Black might prove capable of consoling her after her first grief had passed. He evidently admired her enormously.

Our interview with the lady was painful. She refused vehemently to believe the facts that Poirot advanced, and when she was at last convinced broke down into bitter weeping. An examination of the body turned our suspicions into certainty. Poirot was very sorry for the poor lady, but, after all, he was employed by the insurance company, and what could he do? As he was preparing to leave he said gently to Mrs. Maltravers:

"Madame, you of all people should know that there are no dead!"

"What do you mean?" she faltered, her eyes growing wide.

"Have you never taken part in any spiritualistic séances? You are mediumistic, you know."

"I have been told so. But you do not believe in Spiritualism, surely?"

"Madame, I have seen some strange things. You know that they say in the village that this house is haunted?"

She nodded, and at that moment the parlormaid announced that dinner was ready.

"Won't you just stay and have something to eat?"

We accepted gratefully, and I felt that our presence could not but help distract her a little from her own griefs.

We had just finished our soup, when there was a scream outside the door, and the sound of breaking crockery. We jumped up. The parlormaid appeared, her hand to her heart.

"It was a man—standing in the passage."

Poirot rushed out, returning quickly.

"There is no one there."

"Isn't there, sir?" said the parlormaid weakly. "Oh, it did give me a start!"

"But why?"

She dropped her voice to a whisper.

"I thought—I thought it was the master—it looked like 'im."

I saw Mrs. Maltravers give a terrified start, and my mind flew to the old superstition that a suicide cannot rest. She thought of it too, I am sure, for a minute later, she caught Poirot's arm with a scream.

"Didn't you hear that? Those three taps on the window? That's how *he* always used to tap when he passed round the house."

"The ivy," I cried. "It was the ivy against the pane."

But a sort of terror was gaining on us all. The parlormaid was obviously unstrung, and when the meal was over Mrs. Maltravers besought Poirot not to go at once. She was clearly terrified to be left alone. We sat in the little morning room. The wind was getting up, and moaning round the house in an eerie fashion. Twice the door of the room came unlatched and the door slowly opened, and each time she clung to me with a terrified gasp.

"Ah, but this door, it is bewitched!" cried Poirot angrily at last. He got up and shut it once more, then turned the key in the lock. "I shall lock it, so!"

"Don't do that," she gasped, "if it should come open now—"

And even as she spoke the impossible happened. The locked door slowly swung open. I could not see into the passage from where I sat, but she and Poirot were facing it. She gave one long shriek as she turned to him.

"You saw him—there in the passage?" she cried.

He was staring down at her with a puzzled face, then shook his head.

"I saw him—my husband—you must have seen him too?"

"Madame, I saw nothing. You are not well—unstrung—"

"I am perfectly well, I—Oh, God!"

Suddenly, without any warning, the lights quivered and went out. Out of the darkness came three loud raps. I could hear Mrs. Maltravers moaning.

And then—I saw!

The man I had seen on the bed upstairs stood there facing us, gleaming with a faint ghostly light. There was blood on his lips, and he held his right hand out, pointing. Suddenly a brilliant light seemed to proceed from it. It passed over Poirot and me, and fell on Mrs. Maltravers. I saw her white terrified face, and something else!

"My God, Poirot!" I cried. "Look at her hand, her right hand. It's all red!"

Her own eyes fell on it, and she collapsed in a heap on the floor.

[*Again, let's stop the story for a moment. Poirot is on to something, but what? Does he disbelieve the suicide story? Is there an attempt to defraud the insurance company? What is the truth? Consider these clues:*

1. *the manner of Maltravers' death*
2. *the insurance policy taken out shortly before his death*
3. *the problem of the suicide clause in the policy*
4. *the word association test, with **rook rifle** associated with **farm**, and **shot** with **suicide***

5. *the fact that Maltravers was a Christian Scientist*
6. *Mrs. Maltravers' appearance and behavior*
7. *the terror at the ghostlike figure and the tapping*

Now go on with the story and the surprising conclusion.]

"Blood," she cried hysterically. "Yes, it's blood. I killed him. I did it. He was showing me, and then I put my hand on the trigger and pressed. Save me from him—save me! he's come back!"

Her voice died away in a gurgle.

"Lights," said Poirot briskly.

The lights went on as if by magic.

"That's it," he continued. "You heard, Hastings? And you, Everett? Oh, by the way, this is Mr. Everett, rather a fine member of the theatrical profession. I phoned to him this afternoon. His makeup is good, isn't it? Quite like the dead man, and with a pocket torch and the necessary phosphorescence he made the proper impression. I shouldn't touch her right hand if I were you, Hastings. Red paint marks so. When the lights went out I clasped her hand, you see. By the way, we mustn't miss our train. Inspector Japp is outside the window. A bad night—but he has been able to while away the time by tapping on the window every now and then."

"You see," continued Poirot, as we walked briskly through the wind and rain, "there was a little discrepancy. The doctor seemed to think the deceased was a Christian Scientist, and who could have given him that impression but Mrs. Maltravers? But to us she represented him as being in a grave state of apprehension about his own health. Again, why was she so taken aback by the reappearance of young Black? And lastly, although I know that convention decrees that a woman must make a decent pretense of mourning for her husband, I do not care for such heavily rouged eyelids! You did not observe them, Hastings? No? As I always tell you, you see nothing!

"Well, there it was. There were the two possibilities. Did Black's story suggest an ingenious method of committing suicide to Mr. Maltravers, or did his other listener, the wife, see an equally ingenious method of committing murder? I inclined to the latter view. To shoot himself in the way indicated, he would probably have had to pull the trigger with his toe—or at least so I imagine. Now if Maltravers had been found with one boot off, we should almost certainly have heard of it from someone. An odd detail like that would have been remembered.

"No, as I say, I inclined to the view that it was a case of murder, not suicide, but I realized that I had not a shadow of proof in support of my theory. Hence the elaborate little comedy you saw played tonight."

"Even now I don't quite see all the details of the crime," I said.

"Let us start from the beginning. Here is a shrewd and scheming woman who, knowing of her husband's financial *débâcle* and tired of the elderly mate she has only married for his money, induces him to insure his life for a large sum, and then seeks for the means to accomplish her purpose. An accident gives her that—the young soldier's strange story. The next afternoon when *monsieur le capitaine*, as she thinks, is on the high seas, she and her husband are strolling round the grounds. 'What a curious story that was last night!' she observes. 'Could a man shoot himself in such a way? Do show me if it is possible! ' The poor fool—he shows her. He places the end of the rifle in his mouth. She stoops down, and puts her finger on the trigger, laughing up at him. 'And now, sir,' she says saucily, 'supposing I pull the trigger? '

"And then—and then, Hastings—she pulls it!"

Understanding the Story ————

Main Idea

1. In solving the crime, Hercule Poirot   (a) was momentarily confused   (b) needed his friend Hastings to provide the crucial clue   (c) looked beyond obvious explanations   (d) used an actor to break the case.

Details

2. The name of the attending doctor was   (a) Black (b) Hastings   (c) Everett   (d) Bernard.

3. Black had been in   (a) East Africa   (b) America (c) Australia   (d) Japan.

4. When Mrs. Maltravers saw Captain Black, she was (a) jubilant   (b) upset   (c) indifferent   (d) unfriendly.

5. Black had not taken the ship back because   (a) he had inherited some money   (b) he liked Maltravers too much (c) Poirot asked him to return to Marsdon Manor   (d) his leave had been extended.

Inferences

6. The writer of the story is not surprised when Poirot's missing stick was not discovered because   (a) the writer himself had it   (b) Mrs. Maltravers had hidden it   (c) Poirot didn't have one with him   (d) Black had destroyed it in a fit of anger.

7. The "black-robed figure on the terrace" was   (a) the gardener   (b) Mrs. Maltravers   (c) the ghost of Mr. Maltravers (d) the Inspector.

8. The doctor's attitude toward Poirot can best be described as (a) too pleasant   (b) annoyed   (c) extremely friendly but confused   (d) viciously abrupt.

9. Dr. Bernard found no bullet wounds on the body because the victim   (a) had been poisoned   (b) died of heart failure (c) had been shot through the mouth   (d) died of natural causes.

10. Of Captain Black it may be said he   (a) was a conspirator (b) had been led on by Mrs. Maltravers   (c) tried to confuse Poirot   (d) was an innocent contributor to the crime.

Order of Events

11. Arrange the items in the order in which they occurred. Use letters only.
    A. Poirot gives Black a word-association test.
    B. Poirot interviews Dr. Bernard.
    C. Mrs. Maltravers confesses.
    D. Poirot explains the crime.
    E. Poirot is hired by an insurance company.

Outcomes

12. If Black had not told Mr. and Mrs. Maltravers the story of a suicide,   (a) Maltravers may not have been murdered   (b) Poirot would have solved the case anyway   (c) the actor would have been introduced to Maltravers   (d) Poirot would have gone back to London angry.

Cause and Effect

13. The ghostly vision led to   (a) Everett's arrest   (b) the exposure of Maltravers' suicide   (c) the breakdown of Mrs. Maltravers   (d) Poirot's losing his temper.

Fact or Opinion

Tell whether each of the following is a fact or an opinion.

14. Poirot's methods may be considered at times to be unfair.

15. Captain Black had visited the Maltravers home.

Words in Context _____

1. "If the cause of the death had been heart failure, I should have been more *sanguine*."
   Sanguine (58) means   (a) alert   (b) hopeful   (c) angry   (d) concerned.

2. The doctor became quite *apoplectic*.
   Apoplectic (59) means   (a) apologetic   (b) quiet   (c) enraged   (d) interested.

3. "I cannot tell you how much I regret to *derange* you in this way."
   Derange (60) means   (a) disturb   (b) inform   (c) prevent   (d) compromise.

4. I *essayed* one or two general reflections to which she responded absently.
   Essayed (61) means   (a) deplored   (b) reported
   (c) repeated   (d) attempted.

5. I tried to *dispel* these gloomy fears of his.
   Dispel (61) means   (a) drive away   (b) talk about
   (c) repeat sadly   (d) imagine.

6. "Still, life is full of *discrepancies,* and assuredly the man cannot have taken his own life."
   Discrepancies (61) means   (a) disappointments   (b) happy moments   (c) differences   (d) unexpected events.

7. Our *quarry* swerved and we after him, so that we were witnesses of the meeting.
   Quarry (62) means   (a) mine   (b) prey   (c) leader
   (d) angry person.

8. A few minutes' chat *ensued.*
   Ensued (62) means   (a) erupted   (b) followed   (c) was confusing   (d) made a noise.

9. Poirot *elicited* the fact that Captain Black was putting up at the Anchor Inn.
   Elicited (62) means   (a) drew forth   (b) slyly concealed
   (c) broadcast   (d) was upset by.

10. In about half an hour we *espied* our quarry approaching the inn.
    Espied (63) means   (a) aroused   (b) tried to find
    (c) caught sight of   (d) transported.

11. Poirot went out and *accosted* him.
    Accosted (63) means   (a) stopped and spoke to   (b) saw but overlooked   (c) cleverly avoided   (d) struck and subdued.

12. She refused *vehemently* to believe the facts that Poirot advanced.
    Vehemently (65) means   (a) wickedly   (b) sorrowfully
    (c) constantly   (d) heatedly.

13. The wind was getting up, and moaning round the house in an *eerie* fashion.
    Eerie (66) means   (a) funny   (b) exciting   (c) tiresome
    (d) scary.

14. "Here is a shrewd and scheming woman who, knowing of her husband's financial *débâcle* and tired of the elderly mate she

has only married for his money, induces him to insure his life for a large sum."
Débâcle (69)   means   (a) achievement   (b) disaster (c) enterprise   (d) corruption.

15.   "And now, sir," she says *saucily*, "supposing I pull the trigger."
Saucily (69)   means   (a) mischievously   (b) crudely (c) uncertainly   (d) proudly.

Thinking About the Story _____

1.   Why were Maltravers' boots important to the solution of the story? Since nobody had mentioned the boots, why does Poirot bring them up at all? (This is an easy point to miss. Reread page 68.)

2.   There are laws against the entrapment of suspects. Did Poirot exceed his rights in staging the ghost scene? Do you think it was fair of him to do so? Explain.

3.   Compare the personality of Poirot with the personalities of Sherlock Holmes and Father Brown. Which seems to you the most interesting detective? Which seems most likable?

4.   Sherlock Holmes has his Dr. Watson to tell his stories. Hercule Poirot has his Captain Hastings. Both narrators tell their stories in the first person, with a personal point of view. What advantages are gained by using the first person?

5.   Look again at the list of clues on pages 67–68. Explain how each one helped Poirot to bring the guilty person to justice.

6.   There is an honest-to-goodness mystery in the life of Agatha Christie herself. In December 1926 she vanished from her home without warning. Her car was discovered, abandoned, and a nationwide search for her began. When she was discovered days later at a health resort, she had registered under the name of the woman who later became her husband's second wife. She claimed she remembered nothing of the past days. To this day, no one has ever explained the disappearance. She was accused of staging a publicity stunt since the notoriety brought her to the world's notice, but many experts disagree. At any rate, you may find one of the many books about her as fascinating as a detective story.

The Problem of Cell 13

Jacques Futrelle

♦ "Nothing is impossible," declared The Thinking Machine. "The mind is master of all things. When science fully recognizes that fact, a great advance will have been made."

The "locked room" is a standard set for a great many crime stories. "The Problem of Cell 13" is a crime story with a difference. True, there is a locked room, a maximum-security prison cell from which no one could escape. Or so it was thought. This time, however, there is no crime.

Suppose you had made the rash statement quoted above and your friends took you up on it. Then suppose that, as part of a wager, they placed you in a bare prison cell and challenged you to make your brain get you out of there in a week—if it could! That is just the situation that Professor Van Dusen, nicknamed "The Thinking Machine," found himself in. Yet, by using his brain, he escaped with ease. How did he do it? Read the story to find out.

If you like puzzles, suspense, and surprises, and if you like to match wits with a brilliant detective of fiction, you'll enjoy "The Problem of Cell 13" by Jacques Futrelle. Keep your eyes open. All the clues are presented. Can you outguess the warden? Step up and meet that astounding character, Professor Augustus S.F.X. Van Dusen, Ph.D., LL.D., F.R.S., M.D., M.D.S., etc., better known as "The Thinking Machine."

There is a sad postscript to the story, a bitter irony. The author, Jacques Futrelle, through his main character, declared that nothing is impossible for the brain, that no prison cell can hold a person who keeps his or her thinking processes working. On the night of April 14–15, 1912, Jacques Futrelle went to his death on the luxury steamship *Titanic,* which had been struck by an iceberg.

THE PROBLEM OF CELL 13

Practically all those letters remaining in the alphabet after Augustus S. F. X. Van Dusen was named were afterward acquired by that gentleman in the course of a brilliant scientific career, and, being honorably acquired, were tacked on to the other end. His name, therefore, taken with all that belonged to it, was a wonderfully imposing structure. He was a Ph.D., an LL.D., an F.R.S., an M.D., and an M.D.S. He was also some other things—just what he himself couldn't say—through recognition of his ability by various foreign educational and scientific institutions.

In appearance he was no less striking than in nomenclature. He was slender with the droop of the student in his thin shoulders and the pallor of a close, sedentary life on his clean-shaven face. His eyes wore a perpetual, forbidding squint—of a man who studies little things—and when they could be seen at all through his thick spectacles, were mere slits of watery blue. But above his eyes was his most striking feature. This was a tall, broad brow, almost abnormal in height and width, crowned by a heavy shock of bushy, yellow hair. All these things conspired to give him a peculiar, almost grotesque, personality.

Professor Van Dusen was remotely German. For generations his ancestors had been noted in the sciences; he was the logical result, the master mind. First and above all he was a logician. At least thirty-five years of the half-century or so of his existence had been devoted exclusively to proving that two and two always equal four, except in unusual cases, where they equal three or five, as the case may be. He stood broadly on the general proposition that all things that start must go somewhere, and was able to bring the concentrated mental force of his forefathers to bear on a given problem.

75

Incidentally it may be remarked that Professor Van Dusen wore a No. 8 hat.

The world at large had heard vaguely of Professor Van Dusen as The Thinking Machine. It was a newspaper catch-phrase applied to him at the time of a remarkable exhibition at chess; he had demonstrated then that a stranger to the game might, by the force of inevitable logic, defeat a champion who had devoted a lifetime to its study. The Thinking Machine! Perhaps that more nearly described him than all his honorary initials, for he spent week after week, month after month, in the seclusion of his small laboratory from which had gone forth thoughts that staggered scientific associates and deeply stirred the world at large.

It was only occasionally that The Thinking Machine had visitors, and these were usually men who, themselves high in the sciences, dropped in to argue a point and perhaps convince themselves. Two of these men, Dr. Charles Ransome and Alfred Fielding, called one evening to discuss some theory which is not of consequence here.

"Such a thing is impossible," declared Dr. Ransome emphatically, in the course of the conversation.

"Nothing is impossible," declared The Thinking Machine with equal emphasis. He always spoke petulantly. "The mind is master of all things. When science fully recognizes that fact a great advance will have been made."

"How about the spaceship?" asked Dr. Ransome.

"That's not impossible at all," asserted The Thinking Machine. "It will be invented some time. I'd do it myself, but I'm busy."

Dr. Ransome laughed tolerantly.

"I've heard you say such things before," he said. "But they mean nothing. Mind may be master of matter, but it hasn't yet found a way to apply itself. There are some things that can't be *thought* out of existence, or rather which would not yield to any amount of thinking."

"What, for instance?" demanded The Thinking Machine.

Dr. Ransome was thoughtful for a moment as he smoked. "Well, say prison walls," he replied. "No man can *think* himself out of a cell. If he could, there would be no prisoners."

"A man can so apply his brain and ingenuity that he can leave a cell, which is the same thing," snapped The Thinking Machine.

Dr. Ransome was slightly amused.

"Let's suppose a case," he said, after a moment. "Take a cell where prisoners under sentence of death are confined—men who are desperate and, maddened by fear, would take any chance to escape—suppose you were locked in such a cell. Could you escape?"

"Certainly," declared The Thinking Machine.

"Of course," said Mr. Fielding, who entered the conversation for the first time, "you might wreck the cell with an explosive—but inside, a prisoner, you couldn't have that."

"There would be nothing of that kind," said The Thinking Machine. "You might treat me precisely as you treated prisoners under sentence of death, and I would leave the cell."

"Not unless you entered it with tools prepared to get out," said Dr. Ransome.

The Thinking Machine was visibly annoyed and his blue eyes snapped.

"Lock me in any cell in any prison anywhere at any time, wearing only what is necessary, and I'll escape in a week," he declared, sharply.

Dr. Ransome sat up straight in the chair, interested. Mr. Fielding lighted a new cigar.

"You mean you could actually *think* yourself out?" asked Dr. Ransome.

"I would get out," was the response.

"Are you serious?"

"Certainly I am serious."

Dr. Ransome and Mr. Fielding were silent for a long time.

"Would you be willing to try it?" asked Mr. Fielding, finally.

"Certainly," said Professor Van Dusen, and there was a trace of irony in his voice. "I have done more asinine things than that to convince other men of less important truths."

The tone was offensive and there was an undercurrent strongly resembling anger on both sides. Of course it was an absurd thing, but Professor Van Dusen reiterated his willingness to undertake the escape and it was decided upon.

"To begin now," added Dr. Ransome.

"I'd prefer that it begin tomorrow," said The Thinking Machine, "because—"

"No, now," said Mr. Fielding, flatly. "You are arrested, figuratively, of course, without any warning locked in a cell with no chance to communicate with friends, and left there with identically the same care and attention that would be given to a man under sentence of death. Are you willing?"

"All right, now, then," said The Thinking Machine, and he arose.

"Say, the death-cell in Chisholm Prison."

"The death-cell in Chisholm Prison."

"And what will you wear?"

"As little as possible," said The Thinking Machine. "Shoes, stockings, trousers and a shirt."

"You will permit yourself to be searched, of course?"

"I am to be treated precisely as all prisoners are treated," said The Thinking Machine. "No more attention and no less."

There were some preliminaries to be arranged in the matter of obtaining permission for the test, but all three were influential men and everything was done satisfactorily by telephone, albeit the prison commissioners, to whom the experiment was explained on purely scientific grounds, were sadly bewildered. Professor Van Dusen would be the most distinguished prisoner they had ever entertained.

When The Thinking Machine had donned those things which he was to wear during his incarceration he called the little old woman who was his housekeeper, cook, and maidservant all in one.

"Martha," he said, "it is now twenty-seven minutes past nine o'clock. I am going away. One week from tonight, at half past nine, these gentlemen and one, possibly two, others will take supper with me here. Remember Dr. Ransome is very fond of artichokes."

The three men were driven to Chisholm Prison, where the warden was awaiting them, having been informed of the matter by telephone. He understood merely that the eminent Professor Van Dusen was to be his prisoner, if he could keep him, for one week; that he had committed no crime, but that he was to be treated as all other prisoners were treated.

"Search him," instructed Dr. Ransome.

The Thinking Machine was searched. Nothing was found on him; the pockets of the trousers were empty; the white, stiff-bosomed shirt had no pocket. The shoes and stockings were removed, examined, then replaced. As he watched all these preliminaries— the rigid search and noted the pitiful, childlike physical weakness of the man, the colorless face, and the thin, white hands—Dr. Ransome almost regretted his part in the affair.

"Are you sure you want to do this?" he asked.

"Would you be convinced if I did not?" inquired The Thinking Machine in turn.

"No."

"All right. I'll do it."

What sympathy Dr. Ransome had was dissipated by the tone. It nettled him, and he resolved to see the experiment to the end; it would be a stinging reproof to egotism.

"It will be impossible for him to communicate with anyone outside?" he asked.

"Absolutely impossible," replied the warden. "He will not be permitted writing materials of any sort."

"And your jailers, would they deliver a message from him?"

"Not one word, directly or indirectly," said the warden. "You may rest assured of that. They will report anything he might say or turn over to me anything he might give them."

"That seems entirely satisfactory," said Mr. Fielding, who was frankly interested in the problem.

"Of course, in the event he fails," said Dr. Ransome, "and asks for his liberty, you understand you are to set him free?"

"I understand," replied the warden.

The Thinking Machine stood listening, but had nothing to say until this was all ended, then:

"I should like to make three small requests. You may grant them or not, as you wish."

"No special favors, now," warned Mr. Fielding.

"I am asking none," was the stiff response. "I would like to have some tooth powder—buy it yourself to see that it is tooth powder— and I should like to have one five-dollar and two ten-dollar bills."

Dr. Ransome, Mr. Fielding and the warden exchanged astonished glances. They were not surprised at the request for tooth powder, but were at the request for money.

"Is there any man with whom our friend would come in contact that he could bribe with twenty-five dollars?" asked Dr. Ransome of the warden.

"Not for twenty-five hundred dollars," was the positive reply.

"Well, let him have them," said Mr. Fielding. "I think they are harmless enough."

"And what is the third request?" asked Dr. Ransome.

"I should like to have my shoes polished."

Again the astonished glances were exchanged. This last request was the height of absurdity, so they agreed to it. These things all being attended to, The Thinking Machine was led back into the prison from which he had undertaken to escape.

"Here is Cell 13," said the warden, stopping three doors down the steel corridor. "This is where we keep condemned murderers. No one can leave it without my permission; and no one in it can communicate with the outside. I'll stake my reputation on that. It's only three doors back of my office and I can readily hear any unusual noise."

"Will this cell do, gentlemen?" asked The Thinking Machine. There was a touch of irony in his voice.

"Admirably," was the reply.

The heavy steel door was thrown open, there was a great scurrying and scampering of tiny feet, and The Thinking Machine passed into the gloom of the cell. Then the door was closed and double locked by the warden.

"What is that noise in there?" asked Dr. Ransome, through the bars.

"Rats—dozens of them," replied The Thinking Machine, tersely.

The three men, with final good nights, were turning away when The Thinking Machine called:

"What time is it exactly, warden?"

"Eleven seventeen," replied the warden.

"Thanks. I will join you gentlemen in your office at half past eight o'clock one week from tonight," said The Thinking Machine.

"And if you do not?"

"There is no 'if' about it."

Chisholm Prison was a great, spreading structure of granite, four stories in all, which stood in the center of acres of open space. It was surrounded by a wall of solid masonry eighteen feet high, and so smoothly finished inside and out as to offer no foothold to a climber, no matter how expert. Atop of this fence, as a further precaution, was a five-foot fence of steel rods, each terminating in a keen point. This fence in itself marked an absolute deadline between freedom and imprisonment, for, even if a man escaped from his cell, it would seem impossible for him to pass the wall.

The yard, which on all sides of the prison building was twenty-five feet wide, that being the distance from the building to the wall, was by day an exercise ground for those prisoners to whom was granted the boon of occasional semi-liberty. But that was not for those in Cell 13.

At all times of the day there were armed guards in the yard, four of them, one patrolling each side of the prison building.

By night the yard was almost as brilliantly lighted as by day. On each of the four sides was a great arc light which rose above the prison wall and gave to the guards a clear sight. The lights, too, brightly illuminated the spiked top of the wall. The wires which fed the arc lights ran up the side of the prison building on insulators and from the top story led out to the poles supporting the arc lights.

All these things were seen and comprehended by The Thinking Machine, who was only enabled to see out his closely barred cell window by standing on his bed. This was on the morning following his incarceration. He gathered, too, that the river lay over there beyond the wall somewhere, because he heard faintly the pulsation of a motorboat and high up in the air saw a river bird. From that same direction came the shouts of boys at play and the occasional crack of a batted ball. He knew then that between the prison wall and the river was an open space, a playground.

Chisholm Prison was regarded as absolutely safe. No man had ever escaped from it. The Thinking Machine, from his perch on the bed, seeing what he saw, could readily understand why. The walls of the cell, though built he judged twenty years before, were perfectly solid, and the window bars of new iron had not a shadow of rust on them. The window itself, even with the bars out, would be a difficult mode of egress because it was small.

Yet, seeing these things, The Thinking Machine was not discouraged. Instead, he thoughtfully squinted at the great arc light—there was bright sunlight now—and traced with his eyes the wire which led from it to the building. That electric wire, he reasoned, must come down the side of the building not a great distance from his cell. That might be worth knowing.

Cell 13 was on the same floor with the offices of the prison—that is, not in the basement, nor yet upstairs. There were only four steps up to the office floor, therefore the level of the floor must be only three or four feet above the ground. He couldn't see the ground directly beneath his window, but he could see it further out toward the wall. It would be an easy drop from the window. Well and good.

Then The Thinking Machine fell to remembering how he had come to the cell. First, there was the outside guard's booth, a part of the wall. There were two heavily barred gates there, both of steel. At this gate was one man always on guard. He admitted persons to the prison after much clanking of keys and locks, and let them out when ordered to do so. The warden's office was in the prison building, and in order to reach that official from the prison yard one had to pass a gate of solid steel with only a peephole in it. Then coming from that inner office to Cell 13, where he was now, one must pass a heavy wooden door and two steel doors into the corridors of the prison; and always there was the double-locked door to Cell 13 to reckon with.

There were then, The Thinking Machine recalled, seven doors to be overcome before one could pass from Cell 13 into the outer world, a free man. But against this was the fact that he was rarely interrupted. A jailer appeared at his cell door at six in the morning with a breakfast of prison fare; he would come again at noon, and again at six in the afternoon. At nine o'clock at night would come the inspection tour. That would be all.

"It's admirably arranged, this prison system," was the mental tribute paid by The Thinking Machine. "I'll have to study it a little when I get out. I had no idea there was such great care exercised in the prisons."

There was nothing, positively nothing, in his cell, except his iron bed, so firmly put together that no man could tear it to pieces save with sledges or a file. He had neither of these. There was not even a chair, or a small table, or a bit of tin or crockery. Nothing! The jailer stood by when he ate, then took away the wooden spoon and bowl which he had used.

One by one these things sank into the brain of The Thinking Machine. When the last possibility had been considered he began an examination of his cell. From the roof, down the walls on all sides, he examined the stones and the cement between them. He stamped over the floor carefully time after time, but it was cement, perfectly solid. After the examination he sat on the edge of the iron bed and was lost in thought for a long time. For Professor Augustus S. F. X. Van Dusen, The Thinking Machine, had something to think about.

He was disturbed by a rat, which ran across his foot, then scampered away into a dark corner of the cell, frightened at its own daring. After a while The Thinking Machine, squinting steadily into the darkness of the corner where the rat had gone, was able to make out in the gloom many little beady eyes staring at him. He counted six pair, and there were perhaps others; he didn't see very well.

Then The Thinking Machine, from his seat on the bed, noticed for the first time the bottom of his cell door. There was an opening there of two inches between the steel bar and the floor. Still looking steadily at this opening, The Thinking Machine backed suddenly into the corner where he had seen the beady eyes. There was a great scampering of tiny feet, several squeaks of frightened rodents, and then silence.

None of the rats had gone out the door, yet there were none in the cell. Therefore there must be another way out of the cell, however small. The Thinking Machine, on hands and knees, started a search for this spot, feeling in the darkness with his long, slender fingers.

At last his search was rewarded. He came upon a small opening in the floor, level with the cement. It was perfectly round and somewhat larger than a silver dollar. This was the way the rats had gone. He put his fingers deep into the opening; it seemed to be a disused drainage pipe and was dry and dusty.

Having satisfied himself on this point, he sat on the bed again for an hour, then made another inspection of his surroundings through the small cell window. One of the outside guards stood directly opposite, beside the wall, and happened to be looking at the window of Cell 13 when the head of The Thinking Machine appeared. But the scientist didn't notice the guard.

Noon came and the jailer appeared with the prison dinner of repulsively plain food. At home The Thinking Machine merely ate to live; here he took what was offered without comment. Occasionally he spoke to the jailer who stood outside the door watching him.

"Any improvements made here in the last few years?" he asked.

"Nothing particularly," replied the jailer. "New wall was built four years ago."

"Anything done to the prison proper?"

"Painted the woodwork outside, and I believe about seven years ago a new system of plumbing was put in."

"Ah!" said the prisoner. "How far is the river over there?"

"About three hundred feet. The boys have a baseball ground between the wall and the river."

The Thinking Machine had nothing further to say just then, but when the jailer was ready to go he asked for some water.

"I get very thirsty here," he explained. "Would it be possible for you to leave a little water in a bowl for me?"

"I'll ask the warden," replied the jailer, and he went away.

Half an hour later he returned with water in a small earthen bowl.

"The warden says you may keep this bowl," he informed the prisoner. "But you must show it to me when I ask for it. If it is broken, it will be the last."

"Thank you," said The Thinking Machine. "I shan't break it."

The jailer went on about his duties. For just the fraction of a second it seemed that The Thinking Machine wanted to ask a question, but he didn't.

Two hours later this same jailer, in passing the door of Cell No. 13, heard a noise inside and stopped. The Thinking Machine was down on his hands and knees in a corner of the cell, and from that same corner came several frightened squeaks. The jailer looked on interestedly.

"Ah, I've got you," he heard the prisoner say.

"Got what?" he asked, sharply.

"One of these rats," was the reply. "See?" And between the scientist's long fingers the jailer saw a small gray rat struggling. The prisoner brought it over to the light and looked at it closely. "It's a water rat," he said.

"Ain't you got anything better to do than to catch rats?" asked the jailer.

"It's disgraceful that they should be here at all," was the irritated reply. "Take this one away and kill it. There are dozens more where it came from."

The jailer took the wriggling, squirmy rodent and flung it down on the floor violently. It gave one squeak and lay still. Later he reported the incident to the warden, who only smiled.

Still later that afternoon the outside armed guard on Cell 13 side of the prison looked up again at the window and saw the prisoner looking out. He saw a hand raised to the barred window and then something white fluttered to the ground, directly under the window of Cell 13. It was a little roll of linen, evidently of white shirting material, and tied around it was a five-dollar bill. The guard looked up at the window again, but the face had disappeared.

With a grim smile he took the little linen roll and the five-dollar bill to the warden's office. There together they deciphered something which was written on it with a queer sort of ink, frequently blurred. On the outside was this:

"Finder of this please deliver to Dr. Charles Ransome."

"Ah," said the warden, with a chuckle. "Plan of escape number one has gone wrong." Then, as an afterthought: "But why did he address it to Dr. Ransome?"

"And where did he get the pen and ink to write with?" asked the guard.

The warden looked at the guard and the guard looked at the warden. There was no apparent solution of that mystery. The warden studied the writing carefully, then shook his head.

"Well, let's see what he was going to say to Dr. Ransome," he said at length, still puzzled, and he unrolled the inner piece of linen.

"Well, if that—what—what do you think of that?" he asked, dazed.

The guard took the bit of linen and read this:

"Epa cseot d'net niiy awe htto n'si sih. "T."

The warden spent an hour wondering what sort of cipher it was, and half an hour wondering why his prisoner should attempt to communicate with Dr. Ransome, who was the cause of his being there. After this the warden devoted some thought to the question of where the prisoner got writing materials, and what sort of writing materials he had. With the idea of illuminating this point, he examined the linen again. It was a torn part of a white shirt and had ragged edges.

Now it was possible to account for the linen, but what the prisoner had used to write with was another matter. The warden knew it would have been impossible for him to have either pen or pencil, and, besides, neither pen nor pencil had been used in this writing. What, then? The warden decided to personally investigate. The Thinking Machine was his prisoner; he had orders to hold his prisoners; if this one sought to escape by sending cipher messages to persons outside, he would stop it, as he would have stopped it in the case of any other prisoner.

The warden went back to Cell 13 and found The Thinking Machine on his hands and knees on the floor, engaged in nothing more alarming than catching rats. The prisoner heard the warden's step and turned to him quickly.

"It's disgraceful," he snapped, "these rats. There are scores of them."

"Other men have been able to stand them," said the warden. "Here is another shirt for you—let me have the one you have on."

"Why?" demanded The Thinking Machine, quickly. His tone was hardly natural, his manner suggested actual perturbation.

"You have attempted to communicate with Dr. Ransome," said the warden severely. "As my prisoner, it is my duty to put a stop to it."

The Thinking Machine was silent for a moment.

"All right," he said, finally. "Do your duty."

The warden smiled grimly. The prisoner arose from the floor and removed the white shirt, putting on instead a striped convict shirt the warden had brought. The warden took the white shirt eagerly, and then and there compared the pieces of linen on which was written the cipher with certain torn places in the shirt. The Thinking Machine looked on curiously.

"The guard brought *you* those, then?" he asked.

"He certainly did," replied the warden triumphantly. "And that ends your first attempt to escape."

The Thinking Machine watched the warden as he, by comparison, established to his own satisfaction that only two pieces of linen had been torn from the white shirt.

"What did you write this with?" demanded the warden.

"I should think it a part of your duty to find out," said The Thinking Machine, irritably.

The warden started to say some harsh things, then restrained himself and made a minute search of the cell and of the prisoner instead. He found absolutely nothing; not even a match or toothpick which might have been used for a pen. The same mystery surrounded the fluid with which the cipher had been written. Although the warden left Cell 13 visibly annoyed, he took the torn shirt in triumph.

"Well, writing notes on a shirt won't get him out, that's certain," he told himself with some complacency. He put the linen scraps into his desk to await developments. "If that man escapes from that cell I'll—hang it—I'll resign."

On the third day of his incarceration The Thinking Machine openly attempted to bribe his way out. The jailer had brought his dinner and was leaning against the barred door, waiting, when The Thinking Machine began the conversation.

"The drainage pipes of the prison lead to the river, don't they?" he asked.

"Yes," said the jailer.

"I suppose they are very small?"

"Too small to crawl through, if that's what you're thinking about," was the grinning response.

There was silence until The Thinking Machine finished his meal. Then:

"You know I'm not a criminal, don't you?"

"Yes."

"And that I've a perfect right to be freed if I demand it?"

"Yes."

"Well, I came here believing that I could make my escape," said the prisoner, and his squint eyes studied the face of the jailer. "Would you consider a financial reward for aiding me to escape?"

The jailer, who happened to be an honest man, looked at the slender, weak figure of the prisoner, at the large head with its mass of yellow hair, and was almost sorry.

"I guess prisons like these were not built for the likes of you to get out of," he said, at last.

"But would you consider a proposition to help me get out?" the prisoner insisted, almost beseechingly.

"No," said the jailer, shortly.

"Five hundred dollars," urged The Thinking Machine. "I am not a criminal."

"No," said the jailer.

"A thousand?"

"No," again said the jailer, and he started away hurriedly to escape further temptation. Then he turned back. "If you should give me ten thousand dollars I couldn't get you out. You'd have to pass through seven doors, and I only have the keys to two."

Then he told the warden all about it.

"Plan number two fails," said the warden, smiling grimly. "First a cipher, then bribery."

When the jailer was on his way to Cell 13 at six o'clock, again bearing food to The Thinking Machine, he paused, startled by the unmistakable scrape, scrape of steel against steel. It stopped at the sound of his steps, then craftily the jailer, who was beyond the prisoner's range of vision, resumed his tramping, the sound being apparently that of a man going away from Cell 13. As a matter of fact he was in the same spot.

After a moment there came again the steady scrape, scrape, and the jailer crept cautiously on tiptoes to the door and peered between the bars. The Thinking Machine was standing on the iron bed working at the bars of the little window. He was using a file, judging from the backward and forward swing of his arms.

Cautiously the jailer crept back to the office, summoned the warden in person, and they returned to Cell 13 on tiptoes. The steady scrape was still audible. The warden listened to satisfy himself and then suddenly appeared at the door.

"Well?" he demanded, and there was a smile on his face.

The Thinking Machine glanced back from his perch on the bed and leaped suddenly to the floor, making frantic efforts to hide something. The warden went in, with hand extended.

"Give it up," he said.

"No," said the prisoner, sharply.

"Come, give it up," urged the warden. "I don't want to have to search you again."

"No," repeated the prisoner.

"What was it, a file?" asked the warden.

The Thinking Machine was silent and stood squinting at the warden with something very nearly approaching disappointment on his face—nearly, but not quite. The warden was almost sympathetic.

"Plan number three fails, eh?" he asked, good-naturedly. "Too bad, isn't it?"

The prisoner didn't say.

"Search him," instructed the warden.

The jailer searched the prisoner carefully. At last, artfully concealed in the waistband of the trousers, he found a piece of steel about two inches long, with one side curved like a half moon.

"Ah," said the warden, as he received it from the jailer. "From your shoe heel," and he smiled pleasantly.

The jailer continued his search and found, on the other side of the trousers waistband, another piece of steel identical with the first. The edges showed where they had been worn against the bars of the window.

"You couldn't saw a way through those bars with these," said the warden.

"I could have," said The Thinking Machine firmly.

"In six months, perhaps," said the warden, good-naturedly.

The warden shook his head slowly as he gazed into the slightly flushed face of his prisoner.

"Ready to give it up?" he asked.

"I haven't started yet," was the prompt reply.

Then came another exhaustive search of the cell. Carefully the two men went over it, finally turning out the bed and searching that. Nothing. The warden in person climbed upon the bed and examined the bars of the window where the prisoner had been sawing. When he looked he was amused.

"Just made it a little bright by hard rubbing," he said to the prisoner, who stood looking on with a somewhat crestfallen air. The warden grasped the iron bars in his strong hands and tried to shake them. They were immovable, set firmly in the solid granite. He examined each in turn and found them all satisfactory. Finally he climbed down from the bed.

"Give it up, professor," he advised.

The Thinking Machine shook his head and the warden and jailer passed on again. As they disappeared down the corridor The Thinking Machine sat on the edge of the bed with his head in his hands.

"He's crazy to try to get out of that cell," commented the jailer.

"Of course he can't get out," said the warden. "But he's clever. I would like to know what he wrote that cipher with."

It was four o'clock next morning when an awful, heart-racking shriek of terror resounded through the great prison. It came from a cell, somewhere about the center, and its tone told a tale of horror, agony, terrible fear. The warden heard and with three of his men rushed into the long corridor leading to Cell 13.

As they ran there came again that awful cry. It died away in a sort of wail. The white faces of prisoners appeared at cell doors upstairs and down, staring out wonderingly, frightened.

"It's that fool in Cell 13," grumbled the warden.

He stopped and stared in as one of the jailers flashed a lantern. "That fool in Cell 13" lay comfortably on his cot, flat on his back with his mouth open, snoring. Even as they looked there came again the piercing cry, from somewhere above. The warden's face blanched a little as he started up the stairs. There on the top floor he found a man in Cell 43, directly above Cell 13, but two floors higher, cowering in a corner of his cell.

"What's the matter?" demanded the warden.

"Thank God you've come," exclaimed the prisoner, and he cast himself against the bars of his cell.

"What is it?" demanded the warden again.

He threw open the door and went in. The prisoner dropped on his knees and clasped the warden about the body. His face was white with terror, his eyes were widely distended, and he was shuddering. His hands, icy cold, clutched at the warden's.

"Take me out of this cell, please take me out," he pleaded.

"What's the matter with you, anyhow?" insisted the warden, impatiently.

"I heard something—something," said the prisoner, and his eyes roved nervously around the cell.

"What did you hear?"

"I—I can't tell you," stammered the prisoner. Then, in a sudden burst of terror: "Take me out of this cell—put me anywhere—but take me out of here."

The warden and the three jailers exchanged glances.

"Who is this fellow? What's he accused of?" asked the warden.

"Joseph Ballard," said one of the jailers. "He's accused of throwing acid in a woman's face. She died from it."

"But they can't prove it," gasped the prisoner. "They can't prove it. Please put me in some other cell."

He was still clinging to the warden, and that official threw his arms off roughly. Then for a time he stood looking at the cowering wretch, who seemed possessed of all the wild, unreasoning terror of a child.

"Look here, Ballard," said the warden, finally, "if you heard anything, I want to know what it was. Now tell me."

"I can't, I can't," was the reply. He was sobbing.

"Where did it come from?"

"I don't know. Everywhere—nowhere. I just heard it."

"What was it—a voice?"

"Please don't make me answer," pleaded the prisoner.

"You must answer," said the warden, sharply.

"It was a voice—but—but it wasn't human," was the sobbing reply.

"Voice, but not human?" repeated the warden, puzzled.

"It sounded muffled and—and far away—and ghostly," explained the man.

"Did it come from inside or outside the prison?"

"It didn't seem to come from anywhere—it was just here, there, everywhere. I heard it. I heard it."

For an hour the warden tried to get the story, but Ballard had become suddenly obstinate and would say nothing—only pleaded to be placed in another cell, or to have one of the jailers remain near him until daylight. These requests were gruffly refused.

"And see here," said the warden, in conclusion, "if there's any more of this screaming I'll put you in the padded cell."

Then the warden went his way, a sadly puzzled man. Ballard sat at his cell door until daylight, his face, drawn and white with terror, pressed against the bars, and looked out into the prison with wide, staring eyes.

That day, the fourth since the incarceration of The Thinking Machine, was enlivened considerably by the volunteer prisoner, who spent most of his time at the little window of his cell. He began proceedings by throwing another piece of linen down to the guard, who picked it up dutifully and took it to the warden. On it was written:

"Only three days more."

The warden was in no way surprised at what he read; he understood that The Thinking Machine meant only three days more of his imprisonment, and he regarded the note as a boast. But how was the thing written? Where had The Thinking Machine found this new piece of linen? Where? How? He carefully examined the linen. It was white, of fine texture, shirting material. He took the shirt which he had taken and carefully fitted the two original pieces of the linen to the torn places. This third piece was entirely superfluous; it didn't fit anywhere, and yet it was unmistakably the same goods.

"And where—where does he get anything to write with?" demanded the warden of the world at large.

Still later on the fourth day The Thinking Machine, through the window of his cell, spoke to the armed guard outside.

"What day of the month is it?" he asked.

"The fifteenth," was the answer.

The Thinking Machine made a mental astronomical calculation and satisfied himself that the moon would not rise until after nine o'clock that night. Then he asked another question:

"Who attends to those arc lights?"

"Man from the company."

"You have no electricians in the building?"

"No."

"I should think you could save money if you had your own man."

"None of my business," replied the guard.

The guard noticed The Thinking Machine at the cell window frequently during that day, but always the face seemed listless and there was a certain wistfulness in the squint eyes behind the glasses. After a while he accepted the presence of the leonine head as a matter of course. He had seen other prisoners do the same thing; it was the longing for the outside world.

That afternoon, just before the day guard was relieved, the head appeared at the window again, and The Thinking Machine's hand held something out between the bars. It fluttered to the ground and the guard picked it up. It was a five-dollar bill.

"That's for you," called the prisoner.

As usual, the guard took it to the warden. That gentleman looked at it suspiciously; he looked at everything that came from Cell 13 with suspicion.

"He said it was for me," explained the guard.

"It's a sort of a tip, I suppose," said the warden. "I see no particular reason why you shouldn't accept—"

Suddenly he stopped. He had remembered that The Thinking Machine had gone into Cell 13 with one five-dollar bill and two ten-dollar bills; twenty-five dollars in all. Now a five-dollar bill had been tied around the first pieces of linen that came from the cell. The warden still had it, and to convince himself he took it out and looked at it. It was five dollars; yet here was another five dollars, and The Thinking Machine had only had ten-dollar bills.

"Perhaps somebody changed one of the bills for him," he thought at last, with a sigh of relief.

But then and there he made up his mind. He would search Cell 13 as a cell was never before searched in this world. When a man could write at will, and change money, and do other wholly inexplicable things, there was something radically wrong with his prison. He planned to enter the cell at night—three o'clock would be an excellent time. The Thinking Machine must do all the weird things he did some time. Night seemed the most reasonable.

Thus it happened that the warden stealthily descended upon Cell 13 that night at three o'clock. He paused at the door and listened. There was no sound save the steady, regular breathing of the prisoner. The keys unfastened the double locks with scarcely a clank, and the warden entered, locking the door behind him. Suddenly he flashed his dark lantern in the face of the recumbent figure.

If the warden had planned to startle The Thinking Machine he was mistaken, for that individual merely opened his eyes quietly, reached for his glasses and inquired, in a most matter-of-fact tone:

"Who is it?"

It would be useless to describe the search that the warden made. It was minute. Not one inch of the cell or the bed was overlooked. He found the round hole in the floor, and with a flash of inspiration thrust his thick fingers into it. After a moment of fumbling there he drew up something and looked at it in the light of his lantern.

"Ugh!" he exclaimed.

The thing he had taken out was a rat—a dead rat. His inspiration fled as a mist before the sun. But he continued the search.

The Thinking Machine, without a word, arose and kicked the rat out of the cell into the corridor.

The warden climbed on the bed and tried the steel bars in the tiny window. They were perfectly rigid; every bar of the door was the same.

Then the warden searched the prisoner's clothing, beginning at the shoes. Nothing hidden in them! Then the trousers waistband. Still nothing! Then the pockets of the trousers. From one side he drew out some paper money and examined it.

"Five one-dollar bills," he gasped.

"That's right," said the prisoner.

"But the—you had two tens and a five—what the—how do you do it?"

"That's my business," said The Thinking Machine.

"Did any of my men change this money for you—on your word of honor?"

The Thinking Machine paused just a fraction of a second.

"No," he said.

"Well, do you make it?" asked the warden. He was prepared to believe anything.

"That's my business," again said the prisoner.

The warden glared at the eminent scientist fiercely. He felt—he knew—that this man was making a fool of him, yet he didn't know how. If he were a real prisoner he would get the truth—but, then, perhaps, those inexplicable things which had happened would not have been brought before him so sharply. Neither of the men spoke for a long time, then suddenly the warden turned fiercely and left the cell, slamming the door behind him. He didn't dare to speak, then.

He glanced at the clock. It was ten minutes to four. He had hardly settled himself in bed when again came that heartbreaking shriek through the prison. With a few muttered words, which, while not elegant, were highly expressive, he relighted his lantern and rushed through the prison again to the cell on the upper floor.

Again Ballard was crushing himself against the steel door, shrieking, shrieking at the top of his voice. He stopped only when the warden flashed his lamp in the cell.

"Take me out, take me out," he screamed. "I did it, I did it, I killed her. Take it away."

"Take what away?" asked the warden.

"I threw the acid in her face—I did it—I confess. Take me out of here."

Ballard's condition was pitiable; it was only an act of mercy to let him out into the corridor. There he crouched in a corner, like an animal at bay, and clasped his hands to his ears. It took half an hour to calm him sufficiently for him to speak. Then he told incoherently what had happened. On the night before at four o'clock he had heard a voice—a sepulchral voice, muffled and wailing in tone.

"What did it say?" asked the warden, curiously.

"Acid—acid—acid!" gasped the prisoner. "It accused me. Acid! I threw the acid, and the woman died. Oh!" It was a long, shuddering wail of terror.

"Acid?" echoed the warden, puzzled. The case was beyond him.

"Acid. That's all I heard—that one word, repeated several times. There were other things, too, but I didn't hear them."

"That was last night, eh?" asked the warden. "What happened tonight—what frightened you just now?"

"It was the same thing," gasped the prisoner. "Acid—acid—acid." He covered his face with his hands and sat shivering. "It was acid I used on her, but I didn't mean to kill her. I just heard the words. It was something accusing me—accusing me." He mumbled, and was silent.

"Did you hear anything else?"

"Yes—but I couldn't understand—only a little bit—just a word or two."

"Well, what was it?"

"I heard 'acid' three times, then I heard a long, moaning sound, then—then—I heard 'No. 8 hat.' I heard that voice."

"No. 8 hat," repeated the warden. "What the devil—No. 8 hat? Accusing voices of conscience have never talked about No. 8 hats, so far as I ever heard."

"He's insane," said one of the jailers, with an air of finality.

"I believe you," said the warden. "He must be. He probably heard something and got frightened. He's trembling now. No. 8 hat! What the—"

When the fifth day of The Thinking Machine's imprisonment rolled around the warden was wearing a hunted look. He was anxious for the end of the thing. He could not help but feel that his distinguished prisoner had been amusing himself. And if this were so, The Thinking Machine had lost none of his sense of humor. For on this fifth day he flung down another linen note to the outside guard, bearing the words: "Only two days more." Also he flung down half a dollar.

Now the warden knew—he *knew*—that the man in Cell 13 didn't have any half-dollars—he *couldn't* have any half-dollars, no more than he could have pen and ink and linen, and yet he did have them. It was a condition, not a theory; that is one reason why the warden was wearing a hunted look.

That ghastly, uncanny thing, too, about "Acid" and "No. 8 hat" clung to him tenaciously. They didn't mean anything, of course, merely the ravings of an insane murderer who had been driven by fear to confess his crime, still there were so many things that "didn't mean anything" happening in the prison now since The Thinking Machine was there.

On the sixth day the warden received a postal stating that Dr. Ransome and Mr. Fielding would be at Chisholm Prison on the following evening, Thursday, and in the event Professor Van Dusen had not yet escaped—and they presumed he had not because they had not heard from him—they would meet him there.

"In the event he had not yet escaped!" The warden smiled grimly. Escaped!

The Thinking Machine enlivened this day for the warden with three notes. They were on the usual linen and bore generally on the appointment at half past eight o'clock Thursday night, which appointment the scientist had made at the time of his imprisonment.

On the afternoon of the seventh day the warden passed Cell 13 and glanced in. The Thinking Machine was lying on the iron bed, apparently sleeping lightly. The cell appeared precisely as it always did from a casual glance. The warden would swear that no man was going to leave it between that hour—it was then four o'clock—and half past eight o'clock that evening.

On his way back past the cell the warden heard the steady breathing again, and coming close to the door looked in. He wouldn't have done so if The Thinking Machine had been looking, but now—well, it was different.

A ray of light came through the high window and fell on the face of the sleeping man. It occurred to the warden for the first time that his prisoner appeared haggard and weary. Just then The Thinking Machine stirred slightly and the warden hurried on up the corridor guiltily. That evening after six o'clock he saw the jailer.

"Everything all right in Cell 13?" he asked.

"Yes sir," replied the jailer. "He didn't eat much, though."

It was with a feeling of having done his duty that the warden received Dr. Ransome and Mr. Fielding shortly after seven o'clock. He intended to show them the linen notes and lay before them the full story of his woes, which was a long one. But before this came to pass the guard from the river side of the prison yard entered the office.

"The arc light in my side of the yard won't light," he informed the warden.

"Confound it, that man's a hoodoo," thundered the official. "Everything has happened since he's been here."

The guard went back to his post in the darkness, and the warden 'phoned to the electric light company.

"This is Chisholm Prison," he said through the 'phone. "Send three or four men down here quick, to fix an arc light."

The reply was evidently satisfactory, for the warden hung up the receiver and passed out into the yard. While Dr. Ransome and Mr. Fielding sat waiting, the guard at the outer gate came in with a special delivery letter. Dr. Ransome happened to notice the address, and, when the guard went out, looked at the letter more closely.

"By George!" he exclaimed.

"What is it?" asked Mr. Fielding.

Silently the doctor offered the letter. Mr. Fielding examined it closely.

"Coincidence," he said. "It must be."

It was nearly eight o'clock when the warden returned to his office. The electricians had arrived in a wagon, and were now at work. The warden pressed the buzz-button communicating with the man at the outer gate in the wall.

"How many electricians came in?" he asked, over the short 'phone. "Four? Three workmen in jumpers and overalls and the manager? Frock coat and silk hat? All right. Be certain that only four go out. That's all."

He turned to Dr. Ransome and Mr. Fielding. "We have to be careful here—particularly," and there was broad sarcasm in his tone, "since we have scientists locked up."

The warden picked up the special delivery letter carelessly, and then began to open it.

"When I read this I want to tell you gentlemen something about how—Great Caesar!" he ended, suddenly, as he glanced at the letter. He sat with mouth open, motionless, from astonishment.

"What is it?" asked Mr. Fielding.

"A special delivery letter from Cell 13," gasped the warden. "An invitation to supper."

"What?" and the two others arose, unanimously.

The warden sat dazed, staring at the letter for a moment, then called sharply to a guard outside in the corridor.

"Run down to Cell 13 and see if that man's in there."

The guard went as directed, while Dr. Ransome and Mr. Fielding examined the letter.

"It's Van Dusen's handwriting; there's no question of that," said Dr. Ransome. "I've seen too much of it."

Just then the buzz on the telephone from the outer gate sounded, and the warden, in a semi-trance, picked up the receiver.

"Hello! Two reporters, eh? Let 'em come in." He turned suddenly to the doctor and Mr. Fielding. "Why, the man *can't* be out. He must be in his cell."

Just at that moment the guard returned.

"He's still in his cell, sir," he reported. "I saw him. He's lying down."

"There, I told you so," said the warden, and he breathed freely again. "But how did he mail that letter?"

There was a rap on the steel door which led from the jail yard into the warden's office.

"It's the reporters," said the warden. "Let them in," he instructed the guard; then to the two other gentlemen: "Don't say anything about this before them, because I'd never hear the last of it."

The door opened, and the two men from the front gate entered.

"Good evening, gentlemen," said one. That was Hutchinson Hatch; the warden knew him well.

"Well?" demanded the other, irritably. "I'm here."

That was The Thinking Machine.

He squinted belligerently at the warden, who sat with mouth agape. For the moment that official had nothing to say. Dr. Ransome and Mr. Fielding were amazed, but they didn't know what the warden knew. They were only amazed; he was paralyzed. Hutchinson Hatch, the reporter, took in the scene with greedy eyes.

"How—how—how did you do it?" gasped the warden, finally.

"Come back to the cell," said The Thinking Machine, in the irritated voice which his scientific associates knew so well.

The warden, still in a condition bordering on trance, led the way.

"Flash your light in there," directed The Thinking Machine.

The warden did so. There was nothing unusual in the appearance of the cell, and there—there on the bed lay the figure of The Thinking Machine. Certainly! There was the yellow hair! Again the warden looked at the man beside him and wondered at the strangeness of his own dreams.

With trembling hands he unlocked the cell door and The Thinking Machine passed inside.

"See here," he said.

He kicked at the steel bars in the bottom of the cell door and three of them were pushed out of place. A fourth broke off and rolled away in the corridor.

"And here, too," directed the erstwhile prisoner as he stood on the bed to reach the small window. He swept his hand across the opening and every bar came out.

"What's this in the bed?" demanded the warden, who was slowly recovering.

"A wig," was the reply. "Turn down the cover."

The warden did so. Beneath it lay a large coil of strong rope, thirty feet or more, a dagger, three files, ten feet of electric wire, a thin, powerful pair of steel pliers, a small tack hammer with its handle, and—and a Derringer pistol.

"How did you do it?" demanded the warden.

"You gentlemen have an engagement to supper with me at half past nine o'clock," said The Thinking Machine. "Come on, or we shall be late."

"But how did you do it?" insisted the warden.

"Don't ever think you can hold any man who can use his brain," said The Thinking Machine. "Come on; we shall be late."

[*Let's stop the story a moment. The Thinking Machine has escaped, but how? Have you any idea as to how he managed to pass through solid metal bars, thick concrete walls, and seven massive doors? Let's list the important clues:*

1. *The requests he made at the beginning (shoes blackened, etc.)*
2. *The rats in the cell*
3. *The new plumbing*
4. *The river and the playground*
5. *The man in the cell above*

Do they mean anything to you? Don't be discouraged if they don't. Nearly every reader is baffled; yet, at the end of the story, nearly every reader says, "Of course! It was there all the time for me to see!" This is the perfect tribute to any detective story.

Now read The Thinking Machine's explanation.]

It was an impatient supper party in the rooms of Professor Van Dusen and a somewhat silent one. The guests were Dr. Ransome, Albert Fielding, the warden, and Hutchinson Hatch, reporter. The meal was served to the minute, in accordance with Professor Van Dusen's instructions of one week before; Dr. Ransome found the artichokes delicious. At last the supper was finished and The Thinking Machine turned full on Dr. Ransome and squinted at him fiercely.

"Do you believe it now?" he demanded.

"I do," replied Dr. Ransome.

"Do you admit that it was a fair test?"

"I do."

With the others, particularly the warden, he was waiting anxiously for the explanation.

"Suppose you tell us how—" began Mr. Fielding.

"Yes, tell us how," said the warden.

The Thinking Machine readjusted his glasses, took a couple of preparatory squints at his audience, and began the story. He told it from the beginning logically; and no man ever talked to more interested listeners.

"My agreement was," he began, "to go into a cell, carrying nothing except what was necessary to wear, and to leave that cell within a week. I had never seen Chisholm Prison. When I went into the cell I asked for tooth powder, two ten- and one five-dollar bills, and also to have my shoes blacked. Even if these requests had been refused it would not have mattered seriously. But you agreed to them.

"I knew there would be nothing in the cell which you thought I might use to advantage. So when the warden locked the door on me I was apparently helpless, unless I could turn three seemingly innocent things to use. They were things which would have been permitted any prisoner under sentence of death, were they not, warden?"

"Tooth powder and polished shoes, yes, but not money," replied the warden.

"Anything is dangerous in the hands of a man who knows how to use it," went on The Thinking Machine. "I did nothing that first night but sleep and chase rats." He glared at the warden. "When the matter was broached I knew I could do nothing that night, so suggested next day. You gentlemen thought I wanted time to arrange an escape with outside assistance, but this was not true. I knew I could communicate with whom I pleased, when I pleased."

The warden stared at him a moment, then went on smoking solemnly.

"I was aroused next morning at six o'clock by the jailer with my breakfast," continued the scientist. "He told me dinner was at twelve and supper at six. Between these times, I gathered, I would be pretty much to myself. So immediately after breakfast I examined my outside surroundings from my cell window. One look told me it would be useless to try to scale the wall, even should I decide to leave my cell by the window, for my purpose was to leave not only the cell, but the prison. Of course, I could have gone over the wall, but it would have taken me longer to lay my plans that way. Therefore, for the moment, I dismissed all idea of that.

"From this first observation I knew the river was on that side of the prison, and that there was also a playground there. Subsequently these surmises were verified by a keeper. I knew then one important thing—that anyone might approach the prison wall from that side if necessary without attracting any particular attention. That was well to remember. I remembered it.

"But the outside thing which most attracted my attention was the feed wire to the arc light which ran within a few feet—probably three or four—of my cell window. I knew that would be valuable in the event I found it necessary to cut off that arc light."

"Oh, you shut it off tonight, then?" asked the warden.

"Having learned all I could from that window," resumed The Thinking Machine, without heeding the interruption, "I considered the idea of escaping through the prison proper. I recalled just how I had come into the cell, which I knew would be the only way. Seven doors lay between me and the outside. So, also for the time being, I gave up the idea of escaping that way. And I couldn't go through the solid granite walls of the cell."

The Thinking Machine paused for a moment and Dr. Ransome lighted a new cigar. For several minutes there was silence, then the scientific jailbreaker went on:

"While I was thinking about these things a rat ran across my foot. It suggested a new line of thought. There were at least half a dozen rats in the cell—I could see their beady eyes. Yet I had noticed none come under the cell door. I frightened them purposely and watched the cell door to see if they went out that way. They did not, but they were gone. Obviously they went another way. Another way meant another opening.

"I searched for this opening and found it. It was an old drain pipe, long unused and partly choked with dirt and dust. But this was the way the rats had come. They came from somewhere. Where? Drain pipes usually lead outside prison grounds. This one probably led to the river, or near it. The rats must therefore come from that direction. If they came a part of the way, I reasoned that they came all the way, because it was extremely unlikely that a solid iron or lead pipe would have any hole in it except at the exit.

"When the jailer came with my luncheon he told me two important things, although he didn't know it. One was that a new system of plumbing had been put in the prison seven years before; another that the river was only three hundred feet away. Then I knew positively that the pipe was a part of an old system; I knew, too, that it slanted generally toward the river. But did the pipe end in the water or on land?

"This was the next question to be decided. I decided it by catching several of the rats in the cell. My jailer was surprised to see me engaged in this work. I examined at least a dozen of them. They were perfectly dry; they had come through the pipe, and, most important of all, they were *not house rats, but field rats.* The other end of the pipe was on land, then, outside the prison walls. So far, so good.

"Then, I knew that if I worked freely from this point I must attract the warden's attention in another direction. You see, by telling the warden that I had come there to escape you made the test more severe, because I had to trick him by false scents."

The warden looked up with a sad expression in his eyes.

"The first thing was to make him think I was trying to communicate with you, Dr. Ransome. So I wrote a note on a piece of linen I tore from my shirt, addressed it to Dr. Ransome, tied a five-dollar bill around it and threw it out the window. I knew the guard would take it to the warden, but I rather hoped the warden would send it as addressed. Have you that first linen note, warden?"

The warden produced the cipher.

"What the deuce does it mean, anyhow?" he asked.

"Read it backward, beginning with the 'T' signature and disregard the division into words," instructed The Thinking Machine.

The warden did so.

"T-h-i-s, this," he spelled, studied it a moment, then read it off, grinning:

"This is not the way I intend to escape."

"Well, now what do you think o' that?" he demanded, still grinning.

"I knew that would attract your attention, just as it did," said The Thinking Machine, "and, if you really found out what it was, it would be a sort of gentle rebuke."

"What did you write it with?" asked Dr. Ransome, after he had examined the linen and passed it to Mr. Fielding.

"This," said the erstwhile prisoner, and he extended his foot. On it was the shoe he had worn in prison, though the polish was gone—scraped off clean. "The shoe blacking, moistened with water, was my ink; the metal tip of the shoelace made a fairly good pen."

The warden looked up and suddenly burst into a laugh, half of relief, half of amusement.

"You're a wonder," he said, admiringly. "Go on."

"That precipitated a search of my cell by the warden, as I had intended," continued The Thinking Machine. "I was anxious to get the warden into the habit of searching my cell, so that finally, constantly finding nothing, he would get disgusted and quit. This at last happened, practically."

The warden blushed.

"He then took my white shirt away and gave me a prison shirt. He was satisfied that those two pieces of the shirt were all that was missing. But while he was searching my cell I had another piece of that same shirt, about nine inches square, rolled into a small ball in my mouth."

"Nine inches of that shirt?" demanded the warden. "Where did it come from?"

"The bosoms of all stiff white shirts are of triple thickness," was the explanation. "I tore out the inside thickness, leaving the bosom only two thicknesses. I knew you wouldn't see it. So much for that."

There was a little pause, and the warden looked from one to another of the men with a sheepish grin.

"Having disposed of the warden for the time being by giving him something else to think about, I took my first serious step toward freedom," said Professor Van Dusen. "I knew, within reason, that the pipe led somewhere to the playground outside; I knew a great many boys played there; I knew that rats came into my cell from out there. Could I communicate with someone outside with these things at hand?

"First was necessary, I saw, a long and fairly reliable thread, so—but here," he pulled up his trousers legs and showed that the tops of both stockings, of fine, strong lisle, were gone. "I unraveled those—after I got them started it wasn't difficult—and I had easily a quarter of a mile of thread that I could depend on.

"Then on half of my remaining linen I wrote, laboriously enough, I assure you, a letter explaining my situation to this gentleman here," and he indicated Hutchinson Hatch. "I knew he would assist me—for the value of the newspaper story. I tied firmly to this linen letter a ten-dollar bill—there is no surer way of attracting the eye of anyone—and wrote on the linen: 'Finder of this deliver to Hutchinson Hatch, *Daily American*, who will give another ten dollars for the information.'

"The next thing was to get this note outside on that playground where a boy might find it. There were two ways, but I chose the best. I took one of the rats—I became adept in catching them—tied the linen and money firmly to one leg, fastened my lisle thread to another, and turned him loose in the drain pipe. I reasoned that the natural fright of the rodent would make him run until he was outside the pipe and then out on earth he would probably stop to gnaw off the linen and money.

"From the moment the rat disappeared into that dusty pipe I became anxious. I was taking so many chances. The rat might gnaw the string, of which I held one end; other rats might gnaw it; the rat might run out of the pipe and leave the linen and money where they would never be found; a thousand other things might have happened. So began some nervous hours, but the fact that the rat ran on until only a few feet of the string remained in my cell made me think he was outside the pipe. I had carefully instructed Mr. Hatch what to do in case the note reached him. The question was: Would it reach him?

"This done, I could only wait and make other plans in case this one failed. I openly attempted to bribe my jailer, and learned from him that he held the keys to only two of seven doors between me and freedom. Then I did something else to make the warden nervous. I took the steel supports out of the heels of my shoes and made a pretense of sawing the bars of my cell window. The warden raised a pretty row about that. He developed, too, the habit of shaking the bars of my cell window to see if they were solid. They were—then."

Again the warden grinned. He had ceased being astonished.

"With this one plan I had done all I could and could only wait to see what happened," the scientist went on. "I couldn't know whether my note had been delivered or even found, or whether the rat had gnawed it up. And I didn't dare to draw back through the pipe that one slender thread which connected me with the outside.

"When I went to bed that night I didn't sleep, for fear there would come the slight signal twitch at the thread which was to tell me that Mr. Hatch had received the note. At half past three o'clock, I judge, I felt this twitch, and no prisoner actually under sentence of death ever welcomed a thing more heartily."

The Thinking Machine stopped and turned to the reporter.

"You'd better explain just what you did," he said.

"The linen note was brought to me by a small boy who had been playing baseball," said Mr. Hatch. "I immediately saw a big story in it, so I gave the boy another ten dollars, and got several spools of silk, some twine, and a roll of light, pliable wire. The professor's note suggested that I have the finder of the note show me just where it was picked up, and told me to make my search from there, beginning at two o'clock in the morning. If I found the other end of the thread I was to twitch it gently three times, then a fourth.

"I began to search with a small bulb electric light. It was an hour and twenty minutes before I found the end of the drain pipe, half hidden in weeds. The pipe was very large there, say twelve inches across. Then I found the end of the lisle thread, twitched it as directed and immediately I got an answering twitch.

"Then I fastened the silk to this and Professor Van Dusen began to pull it into his cell. I nearly had heart disease for fear the string would break. To the end of the silk I fastened the twine, and when that had been pulled in I tied on the wire. Then that was drawn into the pipe and we had a substantial line, which the rats couldn't gnaw, from the mouth of the drain into the cell."

The Thinking Machine raised his hand and Hatch stopped.

"All this was done in absolute silence," said the scientist. "But when the wire reached my hand I could have shouted. Then we tried another experiment, which Mr. Hatch was prepared for. I tested the pipe as a speaking tube. Neither of us could hear very clearly, but I dared not speak loud for fear of attracting attention in the prison. At last I made him understand what I wanted immediately. He seemed to have great difficulty in understanding when I asked for nitric acid, and I repeated the word 'acid' several times.

"Then I heard a shriek from a cell above me. I knew instantly that someone had overheard, and when I heard you coming, Mr. Warden, I feigned sleep. If you had entered my cell at that moment that whole plan of escape would have ended there. But you passed on. That was the nearest I ever came to being caught.

"Having established this improvised trolley it is easy to see how I got things in the cell and made them disappear at will. I merely dropped them back into the pipe. You, Mr. Warden, could not have reached the connecting wire with your fingers; they are too large. My fingers, you see, are longer and more slender. In addition I guarded the top of that pipe with a rat—you remember how."

"I remember," said the warden, with a grimace.

"I thought that if anyone were tempted to investigate that hole the rat would dampen his ardor. Mr. Hatch could not send me anything useful through the pipe until next night, although he did send me change for ten dollars as a test, so I proceeded with other parts of my plan. Then I evolved the method of escape, which I finally employed.

"In order to carry this out successfully it was necessary for the guard in the yard to get accustomed to seeing me at the cell window. I arranged this by dropping linen notes to him, boastful in tone, to make the warden believe, if possible, one of his assistants was communicating with the outside for me. I would stand at my window for hours gazing out, so the guard could see, and occasionally I spoke to him. In that way I learned that the prison had no electricians of its own, but was dependent upon the lighting company if anything should go wrong.

"That cleared the way to freedom completely. Early in the evening of the last day of my imprisonment, when it was dark, I planned to cut the feed wire which was only a few feet from my window, reaching it with an acid-tipped wire I had. That would make that side of the prison perfectly dark while the electricians were searching for the break. That would also bring Mr. Hatch into the prison yard.

"There was only one more thing to do before I actually began the work of setting myself free. This was to arrange final details with Mr. Hatch through our speaking tube. I did this within half an hour after the warden left my cell on the fourth night of my imprisonment. Mr. Hatch again had serious difficulty in understanding me, and I repeated the word 'acid' to him several times, and later the words: 'Number eight hat'—that's my size—and these were the things which made a prisoner upstairs confess to murder, so one of the jailers told me next day. This prisoner heard our voices, confused of course, through the pipe, which also went to his cell. The cell directly over me was not occupied, hence no one else heard.

"Of course the actual work of cutting the steel bars out of the window and door was comparatively easy with nitric acid, which I got through the pipe in thin bottles, but it took time. Hour after hour on the fifth and sixth and seventh days the guard below was looking at me as I worked on the bars of the window with the acid on a piece of wire. I used the tooth powder to prevent the acid spreading. I looked away abstractedly as I worked and each minute the acid cut deeper into the metal. I noticed that the jailers always tried the door by shaking the upper part, never the lower bars, therefore I cut the lower bars, leaving them hanging in place by thin strips of metal. But that was a bit of daredeviltry. I could not have gone that way so easily."

The Thinking Machine sat silent for several minutes.

"I think that makes everything clear," he went on. "Whatever points I have not explained were merely to confuse the warden and jailers. These things in my bed I brought in to please Mr. Hatch, who wanted to improve the story. Of course, the wig was necessary in my plan. The special delivery letter I wrote and directed in my cell with Mr. Hatch's fountain pen, then sent it out to him and he mailed it. That's all, I think."

"But your actually leaving the prison grounds and then coming in through the outer gate to my office?" asked the warden.

"Perfectly simple," said the scientist. "I cut the electric light wire with acid, as I said, when the current was off. Therefore when the current was turned on the arc didn't light. I knew it would take some time to find out what was the matter and make repairs. When the guard went to report to you the yard was dark. I crept out the window—it was a tight fit, too—replaced the bars by standing on a narrow ledge and remained in a shadow until the force of electricians arrived. Mr. Hatch was one of them.

"When I saw him I spoke and he handed me a cap, a jumper and overalls, which I put on within ten feet of you, Mr. Warden, while you were in the yard. Later Mr. Hatch called me, presumably as a workman, and together we went out the gate to get something out of the wagon. The gate guard let us pass out readily as two workmen who had just passed in. We changed our clothing and reappeared, asking to see you. We saw you. That's all."

There was silence for several minutes. Dr. Ransome was first to speak.

"Wonderful!" he exclaimed. "Perfectly amazing."

"How did Mr. Hatch happen to come with the electricians?" asked Mr. Fielding.

"His father is manager of the company," replied The Thinking Machine.

"But what if there had been no Mr. Hatch outside to help?"

"Every prisoner has one friend outside who would help him escape if he could."

"Suppose—just suppose—there had been no old plumbing system there?" asked the warden, curiously.

"There were two other ways out," said The Thinking Machine, enigmatically.

Ten minutes later the telephone bell rang. It was a request for the warden.

"Light all right, eh?" the warden asked, through the 'phone. "Good. Wire cut beside Cell 13? Yes, I know. One electrician too many? What's that? Two came out?"

The warden turned to the others with a puzzled expression.

"He only let in four electricians, he has let out two and says there are three left."

"I was the odd one," said The Thinking Machine.

"Oh," said the warden. "I see." Then through the 'phone: "Let the fifth man go. He's all right."

Understanding the Story

Main Idea

1. Professor Van Dusen is a man of   (a) many quirks and bad habits   (b) high intelligence and incredible resourcefulness   (c) unexpected good luck and foolishness   (d) pleasing personality and friendly manner.

Details

2. One of the objects requested by Van Dusen was   (a) tooth powder   (b) an explosive device   (c) a telephone   (d) a mousetrap.

3. Cell 13 was usually reserved for   (a) political prisoners   (b) petty thieves   (c) embezzlers   (d) condemned murderers.

4. Van Dusen's "coded message" to his friend Ransome was supposed to be read   (a) in bright light   (b) with the help of a dictionary   (c) with a secret code devised by the warden   (d) backwards.

5. The mysterious "extra electrician" was   (a) Hatch
   (b) Ransome   (c) Van Dusen   (d) Fielding.

Inferences

6. The rats could reasonably be called   (a) deadly enemies of
   the prisoner   (b) Van Dusen's helpers   (c) subjects of Dr.
   Ransome's experiments   (d) pets of Mr. Hatch.

7. Which of the following statements is NOT true?
   (a) The Thinking Machine outguessed the warden.
   (b) He irritated Ransome.
   (c) He meant to drive the man above him into a confession of
       murder.
   (d) He used the guard for his own ends.

8. For his plan of escape, Van Dusen cleverly used   (a) the location of the prison   (b) the thickness of the walls   (c) Dr.
   Ransome's stupidity   (d) the guard's willingness to accept a
   bribe.

9. At the end, the warden's attitude toward Van Dusen was one
   of   (a) hatred   (b) extreme anger   (c) indifference
   (d) respect.

10. The drain   (a) led to the warden's office   (b) distorted Van
    Dusen's voice   (c) was free of rats   (d) was fully opera-
    tional.

Order of Events

11. Arrange the items in the order in which they occurred. Use
    letters only.
    A. Hatch begins to help Van Dusen.
    B. The lights go out in the prison.
    C. Van Dusen walks in with Hatch.
    D. Van Dusen catches a rat.
    E. Van Dusen declares nothing is impossible.

Outcomes

12. If there had been no drain in the cell, Van Dusen probably
    would have   (a) given up   (b) smuggled in a file for cutting
    the bars   (c) succeeded in bribing a guard   (d) found still
    another way.

Cause and Effect

13. As a direct result of using the drain for a speaking tube,
    (a) the lighting system was blacked out   (b) a prisoner con-
    fessed to murder   (c) the warden caught on to Van Dusen's
    plans.   (d) Ransome and Fielding called the challenge off.

Fact or Opinion

Tell whether each of the following is a fact or opinion.

14. There was a playground near the prison.

15. Van Dusen took unfair advantage of the warden's good nature.

Words in Context _____

1. In appearance he was no less striking than in *nomenclature.*
   Nomenclature (75)   means   (a) physique   (b) name
   (c) temperament   (d) features.

2. He was slender with the droop of the student in his thin shoulders and *pallor* of a close, *sedentary* life on his clean-shaven
   face.
   Pallor (75) means   (a) appearance   (b) glow   (c) paleness
   (d) strength.

3. *Sedentary*   (75)   means   (a) inactive   (b) violent
   (c) unhappy   (d) colorful.

4. His eyes wore a *perpetual,* forbidding squint—of a man who
   studies little things.
   Perpetual (75)   means   (a) unpleasant   (b) invisible
   (c) uncertain   (d) continuing.

5. All these things conspired to give him a peculiar, almost *grotesque,* personality.
   Grotesque (75)   means   (a) gloomy   (b) fantastic
   (c) distracted   (d) weak.

6. He always spoke *petulantly.*
   Petulantly (76) means   (a) slowly   (b) clearly   (c) crossly
   (d) seriously.

7. "I have done more *asinine* things than that to convince other
   men of less important truths."
   Asinine (77)   means   (a) hasty   (b) profound
   (c) unexpected   (d) stupid.

8. Professor Van Dusen *reiterated* his willingness to undertake the escape and it was decided upon.
   Reiterated (77) means   (a) repeated   (b) rejected (c) reported   (d) re-evaluated.

9. The Thinking Machine had donned those things which he was to wear during his *incarceration*.
   Incarceration (78) means   (a) lecture   (b) imprisonment (c) investigation   (d) period of schooling.

10. What sympathy Dr. Ransome had was *dissipated* by the tone.
    Dissipated (79) means   (a) destroyed   (b) increased (c) untouched   (d) misdirected.

11. It *nettled* him, and he resolved to see the experiment to the end.
    Nettled (79) means   (a) interested   (b) pleased (c) awakened   (d) annoyed.

12. "Rats—dozens of them," replied The Thinking Machine *tersely*.
    Tersely (80) means   (a) loudly   (b) eagerly   (c) briefly (d) sweetly.

13. Atop of this fence, as a further precaution, was a five-foot fence of steel rods, each *terminating* in a keen point.
    Terminating (80) means   (a) blossoming   (b) ending (c) decorating   (d) unwinding.

14. Noon came and the jailer appeared with the prison dinner of *repulsively* plain food.
    Repulsively (83) means   (a) disgustingly   (b) unattractively (c) unusually   (d) wholesomely.

15. His tone was hardly natural, his manner suggested actual *perturbation*.
    Perturbation (86) means   (a) application   (b) serenity (c) arbitration   (d) anxiety.

16. "Well, writing notes on a shirt won't get him out, that's certain," he told himself with some *complacency*.
    Complacency (86) means   (a) irritation   (b) heat   (c) self-satisfaction   (d) hesitancy.

17. "But would you consider a proposition to help me get out?" the prisoner insisted, almost *beseechingly*.
    Beseechingly (87) means   (a) in a begging manner   (b) with considerable pride   (c) without hesitation   (d) in somewhat of a hurry.

18. Then came another *exhaustive* search of the cell.
    Exhaustive (89) means (a) weary (b) thorough
    (c) confidential (d) bitterly angry.

19. His face was white with terror, his eyes were widely *distended*, and he was shuddering.
    Distended (90) means (a) bloodshot (b) scarred
    (c) expanded (d) vibrating.

20. When a man could write at will, and change money, and do other wholly *inexplicable* things, there was something radically wrong with his prison.
    Inexplicable (92) means (a) bad-tempered (b) easily understood (c) improper (d) unexplainable.

21. Thus it happened that the warden *stealthily* descended upon Cell 13 that night at three o'clock.
    Stealthily (92) means (a) noisily (b) wearily (c) happily (d) slyly.

22. Suddenly he flashed his dark lantern in the face of the *recumbent* figure.
    Recumbent (92) means (a) unconscious (b) recovering (c) lying down (d) untidy.

23. Then he told *incoherently* what had happened.
    Incoherently (94) means (a) unclearly (b) calmly (c) ungrammatically (d) logically.

24. "When the matter was *broached* I knew I could do nothing that night, so suggested next day."
    Broached (100) means (a) disapproved (b) suggested (c) analyzed (d) uncovered.

25. Subsequently these *surmises* were verified by a keeper.
    Surmises (100) means (a) errors (b) guesses (c) difficulties (d) bad thoughts.

26. "If you really found out what it was, it would be a sort of gentle *rebuke*."
    Rebuke (102) means (a) salute (b) reply (c) touch of humor (d) scolding.

27. "That *precipitated* a search of my cell by the warden, as I had intended."
    Precipitated (102) means (a) caused (b) avoided (c) reported (d) concealed.

28. "When I heard you coming, Mr. Warden, I *feigned* sleep."
    Feigned (105) means (a) sought (b) avoided
    (c) pretended (d) enjoyed.

29. "Having established this *improvised* trolley it is easy to see how I got things in the cell and made them disappear at will."
    Improvised (105) means something that is invented (a) after great difficulty (b) without extensive preparation (c) with the help of other people (d) only by a genius.

30. "I thought that if anyone were tempted to investigate that hole the rat would dampen his *ardor*."
    Ardor (105) means (a) fingertips (b) enthusiasm
    (c) cowardice (d) hesitancy.

Thinking About the Story _____

1. How does The Thinking Machine compare with Sherlock Holmes, Hercule Poirot, and Father Brown in method, personality, and appearance? Why does a writer try to make his detective as distinctive, as different as possible from all others?

2. There are at least five important steps in the thought process:
   (a) Identifying the Problem
   (b) Exploring the Problem
   (c) Narrowing the Problem
   (d) Considering Possible Solutions
   (e) Making the Decision and Acting on It.

   Point out how The Thinking Machine followed the five steps in solving his problem.

3. How do we use similar thinking in our everyday living? Mention a typical personal problem that can be solved by careful thought.

4. "There were two other ways out," declared The Thinking Machine. Do you think the author had in mind other possibilities? Do you? Explain.

5. Why does the author make the warden so puzzled and confused? (Hint: put yourself in the warden's place.) What other detectives had assistants or associates whose ignorance was important to the progress of the plot.

6. On page 76, Dr. Ransome asks, "How about the spaceship?" and The Thinking Machine replies, "That's not impossible at all. It will be invented some time. I'd do it myself, but I'm busy."

This story was written half a century before space flight was achieved, but The Thinking Machine's prediction came true. Mention one achievement now considered impossible with modern technology but possible in the future.

Detective Stories

ACTIVITIES

Thinking About the Stories

1. Edgar Allan Poe is credited with originating the following devices, which have since become commonplace in detective fiction. Select any three of these devices and show how they were used by some of the authors read.
   (a) The unusual detective.
   (b) Solution by the process of elimination. When you have eliminated all the impossibilities, then what remains—no matter how improbable it may seem—must be true.
   (c) The admiring assistant.
   (d) The foolish police official.
   (e) The crime in a room locked on the inside.
   (f) The unjustly suspected person.
   (g) The surprise solution.
   (h) The use of reasoning to solve the crime.
   (i) The trick of concealing something by making it overobvious or commonplace.

2. One of the basic requirements of a good detective story is that the writer must play fair; that is, he must not give to the reader fewer clues than he has given to the detective. By discussing one of the stories read, show how the author has provided clues for the keen reader.

3. "My favorite detective story is one in which something happens that should not or supposedly could not happen. I enjoy watching the detective prove the impossible possible." Is that a fairly accurate description of what you look for in a detective story? What kind of detective story do you favor? How do the stories in this unit measure up to your set of standards?

4. Which one of the four detectives met in the preceding stories seems to you to be the most realistic? Which seems the most unusual? Explain.

5. Is a good title important to a detective story? Which story seems to you to have the best title? Explain.

Projects

1. Start a card catalog for short stories. Whenever you read a short story, jot down on a 3×5 card the title, the name of the author, and two or three sentences about the story. In time you'll have a sizable short-story file invaluable in recalling stories you've read and enjoyed.

2. Make a list of the names of detectives you meet in fiction, the titles of the stories in which they appear, and their distinguishing characteristics. For example, for "The Adventure of the Speckled Band" you would have:

Detective	*Story*	*Characteristics*
Sherlock Holmes	"The Adventure of the Speckled Band"	Insists upon the importance of keen observation

3. Watch a television program dealing with crime and law enforcement. Use these standards in judging the program:
   (a) The program should refrain from making crime appear attractive.
   (b) The story should be presented in such a way that the listener tends to identify himself with the forces of law and order.
   (c) The procedures used in solving the crime should be realistic and believable.

4. A certain teacher of journalism used to stage a quarrel before his class, and then ask questions to test the class's powers of observation. Plan such a scene before your own class. Prepare questions in advance; for example, "Was the boy carrying a book or a magazine in his arm at the time?"

5. By referring to stories read thus far, or by recalling other detective stories you have read, discuss the following quotations. Indicate whether you agree with each quotation and present reasons to support your views.

(a) "The detective story is one of the most moral of all types of fiction, for despite the temporary triumph of evil, good always wins out in the end. The moral, 'Crime Does Not Pay' is always implied."

(b) "It is a rare detective-story writer who can rise above his fellows to create a new kind of detective. The eccentric Holmeses and their faithful Watsons, the blind detectives, the men-about-town, the brilliant amateurs, the hard-boiled sergeants—all these are typed characters that weigh down upon the inferior writer like a millstone."

(c) "Detective stories tend to show national characteristics. The French detective is suave, yet painstaking. The British detective, beneath his reserve and calm, follows the scent with bulldog tenacity. The American detective may be a talkative Yankee or a brilliant, inquisitive woman—but the American love for ingenuity motivates the plot."

(d) "The detective in pulp magazines is less a detective than a person to whom all kinds of impossible things can happen. The detective in a well-constructed story is a thoughtful character, a man who straightens out all the kinks without resorting to gunplay, without relying upon sudden, accidental strokes of fortune."

Additional Readings

Short Stories

"The Purloined Letter" by Edgar Allan Poe

This is a good companion story to G. K. Chesterton's "The Invisible Man." The theme of both is that we have eyes but see not.

"The Footprint in the Sky" by Carter Dickson

Carter Dickson, also known as John Dickson Carr, is one of the finest writers of the puzzle detective tale, of the story that cannot possibly be true. . .but is. This is an excellent example.

"The Disappearance of Mrs. Leigh Gordon" by Agatha Christie

A good example of the humorous detective story, cleverly plotted and fairly presented.

"The Absent-Minded Coterie" by Robert Barr

Barr proves that it doesn't pay to be forgetful.

"The Cyprian Bees" by Anthony Wynne

In this, as in *A Taste of Honey* by H. F. Heard, bees play a leading role.

"The Avenging Chance" by Anthony Berkeley

Roger Sheringham destroys one of the best alibis ever manufactured in "as nearly a perfectly plotted short story as has been written." (Ellery Queen)

Anthologies

101 Years' Entertainment edited by Ellery Queen

An older collection but still one of the best. It contains several of the stories mentioned above.

The Complete Sherlock Holmes by A. Conan Doyle

All the Sherlock Holmes stories in one volume. If you liked "The Speckled Band," try "The Red-Headed League" and "The Blue Carbuncle."

The Father Brown Omnibus by G. K. Chesterton

All the Father Brown stories in one volume. If you haven't already read them, try "The Hammer of God" and "The Blast of the Book." Father Brown unravels the most knotted mysteries.

Studies

Whodunit? Edited by H. R. F. Keating

This excellent guide to crime, suspense, and spy fiction has an alphabetical listing of writers and a separate section on characters. Here you will find James Bond, Charlie Chan, Adam Dalgliesh, Miss Marple, Perry Mason, and Lord Peter Wimsey.

Murder Ink edited by Dilys Winn

This contains amusing articles on detective fiction.

Crime on Her Mind edited by Michele B. Slung

This contains 15 stories of female detectives from the Victorian Era to the 1940s. It also catalogs 100 fictional women detectives.

2 STORIES OF SUSPENSE AND TERROR

Moviegoers seem to love a good scary movie. Year after year, horror films do well at the box office. Though often made with low budgets, they attract a loyal following, and make fortunes for their producers. Why should anyone pay money to be frightened?

Do you attend these movies? Do you like a good terrifying yarn? Have you ever huddled around a campfire, shivering with delightful terror as someone told a ghost story? Have you ever read a frightening tale late at night with the shades drawn, the lights low, and the house as quiet as a tomb?

If you are like most people, you enjoy being frightened—safely. You may relish the hair-raising activities of ghosts, werewolves, vampires, zombies, witches, uncontrolled robots—but you prefer them at a distance. Stories of suspense and terror are always popular, whether they are on television, on the movie screen, or in a book.

The stories you are about to read will give you a few chills, but you'll enjoy them. No one can tell which you will find most full of suspense, for tastes differ, but it is certain that none of them will be easily forgotten. The tales vary. Here you will find a man who volunteers to spend the night in the silent company of known murderers, a man and a woman who work out their fatal destiny in an African game reserve, an incredible custom that ends in death for an unwilling victim, and an open window that leads out onto a . . . but that would be telling.

Here, then, are four of the finest stories of their kind, tales of suspense and the extraordinary, guaranteed to entertain you and set you thinking at the same time.

The Fever Tree

Ruth Rendell

♦ She picked at her food, thinking how he had meant to kill her. She would never be safe now, for having failed once he would try again. Not the same method perhaps but some other. How was she to know he hadn't already tried?

On the honor roll of modern mystery writers, the name Ruth Rendell stands near the top. Her detective stories, many of them featuring the personable detective, Inspector Wexford, are well plotted, worthy of the tradition of Agatha Christie and A. Conan Doyle. She also writes another kind of story: tales of suspense and the terror that can lurk beneath innocent surfaces.

"The Fever Tree" is in her second mode, a tale of suspense that encourages readers to turn pages even faster to find out how things turn out. There are only two main characters, though a third character, Marguerite, plays an important role offstage.

Imagine yourself in an African game reserve. You are traveling with a companion in a rented car. You have been warned to stay in the car and get back to camp by nightfall. You are safe as long as you stay inside the car and get back before dark. But what if you get out of the car? What if you have to face the terrors of the night alone? What if there should be a motive for foul play? What if . . . ?

Ruth Rendell takes these questions in stride and describes an experience you are not likely to forget. Safari, anyone?

THE FEVER TREE

Where malaria is, there grows the fever tree.

It has the feathery fernlike leaves, fresh green and tender, that are common to so many trees in tropical regions. Its shape is graceful with an air of youth, as if every fever tree is still waiting to grow up. But the most distinctive thing about it is the color of its bark which is the yellow of an unripe lemon. The fever trees stand out from among the rest because of their slender yellow trunks.

Ford knew what the tree was called and he could recognize it but he didn't know what its botanical name was. Nor had he ever heard why it was called the fever tree, whether the tribesmen used its leaves or bark or fruit as a specific against malaria or if it simply took its name from its warning presence wherever the malaria-carrying mosquito was. The sight of it in Ntsukunyane seemed to promote a fever in his blood.

An African in khaki shorts and shirt lifted up the bar for them so that their car could pass through the opening in the fence. Inside it looked no different from outside, the same bush, still, silent, unstirred by wind, stretching away on either side. Ford, driving the two miles along the tarmac road to the reception hut, thought of how it would be if he turned his head and saw Marguerite in the passenger seat beside him. It was an illusion he dared not have but was allowed to keep for only a minute. Tricia shattered it. She began to belabor him with schoolgirl questions, uttered in a bright and desperate voice.

Another African, in a fancier, more decorated uniform, took their booking voucher and checked it against a ledger. You had to pay weeks in advance for the privilege of staying here. Ford had booked the day after he had said good-bye to Marguerite and returned, for ever, to Tricia.

"My wife wants to know the area of Ntsukunyane," he said.

"Four million acres."

Ford gave the appropriate whistle. "Do we have a chance of seeing a leopard?"

The man shrugged, smiled, "Who knows? You may be lucky. You're here a whole week so you should see lion, elephant, hippo, cheetah maybe. But the leopard is nocturnal and you must be back in camp by six p.m." He looked at his watch. "I advise you to get on now, sir, if you're to make Thaba before they close the gates."

Ford got back into the car. It was nearly four. The sun of Africa, a living presence, a personal god, burned through a net of haze. There was no wind. Tricia, in a pale yellow sundress with frills, had hung her arm outside the open window and the fair downy skin was glowing red. He told her what the man had said and he told her about the notice pinned inside the hut: *It is strictly forbidden to bring firearms into the game reserve, to feed the animals, to exceed the speed limit, to litter.*

"And most of all you mustn't get out of the car," said Ford.

"What, not ever?" said Tricia, making her pale blue eyes round and naive and marble-like.

"That's what it says."

She pulled a face. "Silly old rules!"

"They have to have them," he said.

In here as in the outside world. It is strictly forbidden to fall in love, to leave your wife, to try to begin anew. He glanced at Tricia to see if the same thoughts were passing through her mind. Her face wore its arch expression, winsome.

"A prize," she said, "for the first one to see an animal."

"All right." He had agreed to this reconciliation, to bring her on this holiday, this second honeymoon, and now he must try. He must work at it. It wasn't just going to happen as love had sprung between him and Marguerite, unsought and untried for. "Who's going to award it?" he said.

"You are if it's me and I am if it's you. And if it's me I'd like a presey from the camp shop. A very nice pricey presey."

Ford was the winner. He saw a single zebra come out from among the thorn trees on the right-hand side, then a small herd. "Do I get a present from the shop?"

He could sense rather than see her shake her head with calculated coyness. "A kiss," she said and pressed warm dry lips against his cheek.

It made him shiver a little. He slowed down for the zebra to cross the road. The thornbushes had spines on them two inches long. By the roadside grew a species of wild zinnia with tiny flowers, coral-red, and these made red drifts among the coarse, pale grass. In the bush were red anthills with tall peaks like towers on a castle in a fairy story. It was thirty miles to Thaba. He drove on just within the speed limit, ignoring Tricia as far as he could whenever she asked him to slow down. They weren't going to see one of the big predators, anyway not this afternoon, he was certain of that, only impala and zebra and maybe a giraffe. On business trips in the past he'd taken time off to go to Serengeti and Kruger and he knew. He got the binoculars out for Tricia and adjusted them and hooked them round her neck, for he hadn't forgotten the binoculars and cameras she had dropped and smashed in the past through failing to do that, and her tears afterwards. The car wasn't air-conditioned and the heat lay heavy and still between them. Ahead of them, as they drove westward,, the sun was sinking in a dull yellow glare. The sweat flowed out of Ford's armpits and between his shoulder blades, soaking his already wet shirt and laying a cold sticky film on his skin.

A stone pyramid with arrows on it, set in the middle of a junction of roads, pointed the way to Thaba, to the main camp at Waka-suthu and to Hippo Bridge over the Suthu River. On top of it sat a baboon with her gray fluffy infant on her knees. Tricia yearned for it, stretching out her arms. She had never had a child. The baboon began picking fleas out of its baby's scalp. Tricia gave a little nervous scream, half disgusted, half joyful. Ford drove down the road to Thaba and in through the entrance to the camp ten minutes before they closed the gates for the night.

The dark comes down fast in Africa. Dusk is of short duration; no sooner have you noticed it than it has gone and night has fallen. In the few moments of dusk, pale things glimmer brightly and birds make a soft murmuring. In the camp at Thaba were a restaurant and a shop, round huts with thatched roofs and wooden chalets with porches. Ford and Tricia had been assigned a chalet on the northern perimeter and from their porch, beyond the high wire fence, you could see the Suthu River flowing smoothly and silently between banks of tall reeds. Dusk had just come as they walked up the wooden steps, Ford carrying their cases. It was then that he saw the fever trees, two of them, their ferny leaves bleached to gray by the twilight but their trunks a sharper, stronger yellow than in the day.

"Just as well we took our anti-malaria pills," said Ford as he pushed open the door. When the light was switched on he could see two mosquitoes on the opposite wall. "Anopheles is the malaria carrier but unfortunately they don't announce whether they're anopheles or not."

Twin beds, a table, lamps, an air conditioner, a fridge, a door, standing open, to lavatory and shower. Tricia dropped her makeup case, without which she went nowhere, on to the bed by the window. The light wasn't very bright. None of the lights in the camp were because the electricity came from a generator. They were a small colony of humans in a world that belonged to the animals, a reversal of the usual order of things. From the window you could see other chalets, other dim lights, other parked cars. Tricia talked to the two mosquitoes.

"Is your name Anna Phyllis? No. Darling, you're quite safe. She says she's Mary Jane and her husband's John Henry."

Ford managed to smile. He had accepted and grown used to Tricia's facetiousness until he had encountered Marguerite's wit. He shoved his case, without unpacking it, into the cupboard and went to have a shower. Tricia stood on the porch, listening to the cicadas, thousands of them. It had gone pitch dark while she was hanging up her dresses and the sky was punctured all over with bright stars.

She had got Ford back from that woman and now she had to keep him. She had lost some weight, bought a lot of new clothes and had had highlights put in her hair. Men had always made her feel frightened, starting with her father when she was a child. It was then, when a child, that she had purposely begun *playing* the child with its winning little ways. She had noticed that her father was kinder and more forbearing toward little girls than toward her mother. Ford had married a little girl, clinging and winsome, and had liked it well enough till he had met a grown woman. Tricia knew all that, but now she knew no better how to keep him than she did then; the old methods were as weary and stale to her as she guessed they might be to him. Standing there on the porch, she half-wished she were alone and didn't have to have a husband, didn't, for the sake of convention and of pride, for support and society, have to hold tight on to him. She listened wistfully for a lion to roar out there in the bush beyond the fence, but there was no sound except the cicadas.

Ford came out in a toweling robe. "What did you do with the mosquito stuff? The spray?"

Frightened at once, she said, "I don't know."

"What do you mean, you don't know? You must know. I gave you the aerosol at the hotel and said to put it in that makeup case of yours."

She opened the case, though she knew the mosquito stuff wasn't there. Of course it wasn't. She could see it on the bathroom shelf in the hotel, left behind because it was too bulky. She bit her lip, looked sideways at Ford. "We can get some more at the shop."

"Tricia, the shop closes at seven and it's now ten past."

"We can get some in the morning."

"Mosquitoes happen to be most active at night." He rummaged among the bottles and jars in the case. "Look at all this useless rubbish. 'Skin cleanser,' 'pearlized foundation,' 'moisturizer'—like some young model girl. I suppose it didn't occur to you to bring the anti-mosquito spray and leave the 'pearlized foundation' behind."

Her lip trembled. She could feel herself, almost involuntarily, rounding her eyes, forming her mouth into the shape for lisping. "We did 'member to take our pills."

"That won't stop the damn' things biting." He went back into the shower and slammed the door.

Marguerite wouldn't have forgotten to bring that aerosol. Tricia knew he was thinking of Marguerite again, that his head was full of her, that she had entered his thoughts powerfully and insistently on the long drive to Thaba. She began to cry. The water went on running out of her eyes and wouldn't stop, so she changed her dress while she cried and the tears came through the powder she put on her face.

They had dinner in the restaurant. Tricia, in pink flowered crepe, was the only dressed-up woman there, and while once she would have fancied the other diners looked at her in admiration, now she thought it must be with derision. She ate her small piece of overcooked hake and her large piece of overcooked, bread-crumbed veal, and watched the red weals from mosquito bites coming up on Ford's arms.

There were no lights on in the camp but those which shone from the windows of the main building and from the chalets. Gradually the lights went out and it became very dark. In spite of his mosquito bites, Ford fell asleep at once but the noise of the air-conditioning kept Tricia awake. At eleven she switched it off and opened the window. Then she did sleep but she awoke again at four, lay awake for half an hour, got up and put her clothes on and went out.

It was still dark but the darkness was lifting as if the thickest veil of it had been withdrawn. A heavy dew lay on the grass. As she passed under the merula tree, laden with small green apricot-shaped fruits, a flock of bats flew out from its branches and circled her head. If Ford had been with her she would have screamed and clung to him but because she was alone she kept silent. The camp and the bush beyond the fence were full of sound. The sounds brought to Tricia's mind the paintings of Hieronymus Bosch, imps and demons and dreadful homunculi which, if they had uttered, might have made noises like these, gruntings and soft whistles and chirps and little thin squeals.

She walked about, waiting for the dawn, expecting it to come with drama. But it was only a gray pallor in the sky, a paleness between parting black clouds, and the feeling of letdown frightened her as if it were a symbol or an omen of something more significant in her life than the coming of morning.

Ford woke up, unable at first to open his eyes for the swelling from mosquito bites. There were mosquitoes like threads of thistle-down on the walls, all over the walls. He got up and staggered, half-blind, out of the bedroom and let the water from the shower run on his eyes. Tricia came and stared at his face, giggling nervously and biting her lip.

The camp gates opened at five-thirty and the cars began their exodus. Tricia had never passed a driving test and Ford couldn't see, so they went to the restaurant for breakfast instead. When the shop opened Ford bought two kinds of mosquito repellent and, impatiently, because he could no longer bear her apologies and her pleading eyes, a necklace of ivory beads for Tricia and a skirt with giraffes printed on it. At nine o'clock, when the swelling round

Ford's eyes had subsided a little, they set off in the car, taking the road for Hippo Bridge.

The day was humid and thickly hot. Ford had counted the number of mosquito bites he had and the total was twenty-four. It was hard to believe that two little tablets of quinine would be proof against twenty-four bites, some of which must certainly have been inflicted by anopheles. Hadn't he seen the two fever trees when they arrived last night? Now he drove the car slowly and doggedly, hardly speaking, his swollen eyes concealed behind sunglasses. By the Suthu River and then by a water hole he stopped and they watched. But they saw nothing come to the water's edge unless you counted the log which at last disappeared, thus proving itself to have been a crocodile. It was too late in the morning to see much apart from the marabou storks which stood one-legged, still and hunched, in a clearing or on the gaunt branch of a tree. Through binoculars Ford stared at the bush which stretched in unbroken, apparently untenanted, sameness to the blue ridge of mountains on the far horizon.

There could be no real fever from the mosquito bites. If malaria were to come it wouldn't be yet. But Ford, sitting in the car beside Tricia, nevertheless felt something like a delirium of fever. It came perhaps from the gross irritation of the whole surface of his body, from the tender burning of his skin and from his inability to move without setting up fresh torment. It affected his mind too, so that each time he looked at Tricia a kind of panic rose in him. Why had he done it? Why had he gone back to her? Was he mad? His eyes and his head throbbed as if his temperature were raised. Tricia's pink jeans were too tight for her and the frills on her white voile blouse ridiculous. With the aid of the binoculars she had found a family of small gray monkeys in the branches of a peepul tree and she was cooing at them out of the window. Presently she opened the car door, held it just open and turned to look at him the way a child looks at her father when he has forbidden something she nevertheless longs and means to do.

They hadn't had sight of a big cat or an elephant, they hadn't even seen a jackal. Ford lifted his shoulders.

"O.K. But, if a ranger comes along and catches you, we'll be in dead trouble."

She got out of the car, leaving the door open. The grass which began at the roadside and covered the bush as far as the eye could see was long and coarse. It came up above Tricia's knees. A lioness or a cheetah lying in it would have been entirely concealed. Ford picked up the binoculars and looked the other way to avoid watching Tricia who had once again forgotten to put the camera strap round her neck. She was making overtures to the monkeys who shrank away from her, embracing each other and burying heads in shoulders, like menaced refugees in a sentimental painting. He moved the glasses slowly. About a hundred yards from where a small herd of buck grazed uneasily, he saw the two cat faces close together, the bodies nestled together, the spotted backs. Cheetah. It came into his mind how he had heard that they were the fastest animals on earth.

He ought to call to Tricia and get her back at once into the car. He didn't call. Through the glasses he watched the big cats that reclined there so gracefully, satiated, at rest, yet with open eyes. Marguerite would have liked them, she loved cats, she had a Burmese, as lithe and slim and poised as one of these wild creatures. Tricia got back into the car, exclaiming how sweet the monkeys were. He started the car and drove off without saying anything to her about the cheetahs.

Later, at about five in the afternoon, she wanted to get out of the car again and he didn't stop her. She walked up and down the road, talking to mongooses. In something over an hour it would be dark. Ford imagined starting up the car and driving back to the camp without her. Leopards were nocturnal hunters, waiting till dark. The swelling around his eyes had almost subsided now but his neck and arms and hands ached from the stiffness of the bites. The mongooses fled into the grass as Tricia approached, whispering to them, hands outstretched. A car with four men in it was coming along from the Hippo Bridge direction. It slowed down and the driver put his head out. His face was brick-red, thick-featured, his hair corrugated blond, and his voice had the squashed vowels accent of the white man born in Africa.

"The lady shouldn't be out on the road like that."

"I know," said Ford. "I've told her."

"Excuse me, d'you know you're doing a very dangerous thing, leaving your car?" The voice had a hectoring boom. Tricia blushed. She bridled, smiled, bit her lip, though she was in fact very afraid of this man who was looking at her as if he despised her, as if she disgusted him. When he got back to camp, would he betray her?

"Promise you won't tell on me?" she faltered, her head on one side.

He gave an exclamation of anger and withdrew his head. The car moved forward. Tricia gave a skip and a jump into the passenger seat beside Ford. They had under an hour in which to get back to Thaba. Ford drove back, following the car with the four men in it.

At dinner they sat at adjoining tables. Tricia wondered how many people they had told about her, for she fancied that some of the diners looked at her with curiosity or antagonism. The man with the fair curly hair they called Eric boasted loudly of what he and his companions had seen that day, a whole pride of lions, two rhinoceros, hyena, and the rare sable antelope.

"You can't expect to see much down that Hippo Bridge road, you know," he said to Ford. "All the game's up at Sotingwe. You take the Sotingwe road first thing tomorrow and I'll guarantee you lions."

He didn't address Tricia, he didn't even look at her. Ten years before, men in restaurants had turned their heads to look at her and though she had feared them, she had basked, trembling, in their gaze. Walking across the grass, back to their chalet, she held on to Ford's arm.

"For God's sake, mind my mosquito bites," said Ford.

He lay awake a long while in the single bed a foot away from Tricia's, thinking about the leopard out there beyond the fence that hunted at night. The leopard would move along the branch of a tree and drop upon its prey. Lionesses hunted in the early morning and brought the kill to their mate and the cubs. Ford had seen all that sort of thing on television. How cheetahs hunted he didn't know except that they were very swift. An angry elephant would lean on a car and crush it or smash a windscreen with a blow from its foot. It was too dark for him to see Tricia but he knew she was awake, lying still, sometimes holding her breath. He heard her breath released in an exhalation, a sigh, that was audible above the rattle of the air conditioner.

Years ago he had tried to teach her to drive. They said a husband should never try to teach his wife, he would have no patience with her and make no allowances. Tricia's progress had never been maintained, she had always been liable to do silly, reckless things and then he had shouted at her. She took a driving test and failed and she said this was because the examiner had bullied her. Tricia seemed to think no one should ever raise his voice to her, and at one glance from her all men should fall slaves at her feet.

He would have liked her to be able to take a turn at driving. There was no doubt you missed a lot when you had to concentrate on the road. But it was no use suggesting it. Theirs was one of the first cars in the line to leave the gates at five-thirty, to slip out beyond the fence into the gray dawn, the still bush. At the stone pyramid, on which a family of baboons sat clustered, Ford took the road for Sotingwe.

A couple of miles up they came upon the lions. Eric and his friends were already there, leaning out of the car windows with cameras. The lions, two full-grown lionesses, two lioness cubs and a lion cub with his mane beginning to sprout, were lying on the roadway. Ford stopped and parked the car on the opposite side to Eric.

"Didn't I say you'd be lucky up here?" Eric called to Tricia, "Not got any ideas about getting out and investigating, I hope."

Tricia didn't answer him or look at him. She looked at the lions. The sun was coming up, radiating the sky with a pinkish-orange glow and a little breeze fluttered all the pale green, fernlike leaves. The larger of the adult lionesses, bored rather than alarmed by Eric's elaborate photographic equipment, got up slowly and strolled into the bush, in among the long dry grass and the red zinnias. The cubs followed her, the other lioness followed her. Through his binoculars Ford watched them stalk with proud, lifted heads, walking, even the little ones, in a graceful, measured, controlled way. There were no impala anywhere, no giraffe, no wildebeest. The world here belonged to the lions.

All the game was gathered at Sotingwe, near the water hole. An elephant with ears like punkahs was powdering himself with red earth blown out through his trunk. Tricia got out of the car to photograph the elephant and Ford didn't try to stop her. He scratched his mosquito bites which had passed the burning and entered the itchy stage. Once more Tricia had neglected to pass the camera strap round her neck. She made her way down to the water's edge and stood at a safe distance—was it a safe distance? Was any distance safe in here?—looking at a crocodile. Ford thought, without really explaining to himself or even fully understanding what he meant, that it was the wrong time of day, it was too early. They went back to Thaba for breakfast.

At breakfast and again at lunch Eric was very full of what he had seen. He had taken the dirt road that ran down from Sotingwe to Suthu Bridge and there, up in a tree near the water, had been a leopard. Malcolm had spotted it first, stretched out asleep on a branch, a long way off but quite easy to see through field glasses.

"Massive great fella with your authentic square-type spots," said Eric, smoking a cigar.

Tricia, of course, wanted to go to Suthu Bridge, so Ford took the dirt road after they had had their siesta. Malcolm described exactly where he had seen the leopard which might, for all he knew, still be sleeping on its branch.

"About half a mile up from the bridge. You look over on your left and there's a sort of clearing with one of those trees with yellow trunks in it. This chap was on a branch on the right side of the clearing."

The dirt road was a track of crimson earth between green verges. Ford found the clearing with the single fever tree but the leopard had gone. He drove slowly down to the bridge that spanned the sluggish green river. When he switched off the engine it was silent and utterly still, the air hot and close, nothing moving but the mosquitoes that danced in their haphazard yet regular measure above the surface of the water.

Tricia was getting out of the car as a matter of course now. This time she didn't even trouble to give him the coy glance that asked permission. She was wearing a red and white striped sundress with straps that were too narrow and a skirt that was too tight. She ran down to the water's edge, took off a sandal and dipped in a daring foot. She laughed and twirled her feet, dabbling the dry round stones with water drops. Ford thought how he had loved this sort of thing when he had first met her, and now he was going to have to bear it for the rest of his life. He broke into a sweat as if his temperature had suddenly risen.

She was prancing about on the stones and in the water, holding up her skirt. There were no animals to be seen. All afternoon they had seen nothing but impala, and the sun was moving down now, beginning to color the hazy, pastel sky. Tricia, on the opposite bank, broke another Ntsukunyane rule and picked daisies, tucking one behind each ear. With a flower between her teeth like a Spanish dancer, she swayed her hips and smiled.

Ford turned the ignition key and started the car. It would be dark in just over an hour and long before that they would have closed the gates at Thaba. He moved the car forward, reversed, making what Tricia, no doubt, would call a three-point turn. Facing towards Thaba now, he put the selector into drive, his foot on the accelerator, he took a deep breath as the sweat trickled between his shoulder blades. The heat made mirages on the road and out of them a car was coming. Ford stopped and switched off the engine. It wasn't Eric's car but one belonging to a couple of young Americans on holiday. The boy raised his hand in a salute at Ford.

Ford called out to Tricia, "Come on or we'll be late." She got into the car, dropping her flowers on to the roadway. Ford had been going to leave her there, that was how much he wanted to be rid of her. Her body began to shake and she clasped her hands tightly together so that he shouldn't see. He had been going to drive away and leave her there to the darkness and the lions, the leopard that hunted by night. He had been driving away, only the Americans' car had come along.

She was silent, thinking about it. The Americans turned back soon after they did and followed them up the dirt road. Impala stood around the solitary fever tree, listening perhaps to inaudible sounds or scenting invisible danger. The sky was smoky yellow with sunset. Tricia thought about what Ford must have intended to do, drive back to camp just before they closed the gates, watch the darkness come down, knowing she was out there, say not a word of her absence to anyone—and who would miss her? Eric? Malcolm? Ford wouldn't have gone to the restaurant and in the morning when they opened the gates he would have driven away. No need even to check out at Ntsukunyane where you paid weeks in advance.

The perfect murder. Who would search for her, not knowing there was need for search? And if her bones were found? One set of bones, human, impala, waterbuck, looks very much like another after the jackals have been at them and the vultures. And when he reached home he would have said he had left her for Marguerite. . . .

He was nicer to her that evening, gentler. Because he was afraid she had guessed or might guess the truth of what had happened at Sotingwe?

"We said we'd have champagne one night. How about now? No time like the present."

"If you like," Tricia said. She felt sick all the time, she had no appetite.

Ford toasted them in champagne. "To us!"

He ordered the whole gamut of the menu, soup, fish, Wiener schnitzel, *crème brûlée*. She picked at her food, thinking how he had meant to kill her. She would never be safe now, for having failed once he would try again. Not the same method perhaps but some other. How was she to know he hadn't already tried? Maybe, for instance, he had substituted aspirin for those quinine tablets, or when they were back in the hotel in Mombasa he might try to drown her. She would never be safe unless she left him.

Which was what he wanted, which would be the next best thing to her death. Lying awake in the night, she thought of what that would mean, going back to live with her mother while he went to Marguerite. He wasn't asleep either. She could hear the sound of his irregular wakeful breathing. She heard the bed creak as he moved in it restlessly, the air-conditioning grinding, the whine of a mosquito. Now, if she hadn't already been killed, she might be wandering out there in the bush, in terror in the dark, afraid to take a step but afraid to remain still, fearful of every sound, yet not knowing which sound most to fear. There was no moon. She had taken note of that before she came to bed and had seen in her diary that tomorrow the moon would be new. The sky had been overcast at nightfall and now it was pitch dark. The leopard could see, perhaps by the light of the stars or with an inner instinctive eye more sure than simple vision and would drop silently from its branch to sink its teeth into the lifted throat.

The mosquito that had whined bit Ford in several places on his face and neck and on his left foot. He had forgotten to use the repellent the night before. Early in the morning, at dawn, he got up and dressed and went for a walk round the camp. There was no one about but one of the African staff, hosing down a guest's car. Squeaks and shufflings came from the bush beyond the fence.

Had he really meant to rid himself of Tricia by throwing her, as one might say, to the lions? For a mad moment, he supposed, because fever had got into his blood, poison into his veins. She knew, he could tell that. In a way it might be all to the good, her knowing, it would show her how hopeless the marriage was that she was trying to preserve.

The swellings on his foot, though covered by his sock, were making the instep bulge through the sandal. His foot felt stiff and burning and he became aware that he was limping slightly. Supporting himself against the trunk of a fever tree, his skin against its cool, dampish, yellow bark, he took off his sandal and felt his swollen foot tenderly with his fingertips. Mosquitoes never touched Tricia, they seemed to shirk contact with her pale dry flesh.

She was up when he hobbled in, she was sitting on her bed, painting her fingernails. How could he live with a woman who painted her fingernails in a game reserve?

They didn't go out till nine. On the road to Waka-suthu Eric's car met them, coming back.

"There's nothing down there for miles, you're wasting your time."

"O.K.," said Ford. "Thanks."

"Sotingwe's the place. Did you see the leopard yesterday?" Ford shook his head. "Oh, well, we can't all be lucky."

Elephants were playing in the river at Hippo Bridge, spraying each other with water and nudging heavy shoulders. Ford thought that was going to be the high spot of the morning until they came upon the kill. They didn't actually see it. The kill had taken place some hours before, but the lioness and her cubs were still picking at the carcass, at a blood-blackened rib cage. They sat in the car and watched. After a while the lions left the carcass and walked away in file through the grass, but the little jackals were already gathered, a pack of them, posted behind trees. Ford came back that way again at four and by then the vultures had moved in, picking the bones.

It was a hot day of merciless sunshine, the sky blue and perfectly clear. Ford's foot was swollen to twice its normal size. He noticed that Tricia hadn't once left the car that day, nor had she spoken girlishly to him or giggled or given him a roguish kiss. She thought he had been trying to kill her, a preposterous notion really. The truth was he had only been giving her a fright, teaching her how stupid it was to flout the rules and leave the car. Why should he kill her, anyway? He could leave her, he *would* leave her, and once they were back in Mombasa he would tell her so. The thought of it made him turn to her and smile. He had stopped by the clearing where the fever tree stood, yellow of bark, delicate and fernlike of leaf, in the sunshine like a young sapling in springtime.

"Why don't you get out anymore?"

She faltered, "There's nothing to see."

"No?"

He had spotted the porcupine with his naked eye but he handed her the binoculars. She looked and laughed with pleasure. That was the way she used to laugh when she was young, not from amusement but delight. He shut his eyes. "Oh, the sweetie porky-pine!"

She reached onto the back seat for the camera. And then she hesitated. He could see the fear, the caution in her eyes. Silently he took the key out of the ignition and held it out to her on the palm of his hand. She flushed. He stared at her, enjoying her discomfiture, indignant that she should suspect him of such baseness.

She hesitated but she took the key. She picked up the camera and opened the car door, holding the key by its fob in her left hand, the camera in her right. He noticed that she hadn't passed the strap of the camera, his treasured Pentax, round her neck, she never did. For the thousandth time he could have told her but he lacked the heart to speak. His swollen foot throbbed and he thought of the long days at Ntsukunyane that remained to them. Marguerite seemed infinitely far away, further even than at the other side of the world where she was.

He knew Tricia was going to drop the camera some fifteen seconds before she did so. It was because she had the key in her other hand. If the strap had been round her neck it wouldn't have mattered. He knew how it was when you held something in each hand and lost your grip or your footing. You had no sense then, in that instant, of which of the objects was valuable and mattered and which was not and didn't. Tricia held on to the key and dropped the camera. The better to photograph the porcupine, she had mounted on to the twisted roots of a tree, roots that looked as hard as a flight of stone steps.

She gave a little cry. At the sounds of the crash and the cry the porcupine erected its quills. Ford jumped out of the car, wincing when he put his foot to the ground, hobbling through the grass to

Tricia who stood as if petrified with fear of him. The camera, the pieces of camera, had fallen among the gnarled, stonelike tree roots. He dropped on to his knees, shouting at her, cursing her.

Tricia began to run. She ran back to the car and pushed the key into the ignition. The car was pointing in the direction of Thaba and the clock on the dashboard shelf said five thirty-five. Ford came limping back, waving his arms at her, his hands full of broken pieces of camera. She looked away and put her foot down hard on the accelerator.

The sky was clear orange with sunset, black bars of the coming night lying on the horizon. She found she could drive when she had to, even though she couldn't pass a test. A mile along the road she met the American couple. The boy put his head out. "Anything worth going down there for?"

"Not a thing," said Tricia, "you'd be wasting your time."

The boy turned his car and followed her back. It was two minutes past six when they entered Thaba, the last cars to do so. The gates closed behind them.

Understanding the Story _____

Main Idea

1. The tragedy was brought on by   (a) Ford's dissatisfaction with his own wife   (b) Tricia's flirtation with Eric   (c) Marguerite's appearance at the game reserve   (d) a serious accident.

Details

2. On her last trip outside the car, Tricia probably intended to photograph a(n)   (a) lion   (b) impala   (c) jackal   (d) porcupine.

3. Ford was annoyed because Tricia had forgotten   (a) her makeup kit   (b) her movie camera   (c) the insect repellent   (d) a book he was reading.

4. The person who told Ford where to find the lions was   (a) Malcolm   (b) Eric   (c) Tricia   (d) the game reserve ranger.

5. Ford was disfigured by   (a) the fever tree   (b) malaria   (c) mosquito bites   (d) a gunshot wound.

Inferences

6. After his experience with Marguerite, Ford considered Tricia's actions   (a) cute   (b) cruel   (c) pleasing   (d) immature.

7. When Ford first saw the cheetahs, Tricia was outside the car; yet he said nothing to her because   (a) he seemed to hope the cheetahs would attack her   (b) he had his gun poised and ready   (c) Tricia had seen the big cats and quickly returned to the vehicle   (d) he wanted to get a better picture.

8. Marguerite is a character in the story because   (a) she knew Africa better than Tricia   (b) Ford constantly compared her with Tricia   (c) she was Tricia's best friend   (d) she despised Ford.

9. Ford's thought about murdering his wife   (a) had been planned for half a year   (b) occurred on the spur of the moment   (c) was the reason for his return to Africa   (d) was suspected by Eric.

10. In all probability Tricia dropped the camera   (a) to spite Marguerite   (b) completely accidentally   (c) on purpose (d) because she had been stung by some stinging insect.

Order of Events

11. Arrange the items in the order in which they occurred. Use letters only.
    A. Tricia sees the porcupine.
    B. Eric scolds Tricia.
    C. Ford gets stung by mosquitoes.
    D. Tricia drops the camera.
    E. Ford nearly drives off and leaves Tricia in the reserve.

Outcomes

12. If Tricia had passed her driving test,   (a) she would have won Ford away from Marguerite   (b) the ranger would have given her a game-reserve license   (c) she would never have got out of the car   (d) Ford might not have handed her the key.

Cause and Effect

13. Because of his mosquito bites, Ford   (a) preferred to stay in camp   (b) could not try to overtake the car   (c) refused to take Tricia out to look for animals   (d) went to a physician.

Fact or Opinion

Tell whether each of the following is a fact or an opinion.

14. Tricia drove back to camp without Ford.

15. Tricia did not take the insect repellent to the game reserve.

Words in Context _____

1. She began to *belabor* him with schoolgirl questions, uttered in a bright and desperate voice.
   Belabor (123) means   (a) bother   (b) humor   (c) amuse (d) accuse.

2. "But the leopard is *nocturnal* and you must be back in camp by six p.m."
   Nocturnal (124) means   (a) fierce   (b) stealthy   (c) active at night   (d) slowly aroused.

3. Her face wore its *arch* expression, *winsome*.
   Arch (124) means   (a) angry   (b) mischievous   (c) unusual (d) childish.

4. *Winsome* (124) means   (a) victorious   (b) athletic (c) wrinkled   (d) charming.

5. He had agreed to this *reconciliation*, to bring her on this holiday, this second honeymoon, and now he must try.
   Reconciliation (124) means   (a) renewal of association (b) journey   (c) expression of friendship   (d) first acquaintance.

6. "A very nice *pricey* presey."
   Pricey (124) means   (a) inexpensive   (b) worthless (c) elaborate   (d) costly.

7. He had accepted and grown used to Tricia's *facetiousness* until he had encountered Marguerite's wit.
   Facetiousness (126) means   (a) thoughtfulness   (b) charm (c) inappropriate wittiness   (d) loudness.

8. While once she would have fancied the other diners looked at her in admiration, now she thought it must be with *derision*.
   Derision (127) means   (a) good-natured humor   (b) scorn (c) sidelong glances   (d) gloom.

9. She watched the red *weals* from mosquito bites coming up on Ford's arms.
   Weals (128) means   (a) lumps   (b) deep   scars (c) irritations   (d) fluids.

10. The camp gates opened at five-thirty and the cars began their *exodus*.
    Exodus (128) means   (a) picnic   (b) departure   (c) arrival (d) checkup.

11. Through binoculars Ford stared at the bush which stretched in unbroken, apparently *untenanted*, sameness to the blue ridge of mountains on the far horizon.
    Untenanted (129) means   (a) uncovered   (b) barren (c) unpopulated   (d) colorless.

12. Through the glasses he watched the big cats that reclined there so gracefully, *satiated*, at rest, yet with open eyes.
Satiated (130) means   (a) fully satisfied   (b) exceptionally greedy   (c) fiercely attentive   (d) highly decorative.

13. Marguerite . . . had a Burmese, as *lithe* and slim and poised as one of these wild creatures.
Lithe (130) means   (a) violent   (b) curious   (c) slender   (d) graceful.

14. His face was brick-red, thick-featured—his hair *corrugated* blond.
Corrugated (130) means   (a) dark   (b) straight   (c) unruly   (d) furrowed.

15. The voice had a *hectoring* boom.
Hectoring (130) means   (a) flattering   (b) bullying   (c) quieting   (d) rising and falling.

16. She *bridled*, smiled, bit her lip, though she was in fact very afraid of this man who was looking at her as if he despised her.
Bridled (130) means   (a) jumped up   (b) rode horseback   (c) took offense   (d) laughed aloud.

17. Though she had feared them, she had *basked*, trembling, in their gaze.
Basked (131) means   (a) taken pleasure   (b) backed off   (c) spoken sharply   (d) strutted.

18. The dirt road was a track of crimson earth between green *verges*.
Verges (133) means   (a) paths   (b) borders   (c) streams   (d) shrubs.

19. He noticed that Tricia hadn't once left the car that day, nor had she spoken girlishly to him or giggled or given him a *roguish* kiss.
Roguish (136) means   (a) stolen   (b) warm   (c) requested   (d) mischievous.

20. He stared at her, enjoying her *discomfiture*, indignant that she should suspect him of such baseness.
Discomfiture (137) means   (a) pleasure in little things   (b) wit   (c) uneasiness   (d) comfort.

Thinking About the Story _____

1. Why does Ford compare Tricia unfavorably with Marguerite? Point out some of the distinguishing characteristics of each.

2. Would Ford ultimately have killed Tricia, or would he merely have left her for Marguerite? Point to elements in the story to support your point of view.

3. Which to you is more unexpected, Ford's momentary impulse to kill Tricia or Tricia's resolve to leave Ford to his death in the reserve? Explain.

4. How do the descriptions of the reserve—there is killing all around—help to set the mood of the story?

5. Does the author intend to have Ford die in the reserve? Suppose he managed to survive, what then?

6. How does the author bring to life the minor character, Eric? Point to revealing descriptions and quotations.

The Open Window

"Saki" (H. H. Munro)

♦ "Do you know, sometimes on still, quiet evenings like this, I almost get a creepy feeling that
they will all walk in through that window—"
She broke off with a little shudder.

Welcome to a classic gem of short-story writing by one of the
great yarn-spinners of all time. "Saki" knew how to make the unusual seem commonplace. Talking cats, ladies who become ot-
ters after death, and similar unusual situations were his specialty. He combined fantasy with satire, all blended with a dash
of humor.

"The Open Window" is a blend of fun and sheer terror, all in
a handful of pages. He brings a smile to your face one moment,
and then freezes the marrow in your bones the next. If you aren't
frightened a little when you hear the voices in the distance, then
you are a hardy soul indeed. Keep your eyes on the open window,
for there are surprises ahead. Relish the remarkable ending, which
ties everything together in a delightfully satisfying knot.

THE OPEN WINDOW

My aunt will be down presently, Mr. Nuttel," said a very self-possessed young lady of fifteen; "in the meantime you must try and put up with me."

Framton Nuttel endeavored to say the correct something which should duly flatter the niece of the moment without unduly discounting the aunt that was to come. Privately he doubted more than ever whether these formal visits on a succession of total strangers would do much toward helping the nerve cure which he was supposed to be undergoing.

"I know how it will be," his sister had said when he was preparing to migrate to this rural retreat; "you will bury yourself down there and not speak to a living soul, and your nerves will be worse than ever from moping. I shall just give you letters of introduction to all the people I know there. Some of them, as far as I can remember, were quite nice."

Framton wondered whether Mrs. Sappleton, the lady to whom he was presenting one of the letters of introduction, came into the nice division.

"Do you know many of the people round here?" asked the niece, when she judged that they had had sufficient silent communion.

"Hardly a soul," said Framton. "My sister was staying here, at the rectory, you know, some four years ago, and she gave me letters of introduction to some of the people here."

He made the last statement in a tone of distinct regret.

"Then you know practically nothing about my aunt?" pursued the self-possessed young lady.

"Only her name and address," admitted the caller. He was wondering whether Mrs. Sappleton was in the married or widowed state. An indefinable something about the room seemed to suggest masculine habitation.

"Her great tragedy happened just three years ago," said the child; "that would be since your sister's time."

"Her tragedy?" asked Framton; somehow in this restful country spot tragedies seemed out of place.

"You may wonder why we keep that window wide open on an October afternoon," said the niece, indicating a large French window that opened on to a lawn.

"It is quite warm for the time of the year," said Framton; "but has that window got anything to do with the tragedy?"

"Out through that window, three years ago to a day, her husband and her two young brothers went off for their day's shooting. They never came back. In crossing the moor to their favorite snipe-shooting ground they were all three engulfed in a treacherous piece of bog. It had been that dreadful wet summer, you know, and places that were safe in other years gave way suddenly without warning. Their bodies were never recovered. That was the dreadful part of it." Here the child's voice lost its self-possessed note and became falteringly human. "Poor aunt always thinks that they will come back some day, they and the little brown spaniel that was lost with them, and walk in at that window just as they used to do. That is why the window is kept open every evening till it is quite dusk. Poor dear aunt, she has often told me how they went out, her husband with his white waterproof coat over his arm, and Ronnie, her youngest brother, singing 'Bertie, why do you bound?' as he always did to tease her, because she said it got on her nerves. Do you know, sometimes on still, quiet evenings like this, I almost get a creepy feeling that they will all walk in through that window—"

She broke off with a little shudder. It was a relief to Framton when the aunt bustled into the room with a whirl of apologies for being late in making her appearance.

"I hope Vera has been amusing you?" she said.

"She has been very interesting," said Framton.

"I hope you don't mind the open window," said Mrs. Sappleton briskly; "my husband and brothers will be home directly from shooting, and they always come in this way. They've been out for snipe in the marshes today, so they'll make a fine mess over my poor carpets. So like you menfolks, isn't it?"

She rattled on cheerfully about the shooting and the scarcity of birds, and the prospects for duck in the winter. To Framton it was all purely horrible. He made a desperate but only partially successful effort to turn the talk on to a less ghastly topic; he was conscious that his hostess was giving him only a fragment of her attention, and her eyes were constantly straying past him to the open window and the lawn beyond. It was certainly an unfortunate coincidence that he should have paid his visit on this tragic anniversary.

"The doctors agree in ordering me complete rest, an absence of mental excitement, and avoidance of anything in the nature of violent physical exercise," announced Framton, who labored under the tolerably widespread delusion that total strangers and chance acquaintances are hungry for the least detail of one's ailments and infirmities, their cause and cure. "On the matter of diet they are not so much in agreement," he continued.

"No?" said Mrs. Sappleton, in a voice which only replaced a yawn at the last moment. Then she suddenly brightened into alert attention—but not to what Framton was saying.

"Here they are at last!" she cried. "Just in time for tea, and don't they look as if they were muddy up to the eyes!"

Framton shivered slightly and turned toward the niece with a look intended to convey sympathetic comprehension. The child was staring out through the open window with dazed horror in her eyes. In a chill shock of nameless fear Framton swung round in his seat and looked in the same direction.

In the deepening twilight three figures were walking across the lawn towards the window; they all carried guns under their arms, and one of them was additionally burdened with a white coat hung over his shoulders. A tired brown spaniel kept close at their heels. Noiselessly they neared the house, and then a hoarse young voice chanted out of the dusk: "I said, Bertie, why do you bound?"

Framton grabbed wildly at his stick and hat; the hall door, the gravel drive, and the front gate were dimly noted stages in his headlong retreat. A cyclist coming along the road had to run into the hedge to avoid imminent collision.

"Here we are, my dear," said the bearer of the white mackintosh, coming in through the window, "fairly muddy, but most of it's dry. Who was that who bolted out as we came up?"

"A most extraordinary man, a Mr. Nuttel," said Mrs. Sappleton; "could only talk about his illness, and dashed off without a word of good-bye or apology when you arrived. One would think he had seen a ghost."

"I expect it was the spaniel," said the niece calmly; "he told me he had a horror of dogs. He was once hunted into a cemetery somewhere on the banks of the Ganges by a pack of pariah dogs, and had to spend the night in a newly dug grave with the creatures snarling and grinning and foaming just above him. Enough to make anyone lose their nerve."

Romance at short notice was her specialty.

Understanding the Story ⎯⎯⎯⎯⎯⎯⎯

Main Idea

1. The main idea of the story is summed up in which of the following sentences from the story?
   (a) "You may wonder why we keep that window wide open on an October afternoon," said the niece, indicating a large French window that opened on to a lawn.
   (b) "Here they are at last!" she cried. "Just in time for tea, and don't they look as if they were muddy up to the eyes!"
   (c) Framton grabbed wildly at his stick and hat; the hall door, the gravel drive, and the front gate were dimly noted stages in his headlong retreat.
   (d) Romance at short notice was her specialty.

Details

2. According to the niece the "tragedy" happened   (a) last week   (b) a month ago   (c) exactly a year ago   (d) three years ago.

3. Framton Nuttel was in the country for   (a) business reasons   (b) reestablishing a friendship with Mrs. Sappleton   (c) his health   (d) research.

4. According to the niece, Mrs. Sappleton's husband and her two young brothers (a) were interested in the theater (b) had been engulfed in a bog (c) had just returned from London (d) were enthusiastic sailors.

5. When Mr. Nuttel left Mrs. Sappleton's house, he left (a) in a great hurry (b) without his walking stick (c) with the niece as a guide (d) after tea.

Inferences

6. Apparently, "Bertie, why do you bound?" was (a) a song (b) named for Mrs. Sappleton's husband (c) an expression used in a fox hunt (d) a book title.

7. Mr. Nuttel can best be described as a (a) hunter (b) bore (c) close friend of the Sappleton's (d) suitor for the niece's hand.

8. Mrs. Sappleton's attitude toward Mr. Nuttel's conversation can best be described as (a) excited (b) attentive (c) uninterested (d) amused.

9. The story about Mr. Nuttel's experiences with a pack of dogs was (a) gruesome (b) imaginary (c) accurately reported by the niece (d) enjoyed by Mrs. Sappleton's two brothers.

10. Mr. Nuttel thought he had seen (a) his own long-lost brother (b) the father he hadn't seen in years (c) three persons' ghosts (d) the niece's fiancé.

Order of Events

11. Arrange the items in the order in which they occurred. Use letters only.
    A. The niece tells the story of the dogs.
    B. Mrs. Sappleton greets Mr. Nuttel.
    C. The hunters return.
    D. The niece entertains Mr. Nuttel.
    E. Mr. Nuttel departs.

Outcomes

12. If Mr. Nuttel had stayed longer, he would have (a) learned the truth (b) proposed to the niece (c) quarreled with Mr. Sappleton (d) hunted with the two brothers.

Cause and Effect

13. If Mr. Nuttel had known Mrs. Sappleton well,   (a) he would
    have left sooner   (b) the niece wouldn't have made up the
    story   (c) the brothers would have objected to his presence
    (d) he would not have visited in the first place.

Fact or Opinion

Tell whether each of the following is a fact or an opinion.

14. The three men had not been swallowed by the bog.

15. The niece was a brilliant young lady.

Words in Context

1. "My aunt will be down presently, Mr. Nuttel," said a *self-possessed* young lady of fifteen.
   Self-possessed (145) means   (a) peculiar   (b) confident
   (c) loving   (d) talkative.

2. "My sister was staying here, at the *rectory*, you know, some four
   years ago."
   Rectory (145) means   (a) city   hall   (b) hospital
   (c) boarding school   (d) minister's residence.

3. "He labored under the tolerably widespread delusion that total
   strangers and chance acquaintances are hungry for the least
   detail of one's ailments and *infirmities*, their cause and cure."
   Infirmities (147) means   (a) strong points   (b) desires
   (c) weaknesses   (d) future plans.

4. A cyclist coming along the road had to run into a hedge to avoid
   imminent collision.
   Imminent (147) means   (a) unwanted   (b) threatening
   (c) unexpected   (d) fatal.

5. "He was once hunted into a cemetery somewhere on the banks
   of the Ganges by a pack of *pariah* dogs."
   Pariah (148) means   (a) outcast   (b) well-trained   (c) gentle
   (d) well-fed.

Thinking About the Story _____

1. Though this is a short short story, it brilliantly draws three con-
    trasting characters for us with dialog alone to do the job.
    (a) How is the young man's character revealed to us? Why is he
        made, for the purposes of the story, so timid and nervous?
    (b) What clues to the character of the niece are provided? How
        does the second paragraph from the end of the story reveal
        and confirm what she is like?
    (c) How does Mrs. Sappleton's obvious boredom with Mr. Nut-
        tel reveal her character? How does her final explanation
        show her to be a down-to-earth person entirely absorbed in
        her family?

2. There are two important quotations to note again:
    "My sister was staying here, at the rectory, you know, some
    four years ago." (145)
    "Then you know practically nothing about my aunt?" (145)

    How do these two quotations help us understand why the niece
    told the particular story she made up?

3. The last sentence in the story explains the story, but is it nec-
    essary? Could you have got the point of the story without it?
    Explain.

4. We say something is ironic when a speaker says something that
    is true in an unexpected or opposite way. Mrs. Sappleton says
    of Nuttel, "One would think he had seen a ghost." How is this
    true in a way she does not suspect?

5. What is the high moment of suspense in the story? Did you feel
    a tingle of uneasiness? When did you first realize the niece's
    story was a hoax?

The Waxwork

A. M. Burrage

♦ This was a little too much! It was bad enough that the waxwork effigies of murderers should move when they weren't being watched, but it was intolerable that they should *breathe.* Somebody was breathing.

At one of the world's most famous wax museums, visitors frequently ask questions of a uniformed policeman who stands guard near the entrance. They are somewhat perturbed when, in the half-light that pervades the museum, they see no gesture on the policeman's part and hear no reply. They repeat the question. Some of the more impatient souls take the policeman by the arm, but he does not move. Then, with a start that pays tribute to the artist, they realize suddenly that he cannot move, for he is wax. At this point they begin to feel, in the eeriness of the quiet museum, a little terrified for not being able to tell the difference between living creatures like themselves and the motionless wax figures that stand in strange attitudes everywhere.

Imagine the following situation. For financial reasons you agree to spend the night alone in the dim quietness of a wax museum. You choose the most gruesome section of all, Murderers' Den. You take your position in the dim light, surrounded by the most dangerous of human beings . . . only in wax, of course. Then as you try to compose yourself for the long night ahead, you fancy you catch a slight movement off to the side. When you turn your head, the figures look back at you with the unblinking stares of waxworks. Listen! Do you hear muffled breathing? Oh, no, it's only your imagination. Or is it? You begin to wonder whether you ought to bolt out of the Den at once, but then you would admit defeat. So you settle back, carefully watching the group of notorious murderers who, of course, are only . . . figures of wax. Will the morning never come?

Are you ready to spend the night in Marriner's Waxworks?

THE WAXWORK

While the uniformed attendants of Marriner's Waxworks were ushering the last stragglers through the great glass-paneled double doors, the manager sat in his office interviewing Raymond Hewson.

The manager was a youngish man, stout, blond, and of medium height. He wore his clothes well and contrived to look extremely smart without appearing overdressed. Raymond Hewson looked neither. His clothes, which had been good when new and which were still carefully brushed and pressed, were beginning to show signs of their owner's losing battle with the world. He was a small, spare, pale man, with lank, errant brown hair, and although he spoke plausibly and even forcibly, he had the defensive and somewhat furtive air of a man who was used to rebuffs. He looked what he was, a man gifted somewhat above the ordinary, who was a failure through his lack of self-assertion.

The manager was speaking.

"There is nothing new in your request," he said. "In fact we refuse it to different people—mostly young bloods who have tried to make bets—about three times a week. We have nothing to gain and something to lose by letting people spend the night in our Murderers' Den. If I allowed it, and some young idiot lost his senses, what would be my position? But your being a journalist somewhat alters the case."

Hewson smiled.

"I suppose you mean that journalists have no senses to lose."

"No, no," laughed the manager, "but one imagines them to be responsible people. Besides, here we have something to gain; publicity and advertisement."

"Exactly," said Hewson, "and there I thought we might come to terms."

The manager laughed again.

"Oh," he exclaimed, "I know what's coming. You want to be paid twice, do you? It used to be said years ago that Madame Tussaud's would give a man a hundred pounds for sleeping alone in the Chamber of Horrors. I hope you don't think that we have made any such offer. Er—what is your paper, Mr. Hewson?"

"I am free-lancing at present," Hewson confessed, "working on space for several papers. However, I should find no difficulty in getting the story printed. The *Morning Echo* would use it like a shot. 'A Night with Marriner's Murderers.' No live paper could turn it down."

The manager rubbed his chin.

"Ah! And how do you propose to treat it?"

"I shall make it gruesome, of course; gruesome with just a saving touch of humor."

The other nodded and offered Hewson his cigarette case.

"Very well, Mr. Hewson," he said. "Get your story printed in the *Morning Echo*, and there will be a five-pound note waiting for you here when you care to come and call for it. But first of all, it's no small ordeal that you're proposing to undertake. I'd like to be quite sure about you, and I'd like you to be quite sure about yourself. I own I shouldn't care to take it on. I've seen those figures dressed and undressed, I know all about the process of their manufacture, I can walk about in company downstairs as unmoved as if I were walking among so many skittles, but I should hate having to sleep down there alone among them."

"Why?" asked Hewson.

"I don't know. There isn't any reason. I don't believe in ghosts. If I did I should expect them to haunt the scene of their crimes or the spot where their bodies were laid, instead of a cellar which happens to contain their waxwork effigies. It's just that I couldn't sit alone among them all night, with their seeming to stare at me in the way they do. After all, they represent the lowest and most appalling types of humanity, and—although I would not own it publicly—the people who come to see them are not generally charged with the very highest motives. The whole atmosphere of the place is unpleasant, and if you are susceptible to atmosphere, I warn you that you are in for a very uncomfortable night."

Hewson had known that from the moment when the idea had first occurred to him. His soul sickened at the prospect, even while he smiled casually upon the manager. But he had a wife and family to keep, and for the past month he had been living on paragraphs, eked out by his rapidly dwindling store of savings. Here was a chance not to be missed—the price of a special story in the *Morning Echo*, with a five-pound note to add to it. It meant comparative wealth and luxury for a week, and freedom from the worst anxieties for a fortnight. Besides, if he wrote the story well, it might lead to an offer of regular employment.

"The way of transgressors—and newspapermen—is hard," he said. "I have already promised myself an uncomfortable night because your Murderers' Den is obviously not fitted up as a hotel bedroom. But I don't think your waxworks will worry me much."

"You're not superstitious?"

"Not a bit," Hewson laughed.

"But you're a journalist; you must have a strong imagination."

"The news editors for whom I've worked have always complained that I haven't any. Plain facts are not considered sufficient in our trade, and the papers don't like offering their readers unbuttered bread."

The manager smiled and rose.

"Right," he said. "I think the last of the people have gone. Wait a moment. I'll give orders for the figures downstairs not to be draped, and let the night people know that you'll be here. Then I'll take you down and show you round."

He picked up the receiver of a house telephone, spoke into it and presently replaced it.

"One condition I'm afraid I must impose on you," he remarked. "I must ask you not to smoke. We had a fire scare down in the Murderers' Den this evening. I don't know who gave the alarm, but whoever it was, it was a false one. Fortunately there were very few people down there at the time, or there might have been a panic. And now, if you're ready, we'll make a move."

Hewson followed the manager through half a dozen rooms where attendants were busy shrouding the kings and queens of England, the generals and prominent statesmen of this and other generations, all the mixed herd of humanity whose fame or notoriety had rendered them eligible for this kind of immortality. The manager stopped once and spoke to a man in uniform, saying something about an armchair in the Murderers' Den.

"It's the best we can do for you, I'm afraid," he said to Hewson. "I hope you'll be able to get some sleep."

He led the way through an open barrier and down ill-lit stone stairs which conveyed a sinister impression of giving access to a dungeon. In a passage at the bottom were a few preliminary horrors, such as relics of the Inquisition, a rack taken from a medieval castle, branding irons, thumbscrews, and other mementoes of man's onetime cruelty to man. Beyond the passage was the Murderers' Den.

It was a room of irregular shape with a vaulted roof, and dimly lit by electric lights burning behind inverted bowls of frosted glass. It was, by design, an eerie and uncomfortable chamber—a chamber whose atmosphere invited its visitors to speak in whispers. There was something of the air of a chapel about it, but a chapel no longer devoted to the practice of piety and given over now for base and impious worship.

The waxwork murderers stood on low pedestals with numbered tickets at their feet. Seeing them elsewhere, and without knowing whom they represented, one would have thought them a dull-looking crew, chiefly remarkable for the shabbiness of their clothes, and as evidence of the changes of fashion even among the unfashionable.

Recent notorieties rubbed dusty shoulders with the old "favorites." Thurtell, the murderer of Weir, stood as if frozen in the act of making a shop window gesture to young Bywaters. There was Lefroy, the poor half-baked little snob who killed for gain so that he might ape the gentleman. Within five yards of him sat Mrs. Thompson, that erotic romanticist, hanged to propitiate British middle-class matronhood. Charles Peace, the only member of that vile company who looked uncompromisingly and entirely evil, sneered across a gangway at Norman Thorne. Browne and Kennedy, the two most recent additions, stood between Mrs. Dyer and Patrick Mahon.

The manager, walking around with Hewson, pointed out several of the more interesting of these unholy notabilities.

"That's Crippen; I expect you recognize him. Insignificant little beast who looks as if he couldn't tread on a worm. That's Armstrong. Looks like a decent, harmless country gentleman, doesn't he? There's old Vaquier; you can't miss him because of his beard. And of course this—"

"Who's that?" Hewson interrupted in a whisper, pointing.

"Oh, I was coming to him," said the manager in a light undertone. "Come and have a good look at him. This is our star turn. He's the only one of the bunch that hasn't been hanged."

The figure which Hewson had indicated was that of a small, slight man not much more than five feet in height. It wore a little waxed moustache, large spectacles, and a caped coat. There was something so exaggeratedly French in its appearance that it reminded Hewson of a stage caricature. He could not have said precisely why the mild-looking face seemed to him so repellent, but he had already recoiled a step and, even in the manager's company, it cost him an effort to look again.

"But who is he?" he asked.

"That," said the manager, "is Dr. Bourdette."

Hewson shook his head doubtfully.

"I think I've heard the name," he said, "but I forget in connection with what."

The manager smiled.

"You'd remember better if you were a Frenchman," he said. "For some long while that man was the terror of Paris. He carried on his work of healing by day, and of throat cutting by night, when the fit was on him. He killed for the sheer devilish pleasure it gave him to kill, and always in the same way—with a razor. After his last crime he left a clue behind him which set the police upon his track. One clue led to another, and before very long they knew that they were on the track of the Parisian equivalent of our Jack the Ripper, and had enough evidence to send him to the madhouse or the guillotine on a dozen capital charges.

"But even then our friend here was too clever for them. When he realized that the toils were closing about him, he mysteriously disappeared, and ever since the police of every civilized country have been looking for him. There is no doubt that he managed to make away with himself, and by some means which has prevented his body coming to light. One or two crimes of a similar nature have taken place since his disappearance, but he is believed almost for certain to be dead, and the experts believe these recrudescences to be the work of an imitator. It's queer, isn't it, how every notorious murderer has imitators?"

Hewson shuddered and fidgeted with his feet.

"I don't like him at all," he confessed. "Ugh! What eyes he's got!"

"Yes, this figure's a little masterpiece. You find the eyes bite into you? Well, that's excellent realism, then, for Bourdette practiced mesmerism, and was supposed to mesmerize his victims before dispatching them. Indeed, had he not done so, it is impossible to see how so small a man could have done his ghastly work. There were never any signs of a struggle."

"I thought I saw him move," said Hewson with a catch in his voice.

The manager smiled.

"You'll have more than one optical illusion before the night's out, I expect. You shan't be locked in. You can come upstairs when you've had enough of it. There are watchmen on the premises, so you'll find company. Don't be alarmed if you hear them moving about. I'm sorry I can't give you any more light, because all the lights are on. For obvious reasons we keep this place as gloomy as possible. And now I think you had better return with me to the office and have a tot of whisky before beginning your night's vigil."

The member of the night staff who placed the armchair for Hewson was inclined to be facetious.

"Where will you have it, sir?" he asked, grinning. "Just 'ere, so as you can 'ave a little talk with Crippen when you're tired of sitting still? Or there's old Mother Dyer over there, making eyes and looking as if she could do with a bit of company. Say where, sir."

Hewson smiled. The man's chaff pleased him if only because, for the moment at least, it lent the proceedings a much desired air of the commonplace.

"I'll place it myself, thanks," he said. "I'll find out where the drafts come from first."

"You won't find any down here. Well, good night, sir. I'm upstairs if you want me. Don't let 'em sneak up be'ind you and touch your neck with their cold and clammy 'ands. And you look out for that old Mrs. Dyer; I b'lieve she's taken a fancy to you."

Hewson laughed and wished the man good night. It was easier than he had expected. He wheeled the armchair—a heavy one upholstered in plush—a little way down the central gangway, and deliberately turned it so that its back was toward the effigy of Dr. Bourdette. For some undefined reason he liked Dr. Bourdette a great deal less than his companions. Busying himself with arranging the chair he was almost lighthearted, but when the attendant's footfalls had died away and a deep hush stole over the chamber, he realized that he had no slight ordeal before him.

The dim unwavering light fell on the rows of figures which were so uncannily like human beings that the silence and the stillness seemed unnatural and even ghastly. He missed the sound of breathing, the rustling of clothes, the hundred and one minute noises one hears when even the deepest silence has fallen upon a crowd. But the air was as stagnant as water at the bottom of a standing pond. There was not a breath in the chamber to stir a curtain or rustle a hanging drapery or start a shadow. His own shadow, moving in response to a shifted arm or leg, was all that could be coaxed into motion. All was still to the gaze and silent to the ear. "It must be like this at the bottom of the sea," he thought, and wondered how to work the phrase into his story on the morrow.

He faced the sinister figures boldly enough. They were only waxworks. So long as he let that thought dominate all others he promised himself that all would be well. It did not, however, save him long from the discomfort occasioned by the waxen stare of Dr. Bourdette, which, he knew, was directed upon him from behind. The eyes of the little Frenchman's effigy haunted and tormented him, and he itched with the desire to turn and look.

"Come!" he thought, "my nerves have started already. If I turn and look at that dressed-up dummy it will be an admission of funk."

And then another voice in his brain spoke to him.

"It's because you're afraid that you won't turn and look at him."

The two Voices quarreled silently for a moment or two, and at last Hewson slewed his chair round a little and looked behind him.

Among the many figures standing in stiff, unnatural poses, the effigy of the dreadful little doctor stood out with a queer prominence, perhaps because a steady beam of light beat straight down upon it. Hewson flinched before the parody of mildness which some fiendishly skilled craftsman had managed to convey in wax, met the eyes for one agonized second, and turned again to face the other direction.

"He's only a waxwork like the rest of you," Hewson muttered defiantly. "You're all only waxworks."

They were only waxworks, yes, but waxworks don't move. Not that he had seen the least movement anywhere, but it struck him that, in the moment or two while he had looked behind him, there had been the least subtle change in the grouping of the figures in front. Crippen, for instance, seemed to have turned at least one degree to the left. Or, thought Hewson, perhaps the illusion was due to the fact that he had not slewed his chair back into its exact original position. And there were Field and Grey, too; surely one of them had moved his hands. Hewson held his breath for a moment, and then drew his courage back to him as a man lifts a weight. He remembered the words of more than one news editor and laughed savagely to himself.

"And they tell me I've got no imagination!" he said beneath his breath.

He took a notebook from his pocket and wrote quickly.

"Mem.—Deathly silence and unearthly stillness of figures. Like being bottom of sea. Hypnotic eyes of Dr. Bourdette. Figures seem to move when not being watched."

He closed the book suddenly over his fingers and looked round quickly and awfully over his right shoulder. He had neither seen nor heard a movement, but it was as if some sixth sense had made him aware of one. He looked straight into the vapid countenance of Lefroy which smiled vacantly back as if to say, "It wasn't I!"

Of course it wasn't he, or any of them; it was his own nerves. Or was it? Hadn't Crippen moved again during that moment when his attention was directed elsewhere. You couldn't trust that little man! Once you took your eyes off him he took advantage of it to shift his position. That was what they were all doing, if he only knew it, he told himself; and half rose out of his chair. This was not quite good enough! He was going. He wasn't going to spend the night with a lot of waxworks which moved while he wasn't looking.

...Hewson sat down again. This was very cowardly and very absurd. They *were* only waxworks and they *couldn't* move; let him hold that thought and all would yet be well. Then why all that silent unrest about him?—a subtle something in the air which did not quite break the silence and happened, whichever way he looked, just beyond the boundaries of his vision.

He swung round quickly to encounter the mild but baleful stare of Dr. Bourdette. Then, without warning, he jerked his head back to stare straight at Crippen. Ha! he'd nearly caught Crippen that time! "You'd better be careful, Crippen—and all the rest of you! If I do see one of you move I'll smash you to pieces! Do you hear?"

He ought to go, he told himself. Already he had experienced enough to write his story, or ten stories, for the matter of that. Well, then, why not go? The *Morning Echo* would be none the wiser as to how long he had stayed, nor would it care so long as his story was a good one. Yes, but that night watchman upstairs would chaff him.

And the manager—one never knew—perhaps the manager would quibble over that five pound note which he needed so badly. He wondered if Rose were asleep or if she were lying awake and thinking of him. She'd laugh when he told her that he had imagined . . .

This was a little too much! It was bad enough that the waxwork effigies of murderers should move when they weren't being watched, but it was intolerable that they should *breathe.* Somebody was breathing. Or was it his own breath which sounded to him as if it came from a distance? He sat rigid, listening and straining until he exhaled with a long sigh. His own breath after all, or—if not, Something had divined that he was listening and had ceased breathing simultaneously.

Hewson jerked his head swiftly around and looked all about him out of haggard and hunted eyes. Everywhere his gaze encountered the vacant waxen faces, and everywhere he felt that by just some least fraction of a second had he missed seeing a movement of hand or foot, a silent opening or compression of lips, a flicker of eyelids, a look of human intelligence now smoothed out. They were like naughty children in a class, whispering, fidgeting and laughing behind their teacher's back, but blandly innocent when his gaze was turned upon them.

This would not do! This distinctly would not do! He must clutch at something, grip with his mind upon something which belonged essentially to the workaday world, to the daylight London streets. He was Raymond Hewson, an unsuccessful journalist, a living and breathing man, and these figures grouped around him were only dummies, so they could neither move nor whisper. What did it matter if they were supposed to be lifelike effigies of murderers? They were only made of wax and sawdust, and stood there for the entertainment of morbid sightseers and orange-sucking trippers. That was better! Now what was that funny story which somebody had told him in the Falstaff yesterday? . . .

He recalled part of it, but not all, for the gaze of Dr. Bourdette, urged, challenged, and finally compelled him to turn.

Hewson half turned, and then swung his chair so as to bring him face to face with the wearer of those dreadful hypnotic eyes. His own eyes were dilated, and his mouth, at first set in a grin of terror, lifted at the corners in a snarl. Then Hewson spoke and woke a hundred sinister echoes.

"You moved, damn you!" he cried. "Yes, you did, damn you! I saw you!"

Then he sat quite still, staring straight before him, like a man found frozen in the Arctic snows.

Dr. Bourdette's movements were leisurely. He stepped off his pedestal with the mincing care of a lady alighting from a bus. The platform stood about two feet from the ground, and above the edge of it a plush-covered rope hung in arc-like curves. Dr. Bourdette lifted up the rope until it formed an arch for him to pass under, stepped off the platform and sat down on the edge facing Hewson. Then he nodded and smiled and said "Good evening."

"I need hardly tell you," he continued, in perfect English in which was traceable only the least foreign accent, "that not until I overheard the conversation between you and the worthy manager of this establishment, did I suspect that I should have the pleasure of a companion here for the night. You cannot move or speak without my bidding, but you can hear me perfectly well. Something tells me that you are—shall I say nervous? My dear sir, have no illusions. I am not one of these contemptible effigies miraculously come to life: I am Dr. Bourdette himself."

He paused, coughed, and shifted his legs.

"Pardon me," he resumed, "but I am a little stiff. And let me explain. Circumstances with which I need not fatigue you, have made it desirable that I should live in England. I was close to this building this evening when I saw a policeman regarding me a thought too curiously. I guessed that he intended to follow and perhaps ask me embarrassing questions, so I mingled with the crowd and came in here. An extra coin bought my admission to the chamber in which we now meet, and an inspiration showed me a certain means of escape.

"I raised a cry of fire, and when all the fools had rushed to the stairs I stripped my effigy of the caped coat which you behold me wearing, donned it, hid my effigy under the platform at the back, and took its place on the pedestal.

"I own that I have since spent a very fatiguing evening, but fortunately I was not always being watched and had opportunities to draw an occasional deep breath and ease the rigidity of my pose. One small boy screamed and exclaimed that he saw me moving. I understood that he was to be whipped and put straight to bed on his return home, and I can only hope that the threat has been executed to the letter.

"The manager's description of me, which I had the embarrassment of being compelled to overhear, was biased but not altogether inaccurate. Clearly I am not dead, although it is as well that the world thinks otherwise. His account of my hobby, which I have indulged for years, although, through necessity, less frequently of late, was in the main true although not intelligently expressed. The world is divided between collectors and noncollectors. With the noncollectors we are not concerned. The collectors collect anything, according to their individual tastes, from money to cigarette cards, from moths to matchboxes. I collect throats."

He paused again and regarded Hewson's throat with interest mingled with disfavor.

"I am obliged to the chance which brought us together tonight," he continued, "and perhaps it would seem ungrateful to complain. From motives of personal safety my activities have been somewhat curtailed of late years, and I am glad of this opportunity of gratifying my somewhat unusual whim. But you have a skinny neck, sir, if you will overlook a personal remark. I should never have selected you from choice. I like men with thick necks . . . thick red necks . . ."

He fumbled in an inside pocket and took out something which he tested against a wet forefinger and then proceeded to pass gently to and fro across the palm of his left hand.

"This is a little French razor," he remarked blandly. "They are not much used in England, but perhaps you know them? One strops them on wood. The blade, you will observe, is very narrow. They do not cut very deep, but deep enough. In just one little moment you shall see for yourself. I shall ask you the little civil question of all the polite barbers: Does the razor suit you, sir?"

He rose up, a diminutive but menacing figure of evil, and approached Hewson with the silent, furtive step of a hunting panther.

"You will have the goodness," he said, "to raise your chin a little. Thank you, and a little more. Just a little more. Ah, thank you! . . . *Merci, m'sieur . . . Ah, merci . . . merci. . . .*"

Over one end of the chamber was a thick skylight of frosted glass which, by day, let in a few sickly and filtered rays from the floor above. After sunrise these began to mingle with the subdued light from the electric bulbs, and this mingled illumination added a certain ghastliness to a scene which needed no additional touch of horror.

The waxwork figures stood apathetically in their places, waiting to be admired or execrated by the crowds who would presently wander fearfully among them. In their midst, in the center gangway, Hewson sat still, leaning far back in his armchair. His chin was uptilted as if he were waiting to receive attention from a barber, and although there was not a scratch upon his throat, nor anywhere upon his body, he was cold and dead. His previous employers were wrong in having him credited with no imagination.

Dr. Bourdette on his pedestal watched the dead man unemotionally. He did not move, nor was he capable of motion. But then, after all, he was only a waxwork.

Understanding the Story ———————

Main Idea

1. Which of the following best expresses the main idea of the story?
   (a) Raymond Hewson was a man without imagination or creative talent.
   (b) Dr. Bourdette was a successful mass murderer.
   (c) The manager shouldn't have agreed to Hewson's plan.
   (d) Hewson had an overactive imagination.

Details

2. Hewson was   (a) a reporter for the *Morning Echo*   (b) an outstanding journalist   (c) not working for any paper (d) financially successful.

3. Hewson planned to stay overnight in   (a) Madame Tussaud's (b) the Chamber of Horrors   (c) the *Morning Echo* office (d) the Murderers' Den.

4. Hewson sought the job for   (a) financial reasons
   (b) publicity   (c) a thrill   (d) curiosity.

5. The only murderer who hadn't been hanged was   (a) Crippen
   (b) Norman Thorne   (c) Mrs. Dyer   (d) Dr. Bourdette.

Inferences

6. The interior of Murderers' Den could best be compared with
   that of a   (a) newspaper conference room   (b) tomb
   (c) middle-class living room   (d) submarine.

7. In his presentation of the possible difficulties associated with
   a night in the Waxworks, the manager was   (a) untruthful
   (b) optimistic   (c) unsympathetic   (d) honest.

8. The breathing that Hewson heard in the still of the night
   (a) was imagined   (b) belonged to Dr. Bourdette   (c) was
   that of the night watchman   (d) was an echo of his own.

9. In death, Hewson's chin was uptilted because he thought
   (a) he could see better at that angle   (b) he fell just before
   he died   (c) he expected to have his throat slashed   (d) he
   struggled with Dr. Bourdette.

10. The two Voices that Hewson heard were   (a) those of Dr.
    Bourdette and Crippen   (b) his own   (c) tape recordings to
    frighten him   (d) those of the manager and the night watch-
    man.

Order of Events

11. Arrange the items in the order in which they occurred. Use
    letters only.
    A. Dr. Bourdette seems to threaten Hewson.
    B. Hewson presents his proposition to the manager.
    C. Hewson is discovered dead in the morning.
    D. The night watchman teases Hewson.
    E. Hewson is escorted to Murderers' Den.

Outcomes

12. If Hewson had left the Waxworks when he first became fright-
    ened,
    (a) he'd have discovered that all the waxworks were really just
        waxworks.
    (b) Dr. Bourdette would have followed him anyway.

(c) the manager would have charged him for the full admission price.

(d) the manager would have doubled the five pounds he promised him.

Cause and Effect

13. The atmosphere of Murderers' Den   (a) made most visitors chuckle   (b) frightened the night watchman away from his post   (c) had little effect on Hewson   (d) caused Hewson to hypnotize himself.

Fact or Opinion

Tell whether each of the following is a fact or an opinion.

14. Hewson could not get a regular job on a newspaper.

15. Dr. Bourdette was only a waxwork.

Words in Context ⸻

1. He wore his clothes well and *contrived* to look extremely smart without appearing overdressed.
   Contrived (153) means   (a) hoped   (b) managed   (c) tried unsuccessfully   (d) liked.

2. He was a small, *spare*, pale man, with lank, *errant* brown hair.
   Spare (153) means   (a) lean   (b) chunky   (c) nervous (d) quiet.

3. *Errant* (153) means   (a) dark   (b) straight   (c) straying (d) orderly.

4. He had the defensive and somewhat *furtive* air of a man who was used to *rebuffs*.
   Furtive (153) means   (a) strong-minded   (b) shifty (c) open   (d) cruel.

5. *Rebuffs* (153) means   (a) kindnesses   (b) opportunities (c) challenges   (d) snubs.

6. He looked what he was, a man gifted somewhat above the ordinary, who was a failure through his lack of *self-assertion*.
   Self-assertion (153) means   (a) sticking up for one's rights

(b) trying to take advantage of other people   (c) hoping for a better time in the future   (d) continuing to learn after formal schooling is over.

7. "If I did I should expect them to haunt the scene of their crimes or the spot where their bodies were laid, instead of a cellar which happens to contain their waxwork *effigies.*"
Effigies (154) means   (a) clothes   (b) evil deeds
(c) accounts   (d) copies.

8. "If you are *susceptible* to atmosphere, I warn you that you are in for a very uncomfortable night."
Susceptible   (154)   means   (a) immune   (b) oblivious
(c) sensitive   (d) impartial.

9. For the past month he had been living on paragraphs, *eked out* by his rapidly dwindling store of savings.
Eked   out   (155)   means   (a) drained   (b) budgeted
(c) accounted for   (d) supplemented.

10. "The way of *transgressors*—and newspapermen—is hard."
Transgressors (155) means   (a) artists   (b) communications people   (c) drivers   (d) sinners.

11. Hewson followed the manager through half a dozen rooms where attendants were busy *shrouding* the kings and queens of England, the generals and prominent statesmen of this and other generations, all the mixed herd of humanity whose fame or *notoriety* had rendered them eligible for this kind of immortality.
Shrouding (155) means   (a) covering   (b) photographing
(c) dusting   (d) inventorying.

12. *Notoriety* (155) means   (a) ability   (b) ill fame
(c) achievement   (d) glamor.

13. There was something of the air of a chapel about it, but a chapel no longer devoted to the practice of piety and given over now for base and *impious* worship.
Impious (156) means   (a) violent   (b) religious   (c) unholy
(d) sacred.

14. Charles Peace, the only member of that *vile* company who looked uncompromisingly and entirely evil, sneered across a gangway at Norman Thorne.
Vile (156) means   (a) well advertised   (b) dull   (c) spirited
(d) evil.

15. There was something so exaggeratedly French in its appearance that it reminded Hewson of a stage *caricature.*
Caricature (157) means   (a) exaggerated representation
(b) understated   imitation   (c) accurate   presentation
(d) good-hearted indication.

16. "When he realized that the *toils* were closing about him he
mysteriously disappeared."
Toils (157) means   (a) workers   (b) opportunities   (c) nets
(d) labors.

17. "He is believed almost for certain to be dead, and the experts
believe these *recrudescences* to be the work of an imitator."
Recrudescences (157) means   (a) crude crimes
(b) reappearances   (c) attempts to seek publicity
(d) innocent actions.

18. "Bourdette practiced *mesmerism,* and was supposed to mesmerize his victims before *dispatching* them."
Mesmerism (157)   means   (a) black   arts   (b) voodoo
(c) hypnotism   (d) use of a sharp weapon.

19. *Dispatching*   (157)   means   (a) killing   (b) amusing
(c) releasing   (d) wearying.

20. "And now I think you had better return with me to the office
and have a tot of whisky before beginning your night's *vigil.*"
Vigil (158) means   (a) entertainment   (b) deep sleep
(c) experience   (d) watch.

21. The dim *unwavering* light fell on the rows of figures which
were so uncannily like human beings that the silence and the
stillness seemed unusual and even ghastly.
Unwavering (158) means   (a) obscure   (b) steady   (c) pale
(d) rosy red.

22. He swung round quickly to encounter the mild but *baleful*
stare of Dr. Bourdette.
Baleful (160) means   (a) penetrating   (b) evil   (c) amused
(d) glassy.

23. Yes, but that night watchman would *chaff* him.
Chaff (160)   means   (a) hate   (b) tease   (c) admire
(d) injure.

24. Hewson jerked his head swiftly around and looked all about
him out of *haggard* and hunted eyes.
Haggard (161) means   (a) exhausted   (b) bright   (c) dark
brown   (d) sparkling.

25. They were like naughty children in a class, whispering, fidgeting and laughing behind their teacher's back, but *blandly* innocent when his gaze was turned upon them.
    Blandly (161) means (a) annoyingly (b) guiltily (c) calmly (d) strangely.

26. His own eyes were *dilated,* and his mouth, at first set in a grin of terror, lifted at the corners in a snarl.
    Dilated (161) means (a) squinting (b) mildly irritated (c) blinking (d) opened wide.

27. He stepped off his pedestal with the *mincing* care of a lady alighting from a bus.
    Mincing (162) means (a) affectedly refined (b) amusedly tolerant (c) grossly exaggerated (d) unusually heavy.

28. He rose up, a *diminutive* but menacing figure of evil.
    Diminutive (163) means (a) deceptive (b) gentle (c) small (d) muscular.

29. The waxwork figures stood *apathetically* in their places, waiting to be admired or *execrated* by the crowds who would presently wander fearfully among them.
    Apathetically (164) means (a) showing no interest (b) exactly (c) in strange poses (d) loosely.

30. *Execrated* (164) means (a) admired (b) detested (c) avoided (d) scolded.

Thinking About the Story

1. This is a story of atmosphere. Everything depends upon a vivid description of the setting to set the mood and get us ready for what happens. Point out examples of what you consider especially good description.

2. A short story doesn't have time for the introduction of extraneous details. Everything must count, as in the following examples.
   (a) How did the false alarm supposedly play a role in the outcome?
   (b) What details about Dr. Bourdette did the manager give Hewson, details which later played a part in the tragedy?
   (c) Why was the night watchman introduced? What did he add to the story?

3. Plays must rely solely on dialog to develop character and plot. The opening dialog between Hewson and the manager is like a play. How does it provide clues to the personalities of the two men?

4. Are there two possible interpretations to the events in this story? The questions above suggest that Hewson died of fright, purely because of an overactive imagination. Is it possible that Dr. Bourdette was actually in Marriner's Waxworks? Did he actually say all those things to Hewson? Which version do you prefer? What arguments can you supply for your point of view?

5. When we read a book or watch a play or movie, we tend to identify with one or more of the characters. When we identify with a character, we care more about what happens to him or her. We become interested in the fate of the character we identify with. The young man in the story is likable, responsible for the support of a family, but poor. He is apparently either not too talented or just unlucky. Did you find yourself identifying with him? Explain why or why not.

6. Two useful words are *sympathy* and *empathy*. Sympathy is a spontaneous feeling of pity for another living creature. A swan that has lost young ones to a hawk excites our sympathy. Empathy is the projection of one's feelings or personality into that of another for better understanding. Empathy may also be used in describing reactions to a painting, a building or some other inanimate object. Which word better describes your feelings about Hewson? Explain.

The Lottery

Shirley Jackson

♦ Mr. Summers, holding his slip of paper in the air, said, "All right, fellows." For a minute, no one moved, and then all the slips of paper were opened. Suddenly, all the women began to speak at once, saying, "Who is it?" "Who's got it?" "Is it the Dunbars?" "Is it the Watsons?"

The story you are about to read is one of the most unusual ever written. When it first appeared in the *New Yorker* on June 28, 1948, it proved to be a bombshell. The author, Shirley Jackson, had some inkling of the excitement to come when a friend on the *New Yorker* staff wrote, "Your story has kicked up quite a fuss around the office." Then the phone calls and letters started to pour in.

Readers wrote in not only to complain; many asked for explanations. Some wanted to find out where the lotteries were being held. It was not enough for Shirley Jackson to say the story was pure fiction, that it came out of her imagination without any tie-in with reality, that it is a kind of morality tale never intended as a picture of an actual custom.

Readers did not believe her. The story is written with such journalistic skill it seems it *must* describe a real event.

Since its publication, "The Lottery" has continued to fascinate readers. In later years, the letters were more respectful. As the fame of "The Lottery" spread, however, readers continued to ask for explanations—which Ms. Jackson never provided. How could she? "The Lottery" has a life all its own. Though the author wrote many stories before and after, *this* is the one that has made her name immortal.

You are about to share a unique experience, one that you'll never forget. Though there is terror between the lines, the story is told with such matter-of-fact understatement, such folksy friendliness, that you'll come to the end with a feeling of shock.

THE LOTTERY

The morning of June 27th was clear and sunny, with the fresh warmth of a full-summer day; the flowers were blossoming profusely and the grass was richly green. The people of the village began to gather in the square, between the post office and the bank, around ten o'clock; in some towns there were so many people that the lottery took two days and had to be started on June 26th, but in this village, where there were only about three hundred people, the whole lottery took less than two hours, so it could begin at ten o'clock in the morning and still be through in time to allow the villagers to get home for noon dinner.

The children assembled first, of course. School was recently over for the summer, and the feeling of liberty sat uneasily on most of them; they tended to gather together quietly for a while before they broke into boisterous play, and their talk was still of the classroom and the teacher, of books and reprimands. Bobby Martin had already stuffed his pockets full of stones, and the other boys soon followed his example, selecting the smoothest and roundest stones; Bobby and Harry Jones and Dickie Delacroix—the villagers pronounced this name "Dellacroy"—eventually made a great pile of stones in one corner of the square and guarded it against the raids of the other boys. The girls stood aside, talking among themselves, looking over their shoulders at the boys, and the very small children rolled in the dust or clung to the hands of their older brothers or sisters.

Soon the men began to gather, surveying their own children, speaking of planting and rain, tractors and taxes. They stood together, away from the pile of stones in the corner, and their jokes were quiet and they smiled rather than laughed. The women, wearing faded housedresses and sweaters, came shortly after their menfolk. They greeted one another and exchanged bits of gossip as they went to join their husbands. Soon the women, standing by their husbands, began to call to their children, and the children came reluctantly, having to be called four or five times. Bobby Martin ducked under his mother's grasping hand and ran, laughing, back to the pile of stones. His father spoke up sharply, and Bobby came quickly and took his place between his father and his oldest brother.

The lottery was conducted—as were the square dances, the teenage club, the Halloween program—by Mr. Summers, who had time and energy to devote to civic activities. He was a round-faced, jovial man and he ran the coal business, and people were sorry for him, because he had no children and his wife was a scold. When he arrived in the square, carrying the black wooden box, there was a murmur of conversation among the villagers, and he waved and called, "Little late today, folks." The postmaster, Mr. Graves, followed him, carrying a three-legged stool, and the stool was put in the center of the square and Mr. Summers set the black box down on it. The villagers kept their distance, leaving a space between themselves and the stool, and when Mr. Summers said, "Some of you fellows want to give me a hand?" there was a hesitation before two men, Mr. Martin and his oldest son, Baxter, came forward to hold the box steady on the stool while Mr. Summers stirred up the papers inside it.

The original paraphernalia for the lottery had been lost long ago, and the black box now resting on the stool had been put into use even before Old Man Warner, the oldest man in town, was born. Mr. Summers spoke frequently to the villagers about making a new box, but no one liked to upset even as much tradition as was represented by the black box. There was a story that the present box had been made with some pieces of the box that had preceded it, the one that had been constructed when the first people settled down to make a village here. Every year, after the lottery, Mr. Summers began talking again about a new box, but every year the subject was allowed to fade off without anything's being done. The black box grew shabbier each year; by now it was no longer completely black but splintered badly along one side to show the original wood color, and in some places faded or stained.

Mr. Martin and his oldest son, Baxter, held the black box securely on the stool until Mr. Summers had stirred the papers thoroughly with his hand. Because so much of the ritual had been forgotten or discarded, Mr. Summers had been successful in having slips of paper substituted for the chips of wood that had been used for generations. Chips of wood, Mr. Summers had argued, had been all very well when the village was tiny, but now that the population was more than three hundred and likely to keep on growing, it was necessary to use something that would fit more easily into the black box. The night before the lottery, Mr. Summers and Mr. Graves made up the slips of paper and put them in the box, and it was then taken to the safe of Mr. Summers's coal company and locked up until Mr. Summers was ready to take it to the square next morning. The rest of the year, the box was put away, sometimes one place, sometimes another; it had spent one year in Mr. Graves' barn and another year underfoot in the post office, and sometimes it was set on a shelf in the Martin grocery and left there.

There was a great deal of fussing to be done before Mr. Summers declared the lottery open. There were the lists to make up—of heads of families, heads of households in each family, members of each household in each family. There was the proper swearing-in of Mr. Summers by the postmaster, as the official of the lottery; at one time, some people remembered, there had been a recital of some sort, performed by the official of the lottery, a perfunctory, tuneless chant that had been rattled off duly each year; some people believed that the official of the lottery used to stand just so when he said or sang it, others believed that he was supposed to walk among the people, but years and years ago this part of the ritual had been allowed to lapse. There had been, also, a ritual salute, which the official of the lottery had had to use in addressing each person who came up to draw from the box, but this also had changed with time, until now it was felt necessary only for the official to speak to each person approaching. Mr. Summers was very good at all this; in his clean white shirt and blue jeans, with one hand resting carelessly on the black box, he seemed very proper and important as he talked interminably to Mr. Graves and the Martins.

Just as Mr. Summers finally left off talking and turned to the assembled villagers, Mrs. Hutchinson came hurriedly along the path to the square, her sweater thrown over her shoulders, and slid into place in the back of the crowd. "Clean forgot what day it was," she said to Mrs. Delacroix, who stood next to her, and they both laughed softly. "Thought my old man was out back stacking wood," Mrs. Hutchinson went on, "and then I looked out the window and the kids was gone, and then I remembered it was the twenty-seventh and came a-running." She dried her hands on her apron, and Mrs. Delacroix said, "You're in time, though. They're still talking away up there."

Mrs. Hutchinson craned her neck to see through the crowd and found her husband and children standing near the front. She tapped Mrs. Delacroix on the arm as a farewell and began to make her way through the crowd. The people separated good-humoredly to let her through; two or three people said, in voices just loud enough to be heard across the crowd, "Here comes your Missus, Hutchinson," and "Bill, she made it after all." Mrs. Hutchinson reached her husband, and Mr. Summers, who had been waiting, said cheerfully, "Thought we were going to have to get on without you, Tessie." Mrs. Hutchinson said, grinning, "Wouldn't have me leave m'dishes in the sink, now, would you, Joe?" and soft laughter ran through the crowd as the people stirred back into position after Mrs. Hutchinson's arrival.

"Well, now," Mr. Summers said soberly, "guess we better get started, get this over with, so's we can go back to work. Anybody ain't here?"

"Dunbar," several people said. "Dunbar, Dunbar."

Mr. Summers consulted his list. "Clyde Dunbar," he said. "That's right. He's broke his leg, hasn't he? Who's drawing for him?"

"Me, I guess," a woman said, and Mr. Summers turned to look at her. "Wife draws for her husband," Mr. Summers said. "Don't you have a grown boy to do it for you, Janey?" Although Mr. Summers and everyone else in the village knew the answer perfectly well, it was the business of the official of the lottery to ask such questions formally. Mr. Summers waited with an expression of polite interest while Mrs. Dunbar answered.

"Horace's not but sixteen yet," Mrs. Dunbar said regretfully. "Guess I gotta fill in for the old man this year."

"Right," Mr. Summers said. He made a note on the list he was holding. Then he asked, "Watson boy drawing this year?"

A tall boy in the crowd raised his hand. "Here," he said. "I'm drawing for m'mother and me." He blinked his eyes nervously and ducked his head as several voices in the crowd said things like "Good fellow, Jack," and "Glad to see your mother's got a man to do it."

"Well," Mr. Summers said, "guess that's everyone. Old Man Warner make it?"

"Here," a voice said, and Mr. Summers nodded.

A sudden hush fell on the crowd as Mr. Summers cleared his throat and looked at the list. "All ready?" he called. "Now, I'll read the names—heads of families first—and the men come up and take a paper out of the box. Keep the paper folded in your hand without looking at it until everyone has had a turn. Everything clear?"

The people had done it so many times that they only half listened to the directions; most of them were quiet, wetting their lips, not looking around. Then Mr. Summers raised one hand high and said, "Adams." A man disengaged himself from the crowd and came forward. "Hi, Steve," Mr. Summers said, and Mr. Adams said, "Hi, Joe." They grinned at one another humorlessly and nervously. Then Mr. Adams reached into the black box and took out a folded paper. He held it firmly by one corner as he turned and went hastily back to his place in the crowd, where he stood a little apart from his family, not looking down at his hand.

"Allen," Mr. Summers said. "Anderson . . . Bentham."

"Seems like there's no time at all between lotteries anymore," Mrs. Delacroix said to Mrs. Graves in the back row. "Seems like we got through with the last one only last week."

"Time sure goes fast," Mrs. Graves said.

"Clark . . . Delacroix."

"There goes my old man," Mrs. Delacroix said. She held her breath while her husband went forward.

"Dunbar," Mr. Summers said, and Mrs. Dunbar went steadily to the box while one of the women said, "Go on, Janey," and another said, "There she goes."

"We're next," Mrs. Graves said. She watched while Mr. Graves came around from the side of the box, greeted Mr. Summers gravely, and selected a slip of paper from the box. By now, all through the crowd there were men holding the small folded papers in their large hands, turning them over and over nervously. Mrs. Dunbar and her two sons stood together, Mrs. Dunbar holding the slip of paper.

"Harburt . . . Hutchinson."

"Get up there, Bill," Mrs. Hutchinson said, and the people near her laughed.

"Jones."

"They do say," Mr. Adams said to Old Man Warner, who stood next to him, "that over in the north village they're talking of giving up the lottery."

Old Man Warner snorted. "Pack of crazy fools," he said. "Listening to the young folks, nothing's good enough for *them*. Next thing you know, they'll be wanting to go back to living in caves, nobody work anymore, live *that* way for a while. Used to be a saying about 'Lottery in June, corn be heavy soon.' First thing you know, we'd all be eating stewed chickweed and acorns. There's *always* been a lottery," he added petulantly. "Bad enough to see young Joe Summers up there joking with everybody."

"Some places have already quit lotteries," Mrs. Adams said.

"Nothing but trouble in *that*," Old Man Warner said stoutly. "Pack of young fools."

"Martin." And Bobby Martin watched his father go forward. "Overdyke . . . Percy."

"I wish they'd hurry," Mrs. Dunbar said to her older son. "I wish they'd hurry."

"They're almost through," her son said.

"You get ready to run tell Dad," Mrs. Dunbar said.

Mr. Summers called his own name and then stepped forward precisely and selected a slip from the box. Then he called, "Warner."

"Seventy-seventh year I been in the lottery," Old Man Warner said as he went through the crowd. "Seventy-seventh time."

"Watson." The tall boy came awkwardly through the crowd. Someone said, "Don't be nervous, Jack," and Mr. Summers said, "Take your time, son."

"Zanini."

After that, there was a long pause, a breathless pause, until Mr. Summers, holding his slip of paper in the air, said, "All right, fellows." For a minute, no one moved, and then all the slips of paper were opened. Suddenly, all the women began to speak at once, saying, "Who is it?" "Who's got it?" "Is it the Dunbars?" "Is it the Watsons?" Then the voices began to say, "It's Hutchinson. It's Bill," "Bill Hutchinson's got it."

"Go tell your father," Mrs. Dunbar said to her older son.

People began to look around to see the Hutchinsons. Bill Hutchinson was standing quiet, staring down at the paper in his hand. Suddenly, Tessie Hutchinson shouted to Mr. Summers, "You didn't give him time enough to take any paper he wanted. I saw you. It wasn't fair!"

"Be a good sport, Tessie," Mrs. Delacroix called, and Mrs. Graves said, "All of us took the same chance."

"Shut up, Tessie," Bill Hutchinson said.

"Well, everyone," Mr. Summers said, "that was done pretty fast, and now we've got to be hurrying a little more to get done in time." He consulted his next list. "Bill," he said, "You draw for the Hutchinson family. You got any other households in the Hutchinsons?"

"There's Don and Eva," Mrs. Hutchinson yelled. "Make *them* take their chance!"

"Daughters draw with their husbands' families, Tessie," Mr. Summers said gently. "You know that as well as anyone else."

"It wasn't *fair*," Tessie said.

"I guess not, Joe," Bill Hutchinson said regretfully. "My daughter draws with her husband's family, that's only fair. And I've got no other family except the kids."

"Then, as far as drawing for families is concerned, it's you," Mr. Summers said in explanation, "and as far as drawing for households is concerned, that's you, too. Right?"

"Right," Bill Hutchinson said.

"How many kids, Bill?" Mr. Summers asked formally.

"Three," Bill Hutchinson said. "There's Bill, Jr., and Nancy, and little Dave. And Tessie and me."

"All right, then," Mr. Summers said. "Harry, you got their tickets back?"

Mr. Graves nodded and held up the slips of paper. "Put them in the box, then," Mr. Summers directed. "Take Bill's and put it in."

"I think we ought to start over," Mrs. Hutchinson said, as quietly as she could. "I tell you it wasn't *fair*. You didn't give him time enough to choose. *Every*body saw that."

Mr. Graves had selected the five slips and put them in the box, and he dropped all the papers but those onto the ground, where the breeze caught them and lifted them off.

"Listen, everybody," Mrs. Hutchinson was saying to the people around her.

"Ready, Bill?" Mr. Summers asked, and Bill Hutchinson, with one quick glance around at his wife and children, nodded.

"Remember," Mr. Summers said, "take the slips and keep them folded until each person has taken one. Harry, you help little Dave." Mr. Graves took the hand of the little boy, who came willingly with him up to the box. "Take a paper out of the box, Davy," Mr. Summers said. Davy put his hand into the box and laughed. "Take just *one* paper," Mr. Summers said. "Harry, you hold it for him." Mr. Graves took the child's hand and removed the folded paper from the tight fist and held it while little Dave stood next to him and looked up at him wonderingly.

"Nancy next," Mr. Summers said. Nancy was twelve, and her school friends breathed heavily as she went forward, switching her skirt, and took a slip daintily from the box. "Bill, Jr.," Mr. Summers said, and Billy, his face red and his feet overlarge, nearly knocked the box over as he got a paper out. "Tessie," Mr. Summers said. She hesitated for a minute, looking around defiantly, and then set her lips and went up to the box. She snatched a paper out and held it behind her.

"Bill," Mr. Summers said, and Bill Hutchinson reached into the box and felt around, bringing his hand out at last with the slip of paper in it.

The crowd was quiet. A girl whispered, "I hope it's not Nancy," and the sound of the whisper reached the edges of the crowd.

"It's not the way it used to be," Old Man Warner said clearly. "People ain't the way they used to be."

"All right," Mr. Summers said. "Open the papers. Harry, you open little Dave's."

Mr. Graves opened the slip of paper and there was a general sigh through the crowd as he held it up and everyone could see that it was blank. Nancy and Bill, Jr., opened theirs at the same time, and both beamed and laughed, turning around to the crowd and holding their slips of paper above their heads.

"Tessie," Mr. Summers said. There was a pause, and then Mr. Summers looked at Bill Hutchinson, and Bill unfolded his paper and showed it. It was blank.

"It's Tessie," Mr. Summers said, and his voice was hushed. "Show us her paper, Bill."

Bill Hutchinson went over to his wife and forced the slip of paper out of her hand. It had a black spot on it, the black spot Mr.

Summers had made the night before with the heavy pencil in the coal-company office. Bill Hutchinson held it up, and there was a stir in the crowd.

"All right, folks," Mr. Summers said. "Let's finish quickly."

Although the villagers had forgotten the ritual and lost the original black box, they still remembered to use stones. The pile of stones the boys had made earlier was ready; there were stones on the ground with the blowing scraps of paper that had come out of the box. Mrs. Delacroix selected a stone so large she had to pick it up with both hands and turned to Mrs. Dunbar. "Come on," she said. "Hurry up."

Mrs. Dunbar had small stones in both hands, and she said, gasping for breath, "I can't run at all. You'll have to go ahead and I'll catch up with you."

The children had stones already, and someone gave little Davy Hutchinson a few pebbles.

Tessie Hutchinson was in the center of a cleared space by now, and she held her hands out desperately as the villagers moved in on her. "It isn't fair," she said. A stone hit her on the side of the head.

Old Man Warner was saying, "Come on, come on, everyone." Steve Adams was in the front of the crowd of villagers, with Mrs. Graves beside him.

"It isn't fair, it isn't right," Mrs. Hutchinson screamed, and then they were upon her.

Understanding the Story ―――――――――

Main Idea

1. The lottery continued to be held because   (a) Mr. Summers made a living from his activities as leader   (b) that's the way it was always done   (c) a few select families stood to benefit by it   (d) the group wanted to be rid of certain people.

Details

2. Names were pulled from a(n)   (a) hat   (b) aluminum tub   (c) black box   (d) drum.

3. The oldest man in town was named   (a) *Delacroix*   (b) *Dunbar*   (c) *Jones*   (d) *Warner*.

4. Names were read   (a) in alphabetical order   (b) in order of wealth   (c) in order of age   (d) in no particular order.

5. The Martins   (a) assisted Mr. Summers   (b) had their names drawn first   (c) were the first to stone Tessie   (d) refused to take part in the lottery.

Inferences

6. "By now, all through the crowd there were men holding the small folded papers in their large hands, turning them over and over nervously." The men were nervous because they (a) did not want to speak to the crowd   (b) hoped to win the lottery   (c) did not want to be chosen   (d) were basically shy.

7. "The villagers kept their distance, leaving a space between themselves and the stool." This sentence suggests that the people   (a) were afraid of what was going to happen   (b) would rather have had Mr. Graves as leader   (c) were not aggressive, pushy people   (d) looked forward to the lottery each year.

8. "No one liked to upset even as much tradition as was represented by the black box." This suggests that the villagers were (a) all kind and gentle folk (b) all cruel, violent people (c) sensible, hardworking citizens   (d) slaves to tradition.

9. The first person to object to the procedure was   (a) Mrs. Dunbar   (b) Janey   (c) Tessie   (d) Mr. Zanini.

10. All the following are true EXCEPT
    (a) The children looked upon the lottery as a game.
    (b) Friends turned on a friend.
    (c) Mr. Summers was a thoroughly evil man.
    (d) Bill Hutchinson forced his wife to conform.

Order of Events

11. Arrange the items in the order in which they occurred. Use letters only.
    A. Mrs. Hutchinson gets the black spot.
    B. Mr. Summers is late for the lottery.
    C. The Hutchinson family is singled out for the lottery.
    D. Mrs. Hutchinson is late for the lottery.
    E. Jack Watson draws for his family.

Outcomes

12. If the black spot had been drawn for little Dave Hutchinson, (a) the lottery would have been called off   (b) his father would have stood in for him   (c) he'd have been honored at a special banquet   (d) he'd have been stoned.

Cause and Effect

13. If enough people had the courage and sense to rebel,   (a) the postmaster would have taken over for Mr. Summers   (b) the Hutchinson children would have been taken away from their parents   (c) the lottery would have been ended   (d) prison would have been substituted for stoning.

Fact or Opinion

Tell whether each of the following is a fact or an opinion.

14. Tessie Hutchinson was cowardly.

15. Even young children took their turn in the lottery.

Words in Context _____

1. The flowers were blooming *profusely* and the grass was richly green.
   Profusely (172) means (a) early (b) moderately (c) abundantly (d) late.

2. The original *paraphernalia* for the lottery had been lost long ago.
   Paraphernalia (173) means (a) plan (b) equipment (c) advertising (d) membership rolls.

3. At one time there had been a recital of some sort, a *perfunctory*, tuneless chant that had been rattled off duly each year.
   Perfunctory (174) means (a) loud (b) easily memorized (c) harmonious (d) unenthusiastic.

4. Years and years ago this part of the ritual had been allowed to *lapse*.
   Lapse (174) means (a) expand (b) change (c) reappear (d) cease.

5. He seemed very proper and important as he talked *interminably* to Mr. Graves and the Martins.
   Interminably (174) means (a) suitably (b) endlessly (c) forcefully (d) gently.

Thinking About the Story _____

1. Why do you think so many people were bitter about this story when it first appeared?

2. Modern horror movies delight in vivid, gory scenes, realistically portrayed. Yet many of these go over the line and become simply ridiculous. Shirley Jackson, on the other hand, suggests horror with what seem like very sweet and gentle touches. For example, when Nancy and Bill Hutchinson, Jr., do not get the black spot, "they both beamed and laughed, turning around to the crowd and holding their slips of paper above their heads." What is the understated horror in this simple, happy description? Or consider this little touch: "The children had stones already, and someone gave Davy Hutchinson a few pebbles." Was

anything in "The Waxwork" more horrible than this? Explain. Point out other examples.

3. Part of the punch in this story is that under certain conditions, who knows what might happen? Many primitive peoples use human sacrifice to insure the fertility of their land and the abundance of their crops. Point out touches showing people behaving as any of us might behave in similar circumstances.

4. Why did Mrs. Hutchinson yell, "There's Don and Eva. Make *them* take their chance." What does this say about what the lottery has done to the people of the village?

5. Apart from the horror, this story has something valuable to say today. Peer pressure, the unwillingness to challenge the crowd, brought the villagers to degradation. How does peer pressure induce young people to indulge in drugs, alcohol, or tobacco in various forms? How does peer pressure affect the formation of gangs and the committing of criminal acts? How can peer pressure be challenged?

6. Many years ago a book called *The Sabertooth Curriculum* criticized educational programs that retained out-of-date practices just because they had been done before. The book described a primitive society as a way of telling the story. The elders of that society kept teaching the young how to fight the sabertooth tiger long after the tiger had disappeared. Can you mention any customs you consider foolish, customs still honored though out of date? Compare your list with the lists of your classmates and prepare to defend your choices.

7. A democracy requires its citizens to think for themselves. Those who fail to do so may be led to do terrible things ordered by their leaders. How does "The Lottery" prove the truth of this statement and demonstrate the dangers of an unthinking acceptance of custom?

8. A scapegoat is a person who is made to take the blame for the mistakes of others. Who was the scapegoat in "The Lottery"? What was her "crime"? Why was she punished? (Look up the origin of the word *scapegoat* in an unabridged dictionary or a book of word origins like William and Mary Morris's *Dictionary of Word and Phrase Origins, Volume II.*)

Stories of Suspense and Terror

ACTIVITIES

Thinking About the Stories

1. Which stories use the surprise-ending device? What does the author gain by using this device?
2. Which story introduces humor as well as horror? Do you feel that the introduction of humor strengthens the story? Prove.
3. Which story did you consider most frightening? Why?
4. Which story could best be dramatized for television? Justify your choice.
5. How do the authors of these stories achieve suspense?

Projects

1. From the class select a group of actors who will present Saki's "The Open Window" in dramatized form. Decide in advance what type of person should play the girl, her aunt, and the nervous young man.
2. From a newspaper or a magazine, find a true-life story that might be used as the basis of a story of suspense. Be ready to discuss the reasons for your choice, and tell how it might be developed into a short story.
3. Prepare to tell in class a ghost story or some other story of suspense. Rehearse carefully to bring out all the shivery details. Try to hold your audience spellbound.
4. Horror movies always seem to have an audience. Teenagers especially seem to support horror movies and their endless sequels. Have a class discussion to consider why these movies have such a special appeal for a teenage audience.

5.   Pretend you are the author of "The Lottery." Someone has writ-
     ten to you angrily, criticizing you for writing such a story. How
     would you answer the letter writer?

Additional Readings

Short Stories

"Leiningen Versus the Ants" by Carl Stephenson

> There is almost unbearable suspense in this story of a man's
> battle against the forces of nature.

"The Most Dangerous Game" by Richard Connell

> Some hunters consider lions the most dangerous game; oth-
> ers declare tigers are more deadly. Richard Connell suggests
> another surprising "animal" in this story of terror and pursuit.

"The Open Boat" by Stephen Crane

> What is it like to be adrift in the open sea, with diminishing
> hope of rescue? Share the experiences of four men as they face
> the possibility of starvation or drowning.

"The Hands of Mr. Ottermole" by Thomas Burke

> The creators of Ellery Queen praised this story in this way:
> "No finer crime story has ever been written, period."

"The Fall of the House of Usher" by Edgar Allan Poe

> For sheer terror, this is one of the most gripping of all stories
> written by the master storyteller. Here there are eerie foot-
> steps, strange noises, and a startling climax.

"August Heat" by W. F. Harvey

> The climax of this brilliant tale of suspense comes after the
> events of the story have unfolded, but the tragedy is clear.

"A Struggle for Life" by Thomas Bailey Aldrich

> This is a fine companion story to "The Waxwork." It is the
> story of a man imprisoned in a tomb. Be on guard. There are
> two surprises.

"Dr. Heidegger's Experiment" by Nathaniel Hawthorne

Four old people are given a chance to regain their youth. What do they do with the opportunity?

Anthologies

The Complete Novels and Selected Tales of Nathaniel Hawthorne

Though more than a century old, many of the stories of Nathaniel Hawthorne can bring a shiver to modern readers.

The Touch of Nutmeg by John Collier

Stories that combine unusual situations with a wicked sense of humor captivate the reader.

3

Out of This World

"Let's make believe." As a child, you probably used this expression often. You enjoyed pretending, playacting, picturing yourself in a variety of imaginative, unreal, impossible situations. As you've grown older, you've not entirely lost this quality. You still enjoy imaginative tales that take you "out of this world."

The four stories in this section range from fantasy to science fiction. Fantasy and science fiction differ in one important respect. Fantasy doesn't pretend to have a scientific background. Science fiction does. Yet both types of literature are challenging, leading you to worlds that do not exist—at least not yet.

In this unit you will meet a fanciful imp that grants wishes for wealth and fame, but as in all such situations, there is a catch. Then you will sympathize with an ancient creature from the deep that seeks companionship of its kind. In both stories a strong element of make-believe exists.

The two remaining stories are science fiction—set in a very possible future. Though the first two stories are not likely ever to be true, the second two stories are quite probable. In the first, a young girl 200 years from now compares the school systems of that time with school systems now. Her conclusions may surprise you. In the second story, explorers and scientists have conquered the moon and live on its surface. They uncover a secret that should be the best news humanity has had for a long time, but like the gifts of the bottle imp, this gift has a deadly catch.

All four stories will challenge your imagination, take you outside the realm of the everyday, the commonplace. They will quite literally take your imagination out of this world.

The Bottle Imp

Robert Louis Stevenson

♦ "I must tell you, although I appear to you so rich and fortunate, all my fortune, and this house itself and its garden, came out of a bottle not much bigger than a pint. This is it."

There are two kinds of folk tales with related themes. In both types, someone enjoys instant wealth and the fulfillment of every wish. How? At a price. In one type, an imp, a devil, a mysterious force grants wishes. It may be a genie in a bottle or it may be something like a charm or even a mysterious monkey's paw. Wishes are granted, but there is usually a catch.

In the second type a person makes a direct pact with the devil. For a while he enjoys wealth and all that money can buy, but in the end he must give up his soul. The Faust legend is a good example of this type. Stephen Vincent Benet's "The Devil and Daniel Webster" is a delightful variation on this age-old theme.

Now you are about to meet the mischievous bottle imp in a story that combines both threads. A mysterious imp grants wishes, but behind it all is a kind of pact with the devil himself. The prize? A person's soul. In "The Bottle Imp" the full impact of the bargain is not apparent at once. The conditions are most unusual, and the suspense grows.

Tales of a bottle imp appear in the folklore of many nations and peoples. Arabian, Estonian, Finnish, Swedish, Swiss, Hebrew, and Philippine folktales tell of bottle imps that give people what they wish. Stevenson's version adds a personal concern lacking in most of the others.

Here you will find many ingredients, not the least of which is love between a man and a woman. Each is willing to sacrifice his or her immortal soul to save the other. The situation seems hopeless. How can either be saved? Let Robert Louis Stevenson spin an ingenious plot.

THE BOTTLE IMP

There was a man in the island of Hawaii, whom I shall call Keawe; for the truth is, he still lives, and his name must be kept secret; but the place of his birth was not far from Honaunau, where the bones of Keawe the Great lie hidden in a cave. This man was poor, brave, and active; he could read and write like a schoolmaster; he was a first-rate mariner besides, sailed for some time in the island steamers, and steered a whaleboat on the Hamakua coast. At length it came in Keawe's mind to have a sight of the great world and foreign cities, and he shipped on a vessel bound to San Francisco.

This is a fine town, with a fine harbor, and rich people uncountable; and, in particular, there is one hill which is covered with palaces. Upon this hill Keawe was one day taking a walk, with his pocket full of money, viewing the great houses upon either hand with pleasure. "What fine houses they are!" he was thinking, "and how happy must these people be who dwell in them, and take no care for the morrow!" The thought was in his mind when he came abreast of a house that was smaller than some others, but all finished and beautified like a toy; the steps of that house shone like silver, and the borders of the garden bloomed like garlands, and the windows were bright like diamonds; and Keawe stopped and wondered at the excellence of all he saw. So stopping, he was aware of a man that looked forth upon him through a window, so clear that Keawe could see him as you see a fish in a pool upon the reef. The man was elderly, with a bald head and a black beard; and his face was heavy with sorrow, and he bitterly sighed. And the truth of it is, that as Keawe looked in upon the man, and the man looked out upon Keawe, each envied the other.

All of a sudden the man smiled and nodded, and beckoned Keawe to enter, and met him at the door of the house.

"This is a fine house of mine," said the man, and bitterly sighed. "Would you not care to view the chambers?"

So he led Keawe all over it, from the cellar to the roof, and there was nothing there that was not perfect of its kind, and Keawe was astonished.

"Truly," said Keawe, "this is a beautiful house; if I lived in the like of it, I should be laughing all day long. How comes it, then, that you should be sighing?"

"There is no reason," said the man, "why you should not have a house in all points similar to this, and finer, if you wish. You have some money, I suppose?"

"I have fifty dollars," said Keawe, "but a house like this will cost more than fifty dollars."

The man made a computation. "I am sorry you have no more," said he, "for it may raise you trouble in the future; but it shall be yours at fifty dollars."

"The house?" asked Keawe.

"No, not the house," replied the man; "but the bottle. For, I must tell you, although I appear to you so rich and fortunate, all my fortune, and this house itself and its garden, came out of a bottle not much bigger than a pint. This is it."

And he opened a lock-fast place, and took out a round-bellied bottle with a long neck; the glass of it was white like milk, with changing rainbow colors in the grain. Withinsides something obscurely moved, like a shadow and a fire.

"This is the bottle," said the man; and, when Keawe laughed, "You do not believe me?" he added. "Try, then, for yourself. See if you can break it."

So Keawe took the bottle up and dashed it on the floor till he was weary; but it jumped on the floor like a child's ball, and was not injured.

"This is a strange thing," said Keawe. "For by the touch of it, as well as by the look, the bottle should be of glass."

"Of glass it is," replied the man, sighing more heavily than ever; "but the glass of it was tempered in the flames of hell. An imp lives in it, and that is the shadow we behold there moving; or, so I suppose. If any man buys this bottle the imp is at his command; all that he desires—love, fame, money, houses like this house, ay, or a city like this city—all are his at the word uttered. Napoleon had this bottle, and by it he grew to be the king of the world; but he sold it at the last and fell. Captain Cook had this bottle, and by it he found his way to so many islands; but he, too, sold it, and was slain upon Hawaii. For, once it is sold, the power goes and the protection; and unless a man remain content with what he has, ill will befall him."

"And yet you talk of selling it yourself?" Keawe said.

"I have all I wish, and I am growing elderly," replied the man. "There is one thing the imp cannot do—he cannot prolong life; and, it would not be fair to conceal from you there is a drawback to the bottle; for if a man die before he sells it, he must burn in hell forever."

"To be sure, that is a drawback and no mistake," cried Keawe. "I would not meddle with the thing. I can do without a house, thank God; but there is one thing I could not be doing with one particle, and that is to be damned."

"Dear me, you must not run away with things," returned the man. "All you have to do is to use the power of the imp in moderation, and then sell it to someone else, as I do to you, and finish your life in comfort."

"Well, I observe two things," said Keawe. "All the time you keep sighing like a maid in love, that is one; and, for the other, you sell this bottle very cheap."

"I have told you already why I sigh," said the man. "It is because I fear my health is breaking up; and, as you said yourself, to die and go to the devil is a pity for anyone. As for why I sell so cheap, I must explain to you there is a peculiarity about the bottle. Long ago, when the devil brought it first upon earth, it was extremely expensive, and was sold first of all to Prester John for many millions of dollars; but it cannot be sold at all, unless sold at a loss. If you sell it for as much as you paid for it, back it comes to you again like a homing pigeon. It follows that the price has kept falling in these centuries, and the bottle is now remarkably cheap. I bought it myself from one of my great neighbors on this hill, and the price I paid was ninety dollars. I could sell it for as high as eighty-nine dollars and ninety-nine cents, but not a penny dearer, or back the thing must come to me. Now, about this there are two bothers. First, when you offer a bottle so singular for eighty-odd dollars, people suppose you to be jesting. And second—but there is no hurry about that—and I need not go into it. Only remember it must be coined money that you sell it for."

"How am I to know that this is all true?" asked Keawe.

"Some of it you can try at once," replied the man. "Give me your fifty dollars, take the bottle, and wish your fifty dollars back into your pocket. If that does not happen, I pledge you my honor I will cry off the bargain and restore your money."

"You are not deceiving me?" said Keawe.

The man bound himself with a great oath.

"Well, I will risk that much," said Keawe, "for that can do no harm," and he paid over his money to the man, and the man handed him the bottle.

"Imp of the bottle," said Keawe, "I want my fifty dollars back." And sure enough, he had scarce said the word before his pocket was as heavy as ever.

"To be sure this is a wonderful bottle," said Keawe.

"And now good morning to you, my fine fellow, and the devil go with you for me," said the man.

"Hold on," said Keawe, "I don't want any more of this fun. Here, take your bottle back."

"You have bought it for less than I paid for it," replied the man, rubbing his hands. "It is yours now; and, for my part, I am only concerned to see the back of you." And with that he rang for his Chinese servant, and had Keawe shown out of the house.

Now, when Keawe was in the street, with the bottle under his arm, he began to think. "If all is true about this bottle, I may have made a losing bargain," thinks he. "But, perhaps the man was only fooling me." The first thing he did was to count his money; the sum was exact—forty-nine dollars American money, and one Chili piece. "That looks like the truth," said Keawe. "Now I will try another part."

The streets in that part of the city were as clean as a ship's decks, and though it was noon, there were no passengers. Keawe set the bottle in the gutter and walked away. Twice he looked back, and there was the milky, round-bellied bottle where he left it. A third time he looked back, and turned a corner; but he had scarce done so, when something knocked upon his elbow, and behold! it was the long neck sticking up; and as for the round belly, it was jammed into the pocket of his pilot-coat.

"And that looks like the truth," said Keawe.

The next thing he did was to buy a corkscrew in a shop, and go apart into a secret place in the fields. And there he tried to draw the cork, but as often as he put the screw in, out it came again, and the cork was as whole as ever.

"This is some new sort of cork," said Keawe, and all at once he began to shake and sweat, for he was afraid of that bottle.

On his way back to the port side he saw a shop where a man sold shells and clubs from the wild islands, old heathen deities, old coined money, pictures from China and Japan, and all manner of things that sailors bring in their sea chests. And here he had an idea. So he went in and offered the bottle for a hundred dollars. The man of the shop laughed at him at first, and offered him five, but, indeed, it was a curious bottle, such glass was never blown in any human glassworks, so prettily the colors shone under the milky white, and so strangely the shadow hovered in the midst; so, after he had disputed a while after the manner of his kind, the shopman gave Keawe sixty silver dollars for the thing and set it on a shelf in the midst of his window.

"Now," said Keawe, "I have sold that for sixty which I bought for fifty—or, to say truth, a little less, because one of my dollars was from Chili. Now I shall know the truth upon another point."

So he went back on board his ship, and when he opened his chest, there was the bottle, and had come more quickly than himself. Now Keawe had a mate on board whose name was Lopaka.

"What ails you," said Lopaka, "that you stare in your chest?"

They were alone in the ship's forecastle, and Keawe bound him to secrecy, and told all.

"This is a very strange affair," said Lopaka; "and I fear you will be in trouble about this bottle. But there is one point very clear—that you are sure of the trouble, and you had better have the profit in the bargain. Make up your mind what you want with it; give the order, and if it is done as you desire, I will buy the bottle myself; for I have an idea of my own to get a schooner, and go trading through the island."

"That is not my idea," said Keawe; "but to have a beautiful house and garden on the Kona Coast, where I was born, the sun shining in at the door, flowers in the garden, glass in the windows, pictures on the walls, and toys and fine carpets on the table, for all the world like the house I was in this day—only a story higher, and with balconies all about like the King's palace; and to live there without care and make merry with my friends and relatives."

"Well," said Lopaka, "let us carry it back with us to Hawaii; and if all comes true, as you suppose, I will buy the bottle, as I said, and ask a schooner."

Upon that they were agreed, and it was not long before the ship returned to Honolulu, carrying Keawe and Lopaka, and the bottle. They were scarce come ashore when they met a friend upon the beach, who began at once to condole with Keawe.

"I do not know what I am to be condoled about," said Keawe.

"Is it possible you have not heard," said the friend, "your uncle—that good old man—is dead, and your cousin—that beautiful boy—was drowned at sea?"

Keawe was filled with sorrow, and, beginning to weep and to lament, he forgot about the bottle. But Lopaka was thinking to himself, and presently, when Keawe's grief was a little abated, "I have been thinking," said Lopaka, "had not your uncle lands in Hawaii, in the district of Kaü?"

"No," said Keawe; "not in Kaü: they are on the mountainside—a little be-south Hookena."

"These lands will now be yours?" asked Lopaka.

"And so they will," says Keawe, and began again to lament for his relatives.

"No," said Lopaka, "do not lament at present. I have a thought in my mind. How if this should be the doing of the bottle? For here is the place ready for your house."

"If this be so," cried Keawe, "it is a very ill way to serve me by killing my relatives. But it may be, indeed; for it was in just such a station that I saw the house with my mind's eye."

"The house, however, is not yet built," said Lopaka.

"No, nor like to be!" said Keawe; "for though my uncle has some coffee and ava and bananas, it will not be more than will keep me in comfort; and the rest of that land is the black lava."

"Let us go to the lawyer," said Lopaka; "I have still this idea in my mind."

Now, when they came to the lawyer's, it appeared Keawe's uncle had grown monstrous rich in the last days, and there was a fund of money.

"And here is the money for the house!" cried Lopaka.

"If you are thinking of a new house," said the lawyer, "here is the card of a new architect of whom they tell me great things."

"Better and better!" cried Lopaka. "Here is all made plain for us. Let us continue to obey orders."

So they went to the architect, and he had drawings of houses on his table.

"You want something out of the way?" said the architect. "How do you like this?" and he handed a drawing to Keawe.

Now, when Keawe set eyes on the drawing, he cried out aloud, for it was the picture of his thought exactly drawn.

"I am in for this house," thought he. "Little as I like the way it comes to me, I am in for it now, and I may as well take the good along with the evil."

So he told the architect all that he wished, and how he would have that house furnished, and about the pictures on the walls and the knickknacks on the tables; and he asked the man plainly for how much he would undertake the whole affair.

The architect put many questions, and took his pen and made a computation; and when he had done he named the very sum that Keawe had inherited.

Lopaka and Keawe looked at one another and nodded.

"It is quite clear," thought Keawe, "that I am to have this house, whether or no. It comes from the devil, and I fear I will get little good by that; and of one thing I am sure, I will make no more wishes as long as I have this bottle. But with the house I am saddled, and I may as well take the good along with the evil."

So he made his terms with the architect, and they signed a paper; and Keawe and Lopaka took ship again and sailed to Australia; for it was concluded between them they should not interfere at all, but leave the architect and the bottle imp to build and to adorn the house at their own pleasure.

The voyage was a good voyage, only all the time Keawe was holding in his breath, for he had sworn he would utter no more wishes, and take no more favors, from the devil. The time was up when they got back. The architect told them that the house was ready, and Keawe and Lopaka took a passage in the *Hall,* and went down Kona way to view the house, and see if all had been done fitly according to the thought that was in Keawe's mind.

Now, the house stood on the mountainside, visible to ships. Above, the forest ran up into the clouds of rain; below, the black lava fell in cliffs, where the kings of old lay buried. A garden bloomed about that house with every hue of flowers; and there was an orchard of papaya on the one hand and an orchard of breadfruit on the other, and right in front, towards the sea, a ship's mast had been rigged up and bore a flag. As for the house, it was three stories high, with great chambers and broad balconies on each. The windows were of glass, so excellent that it was clear as water and as bright as day. All manner of furniture adorned the chambers. Pictures hung upon the walls in golden frames—pictures of ships, and men fighting, and of the most beautiful women, and of singular places; nowhere in the world are these pictures of so bright a color as those Keawe found hanging in his house. As for the knickknacks, they were extraordinarily fine: chiming clocks and musical boxes, little men with nodding heads, books filled with pictures, weapons of price from all quarters of the world, and the most elegant puzzles to entertain the leisure of a solitary man. And as no one would care to live in such chambers, only to walk through and view them, the balconies were made so broad that a whole town might have lived upon them in delight; and Keawe knew not which to prefer, whether the back porch, where you got the land breeze and looked upon the orchards and the flowers, or the front balcony, where you could drink the wind of the sea, and look down the steep wall of the mountain and see the *Hall* going by once a week or so between Hookena and the hills of Pele, or the schooners plying up the coast for wood and ava and bananas.

When they had viewed all, Keawe and Lopaka sat on the porch.

"Well," asked Lopaka, "is it all as you designed?"

"Words cannot utter it," said Keawe. "It is better than I dreamed, and I am sick with satisfaction."

"There is but one thing to consider," said Lopaka, "all this may be quite natural, and the bottle imp have nothing whatever to say to it. If I were to buy the bottle, and got no schooner after all, I should have put my hand in the fire for nothing. I gave you my word, I know; but yet I think you would not grudge me one more proof."

"I have sworn I would take no more favors," said Keawe. "I have gone already deep enough."

"This is no favor I am thinking of," replied Lopaka. "It is only to see the imp himself. There is nothing to be gained by that, and so nothing to be ashamed of, and yet, if I once saw him, I should be sure of the whole matter. So indulge me so far, and let me see the imp; and, after that, here is the money in my hand, and I will buy it."

"There is only one thing I am afraid of," said Keawe. "The imp may be very ugly to view, and if you once set eyes upon him you might be very undesirous of the bottle."

"I am a man of my word," said Lopaka. "And here is the money betwixt us."

"Very well," replied Keawe, "I have a curiosity myself. So come, let us have one look at you, Mr. Imp."

Now as soon as that was said, the imp looked out of the bottle, and in again, swift as a lizard; and there sat Keawe and Lopaka turned to stone. The night had quite come, before either found a thought to say or voice to say it with; and then Lopaka pushed the money over and took the bottle.

"I am a man of my word," said he, "and had need to be so, or I would not touch this bottle with my foot. Well, I shall get my schooner and a dollar or two for my pocket; and then I will be rid of this devil as fast as I can. For to tell you the plain truth, the look of him has cast me down."

"Lopaka," said Keawe, "do not you think any worse of me than you can help; I know it is night, and the roads bad, and the pass by the tombs an ill place to go by so late, but I declare since I have seen that little face, I cannot eat or sleep or pray till it is gone from me. I will give you a lantern, and a basket to put the bottle in, and any picture or fine thing in all my house that takes your fancy; and be gone at once, and go sleep at Hookena with Nahinu."

"Keawe," said Lopaka, "many a man would take this ill; above all, when I am doing you a turn so friendly, as to keep my word and buy the bottle; and for that matter, the night and the dark, and the way by the tombs, must be all tenfold more dangerous to a man with such a sin upon his conscience and such a bottle under his arm. But for my part, I am so extremely terrified myself, I have not the heart to blame you. Here I go, then; and I pray God you may be happy in your house, and I fortunate with my schooner, and both get to heaven in the end in spite of the devil and his bottle."

So Lopaka went down the mountain; and Keawe stood in his front balcony, and listened to the clink of the horse's shoes, and watched the lantern go shining down the path, and along the cliff of caves where the old dead are buried; and all the time he trembled and clasped his hands, and prayed for his friend, and gave glory to God that he himself was escaped out of that trouble.

But the next day came very brightly, and that new house of his was so delightful to behold that he forgot his terrors. One day followed another, and Keawe dwelt there in perpetual joy. He had his place on the back porch; it was there he ate and lived, and read the stories in the Honolulu newspapers; but when anyone came by they would go in and view the chambers and the pictures. And the fame of the house went far and wide; it was called *Ka-Hale Nui*—the Great House—in all Kona; and sometimes the Bright House, for Keawe kept a Chinaman, who was all day dusting and furbishing; and the glass, and the gilt, and the fine stuffs, and the pictures, shone as bright as the morning. As for Keawe himself, he could not walk in the chambers without singing, his heart was so enlarged; and when ships sailed by upon the sea, he would fly his colors on the mast.

So time went by, until one day Keawe went upon a visit as far as Kailua to certain of his friends. There he was well feasted; and left as soon as he could the next morning, and rode hard, for he was impatient to behold his beautiful house; and, besides, the night then coming on was the night in which the dead of old days go abroad in the sides of Kona; and having already meddled with the devil, he was the more chary of meeting with the dead. A little beyond Honaunau, looking far ahead, he was aware of a woman bathing in the edge of the sea; and she seemed a well-grown girl, but he thought no more of it. Then he saw her white shift flutter as she put it on, and then her red holoku; and by the time he came abreast of her she was done with her toilet, and had come up from the sea, and stood by the trackside in her red holoku, and she was all freshened with the bath, and her eyes shone and were kind. Now Keawe no sooner beheld her than he drew rein.

"I thought I knew everyone in this country," said he. "How comes it that I do not know you?"

"I am Kokua, daughter of Kiano," said the girl, "and I have just returned from Oahu. Who are you?"

"I will tell you who I am in a little," said Keawe, dismounting from his horse, "but not now. For I have a thought in my mind, and if you knew who I was, you might have heard of me, and would not give me a true answer. But tell me, first of all, one thing: are you married?"

At this Kokua laughed out aloud. "It is you who asks questions," she said. "Are you married yourself?"

"Indeed, Kokua, I am not," replied Keawe, "and never thought to be until this hour. But here is the plain truth. I have met you here at the road side, and I saw your eyes, which are like the stars, and my heart went to you as swift as a bird. And so now, if you want none of me, say so, and I will go on to my own place; but if you think me no worse than any other young man, say so, too, and I will turn aside to your father's for the night, and tomorrow I will talk with the good man."

Kokua said never a word, but she looked at the sea and laughed.

"Kokua," said Keawe, "if you say nothing, I will take that for the good answer; so let us be stepping to your father's door."

She went on ahead of him, still without speech; only sometimes she glanced back and glanced away again, and she kept the strings of her hat in her mouth.

Now, when they had come to the door, Kiano came out on his veranda, and cried out and welcomed Keawe by name. At that the girl looked over, for the fame of the great house had come to her ears; and, to be sure, it was a great temptation. All that evening they were very merry together; and the girl was as bold as brass under the eyes of her parents, and made a mark of Keawe, for she had a quick wit. The next day he had a word with Kiano, and found the girl alone.

"Kokua," said he, "you made a mark of me all the evening; and it is still time to bid me go. I would not tell you who I was, because I have so fine a house, and I feared you would think too much of that house and too little of the man that loves you. Now you know all, and if you wish to have seen the last of me, say so at once."

"No," said Kokua, but this time she did not laugh, nor did Keawe ask for more.

This was the wooing of Keawe; things had gone quickly; but so an arrow goes, and the ball of a rifle swifter still, and yet both may strike the target. Things had gone fast, but they had gone far also, and the thought of Keawe rang in the maiden's head; she heard his voice in the breach of the surf upon the lava, and for this young man that she had seen but twice she would have left father and mother and her native islands. As for Keawe himself, his horse flew up the path of the mountain under the cliff of tombs, and the sound of the hoofs, and the sound of Keawe singing to himself for pleasure, echoed in the caverns of the dead. He came to the Bright House, and still he was singing. He sat and ate in the broad balcony, and the Chinaman wondered at his master, to hear how he sang between the mouthfuls. The sun went down into the sea, and the night came; and Keawe walked the balconies by lamplight, high on the mountains, and the voice of his singing startled men on ships.

"Here am I now upon my high place," he said to himself. "Life may be no better; this is the mountaintop; and all shelves about me toward the worse. For the first time I will light up the chambers, and bathe in my fine bath with the hot water and the cold, and sleep above in the bed of my bridal chamber."

So the Chinaman had word, and he must rise from sleep and

light the furnaces; and as he walked below, beside the boilers, he heard his master singing and rejoicing above him in the lighted chambers. When the water began to be hot the Chinaman cried to his master: and Keawe went into the bathroom; and the Chinaman heard him sing as he filled the marble basin; and heard him sing, and the singing broken, as he undressed; until of a sudden, the song ceased. The Chinaman listened, and listened; he called up the house to Keawe to ask if all were well, and Keawe answered him "Yes," and bade him go to bed; but there was no more singing in the Bright House; and all night long the Chinaman heard his master's feet go round and round the balconies without repose.

Now, the truth of it was this: as Keawe undressed for his bath, he spied upon his flesh a patch like a patch of lichen on a rock, and it was then that he stopped singing. For he knew the likeness of that patch, and knew that he was fallen in the Chinese Evil.*

Now, it is a sad thing for any man to fall into this sickness. And it would be a sad thing for anyone to leave a house so beautiful and so commodious, and depart from all his friends to the north coast of Molokai, between the mighty cliff and the sea breakers. But what was that to the case of the man Keawe, he who had met his love but yesterday and won her but that morning, and now saw all his hopes break, in a moment, like a piece of glass?

A while he sat upon the edge of the bath, then sprang, with a cry, and ran outside; and to and fro, to and fro, along the balcony, like one despairing.

"Very willingly could I leave Hawaii, the home of my fathers," Keawe was thinking. "Very lightly could I leave my house, the high-placed, the many-windowed, here upon the mountains. Very bravely could I go to Molokai, to Kalaupapa by the cliffs, to live with the smitten and to sleep there, far from my fathers. But what wrong have I done, what sin lies upon my soul, that I should have encountered Kokua coming cool from the seawater in the evening? Kokua, the soul ensnarer! Kokua, the light of my life! Her may I never wed, her may I look upon no longer, her may I no more handle with my loving hand; and it is for this, it is for you, O Kokua! that I pour my lamentations!"

Now you are to observe what sort of a man Keawe was, for he might have dwelt there in the Bright House for years, and no one

---

* Leprosy.

been the wiser of his sickness; but he reckoned nothing of that, if he must lose Kokua. And again he might have wed Kokua even as he was; and so many would have done, because they have the soul of pigs; but Keawe loved the maid manfully, and he would do her no hurt and bring her in no danger.

A little beyond the midst of the night, there came in his mind the recollection of that bottle. He went round the back porch, and called to memory the day when the devil had looked forth; and at the thought ice ran in his veins.

"A dreadful thing is the bottle," thought Keawe, "and dreadful is the imp, and it is a dreadful thing to risk the flames of hell. But what other hope have I to cure my sickness or to wed Kokua? What!" he thought, "would I beard the devil once, only to get me a house, and not face him again to win Kokua?"

Thereupon he called to mind it was the next day the *Hall* went by on her return to Honolulu. "There must I go first," he thought, "and see Lopaka. For the best hope that I have now is to find that same bottle I was so pleased to be rid of."

Never a wink could he sleep; the food stuck in his throat; but he sent a letter to Kiano, and about the time when the steamer would be coming, rode down beside the cliff of the tombs. It rained; his horse went heavily, he looked up at the black mouths of the caves, and he envied the dead that slept there and were done with trouble; and called to mind how he had galloped by the day before, and was astonished. So he came down to Hookena, and there was all the country gathered for the steamer as usual. In the shed before the store they sat and jested and passed the news; but there was no matter of speech in Keawe's bosom, and he sat in their midst and looked without on the rain falling on the houses, and the surf beating among the rocks, and the sighs arose in his throat.

"Keawe of the Bright House is out of spirits," said one to another. Indeed, and so he was, and little wonder.

Then the *Hall* came, and the whale boat carried him on board. The afterpart of the ship was full of Haoles*—who had been to visit the volcano, as their custom is; and the midst was crowded with Kanakas, and the forepart with wild bulls from Hilo and horses from Kaü; but Keawe sat apart from all in his sorrow, and watched for the house of Kiano. There it sat low upon the shore in the black

* Whites.

rocks, and shaded by the cocoa palms, and there by the door was a red holoku,* no greater than a fly, and going to and fro with a fly's busyness. "Ah, queen of my heart," he cried, "I'll venture my dear soul to win you!"

Soon after darkness fell and the cabins were lit up, and the Haoles sat and played at the cards and drank whiskey as their custom is; but Keawe walked the deck all night; and all the next day, as they steamed under the lea of Maui or of Molokai, he was still pacing to and fro like a wild animal in a menagerie.

Towards evening they passed Diamond Head, and came to the pier of Honolulu. Keawe stepped out among the crowd and began to ask for Lopaka. It seemed he had become the owner of a schooner—none better in the islands—and was gone upon an adventure as far as Pola-Pola or Kahiki; so there was no help to be looked for from Lopaka. Keawe called to mind a friend of his, a lawyer in the town (I must not tell his name), and inquired of him. They said he was grown suddenly rich, and had a fine new house upon Waikiki shore; and this put a thought in Keawe's head, and he called a hack and drove to the lawyer's house.

The house was all brand-new, and the trees in the garden no greater than walking sticks, and the lawyer, when he came, had the air of a man well pleased.

"What can I do to serve you?" said the lawyer.

"You are a friend of Lopaka's," replied Keawe, "and Lopaka purchased from me a certain piece of goods that I thought you might enable me to trace."

The lawyer's face became very dark. "I do not profess to misunderstand you, Mr. Keawe," said he, "though this is an ugly business to be stirring in. You may be sure I know nothing, but yet I have a guess, and if you would apply in a certain quarter I think you might have news."

And he named the name of a man, which, again, I had better not repeat. So it was for days, and Keawe went from one to another, finding everywhere new clothes and carriages, and fine new houses and men everywhere in great contentment, although, to be sure, when he hinted at his business their faces would cloud over.

"No doubt I am upon the track," thought Keawe. "The new clothes and carriages are all the gifts of the little imp, and these

* Long gown

glad faces are the faces of men who have taken their profit and got rid of the accursed thing in safety. When I see pale cheeks and hear sighing, I shall know that I am near the bottle."

So it befell at last he was recommended to a Haole in Beritania Street. When he came to the door, about the hour of the evening meal, there were the usual marks of the new house, and the young garden, and the electric light shining in the windows; but when the owner came, a shock of hope and fear ran through Keawe; for here was a young man, white as a corpse, and black about the eyes, the hair shedding from his head, and such a look in his countenance as a man may have when he is waiting for the gallows.

"Here it is, to be sure," thought Keawe, and so with this man he noways veiled his errand. "I am come to buy the bottle," said he.

At the word, the young Haole of Beritania Street reeled against the wall.

"The bottle!" he gasped. "To buy the bottle!" Then he seemed to choke, and seizing Keawe by the arm, carried him into a room and poured out wine in two glasses.

"Here is my respects," said Keawe, who had been much about with Haoles in his time. "Yes," he added, "I am come to buy the bottle. What is the price by now?"

At that word the young man let his glass slip through his fingers, and looked upon Keawe like a ghost.

"The price," says he; "the price! You do not know the price?"

"It is for that I am asking you," returned Keawe. "But why are you so much concerned? Is there anything wrong about the price?"

"It has dropped a great deal in value since your time, Mr. Keawe," said the young man, stammering.

"Well, well, I shall have the less to pay for it," says Keawe. "How much did it cost you?"

The young man was as white as a sheet. "Two cents," said he.

"What?" cried Keawe, "two cents? Why, then, you can only sell it for one. And he who buys it—" The words died upon Keawe's tongue; he who bought it could never sell it again, the bottle and the bottle imp must abide with him until he died, and when he died must carry him to the red end of hell.

The young man of Beritania Street fell upon his knees. "For God's sake, buy it!" he cried. "You can have all my fortune in the bargain. I was mad when I bought it at that price. I had embezzled money at my store; I was lost else; I must have gone to jail."

"Poor creature," said Keawe, "you would risk your soul upon so desperate an adventure, and to avoid the proper punishment of your own disgrace; and you think I could hesitate with love in front of me. Give me the bottle, and the change which I make sure you have all ready. Here is a five-cent piece."

It was as Keawe supposed; the young man had the change ready in a drawer; the bottle changed hands, and Keawe's fingers no sooner clasped upon the stalk than he had breathed his wish to be a clean man. And, sure enough, when he got home to his room, and stripped himself before a glass, his flesh was whole like an infant's. And here was the strange thing: he had no sooner seen this miracle than his mind was changed within him, and he cared naught for the Chinese Evil, and little enough for Kokua; and had but the one thought, that here he was bound to the bottle imp for time and for eternity, and had no better hope but to be a cinder for ever in the flames of hell. Away ahead of him he saw them blaze with his mind's eye, and his soul shrank, and darkness fell upon the light.

When Keawe came to himself a little, he was aware it was the night when the band played at the hotel. Thither he went, because he feared to be alone; and there, among happy faces, walked to and fro, and heard the tunes go up and down, and saw Berger beat the measure, and all the while he heard the flames crackle and saw the red fire burning in the bottomless pit. Of a sudden the band played *Hiki-ao-ao;* that was a song that he had sung with Kokua, and at the strain courage returned to him.

"It is done now," he thought, "and once more let me take the good along with the evil."

So it befell that he returned to Hawaii by the first steamer, and as soon as it could be managed he was wedded to Kokua, and carried her up the mountainside to the Bright House.

Now it was so with these two, that when they were together Keawe's heart was stilled; but as soon as he was alone he fell into a brooding horror, and heard the flames crackle, and saw the red fire burn in the bottomless pit. The girl, indeed, had come to him wholly; her heart leaped in her side at sight of him, her hand clung to his; and she was so fashioned, from the hair upon her head to the nails upon her toes, that none could see her without joy. She was pleasant in her nature. She had the good word always. Full of song she was, and went to and fro in the Bright House, the brightest thing in its three stories, caroling like the birds. And Keawe beheld and heard her with delight, and then must shrink upon one side, and weep and groan to think upon the price that he had paid for her; and then he must dry his eyes, and wash his face, and go and sit with her on the broad balconies, joining in her songs, and, with a sick spirit, answering her smiles.

There came a day when her feet began to be heavy and her songs more rare; and now it was not Keawe only that would weep apart, but each would sunder from the other and sit in opposite balconies with the whole width of the Bright House betwixt. Keawe was so sunk in his despair, he scarce observed the change, and was only glad he had more hours to sit alone and brood upon his destiny, and was not so frequently condemned to pull a smiling face on a sick heart. But one day, coming softly through the house, he heard the sound of a child sobbing, and there was Kokua rolling her face upon the balcony floor, and weeping like the lost.

"You do well to keep in this house, Kokua," he said. "And yet I would give the head off my body that you (at least) might have been happy."

"Happy!" she cried. "Keawe, when you lived alone in your Bright House you were the word of the island for a happy man; laughter and song were in your mouth, and your face was as bright as the sunrise. Then you wedded poor Kokua; and the good God knows what is amiss in her—but from that day you have not smiled. Oh!" she cried, "what ails me? I thought I was pretty, and I knew I loved him. What ails me, that I throw this cloud upon my husband?"

"Poor Kokua," said Keawe. He sat down by her side, and sought to take her hand; but that she plucked away. "Poor Kokua," he said again. "My poor child—my pretty. And I had thought all this while to spare you! Well, you shall know all. Then, at least, you will pity poor Keawe; then you will understand how much he loved you in the past—that he dared hell for your possession—and how much he loves you still (the poor condemned one), that he can yet call up a smile when he beholds you."

With that he told her all, even from the beginning.

"You have done this for me?" she cried. "Ah, well, then what do I care!" and she clasped and wept upon him.

"Ah, child!" said Keawe; "and yet, when I consider of the fire of hell, I care a good deal!"

"Never tell me," said she, "no man can be lost because he loved

Kokua, and no other fault. I tell you, Keawe, I shall save you with these hands, or perish in your company. What! you loved me and gave your soul, and you think I will not die to save you in return?"

"Ah, my dear, you might die a hundred times, and what difference would that make," he cried, "except to leave me lonely till the time comes for my damnation?"

"You know nothing," said she. "I was educated in a school in Honolulu, I am no common girl. And I tell you I shall save my lover. What is this you say about a cent? But all the world is not American. In England they have a piece they call a farthing, which is about half a cent. Ah! sorrow!" she cried, "that makes it scarcely better, for the buyer must be lost, and we shall find none so brave as my Keawe! But, then, there is France; they have a small coin there which they call a centime, and these go five to the cent, or thereabout. We could not do better. Come, Keawe, let us go to the French islands; let us go to Tahiti, as fast as ships can bear us. There we have four centimes, three centimes, two centimes, one centime; four possible sales to come and go on; and two of us to push the bargain. Come, my Keawe! kiss me, and banish care. Kokua will defend you."

"Gift of God!" he cried. "I cannot think that God will punish me for desiring aught so good. Be it as you will, then, take me where you please: I put my life and my salvation in your hands."

Early the next day Kokua went about her preparations. She took Keawe's chest that he went with sailoring; and first she put the bottle in a corner, and then packed it with the richest of their clothes and the bravest of the knickknacks in the house. "For," said she, "we must seem to be rich folks, or who would believe in the bottle?" All the time of her preparation she was as gay as a bird; only when she looked upon Keawe the tears would spring in her eye, and she must run and kiss him. As for Keawe, a weight was off his soul; now that he had his secret shared, and some hope in front of him, he seemed like a new man, his feet went lightly on the earth, and his breath was good to him again. Yet was terror still at his elbow; and ever and again, as the wind blows out a taper, hope died in him, and he saw the flames toss and red fire burn in hell.

It was given out in the country they were gone pleasuring to the States, which was thought a strange thing, and yet not so strange as the truth, if any could have guessed it. So they went to Honolulu in the *Hall*, and thence in the *Umatilla* to San Francisco with a crowd of Haoles, and at San Francisco took their passage by the mail brigantine, the *Tropic Bird,* for Papeete, the chief place of the French in the south islands. Thither they came, after a pleasant voyage, on a fair day of the Trade Wind, and saw the reef with the surf breaking and Motuiti with its palms, and the schooner riding within inside, and the white houses of the town low down along the shore among green trees, and overhead the mountains and the clouds of Tahiti, the wise island.

It was judged the most wise to hire a house, which they did accordingly, opposite the British Consul's to make a great parade of money, and themselves conspicuous with carriages and horses. This it was very easy to do, so long as they had the bottle in their possession; for Kokua was more bold than Keawe, and whenever she had a mind, called on the imp for twenty or a hundred dollars. At this rate they soon grew to be remarked in the town; and the strangers from Hawaii, their riding and their driving, the fine holokus, and the rich lace of Kokua, became the matter of much talk.

They got on well after the first with the Tahitian language, which is indeed like to the Hawaiian, with a change of certain letters; and as soon as they had any freedom of speech, began to push the bottle. You are to consider it was not an easy subject to introduce; it was not easy to persuade people you are in earnest, when you offer to sell them for four centimes the spring of health and riches inexhaustible. It was necessary besides to explain the dangers of the bottle; and either people disbelieved the whole thing and laughed, or they thought the more of the darker part, became overcast with gravity, and drew away from Keawe and Kokua, as from persons who had dealings with the devil. So far from gaining ground, these two began to find they were avoided in the town; the children ran away from them screaming, a thing intolerable to Kokua; Catholics crossed themselves as they went by; and all persons began with one accord to disengage themselves from their advances.

Depression fell upon their spirits. They would sit at night in their new house, after a day's weariness, and not exchange one word, or the silence would be broken by Kokua bursting suddenly into sobs. Sometimes they would pray together; sometimes they would have the bottle out upon the floor, and sit all evening watching how the shadow hovered in the midst. At such times they would be afraid to go to rest. It was long ere slumber came to them, and, if either dozed off, it would be to wake and find the other silently weeping in the dark, or, perhaps, to wake alone, the other having fled from the house and the neighborhood of that bottle, to pace under the bananas in the little garden, or to wander on the beach by moonlight.

One night it was so when Kokua awoke. Keawe was gone. She felt in the bed and his place was cold. Then fear fell upon her, and she sat up in bed. A little moonshine filtered through the shutters. The room was bright, and she could spy the bottle on the floor. Outside it blew high, the great trees of the avenue cried aloud, and the fallen leaves rattled in the veranda. In the midst of this Kokua was aware of another sound; whether of a beast or of man she could scarce tell, but it was as sad as death, and cut her to the soul. Softly she arose, set the door ajar, and looked forth into the moonlit yard. There, under the bananas, lay Keawe, his mouth in the dust, and as he lay he moaned.

It was Kokua's first thought to run forward and console him; her second potently withheld her. Keawe had borne himself before his wife like a brave man; it became her little in the hour of weakness to intrude upon his shame. With the thought she drew back into the house.

"Heaven," she thought, "how careless have I been—how weak! It is he, not I, that stands in this eternal peril; it was he, not I, that took the curse upon his soul. It is for my sake, and for the love of a creature of so little worth and such poor help, that he now beholds so close to him the flames of hell—ay, and smells the smoke of it, lying without there in the wind and moonlight. Am I so dull of spirit that never till now I surmised my duty, or have I seen it before and turned aside? But now, at least, I take up my soul in both the hands of my affection; now I say farewell to the white steps of heaven and the waiting faces of my friends. A love for a love, and let mine be equaled with Keawe's! A soul for a soul, and be it mine to perish!"

She was a deft woman with her hands, and was soon appareled. She took in her hands the change—the precious centimes they kept ever at their side; for this coin is little used, and they had made provision at a government office. When she was forth in the avenue clouds came on the wind, and the moon was blackened. The town slept, and she knew not whither to turn till she heard one coughing in the shadow of the trees.

"Old man," said Kokua, "what do you here abroad in the cold night?"

The old man could scarce express himself for coughing, but she made out that he was old and poor, and a stranger in the island.

"Will you do me a service?" said Kokua. "As one stranger to another, and as an old man to a young woman, will you help a daughter of Hawaii?"

"Ah," said the old man. "So you are the witch from the Eight Islands, and even my old soul you seek to entangle. But I have heard of you, and defy your wickedness."

"Sit down here," said Kokua, "and let me tell you a tale." And she told him the story of Keawe from the beginning to the end.

"And now," said she, "I am his wife, whom he bought with his soul's welfare. And what should I do? If I went to him myself and offered to buy it, he will refuse. But if you go, he will sell it eagerly; I will await you here; you will buy it for four centimes, and I will buy it again for three. And the Lord strengthen a poor girl!"

"If you meant falsely," said the old man, "I think God would strike you dead."

"He would!" cried Kokua. "Be sure he would. I could not be so treacherous; God would not suffer it."

"Give me the four centimes and await me here," said the old man.

Now, when Kokua stood alone in the street, her spirit died. The wind roared in the trees, and it seemed to her the rushing of the flames of hell; the shadows towered in the light of the street lamp, and they seemed to her the snatching hands of evil ones. If she had had the strength, she must have run away, and if she had had the breath, she must have screamed aloud; but, in truth, she could do neither, and stood and trembled in the avenue, like an affrighted child.

Then she saw the old man returning, and he had the bottle in his hand.

"I have done your bidding," said he, "I left your husband weeping like a child; tonight he will sleep easy." And he held the bottle forth.

"Before you give it me," Kokua panted, "take the good with the evil—ask to be delivered from your cough."

"I am an old man," replied the other, "and too near the gate of the grave to take a favor from the devil. But what is this? Why do you not take the bottle? Do you hesitate?"

"Not hesitate!" cried Kokua. "I am only weak. Give me a moment. It is my hand resists, my flesh shrinks back from the accursed thing. One moment only!"

The old man looked upon Kokua kindly. "Poor child!" said he, "you fear: your soul misgives you. Well, let me keep it. I am old, and can never more be happy in this world, and as for the next—"

"Give it me!" gasped Kokua. "There is your money. Do you think I am so base as that? Give me the bottle."

"God bless you, child," said the old man.

Kokua concealed the bottle under her holoku, said farewell to the old man, and walked off along the avenue, she cared not whither. For all roads were now the same to her, and led equally to hell. Sometimes she walked, and sometimes ran; sometimes she screamed out loud in the night, and sometimes lay by the wayside in the dust and wept. All that she had heard of hell came back to her; she saw the flames blaze, and she smelled the smoke, and her flesh withered on the coals.

Near day she came to her mind again, and returned to the house. It was even as the old man said—Keawe slumbered like a child. Kokua stood and gazed upon his face.

"Now, my husband," said she, "it is your turn to sleep. When you wake it will be your turn to sing and laugh. But for poor Kokua, alas! that meant no evil—for poor Kokua no more sleep, no more singing, no more delight, whether in earth or heaven."

With that she lay down in the bed by his side, and her misery was so extreme that she fell in a deep slumber instantly.

Late in the morning her husband woke her and gave her the good news. It seemed he was silly with delight, for he paid no heed to her distress, ill though she dissembled it. The words stuck in her mouth, it mattered not; Keawe did the speaking. She ate not a bite, but who was to observe it? For Keawe cleared the dish. Kokua saw and heard him, like some strange thing in a dream; there were times when she forgot or doubted, and put her hands to her brow; to know herself doomed and hear her husband babble, seemed so monstrous.

All the while Keawe was eating and talking, and planning the time of their return, and thanking her for saving him and fondling her, and calling her the true helper after all. He laughed at the old man that was fool enough to buy that bottle.

"A worthy old man he seemed," Keawe said. "But no one can judge by appearances. For why did the old reprobate require the bottle?"

"My husband," said Kokua, humbly, "his purpose may have been good."

Keawe laughed like an angry man.

"Fiddle-de-dee!" cried Keawe. "An old rogue, I tell you; and an old ass to boot. For the bottle was hard enough to sell at four centimes; and at three it will be quite impossible. The margin is not broad enough, the thing begins to smell of scorching—brrr!" said he, and shuddered. "It is true I bought it myself at a cent, when I knew not there were smaller coins. I was a fool for my pains; there will never be found another, and whoever has that bottle now will carry it to the pit."

"O my husband!" said Kokua. "Is it not a terrible thing to save oneself by the eternal ruin of another? It seems to me I could not laugh. I would be humbled. I would be filled with melancholy. I would pray for the poor holder."

Then Keawe, because he felt the truth of what she said, grew the more angry. "Heighty-teighty!" cried he. "You may be filled with melancholy if you please. It is not the mind of a good wife. If you thought at all of me, you would sit charmed."

Thereupon he went out, and Kokua was alone.

What chance had she to sell that bottle at two centimes? None, she perceived. And if she had any, here was her husband hurrying her away to a country where there was nothing lower than a cent. And here—on the morrow of her sacrifice—was her husband leaving her and blaming her.

She would not even try to profit by what time she had, but sat in the house, and now had the bottle out and viewed it with unutterable fear, and now, with loathing, hid it out of sight.

By and by, Keawe came back, and would have her take a drive.

"My husband, I am ill," she said. "I am out of heart. Excuse me, I can take no pleasure."

Then was Keawe more wroth than ever. With her, because he thought she was brooding over the case of the old man; and with himself, because he thought she was right and was ashamed to be so happy.

"This is your truth," cried he, "and this your affection! Your husband is just saved from eternal ruin, which he encountered for the love of you—and you can take no pleasure! Kokua, you have a disloyal heart."

He went forth again furious, and wandered in the town all day. He met friends, and drank with them; they hired a carriage and drove into the country, and there drank again. All the time Keawe was ill at ease, because he was taking this pastime while his wife was sad, and because he knew in his heart that she was more right than he; and the knowledge made him drink the deeper.

Now there was an old brutal Haole drinking with him, one that had been a boatswain of a whaler—a runaway, a digger in gold mines, a convict in prisons. He had a low mind and a foul mouth; he loved to drink and to see others drunken; and he pressed the glass upon Keawe. Soon there was no more money in the company.

"Here, you!" says the boatswain, "you are rich, you have been always saying. You have a bottle or some foolishness."

"Yes," says Keawe, "I am rich; I will go back and get some money from my wife, who keeps it."

"That's a bad idea, mate," said the boatswain. "Never you trust a petticoat with dollars. They're all as false as water; you keep an eye on her."

Now this word struck in Keawe's mind; for he was muddled with what he had been drinking.

"I should not wonder but she was false, indeed," thought he. "Why else should she be so cast down at my release? But I will show her I am not the man to be fooled. I will catch her in the act."

Accordingly, when they were back in town, Keawe bade the boatswain wait for him at the corner, by the old calaboose, and went forward up the avenue alone to the door of his house. The night had come again; there was a light within, but never a sound; and Keawe crept about the corner, opened the back door softly, and looked in.

There was Kokua on the floor, the lamp at her side; before her was a milk-white bottle, with a round belly and a long neck; and as she viewed it, Kokua wrung her hands.

A long time Keawe stood and looked in the doorway. At first he was struck stupid; and then fear fell upon him that the bargain had been made amiss, and the bottle had come back to him as it came at San Francisco; and at that his knees were loosened, and the fumes of the wine departed from his head like mists off a river in the morning. And then he had another thought; and it was a strange one, that made his cheeks to burn.

"I must make sure of this," thought he.

So he closed the door, and went softly round the corner again, and then came noisily in, as though he were but now returned. And, lo! by the time he opened the front door no bottle was to be seen; and Kokua sat in a chair and started up like one awakened out of sleep.

"I have been drinking all day and making merry," said Keawe. "I have been with good companions, and now I only came back for money, and return to drink and carouse with them again."

Both his face and voice were as stern as judgment, but Kokua was too troubled to observe.

"You do well to use your own, my husband," said she, and her words trembled.

"Oh, I do well in all things," said Keawe, and he went straight to the chest and took out money. But he looked besides in the corner where they kept the bottle, and there was no bottle there.

At that the chest heaved upon the floor like a sea-billow, and the house span about him like a wreath of smoke, for he saw she was lost now, and there was no escape. "It is what I feared," he thought. "It was she who has bought it."

And then he came to himself a little and rose up; but the sweat streamed on his face as thick as the rain and as cold as the well water.

"Kokua," said he, "I said to you today what ill became me. Now I return to house with my jolly companions," and at that he laughed a little quietly. "I will take more pleasure in the cup if you forgive me."

She clasped his knees in a moment, she kissed his knees with flowing tears.

"Oh," she cried, "I ask but a kind word!"

"Let us never one think hardly of the other," said Keawe, and was gone out of the house.

Now, the money that Keawe had taken was only some of that store of centime pieces they had laid in at their arrival. It was very sure he had no mind to be drinking. His wife had given her soul for him, now he must give his for hers; no other thought was in the world with him.

At the corner, by the old calaboose, there was the boatswain waiting.

"My wife has the bottle," said Keawe, "and, unless you help me to recover it, there can be no more money and no more liquor to-night."

"You do not mean to say you are serious about that bottle?" cried the boatswain.

"There is the lamp," said Keawe. "Do I look as if I was jesting?"

"That is so," said the boatswain. "You look as serious as a ghost."

"Well, then," said Keawe, "here are two centimes; you just go to my wife in the house, and offer her these for the bottle, which (if I am not much mistaken) she will give you instantly. Bring it to me here, and I will buy it back from you for one; for that is the law with this bottle that it still must be sold for a less sum. But whatever you do, never breathe a word to her that you have come from me."

"Mate, I wonder are you making a fool of me?" asked the boatswain.

"It will do you no harm if I am," returned Keawe.

"That is so, mate," said the boatswain.

"And if you doubt me," added Keawe, "you can try. As soon as you are clear of the house, wish to have your pocket full of money, or a bottle of the best rum, or what you please, and you will see the virtue of the thing."

"Very well, Kanaka," says the boatswain. "I will try; but if you are having your fun out of me, I will take my fun out of you with a sledgehammer."

So the whaler man went off up the avenue; and Keawe stood and waited. It was near the same spot where Kokua had waited the night before; but Keawe was more resolved, and never faltered in his purpose; only his soul was bitter with despair.

It seemed a long time he had to wait before he heard a voice singing in the darkness of the avenue. He knew the voice to be the boatswain's; but it was strange how drunken it appeared upon a sudden.

Next the man himself came stumbling into the light of the lamp. He had the devil's bottle buttoned in his coat; another bottle was in his hand; and even as he came in view he raised it to his mouth and drank.

"You have it," said Keawe. "I see that."

"Hands off!" cried the boatswain, jumping back. "Take a step near me, and I'll smash your mouth. You thought you could make a catspaw of me, did you?"

"What do you mean?" cried Keawe.

"Mean?" cried the boatswain. "This is a pretty good bottle, this is; that's what I mean. How I got it for two centimes I can't make out; but I am sure you sha'nt have it for one."

"You mean you won't sell?" gasped Keawe.

"No, sir," cried the boatswain. "But I'll give you a drink of the rum, if you like."

"I tell you," said Keawe, "the man who has that bottle goes to hell."

"I reckon I'm going anyway," returned the sailor; "and this bottle's the best thing to go with I've struck yet. No sir!" he cried again, "this is my bottle now, and you can go and fish for another."

"Can this be true?" Keawe cried. "For your own sake, I beseech you, sell it me!"

"I don't value any of your talk," replied the boatswain. "You thought I was a flat, now you see I'm not; and there's an end. If you won't have a swallow of the rum, I'll have one myself. Here's your health, and goodnight to you!"

So off he went down the avenue towards town, and there goes the bottle out of the story.

But Keawe ran to Kokua light as the wind; and great was their joy that night; and great, since then, has been the peace of all their days in the Bright House.

Understanding the Story _____

Main Idea

1. Which of the following best states the main idea of the story?
    (a) Keawe used the bottle imp to provide himself a beautiful house.
    (b) Kokua loved Keawe more than she loved herself.
    (c) Love led the lovers to be trapped by the imp, and love saved them.
    (d) Famous people had once availed themselves of the powers of the bottle imp.

Details

2. Keawe first bought the bottle for   (a) ninety dollars
    (b) eighty dollars   (c) fifty dollars   (d) forty-nine dollars.

3. The bottle was actually made of   (a) marble   (b) very fine wood   (c) alabaster   (d) glass.

4. The two places that provide the setting for most of the story are   (a) Hawaii and Tahiti   (b) Tahiti and Boston
    (c) Hawaii and France   (d) Tahiti and France.

5. The second time Keawe bought the bottle he paid   (a) fifty dollars   (b) a dollar   (c) two cents   (d) one cent.

Inferences

6. Keawe bought the bottle the first time through
    (a) advertising   (b) a persuasive seller   (c) a trick
    (d) superior force.

7. Keawe and Kokua moved to the French island because they needed   (a) coins of lesser value   (b) a new fishing boat
    (c) practice in speaking French   (d) a house in classical style.

8. The final owner of the bottle was   (a) Lopaka   (b) Keawe
    (c) Kokua   (d) the boatswain.

9. Because of her love for Keawe, Kokua arranged   (a) a great party for their anniversary   (b) to buy the bottle   (c) to bring Lopaka back for a visit   (d) to give up her fortune.

10. The bottle would return if it were sold   (a) for more than the previous transaction   (b) to a person under 21   (c) to a poor person   (d) to a person who didn't need the wishes anyway.

Order of Events

11. Arrange the items in the order in which they occurred. Use letters only.
    A. Lopaka buys the bottle.
    B. Keawe marries Kokua.
    C. Captain Cook buys the bottle.
    D. Keawe buys the bottle the second time.
    E. Kokua buys the bottle.

Outcomes

12. If Kokua had not thought of the French centime, Keawe might have (a) been a much happier man (b) settled in San Francisco (c) lost his immortal soul (d) forced Kokua to take the bottle imp.

Cause and Effect

13. Keawe's deep depression arose from (a) a fight with Kokua (b) loss of his friend Lopaka (c) his possession of the bottle (d) the sinking of his favorite ship.

Fact or Opinion

Tell whether each of the following is a fact or an opinion.

14. In every respect Kokua's devotion to Keawe matched his devotion to her.

15. Kokua and Keawe lived in the Bright House.

Words in Context

1. The man made a *computation*. "I am sorry you have no more," said he, "for it may raise you trouble in the future; but it shall be yours at fifty dollars."
   Computation (192) means (a) offer (b) calculation (c) sorrowful face (d) hasty answer.

2. Withinsides something *obscurely* moved, like a shadow and a fire.
   Obscurely (192) means (a) rapidly (b) brightly (c) routinely (d) not clearly.

3. They were scarce come ashore when they met a friend upon the beach, who began at once to *condole* with Keawe.
   Condole (196) means   (a) sympathize   (b) argue
   (c) converse   (d) play.

4. "And so they will," says Keawe, and began again to *lament* for his relatives.
   Lament (196) means   (a) inquire   (b) speak cheerfully
   (c) mourn   (d) search.

5. "So *indulge* me so far, and let me see the imp."
   Indulge (198) means   (a) enrich   (b) humor   (c) force
   (d) persuade.

6. "Kokua, the soul *ensnarer!* Kokua, the light of my life."
   Ensnarer (202) means one who   (a) traps   (b) amuses
   (c) destroys   (d) renews.

7. It was Kokua's first thought to run forward and console him; her second *potently* withheld her.
   Potently (210) means   (a) quietly   (b) eagerly
   (c) powerfully   (d) scarcely.

8. "Am I so dull of spirit that never till now I *surmised* my duty, or have I seen it before and turned aside?"
   Surmised (210) means   (a) overlooked   (b) discussed
   (c) enjoyed   (d) realized.

9. She was a *deft* woman with her hands, and was soon *appareled.*
   Deft (210) means   (a) clumsy   (b) eager   (c) nervous
   (d) skillful.

10. *Appareled* (210) means   (a) clothed   (b) impressed
    (c) annoyed   (d) determined.

11. "Poor child!" said he, "you fear: your soul *misgives* you."
    Misgives (212) means   (a) intrigues   (b) frightens
    (c) glorifies   (d) leaves.

12. Kokua concealed the bottle under her holoku, said farewell to the old man, and walked off along the avenue, she cared not *whither.*
    Whither (212) means   (a) when   (b) why   (c) to what
    place   (d) for what purpose.

13. He paid no heed to her distress, ill though she *dissembled* it.
    Dissembled (212) means   (a) announced   (b) disguised
    (c) discussed   (d) rejected.

14. "A worthy old man he seemed," Keawe said. "But no one can judge by appearances. For why did the old *reprobate* require the bottle?"
Reprobate (213) means (a) sailor (b) traitor (c) dreamer (d) scoundrel.

15. She now had the bottle out and viewed it with *unutterable* fear, and now, with *loathing*, hid it out of sight.
Unutterable (213) means unable to be (a) spoken (b) imagined (c) disregarded (d) completed.

16. *Loathing* (213) means (a) quickness of action (b) affection (c) bitter hatred (d) some hesitation.

17. "Then was Keawe more *wroth* than ever."
Wroth (213) means (a) understanding (b) fearful (c) angry (d) curious.

18. "I have been with good companions, and now I only came back for money, and return to drink and *carouse* with them again."
Carouse (215) means (a) converse quietly (b) frolic noisily (c) walk directly (d) hunt fearlessly.

19. "You thought you could make a *catspaw* of me, did you?"
Catspaw (217) means (a) dupe (b) friend (c) winner (d) talker.

20. "For your own sake, I *beseech* you, sell it me!"
Beseech (217) means (a) talk rapidly (b) scold bitterly (c) amuse cheerfully (d) beg earnestly.

Thinking About the Story ⎯⎯⎯⎯⎯⎯

1. The bottle was sold originally to Prester John, a mythical king, for millions of dollars. Why is it being sold for a handful of dollars when Keawe first learns of it?

2. A common theme in literature and folklore is that everything comes at a price. Napoleon and Captain Cook once owned the bottle; yet they paid a price at the end. What price did both Kokua and Keawe pay for their ownership of the bottle?

3. On page 192, the man says, "I am sorry you have not more, for it may raise you trouble in the future; but it shall be yours at fifty dollars." Why may that sum raise trouble in the future?

Why would it have been better if Keawe had had more than fifty dollars?

4. Why was the restriction about coined money (page 193) put into the pact with the bottle imp?

5. What effect does the sight of the bottle imp have on Lopaka and Keawe? How does this brief vision add tension to the story?

6. Suppose you were given three wishes, with no apparent strings attached? Would you make them? What would you wish for? Or would you prefer not to make the wishes since there might be a catch after all? Explain.

The Fog Horn

Ray Bradbury

♦ The Fog Horn blew. The monster roared again. The Fog Horn blew. The monster opened its great toothed mouth and the sound that came from it was the sound of the Fog Horn itself. Lonely and vast and faraway. The sound of isolation, a viewless sea, a cold night, apartness. That was the sound.

The deeps of the seas are almost as mysterious and challenging as the deeps of outer space. We already know that strange creatures live on the sea bottom under unbelievably unfavorable conditions. There, for example, bacteria flourish at temperatures above 600 degrees Fahrenheit—hot enough in air to burn paper. Who knows what creatures may still flourish in the largely unexplored depths? The coelacanth, for example, a creature thought to have died out millions of years ago, sometimes appears in the nets of Madagascar fisherfolk. People enjoy stories of undiscovered creatures. We would like to believe, for example, that the Loch Ness monster in Scotland really exists.

Science-fiction writing and movies have played upon the mystery and the fear that mystery sometimes generates. Creatures like Godzilla rise from the sea to stalk the land and terrorize inhabitants. In sequels to the original movie, Godzilla reformed and became friend of humankind. Most sea monsters, however, are simply evil, threatening to destroy all creatures of the land.

In "The Fog Horn," the veteran science-fiction writer Ray Bradbury takes a familiar theme, but he makes of it a thing of beauty. His descriptions of the lonely seacoast bring the scene to vivid life. His evocation of the mysterious sound of the fog horn helps his readers share the experience. Above all, his interpretation of the sea monster is altogether new and wonderful.

This is no vicious monster out for mindless destruction but a lonely creature with whom we sympathize. Be ready to hear the fog horn and share an incredible experience.

THE FOG HORN

Out there in the cold water, far from land, we waited every night for the coming of the fog, and it came, and we oiled the brass machinery and lit the fog light up in the stone tower. Feeling like two birds in the gray sky, McDunn and I sent the light touching out, red, then white, then red again, to eye the lonely ships. And if they did not see our light, then there was always our Voice, the great deep cry of our Fog Horn shuddering through the rags of mist to startle the gulls away like decks of scattered cards and make the waves turn high and foam.

"It's a lonely life, but you're used to it now, aren't you?" asked McDunn.

"Yes," I said. "You're a good talker, thank the Lord."

"Well, it's your turn on land tomorrow," he said, smiling, "to dance the ladies and drink gin."

"What do you think, McDunn, when I leave you out here alone?"

"On the mysteries of the sea." McDunn lit his pipe. It was a quarter past seven of a cold November evening, the heat on, the light switching its tail in two hundred directions, the Fog Horn bumbling in the high throat of the tower. There wasn't a town for a hundred miles down the coast, just a road which came lonely through dead country to the sea, with few cars on it, a stretch of two miles of cold water out to our rock, and rare few ships.

"The mysteries of the sea," said McDunn thoughtfully. "You know, the ocean's the biggest damned snowflake ever? It rolls and swells a thousand shapes and colors, no two alike. Strange. One night, years ago, I was here alone, when all of the fish of the sea surfaced out there. Something made them swim in and lie in the bay, sort of trembling and staring up at the tower light going red, white, red, white across them so I could see their funny eyes. I turned cold. They were like a big peacock's tail, moving out there until midnight. Then, without so much as a sound, they slipped away, the million of them was gone. I kind of think maybe, in some sort of way, they came all those miles to worship. Strange. But think how the tower must look to them, standing seventy feet above the water, the Godlight flashing out from it, and the tower declaring itself with a monster voice. They never came back, those fish, but don't you think for a while they thought they were in the Presence?"

I shivered. I looked out at the long gray lawn of the sea stretching away into nothing and nowhere.

"Oh, the sea's full." McDunn puffed his pipe nervously, blinking. He had been nervous all day and hadn't said why. "For all our engines and so-called submarines, it'll be ten thousand centuries before we set foot on the real bottom of the sunken lands, in the fairy kingdoms there, and know *real* terror. Think of it, it's still the year 300,000 Before Christ down under there. While we've paraded around with trumpets, lopping off each other's countries and heads, they have been living beneath the sea twelve miles deep and cold in a time as old as the beard of a comet."

"Yes, it's an old world."

"Come on. I got something special I been saving up to tell you."

We ascended the eighty steps, talking and taking our time. At the top, McDunn switched off the room lights so there'd be no reflection in the plate glass. The great eye of the light was humming, turning easily in its oiled socket. The Fog Horn was blowing steadily, once every fifteen seconds.

"Sounds like an animal, don't it?" McDunn nodded to himself. "A big lonely animal crying in the night. Sitting here on the edge of ten billion years calling out to the Deeps, I'm here, I'm here, I'm here. And the Deeps *do* answer, yes, they do. You been here now for three months, Johnny, so I better prepare you. About this time of year," he said, studying the murk and fog, "something comes to visit the lighthouse."

"The swarms of fish like you said?"

"No, this is something else. I've put off telling you because you might think I'm daft. But tonight's the latest I can put it off, for if my calendar's marked right from last year, tonight's the night it comes. I won't go into detail, you'll have to see it yourself. Just sit down there. If you want, tomorrow you can pack your duffel and take the motorboat in to land and get your car parked there at the dinghy pier on the cape and drive on back to some little inland town and keep your lights burning nights, I won't question or blame you. It's happened three years now, and this is the only time anyone's been here with me to verify it. You wait and watch."

Half an hour passed with only a few whispers between us. When we grew tired waiting, McDunn began describing some of his ideas to me. He had some theories about the Fog Horn itself.

"One day many years ago a man walked along and stood in the sound of the ocean on a cold sunless shore and said, 'We need a voice to call across the water, to warn ships; I'll make one. I'll make a voice like all of time and all of the fog that ever was; I'll make a voice that is like an empty bed beside you all night long, and like an empty house when you open the door, and like trees in autumn with no leaves. A sound like the birds flying south, crying, and a sound like November wind and the sea on the hard, cold shore. I'll make a sound that's so alone that no one can miss it, that whoever hears it will weep in their souls, and hearths will seem warmer, and being inside will seem better to all who hear it in the distant towns. I'll make me a sound and an apparatus and they'll call it a Fog Horn and whoever hears it will know the sadness of eternity and the briefness of life.' "

The Fog Horn blew.

"I made up that story," said McDunn quietly, "to try to explain why this thing keeps coming back to the lighthouse every year. The Fog Horn calls it, I think, and it comes. . . ."

"But—" I said.

"Sssst!" said McDunn. "There!" He nodded out to the Deeps.

Something was swimming toward the lighthouse tower.

It was a cold night, as I have said; the high tower was cold, the light coming and going, and the Fog Horn calling and calling through the raveling mist. You couldn't see far and you couldn't see plain, but there was the deep sea moving on its way about the night earth, flat and quiet, the color of gray mud, and here were the two of us alone in the high tower, and there, far out at first, was a ripple, followed by a wave, a rising, a bubble, a bit of froth. And then, from the surface of the cold sea came a head, a large head, dark-colored, with immense eyes, and then a neck. And then—not a body—but more neck and more! The head rose a full forty feet above the water on a slender and beautiful dark neck. Only then did the body, like a little island of black coral and shells and crayfish, drip up from the subterranean. There was a flicker of tail. In all, from head to tip of tail, I estimated the monster at ninety or a hundred feet.

I don't know what I said. I said something.

"Steady, boy, steady," whispered McDunn.

"It's impossible!" I said.

"No, Johnny, *we're* impossible. *It's* like it always was ten million years ago. *It* hasn't changed. It's *us* and the land that've changed, become impossible. *Us!*"

It swam slowly and with a great dark majesty out in the icy waters, far away. The fog came and went about it, momentarily erasing its shape. One of the monster eyes caught and held and flashed back our immense light, red, white, red, white, like a disk held high and sending a message in primeval code. It was as silent as the fog through which it swam.

"It's a dinosaur of some sort!" I crouched down, holding to the stair rail.

"Yes, one of the tribe."

"But they died out!"

"No, only hid away in the Deeps. Deep, deep down in the deepest Deeps. Isn't *that* a word now, Johnny, a real word, it says so much: the Deeps. There's all the coldness and darkness and deepness in the world in a word like that."

"What'll we do?"

"Do? We got our job, we can't leave. Besides, we're safer here than in any boat trying to get to land. That thing's as big as a destroyer and almost as swift."

"But here, why does it come *here?*"

The next moment I had my answer.

The Fog Horn blew.

And the monster answered.

A cry came across a million years of water and mist. A cry so anguished and alone that it shuddered in my head and my body. The monster cried out at the tower. The Fog Horn blew. The monster roared again. The Fog Horn blew. The monster opened its great toothed mouth and the sound that came from it was the sound of the Fog Horn itself. Lonely and vast and far away. The sound of isolation, a viewless sea, a cold night, apartness. That was the sound.

"Now," whispered McDunn, "do you know why it comes here?"
I nodded.

"All year long, Johnny, that poor monster there lying far out, a thousand miles at sea, and twenty miles deep maybe, biding its time, perhaps it's a million years old, this one creature. Think of it, waiting a million years; could *you* wait that long? Maybe it's the last of its kind. I sort of think that's true. Anyway, here come men on land and build this lighthouse, five years ago. And set up their Fog Horn and sound it and sound it out toward the place where you bury yourself in sleep and sea memories of a world where there were thousands like yourself, but now you're alone, all alone in a world not made for you, a world where you have to hide.

"But the sound of the Fog Horn comes and goes, comes and goes, and you stir from the muddy bottom of the Deeps, and your eyes open like the lenses of two-foot cameras and you move, slow, slow, for you have the ocean sea on your shoulders, heavy. But that Fog Horn comes through a thousand miles of water, faint and familiar, and the furnace in your belly stokes up, and you begin to rise, slow, slow. You feed yourself on great slakes of cod and minnow, on rivers of jellyfish, and you rise slow through the autumn months, through September when the fogs started, through October with more fog and the horn still calling you on, and then, late in November, after pressurizing yourself day by day, a few feet higher every hour, you are near the surface and still alive. You've got to go slow; if you surfaced all at once you'd explode. So it takes you all of three months to surface, and then a number of days to swim through the cold waters to the lighthouse. And there you are, out there, in the night, Johnny, the biggest damn monster in creation. And here's the lighthouse calling to you, with a long neck like your neck sticking way up out of the water, and a body like your body, and, most important of all, a voice like your voice. Do you understand now, Johnny, do you understand?"

The Fog Horn blew.

The monster answered.

I saw it all, I knew it all—the million years of waiting alone, for someone to come back who never came back. The million years of isolation at the bottom of the sea, the insanity of time there, while the skies cleared of reptile-birds, the swamps dried on the continental lands, the sloths and saber-tooths had their day and sank in tar pits, and men ran like white ants upon the hills.

The Fog Horn blew.

"Last year," said McDunn, "that creature swam round and round, round and round, all night. Not coming too near, puzzled, I'd say. Afraid, maybe. And a bit angry after coming all this way. But the next day, unexpectedly, the fog lifted, the sun came out fresh, the sky was as blue as a painting. And the monster swam off away from the heat and the silence and didn't come back. I suppose it's been brooding on it for a year now, thinking it over from every which way."

The monster was only a hundred yards off now, it and the Fog Horn crying at each other. As the lights hit them, the monster's eyes were fire and ice, fire and ice.

"That's life for you," said McDunn. "Someone always waiting for someone who never comes home. Always someone loving some thing more than that thing loves them. And after a while you want to destroy whatever that thing is, so it can't hurt you no more."

The monster was rushing at the lighthouse.

The Fog Horn blew.

"Let's see what happens," said McDunn.

He switched the Fog Horn off.

The ensuing minute of silence was so intense that we could hear our hearts pounding in the glassed area of the tower, could hear the slow greased turn of the light.

The monster stopped and froze. Its great lantern eyes blinked. Its mouth gaped. It gave a sort of rumble, like a volcano. It twitched its head this way and that, as if to seek the sounds now dwindled off into the fog. It peered at the lighthouse. It rumbled again. Then its eyes caught fire. It reared up, threshed the water, and rushed at the tower, its eyes filled with angry torment.

"McDunn!" I cried. "Switch on the horn!"

McDunn fumbled with the switch. But even as he flicked it on, the monster was rearing up. I had a glimpse of its gigantic paws, fishskin glittering in webs between the fingerlike projections, clawing at the tower. The huge eye on the right side of its anguished head glittered before me like a caldron into which I might drop, screaming. The tower shook. The Fog Horn cried; the monster cried. It seized the tower and gnashed at the glass, which shattered in upon us.

McDunn seized my arm. "Downstairs!"

The tower rocked, trembled, and started to give. The Fog Horn and the monster roared. We stumbled and half fell down the stairs. "Quick!"

We reached the bottom as the tower buckled down toward us. We ducked under the stairs into the small stone cellar. There were a thousand concussions as the rocks rained down; the Fog Horn stopped abruptly. The monster crashed upon the tower. The tower fell. We knelt together, McDunn and I, holding tight, while our world exploded.

Then it was over, and there was nothing but darkness and the wash of the sea on the raw stones.

That and the other sound.

"Listen," said McDunn quietly. "Listen."

We waited a moment. And then I began to hear it. First a great vacuumed sucking of air, and then the lament, the bewilderment, the loneliness of the great monster, folded over and upon us, above us, so that the sickening reek of its body filled the air, a stone's thickness away from our cellar. The monster gasped and cried. The tower was gone. The light was gone. The thing that had called to it across a million years was gone. And the monster was opening its mouth and sending out great sounds. The sounds of a Fog Horn, again and again. And ships far at sea, not finding the light, not seeing anything, but passing and hearing late that night, must've thought: There it is, the lonely sound, the Lonesome Bay horn. All's well. We've rounded the cape.

And so it went for the rest of that night.

The sun was hot and yellow the next afternoon when the rescuers came out to dig us from our stoned-under cellar.

"It fell apart, is all," said Mr. McDunn gravely. "We had a few bad knocks from the waves and it just crumbled." He pinched my arm.

There was nothing to see. The ocean was calm, the sky blue. The only thing was a great algaic stink from the green matter that covered the fallen tower stones and the shore rocks. Flies buzzed about. The ocean washed empty on the shore.

The next year they built a new lighthouse, but by that time I had a job in the little town and a wife and a good small warm house that glowed yellow on autumn nights, the doors locked, the chimney puffing smoke. As for McDunn, he was master of the new lighthouse, built to his own specifications, out of steel-reinforced concrete. "Just in case," he said.

The new lighthouse was ready in November. I drove down alone

one evening late and parked my car and looked across the gray waters and listened to the new horn sounding, once, twice, three, four times a minute far out there, by itself.

The monster?

It never came back.

"It's gone away," said McDunn. "It's gone back to the Deeps. It's learned you can't love anything too much in this world. It's gone into the deepest Deeps to wait another million years. Ah, the poor thing! Waiting out there, and waiting out there, while man comes and goes on this pitiful little planet. Waiting and waiting."

I sat in my car, listening. I couldn't see the lighthouse or the light standing out in Lonesome Bay. I could only hear the Horn, the Horn, the Horn. It sounded like the monster calling.

I sat there wishing there was something I could say.

Understanding the Story ⸺

Main Idea

1. The sea monster is   (a) a bloodthirsty creature intent on wrecking lighthouses .   (b) a poor lonely creature from another time   (c) a creature of McDunn's imagination   (d) probably a tremendous whale.

Details

2. The explanation of the creature's appearance is given by (a) Johnny   (b) an old sailor   (c) McDunn   (d) the builder of the lighthouse.

3. The interval between the monster's two appearances was a (a) week   (b) month   (c) year   (d) decade.

4. The monster had to come to the surface   (a) rapidly (b) moderately rapidly   (c) very slowly   (d) on the night of the full moon.

5. The lights that flash at each other like a code are the beacon

on the lighthouse and the   (a) beacon on the opposite shore
(b) monster's eye   (c) light from a passing ship   (d) none
of these.

Inferences

6. The basic emotion of McDunn toward the monster was one of
   (a) fear   (b) anger   (c) pity   (d) laughter.

7. The attitude of the monster at the end was one of
   (a) fulfillment   (b) frustration   (c) delight   (d) amused
   curiosity.

8. The location of the lighthouse can best be described as
   (a) isolated   (b) congested   (c) ugly   (d) popular.

9. When McDunn says, "Something comes to visit the lighthouse," he is referring to   (a) an inspector   (b) a great
   white shark   (c) a naval squadron   (d) a dinosaur.

10. The fog horn is mistaken for   (a) the call of a sea creature
    (b) a truck horn   (c) a distress call by a sinking ship   (d) an
    overheard radio broadcast.

Order of Events

11. Arrange the items in the order in which they occurred. Use
    letters only.
    A. The lighthouse is rebuilt.
    B. The sea creature returns.
    C. McDunn tells Johnny about the coming visit.
    D. The lighthouse is smashed.
    E. The creature first hears the fog horn.

Outcomes

12. If the men had stayed high up in the tower, they probably
    would have   (a) made friends with the creature   (b) learned
    where the creature had come from   (c) been killed
    (d) radioed scientists about the creature.

Cause and Effect

13. The creature's disappointment led him to   (a) kill McDunn
    (b) call for help   (c) disappear for good   (d) try again three
    years later.

Fact or Opinion

Tell whether each of the following is a fact or an opinion.

14. Johnny gave up his lighthouse job.

15. McDunn was a braver person than Johnny.

Words in Context

1. "About this time of year," he said, studying the *murk* and fog, "something comes to visit the lighthouse."
   Murk (225) means (a) wetness (b) moonlight (c) darkness (d) sea.

2. "I've put off telling you because you might think I'm *daft*."
   Daft (225) means (a) insane (b) uninformed (c) too clever (d) impatient.

3. "If you want, tomorrow you can. . .get your car parked there at the *dinghy* pier on the cape."
   Dinghy (226) means (a) automobile (b) concession stand (c) small boat (d) dilapidated breakwater.

4. The high tower was cold, the Fog Horn calling and calling through the *raveling* mist.
   Raveling (226) means (a) thickening (b) untangling (c) darkening (d) moistening.

5. One of the monster eyes caught and held and flashed back our immense light, red, white, red, white, like a disk held high and sending a message in *primeval* code.
   Primeval (227) means (a) confusing (b) rapid-fire (c) ancient (d) Morse.

6. A cry so *anguished* and alone that it shuddered in my head and my body.
   Anguished (227) means (a) tortured (b) optimistic (c) loud (d) soft.

7. The *ensuing* minute of silence was so intense that we could hear our hearts pounding in the glassed area of the tower.
   Ensuing (229) means (a) quickening (b) deadening (c) following (d) vibrating.

8. The huge eye on the right side of its anguished head glittered before me like a *caldron* into which I might drop, screaming.

Caldron (229) means   (a) bright light   (b) large kettle
(c) intense fire   (d) shiny mirror.

9. First a great vacuumed sucking of air and then the *lament,* the
bewilderment, the loneliness of the great monster, folded over
and upon us, above us, so that the sickening *reek* of its body
filled the air.
Lament (230)   means   (a) laughter   (b) excitement
(c) irritation   (d) wailing.

10. *Reek* (230) means   (a) disagreeable odor   (b) vibrating
noise   (c) heavy perfume   (d) massive appearance.

Thinking About the Story _____

1. How does this story differ from usual "monster stories" as in
fiction, television, and the movies?

2. This story is noteworthy for its excellent descriptions. Select
one vivid picture to read aloud.

3. McDunn says, "It's learned you can't love anything too much in
this world." What does this statement mean to you? Do you
agree with it? Why or why not?

4. Even in our sophisticated society, discovery of an animal hitherto unknown to science makes headlines. Why?

5. Does your own taste in entertainment run to make-believe and
fantasy, or do you prefer solid, realistic stories of life as it is?
Explain your preference.

6. Needless to say, an animal that has lived a million years is so
unlikely as to be virtually an impossibility. We recognize the
impossibility. Yet we get caught up in the story. We feel sorry
for this creature who does not, cannot, exist. Why?

The Secret

Arthur C. Clarke

♦ "I've convinced the Doctor that there's only
one way to keep you quiet—and that's to tell you
everything."

The movie *2001: A Space Odyssey* made the name of Arthur
C. Clarke famous around the world. In science-fiction circles,
however, that name had already commanded respect for many
years.

Fantasies about the moon and moon travel go back at least
to the days of the Romans. The Greek writer Lucian, in the second
century, fantasized about men from the moon. The great German
astronomer Johannes Kepler wrote a moon story in 1634. Francis
Godwin, an Anglican bishop, sent his hero to the moon in *The Man
in the Moon,* published in 1638. Cyrano de Bergerac's *A Voyage
to the Moon* went into nine French editions and two English editions between 1650 and 1687.

Speculation continued. Joseph Atterley's *A Voyage to the
Moon,* published in 1827, inspired Edgar Allan Poe's *The Moon
Hoax,* first published in 1835. Jules Verne wrote *A Trip to the Moon*
in 1865. In 1901 H. G. Wells wrote *The First Men in the Moon.*

In 1969 two Americans set foot on the moon. Five other American lunar landings made the surface of the moon almost as familiar as the Southwest desert. The mysterious "other side" of the
moon has been shown to be very much like the visible side. Many
lunar mysteries have evaporated, but writers continue to write
science fiction about the moon.

"The Secret" takes you to the moon, at a time when colonies
have already been established on the surface. Such an achievement could only be managed by a technologically advanced civ-
ilization. Yet, despite all the scientific know-how, there is a terrible secret that has given several scientists nervous breakdowns.

The nature of the secret is disclosed only at the end. No matter what you expect, you'll not anticipate this. Arthur C. Clarke
doesn't take the easy way out: mysterious plagues, horrible monsters, alien invaders. His secret is . . . different!

THE SECRET

Henry Cooper had been on the Moon for almost two weeks before he discovered that something was wrong. At first it was only an ill-defined suspicion, the sort of hunch that a hardheaded science reporter would not take too seriously. He had come here, after all, at the United Nations Space Administration's own request. UNSA had always been hot on public relations—especially just before budget time, when an overcrowded world was screaming for more roads and schools and sea farms, and complaining about the billions being poured into space.

So here he was, doing the lunar circuit for the second time, and beaming back two thousand words of copy a day. Although the novelty had worn off, there still remained the wonder and mystery of a world as big as Africa, thoroughly mapped, yet almost completely unexplored. A stone's throw away from the pressure domes, the labs, the spaceports, was a yawning emptiness that would challenge men for centuries to come.

Some parts of the Moon were almost too familiar, of course. Who had not seen that dusty scar in the Mare Imbrium, with its gleaming metal pylon and the plaque that announced in the three official languages of Earth:

ON THIS SPOT
AT 2001 UT
13 SEPTEMBER 1959
THE FIRST MAN-MADE OBJECT REACHED ANOTHER WORLD

Cooper had visited the grave of Lunik II—and the more famous tomb of the men who had come after it. But these things belonged

236

to the past; already, like Columbus and the Wright brothers, they were receding into history. What concerned him now was the future.

When he had landed at Archimedes Spaceport, the Chief Administrator had been obviously glad to see him, and had shown a personal interest in his tour. Transportation, accommodation, and official guide were all arranged. He could go anywhere he liked, ask any questions he pleased. UNSA trusted him, for his stories had always been accurate, his attitude friendly. Yet the tour had gone sour; he did not know why, but he was going to find out.

He reached for the phone and said: "Operator? Please get me the Police Department. I want to speak to the Inspector General."

Presumably Chandra Coomaraswamy possessed a uniform, but Cooper had never seen him wearing it. They met, as arranged, at the entrance to the little park that was Plato City's chief pride and joy. At this time in the morning of the artificial twenty-four-hour "day" it was almost deserted, and they could talk without interruption.

As they walked along the narrow gravel paths, they chatted about old times, the friends they had known at college together, the latest developments in interplanetary politics. They had reached the middle of the park, under the exact center of the great blue-painted dome, when Cooper came to the point.

"You know everything that's happening on the Moon, Chandra," he said. "And you know that I'm here to do a series for UNSA—hope to make a book out of it when I get back to Earth. So why should people be trying to hide things from me?"

It was impossible to hurry Chandra. He always took his time to answer questions, and his few words escaped with difficulty around the stem of his hand-carved Bavarian pipe.

"What people?" he asked at length.

"You've really no idea?"

The Inspector General shook his head.

"Not the faintest," he answered; and Cooper knew that he was telling the truth. Chandra might be silent, but he would not lie.

"I was afraid you'd say that. Well, if you don't know any more than I do, here's the only clue I have—and it frightens me. Medical Research is trying to keep me at arm's length."

"Hmm," replied Chandra, taking his pipe from his mouth and looking at it thoughtfully.

"Is that all you have to say?"

"You haven't given me much to work on. Remember, I'm only a cop; I lack your vivid journalistic imagination."

"All I can tell you is that the higher I get in Medical Research, the colder the atmosphere becomes. Last time I was here, everyone was very friendly, and gave me some fine stories. But now, I can't even meet the Director. He's always too busy, or on the other side of the Moon. Anyway, what sort of man is he?"

"Dr. Hastings? Prickly little character. Very competent, but not easy to work with."

"What could he be trying to hide?"

"Knowing you, I'm sure you have some interesting theories."

"Oh, I thought of narcotics, and fraud, and political conspiracies—but they don't make sense, in these days. So what's left scares the hell out of me."

Chandra's eyebrows signaled a silent question mark.

"Interplanetary plague," said Cooper bluntly.

"I thought that was impossible."

"Yes—I've written articles myself proving that the life forms on other planets have such alien chemistries that they can't react with us, and that all our microbes and bugs took millions of years to adapt to our bodies. But I've always wondered if it was true. Suppose a ship has come back from Mars, say, with something *really* vicious—and the doctors can't cope with it?"

There was a long silence. Then Chandra said: "I'll start investigating. *I* don't like it either, for here's an item you probably don't know. There were three nervous breakdowns in the Medical Division last month—and that's very, very unusual."

He glanced at his watch, then at the false sky, which seemed so distant, yet which was only two hundred feet above their heads.

"We'd better get moving," he said. "The morning shower's due in five minutes."

The call came two weeks later, in the middle of the night—the real lunar night. By Plato City time, it was Sunday morning.

"Henry? Chandra here. Can you meet me in half an hour at air lock five? Good—I'll see you."

This was it, Cooper knew. Air lock five meant that they were going outside the dome. Chandra had found something.

The presence of the police driver restricted conversation as the tractor moved away from the city along the road roughly bulldozed across the ash and pumice. Low in the south, Earth was almost full, casting a brilliant blue-green light over the infernal landscape. However hard one tried, Cooper told himself, it was difficult to make the Moon appear glamorous. But nature guards her greatest secrets well; to such places men must come to find them.

The multiple domes of the city dropped below the sharply curved horizon. Presently, the tractor turned aside from the main road to follow a scarcely visible trail. Ten minutes later, Cooper saw a single glittering hemisphere ahead of them, standing on an isolated ridge of rock. Another vehicle, bearing a red cross, was parked beside the entrance. It seemed that they were not the only visitors.

Nor were they unexpected. As they drew up to the dome, the flexible tube of the air-lock coupling groped out toward them and snapped into place against their tractor's outer hull. There was a brief hissing as pressure equalized. Then Cooper followed Chandra into the building.

The air-lock operator led them along curving corridors and radial passageways toward the center of the dome. Sometimes they caught glimpses of laboratories, scientific instruments, computers—all perfectly ordinary, and all deserted on this Sunday morning. They must have reached the heart of the building, Cooper told himself when their guide ushered them into a large circular chamber and shut the door softly behind them.

It was a small zoo. All around them were cages, tanks, jars containing a wide selection of the fauna and flora of Earth. Waiting at its center was a short, gray-haired man, looking very worried, and very unhappy.

"Dr. Hastings," said Coomaraswamy, "meet Mr. Cooper." The Inspector General turned to his companion and added, "I've convinced the Doctor that there's only one way to keep you quiet—and that's to tell you everything."

"Frankly," said Hastings, "I'm not sure if I give a damn any more." His voice was unsteady, barely under control, and Cooper thought, Hello! There's another breakdown on the way.

The scientist wasted no time on such formalities as shaking hands. He walked to one of the cages, took out a small bundle of fur, and held it toward Cooper.

"Do you know what this is?" he asked abruptly.

"Of course. A hamster—the commonest lab animal."

"Yes," said Hastings. "A perfectly ordinary golden hamster. Except that this one is five years old—like all the others in this cage."

"Well? What's odd about that?"

"Oh, nothing, nothing at all . . . except for the trifling fact that hamsters live for only two years. And we have some here that are getting on for ten."

For a moment no one spoke; but the room was not silent. It was full of rustlings and slitherings and scratchings, of faint whimpers and tiny animal cries. Then Cooper whispered: "My God—you've found a way of prolonging life!"

"No," retorted Hastings. "We've not found it. The Moon has given it to us . . . as we might have expected, if we'd looked in front of our noses."

He seemed to have gained control over his emotions—as if he was once more the pure scientist, fascinated by a discovery for its own sake and heedless of its implications.

"On Earth," he said, "we spend our whole lives fighting gravity. It wears down our muscles, pulls our stomachs out of shape. In seventy years, how many tons of blood does the heart lift through how many miles? And all that work, all that strain is reduced to a sixth here on the Moon, where a one-hundred-and-eighty-pound human weighs only thirty pounds."

"I see," said Cooper slowly. "Ten years for a hamster—and how long for a man?"

"It's not a simple law," answered Hastings. "It varies with the size and the species. Even a month ago, we weren't certain. But now we're quite sure of this: on the Moon, the span of human life will be at least two hundred years."

"And you've been trying to keep it secret!"

"You fool! Don't you understand?"

"Take it easy, Doctor—take it easy," said Chandra softly.

With an obvious effort of will, Hastings got control of himself again. He began to speak with such icy calm that his words sank like freezing raindrops into Cooper's mind.

"Think of them up there," he said, pointing to the roof, to the invisible Earth, whose looming presence no one on the Moon could ever forget. "Six billion of them, packing all the continents to the edges—and now crowding over into the sea beds. And here—" he pointed to the ground—"only a hundred thousand of *us*, on an almost empty world. But a world where we need miracles of technology and engineering merely to exist, where a man with an I.Q. of only a hundred and fifty can't even get a job.

"And now we find that we can live for two hundred years. Imagine how they're going to react to *that* news! This is your problem now, Mister Journalist; you've asked for it, and you've got it. Tell me this, please—I'd really be interested to know—*just how are you going to break it to them?*"

He waited, and waited. Cooper opened his mouth, then closed it again, unable to think of anything to say.

In the far corner of the room, a baby monkey started to cry.

Understanding the Story _____

Main Idea

1. Which of these best expresses the main idea of the story?
   (a) Security on the moon is unnecessarily tight.
   (b) What should be good news has dangerous possibilities.
   (c) A plague threatens all life on earth.
   (d) Henry Cooper never does learn the secret.

Details

2. The Inspector General is named   (a) Hastings   (b) Cooper
   (c) Coomaraswamy   (d) Archimedes.

3. The number of times Cooper visited the moon was   (a) once
   (b) twice   (c) three times   (d) four times.

4. The age of the golden hamster was   (a) two months   (b) a
   year   (c) two years   (d) five years.

5. The dome that Cooper visited contained a   (a) zoo
   (b) radiation   laboratory   (c)   motion   picture   theater
   (d) building for moon vehicles.

Inferences

6. We may assume that a great many people on earth
   (a) already knew the secret   (b) refused to read Cooper's reports   (c) disapproved expenditures for moon exploration
   (d) had visited the moon dozens of times.

7. In the expression *Twenty-four-hour "day,"* *day* is in quotation
   marks because the "day" is   (a) actually shorter than 24
   hours   (b) longer than 24 hours   (c) artificially maintained
   (d) sunny all the time.

8. Three nervous breakdowns in the Medical Division suggested
   (a) some mysterious microbe   (b) unusual stress   (c) poor
   communications   (d) a shortage of doctors.

9. When Cooper presented his concerns, Chandra   (a) was also
   worried   (b) already knew the secret   (c) refused to coop-
   erate   (d) had Cooper sent back to earth.

10. A major problem with the discovery of extended life is
    (a) the limited amount of life serum   (b) the danger of the

plague   (c) the moon's limited ability to support large pop-
ulations   (d) the constant wars being waged on earth.

Order of Events

11. Arrange the items in the order in which they occurred. Use
    letters only.
    A. Cooper tells Chandra his worries.
    B. Hastings shows Cooper the hamster.
    C. Chandra investigates the problem in the Medical Division.
    D. Cooper lands at Archimedes Spaceport.
    E. Hastings tells Cooper and Chandra the secret.

Outcomes

12. If Cooper had not pestered Chandra,   (a) the secret might
    not have come out (b) the three nervous breakdowns might not
    have happened   (c) Chandra might have given up his official
    position   (d) Cooper would have had an even better story.

Cause and Effect

13. The moon's lessened gravity   (a) was a burden for earth vis-
    itors   (b) made sports on the moon quite difficult   (c) caused
    Cooper some embarrassing falls   (d) extended the life span
    of creatures living on the moon.

Fact or Opinion

Tell whether each of the following is a fact or an opinion.

14. The moon was administered by an international organization,
    UNSA.

15. Dr. Hastings was too dramatic for a cool scientist.

Words in Context

1. At first it was only an *ill-defined* suspicion, the sort of hunch
   that a hardheaded science reporter would not take too seriously.
   Ill-defined   (236)   means   (a) exciting   (b) probable
   (c) vague   (d) powerful.

2. Who had not seen that dusty scar in the Mare Imbrium, with its gleaming metal *pylon?*
    Pylon (236) means   (a) towerlike structure   (b) moon vehicle   (c) advertisement   (d) airplane.

3. The *multiple* domes of the city dropped below the sharply curved horizon.
    Multiple (239) means   (a) curved   (b) immense   (c) many   (d) easily visible.

4. All around them were cages, tanks, jars, containing a wide selection of the *fauna and flora* of Earth.
    Fauna and flora (239) means   (a) animals and minerals   (b) minerals and plants   (c) products and flowers   (d) animals and plants.

5. It was full of rustlings and *slitherings* and scratchings, of faint whimpers and tiny animal cries.
    Slitherings (240) means   (a) cries   (b) slidings   (c) roars   (d) moans.

Thinking About the Story _____

1. Why was Dr. Hastings so concerned about keeping the secret? Why did he fear the good news?

2. This was written in 1963, 6 years before the moon landing. Is Clarke's picture of how the moon might be settled an accurate one? Explain.

3. When Cooper says, "My God—you've found a way of prolonging life!" Hastings says, "No!" Why does he say "No?" Isn't human life being prolonged?

4. Clarke talks about the moon as "thoroughly mapped, yet almost completely unexplored." What does he mean?

5. Suppose you had the opportunity to go to the moon to live your life under conditions described in the story. Suppose that doing so would help you live 200 years. Would you go? Explain.

The Fun They Had

Isaac Asimov

♦ She was thinking about the old schools they had when her grandfather's grandfather was a little boy. All the kids from the whole neighborhood came, laughing and shouting in the schoolyard, sitting together in the schoolroom, going home together at the end of the day.

Every human institution has its critics, and the schools have theirs. In this age of modern technology, schools are sometimes criticized if they do not make full use of the many electronic aids now available. Yet it may be possible to go too far in installing electronic and mechanical aids.

"The Fun They Had" takes us two centuries into the future. Computer education has completely taken over. Books are almost unknown, a curiosity when they are found. Students learn in isolation, tied to a computer "teacher." The flesh-and-blood teacher has been completely replaced by a computer screen and a great number of adjustable programs. Without distractions from other students, without personality conflicts with teachers and students, the learners of the future should be efficient and completely happy. But there may be some disadvantages, too, as "The Fun They Had" suggests.

Isaac Asimov is one of the most respected science fiction authors of our day. In his "Foundation" novels he has created an exotic universe and an exciting plot line. His science fiction short stories, like this one, are reprinted in many anthologies. Yet Asimov is more than a writer of fiction. He is a science writer with excellent credentials. He is a student of language. He has written authoritative books on Shakespeare and the Bible.

Let Isaac Asimov take you to a time in the future when all educational problems have been solved . . . or have they?

THE FUN THEY HAD

Margie even wrote about it that night in her diary. On the page headed May 17, 2157, she wrote, "Today Tommy found a real book!"

It was a very old book. Margie's grandfather once said that when he was a little boy *his* grandfather told him that there was a time when all stories were printed on paper.

They turned the pages, which were yellow and crinkly, and it was awfully funny to read words that stood still instead of moving the way they were supposed to—on a screen, you know. And then, when they turned back to the page before, it had the same words on it that it had had when they read it the first time.

"Gee," said Tommy, "what a waste. When you're through with the book, you just throw it away, I guess. Our television screen must have had a million books on it and it's good for plenty more. I wouldn't throw *it* away."

"Same with mine," said Margie. She was eleven and hadn't seen as many telebooks as Tommy had. He was thirteen.

She said, "Where did you find it?"

"In my house." He pointed without looking, because he was busy reading. "In the attic."

"What's it about?"

"School."

Margie was scornful. "School? What's there to write about school? I hate school."

Margie always hated school, but now she hated it more than ever. The mechanical teacher had been giving her test after test in geography and she had been doing worse and worse until her mother had shaken her head sorrowfully and sent for the County Inspector.

He was a round little man with a red face and a whole box of tools with dials and wires. He smiled at Margie and gave her an apple, then took the teacher apart. Margie had hoped he wouldn't know how to put it together again, but he knew how all right, and, after an hour or so, there it was again, large and black and ugly, with a big screen on which all the lessons were shown and the questions were asked. That wasn't so bad. The part Margie hated most was the slot where she had to put homework and test papers. She always had to write them out in a punch code they made her learn when she was six years old, and the mechanical teacher calculated the mark in no time.

The Inspector had smiled after he was finished and patted Margie's head. He said to her mother, "It's not the little girl's fault, Mrs. Jones. I think the geography sector was geared a little too quick. Those things happen sometimes. I've slowed it up to an average ten-year level. Actually, the over-all pattern of her progress is quite satisfactory." And he patted Margie's head again.

Margie was disappointed. She had been hoping they would take the teacher away altogether. They had once taken Tommy's teacher away for nearly a month because the history sector had blanked out completely.

So she said to Tommy, "Why would anyone write about school?"

Tommy looked at her with very superior eyes. "Because it's not our kind of school, stupid. This is the old kind of school that they had hundreds and hundreds of years ago." He added loftily, pronouncing the word carefully, "*Centuries* ago."

Margie was hurt. "Well, I don't know what kind of school they had all that time ago." She read the book over his shoulder for a while, then said, "Anyway, they had a teacher."

"Sure they had a teacher, but it wasn't a *regular* teacher. It was a man."

"A man? How could a man be a teacher?"

"Well, he just told the boys and girls things and gave them homework and asked them questions."

"A man isn't smart enough."

"Sure he is. My father knows as much as my teacher."

"He can't. A man can't know as much as a teacher."

"He knows almost as much, I betcha."

Margie wasn't prepared to dispute that. She said, "I wouldn't want a strange man in my house to teach me."

Tommy screamed with laughter. "You don't know much, Margie. The teachers didn't live in the house. They had a special building and all the kids went there."

"And all the kids learned the same thing?"

"Sure, if they were the same age."

"But my mother says a teacher has to be adjusted to fit the mind of each boy and girl it teaches and that each kid has to be taught differently."

"Just the same they didn't do it that way then. If you don't like it, you don't have to read the book."

"I didn't say I didn't like it," Margie said quickly. She wanted to read about those funny schools.

They weren't even half-finished when Margie's mother called, "Margie! School!"

Margie looked up. "Not yet, Mamma."

"Now!" said Mrs. Jones. "And it's probably time for Tommy, too."

Margie said to Tommy, "Can I read the book some more with you after school?"

"Maybe," he said nonchalantly. He walked away whistling, the dusty old book tucked beneath his arm.

Margie went into the schoolroom. It was right next to her bedroom, and the mechanical teacher was on and waiting for her. It was always on at the same time every day except Saturday and Sunday, because her mother said little girls learned better if they learned at regular hours.

The screen was lit up, and it said: "Today's arithmetic lesson is on the addition of proper fractions. Please insert yesterday's homework in the proper slot."

Margie did so with a sigh. She was thinking about the old schools they had when her grandfather's grandfather was a little boy. All the kids from the whole neighborhood came, laughing and shouting in the schoolyard, sitting together in the schoolroom, going home together at the end of the day. They learned the same things, so they could help one another on the homework and talk about it.

And the teachers were people. . . .

The mechanical teacher was flashing on the screen: "When we add the fractions $\frac{1}{2}$ and $\frac{1}{4}$—"

Margie was thinking about how the kids must have loved it in the old days. She was thinking about the fun they had.

Understanding the Story ────────────

Main Idea

1. The main idea of the story is summed up in which of the following statements?
   (a) The education of the future will make children happy.
   (b) It's fun to play with computers.
   (c) Books can and should be replaced by computers.
   (d) A computerized, impersonal education may have disadvantages.

Details

2. May 17, 2157, is   (a) the date when the last book in the world was found   (b) the day of the story   (c) a day when teachers replaced computers   (d) Margie's birthday.

3. Margie had been doing poorly in   (a) geography (b) mathematics   (c) reading   (d) social studies.

4. "The man with a red face" was   (a) a teacher of reading (b) the County Inspector   (c) Margie's father   (d) a robot teacher.

5. The computer was adjusted to   (a) go a little more slowly (b) help Margie with her spelling   (c) teach history after geography   (d) teach reading.

6. Margie's attitude toward the computer was one of   (a) dislike   (b) curiosity   (c) amusement   (d) affection.

7. To the children in this story *teacher* means   (a) County Inspector   (b) supervisor   (c) friend   (d) computer.

8. A major problem with teaching computers was   (a) cost   (b) bulkiness   (c) mechanical breakdowns   (d) convenience of use.

9. One thing that Margie envied about the good old days was   (a) the geography lessons   (b) the social life of children   (c) improved instruction   (d) being able to be taught at home.

10. Tommy thought books   (a) were generally better than computers   (b) taught one subject more efficiently than computers   (c) were wasteful and inefficient   (d) would someday replace computers.

Order of Events

11. Arrange the items in the order in which they occurred. Use letters only.
    A. Margie looks at a book for the first time.
    B. Margie does poorly in geography.
    C. Margie daydreams about life centuries before.
    D. Tommy finds the book.
    E. The County Inspector adjusts the computer.

Outcomes

12. If Margie had gone to school outside the home, probably she would have   (a) never worked with a computer again   (b) been happier   (c) been separated from Tommy   (d) done poorly in geography.

Cause and Effect

13. An important solution for poor progress with the computer was   (a) insistence on work Saturdays and Sundays   (b) adjustment of speed of instruction   (c) change to a different brand name of computer   (d) punishment of the slow learner.

Fact or Opinion

Tell whether each of the following is a fact or an opinion.

14. The book's pages were yellow with age.

15. Older methods of instruction were better than the newer.

Words in Context

1. They turned the pages, which were yellow and *crinkly*.
   Crinkly (246) means   (a) wrinkled   (b) stiff   (c) smooth
   (d) shredded.

2. "I think the geography *sector* was *geared* a little too quick."
   Sector (247) means   (a) book   (b) explanation   (c) section
   (d) page.

3. *Geared* (247) means   (a) tried   (b) set   (c) omitted
   (d) committed.

4. He added *loftily*, pronouncing the word carefully, "Centuries
   ago."
   Loftily (247) means   (a) without hesitation   (b) after a moment's delay   (c) with considerable force   (d) in a superior
   manner.

5. "Maybe," he said *nonchalantly*. He walked away whistling, the
   dusty old book tucked beneath his arm.
   Nonchalantly (248) means   (a) casually   (b) slowly
   (c) mysteriously   (d) unexpectedly.

Thinking About the Story

1. Some educators believe that the social values of school are extremely valuable. Much is learned from the interaction of personalities: student-student; student-teacher. Do you agree? Explain. How does the "school" in this story differ from present-
   day schools?

2. What advantages do printed books have over computer books?
   What disadvantages?

3. Would you like to have the kind of instruction Margie had? Explain.

4. Have you used computers for instruction? Entertainment? What was your reaction?

5. Some people prefer to watch movies on television or on VCR's. Others prefer to go to a movie theater. Which do you prefer? Why?

Out of This World

ACTIVITIES

Thinking About the Stories

1. Though all four stories in this unit are quite different, they do have one element in common. What is that element? Explain.

2. Within the past generation, movies using science fiction themes have improved visually. Special effects and the use of computer-generated graphics have added an extra dimension to film making. Tell about a science fiction movie you saw recently in the movies or on television. How were special effects used to create a world of imagination?

3. Which story do you think is the most effective? Why?

4. Although science fiction stories are often set in the future, they deal with problems that are contemporary. What two contemporary problems do "The Secret" and "The Fun They Had" deal with?

5. Even though stories are "way out," they must still create realistic characters. If characters are unrealistic, we lose all interest. Are the major characters in the four stories believable? Explain.

Projects

1. Read a story in one of the anthologies listed on page 255 or in some other collection. Prepare to tell the story to the class. Rehearse the narration carefully so that the attention of your audience will be held throughout.

2. Television programs like *Amazing Stories* and *The Twilight Zone* specialize in stories of the imagination. If you were asked to select one of the stories in this unit for dramatization on television, which would you choose? Consider such problems as (a) the extent to which dialog keeps the story moving, (b) presentation of atmosphere, (c) length, and (d) characterization.

3. Select any of the stories from this unit and compare it with a motion picture of science fiction or imagination you have seen recently. Consider the ingenuity of the plot and the stimulation of imagination.

4. If you have seen one of the *Star Trek* television series or one of the *Star Trek* movies, be ready to tell about it. What makes this series so special? Why do Trekkies (*Star Trek* fans) have get-togethers from time to time?

5. Steven Spielberg and George Lucas are prominent creators of stories of the imagination. Select one of these and prepare to make an oral report on the person of your choice. Use the *Readers' Guide* and *Current Biography* for information about your subject.

Additional Readings ⸺⸺⸺⸺⸺

Short Stories

"The Lady or the Tiger?" by Frank Stockton

This is the most famous puzzle tale of all time. No one has ever satisfactorily answered the title's question, but each reader thinks he knows.

"A. V. Laider" by Max Beerbohm

There is a puzzle in this famous tale also, but the dimensions of the puzzle aren't perfectly clear until the last line of the story.

"The Man and the Snake" by Ambrose Bierce

Can a snake hypnotize birds, animals, even men? This story, by an unusual short story writer, provides an unforgettable answer.

"The Monkey's Paw" by W. W. Jacobs

This has the wish-fulfillment theme of "The Bottle Imp," but it is handled in an altogether different way. Suppose you were granted three wishes and could gain the three things you desired most. Would you be happy?

"Satan and Sam Shay" by Robert Arthur

Another variation on the Faust theme. This time the Devil has to do a mortal's bidding.

Anthologies

Out of This World edited by Julius Fast

This is an older but still excellent collection of fantasies and stories that will make you shiver.

The Short Stories of Saki by "Saki" (H.H. Munro)

The collected stories of the writer who excelled in combining the humorous with the unusual.

The Arbor House Treasury of Modern Science Fiction compiled by Robert Silverberg and Martin H. Greenberg

A recent anthology of science fiction with a solid representation of the best creative writers of recent times.

Histories and Studies

Explorers of the Infinite by Sam Moskowitz

A comprehensive history of science fiction, beginning with an interesting study of Cyrano de Bergerac, often forgotten as a writer of science fiction.

The Visual Encyclopedia of Science Fiction edited by Brian Ash

An illustrated reference book for science fiction fans.

4 *Boy Meets Girl*

Romance is the dominant theme of most fiction. The setting may be Central Africa or Silicon Valley, the Dark Ages or the Planets of Outer Space; and the characters may be rich or poor, beautiful or plain, strong or weak. But none of these differences really matters because almost all these stories boil down to the inevitable formula—

1. Boy and girl meet.
2. Boy and girl are separated.
3. Boy and girl are united.

Conflict, suspense, and final success—what more can a reader ask for?

What more? Much more! There is no need to assume that the plots are all alike. The four stories that follow show some of the interesting variations that can be made on the romance formula. In the first story, according to convention, they meet, they are separated, and finally they are united—but count on O. Henry to turn the tables on the reader. The second story is scarcely a formula story at all; the "boy" in the formula is still very much in the future. Yet this tale of a starry-eyed girl at her first dance has more real emotion than a dozen TV yarns of the more obvious variety. In the third story, which is a hilarious account of young love, boy and girl meet. They share a glowing, romantic moment and then . . . But let Herman Wouk tell the tale. And the fourth story! Leave it to John Collier, master of the chill-down-your-spine story, to give a different twist to the formula.

Stories of romance need not be standardized. Those you are about to read are to be sure "love stories," but they are certainly not stereotyped or dull.

The Higher Pragmatism

O. Henry

♦ "I suppose Mack and I always will be hopeless amateurs. But, as the thing has turned out in my case, I'm mighty glad of it."

In "The Higher Pragmatism," O.Henry introduces us to two characters from widely separated sections of society. Each has been thrown for a loss for the same reason—the total loss of self-confidence in the presence of someone who is known to have "class." Mack, the park-bench hobo, couldn't win a fight in the professional ring, even though he had knocked out the middle-weight champion of the world. Jack (Philip Arden) is having insurmountable difficulties with his love affair because, in the presence of the beautiful Mildred Telfair, he behaves like a frightened "amateur."

The hobo advises Jack to be pragmatic; that is, to be practical, accept his fate, and stop trying. Jack becomes angry enough to set out to prove that he is not a failure. He "climbs through the ropes" and starts swinging. He will prove the hobo wrong!

What happens to him from this point on is an excellent example of O. Henry's mastery of the surprise-ending technique. O. Henry reveals a higher pragmatism, what can happen when fate becomes practical!

THE HIGHER PRAGMATISM

Once upon a time I found a ten-cent magazine lying on a bench in a little city park. Anyhow, that was the amount he asked me for when I sat on the bench next to him. He was a musty, dingy, and tattered magazine, with some queer stories bound in him, I was sure. He turned out to be a scrapbook.

"I am a newspaper reporter," I said to him, to try him. "I have been detailed to write up some of the experiences of the unfortunate ones who spend their evenings in this park. May I ask you to what you attribute your downfall in—"

I was interrupted by a laugh from my purchase—a laugh so rusty and unpracticed that I was sure it had been his first for many a day.

"Oh, no, no," said he. "You ain't a reporter. Reporters don't talk that way. They pretend to be one of us, and say they've just got on the blind baggage from St. Louis. I can tell a reporter on sight. Us park bums get to be fine judges of human nature. We sit here all day and watch the people go by. I can size up anybody who walks past my bench in a way that would surprise you."

"Well," I said, "go on and tell me. How do you size me up?"

"I should say," said the student of human nature with unpardonable hesitation, "that you was, say, in the contracting business—or maybe worked in a store—or was a signpainter. You stopped in the park to finish your cigar, and thought you'd get a little free monolog out of me. Still, you might be a plasterer or a lawyer—it's getting kind of dark, you see. And your wife won't let you smoke at home."

I frowned gloomily.

"But, judging again," went on the reader of men, "I'd say you ain't got a wife."

"No," said I, rising restlessly. "No, no, no, I ain't. But I *will* have, by the arrows of Cupid. That is if—"

My voice must have trailed away and muffled itself in uncertainty and despair.

"I see you have a story yourself," said the dusty vagrant—imprudently, it seemed to me. "Suppose you take your dime back and spin your yarn for me. I'm interested myself in the ups and downs of unfortunate ones who spend their evenings in the park."

Somehow, that amused me. I looked at the frowsy derelict with more interest. I did have a story. Why not tell it to him? I had told none of my friends. I had always been a reserved and bottled-up man. It was psychical timidity or sensitiveness—perhaps both. And I smiled to myself in wonder when I felt an impulse to confide in this stranger and vagabond.

"Jack," said I.

"Mack," said he.

"Mack," said I, "I'll tell you."

"Do you want the dime back in advance?" said he. I handed him a dollar.

"The dime," said I, "was the price of listening to *your* story."

"Right on the point of the jaw," said he. "Go on."

And then, incredible as it may seem to the lovers in the world who confide their sorrows only to the night wind and the gibbous moon, I laid bare my secret to that wreck of all things that you would have supposed to be in sympathy with love.

I told him of the days and weeks and months that I had spent in adoring Mildred Telfair. I spoke of my despair, my grievous days and wakeful nights, my dwindling hopes and distress of mind. I even pictured to this night-prowler her beauty and dignity, the great sway she had in society, and the magnificence of her life as the elder daughter of an ancient race whose pride overbalanced the dollars of the city's millionaires.

"Why don't you cop the lady out?" asked Mack, bringing me down to earth and dialect again.

I explained to him that my worth was so small, my income so minute, and my fears so large, that I hadn't the courage to speak to her of my worship. I told him that in her presence I could only blush and stammer, and that she looked upon me with a wonderful, maddening smile of amusement.

"She kind of moves in the professional class, don't she?" asked Mack.

"The Telfair family—" I began, haughtily.

"I mean professional beauty," said my hearer.

"She is greatly and widely admired," I answered, cautiously.

"Any sisters?"

"One."

"You know any more girls?"

"Why, several," I answered. "And a few others."

"Say," said Mack, "tell me one thing—can you hand out the dope to other girls? Can you chin 'em and make matinée eyes at 'em and squeeze 'em? You know what I mean. You're just shy when it comes to this particular dame—the professional beauty—ain't that right?"

"In a way you have outlined the situation with approximate truth," I admitted.

"I thought so," said Mack, grimly. "Now, that reminds me of my own case. I'll tell you about it."

I was indignant, but concealed it. What was this loafer's case or anybody's case compared with mine? Besides, I had given him a dollar and ten cents.

"Feel my muscle," said my companion, suddenly flexing his biceps. I did so mechanically. His arm was as hard as cast iron.

"Four years ago," said Mack, "I could lick any man in New York outside of the professional ring. Your case and mine is just the same. I come from the West Side—between Thirteenth and Fourteenth—and I won't give the number on the door. I was a scrapper when I was ten, and when I was twenty no amateur in the city could stand up four rounds with me. 'S a fact. You know Bill McCarty? No? He managed the smokers for some of them swell clubs. Well, I knocked out everything Bill brought up before me. I was a middleweight, but could train down to a welter when necessary. I boxed all over the West Side at bouts and benefits and private entertainments, and was never put out once.

"But, say, the first time I put my foot in the ring with a professional I was no more than a canned lobster. I dunno how it was—I seemed to lose heart. I guess I got too much imagination. There was a formality and publicness about it that kind of weakened my nerve. I never won a fight in the ring. Lightweights and all kinds of scrubs used to sign up with my manager and then walk up and tap me on the wrist and see me fall. The minute I seen the crowd and a lot of gents in evening clothes down in front, and seen a professional come inside the ropes, I got as weak as ginger ale.

"Of course, it wasn't long till I couldn't get no backers, and I didn't have any more chances to fight a professional—or many amateurs, either. But lemme tell you—I was as good as most men inside the ring or out. It was just that dumb, dead feeling I had when I was up against a regular that always done me up.

"Well, sir, after I had got out of the business, I got a mighty grouch on. I used to go round town licking private citizens and all kinds of unprofessionals just to please myself. I'd lick cops in dark streets and car conductors and cabdrivers and draymen whenever I could start a row with 'em. It didn't make any difference how big they were, or how much science they had, I got away with 'em. If I'd only just have had the confidence in the ring that I had beating up the best men outside of it, I'd be wearing black pearls and heliotrope silk socks today.

"One evening I was walking along near the Bowery, thinking about things, when along comes a slumming-party. About six or seven they was, all in swallowtails, and these silk hats that don't shine. One of the gang kind of shoves me off the sidewalk. I hadn't had a scrap in three days, and I just says, 'De-light-ed' and hits him back of the ear.

"Well, we had it. That Johnnie put up as decent a little fight as you'd want to see in the moving pictures. It was on a side street, and no cops around. The other guy had a lot of science but it only took me about six minutes to lay him out.

"Some of the swallowtails dragged him up against some steps and began to fan him. Another one of 'em comes over to me and says:

" 'Young man, do you know what you've done?'

" 'Oh, beat it,' says I. 'I've done nothing but a little punching-bag work. Take Freddy back to Yale and tell him to quit studying sociology on the wrong side of the sidewalk.'

" 'My good fellow,' says he, 'I don't know who you are, but I'd like to. You've knocked out Reddy Burns, the champion middleweight of the world! He came to New York yesterday, to try to get a match on with Jim Jeffries. If you—'

"But when I come out of my faint I was laying on the floor in a drugstore saturated with aromatic spirits of ammonia. If I'd known that was Reddy Burns, I'd have got down in the gutter and crawled past him instead of handing him one like I did. Why, if I'd ever been in a ring and seen him climbing over the ropes, I'd have been all to the sal volatile.

"So that's what imagination does," concluded Mack. "And as I said, your case and mine is simultaneous. You'll never win out. You can't go up against the professionals. I tell you, it's a park bench for yours in this romance business."

Mack, the pessimist, laughed harshly.

"I'm afraid I don't see the parallel," I said, coldly. "I have only a very slight acquaintance with the prize ring."

The derelict touched my sleeve with his forefinger, for emphasis, as he explained his parable.

"Every man," said he, with some dignity, "has got his lamps on something that looks good to him. With you, it's this dame that you're afraid to say your say to. With me, it was to win out in the ring. Well, you'll lose just like I did."

"Why do you think I shall lose?" I asked, warmly.

" 'Cause," said he, "you're afraid to go in the ring. You dassen't stand up before a professional. Your case and mine is just the same. You're a amateur; and that means that you'd better keep outside of the ropes."

"Well, I must be going," I said, rising and looking with elaborate care at my watch.

When I was twenty feet away the park-bencher called to me.

"Much obliged for the dollar," he said. "And for the dime. But you'll never get 'er. You're in the amateur class."

"Serves you right," I said to myself, "for hobnobbing with a tramp. His impudence!"

But, as I walked, his words seemed to repeat themselves over and over again in my brain. I think I even grew angry at the man.

"I'll show him!" I finally said, aloud. "I'll show him that I can fight Reddy Burns, too—even knowing who he is."

I hurried to a telephone booth and rang up the Telfair residence.

A soft, sweet voice answered. Didn't I know that voice? My hand holding the receiver shook.

"Is that *you?*" said I, employing the foolish words that form the vocabulary of every talker through the telephone.

"Yes, this is I," came back the answer in the low, clear-cut tones that are an inheritance of Telfairs. "Who is it, please?"

"It's me," said I, less ungrammatically than egotistically. "It's me, and I've got a few things that I want to say to you right now and immediately and straight to the point."

"*Dear* me," said the voice. "Oh, it's you, Mr. Arden!"

I wondered if any accent on the first word was intended. Mildred was fine at saying things that you had to study out afterward.

"Yes," said I, "I hope so. And now to come down to brass tacks." I thought that rather a vernacularism, if there is such a word, as soon as I had said it; but I didn't stop to apologize. "You know, of course, that I love you, and that I have been in that idiotic state for a long time. I don't want any more foolishness about it—that is, I mean I want an answer from you right now. Will you marry me or not? Hold the wire, please. Keep out, Central. Hello, hello! Will you, or will you *not?*"

That was just the uppercut for Reddy Burns' chin. The answer came back:

"Why, Phil, dear, of course I will! I didn't know that you—that is, you never said—oh, come up to the house, please—I can't say what I want to over the 'phone. You are so importunate. But please come up to the house, won't you?"

Would I?

I rang the bell of the Telfair house violently. Some sort of a human came to the door and shooed me into the drawing room.

"Oh, well," said I to myself, looking at the ceiling, "anyone can learn from anyone. That was a pretty good philosophy of Mack's, anyhow. He didn't take advantage of his experience, but I get the benefit of it. If you want to get into the professional class, you've got to—"

I stopped thinking then. Someone was coming down the stairs. My knees began to shake. I knew then how Mack had felt when a professional began to climb over the ropes. I looked around foolishly for a door or a window by which I might escape. If it had been any other girl approaching, I mightn't have—

But just then the door opened, and Bess, Mildred's younger sister, came in. I'd never seen her look so much like a glorified angel. She walked straight up to me, and—and—

I'd never noticed before what perfectly wonderful eyes and hair Elizabeth Telfair had.

"Phil," she said, in the Telfair sweet, thrilling tones, "why didn't you tell me about it before? I thought it was sister you wanted all the time, until you telephoned to me a few minutes ago!"

I suppose Mack and I always will be hopeless amateurs. But, as the thing has turned out in my case, I'm mighty glad of it.

Understanding the Story

Main Idea

1. Which of the following bits of dialog best expresses the main idea of the story?
   (a) "The dime was the price of listening to *your* story."
   (b) "Every man has got his lamps on something that looks good to him."
   (c) "You're an amateur; and that means you'd better keep outside the ropes."
   (d) "I'll show him that I can fight Reddy Burns, too—even knowing who he is."

Details

2. This story takes place mainly   (a) in a gymnasium   (b) on a park bench   (c) in a night club   (d) in a boxing ring.

3. Mr. Arden gives Mack a dollar   (a) because he feels sorry for him   (b) to have Mack tell of his misfortunes   (c) to have Mack listen to his story   (d) to get rid of him.

4. Which of the following statements is *not* true?
   (a) Mr. Arden is in love with a famous beauty.
   (b) Both men have been disappointed in love.
   (c) Mr. Arden tries to prove Mack's theory wrong.
   (d) Both men reveal their thoughts to a stranger.

5. Which of the following statements is *not* true?
   (a) Mack was knocked out by third-rate fighters.
   (b) Mack knocked out the middleweight champion of the world.
   (c) As an amateur, Mack had been sensational.
   (d) Mack is really a newsreporter in disguise.

Inferences

6. By an "amateur" Mack means a person   (a) who never fights well   (b) who is an apprentice   (c) who defeats himself when he faces a "professional"   (d) who will eventually succeed.

Cause and Effect

7. After speaking to Mack, Mr. Arden   (a) goes home   (b) makes a telephone call   (c) takes back his dollar   (d) decides to give Mack a job.

8. After the talk with Mack, Mr. Arden is   (a) angry but determined   (b) calm but resigned   (c) puzzled but relieved   (d) pleased but tired.

Outcomes

9. At the end of the story,   (a) Mr. Arden proves Mack wrong   (b) Mack is sorry that he met Mr. Arden   (c) Mack's analysis of Mr. Arden remains valid   (d) Mack goes back to professional fighting.

10. Years later, when he thinks about the results of his telephone call, Mr. Arden is   (a) regretful   (b) resigned   (c) pleased   (d) concerned.

Words in Context

1. "May I ask you to what you *attribute* your downfall."
   Attribute (259) means   (a) refer   (b) blame   (c) consign   (d) reserve.

2. "You . . . thought you'd get a free *monolog* out of me."
   Monolog (259) means   (a) meal   (b) gift   (c) complaint   (d) story.

3. " . . . you have a story yourself," said the dusty *vagrant—imprudently.*
    Vagrant—imprudently (260) means   (a) visitor quickly
    (b) young man loudly   (c) homeless person rashly   (d) tall
    stranger proudly.

4. I looked at the *frowsy derelict* with more interest.
    Frowsy derelict (260) means   (a) talkative intruder   (b) old-
    fashioned boat   (c) poorly dressed tramp   (d) lonely bench
    warmer.

5. I had always been a *reserved* and bottled-up man.
    Reserved (260) means   (a) showy   (b) quiet in manner
    (c) popular   (d) fast-talking.

6. I told . . . my *dwindling* hopes and distress of mind.
    Dwindling (260) means   (a) ambitious   (b) foolish
    (c) shrinking   (d) high.

7. I was . . . *saturated with aromatic* spirits of ammonia.
    Saturated with aromatic (263) means   (a) smelling the
    strong   (b) drinking sips of   (c) overcome by powerful
    (d) drenched with strong-smelling.

8. " . . . your case and mine *is simultaneous.*"
    Instead of *is simultaneous* (263) Mack should have said
    (a) are different   (b) are unusual   (c) are difficult   (d) are
    similar.

9. The derelict . . . explained his *parable.*
    Parable (263) means a story that   (a) reveals courage   (b) is
    overlong   (c) is very brief   (d) has a moral.

10. Mack the *pessimist* laughed harshly.
    Pessimist (263) is a person who has   (a) a fighting spirit
    (b) much to say   (c) a gloomy outlook   (d) a lucky past.

Thinking About the Story ───────────

1. How does Mack, from the very first moment of the story, reveal
    that he is an unusual person? What qualities did he have that
    should have led to success? What was the flaw or weakness that
    caused his downfall? Could he have prevented his failure? Do
    you think some people are born failures? Explain your opinion.

2. Why does Mr. Arden tell his story? Why does Mack tell his? Is there any advantage to telling others of our failures? Explain. What should we learn from telling others of our disappointments?

3. What do you think of Mack's theory that people are either amateurs or professionals? Have you met any people—in real life, or in stories other than this one—whom you would classify as either amateurs or professionals in their approach to life?

4. How does the author make use of dialog to show the difference between the two men? To what extent is it fair to judge a person on his speech pattern?

5. What are some of the unexpected twists in the story? Are they true to life or based on coincidences that are farfetched? What makes O. Henry so outstanding as an author?

Her First Ball

Katherine Mansfield

♦ But deep inside her a little girl threw her pinafore over her head and sobbed. Why had he
spoiled it all?

"Her First Ball" is the story of a girl at her first formal dance.
But it is not merely a "girl's" story. A few simple word changes
mentally made here and there in the story make it just as applicable to boys Leila's age.

"Her First Ball" is an analysis of emotion, the emotion of
youth. It tells you something about the vitality of youth that you
can prove from your own experience. It is a thoughtful presentation of the desire of youth for happiness, of the inability of youth
to be unhappy, even in the knowledge that happiness may be
fragile and of brief duration. The final paragraph is worth reading
several times.

This beautifully told story has humor, tenderness, sympathy,
and warmth. It has, too, that great quality of being unforgettable,
as you'll discover when you find it popping into your head at odd
moments a month, six months, and ten years from now.

HER FIRST BALL

Exactly when the ball began Leila would have found it hard to say. Perhaps her first real partner was the cab. It did not matter that she shared the cab with the Sheridan girls and their brother. She sat back in her own little corner of it, and the bolster on which her hand rested felt like the sleeve of an unknown young man's dress suit; and away they bowled, past waltzing lampposts and houses and fences and trees.

"Have you really never been to a ball before, Leila? But, my child, how too weird—" cried the Sheridan girls.

"Our nearest neighbor was fifteen miles," said Leila softly, gently opening and shutting her fan.

Oh, dear, how hard it was to be indifferent like the others! She tried not to smile too much; she tried not to care. But every single thing was so new and exciting . . . Meg's tuberoses, Jose's long loop of amber, Laura's little dark head, pushing above her white fur like a flower through snow. She would remember forever. It even gave her a pang to see her cousin Laurie throw away the wisps of tissue paper he pulled from the fastenings of his new gloves. She would like to have kept those wisps as a keepsake, as a remembrance. Laurie leaned forward and put his hand on Laura's knee.

"Look here, darling," he said. "The third and the ninth as usual. Twig?"

Oh, how marvelous to have a brother! In her excitement Leila felt that if there had been time, if it hadn't been impossible, she couldn't have helped crying because she was an only child, and no brother had ever said "Twig?" to her; no sister would ever say, as Meg said to Jose that moment, "I've never known your hair go up more successfully than it has tonight!"

But, of course, there was no time. They were at the drill hall already; there were cabs in front of them and cabs behind. The road was bright on either side with moving fanlike lights, and on the pavement happy couples seemed to float through the air; little satin shoes chased each other like birds.

"Hold on to me, Leila; you'll get lost," said Laura.

"Come on, girls, let's make a dash for it," said Laurie.

Leila put two fingers on Laura's pink velvet cloak, and they were somehow lifted past the big golden lantern, carried along the passage, and pushed into the little room marked "Ladies." Here the crowd was so great there was hardly space to take off their things; the noise was deafening. Two benches on either side were stacked high with wraps. Two old women in white aprons ran up and down tossing fresh armfuls. And everybody was pressing forward trying to get at the little dressing table and mirror at the far end.

A great quivering jet of gas lighted the ladies' room. It couldn't wait; it was dancing already. When the door opened again and there came a burst of tuning from the drill hall, it leaped almost to the ceiling.

Dark girls, fair girls were patting their hair, tying ribbons again, tucking handkerchiefs down the fronts of their bodices, smoothing marble-white gloves. And because they were all laughing it seemed to Leila that they were all lovely.

"Aren't there any invisible hairpins?" cried a voice. "How most extraordinary! I can't see a single invisible hairpin."

"Powder my back, there's a darling," cried someone else.

"But I must have a needle and cotton. I've torn simply miles and miles of the frill," wailed a third.

Then, "Pass them along, pass them along!" The straw basket of programs was tossed from arm to arm. Darling little pink-and-silver programs, with pink pencils and fluffy tassels. Leila's fingers shook as she took one out of the basket. She wanted to ask someone, "Am I meant to have one too?" but she had just time to read: "Waltz 3. *Two, Two in a Canoe.* Polka 4. *Making the Feathers Fly,*" when Meg cried, "Ready, Leila?" and they pressed their way through the crush in the passage towards the big double doors of the drill hall.

Dancing had not begun yet, but the band had stopped tuning, and the noise was so great it seemed that when it did begin to play it would never be heard. Leila, pressing close to Meg, looking over Meg's shoulder, felt that even the little quivering colored flags strung across the ceiling were talking. She quite forgot to be shy; she forgot how in the middle of dressing she had sat down on the bed with one shoe off and one shoe on and begged her mother to ring up her cousins and say she couldn't go after all. And the rush of longing she had had to be sitting on the veranda of their forsaken up-country home, listening to the baby owls crying "More pork" in the moonlight, was changed to a rush of joy so sweet that it was hard to bear alone. She clutched her fan, and, gazing at the gleaming, golden floor, the azaleas, the lanterns, the stage at one end with its red carpet and gilt chairs and the band in a corner, she thought breathlessly, "How heavenly; how simply heavenly!"

All the girls stood grouped together at one side of the doors, the men at the other, and the chaperones in dark dresses, smiling rather foolishly, walked with little careful steps over the polished floor towards the stage.

"This is my little country cousin Leila. Be nice to her. Find her partners; she's under my wing," said Meg, going up to one girl after another.

Strange faces smiled at Leila—sweetly, vaguely. Strange voices answered, "Of course, my dear." But Leila felt the girls didn't really see her. They were looking towards the men. Why didn't the men begin? What were they waiting for? There they stood, smoothing their gloves, patting their glossy hair and smiling among themselves. Then, quite suddenly, as if they had only just made up their minds that that was what they had to do, the men came gliding over the parquet. There was a joyful flutter among the girls. A tall, fair man flew up to Meg, seized her program, scribbled something; Meg passed him on to Leila. "May I have the pleasure?" He ducked and smiled. There came a dark man wearing an eyeglass, then cousin Laurie with a friend, and Laura with a little freckled fellow whose tie was crooked. Then quite an old man—fat, with a big bald patch on his head—took her program, and murmured, "Let me see, let me see!" And he was a long time comparing his program, which looked black with names, with hers. It seemed to give him so much trouble that Leila was ashamed. "Oh, please don't bother," she said eagerly. But instead of replying the fat man wrote something, glanced at her again. "Do I remember this bright little face?" he said softly. "Is it known to me of yore?" At that moment the band began playing; the fat man disappeared. He was tossed away on a great wave of music that came flying over the gleaming floor, breaking the groups up into couples, scattering them, sending them spinning . . .

Leila had learned to dance at boarding school. Every Saturday afternoon the boarders were hurried off to a little corrugated iron mission hall where Miss Eccles (of London) held her "select" classes. But the difference between that dusty-smelling hall—with calico texts on the walls, the poor terrified little woman in a brown velvet toque with rabbit's ears thumping the cold piano, Miss Eccles poking the girls' feet with her long white wand—and this was so tremendous that Leila was sure if her partner didn't come and she had to listen to that marvelous music and to watch the others sliding, gliding over the golden floor, she would die at least, or faint, or lift her arms and fly out of one of those dark windows that showed the stars.

"Ours, I think—" Someone bowed, smiled, and offered her his arm; she hadn't to die after all. Someone's hand pressed her waist, and she floated away like a flower that is tossed into a pool.

"Quite a good floor, isn't it?" drawled a faint voice close to her ear.

"I think it's most beautifully slippery," said Leila.

"Pardon!" The faint voice sounded surprised. Leila said it again. And there was a tiny pause before the voice echoed, "Oh, quite!" and she was swung round again.

He steered so beautifully. That was the great difference between dancing with girls and men, Leila decided. Girls banged into each other, and stamped on each other's feet; the girl who was gentleman always clutched you so.

The azaleas were separate flowers no longer; they were pink and white flags streaming by.

"Were you at the Bells' last week?" the voice came again. It sounded tired. Leila wondered whether she ought to ask him if he would like to stop.

"No, this is my first dance," said she.

Her partner gave a little gasping laugh. "Oh, I say," he protested.

"Yes, it is really the first dance I've ever been to." Leila was most fervent. It was such a relief to be able to tell somebody. "You see, I've lived in the country all my life up until now . . ."

At that moment the music stopped, and they went to sit on two chairs against the wall. Leila tucked her pink satin feet under and fanned herself, while she blissfully watched the other couples passing and disappearing through the swing doors.

"Enjoying yourself, Leila?" asked Jose, nodding her golden head.

Laura passed and gave her the faintest little wink; it made Leila wonder for a moment whether she was quite grown up after all. Certainly her partner did not say very much. He coughed, tucked his handkerchief away, pulled down his waistcoat, took a minute thread off his sleeve. But it didn't matter. Almost immediately the band started, and her second partner seemed to spring from the ceiling.

"Floor's not bad," said the new voice. Did one always begin with the floor? And then, "Were you at the Neaves' on Tuesday?" And again Leila explained. Perhaps it was a little strange that her partners were not more interested. For it was thrilling. Her first ball! She was only at the beginning of everything. It seemed to her that she had never known what the night was like before. Up till now it had been dark, silent, beautiful very often—oh, yes—but mournful somehow. Solemn. And now it would never be like that again—it had opened dazzling bright.

"Care for an ice?" said her partner. And they went through the swing doors, down the passage, to the supper room. Her cheeks burned, she was fearfully thirsty. How sweet the ices looked on little glass plates, and how cold the frosted spoon was, iced too! And when they came back to the hall there was the fat man waiting for her by the door. It gave her quite a shock again to see how old he was; he ought to have been on the stage with the fathers and mothers. And when Leila compared him with her other partners he looked shabby. His waistcoat was creased, there was a button off his glove, his coat looked as if it was dusty with French chalk.

"Come along, little lady," said the fat man. He scarcely troubled to clasp her, and they moved away so gently, it was more like walking than dancing. But he said not a word about the floor. "Your first dance, isn't it?" he murmured.

"How *did* you know?"

"Ah," said the fat man, "that's what it is to be old!" He wheezed faintly as he steered her past an awkward couple. "You see, I've been doing this kind of thing for the last thirty years."

"Thirty years?" cried Leila. Twelve years before she was born!

"It hardly bears thinking about, does it?" said the fat man gloomily. Leila looked at his bald head, and she felt quite sorry for him.

"I think it's marvelous to be still going on," she said kindly.

"Kind little lady," said the fat man, and he pressed her a little closer, and hummed a bar of the waltz. "Of course," he said, "you can't hope to last anything like as long as that. No-o," said the fat man, "long before that you'll be sitting up there on the stage, looking on, in your nice black velvet. And these pretty arms will have turned into little short fat ones, and you'll beat time with such a different kind of fan—a black bony one." The fat man seemed to shudder. "And you'll smile away like the poor old dears up there, and point to your daughter, and tell the elderly lady next to you how some dreadful man tried to kiss her at the club ball. And your heart will ache, ache"—the fat man squeezed her closer still, as if he really was sorry for that poor heart—"because no one wants to kiss you now. And you'll say how unpleasant these polished floors are to walk on, how dangerous they are. Eh, Mademoiselle Twinkletoes?" said the fat man softly.

Leila gave a light little laugh, but she did not feel like laughing. Was it—could it all be true? It sounded terribly true. Was this first ball only the beginning of her last ball after all? At that the music seemed to change; it sounded sad, sad; it rose upon a great sigh. Oh, how quickly things changed! Why didn't happiness last forever? Forever wasn't a bit too long.

"I want to stop," she said in a breathless voice. The fat man led her to the door.

"No," she said, "I won't go outside. I won't sit down. I'll just stand here, thank you." She leaned against the wall, tapping with her foot, pulling up her gloves and trying to smile. But deep inside her a little girl threw her pinafore over her head and sobbed. Why had he spoiled it all?

"I say, you know," said the fat man, "you mustn't take me seriously, little lady."

"As if I should!" said Leila, tossing her small dark head and sucking her underlip . . .

Again the couples paraded. The swing doors opened and shut. Now new music was given out by the bandmaster. But Leila didn't want to dance anymore. She wanted to be home, or sitting on the veranda listening to those baby owls. When she looked through the dark windows at the stars, they had long beams like wings . . .

But presently a soft, melting, ravishing tune began, and a young man with curly hair bowed before her. She would have to dance, out of politeness, until she could find Meg. Very stiffly she walked into the middle; very haughtily she put her arm on his sleeve. But in one minute, in one turn, her feet glided, glided. The lights, the azaleas, the dresses, the pink faces, the velvet chairs, all became one beautiful flying wheel. And when her next partner bumped her into the fat man and he said, "Par*don*," she smiled at him more radiantly than ever. She didn't even recognize him again.

Understanding the Story _____

Main Idea

1. Which of the following quotations best expresses the main idea of the story?
   (a) "Have you really never been to a ball before, Leila? But, my child, how too weird—"
   (b) And because they were all laughing, it seemed to Leila that they were all lovely.
   (c) It sounded terribly true. Was this first ball only the beginning of her last ball after all?
   (d) "Do I remember the bright little face? Is it known to me of yore?"

Details

2. Leila goes to the dance with   (a) her parents   (b) her brothers and sisters   (c) her neighbors   (d) her cousins.

3. The dance is held in   (a) a hall   (b) the country   (c) a barn
   (d) a nightclub.

4. The Sheridans reveal their kindness by   (a) dancing with
   Leila   (b) seeing that her card is filled   (c) getting her ices
   (d) sitting out the dances with her.

5. Which one of the following statements is not true?
   (a) Previously, Leila had danced only with girls as partners.
   (b) Leila has no difficulty in filling her program.
   (c) Leila dances poorly.
   (d) Leila reveals to her partners that this is her first formal
   dance.

Inferences

6. When the first dance ends, Leila's partner has little to say because   (a) he is too busy eating   (b) he is indifferent
   (c) Leila doesn't try to make conversation   (d) Leila wants
   him to leave quickly.

Cause and Effect

7. Her elderly partner almost spoils the dance for Leila by
   (a) stepping on her dress   (b) making a spectacle of himself
   (c) telling her that she too will be old someday   (d) telling
   her about her mother.

8. After dancing with the elderly partner, Leila   (a) wants to go
   home   (b) feels contented   (c) pities him   (d) quarrels
   with him.

Order of Events

9. Arrange the items in the order in which they occurred. Use
   letters only.
   A. The basket of programs arrives.
   B. Laura agrees to dance the third and ninth with her brother.
   C. Meg asks the other girls to keep an eye on Leila.
   D. Leila does not recognize the elderly man.
   E. Leila samples the refreshments.

Outcomes

10. The elderly man in the story   (a) takes Leila home
    (b) serves as a contrast to Leila   (c) tells others about Leila
    (d) is her escort at the dinner.

Words in Context

1. Oh, dear, how hard it was to be *indifferent* like the others!
   Indifferent (270) means   (a) excited   (b) unconcerned
   (c) talkative   (d) beautiful.

2. But every single thing was so new and exciting . . . Meg's
   tuberoses, Jose's long loop of amber.
   Tuberoses (270) means   (a) flowers   (b) dress   (c) hairdo
   (d) makeup.

3. It even gave her a *pang.*
   Pang (270) means   (a) satisfaction   (b) sharp pain   (c) a
   feeling of jealousy   (d) sense of security.

4. And the rush of longing she had to be sitting on the *veranda* . . .
   Veranda (272) means   (a) porch   (b) living   room
   (c) foyer   (d) formal sitting room.

5. She clutched her fan, and gazing at . . . the red carpet and *gilt*
   chairs . . .
   Gilt (272) means   (a) covered   (b) delicately   carved
   (c) gold-colored   (d) high-backed.

6. Leila was most *fervent.*
   Fervent (273) means   (a) enthusiastic   (b) in   tears
   (c) shouting   (d) overcome.

7. He *wheezed* faintly as he steered her past an awkward couple.
   Wheezed (274)   means   (a) smiled   (b) frowned
   (c) squeezed her hand   (d) breathed aloud.

8. But deep inside her a little girl threw her *pinafore* over her
   head and sobbed.
   Pinafore (275) means   (a) outer coat   (b) large handkerchief   (c) apron-like garment   (d) small blanket.

9. . . . very *haughtily* she put her arm on his sleeve.
   Haughtily (276) means   (a) proudly   (b) quickly
   (c) slowly   (d) cautiously.

10.   . . . she smiled at him more *radiantly* than ever.
   Radiantly (276)   means   (a) gloomily   (b) joyously
   (c) reluctantly   (d) purposely.

Thinking About the Story

1.   How did the Sheridans show that they understood how Leila
   felt? Were they overprotective or did they give her a chance to
   learn—and grow? Explain. How would you have treated her if
   she were your charge?

2.   Formal dances have many conventions. What were some of the
   customs that Leila had learned to expect? How do the customs
   of the dance that Leila attended compare with those of formal
   dances of today? Have the changes been for the better? Explain.

3.   Not knowing the conventions is so important! What mistakes
   did Leila make when talking to her partners, mistakes that more
   experienced party-goers avoid? Reread the dialogs on pages
   273–275. How should she have responded to her partners' open-
   ers? Why wasn't she more aware? Why weren't the partners
   more aware?

4.   The fat older man is in sharp contrast to Leila. Why did she feel
   that he spoiled the evening for her? Who has the more realistic
   attitude toward the dance, Leila or he? Why doesn't Leila even
   recognize the fat man when she is dancing with her next partner? Why did he tell her what he did? Since he feels the way he
   does, why does he attend the dance?

5.   Although the time and place are different, going to a dance can
   be just as momentous today. How did your experiences at your
   first dance compare with Leila's? Did your friends or relatives
   play the same role for you that the Sheridans played for Leila?
   Were you as serious as Leila, or were you as carefree as some
   of the other characters in the story? Which is the better attitude
   to have? Explain.

The Party

Herman Wouk

♦ There, it was done. The ardent look which went
with these words made them a plain declaration
of love. Lucille rewarded him by timidly putting
her little hand into his and returning his look of
tenderness. What were golden thrones or underground palaces now, compared to the rosy glory
of this moment?

Childhood crushes seldom last, but while they do, they can
be intense. This is the story of Herbie Bookbinder, captain of the
school patrol, daydreamer, and devoted lover . . . in his imagination. Herbie is potentially one of the great lovers of history, but
the course of true love seldom runs smooth. The reason for Herbie's downfall is unique in all the history of romantic love, as you
will soon discover.

"The Party" deals with events of several generations ago. You
will smile at the fuss over silk stockings and short pants. You will
chuckle at the fuss made over an automobile, when automobiles
were not so commonplace. You will recognize in this a delightful
period piece, but you will also recognize human truths.

Tragic young love is the subject of Shakespeare's *Romeo and
Juliet.* Mark Twain's *Tom Sawyer* describes the young love of Tom
and Becky. Classics like Booth Tarkington's *Penrod* show a young
person's romantic fantasies. The subject is, of course, an important element in the latest teenage novels. All these show young
people in love, or at least in love with the idea of love. Herbie
Bookbinder joins an illustrious company.

THE PARTY

Herbie stood before a mirror in his room the following Sunday, preening and preening and preening himself for a visit to Lucille Glass's home.

He had been at work on himself for an hour. It was not in the matter of washing that his new zeal had broken forth. No, Mrs. Bookbinder had compelled him to take off his tie after he had retied it ten times, and had gone over his neck and ears with a soapy washcloth. After submitting to this indignity, which he regarded as an adult superstition, Herbert went through all the tie trouble again, and then shifted his efforts to his thick curly black hair. He parted it once, twice, a half-dozen times, and each time rejected the result, because of a stray strand that crossed the white line, or because of a tiny jaggedness here or there, or because the part seemed too low or too high. On an ordinary school day, one swipe with a comb was the rule. Two made him feel noble. Three meant that he was in trouble with his teacher and was making a mighty effort to please.

The cause of all this care, an invitation engraved on thick white paper, was propped before him on the dresser:

Mr. and Mrs. Louis Glass

cordially invite you

to their Housewarming

at 2645 Mosholu Parkway, the Bronx

1 p.m., Sunday, May 15th

R.S.V.P.

At the bottom of the sheet these words were added by hand: "There will be a children's party in the playroom, and Lucille cordially invites Felicia and Herbie to attend."

This first visit to an actual Private House, a structure raised by man for only one family to inhabit, would in itself have been a marvel. But happening in this way, it was dwarfed by a vaster event. He was going to spend a whole real-life afternoon with his underground queen.

Herbie reigned each night before falling asleep in a splendid imaginary palace which he had discovered one night by falling through a trapdoor (in imagination) in the floor of the old "haunted house" on Tennyson Avenue—a device borrowed from *Alice in Wonderland* without acknowledgment. The girls with whom he was smitten succeeded one another as queen of this subterranean pleasure dome. Diana Vernon had been dethroned. Lucille's coronation, a spectacle of incredible magnificence, had already taken place, and she now held court nightly beside him.

But it was not only in such fantasies that he had seen her. There had been several meetings on the third-floor landing of the girls' staircase at P.S. 50 since the first one. In the entire maze of the school, that landing was the one space Captain Bookbinder never failed to inspect daily at lunch time, and of all possible posts along six flights of the girls' staircase, it was the one area that Policewoman Glass deemed most likely to be the scene of an outbreak of crime. These two guardians of the law therefore managed to greet each other daily. The conversations were brief and weak. Herbie was rendered speechless by romance—an unlucky foible, since nothing else had the same effect on him except acute tonsillitis.

The strange part was that he found no difficulty at all in having long, tender talks with Lucille when they sat on their golden double throne under the haunted house, eating chocolate frappés on silver salvers and carelessly viewing the gorgeous pageants staged in the great hall for their amusement (the pageants, except for the quantity of gold, diamonds, rubies, and silk in the costumes, were very much like the vaudeville shows at Loew's Boulevard). He not only managed brilliant chatter for himself but also invented the queen's affectionate answers. Something about the light of day, the matter-of-fact iron and concrete of the staircase, and the girl's appearance in street clothes instead of a robe of state, dried up his eloquence.

As he combed and recombed his hair, he pictured himself

strolling with Lucille in the gardens of 2645 Mosholu Parkway, an
edifice he had never seen. From the grand sound of the words
"Mosholu Parkway," he imagined it to be something like an English
castle in the movies. There, under arching old trees, amid the flower
beds, deliciously alone, could Herbie and Lucille fail to come at last
to the sweet mutual pledges of love?

It suddenly struck Herbert that he would look older if he
combed his hair straight back without a part, as Lennie Krieger
did. He tried the experiment. The result appeared so strange to him
that he hastily erased it with the comb. He next attempted, for the
first time in his life, a part on the right side of his face instead of
the left. This was hard to do, because the heavy hair, trained in one
direction, sprang back from under the comb and stood up defiantly
in the middle of his head. By soaking it with water he succeeded in
bending it to his will, and surveyed the outcome with satisfaction.
It seemed to give his face a new dignity which added years.

In his mother's bedroom he could hear the silk-stockings con-
troversy raging. Since the hour of the arrival of the invitation, Felicia had been waging a campaign for her first pair of ladies' ho-
siery. The two-year advantage in age she had over Lucille Glass
made her feel that she had been insulted by being asked to "a baby's
party," and although she was perishing to go, she felt she could not
appear at 2645 Mosholu Parkway without some token of her mature
years. With silk stockings on, she reasoned, she could carelessly
wander into the playroom and consume all the ice cream, cake, and
candy that came to her hand, in the guise of a kindly visitor from
the adult world.

Now, this was close logic, but Felicia knew that it was not likely
to penetrate the opaque mind of a parent. Her lines of attack on her
mother were three:

1. If I can't wear silk stockings, I *won't go* to the old party, and
   you can't *make* me.
2. Every girl in my class has at least *five* pairs of silk stockings,
   and even kids a year *below* me have them.
3. Herbie gets *everything* in this house, and I get *nothing.*

Mrs. Bookbinder had doggedly held out, because she resisted
by instinct every move of the children toward maturity. She knew
that in the end Felicia would go to the party in rubber rompers if

necessary. But with all her edge of experience, insight, and authority, she made a slip that cost her the victory.

Felicia howled, "Why, why, *why* can't I wear silk stockings?"

The mother answered, "Felicia, for the last time, it's too late now to argue. The stores are closed today, and I can't buy the stockings anyway."

Felicia pounced. "I can borrow a pair from Emily."

"They won't fit."

"Oh, won't they?"

The girl flashed open a lower drawer of the dresser, and from under a pile of her blouses pulled out a pair of the sheer hose. Before the astonished parent could protest, she kicked off her slippers and pulled the stockings on, saying rapidly, "I borrowed them Friday, just in case. I wasn't going to wear them without your permission. But do they fit or don't they? Look. Look!" She jumped up and pirouetted. They fitted.

"Well, anyway, Papa won't stand for it," said the trapped mother.

"I'll go ask him. Whatever he says goes. All right?" The girl was at the door of the bedroom, on her way to the parlor, where her father was poring over *Refrigerating Engineering.*

To have her veto overridden was a worst defeat for the mother than plain surrender, and she knew it. Dialogues between the children and the father always went so:

CHILD: Pa, can I do so-and-so?
FATHER: I'm busy. Ask your mother.
CHILD: She says it's up to you.
FATHER: Oh. (*Brief glance at the child, standing by him humbly with a winning smile.*) I guess so, yes.
CHILD: (*Top of lungs*) Ma! Pa says it's all right.

He had thus given consent even to things of which he later disapproved, growling, when the mother cited his permission, "Well, why do you send them to me?"

Mrs. Bookbinder said, "Never mind. You can wear them, just this once, and you'll return them in the morning."

The girl hugged her mother, agreeing with joyous hypocrisy. Her foot was inside the door of grownup life at last, and she knew she would not be driven out again by fire or bayonet. Nor was she. From that day forward she wore silk stockings.

Half past twelve, and the family assembled in the parlor for a final review before leaving.

"Herbert, there's something funny about the way you look." The mother examined him up and down, and her eyes finally came to rest on his hair. "What is it?"

The boy quickly put his cake-eater hat on. "Nothing, Mom. I'm just dressed up."

"Take your hat off in the house."

The boy reluctantly obeyed.

"Papa, can you tell what it is?"

The father inspected him. "He looks older, somehow. What's the difference? Let's go."

At the word "older," Herbert felt all warm inside, as though he had drunk wine.

"Ma, I see what it is," cried Felicia, and giggled. "He's parted his hair on the wrong side. Isn't that silly?"

"All right for you, Silk Stockings," snarled Herbert. In a red flash he considered informing his mother that Felicia had bought, not borrowed, the hose, with nickels and dimes fished out of her pig bank with a bread knife, but talebearing revolted him. "What's the difference which side I part it on, anyway?" he appealed to his parents.

"As long as it makes no difference, go back and comb it the right way," said the mother.

Mrs. Bookbinder was fertile in these argumentative dead ends. Herbert slunk off muttering, and combed away precious years of ripeness, but not before he had postured before the mirror for a couple of minutes, boiling at the injustice that forced him to mar the handsome world-weary effect he had stumbled on.

As soon as the secondhand Chevrolet that was the official car of the Bronx River Ice Company brought the family to 2645 Mosholu Parkway, Herbie began revising his plans of gallantry. The kiss in the garden was definitely not practical. The Glass castle was a two-story redbrick house, flanked on either side by similar castles, with only narrow cement driveways separating them. The garden consisted of two squares of grass on either side of the entrance, each about as large as the carpet in the Bookbinder parlor. The little hedges surrounding these compressed meadows would not have provided enough privacy for a pair of romantically inclined cats.

"What a dump!" said Felicia, with ladylike tugs through her skirt at the tops of her stockings, which were tending to slide down her bony legs.

"Don't you dare say anything like that! It isn't polite," cried Mrs. Bookbinder. "And don't you dare fool with those stockings when anybody is looking."

Herbie, whose disappointment quickly melted in the anticipation of seeing Lucille, could hardly breathe as he ran up the white plaster steps and rang the bell. He managed to say thickly to Felicia, "Bet it's a rotten party."

"Oh, sure," sneered the sister, "you don't want to see that red-headed infant. Not much. I hope they have a team of horses to pull you through the door."

So when Lucille opened the door Herbie's face was red, but not nearly as red as the girl's instantly became under his intense, devouring look of admiration. And Felicia's face was reddest of all when, as the children entered the house, Herbie glanced back into Felicia's eyes, then at her legs, and burst out laughing.

Lucille Glass, eleven years old, her parents' spoiled darling, was also wearing silk stockings.

The children's party was at its full fury when the Bookbinders came. The basement of the Glass home, gaily decorated and finished as a game room, echoed with squeals, shouts, laughter, complaints, and clatter. Large piles of delicatessen sandwiches were vanishing under the onslaught of fifteen or twenty hungry children, and two temporary maids and a harassed aunt of Lucille were trying to serve ice cream and cake on paper plates amid a tangle of clutching hands and glittering eyes. The parents were feeding upstairs in the placid manner of well-broken-in human beings, while their young cavorted below like pygmies around a kill. Fortunately, there was much too much icecream for everyone, and it was not long before the clamor began to subside, the hands to cease clutching, and the glitter to fade slowly into a glaze.

Herbie emerged from the basement washroom in a happy fog, water seeping down the sides of his face from his hair, which he had plastered back again with the wrong side parted. He was in Lucille Glass's home. He had shaken her hand. He had sat beside

her on a sofa for ten minutes, eating corned-beef sandwiches and
no more aware of the taste than if he had been chewing straw. The
girl, in her blue and white party dress, with a white bow in her hair,
seemed not of this world, but a changeling fallen from a star. Time
had slowed down as in dreams. He had been at the party sixty minutes, but it was like a week of ordinary living. There stretched ahead
the rich years and years before five o'clock when he would have to
go home.

Lucille emerged from the knot of children at the table and came
to him with two plates of chocolate ice cream in her hands. "You
almost missed this," she said. "Want some?"

He took the plate gratefully and was digging the paper spoon
into the sweet brown mound when she laid her hand for a moment
shyly on his arm. "Don't eat it here," she said. "Come where it's
quiet." She slipped away, threading through the crowded basement, and he followed, wondering. They passed Felicia and Lennie
near the table wolfing huge chunks of a white cake, and Herbie tried
to avoid them, but the sharp-eyed sister called out, "When's the
wedding, Herbie?" and Lennie graciously added, "Hooray for the
sheik in short pants." (His own trousers were long.) Herbie said
nothing, and hurried out through the little door at the back where
Lucille had disappeared.

To his astonishment he was in a gloomy garage. Lucille climbed
into the back seat of her father's new Chrysler and beckoned him
to follow. Herbie had never been in any kind of automobile but a
Chevrolet, and as he sat down on the soft gray upholstery he became dizzy with pleasure. Ice cream, cool dimness, solitude, a
Chrysler, and Lucille! The world of fact was uncovering its treasures, and all his daydreams seemed tawdry. The underground palace crumbled in his mind.

The children ate their ice cream slowly.

"What are you going to be when you grow up?" said Lucille at
last, putting her well-cleaned paper plate and spoon on the floor.

"An astronomer," said Herbie.

"You mean look at the stars through a telescope?"

"That's right. I can pick out first-magnitude stars right now. I'll
show them to you some night."

"What are their names?"

"Well, there's lots. Orion, Sirius, Betelgeuse, Andromeda, Gem-
ini . . ." He paused. Herbie did much reading about stars, but very

little looking at them. The figures of their sizes and distances fascinated him, but they all looked pretty nearly alike in the sky, and anyway, they were none too visible beyond the street lights of Homer Avenue. He was not sure of the difference between a star and a constellation and was fairly confident that his listener wasn't either, so he reeled off any names out of the jumble he remembered. It worked.

"Gee, those names are beautiful."

"I know lots more."

"Can you make money that way?" asked the girl. "Just looking at stars?"

"Sure. Plenty."

"Enough to get married and have a family?"

"Easy."

The girl pondered for a moment, then said doubtfully, "How?"

Herbie hadn't the least idea. But he was not the first male to be challenged by a woman's common sense, nor the first to override it. "By discovering new stars, of course," he said promptly.

"Then what happens?" inquired the girl.

"Why, you win a prize," said Herbie.

"How much?"

"I forget. A million dollars—maybe ten million. Something like that."

"For *one* star?"

"I'll show it to you in the encyclopedia if you don't believe me," said Herbie. "What can a guy do that's more important than finding a new star?"

Lucille was convinced, and silenced. There was a pause.

"This is a swell car," said Herbie. The remark fell into the silence like a stone into a pond and vanished, leaving ripples of self-consciousness in the air. The boy and girl happened to look into each other's eyes. Both blushed.

"Are you—are you going to get married?" said Lucille.

"Not till I'm old," said Herbie.

"How old?"

"Real old."

"How old is that?"

"I don't know."

"Twenty-five?"

"Older than that."

"Thirty?"

"Fifty-five, more likely," said Herbie. The tendency to go higher was irresistible. Lucille seemed properly awed at being in the presence of a man who was not going to marry until he was fifty-five. She was still for a moment, then said, "Have you got a girl?"

"No," said Herbie. "Have you got a fellow?"

"No. What kind of girl are you going to marry?"

"I don't know," said Herbie. Then, with a burst of audacious gallantry, "But she's gonna have to have red hair!"

There, it was done. The ardent look which went with these words made them a plain declaration of love. Lucille rewarded him by timidly putting her little hand into his and returning his look of tenderness. What were golden thrones or underground palaces now, compared to the rosy glory of this moment? Here in an attached garage was a corner of heaven, upholstered in gray. Herbert had not known there was room for such swelling bliss in his heart.

But the tenderness was fading from Lucille's glance. She was no longer gazing into his eyes, but above them.

"Gosh! Lookit your hair," she said.

Herbert put his hand to his head and felt his hair still damp, standing away from his scalp, straight up. Ten minutes of drying and it was full of fight again, thrusting back toward its old place. Herbie pressed it down. It sprang back erect, like good turf. Twice he did this, and an awful thing happened. Lucille Glass giggled.

"That's funny, the way it jumps up," she said.

"Aw, it's nothing. I can fix it," stammered Herbie, and began thrusting the locks downward, palm over palm. Drops of water ran down his forehead from under his fingers. In effect he was pressing his hair dry. When he stopped at last and took his hands away, the hair rose, and stood straight out in all directions. He looked somewhat like a boy being electrocuted. Lucille fell back in the seat, exploding with laughter, her hands over her mouth. Herbie wiped his oozing palms on his breeches, and muttering, "Dunno what's wrong with this crazy old mop," he began to comb his hair furiously with his fingers. This frantic clawing at his head looked extremely strange.

An unwelcome voice spoke through the car window: "What's the matter, Fatso? Got cooties?"

Lennie Krieger and Felicia were grinning through the glass.

"My clever brother," said Felicia. "Combs his hair on the wrong side 'cause he thinks it makes him look older. How you doing, Grandpa?"

Herbie's cheeks were on fire. He turned with a feeble smile to Lucille, but he saw only her back as she clambered out of the car. "Auntie must be screaming for me," she said and was gone.

Back before a mirror in the bathroom once more, Herbie fumed and agonized as he put his treacherous hair to rights. He blamed Felicia for the blasted afternoon, blamed Lennie, blamed his mother, blamed everyone and everything except himself. He murmured aloud, "I'll show 'em! I'll get even! Try to make a fool out of *me*, will they?" and lashed himself into such a state of indignation at a plotting world that he soon felt much better.

Not for long, though. When he stepped out into the party room, he was surprised and sickened. In the middle of a circle of children, Lennie Krieger was dancing with Lucille to music from a radio. The little girl's movements were stiff, and her face intently serious, as she followed the adept boy's steps. Herbie joined the circle and heard the low comments—envious and jeering from the boys, admiring from the girls—and tasted the gall of jealousy. He tried to catch Lucille's eye. Once she looked at him with unseeing gravity as though he were a piece of furniture, and spun away. Felicia came to his side and said, "Hello, sheik," but the heart was not in her spite, for she was suffering, too. Lennie was her admirer, and snubbing him was the food of her feminine nature, but for once he had snubbed her when the music started, to ask the "baby" to dance.

A game of pin-the-tail-on-the-donkey was next played. Herbie, blindfolded, fell over a chair on his face, and caused roars of merriment. When Lennie's turn came he worked loose the bandage on his eyes, pretended to grope to the donkey, and pinned the tail squarely where it belonged, to great applause. Herbie detected the cheat, but felt powerless to do anything about it. They played a number of kissing games under the watchful eye of the aunt. Somehow it happened that Lennie kissed Lucille three times and she kissed him twice. Herbie only had one chance to do any kissing, and then it fell to his lot to kiss Felicia. It was a thoroughly ghastly afternoon. And when, at a quarter to five, Herbie managed to corner the red-headed girl, and whispered, "Come on back out in the garage a minute," she froze him with, "I can't. I promised to show Lennie my camp pictures," and dashed away.

From the demeanor of the four members of the Bookbinder family when they rode home, 2645 Mosholu Parkway might have been the address of Woodlawn Cemetery. Jacob Bookbinder broke the bleak silence once to say, "If you ask me, Louis Glass is being paid by Powers to say the blue paper is no good—" but his wife said, "Please. Even in front of the children do we need to discuss it?" No further sound was heard, except the rattling song of the Chevrolet, until it drew to a stop on Homer Avenue.

As she opened the door, Mrs. Bookbinder said to the children in the back seat, "Why so quiet? Did you enjoy the party?"

"Party!" sniffed Felicia. "Please, Mom, don't drag me to any more nurseries."

Herbie said nothing. He was already out of the car, on his way to the highest rock in the vacant lot, where he often sought solitude. There in the sunset he undertook some emergency repair work. For an hour he tried to rebuild the ruins of the underground palace, but it was wrecked forever. Nothing was left but its queen, and she no longer wore crown and robe, but a white bow and a party frock. And he could not even compel her to sit by his side. Her faithless Majesty went on and on dancing with Lennie.

Understanding the Story _____

Main Idea

1. Which of the following best expresses the main idea of the
   story?
   (a) The Bookbinder family was an unusually close family.
   (b) The daydreams of youth are sometimes shattered by reality.
   (c) Lucille Glass was unnecessarily cruel in her treatment of
   Herbie.
   (d) The relationship of Felicia and Herbie was an example of
   family rivalry.

Details

2. Herbie confesses that he will lose his heart to a girl   (a) like
   Felicia   (b) who lives in Brooklyn   (c) with red hair
   (d) like her mother.

3. The party is held in   (a) a rented ballroom   (b) an apartment house   (c) the basement of a school   (d) a private
   house.

4. Lucille and Herbie have their heart-to-heart talk   (a) in a garage   (b) in the cellar   (c) in a schoolroom   (d) upstairs
   with the adults.

5. Herbie parts his hair on the other side to   (a) please his
   mother   (b) conceal a scar   (c) look older   (d) annoy Felicia.

Inferences

6. Felicia is allowed to wear silk stockings as the result of
   (a) her mother's pride in her daughter   (b) an oversight on
   her brother's part   (c) her father's annoyance at Herbie
   (d) a clever campaign she waged.

7. In talking about astronomy, Herbie actually   (a) doesn't
   know as much as he pretends   (b) does not try to impress
   Lucille   (c) is an expert   (d) shows that he has often looked
   at the stars.

8. For Herbie the party proves to be a (a) reminder of his last party   (b) disappointment   (c) moderate success   (d) triumph.

9. Actually, the silk stockings (a) belonged to Mrs. Bookbinder   (b) had been bought in advance   (c) were an inferior type of stocking   (d) cost Herbie a week's allowance.

10. Herbie has met Lucille on the third-floor landing   (a) by accident   (b) because of the principal's assignment   (c) to see her every day   (d) to ask Lucille to the party.

Order of Events

11. Arrange the items in the order in which they occurred. Use letters only.
    A. Felicia persuades her parents to allow her to wear silk stockings.
    B. Herbie and Lucille have a heart-to-heart talk.
    C. Lucille tells Herbie she's going to show Lennie her camp pictures.
    D. Herbie works on his hair for an hour.
    E. The Bookbinders arrive at the Glasses' house.

Outcomes

12. If Herbie's hair had stayed down,   (a) Felicia would have rejoiced   (b) Herbie would have been unhappy   (c) the children would not have played games   (d) Lucille would not have laughed.

Cause and Effect

13. A major part of Herbie's problem was   (a) trying to look older   (b) arguing with his mother   (c) forgetting to talk to Lucille   (d) taking sides in the argument over silk stockings.

Fact or Opinion

Tell whether each of the following is a fact or an opinion.

14. Lucille was the most beautiful girl at the party.

15. To impress Lucille, Herbie made up astronomical information.

Words in Context _____

1. Herbie stood before a mirror . . . *preening himself* for a visit
    to Lucille Glass's home.
    Preening himself (281) means   (a) inviting   (b) dressing
    with care   (c) hurrying   (d) arriving.

2. After submitting to this *indignity* . . . Herbert went through all
    the tie trouble again.
    Indignity   (281)   means   (a) remark   (b) insult
    (c) repetition   (d) joking.

3. The girls with whom he was *smitten* succeeded one another as
    queen of this *subterranean* pleasure dome.
    Smitten (282) means   (a) afraid of   (b) acquainted
    (c) having a crush on   (d) going to school with.

4. *Subterranean* (282) means   (a) magnificent   (b) secret
    (c) well-fortified   (d) subtle.

5. It was the one area that Policewoman Glass *deemed* most likely
    to be the scene of an outbreak of crime.
    Deemed   (282)   means   (a) considered   (b) boasted
    (c) required   (d) referred to as.

6. Herbie was rendered speechless by romance—an unlucky
    foible.
    Foible   (282)   means   (a) accident   (b) acquaintance
    (c) weakness   (d) story.

7. Their young *cavorted* below like pygmies around a kill.
    Cavorted (286) means   (a) yelled   (b) romped   (c) dressed
    (d) ate.

8. The world of fact was uncovering its treasures, and all his day-
    dreams seemed *tawdry.*
    Tawdry (287) means   (a) bright and sparkling   (b) dull and
    gloomy   (c) cheap and showy   (d) bitter and cruel.

9. Then, with a burst of *audacious gallantry,* "But she's gonna
    have to have red hair!"
    Audacious gallantry (289) means   (a) fierce pride   (b) bold
    courtesy   (c) daring rudeness   (d) quiet humility.

10. From the *demeanor* of the four members of the Bookbinder
    family when they rode home, 2645 Mosholu Parkway might
    have been the address of Woodlawn Cemetery.
    Demeanor (291) means   (a) nastiness   (b) pride   (c) haste
    (d) behavior.

Thinking About the Story

1. Many things have changed since the time described in the story. Many customs are different now. Point out differences between then and now. Consider such things as dress and parent-child relationships.

2. One of Herbie's greatest problems is his self-consciousness. Why do young people tend to be excessively self-conscious? How can this feeling be managed or overcome?

3. The relationship between Herbie and his sister Felicia rings true. There does tend to be frequent disagreement between brother and sister (or between any two children in a family). Why does the rivalry arise? Can this rivalry be beneficial? Harmful? Explain.

4. How does the author show his descriptive skill, as well as his understanding of human nature, in his description of the party? The preparation for the party? The attitude of the Bookbinders toward the party? The behavior of the children?

5. What kind of person is Herbie? Describe him. Tell whether you think he is a "typical" boy. If you have read *Tom Sawyer*, compare Herbie with Tom. ("The Party" is a chapter from *City Boy*. If you enjoyed the story, you'll be delighted with the other adventures of the Bookbinder family.)

6. In a sound, classic short story, there are six important elements:
    a. Situation. Somebody wants something or is dissatisfied with things as they are.
    b. Complication. Something gets in the way of that satisfaction.
    c. Conflict. Because of the complication, there is a conflict, the heart of a short story. Difficulties bother the main character.
    d. Development. One incident follows another, as the plot unfolds.
    e. Climax. Matters come to a head. At the climax, the reader begins to sense the ending.
    f. Outcome. Matters are resolved. The main character does or does not get satisfaction from events.

    Identify the six important elements in "The Party."

The Chaser

John Collier

♦ "Do you mean it is a poison?" cried Alan, very much horrified.

"Call it cleaning fluid if you like," said the old man indifferently. "Lives need cleaning. Call it a spot-remover . . . "

"The Chaser" is another love story—with a difference! It opens, as is typical for a John Collier story, with a most ordinary setting. Two men meet to transact some business. They come together in a drab, bare office in the older part of town. Both men are willing, and the deal is quickly completed.

But surprise! The trap has been sprung. With his usual mixture of understatement—and horror—the author has combined the tender yearning of young love with the grim reality of the perfect weapon for murder.

Whether the title "The Chaser" means the young man's hunt for a solution to his present misery or the ultimate solution as offered by the old man, the ending of this story gives the reader chilling afterthoughts—a chaser after reading the story—that will continue to haunt long after you have read this seemingly simple story. The twist in the last sentence is sufficient to make you a John Collier fan forever!

THE CHASER

Alan Austen, as nervous as a kitten, went up certain dark and creaky stairs in the neighborhood of Pell Street, and peered about for a long time on the dim landing before he found the name he wanted written obscurely on one of the doors.

He pushed open this door, as he had been told to do, and found himself in a tiny room, which contained no furniture but a plain kitchen table, rocking chair, and an ordinary chair. On one of the dirty buff-colored walls were a couple of shelves, containing in all perhaps a dozen bottles and jars.

An old man sat in the rocking chair, reading a newspaper. Alan, without a word, handed him the card he had been given. "Sit down, Mr. Austen," said the old man very politely. "I am glad to make your acquaintance."

"Is it true," asked Alan, "that you have a certain mixture that has—er—quite extraordinary effects?"

"My dear sir," replied the old man, "my stock in trade is not very large—I don't deal in laxatives and teething mixtures—but such as it is, it is varied. I think nothing I sell has effects which could be precisely described as ordinary."

"Well, the fact is—" began Alan.

"Here, for example," interrupted the old man reaching for a bottle from the shelf. "Here is a liquid as colorless as water, almost tasteless, quite imperceptible in coffee, milk, wine, or any other beverage. It is also quite imperceptible to any known method of autopsy."

"Do you mean it is a poison?" cried Alan, very much horrified.

"Call it cleaning fluid if you like," said the old man indifferently. "Lives need cleaning. Call it a spot-remover. 'Out, damned spot!' Eh? 'Out, brief candle!' "

"I want nothing of that sort," said Alan.

"Probably it is just as well," said the old man. "Do you know the price of this? For one teaspoonful, which is sufficient, I ask five thousand dollars. Never less. Not a penny less."

"I hope all your mixtures are not as expensive," said Alan apprehensively.

"Oh, dear, no," said the old man. "It would be no good charging that sort of price for a love potion, for example. Young people who need a love potion very seldom have five thousand dollars. Otherwise they would not need a love potion."

"I'm glad to hear you say so," said Alan.

"I look at it like this," said the old man. "Please a customer with one article, and he will come back when he needs another. Even if it *is* more costly. He will save up for it, if necessary."

"So," said Alan, "you really do sell love potions?"

"If I did not sell love potions," said the old man, reaching for another bottle, "I should not have mentioned the other matter to you. It is only when one is in a position to oblige that one can afford to be so confidential."

"And these potions," said Alan. "They are not just—just—er—"

"Oh, no," said the old man. "Their effects are permanent, and extend far beyond the mere casual impulse. But they include it. Oh yes, they include it. Bountifully. Insistently. Everlastingly."

"Dear me!" said Alan, attempting a look of scientific detachment. "How very interesting!"

"But consider the spiritual side," said the old man.

"I do, indeed," said Alan.

"For indifference," said the old man, "they substitute devotion. For scorn, adoration. Give one tiny measure of this to the young lady—its flavor is imperceptible in orange juice, soup, or cocktails—and however fun-loving and giddy she is, she will change altogether. She'll want nothing but solitude, and you."

"I can hardly believe it," said Alan. "She is so fond of parties."

"She will not like them any more," said the old man. "She'll be afraid of the pretty girls you may meet."

"She'll actually be jealous?" cried Alan in a rapture. "Of me?"

"Yes, she will want to be everything to you."

"She is, already. Only she doesn't care about it."

"She will, when she has taken this. She will care intensely. You'll be her sole interest in life."

"Wonderful!" cried Alan.

"She'll want to know all you do," said the old man. "All that has happened to you during the day. Every word of it. She'll want to know what you are thinking about, why you smile suddenly, why you are looking sad."

"That is love!" cried Alan.

"Yes," said the old man. "How carefully she'll look after you! She'll never allow you to be tired, to sit in a draft, to neglect your food. If you are an hour late, she'll be terrified. She'll think you are killed, or that some siren has caught you."

"I can hardly imagine Diana like that!" cried Alan.

"You will not have to use your imagination," said the old man. "And by the way, since there are always sirens, if by any chance you *should*, later on, slip a little, you need not worry. She will forgive you, in the end. She'll be terribly hurt, of course, but she'll forgive you—in the end."

"That will not happen," said Alan fervently.

"Of course not," said the old man. "But, if it does, you need not worry. She'll never divorce you. Oh, no! And, of course, she herself will never give you the least grounds for—not divorce, of course—but even uneasiness."

"And how much," said Alan, "how much is this wonderful mixture?"

"It is not so dear," said the old man, "as the spot-remover, as I think we agreed to call it. No. That is five thousand dollars; never a penny less. One has to be older than you are, to indulge in that sort of thing. One has to save up for it."

"But the love potion?" said Alan.

"Oh, that," said the old man, opening the drawer in the kitchen table, and taking out a tiny, rather dirty-looking vial. "That is just a dollar."

"I can't tell you how grateful I am," said Alan, watching him fill it.

"I like to oblige," said the old man. "Then customers come back, later in life, when they are rather better off, and want more expensive things. Here you are. You will find it very effective."

"Thank you again," said Alan. "Good-bye."

"*Au revoir,*" said the old man.

Understanding the Story ⸺⸺⸺

Main Idea

1. The main idea of this story is that   (a) love can be made to last for a lifetime   (b) the love a young man desires can destroy the relationship between older people   (c) chemicals can create and modify love   (d) love potions are inexpensive.

Inference

2. Alan Austen has come to the small office because he is (a) looking for excitement   (b) desperate   (c) wealthy (d) angry.

3. The very effective love potion that Alan buys does not (a) make a person permanently in love with another (b) change indifference to romantic love   (c) make the loved one give up friends   (d) change the buyer's affection.

Details

4. The author does *not* describe   (a) how Alan felt when he paid for the potion   (b) the appearance of both men   (c) the appearance of the office   (d) the container for the love potion.

5. The old man calls the expensive potion a cleaning fluid because it   (a) has   many   uses   (b) removes   people (c) removes affection   (d) improves life for both lover and loved one.

6. All of the following are true except   (a) Alan is afraid that he will lose the girl he loves   (b) the old man sells a limited number of drugs   (c) Alan does not question the effectiveness of the potion   (d) Alan is not told the name of the expensive drug.

7. The love potion is low in price because the old man   (a) is sympathetic toward poor lovers   (b) expects a later purchase   (c) sells so much of it   (d) knows it is inexpensive to make.

Order of Events

8. Arrange the items in the order in which they occurred. Use letters only.
   A. Alan decides to buy the love potion.

B. Alan may have to decide what to do with $5000.
C. Alan falls in love.
D. Alan meets the old man.
E. Alan is ignored by Diana.

Cause and Effect

9. Which of the following is *not* true of the love potion?
    (a) It destroys the receiver's independence.
    (b) It changes the receiver's personality.
    (c) It is administered in one dose.
    (d) It leads to mutual respect and trust.

Outcome

10. By giving Alan the quality of love he expects from Diana, the old man anticipates   (a) that Alan will recommend other customers   (b) that Alan will live happily ever after   (c) that Diana will come to him for a potion for Alan   (d) that Alan will be dissatisfied in time.

Words in Context

1. He found the name he wanted written *obscurely* on one of the doors.
   Obscurely (297) means   (a) carelessly   (b) unclearly   (c) in gold letters   (d) in large letters.

2. "Here is a liquid as colorless as water, almost tasteless, quite *imperceptible* in coffee, milk, wine, or any other beverage."
   Imperceptible (297) means   (a) distinct   (b) pleasing   (c) cool   (d) undetectable.

3. "Call it cleaning fluid if you like," said the old man *indifferently*.
   Indifferently (297) means   (a) eagerly   (b) hastily   (c) nonchalantly   (d) slowly.

4. "I hope all your mixtures are not as expensive," said Alan *apprehensively*.
   Apprehensively (298) means   (a) anxiously   (b) loudly   (c) greedily   (d) understandingly.

5. "It would be no good charging that sort of price for a love *potion*."
   Potion (298) means   (a) liquid mixture   (b) deadly poison   (c) magical charm   (d) protective power.

6. "Their effects are permanent, and extend far beyond the mere *casual* impulse."
    Casual (298)   means   (a) deliberate   (b) planned
    (c) infrequent   (d) unplanned.

7. "Oh yes, they include it. *Bountifully.*"
    Bountifully (298) means   (a) fatally   (b) generously abundantly   (c) overly expensively   (d) extremely dangerously.

8. "She'll think you are killed, or that some *siren* has caught you."
    Siren (299) means   (a) police car horn   (b) warning signal
    (c) fire gong   (d) scheming woman.

9. "That will not happen," said Alan *fervently.*
    Fervently (299) means   (a) very gleefully   (b) quietly
    (c) very earnestly   (d) suddenly.

10. "*Au revoir*," said the old man.
    Au revoir (299) means   (a) Good luck   (b) Have a good day
    (c) Until we meet again   (d) Enjoy.

Thinking About the Story

1. Why does Alan turn to the old man for a solution to his problem? Is it fair to Diana, the girl in the story? How far should we go in real life to win the love of another?

2. When did you realize the tie-in sale aspect of the story? When did you realize the evil in the old man? One of the favorite themes of medieval literature was the temptations of Satan. Is this a dated story or could it happen today? Why is Alan oblivious to the one-two danger in his purchase? Would you purchase such a potion? Explain.

3. The old man is a shrewd psychologist. Through his temptations, what traits of Alan's character does the old man expose? Would you find Alan someone you would like to know? Explain.

4. How does the marriage resulting from the first potion compare with your own picture of what an ideal marriage should be like?

5. The last sentence homes in on the message in the story.
    "*Au revoir*," said the old man.
    Is it too obvious or is it the door-opener to horror? Explain.

6. This is a story of sharp contrasts. How did Collier combine these contrasts to achieve a sense of frustration at first and finally a sense of horror? Could this story be converted into an effective TV drama? Explain.

Boy Meets Girl

ACTIVITIES

Thinking About the Stories

1. Which story do you think is the most effective? Why?

2. Which character in these stories would you most like to meet? Give the reasons for your choice.

3. Compare these stories with typical TV situation comedies in respect to novelty of plot, choice of characters, and approach to life.

4. Which scene did you find most humorous? Which scene did you find reveals most of human nature? Explain.

5. How does this group of stories compare with those in the first three sections of the book? Compare the two groups in respect to realism, suspense, interesting characters, and application to the problems of life.

Projects

1. Read one of the stories listed on pages 304–305 and prepare to tell it in class. Rehearse the narration so that the story will hold the interest of your listeners.

2. Choose a newspaper item that could form the basis of a boy-meets-girl story. Be prepared to tell how it might be developed into a short story.

3. Many modern writers, including O. Henry, describe their characters in brief, well-turned phrases. Select two people whom you know, and try to describe them in imitation of O. Henry's style.

4. Write the plot of an original short story based on one of the following.
   (a) My first dance.

(b) I stepped outside my "class" that time.

(c) My first date's father.

(d) They all laughed when I said that I could dance better than anyone else in the group.

(e) A book on etiquette couldn't help me out of this one.

(f) Best friends and dates don't mix.

(g) Who ever thought that going to a movie could become so complicated?

(h) The voice of experience was stilled, and the voice of temptation led me on.

5. Occasionally, actual incidents in real life are climaxed by the kind of surprise ending for which O. Henry's stories are noted. Write the plot of one such incident that you heard about or that happened to you.

Additional Readings

Short Stories

"The Third Ingredient" by O. Henry

> Three people were made happy as the result of the search for an onion.

"Piano" by William Saroyan

> When he sat down to play, she fell more deeply in love with him.

"The Outcasts of Poker Flat" by Bret Harte

> Storms make strange companions.

"Sixteen" by Maureen Daly

> Heartbreak at the telephone.

"The Waltz" by Dorothy Parker

> Reveals the contrast between the girl's thoughts and what she said to her dancing partner.

"Sam Small's Better Half" by Eric Knight

> Sam Small and his better self fight for his better half.

"Early Marriage" by Conrad Richter

A girl of seventeen travels by wagon to meet her bridegroom, 170 miles away.

Novels

Laughing Boy by Oliver LaFarge

An American Indian struggles in vain to learn the ways of his fellow Americans.

Seventeenth Summer by Maureen Daly

Love and a sensitive girl of seventeen.

Seventeen by Booth Tarkington

Fun poked goodnaturedly at the serious young man of seventeen who falls in love with a glamour girl.

Alice Adams by Booth Tarkington

Alice grows up when she realizes that her parents are not wealthy.

Portrait of Jennie by Robert Nathan

The artist falls in love with the strange girl who sits for his masterpiece.

Wuthering Heights by Emily Brontë

The handsome gypsy, Heathcliff, and the well-born Catherine fall in love but cannot marry.

Collections

That Man is Here Again by Arthur Kober

Alibi Ike; You Know Me, Al by Ring Lardner

Runyon à la Carte by Damon Runyon

The Four Million by O. Henry

The Garden Party; Bliss by Katherine Mansfield

5 Courageous Company

At a crisis in life, what makes some people rise to the occasion, move fearlessly ahead, tackle the problems? The newspapers report such incidents with admiration: the passerby who saves an old man from a burning building, the swimmer who risks his own life to save a drowning child. You probably read such stories and wonder, "Would I have done the same?" Only experiencing such an incident will tell.

Courage has many faces. Challenges can be spiritual or physical. Moral courage is as admirable as physical courage. The senator who casts an unpopular vote against his party and his constituents may be as brave as the man who prevents a robbery. Courage—like ambition and loyalty, like honesty, beauty and humor—may be "all things to all men." There are so many different kinds of courage. Which character in the stories to come seems to you most courageous?

Why do some people come through when others fail? What special qualities does the gallant person possess? What inner struggles does such a person face and overcome? A good story can help others understand.

The four stories in this unit are quite different. Three have a common core. Why didn't Jack London's boxer quit fighting? Why did the two women in "Fire in the Bush" behave as they did? Why did a lonely man face two trespassers and possible danger in "Sixty Acres"?

The third story, "Death of Red Peril," is a welcome change of pace. What happens when loyalty, love, pride, and humor get all mixed up with courage, a caterpillar, a vengeful lock tender, and the Erie Canal?

A Piece of Steak

Jack London

♦ The house by this time had gone mad, and it was his house, nearly every voice yelling: "Go it, Tom!" "Get 'im! Get 'im!" "You've got 'im, Tom! You've got 'im!" It was to be a whirlwind finish, and that was what a ringside audience paid to see.

Outstanding athletes in every sport are the heroes of our time. Quarterbacks, pitchers, centers, goalies—the great ones command astronomical salaries and the intense loyalty of millions of fans. There are other athletes, men and women who make the sports possible, yet who do not make headlines.

The outstanding as well as the average athletes all face a common fate: final retirement from the sport because of injury or age. Some highly paid athletes save their money, make sound investments, and live comfortably after retirement. Often they take on other jobs like coaching or acting as a television commentator. But there are others who find themselves at the end of their careers with little money and poor prospects. Jack London could sympathize with these unfortunates. He had known at firsthand the pangs of hunger, for his own childhood had been poverty-stricken.

People ask, "Whatever became of . . . ?" and they sometimes uncover a sad answer: obscurity, frustration, and sometimes poverty.

"A Piece of Steak" tells of an athlete past his prime, a former great who thought the applause and money would last forever. It is the story of Tom King trying to make enough money from boxing to support his family. It is more than a character study, though. It is also a picture of youth and age, of conflicting attitudes toward life, of harsh and uncompromising realities.

Even if you are not a boxing enthusiast, you'll be caught up in Tom King's greatest challenge as he tries to win just one more time. You'll also learn the significance of the title, "A Piece of Steak."

A Piece of Steak

With the last morsel of bread Tom King wiped his plate clean of the last particle of flour gravy and chewed the resulting mouthful in a slow and meditative way. When he arose from the table, he was oppressed by the feeling that he was distinctly hungry. Yet he alone had eaten. The two children in the other room had been sent early to bed in order that in sleep they might forget they had gone supperless. His wife had touched nothing, and had sat silently and watched him with solicitous eyes. She was a thin, worn woman of the working class, though signs of an earlier prettiness were not wanting in her face. The flour for the gravy she had borrowed from the neighbor across the hall. The last two ha'pennies had gone to buy the bread.

He sat down by the window on a rickety chair that protested under his weight, and quite mechanically he put his pipe in his mouth and dipped into the side pocket of his coat. The absence of any tobacco made him aware of his action, and with a scowl for his forgetfulness he put the pipe away. His movements were slow, almost hulking, as though he were burdened by the heavy weight of his muscles. He was a solid-bodied, stolid-looking man, and his appearance did not suffer from being overprepossessing. His rough clothes were old and slouchy. The uppers of his shoes were too weak to carry the heavy resoling that was itself of no recent date. And his cotton shirt, a cheap, two-shilling affair, showed a frayed collar and ineradicable paint stains.

But it was Tom King's face that advertised him unmistakably for what he was. It was the face of a typical prizefighter; of one who had put in long years of service in the squared ring and, by that means, developed and emphasized all the marks of the fighting beast. It was distinctly a lowering countenance, and, that no feature of it might escape notice, it was clean-shaven. The lips were shapeless and constituted a mouth harsh to excess, that was like a gash in his face. The jaw was aggressive, brutal, heavy. The eyes, slow of movement and heavy-lidded, were almost expressionless under the shaggy, indrawn brows. Sheer animal that he was, the eyes were the most animal-like feature about him. They were sleepy, lion-like—the eyes of a fighting animal. The forehead slanted quickly back to the hair, which, clipped close, showed every bump of a villainous-looking head. A nose, twice broken and molded variously by countless blows, and a cauliflower ear, permanently swollen and distorted to twice its size, completed his adornment, while the beard, fresh-shaven as it was, sprouted in the skin and gave the face a blue-black stain.

Altogether, it was the face of a man to be afraid of in a dark alley or lonely place. And yet Tom King was not a criminal, nor had he ever done anything criminal. Outside of brawls, common to his walk in life, he had harmed no one. Nor had he ever been known to pick a quarrel. He was a professional, and all the fighting brutishness of him was reserved for his professional appearances. Outside the ring he was slow-going, easy-natured, and, in his younger days, when money was flush, too openhanded for his own good. He bore no grudges and had few enemies. Fighting was a business with him. In the ring he struck to hurt, struck to maim, struck to destroy; but there was no animus in it. It was a plain business proposition. Audiences assembled and paid for the spectacle of men knocking each other out. The winner took the big end of the purse. When Tom King faced the Woolloomoolloo Gouger, twenty years before, he knew that the Gouger's jaw was only four months healed after having been broken in a Newcastle bout. And he had played for that jaw and broken it again in the ninth round, not because he bore the Gouger any ill will, but because that was the surest way to put the Gouger out and win the big end of the purse. Nor had the Gouger borne him any ill will for it. It was the game, and both knew the game and played it.

Tom King had never been a talker, and he sat by the window, morosely silent, staring at his hands. The veins stood out on the backs of the hands, large and swollen; and the knuckles, smashed and battered and malformed, testified to the use to which they had been put. He had never heard that a man's life was the life of his arteries, but well he knew the meaning of those big, upstanding veins. His heart had pumped too much blood through them at top pressure. They no longer did the work. He had stretched the elasticity out of them, and with their distention had passed his endurance. He tired easily now. No longer could he do a fast twenty rounds, hammer and tongs, fight, fight, fight, from gong to gong, with fierce rally on top of fierce rally, beaten to the ropes and in turn beating his opponent to the ropes, and rallying fiercest and fastest of all in that last, twentieth round, with the house on its feet and yelling, himself rushing, striking, ducking, raining showers of blows upon showers of blows and receiving showers of blows in return, and all the time the heart faithfully pumping the surging blood through the adequate veins. The veins, swollen at the time, had always shrunk down again, though not quite—each time, imperceptibly at first, remaining just a trifle larger than before. He stared at them and at his battered knuckles, and, for the moment, caught a vision of the youthful excellence of those hands before the first knuckle had been smashed on the head of Benny Jones, otherwise known as the Welsh Terror.

The impression of his hunger came back to him.

"Blimey, but couldn't I go a piece of steak!" he muttered aloud, clenching his huge fists and spitting out a smothered oath.

"I tried both Burke's an' Sawley's," his wife said half apologetically.

"An' they wouldn't?" he demanded.

"Not a ha'penny. Burke said—" She faltered.

"G'wan! Wot'd he say?"

"As how 'e was thinkin' Sandel 'ud do ye tonight, an' as how yer score was comfortable big as it was."

Tom King grunted but did not reply. He was busy thinking of the bull terrier he had kept in his younger days to which he had fed steaks without end. Burke would have given him credit for a thousand steaks—then. But times had changed. Tom King was getting old; and old men, fighting before second-rate clubs, couldn't expect to run bills of any size with the tradesmen.

He had got up in the morning with a longing for a piece of steak, and the longing had not abated. He had not had a fair training for this fight. It was a drought year in Australia, times were hard, and even the most irregular work was difficult to find. He had had no sparring partner, and his food had not been of the best nor always sufficient. He had done a few days' navvy work when he could get it, and he had run around the Domain in the early mornings to get his legs in shape. But it was hard, training without a partner and with a wife and two kiddies that must be fed. Credit with the tradesmen had undergone very slight expansion when he was matched with Sandel. The secretary of the Gayety Club had advanced him three pounds—the loser's end of the purse—and beyond that had refused to go. Now and again he had managed to borrow a few shillings from old pals, who would have lent more only that it was a drought year and they were hard put themselves. No—and there was no use in disguising the fact—his training had not been satisfactory. He should have had better food and no worries. Besides, when a man is forty, it is harder to get into condition than when he is twenty.

"What time is it, Lizzie?" he asked.

His wife went across the hall to inquire, and came back.

"Quarter before eight."

"They'll be startin' the first bout in a few minutes," he said. "Only a tryout. Then there's a four-round spar 'tween Dealer Wells an' Gridley, an' a ten-round go 'tween Starlight an' some sailor bloke. I don't come on for over an hour."

At the end of another silent ten minutes he rose to his feet.

"Truth is, Lizzie, I ain't had proper trainin'."

He reached for his hat and started for the door. He did not offer to kiss her—he never did on going out—but on this night she dared to kiss him, throwing her arms around him and compelling him to bend down to her face. She looked quite small against the massive bulk of the man.

"Good luck, Tom," she said. "You gotter do 'im."

"Ay, I gotter do 'im," he repeated. "That's all there is to it. I jus' gotter do 'im."

He laughed with an attempt at heartiness, while she pressed more closely against him. Across her shoulders he looked around the bare room. It was all he had in the world, with the rent overdue, and her and the kiddies. And he was leaving it to go out into the night to get meat for his mate and cubs—not like a modern workingman going to his machine grind, but in the old, primitive, royal, animal way, by fighting for it.

"I gotter do 'im," he repeated, this time a hint of desperation in his voice. "If it's a win, it's thirty quid—an' I can pay all that's owin', with a lump o' money left over. If it's a lose, I get naught—

not even a penny for me to ride home on the tram. The secretary's give all that's comin' from a loser's end. Good-by, old woman. I'll come straight home if it's a win."

"An' I'll be waitin' up," she called to him along the hall.

It was full two miles to the Gayety, and as he walked along he remembered how in his palmy days—he had once been the heavyweight champion of New South Wales—he would have ridden in a cab to the fight, and how, most likely, some heavy backer would have paid for the cab and ridden with him. There were Tommy Burns and that Yankee, Jack Johnson—they rode about in motorcars. And he walked! And, as any man knew, a hard two miles was not the best preliminary to a fight. He was an old un, and the world did not wag well with old uns. He was good for nothing now except navvy work, and his broken nose and swollen ear were against him even in that. He found himself wishing that he had learned a trade. It would have been better in the long run. But no one had told him, and he knew, deep down in his heart, that he would not have listened if they had. It had been so easy. Big money—sharp, glorious fights—periods of rest and loafing in between—a following of eager flatterers, the slaps on the back, the shakes of the hand, the toffs glad to buy him a drink for the privilege of five minutes' talk—and the glory of it, the yelling houses, the whirlwind finish, the referee's "King wins!" and his name in the sporting columns next day.

Those had been times! But he realized now, in his slow, ruminating way, that it was the old uns he had been putting away. He was Youth, rising; and they were Age, sinking. No wonder it had been easy—they with their swollen veins and battered knuckles and weary in the bones of them from the long battles they had already fought. He remembered the time he put out old Stowsher Bill, at Rush-Cutters Bay, in the eighteenth round, and how old Bill had cried afterward in the dressing room like a baby. Perhaps old Bill's rent had been overdue. Perhaps he'd had at home a missus an' a couple of kiddies. And perhaps Bill, that very day of the fight, had had a hungering for a piece of steak. Bill had fought game and taken incredible punishment. He could see now, after he had gone through the mill himself, that Stowsher Bill had fought for a bigger stake, that night twenty years ago, than had young Tom King, who had fought for glory and easy money. No wonder Stowsher Bill had cried afterward in the dressing room.

Well, a man had only so many fights in him, to begin with. It was the iron law of the game. One man might have a hundred hard fights in him, another man only twenty; each, according to the make of him and the quality of his fiber, had a definite number, and when he had fought them he was done. Yes, he had had more fights in him than most of them, and he had had far more than his share of the hard, grueling fights—the kind that worked the heart and lungs to bursting, that took the elastic out of the arteries and made hard knots of muscle out of youth's sleek suppleness, that wore out nerve and stamina and made brain and bones weary from excess of effort and endurance overwrought. Yes, he had done better than all of them. There was none of his old fighting partners left. He was the last of the old guard. He had seen them all finished, and he had had a hand in finishing some of them.

They had tried him out against the old uns, and one after another he had put them away—laughing when, like old Stowsher Bill, they cried in the dressing room. And now he was an old un, and they tried out the youngsters on him. There was that bloke Sandel. He had come over from New Zealand with a record behind him. But nobody in Australia knew anything about him, so they put him up against old Tom King. If Sandel made a showing, he would be given better men to fight, with bigger purses to win; so it was to be depended upon that he would put up a fierce battle. He had everything to win by it—money and glory and career; and Tom King was the grizzled old chopping block that guarded the highway to fame and fortune. And he had nothing to win except thirty quid, to pay to the landlord and the tradesmen. And as Tom King thus ruminated, there came to his stolid vision the form of youth, glorious youth, rising exultant and invincible, supple of muscle and silken of skin, with heart and lungs that had never been tired and torn and that laughed at limitation of effort. Yes, youth was the nemesis. It destroyed the old uns and recked not that, in so doing, it destroyed itself. It enlarged its arteries and smashed its knuckles, and was in turn destroyed by youth. For youth was ever youthful. It was only age that grew old.

At Castlereagh Street he turned to the left, and three blocks along came to the Gayety. A crowd of young larrikins hanging outside the door made respectful way for him, and he heard one say to another: "That's 'im! That's Tom King!"

Inside, on the way to his dressing room, he encountered the

secretary, a keen-eyed, shrewd-faced young man, who shook his hand.

"How are you feelin', Tom?" he asked.

"Fit as a fiddle," King answered, though he knew that he lied, and that if he had a quid he would give it right there for a good piece of steak.

When he emerged from the dressing room, his seconds behind him, and came down the aisle to the squared ring in the center of the hall, a burst of greeting and applause went up from the waiting crowd. He acknowledged salutations right and left, though few of the faces did he know. Most of them were the faces of kiddies unborn when he was winning his first laurels in the squared ring. He leaped lightly to the raised platform and ducked through the ropes to his corner, where he sat down on a folding stool. Jack Ball, the referee, came over and shook his hand. Ball was a broken-down pugilist who for over ten years had not entered the ring as a principal. King was glad that he had him for referee. They were both old uns. If he should rough it with Sandel a bit beyond the rules, he knew Ball could be depended upon to pass it by.

Aspiring young heavyweights, one after another, were climbing into the ring and being presented to the audience by the referee. Also he issued their challenges for them.

"Young Pronto," Ball announced, "from North Sydney, challenges the winner for fifty pounds side bet."

The audience applauded, and applauded again as Sandel himself sprang through the ropes and sat down in his corner. Tom King looked across the ring at him curiously, for in a few minutes they would be locked together in merciless combat, each trying with all the force of him to knock the other into unconsciousness. But little could he see, for Sandel, like himself, had trousers and sweater on over his ring costume. His face was strongly handsome, crowned with a curly mop of yellow hair, while his thick, muscular neck hinted at bodily magnificence.

Young Pronto went to one corner and then the other, shaking hands with the principals and dropping down out of the ring. The challenges went on. Ever youth climbed through the ropes—youth unknown but insatiable, crying out to mankind that with strength and skill it would match issues with the winner. A few years before, in his own heyday of invincibleness, Tom King would have been amused and bored by these preliminaries. But now he sat fascinated, unable to shake the vision of youth from his eyes. Always were these youngsters rising up in the boxing game, springing through the ropes and shouting their defiance; and always were the old uns going down before them. They climbed to success over the bodies of the old uns. And ever they came, more and more young-sters—youth unquenchable and irresistible—and ever they put the old uns away, themselves becoming old uns and traveling the same downward path, while behind them, ever pressing on them, was youth eternal—the new babies, grown lusty and dragging their el-ders down, with behind them more babies to the end of time—youth that must have its will and that will never die.

King glanced over to the press box and nodded to Morgan, of the *Sportsman*, and Corbett, of the *Referee*. Then he held out his hands, while Sid Sullivan and Charley Bates, his seconds, slipped on his gloves and laced them tight, closely watched by one of San-del's seconds, who first examined critically the tapes on King's knuckles. A second of his own was in Sandel's corner, performing a like office. Sandel's trousers were pulled off, and as he stood up his sweater was skinned off over his head. And Tom King, looking, saw youth incarnate, deep-chested, heavy-thewed, with muscles that slipped and slid like live things under the white satin skin. The whole body was acrawl with life, and Tom King knew that it was a life that had never oozed its freshness out through the aching pores during the long fights wherein youth paid its toll and departed not quite so young as when it entered.

The two men advanced to meet each other, and as the gong sounded and the seconds clattered out of the ring with the folding stools, they shook hands and instantly took their fighting attitudes. And instantly, like the mechanism of steel and springs balanced on a hair trigger, Sandel was in and out and in again, landing a left to the eyes, a right to the ribs, ducking a counter, dancing lightly away and dancing menacingly back again. He was swift and clever. It was a dazzling exhibition. The house yelled its approbation. But King was not dazzled. He had fought too many fights and too many youngsters. He knew the blows for what they were—too quick and too deft to be dangerous. Evidently Sandel was going to rush things from the start. It was to be expected. It was the way of youth, ex-pending its splendor and excellence in wild insurgence and furious onslaught, overwhelming opposition with its own unlimited glory of strength and desire.

Sandel was in and out, here, there, and everywhere, light-footed and eager-hearted, a living wonder of white flesh and stinging muscle that wove itself into a dazzling fabric of attack, slipping and leaping like a flying shuttle from action to action through a thousand actions, all of them centered upon the destruction of Tom King, who stood between him and fortune. And Tom King patiently endured. He knew his business, and he knew youth now that youth was no longer his. There was nothing to do till the other lost some of his steam, was his thought, and he grinned to himself as he deliberately ducked so as to receive a heavy blow on the top of his head. It was a wicked thing to do, yet eminently fair according to the rules of the boxing game. A man was supposed to take care of his own knuckles, and if he insisted on hitting an opponent on the top of the head he did so at his own peril. King could have ducked lower and let the blow whiz harmlessly past, but he remembered his own early fights and how he smashed his first knuckle on the head of the Welsh Terror. He was but playing the game. That duck had accounted for one of Sandel's knuckles. Not that Sandel would mind it now. He would go on, superbly regardless, hitting as hard as ever throughout the fight. But later on, when the long ring battles had begun to tell, he would regret that knuckle and look back and remember how he smashed it on Tom King's head.

The first round was all Sandel's, and he had the house yelling with the rapidity of his whirlwind rushes. He overwhelmed King with avalanches of punches, and King did nothing. He never struck once, contenting himself with covering up, blocking and ducking and clinching to avoid punishment. He occasionally feinted, shook his head when the weight of a punch landed, and moved stolidly about, never leaping or springing or wasting an ounce of strength. Sandel must foam the froth of youth away before discreet age could dare to retaliate. All King's movements were slow and methodical, and his heavy-lidded, slow-moving eyes gave him the appearance of being half asleep or dazed. Yet they were eyes that saw everything, that had been trained to see everything through all his twenty years and odd in the ring. They were eyes that did not blink or waver before an impending blow, but that coolly saw and measured distance.

Seated in his corner for the minute's rest at the end of the round, he lay back with outstretched legs, his arms resting on the right angle of the ropes, his chest and abdomen heaving frankly and deeply as he gulped down the air driven by the towels of his seconds. He listened with closed eyes to the voices of the house, "Why don't yeh fight, Tom?" many were crying. "Yeh ain't afraid of 'im, are yeh?"

"Muscle-bound," he heard a man on a front seat comment. "He can't move quicker. Two to one on Sandel, in quids."

The gong struck and the two men advanced from their corners. Sandel came forward fully three quarters of the distance, eager to begin again; but King was content to advance the shorter distance. It was in line with his policy of economy. He had not been well trained, and he had not had enough to eat, and every step counted. Besides, he had already walked two miles to the ringside. It was a repetition of the first round, with Sandel attacking like a whirlwind and with the audience indignantly demanding why King did not fight. Beyond feinting and several slowly delivered and ineffectual blows he did nothing save block and stall and clinch. Sandel wanted to make the pace fast, while King, out of his wisdom, refused to accommodate him. He grinned with a certain wistful pathos in his ring-battered countenance, and went on cherishing his strength with the jealousy of which only age is capable. Sandel was youth, and he threw his strength away with the munificent abandon of youth. To King belonged the ring generalship, the wisdom bred of long, aching fights. He watched with cool eyes and head, moving slowly and waiting for Sandel's froth to foam away. To the majority of the onlookers it seemed as though King was hopelessly outclassed, and they voiced their opinion in offers of three to one on Sandel. But there were wise ones, a few, who knew King of old time, and who covered what they considered easy money.

The third round began as usual, one-sided, with Sandel doing all the leading and delivering all the punishment. A half minute had passed when Sandel, overconfident, left an opening. King's eyes and right arm flashed in the same instant. It was his first real blow—a hook, with the twisted arch of the arm to make it rigid, and with all the weight of the half-pivoted body behind it. It was like a sleepy-seeming lion suddenly thrusting out a lightning paw. Sandel, caught on the side of the jaw, was felled like a bullock. The audience gasped and murmured awe-stricken applause. The man was not muscle-bound, after all, and he could drive a blow like a trip hammer.

Sandel was shaken. He rolled over and attempted to rise, but the sharp yells from his seconds to take the count restrained him. He knelt on one knee, ready to rise, and waited, while the referee stood over him, counting the seconds loudly in his ear. At the ninth he rose in fighting attitude, and Tom King, facing him, knew regret that the blow had not been an inch nearer the point of the jaw. That would have been a knockout, and he could have carried the thirty quid home to the missus and the kiddies.

The round continued to the end of its three minutes, Sandel for the first time respectful of his opponent and King slow of movement and sleepy-eyed as ever. As the round neared its close, King, warned of the fact by sight of the seconds crouching outside ready for the spring in through the ropes, worked the fight around to his own corner. And when the gong struck, he sat down immediately on the waiting stool, while Sandel had to walk all the way across the diagonal of the square to his own corner. It was a little thing, but it was the sum of little things that counted. Sandel was compelled to walk that many more steps, to give up that much energy, and to lose a part of the precious minute of rest. At the beginning of every round King loafed slowly out from his corner, forcing his opponent to advance the greater distance. The end of every round found the fight maneuvered by King into his own corner so that he could immediately sit down.

Two more rounds went by, in which King was parsimonious of effort and Sandel prodigal. The latter's attempt to force a fast pace made King uncomfortable, for a fair percentage of the multitudinous blows showered upon him went home. Yet King persisted in his dogged slowness, despite the crying of the young hotheads for him to go in and fight. Again, in the sixth round, Sandel was careless, again Tom King's fearful right flashed out to the jaw, and again Sandel took the nine seconds' count.

By the seventh round Sandel's pink of condition was gone, and he settled down to what he knew was to be the hardest fight in his experience. Tom King was an old un, but a better old un than he had ever encountered—an old un who never lost his head, who was remarkably able at defense, whose blows had the impact of a knotted club, and who had a knockout in either hand. Nevertheless, Tom King dared not hit often. He never forgot his battered knuckles, and knew that every hit must count if the knuckles were to last out the fight. As he sat in his corner, glancing across at his opponent, the thought came to him that the sum of his wisdom and Sandel's youth would constitute a world's champion heavyweight. But that was the trouble. Sandel would never become a world champion. He lacked the wisdom, and the only way for him to get it was to buy it with youth; and when wisdom was his, youth would have been spent in buying it.

King took every advantage he knew. He never missed an opportunity to clinch, and in effecting most of the clinches his shoulder drove stiffly into the other's ribs. In the philosophy of the ring a shoulder was as good as a punch so far as damage was concerned, and a great deal better so far as concerned expenditure of effort. Also in the clinches King rested his weight on his opponent, and was loath to let go. This compelled the interference of the referee, who tore them apart, always assisted by Sandel, who had not yet learned to rest. He could not refrain from using those glorious flying arms and writhing muscles of his, and when the other rushed into a clinch, striking shoulder against ribs, and with head resting under Sandel's left arm, Sandel almost invariably swung his right behind his own back and into the projecting face. It was a clever stroke, much admired by the audience, but it was not dangerous, and was, therefore, just that much wasted strength. But Sandel was tireless and unaware of limitations, and King grinned and doggedly endured.

Sandel developed a fierce right to the body, which made it appear that King was taking an enormous amount of punishment, and it was only the old ringsters who appreciated the deft touch of King's left glove to the other's biceps just before the impact of the blow. It was true, the blow landed each time; but each time it was robbed of its power by that touch on the biceps. In the ninth round, three times inside a minute, King's right hooked its twisted arch to the jaw; and three times Sandel's body, heavy as it was, was leveled to the mat. Each time he took the nine seconds allowed him and rose to his feet, shaken and jarred, but still strong. He had lost much of his speed, and he wasted less effort. He was fighting grimly; but he continued to draw upon his chief asset, which was youth. King's chief asset was experience. As his vitality had dimmed and his vigor abated, he had replaced them with cunning, with wisdom born of the long fights and with a careful shepherding of strength. Not alone had he learned never to make a superfluous movement, but he had learned how to seduce an opponent into throwing his strength away. Again and again, by feint of foot and hand and body, he continued to inveigle Sandel into leaping back, ducking, or countering. King rested, but he never permitted Sandel to rest. It was the strategy of age.

Early in the tenth round King began stopping the other's rushes with straight lefts to the face, and Sandel, grown wary, responded by drawing the left, then by ducking it and delivering his right in a swinging hook to the side of the head. It was too high up to be vitally effective; but when first it landed King knew the old, familiar descent of the black veil of unconsciousness across his mind. For the instant, or for the slightest fraction of an instant, rather, he ceased. In the one moment he saw his opponent ducking out of his field of vision and the background of white, watching faces; in the next moment he again saw his opponent and the background of faces. It was as if he had slept for a time and just opened his eyes again, and yet the interval of unconsciousness was so microscopically short that there had been no time for him to fall. The audience saw him totter and his knees give, and then saw him recover and tuck his chin deeper into the shelter of his left shoulder.

Several times Sandel repeated the blow, keeping King partially dazed, and then the latter worked out his defense, which was also a counter. Feinting with his left, he took a half step backward, at the same time uppercutting with the whole strength of his right. So accurately was it timed that it landed squarely on Sandel's face in the full, downward sweep of the duck, and Sandel lifted in the air and curled backward, striking the mat on his head and shoulders. Twice King achieved this, then turned loose and hammered his opponent to the ropes. He gave Sandel no chance to rest or to set himself, but smashed blow in upon blow till the house rose to its feet and the air was filled with an unbroken roar of applause. But Sandel's strength and endurance were superb, and he continued to stay on his feet. A knockout seemed certain, and a captain of police, appalled at the dreadful punishment, arose by the ringside to stop the fight. The gong struck for the end of the round and Sandel staggered to his corner, protesting to the captain that he was sound and strong. To prove it, he threw two back air-springs, and the police captain gave in.

Tom King, leaning back in his corner and breathing hard, was disappointed. If the fight had been stopped, the referee, perforce, would have rendered him the decision and the purse would have been his. Unlike Sandel, he was not fighting for glory or career, but for thirty quid. And now Sandel would recuperate in the minute of rest.

Youth will be served—this saying flashed into King's mind, and he remembered the first time he had heard it, the night when he had put away Stowsher Bill. The toff who had bought him a drink after the fight and patted him on the shoulder had used those words. Youth will be served! The toff was right. And on that night in the long ago he had been youth. Tonight youth sat in the opposite corner. As for himself, he had been fighting for half an hour now, and he was an old man. Had he fought like Sandel, he would not have lasted fifteen minutes. But the point was that he did not recuperate. Those upstanding arteries and that sorely tried heart would not enable him to gather strength in the intervals between the rounds. And he had not had sufficient strength in him to begin with. His legs were heavy under him and beginning to cramp. He should not have walked those two miles to the fight. And there was the steak which he had got up longing for that morning. A great and terrible hatred rose up in him for the butchers who had refused him credit. It was hard for an old man to go into a fight without enough to eat. And a piece of steak was such a little thing, a few pennies at best; yet it meant thirty quid to him.

With the gong that opened the eleventh round Sandel rushed, making a show of freshness which he did not really possess. King knew it for what it was—a bluff as old as the game itself. He clinched to save himself, then, going free, allowed Sandel to get set. This was what King desired. He feinted with his left, drew the answering duck and swinging upward hook, then made the half step backward, delivered the uppercut full to the face and crumpled Sandel over to the mat. After that he never let him rest, receiving punishment himself, but inflicting far more, smashing Sandel to the ropes, hooking and driving all manner of blows into him, tearing away from his clinches or punching him out of attempted clinches, and even when Sandel would have fallen, catching him with one uplifting hand and with the other immediately smashing him into the ropes where he could not fall.

The house by this time had gone mad, and it was his house, nearly every voice yelling: "Go it, Tom!" "Get 'im! Get 'im!" "You've got 'im, Tom! You've got 'im!" It was to be a whirlwind finish, and that was what a ringside audience paid to see.

And Tom King, who for half an hour had conserved his strength, now expended it prodigally in the one great effort he knew he had in him. It was his one chance—now or not at all. His strength was waning fast, and his hope was that before the last of it ebbed out of him he would have beaten his opponent down for the count. And as he continued to strike and force, coolly estimating the weight of his blows and the quality of the damage wrought, he realized how hard a man Sandel was to knock out. Stamina and endurance were his to an extreme degree, and they were the virgin stamina and endurance of youth. Sandel was certainly a coming man. He had it in him. Only out of such rugged fiber were successful fighters fashioned.

Sandel was reeling and staggering, but Tom King's legs were cramping and his knuckles going back on him. Yet he steeled himself to strike the fierce blows, every one of which brought anguish to his tortured hands. Though now he was receiving practically no punishment, he was weakening as rapidly as the other. His blows went home, but there was no longer the weight behind them, and each blow was the result of a severe effort of will. His legs were like lead, and they dragged visibly under him; while Sandel's backers, cheered by this symptom, began calling encouragement to their man.

King was spurred to a burst of effort. He delivered two blows in succession—a left, a trifle too high, to the solar plexus, and a right cross to the jaw. They were not heavy blows, yet so weak and dazed was Sandel that he went down and lay quivering. The referee stood over him, shouting the count of the fatal seconds in his ear. If before the tenth second was called he did not rise, the fight was lost. The house stood in hushed silence. King rested on trembling legs. A mortal dizziness was upon him, and before his eyes the sea of faces sagged and swayed, while to his ears, as from a remote distance, came the count of the referee. Yet he looked upon the fight as his. It was impossible that a man so punished could rise.

Only youth could rise, and Sandel rose. At the fourth second he rolled over on his face and groped blindly for the ropes. By the seventh second he had dragged himself to his knee, where he rested, his head rolling groggily on his shoulders. As the referee cried "Nine!" Sandel stood upright, in proper stalling position, his left arm wrapping about his face, his right wrapped about his stomach. Thus were his vital points guarded, while he lurched forward toward King in the hope of effecting a clinch and gaining more time.

At the instant Sandel rose, King was at him, but the two blows he delivered were muffled on the stalled arms. The next moment Sandel was in the clinch and holding on desperately while the referee strove to drag the two men apart. King helped to force himself free. He knew the rapidity with which youth recovered, and he knew that Sandel was his if he could prevent that recovery. One stiff punch would do it. Sandel was his, undubitably his, He had out-generaled him, outfought him, outpointed him. Sandel reeled out of the clinch, balanced on the hairline between defeat or survival. One good blow would topple him over and down and out. And Tom King, in a flash of bitterness, remembered the piece of steak and wished that he had it then behind that necessary punch he must deliver. He nerved himself for the blow, but it was not heavy enough nor swift enough. Sandel swayed but did not fall, staggering back to the ropes and holding on. King staggered after him, and, with a pang like that of dissolution, delivered another blow. But his body had deserted him. All that was left of him was a fighting intelligence that was dimmed and clouded from exhaustion. The blow that was aimed for the jaw struck no higher than the shoulder. He had willed the blow higher, but the tired muscles had not been able to obey. And, from the impact of the blow, Tom King himself reeled back and nearly fell. Once again he strove. This time his punch missed altogether, and from absolute weakness he fell against Sandel and clinched, holding on to him to save himself from sinking to the floor.

King did not attempt to free himself. He had shot his bolt. He was gone. And youth had been served. Even in the clinch he could feel Sandel growing stronger against him. When the referee thrust them apart, there, before his eyes, he saw youth recuperate. From instant to instant Sandel grew stronger. His punches, weak and fu-tile at first, became stiff and accurate. Tom King's bleared eyes saw the gloved fist driving at his jaw, and he willed to guard it by inter-posing his arm. He saw the danger, willed the act; but the arm was too heavy. It seemed burdened with a hundredweight of lead. It would not lift itself, and he strove to lift it with his soul. Then the gloved fist landed home. He experienced a sharp snap that was like an electric spark, and simultaneously the veil of blackness envel-oped him.

When he opened his eyes again he was in his corner, and he heard the yelling of the audience like the roar of the surf at Bondi Beach. A wet sponge was being pressed against the base of his brain, and Sid Sullivan was blowing cold water in a refreshing spray over his face and chest. His gloves had already been removed, and San-del, bending over him, was shaking his hand. He bore no ill will toward the man who had put him out, and he returned the grip with a heartiness that made his battered knuckles protest. Then Sandel stepped to the center of the ring and the audience hushed its pandemonium to hear him accept young Pronto's challenge and offer to increase the side bet to one hundred pounds. King looked on apathetically while his seconds mopped the streaming water from him, dried his face, and prepared him to leave the ring. He felt hungry. It was not the ordinary, gnawing kind, but a great faintness, a palpitation at the pit of the stomach that communicated itself to all his body. He remembered back into the fight to the moment when he had Sandel swaying and tottering on the hairline balance of defeat. Ah, that piece of steak would have done it! He had lacked just that for the decisive blow, and he had lost. It was all because of the piece of steak.

His seconds were half supporting him as they helped him through the ropes. He tore free from them, ducked through the ropes unaided, and leaped heavily to the floor, following on their heels as they forced a passage for him down the crowded center aisle. Leaving the dressing room for the street, in the entrance to the hall, some young fellow spoke to him.

"W'y didn't yuh go in an' get 'im when yuh 'ad 'im?" the young fellow asked.

"Aw, shut up!" said Tom King, and passed down the steps to the sidewalk.

The doors of the public house at the corner were swinging wide, and he saw the lights and the smiling barmaids, heard the many voices discussing the fight and the prosperous chink of money on the bar. Somebody called to him to have a drink. He hesitated perceptibly, then refused and went on his way.

He had not a copper in his pocket, and the two-mile walk home seemed very long. He was certainly getting old. Crossing the Domain he sat down suddenly on a bench, unnerved by the thought of the missus sitting up for him, waiting to learn the outcome of the fight. That was harder than any knockout, and it seemed almost impossible to face.

He felt weak and sore, and the pain of his smashed knuckles warned him that, even if he could find a job at navvy work, it would be a week before he could grip a pick handle or a shovel. The hunger palpitation at the pit of the stomach was sickening. His wretchedness overwhelmed him, and into his eyes came an unwonted moisture. He covered his face with his hands, and, as he cried, he remembered Stowsher Bill and how he had served him that night in the long ago. Poor old Stowsher Bill! He could understand now why Bill had cried in the dressing room.

Understanding the Story _____

Main Idea

1. The main idea of the story is summed up in which of the following sentences?
   (a) Sandel won the fight through trickery and deceit.
   (b) If Tom King had been properly nourished, he might have squeezed out just one more victory.
   (c) Tom had once been a great fighter and had defeated some of the greatest fighters of his time.
   (d) Worries about his family were really the reason Tom King lost the fight.

Details

2. In advance of the fight, Tom had been given the sum of   (a) a few shillings   (b) three pounds   (c) ten pounds   (d) thirty pounds.

3. This story takes place in   (a) New York   (b) England   (c) New Zealand   (d) Australia.

4. The Woolloomoolloo Gouger was a   (a) referee   (b) trainer   (c) fighter   (d) wrestler.

5. The boxer who had cried in the dressing room was   (a) Stowsher Bill   (b) Jack Johnson   (c) Dealer Wells   (d) the Welsh Terror.

Inferences

6. Tom King's face would have to be considered   (a) handsome   (b) bearded   (c) ugly   (d) comforting.

7. Tom remembered his old bull terrier because of   (a) the ter-

rier's great loyalty to Tom   (b) the low price he sold him for
(c) the dog he owned later   (d) the steaks he had fed the dog.

8. It seems safe to infer that the children were   (a) spoiled and
ill-mannered   (b) noisy when Tom wanted to sleep
(c) poorly nourished   (d) unconsciously disliked by Tom.

9. The fight ended in   (a) a riot at the Gayety   (b) a knockout
of Tom   (c) Sandel's giving up   (d) the referee's awarding
the decision to Tom.

10. During the fight Tom was   (a) cautious and intelligent
(b) generally wild and unrestrained   (c) extremely bitter toward Sandel   (d) resentful toward the referee.

Order of Events

11. Arrange the items in the order in which they occurred. Use
letters only.
A. Tom sits on a bench and thinks back to the past.
B. Lizzie kisses her husband good-bye.
C. Sandel comes out swinging wildly.
D. Tom beats Stowsher Bill.
E. Tom knocks Sandel down.

Outcomes

12. Tom might have won his fight if   (a) his wife had given him
more encouragement   (b) the butcher had given his wife
credit   (c) Sandel had knocked Tom down   (d) the match
had been a fight to the finish.

Cause and Effect

13. Tom probably would not have been fighting at his age if
(a) Sandel had not been his opponent   (b) his children had
asked him not to   (c) there had been a different referee
(d) he had saved his money when young.

Fact or Opinion

Tell whether each of the following is a fact or an opinion.

14. At the end of the fight, the fans still thought Tom was the greatest.

15. The winner of Tom's fight received 30 pounds (quid).

Words in Context

1. He was a solid-bodied, *stolid*-looking man.
   Stolid (309) means   (a) handsome   (b) unemotional
   (c) odd   (d) ordinary.

2. It was distinctly a *lowering countenance*.
   Lowering countenance (309) means   (a) happy appearance
   (b) sensitive profile   (c) gloomy face   (d) fearful expression.

3. In the ring he struck to hurt, struck to maim, struck to destroy; but there was no *animus* in it.
   Animus (310) means   (a) plan   (b) money   (c) joy
   (d) hatred.

4. He had had far more than his share of the hard, grueling fights—the kind that. . .made hard knots of muscle out of youth's *sleek suppleness*.
   Sleek suppleness (314) means   (a) soft fleshiness
   (b) growing strength (c) slight experience   (d) smooth flexibility.

5. There came to his stolid vision the form of youth, glorious youth, rising *exultant and invincible*.
   Exultant and invincible (314) means   (a) endlessly and successfully   (b) jubilant and unbeatable   (c) shouting and victorious   (d) happy and wealthy.

6. And ever they came, more and more youngsters—youth *unquenchable and irresistible*.
   Unquenchable and irresistible (316) means   (a) hesitant and angry   (b) unstoppable and overwhelming   (c) annoying and vengeful   (d) distant and capable.

7. Sandel must foam the froth of youth away before *discreet* age could dare to *retaliate*.
   Discreet . . . retaliate (317) means   (a) confident . . . fight back
   (b) capable . . . escape   (c) weak . . . resign   (d) cautious . . . counterattack.

8. They were eyes that did not blink or *waver* before an *impending* blow.
   Waver . . . impending (317) means   (a) cover up . . . heavy   (b) hesitate . . . coming   (c) tremble . . . tremendous (d) retreat . . . fatal.

9. He grinned with a certain *wistful pathos* in his ring-battered countenance.

Wistful pathos (318) means   (a) sad feeling   (b) clear determination   (c) wise realization   (d) rash concern.

10. Two more rounds went by, in which King was *parsimonious*
of effort and Sandel *prodigal.*
Parsimonious . . . prodigal (319) means   (a) thrifty . . . wasteful   (b) clever . . . foolish   (c) careless . . . cautious
(d) lacking . . . productive.

Thinking About the Story

1. The famous dramatist George Bernard Shaw is supposed to
have said, "Youth is a wonderful thing. What a crime to waste
it on children." What does this mean to you? Do you agree
with it? How does it apply to this story?

2. On page 319, we are taken into Tom King's thoughts. "Sandel
would never become a world champion. He lacked the wisdom, and the only way for him to get it was to buy it with
youth; and when wisdom was his, youth would have been spent
in buying it."
Explain the quotation and tell how it makes a major point
about the story.

3. After the unflattering description of Tom's appearance, how
does your attitude toward Tom gradually change?

4. The story is obviously set in an older time when boxers trained
differently and were handled differently. Yet there is a current
reality in the description of the fight. How does the author convey to the reader the feel of the fight?

5. There are several expressions that have similar meanings. "We
were near and yet so far." "It was a near miss." "We had almost won; then suddenly. . . ." What point in the story comes
closest to these expressions? Is there one point, or more than
one point, when Tom is close to victory? Explain.

6. The story is apparently set in a time when arrangements like
welfare and unemployment insurance were unheard of. How
do these plans help to ease the plight of the poor?

Fire in the Bush

James Warwick

♦ There followed an interval of utter chaos, a nightmare of horror from which she could not wake. Long tongues of flame reached out for her, flaming trees crashed down across her path, and the dense clouds of hot smoke almost suffocated her.

Fire! That cry strikes terror in the hearts of those who hear it. Audiences in a crowded theater have panicked at the sound and lost all sense of reasonable action. Guests in a hotel have jumped to their death although rescue was on the way. Movies like *The Towering Inferno* have shown how fire can change intelligent men and women into terrified, unreasoning victims. Forest fires have swept people and animals to destruction.

A raging fire in any form is something to dread, but there is one fire that has an especially terrifying quality. When fire sweeps across grasslands and scrub after a drought, it travels with such awesome speed that many persons cannot get out of the way. In areas of low rainfall, the sparse vegetation often becomes tinder dry, as in portions of the Australia sheep-grazing country. These areas have just enough vegetation to sustain sheep, but not enough to encourage extensive agriculture. They are particularly subject to the kind of fire described in this story.

We enjoy reading stories of the struggle against the elemental forces of nature. We project ourselves into the stories and become silent partners in the action. We ask ourselves, "What would I have done in that same situation?"

"Fire in the Bush" deserves a place beside other great stories of human courage. Here you will meet two women and their children on an isolated sheep ranch. You will live with them their experiences as the roaring blaze rushes toward their lonely home. How can they survive the onrushing blaze? Follow Jerry Armytage as she faces the tragic loss of all she has cherished.

FIRE IN THE BUSH

Set like a mote in a sea of detachment, looking out upon a sun-scorched sweep of Australian bush, stood a small homestead. It was built upon a low red knoll, after which it was named Red Hill, and, in some fashion not easy of determination, it struck at the heart, for it seemed crushed by the terrific weight of untamed wilderness surrounding it.

A deep creek ran at the back, and a water hole, cool and green under the shadow of tall eucalyptus trees, glimmered at the bottom.

The house was low and roughhewn; about it hung the faint pungency of gum sap, for it had replaced the graceful white gums whose timbers formed its planks and whose ancient companions still remained clustered around it, rustling together, seeming to whisper as they swayed above it, "See what has happened to our fallen friends!"

A tall, spidery windmill stood alone on the bank of the creek and blended its note into their complaints, whining eerily as the sail swept in slow circles this way and that, or groaning and clanking with sudden frantic bursts of energy when the fitful blasts of hot wind from the desert mocked its puny efforts to fill the water tank beneath.

A rough fence of logs, laid one upon another and running in a zigzag fashion surrounded the place, and several small outbuildings stood nearby.

The all-pervading red dust had long since laid its brand on this handwork of man. All had turned a pinkish hue; even the ironwork of the windmill and tank showed the dust's effects, and the corrugated iron roof, whitewashed to reflect the burning rays of the sun, was powdered thickly with it.

The main room of the cabin was in keeping with its exterior. Rough, homemade furniture was scattered about, and two low squatter chairs, with long extended arms for leg rests and curved seats of oxhide, stood near a large table in the center. The legs of everything were set in tins filled with kerosene and water—a protection against the ants which ate their way busily into everything they could get at.

The center of the room was filled by a large mosquito net which, falling from a hoop near the ceiling, formed an inner sanctuary against the flies and insects. It had once been white but, like everything else, had fallen beneath the influence of the red dust. Its pinkish-brown folds hung limply, like the discarded bridal veil of a marriage long since forgotten.

Crack! went the overheated iron of the kitchen roof for the sixth time in five minutes. Jerry Armytage knew: she had counted them. She straightened her back a moment and listened; her face was flushed and damp, the sweat in her eyes smarted, and, when she dabbed at them absently, dark smudges appeared, so that her gray eyes might quite literally have been put in with a smutty finger.

"Drat the thing!" she said, and bent again above the stove which defied her.

Like some sullen black monster it was; a squat malevolent devil, either red hot, roaring and flaming, or half cold and vomiting clouds of acrid smoke.

"Cross-grained brute!" she admonished it, raking and poking with a long, twisted piece of iron until her arms and apron were black with soot, and a great lump dislodged from the flue—which disappeared through a hole in the side of the wall—fell into the soft wood ash in the firebox and almost blinded her in a cloud of dust and sparks.

She washed her face in a bucket, rebuilt the fire, and waited patiently until the steady roar told her it was drawing at last. Then she inspected her bread, put aside the loaves already spoiled beyond hope, and, refilling the oven with a fresh batch, walked to the open window for a breath of air. Standing there very still, with heavy lashes lowered against the glare, she listened to the voices of her children as they played beside the creek.

A fine face, strong. A face reflecting something of the soil—this silent, brooding bush land whose influence ran unbroken through her every memory. As a child she had learned the lessons it had to teach, and learning, found the secret of its stark simplicity; the patient strength with which to meet and conquer the adverse circumstances of an untoward existence.

Her husband had left for town the day before to sign a contract with a shearing company. She was alone, except for the children and a black ginn, Mary, who sometimes helped about the house. Alone, but not lonely. Women born of the solitude, as she had been, have something of that solitude within themselves. The stark monotony of their environment, the almost visible awareness of its terrible indifference, its remoteness from all human affairs, breeds an introspective outlook. Understanding it, they learn acceptance. It stills the tongue and sharpens the perception: a universal language, a spiritual communion with the soil, which serves in place of spoken thought to every dweller in the silent places. All of them are open to its influence, and all of them treasure the thing it stands for individually; it carries them forward day to day, a stream of strength-renewing force, intangible, but steady-flowing as a river.

Already this quality was visible in her children, two silent little mites, a boy and a girl, who sat beside the water hole in rapt contemplation of the dark green water. It was difficult at first sight to tell them apart, for they were dressed alike in worn blue dungarees. Both were blond, and their bright blue eyes stood out in vivid contrast with the dark mahogany of their sunburned faces. They were grave and serious, watching with interest all the varied life which arrived so silently to drink and, having quenched its thirst, so silently departed. Now and then they dipped their fingers in the water, sucking them afterward as though to make sure it was wet, and once, when a parrot of gorgeous pink-and-cream plumage flashed in a vivid circle and then settled and hung head-down from a trailing branch, the boy spoke: "Major Mitchell!" he said, and looked at his sister who nodded and smiled her pleasure, but said nothing.

How quiet it was! The woman listened uneasily. It was always quiet, but today there was something unnatural about its quality. She remained very still, and her eyes, half closed and fixed intently upon a dead stump below the window, had a slumberous, trancelike look about them. She was listening to an inner voice—an instinct—deep-seated, like that strange illusive soul sight known among the Scotch as "fey."

Quite suddenly she unloosened her apron and, opening the door, stepped outside, where again she stood very still, her nostrils quivering slightly, her whole body strung into tense expectancy by the *feel* of something amiss. A moment later she walked across to the creek bank and climbed to the top of the windmill.

Her eyes traveled slowly across the widespread plain. She saw the cockeyed blobs—little dusty spirals, which raced in frantic circles across the shimmering clay pan beyond the creek. Distant clumps of timber had a curiously unreal look, as though set in water and suspended above the earth, where they danced, rootless, liquid and fantastic in a sea of heat. Tufts of spinifex and Mitchell grass, a broken yellow pattern against the reds and grays, gleamed palely, stricken into torpid immobility by the breathless hush.

She traced the creek, its line of feathery white gums a twisted trail into the distance, and, scattered here and there along its banks, her eyes picked out the gray of sheep camped in tiny mobs within the shade.

North, south, and east, the horizon held its usual outline: a wavering, almost indiscernible blending of earth and sky. To the west a dun-colored cloud was slowly spreading, and this she watched intently, studying its outline, the glasslike syrupy effect which hung above and around it. Sand storms sometimes threw up similar hazes—yet this was not like any sand storm she had watched approach. There was nothing of wind in the sky behind it; it had none of the usual ragged edges—streamers tossed like tattered ribbons against a gale. A sinister, creeping movement there was about it, and, allowing for distance, a swiftly spreading one.

Again her nostrils quivered slightly. Her eyes sought her children where they sat beside the pool below; some menace to their well-being perhaps out there . . . They were watching her, and between them sat their friend and playmate, a half-bred kelpie sheepdog named Patch, who also was looking up at her and whining uneasily deep in her throat.

Patch feels it too, she thought; and once again she strained her eyes to catch the hidden significance behind that spreading line of haze, so distant and seemingly innocent, and yet perhaps so fateful to all she loved.

For a while she could see no sign of any change at all; then, faint at first but growing more frequent as her eyes became accustomed to watching for it, she discerned what might have been a heliograph—faint highlights reflected in rapid flashes against a billowing plume of smoke: FIRE.

Her heart leaped to her throat, and a sickening hot sensation stabbed her through the stomach. She caught at the slender girders behind her and for a moment seemed plunged headdown toward the earth. Standing rigid against the tiny steeple of the milltop she fought to hold her reeling senses, willing them back with everything of stubborn courage she could summon in her need, while within, the answer to all the vague uneasiness that had disturbed her was clamoring like a dreadful tocsin through her brain. A bush fire! Most sinister of all the dire curses Nature held like naked swords suspended above her creatures. A bush fire! And she alone to meet the terror of its passage. Red death to all life trapped within its glowing boundaries. Home, children, livelihood—ashes within its greedy maw.

Her mouth grew set, a thin, straight line; she shook herself as though to free the clutching darkness from her brain. Carefully at first, later with growing confidence, she felt her way down the rickety structure and, reaching the ground, ran toward the house. She was ripping off her skirt and blouse as she disappeared, and a few minutes later what might have been a slim young man in moleskin trousers and a bluejean jumper appeared and raced toward the saddle room in the rear. She paused at the open door and, cupping her hands, sent a long-drawn "coo-ee" echoing toward a tiny gunyah which crouched beneath a clump of she-oak near the creek.

A black ginn's head came thrusting through the leaves which closed its entrance, her body followed it, and she stood, a tent-like figure of huge proportions, peering and blinking in the blinding glare of sun.

"Get the black children! Bring 'em up here, quick!" Jerry shouted and, without waiting for an answer, whipped a bridle and a stock whip from a peg, threw a handful of corn into a tin dipper, and ran toward the horse paddock.

Luck was with her. Trixie, a bright bay mare, stood dreaming in the shade beside the gate. Jerry rattled the corn invitingly, calling her softly by name, and Trixie, attracted by the sound, came slowly forward and thrust her nose toward the grain. She let her have a mouthful, then looped the reins about her neck, bitting her, and, without fastening the throat latch, vaulted lightly across her withers. In less than a minute she was galloping bareback down the paddock, and presently the whip began to sing: Crack! crack! crack! Sharp reports like a rifle fire to awaken sluggish animals from their midday dreams.

Back through the scattered timber they came, a thundering

string of geldings, mares and foals, and she behind them in the swirling dust, slim form crouched low above the withers of the mare, her hair whipped back, the long whip sweeping in flying arcs and crack! crack! crack! to drive them ever faster.

Her face was flushed, the gray eyes brilliant, alive to every threatening obstacle in her path. Tree trunks to swing between, low, sweeping branches to dodge, and always the whiplash to watch, to keep clear of branches and of the good mare's flying hoofs.

These physical details she took care of automatically—long practice gives freedom in such things—but the sudden terrific task ahead was another matter, and her brain was racing with schemes and plans with which to meet it—for on her judgment and hers alone rested the fate of all their lives.

Not new this heavy responsibility—more pressing perhaps and swifter to deal destruction. She had seen bush fires before, had helped fight many of them; but this one threatened to outdo anything she had ever encountered. For months no rain had fallen, and the country was parched to tinder dryness; heat alone would ignite the yellow grass. With her mind's eye she could watch it explode and vanish in a gout of flame, a leaping line of fire ahead of fire which often traveled swift as a man could run!

At the horse yards she pulled the bridle from the sweating mare and let her go. She was too soft for the work that lay ahead. Her eyes picked out a raw-boned, flea-bitten gray, a gelding they had christened Fiddle because his head looked like a violin. Deep-chested he was, with clean-run sloping shoulders and long lean quarters, grooved deep with stringy muscle. His ribs stood out like barrel staves, he looked ragged and unkempt, but she knew his worth in any test of courage and endurance, and now she saddled him carefully, telling of her need the while her fingers swiftly drew the buckles tight.

"Fiddle, old man, we're in a fix. You ugly old devil, it's up to you today! Don't fail me, will you? You won't! You never have!"

He nuzzled her arm, and she ran her fingers lightly down his muzzle. They understood each other, these two strong lives.

The yard gates barred, she mounted and trotted toward the house. The horses must wait; she would try to save them later; for the moment there were other things to do.

Mary, the black ginn, with three small black children in tow, stood waiting near the windmill.

"Plurry big fella fire," she grunted when Jerry drew up beside her. "Mine tinkit Missus run all about, no good."

"Mary—" Jerry spoke slowly and distinctly—"get blanket, get anything you can carry—" she pointed to the house—"house burn up maybe. Carry everything longa creek. Watch your children and wait for me."

Her own children had climbed up from the pool and stood wide-eyed, regarding her.

"Dickey, Valentine, you stay with Mary. Do you understand?" They nodded. "Mummy has to leave you for a little while; you stay with her until I get back. Don't forget what Mummy says. Stay with her. I'm trusting you!"

"Mary, you keep children longa you—yes?"

"I keep." Laconic, but she knew the ginn was reliable in any crisis she could understand. She could, must, trust her with the children.

The gray was restless, pawing and circling, fighting to get away. She paid no heed to him; her head was held a little sideways in the listening attitude of an animal, steel-taut and sprung to meet a thrust of fate—a momentary stillness caught from the welter of swiftly milling events.

Faint and far away in the silence she heard a rushing murmur, the muted voice of the advancing foe. It shocked her into instant action.

"Mummy'll be back soon, kids! Here, Patch! to heel!" She gave Fiddle his head and with the dog behind drummed out of sight among the timber.

The black ginn watched the dust of the departure. A heavy, enigmatic figure. She knew the menace of that distant sound, but nothing of its import reflected on her face. Still it was, and watchful. To the innocent questions directed at her by the children the black woman answered nothing, but, when later she gathered them about her and ascended the slope toward the house, her eyes were keen to note their movements, and she muttered at them in aboriginal, broken, throaty sounds, which her own offspring repeated in clattering whispers, pulling at Dickey and Valentine with their little clawlike fingers.

The boy held his sister by the hand, and neither spoke, but as the woman gathered articles together and carried them down to the pool, they took whatever she handed them and followed close behind her. A great black hen and five tiny chicks, up and down the slope . . .

Hi! hi! hi! Crack! crack! Scurrying gray patches moving toward the creek.

"Way back there, Patch! Sool 'em, girl! Hi! hi! hi! Get up there, woolies!" Crack! crack! crack!

Little rivulets of wool, walking, trotting, fleeing in tiny panic when horse or dog approached, settled back into maddening sloth when horse or dog passed on to others farther afield. Her eyes were everywhere, searching the thickets of wattle and mulga, rousing them up and sending them out to join the scattered procession.

Horse, dog, and woman, working together as one unit, cantering tirelessly back and forth . . .

Streamers of sheep drew slowly in toward the creek, ribbons of them, following each other head to tail. Heavy with wool, they were hot and grew quickly weary. The woman harried at them with whip and voice, the dog darted at them, they fled—a hundred, two hundred yards—like a wave which rushes up the beach, then, like the wave, they spent themselves and stood with stupid, hanging heads until the leaders moved again, when they followed, a ponderous, ever-converging progress toward one point: the clay pan.

That was her plan—to drive them to the clay pan. A glimmering surface of hard-baked clay. Devoid of any growth, the fire would ring it, half a mile of safety for anything with sense enough to stay within its boundaries and strength enough to withstand the choking fumes of heat and smoke. That was her plan. The only possible one, for the country would be swept with fire for miles. A swiftly gathered holocaust, for death would reign where it had passed.

A fitful breeze had arisen, warm, soft puffs which set the feathery mulga tips to swaying and ran a rippling sheen of gray toward the west. Her luck: it was against the enemy, not with it.

The country fell away in folds, an almost imperceptible slope toward a broken territory of lignum and ti tree in which the fire was raging fiercely. She could see the rolling clouds of smoke, caught by the tiny puffs, pressed back, and billowing up in great soft plumes to hang high in the air. A slowly spreading cloud which tinged the brilliant sunlight to a murky hue and filled the air with powdery ash.

Fleeting glances; no time to stop and mark its progress. No need. She knew the terrible measure of its advance; its wideflung spreading wings, like fiery horns; the glowing center darting and licking its way from bush to bush! She knew—and knowing, set herself to conquer the panic it engendered, holding her thoughts to the attainment of her end. In saving the sheep, she saved a gleam of hope, for the country would recover when it rained; if the sheep were lost then the charred dead miles would serve as a fitting symbol for the work of years. Black ruin and desolation stared her in the face.

Back and forth and back again!

Up and down the line of pattering gray! Scattered scents of wattle and eucalyptus, of pungent mulga and aromatic undergrowth . . . Vivid memories, like darting shafts of light through darkness. Girlhood pictures of other days and other scenes . . .

Over dry gullies and breakaways! Fallen logs and hidden pitfalls! Dashing through clearings where trembling grasses stood tall and yellow in the murky sunlight, or plunged into gloomy low-growing thickets where black-stemmed brigelow trees forced a slackened pace.

Back and forth and back again!

Mile after mile of it, and always the lagging pattering horde to urge into faster progress with high-pitched Hi! hi! hi's! and lessening Crack! crack! crack's! The cracker on her stock whip was worn to nothing and her arm almost paralyzed from one crashing contact with an overhanging tree.

Fiddle was streaked and lathered with soapy foam, but he held his pace unurged. She was light and a splendid rider, swinging with his every slightest twist to left or right, rising lightly when he jumped or scrambled over obstacles, picking the path ahead and following it, steady seated and light of hand.

The roar of approaching flames was growing louder. Sometimes she glimpsed them, a mile or less away, but she never faltered or slackened her efforts. In every tempting shade the sheep began gathering in knots, dozens of them in closely packed bunches, lying or standing in wooden indifference. She roused them up and sent them running helter-skelter, and Patch kept them to it for a little while . . .

Back and forth and back again!

Eight thousand of them in one huge mob she was driving toward the last. Rams, ewes and wethers. A slow-moving tide of wool. A threading, trickling stream of them in and out among the low bushes of blue and gray, until, as they converged toward the clay pan, it seemed the very ground itself was moving, for gray of wool and gray of mulga bush are blending shades. They flowed down the creek bank in bleating, baa-ing waves. Patch blocked their attempt to follow its course to water, rounding them up and driving the leaders over the opposite bank, while in the rear, with a wall of fire behind her, the woman galloped from group to group of halt and weary and lame.

The flames came wriggling lizard-like among the palely gleaming grass. Fiddle was growing restive; he snorted and plunged in terror when some tree or bush would suddenly ignite, exploding into hissing, crackling fury, a leaping tongue of orange and yellow hate. Her lungs were bursting. She was choked with smoke and dust, but she held on until the last of them were over the creek; then, leaving the tail to struggle after the others, she sped across the open clay pan and milled the leaders in the center.

"Watch 'em, Patch!" she called when it was finished.

The dog lay panting in the dust, with lolling tongue and foam-flecked jaws; she left her there and galloped away toward the homestead, knowing that Patch would stick it out until released from the charge.

Fiddle was nearly foundered when she reached the horse yards. She pulled the saddle and bridle off and let him stand while she bitted another mount. Then she slipped a halter over his head and led him to the creek bank where she left him tied securely in the shade.

Mary and the children were busy near the water hole. The ginn had finished digging a hole waist deep and very wide; with the children helping her, she now began to fill it from a pile of articles close at hand. A bag of flour, two cases of tinned goods and a miscellaneous assortment followed. The children were making a game of it, racing each other and vastly pleased as they staggered under burdens they could scarcely carry at all, tumbling everything into the hole.

Jerry called to them but did not stay; the fire was showing in a dozen places, ringing the slope and creeping up the hill toward the house. She opened the yard gates and drove the rest of the horses back toward the clay pan, which was already almost circled by the flames. She could see Patch in the distance, a tiny dot far out in the middle of the great orange expanse, moving slowly around the restless sheep.

She headed the horses, bunched them, and let them stream onto the clay pan at a walk. They were hard to manage, and she lost some precious time before they settled, but she dared not let them go until they quieted: they might scatter the sheep and undo everything she had worked so hard to win. She watched a moment to see that they did not try to break back, then she wheeled and found herself almost cut off.

The fire was burning toward her rapidly, fanned by the little breeze; the bed of the creek was choked by fallen timber, and she was forced to climb the opposite bank. Once up, there was nothing for it but to head straight for the homestead and trust to speed and luck to carry her through.

There followed an interval of utter chaos, a nightmare of horror from which she could not wake. Long tongues of flame reached out for her, flaming trees crashed down across her path, and the dense clouds of hot smoke almost suffocated her. Her terrified horse plunged and swerved, but she held him straight and forced him on. The smoke had filled her eyes with scalding tears; she closed them and listened in darkness to the roar of blazing timber; the horse bucked away from a burning log and almost unseated her: dizzy and sick, she straightened herself in the saddle and with a great effort forced him over it and out into the open where breathing was easier. Then at racing pace she covered the last half-mile and dropped exhausted from his back beside the water hole.

Mary had finished her work, and a great mound of sand was piled above the things she had salvaged. She came running to help Jerry, who handed over the reins of her mount and ran to unloose Fiddle.

All five of the children were standing beside the water. The little dark ones began to whimper with fright as they watched the flames approach, and Dickey, frightened also, but putting up a bold front, held his sister's hand and eyed them scornfully.

"Scary cats!" he jeered at them. "You're afraid! Lettin' a little weeny fire scare you! Val ain't afraid, are you?"

"N-no-o," said Valentine, "b-but, Dickey, it ain't a weeny fire— it's a b-big one!"

She held a little rag doll crushed under one arm, and she loosed her hand from Dickey's and held the doll up as though to let it see.

"It's a b-big one, ain't it, Sue? You never see'd such a b-big one, I bet!"

A dead tree suddenly caught and exploded with a roar into leaping flames. She caught the doll close, holding it tight with its head against her chest, and now she also began to whimper with fright.

"Augh! Girls!" said Dickey in disgust, but he eyed the fire uneasily, and they both ran eagerly to meet their mother when she approached leading Fiddle by his halter.

A heap of soaking wet blankets lay piled across a log. Jerry flung one across the horse's back, and Mary put one on the other animal. Then, handing a blanket to each of the children, and with the horses following, they waded out until the water reached their waists. Mary looked like a great black tub, her shrieking brood clinging tightly to her wet skirt.

"Cover them up!" Jerry shouted, and the ginn smothered their yells in the wet folds.

The air was filled with rushing blasts of heat and smoke. Each breath was an agony, an effort which seared the lungs. Valentine clung to her mother, choking and crying, but she still held the doll with its head above the water. Dickey faced it with a white, drawn face and trembling lips.

The horses had pulled away and waded to the farther side, where the deeper water almost reached their withers; they were snorting and terrified, but an instinct stronger than fear held them still.

Jerry carefully covered each of the children with wet blankets, drawing them about their heads and shoulders like cowls.

"See, darlings, hold it against your mouth and breathe through it—like this . . ."

She drew the blanket over her shoulders and held it against her mouth, then she knelt beside them so that her head was level with theirs and just above the water.

With an increasing roar the fire swept down toward them. Valentine screamed in terror when an emu dashed down the bank and churned its way across the pool.

"There, there, dear! It won't hurt you," Jerry comforted her. "The poor thing is trying to save its life, just like we are. See, dear, Dickey's not afraid. Are you, Dickey?" But Dickey just choked and squeezed her hand beneath the water: his lungs were too full of smoke to speak.

All kinds of bush life came scuttling down to the water: bush rats, goannas, wallabies and several big kangaroos. They crowded together, thrashing the water to muddy foam and eyeing the little group of human beings fearfully, but panic held them where they were.

Flocks of parrots were flying overhead, great strings of birds whose shrill screeching resounded even above the roar of the fire. One, a galah with lovely plumage of soft dove gray and rose, fell squattering into the water near them. Jerry reached for it and let it cling to a fold of her blanket, and Valentine's sobbing almost ceased as her interest in the poor thing's plight captured her imagination. She carefully put her hand below the fold it clung to and held it steady so that its frantic struggling presently stopped. Soon it regained its strength and flew away.

Jerry's eyes were on her home. The fence was already gone, and the outbuildings were swaying pillars of fire. Flames were beginning to break through the roof of the homestead. Memories, bitter and sweet, were flooding her eyes with smarting tears . . . She had been married under that roof . . . Beneath one of those trees her first-born lay buried; she could see the tiny cross above its grave and knew that it too presently would be gone . . .

Good years and bad years. Hopes and fears. Shearings which followed each other—the yearly highlights, for all their strivings led to and from that busy time . . .

Shearing . . . when the men arrived and the quiet was broken by laughter and song and the whirr of clippers. When the wool teams drew up beside stacks of bales and left again with twenty-seven strong horses almost dwarfed beneath their towering loads! Wagon-loads of hope which slowly drew away and slowly merged into the distance, becoming dwindling puffs of dust which tantalized the eye until they vanished.

Would they come this year? Would there be anything left for the shearers to come to? Could Patch hold the sheep—and if she did, would rain come in time to save their lives? . . . Broken thoughts and broken hopes . . . She turned her eyes away and held her children tightly to her breast.

Showers of sparks and fluttering red and blackened leaves fell all about; little hisses and bubblings came from them as they settled on the water. She saw that the wooden posts in which the iron legs of the windmill were clamped were blazing, and she watched uneasily to see which way it would go. A cloud of sparks rose high above the homestead as the roof caved in, and a moment later the windmill sagged and fell with a splintering crash across the tank beneath it.

The fire passed on and roared into the distance, and in a little while the wild life began dispersing, stealing silently away. The horses waded out and shook themselves, rolling afterward, so that their hides were rough with blackened ash and leaves.

She waited awhile, then slowly followed, clambering stiffly up the bank, a child on either side of her. Mary came grunting after, the three small black children still clinging to her sodden skirt.

It was finished. Red Hill was gone. Nothing remained but a heap of smoldering ashes, black dust and desolation as far as the eye could see. She gazed at it with red-rimmed, weary eyes. What a country! So fatal and tragically swift to destroy! She felt crushed and helpless and, now that it was over, afraid.

The ginn, a stolid, emotionless figure, began ferreting carefully beneath a heap of sand and stones; she watched her disinterestedly, and saw that she uncovered an ax with which she presently began cutting some scattered saplings missed by the fire. As each one fell, her black children dragged it to a spot she pointed out to them. They all worked silently, picking their way lightly between the smoking embers.

"What for you cut bush?" Jerry asked as the ginn passed close in search of suitable branches.

"House burn up. Buildum gunyah. Rain come by'n'by wet everyting." She pointed.

The distant clay pan glimmered dimly beneath the drifting haze of smoke. Crowded near the center were the sheep, a splash of gray, and, scattered here and there across it, little groups of horses stood or moved in idling circles. Beyond, piling up like great black mountains toward the dun-colored ball that was the sun, storm clouds were gathering. A jagged rampart of hope: RAIN.

"You gottum nother fella ax?"

The ginn nodded and uncovered a second shining blade. Jerry took it and ran her thumb along the edge, an edge fine-whetted to do a job.

Her eyes dwelt a moment on the gathering clouds, the distant sheep and horses, the blackened countryside so soon to benefit by that blessed rain.

A fine face, strong. A face reflecting something of the strength that lies unquenchable in the soil.

Despair and weariness were pushed aside, gray eyes grew steady with hope and courage.

"Come, children!" she said, and took her place beside the black ginn. Their axes rose and fell together, a swinging rhythm of glistening steel.

Understanding the Story

Main Idea

1. The main idea of the story is summed up in which of the following statements?
   (a) A forest fire is much more dangerous than a fire in the bush.
   (b) The heroine's main concern was saving the sheep from the ravages of the approaching fire.
   (c) The heroine showed uncommon courage and resourcefulness in facing the dangers of the fire.
   (d) By diverting water from the creek, the two women might have saved the homestead from the fire.

Details

2. "Fire in the Bush" takes place in (a) Canada (b) the southwestern part of the United States (c) Australia (d) New Zealand.

3. Jerry's husband (a) is out in the fields (b) has gone hunting (c) has been ill (d) has gone to town.

4. Jerry tells Mary to (a) be calm (b) guard the children (c) try to save the house (d) call for help.

5. The only way to save the ranch animals is to (a) drive them away from the fire (b) build a counter-fire (c) drive them to the clay pan (d) put out the fire.

Inferences

6. When the danger is past, Mary teaches Jerry how   (a) to accept the loss   (b) to collect the insurance   (c) to get in touch with her husband   (d) they could have saved the house.

7. Which one of the following statements is *true?*
   (a) Jerry doesn't know how to handle the stove.
   (b) She dislikes the loneliness of her life.
   (c) She is a poor rider.
   (d) She is frightened by the approaching fire.

8. The house Jerry lives in resembles a   (a) pioneer log cabin (b) modern cottage   (c) run-down shack   (d) luxurious mansion.

9. When the fire passes,   (a) Jerry weeps over her losses (b) the two women begin to build another dwelling   (c) they go to bring the animals back   (d) the husband returns.

10. The best word to label Fiddle is   (a) reliable   (b) rebellious (c) beautiful   (d) useless.

Order of Events

11. Arrange the items in the order in which they occurred. Use letters only.
    A. Mary says that rain is coming.
    B. Jerry sets Patch to herd the sheep.
    C. Wild animals crowd into the creek.
    D. Mary builds a mound of sand to save the household things.
    E. Jerry first senses the approaching fire.

Outcomes

12. If there had been no clay pan,   (a) the house would have survived   (b) the sheep would have perished   (c) Jerry would have made a clearing for the animals   (d) Mary would have panicked.

Cause and Effect

13. The fire   (a) brought out unusual strength and courage in Jerry   (b) destroyed the entire bird population of the area (c) miraculously left the house untouched   (d) brought on a sharp disagreement between Mary and Jerry.

Fact or Opinion

Tell whether each of the following is a fact or an opinion.

14. Fiddle was braver than Patch.

15. The children and their mothers sought refuge in the creek.

Words in Context _____

1. Set like *a mote in a sea of detachment* . . . stood a small homestead.
   A mote in a sea of detachment (331) means a   (a) child in a world of adults   (b) piece of dust on a plate   (c) package in a storeroom   (d) speck in an isolated vastness.

2. Like some sullen black monster it was; a *squat malevolent* devil.
   Squat and *malevolent* (332) means   (a) long and efficient   (b) ugly and cooperative   (c) low and spiteful   (d) large and unmanageable.

3. "*Cross-grained* brute!" she *admonished* it.
   Cross-grained . . . *admonished* (332) means   (a) ugly . . . shouted   (b) horrible . . . whispered to   (c) stubborn . . . scolded   (d) perverse . . . adjusted.

4. To meet and conquer the *adverse* circumstances of an *untoward* existence.
   Adverse . . . *untoward* (333) means   (a) friendly . . . challenging   (b) unfavorable . . . difficult to manage   (c) complicated . . . made too simple   (d) tragic . . . productive.

5. The almost visible awareness of its terrible *indifference* . . . breeds an *introspective* outlook.
   Indifference . . . *introspective* (333) means   (a) cruelty . . . self-pitying   (b) destruction . . . fearful   (c) isolation . . . distrustful   (d) not caring . . . self-questioning.

6. The horizon held its usual outline: *a wavering, almost indiscernible blending of earth and sky.*
   When she looked toward the horizon (334), she saw   (a) a clearly defined line   (b) a thin border   (c) an indistinct line of separation   (d) a separation by colors.

7. She *discerned* what might have been a *heliograph.*
   Discerned ... heliograph (334) means   (a) heard ... helicopter   (b) made out ... signal by mirror reflecting sunlight   (c) sensed quickly ... heat lightning racing toward her   (d) saw ... bird of prey.

8. A bush fire! Most *sinister* of all the *dire* curses Nature held.
   Sinister ... dire (335) means   (a) fatal ... unexpected   (b) contagious ... horrible   (c) frequent ... common   (d) menacing ... dreadful.

9. He *nuzzled* her arm, and she ran her fingers lightly down his muzzle.
   Nuzzled (336) means   (a) licked   (b) rubbed with his nose   (c) smelled   (d) pushed away.

10. —a momentary stillness caught from the *welter* of swiftly *milling* events.
    Welter ... milling (337) means   (a) sadness ... tragic   (b) confusion ... moving   (c) danger ... occurring   (d) meaning ... unfolding.

Thinking About the Story _____

1. In a few short pages we are introduced to strongly defined characters. Tell briefly your impression of Jerry, Mary, Dickey, Valentine, Fiddle, Patch.

2. The story builds up a feeling of ominous tension even before the fire is spotted. How does the episode of the stove help build this tension?

3. How does the author provide an excellent picture of what life is like on a lonely Australian sheep station. Point out exceptionally good bits of description.

4. Point out several good descriptions of the raging fire. How does the author introduce the heroine's feelings and actions to deepen the terror?

5. This is a pioneer setting. How does this story help to explain the growth of democracy in Australia and in our own West? (Hint: what part does self-reliance play in the development of democracy?)

6. "She felt crushed and helpless and, *now that it was over, afraid* (page 344). Discuss the meaning of this sentence, particularly the italicized words. Have you ever had to act quickly in a dangerous or critical situation? Did the feeling of fear oppress you before, or after, the climax?

Death of Red Peril

Walter D. Edmonds

♦ "Leeza," he says, "I got the fastest caterpillar
in seven counties. It's an act of Providence I seen
him, the way he jumped the ruts."

With mock solemnity and reverent chuckles, we present this
tale of the rise and fall of the most famous caterpillar in American
fiction, that lightning-fast, stout-hearted demon speedster of the
chalk-ring track, known to all and sundry as *Red Peril.*

Now Red Peril may be only a lowly caterpillar, but as you get
into this story, you'll acquire a respect, affection, and sympathy
for this sturdy little creature. You'll begin to think of him as an
intelligent being with feelings and fears. You'll consider him a
worthy member of our courageous company.

Walter D. Edmonds, the author of this folktale, has special-
ized in exploiting the history and legends of upstate New York. In
this tall tale he deals with the relationship between Red Peril and
his owner—an Erie Canal bargeman—and the way they fought for
each other. You may shed an unexpected tear with Pa as a mor-
tally wounded Red Peril tries to win his last race for his master.

The humor in this story may not be as boisterous as the hi-
larity in "The Party," but there is rich laughter to be found here.
Half a dozen colorful characters come to vivid life for you, as they
employ cunning, trickery, and bravado and try to pick a winning
caterpillar. At the center of all that conniving is Red Peril, caterpillar extraordinary, racer without equal. Can Red Peril make that
last chalk line? On to the race.

DEATH OF RED PERIL

A horse race is a handsome thing to watch if a man has his money on a sure proposition. My pa was always a great hand at a horse race. But when he took to a boat and my mother he didn't have no more time for it. So he got interested in another sport.

Did you ever hear of racing caterpillars? No? Well, it used to be a great thing on the canawl. My pa used to have a lot of them insects on hand every fall, and the way he could get them to run would make a man have his eyes examined.

The way we raced caterpillars was to set them in a napkin ring on a table, one facing one way and one the other. Outside the napkin ring was drawed a circle in chalk three feet acrost. Then a man lifted the ring and the handlers was allowed one jab with a darning needle to get their caterpillars started. The one that got outside the chalk circle the first was the one that won the race.

I remember my pa tried out a lot of breeds, and he got hold of some pretty fast steppers. But there wasn't one of them could equal Red Peril. To see him you wouldn't believe he could run. He was all red and kind of stubby, and he had a sort of a wart behind that you'd think would get in his way. There wasn't anything fancy in his looks. He'd just set still studying the ground and make you think he was dreaming about last year's oats; but when you set him in the starting ring he'd hitch himself up behind like a man lifting on his galluses, and then he'd light out for glory.

Pa come acrost Red Peril down in Westernville. Ma's relatives resided there, and it being Sunday we'd all gone in to church. We was riding back in a hired rig with a dandy trotter, and Pa was pushing her right along and Ma was talking sermon and clothes, and me and my sister was setting on the back seat playing poke your nose, when all of a sudden Pa hollers, "Whoa!" and set the horse right down on the breeching. Ma let out a holler and come to rest on the dashboard with her head under the horse. "My gracious land!" she says. "What's happened?" Pa was out on the other side of the road right down in the mud in his Sunday pants, a-wropping up something in his yeller handkerchief. Ma begun to get riled. "What you doing, Pa?" she says. "What you got there?" Pa was putting his handkerchief back into his inside pocket. Then he come back over the wheel and got him a chew. "Leeza," he says, "I got the fastest caterpillar in seven counties. It's an act of Providence I seen him, the way he jumped the ruts." "It's an act of God I ain't laying dead under the back end of that horse," says Ma. "I've gone and spoilt my Sunday hat." "Never mind," says Pa; "Red Peril will earn you a new one." Just like that he named him. He was the fastest caterpillar in seven counties.

When we got back onto the boat, while Ma was turning up the supper, Pa set him down to the table under the lamp and pulled out the handkerchief. "You two devils stand there and there," he says to me and my sister, "and if you let him get by I'll leather the soap out of you."

So we stood there and he undid the handkerchief, and out walked one of them red, long-haired caterpillars. He walked right to the middle of the table, and then he took a short turn and put his nose in his tail and went to sleep.

"Who'd think that insect could make such a break for freedom as I seen him make?" says Pa, and he got out a empty Brandreth box and filled it up with some towel and put the caterpillar inside. "He needs a rest," says Pa. "He needs to get used to his stall. When he limbers up I'll commence training him. Now then," he says, putting the box on the shelf back of the stove, "don't none of you say a word about him."

He got out a pipe and set there smoking and figuring, and we could see he was studying out just how he'd make a world-beater out of that bug. "What you going to feed him?" asks Ma. "If I wasn't afraid of spoiling his stomach," Pa says, "I'd try him out with milkweed."

Next day we hauled up the Lansing Kill Gorge. Ned Kilbourne, Pa's driver, come aboard in the morning, and he took a look at that caterpillar. He took him out of the box and felt his legs and laid him down on the table and went clean over him. "Well," he says, "he don't look like a great lot, but I've knowed some of that red variety could chug along pretty smart." Then he touched him with a pin. It was a sudden sight.

It looked like the rear end of that caterpillar was racing the front end, but it couldn't never quite get by. Afore either Ned or Pa could get a move Red Peril had made a turn around the sugar bowl and run solid aground in the butter dish.

Pa let out a loud swear. "Look out he don't pull a tendon," he says. "Butter's a bad thing. A man has to be careful. Jeepers," he says, picking him up and taking him over to the stove to dry, "I'll handle him myself. I don't want no rum-soaked bezabors dishing my beans."

"I didn't mean harm, Will," says Ned. "I was just curious."

There was something extraordinary about that caterpillar. He was intelligent. It seemed he just couldn't abide the feel of sharp iron. It got so that if Pa reached for the lapel of his coat Red Peril would light out. It must have been he was tender. I said he had a sort of a wart behind, and I guess he liked to find it a place of safety.

We was all terrible proud of that bird. Pa took to timing him on the track. He beat all known time holler. He got to know that as soon as he crossed the chalk he would get back safe in his quarters. Only when we tried sprinting him across the supper table, if he saw a piece of butter he'd pull up short and bolt back where he come from. He had a mortal fear of butter.

Well, Pa trained him three nights. It was a sight to see him there at the table, a big man with a needle in his hand, moving the lamp around and studying out the identical spot that caterpillar wanted most to get out of the needle's way. Pretty soon he found it, and then he says to Ned, "I'll race him agin all comers at all odds." "Well, Will," says Ned, "I guess it's a safe proposition."

We hauled up the feeder to Forestport and got us a load of potatoes. We raced him there against Charley Mack, the bank walker's, Leopard Pillar, one of them tufted breeds with a row of black buttons down the back. The Leopard was well liked and had won several races that season, and there was quite a few boaters around that fancied him. Pa argued for favorable odds, saying he was racing a maiden caterpillar; and there was a lot of money laid out, and Pa and Ned managed to cover the most of it. As for the race, there wasn't anything to it. While we was putting him in the ring—one of them birchbark and sweet-grass ones Indians make—Red Peril didn't act very good. I guess the smell and the crowd kind of upset him. He was nervous and kept fidgeting with his front feet; but they hadn't more'n lifted the ring than he lit out under the edge as tight as he could make it, and Pa touched him with the needle just as he lepped the line. Me and my sister was supposed to be in bed, but Ma had gone visiting in Forestport and we'd snuck in and was under the table, which had a red cloth onto it, and I can tell you there was some shouting. There was some couldn't believe that insect had been inside the ring at all; and there was some said he must be a cross with a dragon fly or a side-hill gouger; but old Charley Mack, that'd worked in the camps, said he guessed Red Peril must be descended from the caterpillars Paul Bunyan used to race. He said you could tell by the bump on his tail, which Paul used to put on all his caterpillars, seeing as how the smallest pointed object he could hold in his hand was a peavey.

Well, Pa raced him a couple of more times and he won just as easy, and Pa cleared up close to a hundred dollars in three races. That caterpillar was a mammoth wonder, and word of him got going and people commenced talking him up everywhere, so it was hard to race him around these parts.

But about that time the lock keeper of Number One on the feeder come across a pretty swift article that the people around Rome thought high of. And as our boat was headed down the gorge, word got ahead about Red Peril, and people began to look out for the race.

We come into Number One about four o'clock, and Pa tied up right there and went on shore with his box in his pocket and Red Peril inside the box. There must have been ten men crowded into the shanty, and as many more again outside looking in the windows and door. The lock tender was a skinny bezabor from Stittville, who thought he knew a lot about racing caterpillars; and, come to think of it, maybe he did. His name was Henry Buscerck, and he had a bad tooth in front he used to suck at a lot.

Well, him and Pa set their caterpillars on the table for the crowd to see, and I must say Buscerck's caterpillar was as handsome a brute as you could wish to look at, bright bay with black points and a short fine coat. He had a way of looking right and left, too, that made him handsome. But Pa didn't bother to look at him. Red Peril was a natural marvel, and he knew it.

Buscerck was a sly, twirpish man, and he must've heard about

Red Peril—right from the beginning, as it turned out; for he laid out the course in yeller chalk. They used Pa's ring, a big silver one he'd bought secondhand just for Red Peril. They laid out a lot of money, and Dennison Smith lifted the ring. The way Red Peril histed himself out from under would raise a man's blood pressure twenty notches. I swear you could see the hair lay down on his back. Why, that black-pointed bay was left nowhere! It didn't seem like he moved. But Red Peril was just gathering himself for a fast finish over the line when he seen it was yeller. He reared right up; he must've thought it was butter, by Jeepers, the way he whirled on his hind legs and went the way he'd come. Pa begun to get scared, and he shook his needle behind Red Peril, but that caterpillar was more scared of butter than he ever was of cold steel. He passed the other insect afore he'd got halfway to the line. By Cripus, you'd ought to 've heard the cheering from the Forestport crews. The Rome men was green. But when he got to the line, danged if that caterpillar didn't shy agin and run around the circle twicet, and then it seemed like his heart had gone in on him, and he crept right back to the middle of the circle and lay there hiding his head. It was the pitifulest sight a man ever looked at. You could almost hear him moaning, and he shook all over.

I've never seen a man so riled as Pa was. The water was running right out of his eyes. He picked up Red Peril and he says, "This here's no race." He picked up his money and he says, "The course was illegal, with that yeller chalk." Then he squashed the other caterpillar, which was just getting ready to cross the line, and he looks at Buscerck and says, "What're you going to do about that?"

Buscerck says, "I'm going to collect my money. My caterpillar would have beat."

"If you want to call that a finish you can," says Pa, pointing to the squashed bay one, "but a baby could see he's still got to reach the line. Red Peril got to wire and come back and got to it again afore your hayseed worm got half his feet on the ground. If it was any other man owned him," Pa says, "I'd feel sorry I squashed him."

He stepped out of the house, but Buscerck laid a-hold of his pants and says, "You got to pay, Hemstreet. A man can't get away with no such excuses in the city of Rome."

Pa didn't say nothing. He just hauled off and sunk his fist, and Buscerck come to inside the lock, which was at low level right then. He waded out the lower end and he says, "I'll have you arrested for this." Pa says, "All right; but if I ever catch you around this lock again I'll let you have a feel with your other eye."

Nobody else wanted to collect money from Pa, on account of his build, mostly, so we went back to the boat. Pa put Red Peril to bed for two days. It took him all of that to get over his fright at the yeller circle. Pa even made us go without butter for a spell, thinking Red Peril might know the smell of it. He was such an intelligent, thinking animal, a man couldn't tell nothing about him.

But next morning the sheriff comes aboard and arrests Pa with a warrant and takes him afore a justice of the peace. That was old Oscar Snipe. He'd heard all about the race, and I think he was feeling pleasant with Pa, because right off they commenced talking breeds. It would have gone off good only Pa'd been having a round with the sheriff. They come in arm in arm, singing a Hallelujah meeting song; but Pa was polite, and when Oscar says, "What's this?" he only says, "Well, well."

"I hear you've got a good caterpillar," says the judge.

"Well, well," says Pa. It was all he could think of to say.

"What breed is he?" says Oscar, taking a chew.

"Well," says Pa, "well, well."

Ned Kilbourne says he was a red one.

"That's a good breed," says Oscar, folding his hands on his stummick and spitting over his thumbs and between his knees and into the sandbox all in one spit. "I kind of fancy the yeller ones myself. You're a connesewer," he says to Pa, "and so'm I, and between connesewers I'd like to show you one. He's as neat a stepper as there is in this county."

"Well, well," says Pa, kind of cold around the eyes and looking at the lithograph of Mrs. Snipe done in a hair frame over the sink.

Oscar slews around and fetches a box out of his back pocket and shows us a sweet little yeller one.

"There she is," he says, and waits for praise.

"She was a good woman," Pa said after a while, looking at the picture, "if any woman that's four times a widow can be called such."

"Not her," says Oscar. "It's this yeller caterpillar."

Pa slung his eyes on the insect which Oscar was holding, and it seemed like he'd just got an idee.

"Fast?" he says, deep down. "That thing run! Why, a snail with the stringhalt could spit in his eye."

Old Oscar come to a boil quick.

"Evidence. Bring me the evidence."

He spit, and he was that mad he let his whole chew get away from him without noticing. Buscerck says, "Here," and takes his hand off'n his right eye.

Pa never took no notice of nothing after that but the eye. It was the shiniest black onion I ever see on a man. Oscar says, "Forty dollars!" And Pa pays and says, "It's worth it."

But it don't never pay to make an enemy in horse racing or caterpillars, as you will see, after I've got around to telling you.

Well, we raced Red Peril nine times after that, all along the Big Ditch, and you can hear to this day—yes, sir—that there never was a caterpillar alive could run like Red Peril. Pa got rich onto him. He allowed to buy a new team in the spring. If he could only've started a breed from that bug, his fortune would've been made and Henry Ford would've looked like a bent nickel alongside of me to-day. But caterpillars aren't built like Ford cars. We beat all the great caterpillars of the year, and it being a time for a late winter, there was some fast running. We raced the Buffalo Big Blue and Fenwick's Night Mail and Wilson's Joe of Barneveld. There wasn't one could touch Red Peril. It was close into October when a crowd got together and brought up the Black Arrer of Ava to race us, but Red Peril beat him by an inch. And after that there wasn't a cater-pillar in the state would race Pa's.

He was mighty chesty them days and had come to be quite a figger down the canawl. People come aboard to talk with him and admire Red Peril; and Pa got the idea of charging five cents a sight, and that made for more money even if there wasn't no more run-ning for the animile. He commenced to get fat.

And then come the time that comes to all caterpillars. And it goes to show that a man ought to be as careful of his enemies as he is lending money to friends.

We was hauling down the Lansing Kill again and we'd just crossed the aqueduct over Stringer Brook when the lock keeper, that minded it and the lock just below, come out and says there was quite a lot of money being put up on a caterpillar they'd collected down in Rome.

Well, Pa went in and he got out Red Peril and tried him out. He was fat and his stifles acted kind of stiff, but you could see with half an eye he was still fast. His start was a mite slower, but he made great speed once he got going.

"He's not in the best shape in the world," Pa says, "and if it was any other bug I wouldn't want to run him. But I'll trust the old brute," and he commenced brushing him up with a toothbrush he'd bought a-purpose.

"Yeanh," says Ned. "It may not be right, but we've got to consider the public."

By what happened after, we might have known that we'd meet up with that caterpillar at Number One Lock; but there wasn't no sign of Buscerck, and Pa was so excited at racing Red Peril again that I doubt if he noticed where he was at all. He was all rigged out for the occasion. He had on a black hat and a new red boating waistcoat, and when he busted loose with his horn for the lock you'd have thought he wanted to wake up all the deef-and-dumbers in seven counties. We tied by the upper gates and left the team to graze; and there was quite a crowd on hand. About nine morning boats was tied along the towpath, and all the afternoon boats waited. People was hanging around, and when they heard Pa whanging his horn they let out a great cheer. He took off his hat to some of the ladies, and then he took Red Peril out of his pocket and everybody cheered some more.

"Who owns this here caterpillar I've been hearing about?" Pa asks. "Where is he? Why don't he bring out his pore contraption?"

A feller says he's in the shanty.

"What's his name?" says Pa.

"Martin Henry's running him. He's called the Horned Demon of Rome."

"Dinged if I ever thought to see him at my time of life," says Pa. And he goes in. Inside there was a lot of men talking and smoking and drinking and laying money faster than leghorns can lay eggs, and when Pa comes in they let out a great howdy, and when Pa put down the Brandreth box on the table they crowded round; and you'd ought to 've heard the mammoth shout they give when Red Peril climbed out of his box. And well they might. Yes, sir!

You can tell that caterpillar's a thoroughbred. He's shining right down to the root of each hair. He's round, but he ain't too fat. He don't look as supple as he used to, but the folks can't tell that. He's got the winner's look, and he prances into the center of the ring with a kind of delicate canter that was as near single footing as I ever see a caterpillar get to. By Jeepers Cripus! I felt proud to be in the same family as him, and I wasn't only a little lad.

Pa waits for the admiration to die down, and he lays out his money, and he says to Martin Henry, "Let's see your ring-boned swivel-hocked imitation of a bug."

Martin answers, "Well, he ain't much to look at, maybe, but you'll be surprised to see how he can push along."

And he lays down the dangedest lump of worm you ever set your eyes on. It's the kind of insect a man might expect to see in France or one of them furrin lands. It's about two and a half inches long and stands only half a thumbnail at the shoulder. It's green and as hairless as a newborn egg, and it crouches down squinting around at Red Peril like a man with sweat in his eye. It ain't natural nor refined to look at such a bug, let alone race it.

When Pa seen it, he let out a shout and laughed. He couldn't talk from laughing.

But the crowd didn't say a lot, having more money on the race than ever was before or since on a similar occasion. It was so much that even Pa commenced to be serious. Well, they put 'em in the ring together and Red Peril kept over on his side with a sort of intelligent dislike. He was the brainiest article in the caterpillar line I ever knowed. The other one just hunkered down with a mean look in his eye.

Millard Thompson held the ring. He counted, "One—two—three—and off." Some folks said it was the highest he knew how to count, but he always got that far anyhow, even if it took quite a while for him to remember what figger to commence with.

The ring come off and Pa and Martin Henry sunk their needles—at least they almost sunk them, for just then them standing close to the course seen that Horned Demon sink his horns into the back end of Red Peril. He was always a sensitive animal, Red Peril was, and if a needle made him start you can think for yourself what them two horns did for him. He cleared twelve inches in one jump—but then he sot right down on his belly, trembling.

"Foul!" bellers Pa. "My 'pillar's fouled."

"It ain't in the rule book," Millard says.

"It's a foul!" yells Pa; and all the Forestport men yell, "Foul! Foul!"

But it wasn't allowed. The Horned Demon commenced walking to the circle—he couldn't move much faster than a barrel can roll uphill, but he was getting there. We all seen two things, then. Red Peril was dying, and he was losing the race. Pa stood there kind of foamy in his beard, and the water running right out of both eyes.

It's an awful thing to see a big man cry in public. But Ned saved us. He seen Red Peril was dying, the way he wiggled, and he figgered, with the money he had on him, he'd make him win if he could.

He leans over and puts his nose into Red Peril's ear, and he shouts, "My Cripus, you've gone and dropped the butter!"

Something got into that caterpillar's brain, dying as he was, and he let out the smallest squeak of a hollering fright I ever listened to a caterpillar make. There was a convulsion got into him. He looked like a three-dollar mule with the wind colic, and then he gave a bound. My holy! How that caterpillar did rise up. When he come down again, he was stone dead, but he lay with his chin across the line. He'd won the race. The Horned Demon was blowing bad and only halfway to the line . . .

Well, we won. But I think Pa's heart was busted by the squeal he heard Red Peril make when he died. He couldn't abide Ned's face after that, though he knowed Ned had saved the day for him. But he put Red Peril's carcase in his pocket with the money and walks out.

And there he seen Buscerck standing at the sluices. Pa stood looking at him. The sheriff was alongside Buscerck and Oscar Snipe on the other side, and Buscerck guessed he had the law behind him.

"Who owns that Horned Demon?" says Pa.

"Me," says Buscerck with a sneer. "He may have lost, but he done a good job doing it."

Pa walks right up to him.

"I've got another forty dollars in my pocket," he says, and he connected sizably.

Buscerck's boots showed a minute. Pretty soon they let down the water and pulled him out. They had to roll a couple of gallons out of him afore they got a grunt. It served him right. He'd played foul. But the sheriff was worried, and he says to Oscar, "Had I ought to arrest Will?" (Meaning Pa.)

Oscar was a sporting man. He couldn't abide low dealing. He looks at Buscerck there, shaping his belly over the barrel, and he says, "Water never hurt a man. It keeps his hide from cracking." So they let Pa alone. I guess they didn't think it was safe to have a man in jail that would cry about a caterpillar. But then they hadn't lived alongside of Red Peril like us.

Understanding the Story _____

Main Idea

1. Red Peril   (a) disliked the sight or smell of butter   (b) was really slower than Horned Demon   (c) was the fastest racing caterpillar in the area   (d) was attacked by another caterpillar.

Details

2. Pa takes up the hobby of caterpillar racing because   (a) he gets the idea from finding Red Peril   (b) he has to give up horse racing   (c) Henry Buscerck challenged him   (d) his wife suggests it.

3. The owner of the last opponent of Red Peril is   (a) a stranger   (b) the man Pa had hit   (c) the Judge   (d) the governor.

4. Red Peril learns to dislike anything yellow because   (a) he had run into a butter dish   (b) he was kept in a yellow cage   (c) all caterpillars dislike yellow   (d) yellow is Pa's favorite color.

5. In his last race, Red Peril   (a) is defeated   (b) kills his opponent   (c) conquers his fear of butter   (d) is killed.

Inferences

6. The judge doesn't fine Pa again because   (a) Buscerck asks him not to   (b) he has won some money on Red Peril   (c) Pa cries   (d) he made a mistake.

7. Henry Buscerck's laying out the course in yellow chalk was   (a) an accident   (b) the usual way to do it   (c) a way of helping Red Peril   (d) an act of trickery.

8. Pa talks and thinks about Red Peril as if the caterpillar might be   (a) immortal   (b) a racehorse   (c) a sheriff   (d) a butterfly.

9. One trouble with Red Peril was that his reputation   (a) scared away many competitors   (b) got worse after his first race   (c) never changed   (d) was never great enough to arouse interest.

10. This story is   (a) a tale of an actual event   (b) a horror story   (c) a story of a scientific experiment   (d) not intended to be true to life.

Order of Events

11. Arrange the items in the order in which they occurred. Use letters only.
    A. Red Peril runs into the butter dish.
    B. Pa gives up horse racing.
    C. The Horned Demon attacks Red Peril.
    D. Pa strikes Henry Buscerck the first time.
    E. Pa finds Red Peril.

Outcomes

12. If the Horned Demon had not attacked Red Peril, Red Peril would have   (a) attacked Horned Demon   (b) won easily   (c) lost in a close race   (d) stayed in the center of the ring without moving.

Cause and Effect

13. Pa struck Henry Buscerck the second time because   (a) he mistook him for someone else   (b) Horned Demon had defeated Red Peril   (c) Oscar Snipe put Pa up to it   (d) Henry Buscerck's caterpillar had killed Red Peril.

Fact or Opinion

Tell whether each of the following is a fact or an opinion.

14. Red Peril avoided butter.

15. Pa was the most hot-blooded man in the Erie Canal.

Words in Context

1. He'd hitch himself up behind like a man lifting on his *galluses,* and then he'd light out for glory.
   Galluses   (351)   means   (a) shoes   (b) trousers (c) suspenders   (d) glasses.

2. We was riding back in a hired *rig* with a dandy *trotter.*
   Rig ... *trotter*   (351)   means   (a) truck ... assistant

(b) tractor ... mule (c) carriage ... horse (d) taxi ... companion.

3. Pa hollers, "Whoa!" and *set the horse right down on the breeching.*
   Set the horse right down on the breeching (352) means (a) stopped the horse in its tracks (b) ran the horse off the road (c) turned the vehicle over (d) stopped the horse on the railroad tracks.

4. "It's an act of *Providence* I seen him."
   Providence (352) means (a) a great dramatist (b) Rhode Island officials (c) Congress (d) Divine assistance.

5. He had a *mortal* fear of butter.
   Mortal (353) means (a) lively (b) occasional (c) mild (d) extreme.

6. The smallest pointed object he could hold was a *peavey.* A *peavey* (354) is a woodsman's (a) watch chain (b) hooked pole (c) rifle (d) heavy jacket.

7. That caterpillar was a *mammoth* wonder.
   Mammoth (354) means (a) temporary (b) dangerous (c) very great (d) completely constant

8. "You're a *connesewer,*" he says to Pa, "and so'm I, and between connesewers I'd like to show you one."
   By *connesewer* (connoisseur) (356) he meant (a) expert (b) contender (c) gambler (d) a winning player.

9. "Well, well," says Pa, kind of cold around the eyes and looking at the *lithograph* of Mrs. Snipe.
   Lithograph (356) means (a) kitchen (b) printed photograph (c) crocheting (d) betting score.

10. He didn't look as *supple* as he used to, but the folks can't tell that.
    Supple (358) means (a) speedy (b) capable (c) fresh (d) flexible.

Thinking About the Story

1. Humor often depends upon contrasts. If a tall, heavy man is walking a toy dog, people will chuckle. Part of the humor in this story comes from the contrast between the tiny caterpillar and

the way he is treated: like a thoroughbred racehorse. Point out examples in the text to show this treatment.

2. The events are seen through the eyes of a boy and are told by him. Why is it an advantage to have the boy tell the story?

3. Why did Red Peril get out of condition? How did Pa make money during his period of inactivity?

4. Though a tall story depends upon exaggeration, it must be told with a straight face. The most outrageous events must be told matter-of-factly, as though they were commonplace. What examples of exaggeration can you find in the story?

5. Most stories have at least three elements: explanation, complication, and resolution. The explanation sets the stage. It introduces the main characters and tells something about them. The complication introduces conflict. Something goes wrong. The resolution ties the ends together and completes the story. For romantic tales, this outline is sometimes abbreviated: boy meets girl; boy loses girl; boy wins girl again. How does this story provide explanation, conflict, and resolution?

Sixty Acres

Raymond Carver

♦ "Whose land do you think this is?" Waite said. "What do you mean, shooting ducks on my land!" One boy turned around cautiously, his hand still in front of his eyes. "What are you going to do?"

Put yourself into this picture. You own 60 acres of choice land on an Indian reservation. Someone calls to tell you that some hunters are shooting ducks on your land. Outsiders are forbidden, by government decree, to hunt on the land. Yet the shots ring out.

The problem falls on you. There is no corner policeman on hand to preserve your rights. If the hunters are going to be turned away, *you* must do the job. Yet the hunters are armed and may be dangerous. Besides, there is just one of you and two of them. What do you do?

This is the story of Lee Waite who faces that possibly dangerous situation with courage. But it is more than a story of a man defending his rights. It is also a complex story of individuals: Lee, his wife, his children, his silent mother. It is a story of personal pressures inside the home reflected in the pressures outside the home. It is a touching picture of one man's life on an Indian reservation.

"Sixty Acres" is a quiet story. Nothing much happens on the surface, yet you will find yourself inside the skin of a brave man who faces possible danger with many human misgivings but with understated courage.

SIXTY ACRES

The call had come an hour ago, when they were eating. Two men were shooting on Lee Waite's part of Toppenish Creek, down below the bridge on the Cowiche Road. It was the third or fourth time this winter someone had been in there, Joseph Eagle reminded Lee Waite. Joseph Eagle was an old Indian who lived on his government allotment in a little place off the Cowiche Road, with a radio he listened to day and night and a telephone in case he got sick. Lee Waite wished the old Indian would let him be about that land, that Joseph Eagle would do something else about it, if he wanted, besides call.

Out on the porch, Lee Waite leaned on one leg and picked at a string of meat between his teeth. He was a small thin man with a thin face and long black hair. If it had not been for the phone call, he would have slept awhile this afternoon. He frowned and took his time pulling into his coat; they would be gone anyway when he got there. That was usually the way. The hunters from Toppenish or Yakima could drive the reservation roads like anyone else; they just weren't allowed to hunt. But they would cruise by that untenanted and irresistible sixty acres of his, two, maybe three times, then, if they were feeling reckless, park down off the road in the trees and hurry through the knee-deep barley and wild oats, down to the creek—maybe getting some ducks, maybe not, but always doing a lot of shooting in the little time before they cleared out. Joseph Eagle sat crippled in his house and watched them plenty of times. Or so he told Lee Waite.

He cleaned his teeth with his tongue and squinted in the late-afternoon winter half-light. He wasn't afraid; it wasn't that, he told himself. He just didn't want trouble.

The porch, small and built on just before the war, was almost dark. The one window glass had been knocked out years before, and Waite had nailed a beet sack over the opening. It hung there next to the cabinet, matted-thick and frozen, moving slightly as the cold air from outside came in around the edges. The walls were crowded with old yokes and harnesses, and up on one side, above the window, was a row of rusted hand tools. He made a last sweep with his tongue, tightened the light bulb into the overhead socket, and opened the cabinet. He took out the old double-barrel from in back and reached into the box on the top shelf for a handful of shells. The brass ends of the shells felt cold, and he rolled them in his hand before dropping them into a pocket of the old coat he was wearing.

"Aren't you going to load it, Papa?" the boy Benny asked from behind.

Waite turned, saw Benny and little Jack standing in the kitchen doorway. Ever since the call they had been after him—had wanted to know if this time he was going to shoot somebody. It bothered him, kids talking like that, like they would enjoy it, and now they stood at the door, letting all the cold air in the house and looking at the large gun up under his arm.

"Get back in that house where the hell you belong," he said.

They left the door open and ran back in where his mother and Nina were and on through to the bedroom. He could see Nina at the table trying to coax bites of squash into the baby, who was pulling back and shaking her head. Nina looked up, tried to smile.

Waite stepped into the kitchen and shut the door, leaned against it. She was plenty tired, he could tell. A beaded line of moisture glistened over her lip, and, as he watched, she stopped to move the hair away from her forehead. She looked up at him again, then back at the baby. It had never bothered her like this when she was carrying before. The other times she could hardly sit still and used to jump up and walk around, even if there wasn't much to do except cook a meal or sew. He fingered the loose skin around his neck and glanced covertly at his mother, dozing since the meal in a chair by the stove. She squinted her eyes at him and nodded. She was seventy and shriveled, but her hair was still crow-black and hung down in front over her shoulders in two long tight braids. Lee Waite was sure she had something wrong with her because sometimes she went two days without saying something, just sitting in the other room by the window and staring off up the valley. It made him shiver when she did that, and he didn't know any more what her little signs and signals, her silences, were supposed to mean.

"Why don't you say something?" he asked, shaking his head. "How do I know what you mean, Mama, if you don't say?" Waite looked at her for a minute and watched her tug at the ends of her braids, waited for her to say something. Then he grunted and crossed by in front of her, took his hat off a nail, and went out.

It was cold. An inch or two of grainy snow from three days past covered everything, made the ground lumpy, and gave a foolish look to the stripped rows of beanpoles in front of the house. The dog came scrabbling out from under the house when it heard the door, started off for the truck without looking back. "Come here!" Waite called sharply, his voice looping in the thin air.

Leaning over, he took the dog's cold, dry muzzle in his hand. "You better stay here this time. Yes, yes." He flapped the dog's ear back and forth and looked around. He could not see the Satus Hills across the valley because of the heavy overcast, just the wavy flatness of sugarbeet fields—white, except for black places here and there where the snow had not gotten. One place in sight—Charley Treadwell's, a long way off—but no lights lit that he could tell. Not a sound anywhere, just the low ceiling of heavy clouds pressing down on everything. He'd thought there was a wind, but it was still.

"Stay here now. You hear?"

He started for the truck, wishing again he did not have to go. He had dreamed last night, again—about what he could not remember—but he'd had an uneasy feeling ever since he woke up. He drove in low gear down to the gate, got out and unhooked it, drove past, got out again and hooked it. He did not keep horses any more—but it was a habit he had gotten into, keeping the gate shut.

Down the road, the grader was scraping toward him, the blade shrieking fiercely every time the metal hit the frozen gravel. He was in no hurry, and he waited the long minutes it took the grader to come up. One of the men in the cab leaned out with a cigaret in his hand and waved as they went by. But Waite looked off. He pulled out onto the road after they passed. He looked over at Charley Treadwell's when he went by, but there were still no lights, and the car was gone. He remembered what Charley had told him a few days ago, about a fight Charley had had last Sunday with some kid who came over his fence in the afternoon and shot into a pond of ducks, right down by the barn. The ducks came in there every afternoon, Charley said. They *trusted* him, he said, as if that mattered. He'd run down from the barn where he was milking, waving his arms and shouting, and the kid had pointed the gun at him. If I could've just got that gun away from him, Charley had said, staring hard at Waite with his one good eye and nodding slowly. Waite hitched a little in the seat. He did not want any trouble like that. He hoped whoever it was would be gone when he got there, like the other times.

Out to the left he passed Fort Simcoe, the white-painted tops of the old buildings standing behind the reconstructed palisade. The gates of the place were open, and Lee Waite could see cars parked around inside and a few people in coats, walking. He never bothered to stop. Once the teacher had brought all the kids out here—a field trip, she called it—but Waite had stayed home from school that day. He rolled down the window and cleared his throat, hawked it at the gate as he passed.

He turned onto Lateral B and then came to Joseph Eagle's place—all the lights on, even the porch light. Waite drove past, down to where the Cowiche Road came in, and got out of the truck and listened. He had begun to think they might be gone and he could turn around and go on back when he heard a grouping of dull far-off shots come across the fields. He waited awhile, then took a rag and went around the truck and tried to wipe off some of the snow and ice in the window edges. He kicked the snow off his shoes before getting in, drove a little farther until he could see the bridge, then looked for the tracks that turned off into the trees, where he knew he would find their car. He pulled in behind the gray sedan and switched the ignition off.

He sat in the truck and waited, squeaking his foot back and forth on the brake and hearing them shoot every now and then. After a few minutes he couldn't sit still any longer and got out, walked slowly around to the front. He had not been down there to do anything in four or five years. He leaned against the fender and looked out over the land. He could not understand where all the time had gone.

He remembered when he was little, wanting to grow up. He

used to come down here often then and trap this part of the creek for muskrat and set night-lines for German brown. Waite looked around, moved his feet inside his shoes. All that was a long time ago. Growing up, he had heard his father say he intended this land for the three boys. But both brothers had been killed. Lee Waite was the one it came down to, all of it.

He remembered: deaths. Jimmy first. He remembered waking to the tremendous pounding on the door—dark, the smell of wood pitch from the stove, an automobile outside with the lights on and the motor running, and a crackling voice coming from a speaker inside. His father throws open the door, and the enormous figure of a man in a cowboy hat and wearing a gun—the deputy sheriff— fills the doorway. *Waite? Your boy Jimmy been stabbed at a dance in Wapato.* Everyone had gone away in the truck and Lee was left by himself. He had crouched, alone the rest of the night, in front of the wood stove, watching the shadows jump across the wall. Later, when he was twelve, another one came, a different sheriff, and only said they'd better come along.

He pushed off from the truck and walked the few feet over to the edge of the field. Things were different now, that's all there was to it. He was thirty-two, and Benny and little Jack were growing up. And there was the baby. Waite shook his head. He closed his hand around one of the tall stalks of milkweed. He snapped its neck and looked up when he heard the soft chuckling of ducks overhead. He wiped his hand on his pants and followed them for a moment, watched them set their wings at the same instant and circle once over the creek. Then they flared. He saw three ducks fall before he heard the shots.

He turned abruptly and started back for the truck.

He took out his gun, careful not to slam the door. He moved into the trees. It was almost dark. He coughed once and then stood with his lips pressed together.

They came thrashing through the brush, two of them. Then, jig- gling and squeaking the fence, they climbed over into the field and crunched through the snow. They were breathing hard by the time they got up close to the car.

"My God, there's a truck there!" one of them said and dropped the ducks he was carrying.

It was a boy's voice. He had on a heavy hunting coat, and in the game pockets Waite could dimly make out the enormous padding of ducks.

"Take it easy, will you!" The other boy stood craning his head around, trying to see. "Hurry up! There's nobody inside. Get the hell in the car!"

Not moving, trying to keep his voice steady, Waite said, "Stand there. Put your guns right there on the ground." He edged out of the trees and faced them, raised and lowered his gun barrels. "Take off them coats now and empty them out."

"O God! *God* almighty!" one of them said.

The other did not say anything but took off his coat and began pulling out the ducks, still looking around.

Waite opened the door of their car, fumbled an arm around inside until he found the headlights. The boys put a hand up to shield their eyes, then turned their backs to the light.

"Whose land do you think this is?" Waite said. "What do you mean, shooting ducks on my land!"

One boy turned around cautiously, his hand still in front of his eyes. "What are you going to do?"

"What do you think I'm going to do?" Waite said. His voice sounded strange to him, light, insubstantial. He could hear the ducks settling on the creek, chattering to other ducks still in the air. "What do you think I'm going to do with you?" he said. "What would you do if you caught boys trespassing on your land?"

"If they said they was sorry and it was the first time, I'd let them go," the boy answered.

"I would too, sir, if they said they was sorry," the other boy said.

"You would? You really think that's what you'd do?" Waite knew he was stalling for time.

They did not answer. They stood in the glare of the headlights and then turned their backs again.

"How do I know you wasn't here before?" Waite said. "The other times I had to come down here?"

"Word of honor, sir, we never been here before. We just drove by. For godsake," the boy sobbed.

"That's the whole truth," the other boy said. "Anybody can make a mistake once in his life."

It was dark now, and a thin drizzle was coming down in front of the lights. Waite turned up his collar and stared at the boys. From down on the creek the strident quacking of a drake carried up to him. He glanced around at the awful shapes of the trees, then back at the boys again.

"Maybe so," he said and moved his feet. He knew he would let them go in a minute. There wasn't much else he could do. He was putting them off the land; that was what mattered. "What's your names, anyway? What's yours? You. Is this here your car or not? What's your name?"

"Bob Roberts," the one boy answered quickly and looked sideways at the other.

"Williams, sir," the other boy said. "Bill Williams, sir."

Waite was willing to understand that they were kids, that they were lying to him because they were afraid. They stood with their backs to him, and Waite stood looking at them.

"You're lying!" he said, shocking himself. "Why you lying to me? You come onto my land and shoot my ducks and then you lie like hell to me!" He laid the gun over the car door to steady the barrels. He could hear branches rubbing in the treetops. He thought of Joseph Eagle sitting up there in his lighted house, his feet on a box, listening to the radio.

"All right, all right," Waite said. "Liars! Just stand there, liars." He walked stiffly around to his truck and got out an old beet sack, shook it open, had them put all the ducks in that. When he stood still, waiting, his knees unaccountably began to shake.

"Go ahead and go. Go on!"

He stepped back as they came up to the car. "I'll back up to the road. You back up along with me."

"Yes, sir," the one boy said as he slid in behind the wheel. "But what if I can't get this thing started now? The battery might be dead, you know. It wasn't very strong to begin with."

"I don't know," Waite said. He looked around. "I guess I'd have to push you out."

The boy shut off the lights, stamped on the accelerator, and hit the starter. The engine turned over slowly but caught, and the boy held his foot down on the pedal and raced the engine before firing up the lights again. Waite studied their pale cold faces staring out at him, looking for a sign from him.

He slung the bag of ducks into his truck and slid the double-barrel across the seat. He got in and backed out carefully onto the road. He waited until they were out, then followed them down to Lateral B and stopped with his motor running, watching their tail-lights disappear toward Toppenish. He had put them off the land. That was all that mattered. Yet he could not understand why he felt something crucial had happened, a failure.

But nothing had happened.

Patches of fog had blown in from down the valley. He couldn't see much over toward Charley's when he stopped to open the gate, only a faint light burning out on the porch that Waite did not remember seeing that afternoon. The dog waited on its belly by the barn, jumped up and began snuffling the ducks as Waite swung them over his shoulder and started up to the house. He stopped on the porch long enough to put the gun away. The ducks he left on the floor beside the cabinet. He would clean them tomorrow or the next day.

"Lee?" Nina called.

Waite took off his hat, loosened the light bulb, and before opening the door he paused a moment in the quiet dark.

Nina was at the kitchen table, the little box with her sewing things beside her on another chair. She held a piece of denim in her hand. Two or three of his shirts were on the table, along with a pair of scissors. He pumped a cup of water and picked up from a shelf over the sink some of the colored rocks the kids were always bringing home. There was a dry pine cone there too and a few big papery maple leaves from the summer. He glanced in the pantry. But he was not hungry. Then he walked over to the doorway and leaned against the jamb.

It was a small house. There was no place to go.

In the back, in one room, all of the children slept, and in the room off from this, Waite and Nina and his mother slept, though sometimes, in the summer, Waite and Nina slept outside. There was never a place to go. His mother was still sitting beside the stove, a blanket over her legs now and her tiny eyes open, watching him.

"The boys wanted to stay up until you came back," Nina said, "but I told them you said they had to go to bed."

"Yes, that's right," he said. "They had to go to bed, all right."

"I was afraid," she said.

"Afraid?" He tried to make it sound as if this surprised him. "Were you afraid too, Mama?"

The old woman did not answer. Her fingers fiddled around the sides of the blanket, tucking and pulling, covering against draft.

"How do you feel, Nina? Feel any better tonight?" He pulled out a chair and sat down by the table.

His wife nodded. He said nothing more, only looked down and began scoring his thumbnail into the table.

"Did you catch who it was?" she said.

"It was two kids," he said. "I let them go."

He got up and walked to the other side of the stove, spat into the woodbox, and stood with his fingers hooked into his back pockets. Behind the stove the wood was black and peeling, and overhead he could see, sticking out from a shelf, the brown mesh of a gill net wrapped around the prongs of a salmon spear. But what was it? He squinted at it.

"I let them go," he said. "Maybe I was easy on them."

"You did what was right," Nina said.

He glanced over the stove at his mother. But there was no sign from her, only the black eyes staring at him.

"I don't know," he said. He tried to think about it, but already it seemed as if it had happened, whatever it was, long ago. "I should've given them more of a scare, I guess." He looked at Nina. "My land," he added. "I could've killed them."

"Kill who?" his mother said.

"Them kids down on the Cowiche Road land. What Joseph Eagle called about."

From where he stood he could see his mother's fingers working in her lap, tracing the raised design in the blanket. He leaned over the stove, wanting to say something else. But he did not know what.

He wandered to the table and sat down again. Then he realized he still had on his coat, and he got up, took a while unfastening it, and then laid it across the table. He pulled up the chair close to his wife's knees, crossed his arms limply, and took his shirt sleeves between his fingers.

"I was thinking maybe I'll lease out that land down there to the hunting clubs. No good to us down there like that. Is it? Our house was down there or it was our land right out here in front would be something different, right?"

In the silence he could hear only the wood snapping in the stove. He laid his hands flat on the table and could feel the pulse jumping in his arms. "I can lease it out to one of the duck clubs from Toppenish. Or Yakima. Any of them would be glad to get hold of land like that, right on the flyway. That's some of the best hunting land in the valley . . . If I could put it to some use someway, it would be different then." His voice trailed off.

She moved in the chair. She said, "If you think we should do it. It's whatever you think. I don't know."

"I don't know, either," he said. His eyes crossed the floor, raised past his mother, and again came to rest on the salmon spear. He got up, shaking his head. As he moved across the little room, the old woman crooked her head and laid her cheek on the chairback, eyes narrowed and following him. He reached up, worked the spear and the mass of netting off the splintery shelf, and turned around behind her chair. He looked at the tiny dark head, at the brown woolen shawl shaped smooth over the hunched shoulders. He turned the spear in his hands and began to unwrap the netting.

"How much would you get?" Nina said.

He knew he didn't know. It even confused him a little. He plucked at the netting, then placed the spear back on the shelf. Outside, a branch scraped roughly against the house.

"Lee?"

He was not sure. He would have to ask around. Mike Chuck had leased out thirty acres last fall for five hundred dollars. Jerome Shinpa leased some of his land every year, but Waite had never asked how much he got.

"Maybe a thousand dollars," he said.

"A thousand dollars?" she said.

He nodded, felt relief at her amazement. "Maybe so. Maybe more. I will have to see. I will have to ask somebody how much." It was a lot of money. He tried to think about having a thousand dollars. He closed his eyes and tried to think.

"That wouldn't be selling it, would it?" Nina asked. "If you lease it to them, that means it's still your land?"

"Yes, yes, it's still my land!" He went over to her and leaned across the table. "Don't you know the difference, Nina? They can't *buy* land on the reservation. Don't you know that? I will lease it to them for them to use."

"I see," she said. She looked down and picked at the sleeve of one of his shirts. "They will have to give it back? It will still belong to you?"

"Don't you understand?" he said. He gripped the table edge. "It is a lease!"

"What will Mama say?" Nina asked. "Will it be all right?"

They both looked over at the old woman. But her eyes were closed and she seemed to be sleeping.

"A thousand dollars," Nina said and shook her head.

A thousand dollars. Maybe more. He didn't know. But even a thousand dollars! He wondered how he would go about it, letting people know he had land to lease. It was too late now for this year— but he could start asking around in the spring. He crossed his arms and tried to think. His legs began to tremble, and he leaned against the wall. He rested there and then let his weight slide gently down the wall until he was squatting.

"It's just a lease," he said.

He stared at the floor. It seemed to slant in his direction; it seemed to move. He shut his eyes and brought his hands against his ears to steady himself. And then he thought to cup his palms, so that there would come that roaring, like the wind howling up from a seashell.

Understanding the Story ────────

Main Idea

1. Even though the hunters turned out to be boys, Lee Waite (a) should have taken them to the local authorities (b) gave up the ducks when they challenged him (c) showed courage in facing them by himself (d) told his family they were men.

Details

2. The one who told Lee Waite about the intruders was (a) Benny (b) little Jack (c) Nina (d) Joseph Eagle.

3. Jimmy's death had been announced by (a) Charley Treadwell (b) a deputy sheriff (c) Lee's father (d) Lee's mother.

4. If Lee leased the hunting rights, he thought he might get (a) a hundred dollars (b) five hundred dollars (c) a thousand dollars (d) ten thousand dollars.

5. Charley Treadwell was bothered because a hunter had (a) shot at his ducks (b) left tire tracks in the fresh mud (c) left papers and cans on his property (d) stolen some crops.

Inferences

6. Lee Waite's attitude toward Fort Simcoe was one of (a) affection (b) indifference (c) scorn (d) relief.

7. The mother's behavior throughout the story could be characterized as (a) intense participation in Lee's problems (b) almost complete withdrawal (c) subtle amusement (d) aroused curiosity.

8. When caught by Lee, the boys were (a) brazen (b) silent (c) violent (d) frightened.

9. Lee's house was (a) poor and small (b) modest but well furnished (c) large and well built (d) spacious but poorly furnished.

10. When one of the boys said, "Hurry up!" we can be sure the two boys (a) knew they were doing wrong (b) had inter-

rupted their shooting (c) knew Lee Waite (d) had taken only one duck.

Order of Events

11. Arrange the items in the order in which they occurred. Use letters only.
    A. Lee meets the road grader.
    B. Charley Treadwell has a run-in with a hunter.
    C. Lee runs the boys off the land.
    D. Lee thinks about leasing part of his land.
    E. Jimmy Waite is killed.

Outcomes

12. If Lee leased out his land, (a) his mother would speak out against the lease (b) it would be considered illegal (c) his poverty would be lessened (d) Charley Treadwell would object.

Cause and Effect

13. Lee had inherited the sixty acres because (a) he was the favorite son (b) his father and mother had been divorced (c) Indian regulation prohibited splitting land holdings (d) his brothers had been killed.

Fact or Opinion

Tell whether each of the following is a fact or an opinion.

14. The mother's behavior showed she was angry and bitter.

15. The dog did not accompany Lee to the meeting with the hunters.

Words in Context _____

1. But they would cruise by that *untenanted and irresistible* sixty acres of his.
   Untenanted and irresistible (366) means (a) wooded and swampy (b) unfarmed and rugged (c) bare and hilly (d) unoccupied and attractive.

2. He fingered the loose skin around his neck and glanced *covertly* at his mother.
   Covertly (367) means (a) lovingly (b) quickly (c) secretly (d) suddenly.

3. Out to the left he passed Fort Simcoe, the white-painted tops of the old buildings standing behind the *reconstructed palisade.*
   Reconstructed palisade (369) means (a) remodeled high wall (b) strengthened cliff (c) rebuilt fence (d) repainted gate.

4. His voice sounded strange to him, light, *insubstantial.*
   Insubstantial (371) means (a) angry (b) frail (c) low-pitched (d) angelic.

5. From down on the creek the *strident* quacking of a *drake* carried up to him.
   Strident ... *drake* (372) means (a) shrill ... goose (b) quiet ... loon (c) harsh ... male duck (d) melodious ... duckling.

6. When he stood still, waiting, his knees *unaccountably* began to shake.
   Unaccountably (372) means (a) unexplainably (b) visibly (c) abruptly (d) comically.

7. Yet he could not understand why he felt something *crucial* had happened, a failure.
   Crucial (373) means (a) fatal (b) decisive (c) trivial (d) unpleasant.

8. Then he walked over to the doorway and leaned against the *jamb.*
   Jamb (373) means (a) knob (b) panel (c) wall (d) frame.

9. He said nothing more, only looked down and began *scoring* his thumbnail into the table.
   Scoring (374) means (a) making a line with (b) rubbing quickly with (c) tapping unevenly with (d) removing the dust with.

10. Overhead he could see, sticking out from a shelf, the brown mesh of a *gill net.*
    Gill net (374) means a device for (a) catching fish (b) cooking fish (c) measuring grain (d) cleaning grain.

Thinking About the Story _____

1. We get only a few glimpses of Nina, Lee's wife. What kind of person is she? How do her activities provide a clue to her character?

2. Why did the deaths of Lee's brothers make him uneasy about going down to face the hunters? What does his decision to go tell about him?

3. How does the isolation of Lee's sixty acres add to the suspense and tension in the story?

4. What kind of picture do we have of Lee? Is he cheerful, happy, free of problems, wealthy? Explain.

5. Besides being the story of a lonely, but brave, man, this is a picture of life on an Indian reservation in the state of Washington. What conclusions can you draw about this kind of life?

6. Why does the author make Lee's mother so strangely silent? What does her behavior add to the tone of the story?

Courageous Company

ACTIVITIES

Thinking About the Stories

1. What type of courage is revealed by each of the main characters in this group of stories? Which character do you admire most? Why?

2. Which story would make the most effective television movie? Explain.

3. Do the stories in this section prove or disprove the validity of each of the following quotations? Justify your answers.
   (a) "A stout heart breaks bad luck."   —CERVANTES
   (b) "To fight aloud is very brave,
       But gallanter I know,
       Who charge within the bosom
       The cavalry of woe."   —EMILY DICKINSON
   (c) "Courage in danger is half the battle."   —PLAUTUS
   (d) "Who has not courage should have legs."   —JOHN RAY
   (e) "True courage is to do without witnesses everything that one is capable of doing before all the world."
       —LA ROCHEFOUCAULD

4. "Qualities other than just courage are needed if we expect to succeed in overcoming the obstacles placed in our paths." Does this statement apply to the stories in this unit? Select one story and show how the statement does or does not apply.

5. How does the humor in "Death of Red Peril" provide a good balance to the other stories in this unit?

Projects

1. Select a news item describing a forest fire or a large fire in a city. Retell the story from the angle of one of the firefighters or of someone who had been caught in the blaze and escaped.

2. Imagine that you are a feature writer assigned by your editor

to interview Tom King in his home immediately after his defeat by Sandel. Make up six questions and imagine Tom's answers to these questions.

3. "Death of Red Peril" is a tall tale. In a collection of folktales, find one that you can retell to the class. It may be about Paul Bunyan, Pecos Bill, John Henry, or another hero, or it may be about some lowly character like Red Peril.

4. Write the news item that might have appeared in the sports section of the newspaper the morning after Tom King's defeat.

5. From the daily newspaper clip an item that reports a heroic deed. For example, a five-year-old boy saves a choking playmate by applying the Heimlich maneuver. Be ready to tell your classmates about the act of heroism.

Additional Readings

Short Stories

"He" by Katherine Anne Porter

> This is a hymn of praise for the courageous life of the rural poor. For a while you will share the life of Mrs. Whipple as she tries to keep her family together.

"Turkey Red" by Francis G. Wood

> A blizzard, a sick child, and no doctor within reach.

"To Build a Fire" by Jack London

> Story of a land where fire is not merely a comfort and a convenience but the very means of survival.

"The Devil and Daniel Webster" by Stephen Vincent Benet

> The Devil seeks to win the soul of Daniel Webster, but he doesn't reckon with the great orator's powers of persuasion.

Anthologies

The World of the Short Story—a 20th Century Collection edited by Clifton Fadiman

> A selection of stories by 20th century writers from Max Beerbohm and Somerset Maugham to Joyce Carol Oates and Ann Beattie.

An Anthology of Famous American Stories edited by Angus Burrell and Bennett Cerf

An older collection but representative of some of the best American short fiction.

A Book of the Short Story edited by E. A. Cross

Some of the greatest short stories from every land. A history and study of the short story is a valuable introduction.

6 *For Lack of a Friend*

Teenage is the time when we loosen the ties to our parents and seek guidelines and companionship among those in our own age group. It is the period in our lives when the need to establish ourselves among our peers becomes a major focus in our lives. How we dress, how we speak, what we eat, how we think—almost everything about us—is set by the standards of the group, the clique, the gang, the set of friends we have.

From the legends of old to the stories in the Bible, from the classics to today's TV teenage tales, friends and friendship have been ever favorite themes of storyland.

The stories in this section explore the role of friends and friendship in the lives of four different groups of people. Bottles Barton takes you into his inner life to show how lack of a friend can affect our lives. Through Tony and Durante we meet a contrast in definitions of how a friend should act when life is endangered. The new kid brings you face to face with some of the meanings of friendship accepted by the early teens. Raymond and his sister tell us how one girl adjusted to her world so filled with family obligations that she had no time to establish friendships.

These four stories can stand on their own as worthwhile reading. But they do more than that. They will help you to explore your own definition of friendship and how it should affect your life.

That's What Happened to Me

Michael Fessier

♦ "I could have pitched no-hit games and I could have made touchdowns from my own ten-yard line. I know I could. I had it all figured out."

Bottles Barton breaks the state scholastic record in the high jump—from a standing position at the bar! He breaks the record in the pole vault—without the use of a pole! No longer the despised butt of his schoolmates' cruel jokes, he becomes the school hero, the idol of the fans, the people's choice, the apple of his employer's eye, the object of the coeds' devotion—and one of the most pathetic figures you have ever come across.

Friendship meant a great deal to Bottles Barton. Sometimes the lack of something as important as friendship can do strange things to the personality of a growing boy.

THAT'S WHAT HAPPENED TO ME

I have done things and had things happen to me and nobody knows about it. So I am writing about it so that people will know. Although there are a lot of things I could tell about, I will just tell about the jumping because that is the most important. It gave me the biggest thrill. I mean high jumping, standing and running. You probably never heard of a standing high jumper but that's what I was. I was the greatest jumper ever was.

I was going to high school and I wasn't on any team. I couldn't be because I had to work for a drugstore and wash bottles and deliver medicine and sweep the floor. So I couldn't go out for any of the teams because the job started soon's school was over. I used to crab to the fellows about how old man Patch made me wash so many bottles and so they got to calling me Bottles Barton and I didn't like it. They'd call me Bottles in front of the girls and the girls'd giggle.

Once I poked one of the fellows for calling me Bottles. He was a big fellow and he played on the football team and I wouldn't have hit him because I was little and couldn't fight very well. But he called me Bottles before Anna Louise Daniels and she laughed and I was so mad I didn't know whether I wanted to hit her or the football player but finally I hit him. He caught my arm and threw me down and sat on me and pulled my nose.

"Look, Anna Louise," he said, "it stretches."

He pulled my nose again and Anna Louise put her arms around herself and jumped up and down and laughed and then I knew that it was her I should have taken the first poke at. I was more mad at her than the football player although it was him pulling my nose and sitting on me.

387

The next day I met Anna Louise in the hall going to the ancient history class and she was with a couple of other girls and I tried to go past without them noticing me. I don't know why but I had a funny feeling like as if somebody was going to throw a rock at me or something. Anna Louise looked at me and giggled.

"Hello, old rubbernose," she said.

The girls giggled and I hurried down the hall and felt sick and mad and kind of like I was running away from a fight, although nobody'd expect me to fight a girl. And so they called me Bottles sometimes and Rubbernose other times and always whoever was near would laugh. They didn't think it was funny because Jimmy Wilkins was called Scrubby or Jack Harris was called Doodles. But they thought it was funny I was called Rubbernose and Bottles and they never got tired of laughing. It was a new joke every time.

Scrubby pitched for the baseball team and Doodles was quarterback of the football team.

I could have pitched for the baseball team or played quarterback on the football team. I could have pitched no-hit games and I could have made touchdowns from my own ten-yard line. I know I could. I had it all figured out. I went over how I'd throw the ball and how the batter'd miss and it was easy. I figured out how to run and dodge and straight-arm and that was easy too. But I didn't get the chance because I had to go right to Patch's Drugstore after school was out.

Old man Patch was a pretty good guy but his wife she was nothing but a crab. I'd wash bottles and old man Patch he would look at them and not say anything. But Mrs. Patch, old lady Patch, she would look at the bottles and wrinkle her nose and make me wash half of them over again. When I swept up at night she'd always find some corner I'd missed and she'd bawl me out. She was fat and her hair was all straggly and I wondered why in the deuce old man Patch ever married her, although I guess maybe she didn't look so awful when she was a girl. She couldn't have been very pretty though.

They lived in back of the drugstore and when people came in at noon or at six o'clock either old man or old lady Patch'd come out still chewing their food and look at the customer and swallow and then ask him what he wanted.

I studied salesmanship at high school and I figured this wasn't very good for business and I wanted to tell them but I never did.

One of the fellows at school was in waiting for a prescription and he saw me working at some of the things I did at the drugstore. So when another fellow asked me what I did this fellow he laughed and said, "Old Bottles! Why, he rates at that store. Yes he does! He rates like an assistant helper's helper."

That's about the way I did rate but I was planning on how I'd someday own a real, modern drugstore and run the Patches out of business so I didn't mind so much.

What I did mind was Anna Louise at school. She was the daughter of a doctor and she thought she was big people and maybe she was but she wasn't any better'n me. Maybe my clothes weren't so good but that was only temporary. I planned on having twenty suits some day.

I wanted to go up to her and say, "Look here, Anna Louise, you're not so much. Your father isn't a millionaire and someday I'm going to be one. I'm going to have a million dollars and twenty suits of clothes." But I never did.

After she laughed at me and started calling me Rubbernose, I began planning on doing things to make her realize I wasn't what she thought I was. That's how the jumping came about.

It was the day before the track meet and everybody was talking about whether or not our school could win. They figured we'd have to win the high jump and pole vault to do it.

"Lord, if we only had old Heck Hansen back!" said Goobers MacMartin. "He'd outjump those Fairfield birds two inches in the high and a foot in the pole vault."

"Yeah," somebody else said, "but we haven't got Heck Hansen. What we got is pretty good but not good enough. Wish we had a jumper."

"We sure need one," I said.

There was a group of them all talking, boys and girls, and I was sort of on the outside listening.

"Who let you in?" Goobers asked me.

Frank Shay grabbed me by the arm and dragged me into the center of the circle.

"The very man we've been looking for," he said. "Yessir. Old Bottles Rubbernose Barton. He can win the jumping events for us."

"Come on, Bottles," they said. "Save the day for us. Be a good old Rubbernose."

Anna Louise was one who laughed the most and it was the third time I'd wanted to pop her on the nose.

I went away from there and didn't turn back when they laughed and called and whistled at me.

"She'd be surprised if I did," I said.

I kept thinking this over and pretty soon I said, "Well, maybe you could."

Then when I was sweeping the drugstore floor I all of a sudden said, "I can!"

"You can what?" Mrs. Patch asked me.

"Nothing," I said.

"You can hurry about sweeping the floor, that's what you can do," she said.

There was a big crowd out for the track meet and we were tied when I went up to our coach. It was just time for the jumping to start.

"What are you doing in a track suit?" he asked me.

"I'm going to save the day for Brinkley," I said. "I'm going to jump."

"No, you aren't," he said. "You run along and start a marble game with some other kid."

I looked him in the eye and I spoke in a cold, level tone of voice.

"Mr. Smith," I said, "the track meet depends on the high jump and the pole vault and unless I am entered we will lose those two events and the meet. I can win and I am willing to do it for Brinkley. Do you want to win the meet?"

He looked amazed.

"Where have you been all the time?" he asked. "You talk like you've got something on the ball."

I didn't say anything, I just smiled.

The crowd all rushed over to the jumping pits and I took my time going over. When everybody had jumped but me the coach turned and said, "Come on now, Barton, let's see what you can do."

"Not yet," I said.

"What do you mean?" he asked.

"I'll wait until the last man has been eliminated," I said. "Then I'll jump."

The crowd laughed but I just stared coldly at them. The coach tried to persuade me to jump but I wouldn't change my mind.

"I stake everything on one jump," I said. "Have faith in me."

He looked at me and shook his head and said, "Have it your own way."

They started the bar a little over four feet and pretty soon it was creeping up toward five feet and a half. That's always been a pretty good distance for high school jumpers. When the bar reached five feet seven inches all our men except one was eliminated. Two from Fairfield were still in the event. They put the bar at five feet nine inches and one man from Fairfield made it. Our man tried hard but he scraped the bar and knocked it off.

The crowd started yelling, thinking Fairfield had won the event.

"Wait a minute," I yelled. "I haven't jumped yet."

The judges looked at their lists and saw it was so. Maybe you think it was against the rules for them to allow me to skip my turn but anyway that's the way it was.

"You can't make that mark," one of the judges said. "Why try? You're not warmed up."

"Never mind," I said.

I walked up close to the jumping standard and stood there.

"Go ahead and jump," one of the judges said.

"I will," I said.

"Well, don't stand there," he said. "Come on back here so's you can get a run at it."

"I don't want any run at the bar," I said. "I'll jump from here."

The judge yelled at the coach and told him to take me out on account of I was crazy.

I swung my arms in back of me and sprung up and down a second and then I jumped over the bar with inches to spare. When I came down it was so silent I could hear my footsteps as I walked across the sawdust pit. The judge that'd crabbed at me just stood and looked. His eyes were bugged out and his mouth hung open.

"Good Lord!" he said. "Almighty most loving Lord!"

Our coach came up and he stood beside the judge and they both looked the same, bug-eyed.

"Did you see that?" the coach asked. "Tell me you didn't. Please do. I'd rather lose this track meet than my mind."

The judge turned slowly and looked at him.

"Good Lord!" he said, "there's two of us."

All of a sudden everybody started yelling and the fellows near me pounded me on the back and tried to shake my hand. I smiled and brushed them aside and walked over to the judge.

"What's the high school record for this state?" I asked.

"Five feet, eleven inches," he said.

"Put her at six," I said.

They put the bar at six and I gathered myself together and gave a heave and went over the bar like I was floating. It was easy. Well, that just knocked the wind out of everybody. They'd thought I couldn't do anything and there I'd broken the state record for the high jump without a running start.

The crowd surrounded me and tried to shake my hand and the coach and judge got off to one side and reached out and pinched each other's cheek and looked at the bar and shook their heads. Frank Shay grabbed my hand and wrung it and said, "Gosh, Bottles, I was just kidding the other day. I didn't know you were such a ring-tailed wonder. Say, Bottles, we're having a frat dance tonight. Will you come?"

"You know what you can do with your frat," I said. "I don't approve of them. They're undemocratic."

A lot of the fellows that'd made fun of me before crowded around and acted as if I'd been their friend all along.

When Anna Louise crowded through the gang and said, "Oh, you're marvelous!" I just smiled at her and said, "Do you think so?" and walked away. She tagged around after me but I talked mostly with two other girls.

They didn't usually have a public address system at our track meets but they started using one then.

"Ladies and gentlemen," the announcer said, "you have just witnessed a record-breaking performance by Bottles Barton."

He went on like that telling them what an astonishing thing I'd done and it came to me I didn't mind being called Bottles any more. In fact, I kind of liked it.

Mr. and Mrs. Patch came up and Mrs. Patch tried to kiss me but I wouldn't let her. Old man Patch shook my hand.

"You've made our drugstore famous," he said. "From now on you're a clerk. No more bottle washing."

"We'll make him a partner," old lady Patch said.

"No, you won't," I said. "I think I'll go over to the McManus Pharmacy."

Then they called the pole vault and I did like I'd done before. I wouldn't jump until our men'd been eliminated. The bar was at eleven feet.

"It's your turn," our coach told me. "Ever use a pole before?"

"Oh, sure," I told him.

He gave me a pole and the crowd cleared away and grew silent. Everyone was watching me.

I threw the pole down and smiled at the crowd. The coach yelled for me to pick up the pole and jump. I picked it up and threw it ten feet away from me. Everybody gasped. Then I took a short run and went over the bar at eleven feet. It was simple.

This time the coach and the judge took pins and poked them in one another's cheeks. The coach grabbed me and said, "When I wake up I'm going to be so mad at you I'm going to give you the beating of your life."

Anna Louise came up and held my arm and said, "Oh, Bottles, you're so wonderful! I've always thought so. Please forgive me for calling you Rubbernose. I want you to come to our party tonight."

"All right," I said. "I'll forgive you but don't you call me Rubbernose again."

They moved the bar up again and the fellow from Fairfield couldn't make it. I took a short run and went over. I did it so easy it came to me I could fly if I wanted to but I decided not to try it on account of people wouldn't think it so wonderful if a fellow that could fly jumped eleven feet without a pole. I'd won the track meet for Brinkley High and the students all came down out of the stand and put me on their shoulders and paraded me around and around the track. A lot of fellows were waving papers at me and asking me to sign them and get $1000 a week as a professional jumper. I signed one which threw in an automobile.

That's what I did once and nobody knows about it, so I am writing about it so people will know.

Understanding the Story

Main Idea

1. The secret of Bottles' "success" is   (a) his ability as an athlete (b) his courage in practicing alone   (c) his need for friends   (d) Anna Louise's admiration for him.

Inference

2. Bottles doesn't go in for school sports on a regular basis because   (a) he spends too much time studying   (b) his mother forbids him to   (c) the coach refuses to allow him to participate   (d) he has never had a chance to.

Cause and Effect

3. Bottles Barton receives his nickname as a result of   (a) his work in the school lab   (b) his interest in chemistry   (c) his work in the drugstore   (d) his short body and long neck.

4. The coach allows Bottles to enter the meet because   (a) the judges ordered him to   (b) the spectators demand it (c) Brinkley High has already won   (d) he is convinced by Bottles' manner.

5. As a result of his achievements in the track meet, Bottles (a) is accepted by his classmates as a friend   (b) receives a great many medals   (c) receives a bid to the Olympics (d) becomes world champion.

Details

6. Which of the following statements is not true?
   (a) Bottles breaks the scholastic record for the high jump.
   (b) Bottles never has any doubt that he will win the events he is entered in.
   (c) Bottles could have jumped higher had he wanted to.
   (d) Bottles takes several practice jumps before entering the contest.

7. After the high jump   (a) Anna Louise still makes fun of him (b) Bottles refuses an invitation to a fraternity dance   (c) the judges disqualify Bottles   (d) Bottles receives a medal.

Order of Events

8. Arrange the items in the order in which they occurred. Use letters only.
   A. The Bartons have to struggle to make ends meet.
   B. Bottles picks a fight with a football type.
   C. Bottles breaks jumping records.
   D. Bottles is attracted to Anna Louise.
   E. Bottles gets a second nickname.

Outcomes

9. In reality, as a result of his entry into the track meet, Bottles (a) forces Anna Louise to apologize   (b) loses his nickname (c) is fired   (d) is as lonely as ever.

10. By this stage in his life, Bottles has learned   (a) how to succeed in real life   (b) not to trust friends   (c) not to accept a weak substitute for achievement   (d) to run away from reality.

Words in Context

1. I had a funny feeling like as if somebody was going to throw a rock at me.
   When Bottles said the above (388), he felt   (a) satisfied (b) sad   (c) fearful   (d) pleased.

2. The girls giggled and I hurried down the hall and felt sick and mad and kind of like I was running away from a fight . . .
   When Bottles said the above (388), he felt   (a) victorious (b) encouraged   (c) frustrated   (d) childish.

3. But Mrs. Patch . . . would look at the bottles and *wrinkle her nose* and make me wash half of them over again.
   The wrinkling of the nose (388) meant   (a) she was going to sneeze   (b) she was dissatisfied   (c) she didn't like the odor (d) she was trying to smile.

4. She was fat and her hair was all *straggly* . . .
   Straggly (388)   means   (a) uncombed   (b) overlong (c) discolored   (d) greasy.

5. "You run along and start a marble game with some other kid." By saying the above to Bottles (390), the coach reveals that (a) he has faith in Bottles   (b) he doesn't believe what he is seeing   (c) he expects to lose   (d) he doesn't know how capable Bottles is.

6. I looked him in the eye and I spoke in a cold, level tone of voice. Bottles' tone of voice (390) shows   (a) fear and dislike   (b) confidence and determination   (c) amazement and sorrow   (d) triumph and greediness.

7. "I'll wait until the last man has been *eliminated,*" I said. "Then I'll jump."
   Eliminated (390) means   (a) selected   (b) executed   (c) weeded out   (d) defeated.

8. "I don't approve of them. They're *undemocratic.*"
   Undemocratic (392) means   (a) Republican   (b) unpopular   (c) prejudiced   (d) expensive.

9. "I *stake* everything on one jump," I said. "Have faith in me."
   Stake (390) means   (a) offer   (b) wager   (c) proportion   (d) post.

10. Our man tried hard but he *scraped* the bar and knocked it off.
    Scraped (391) means   (a) grazed   (b) gashed   (c) seized   (d) bruised.

Thinking About the Story

1. What are the causes of Bottles' feeling of inferiority? What does Anna Louise Daniels stand for in Bottles' mind? To what extent is this a realistic story even though it contains fantasy? Explain.

2. How does Bottles get his "sweet revenge"? How does it happen that he becomes a track star rather than a pitcher or quarterback?

3. Why do some people resent and even dislike this story? Is this a humorous or a tragic story? Explain.

4. Is Bottles' method of solving problems beneficial or harmful to him? Explain. What advice would you give him?

5. Why is the last sentence the key to the explanation of the story? How should the other students have treated him? Have you read any other stories in which a scapegoat is the major character? How do you feel toward such characters? Give your reasons and refer to incidents to support them.

Wine on the Desert

Max Brand

♦ There was really no hurry at all. He had almost twenty-four hours' head start, for they would not find his dead man until this morning.

A killer named Dick Durante hits upon what appears to him to be the perfect getaway. But, as he discovers when it is too late, the ruthless abuse of friendship is followed by consequences more terrible than pursuit by a sheriff's posse. He made the mistake of thinking that those who make no outward show of resistance to criminal aggression are, necessarily, cowards and fools.

Max Brand, the author of "Wine on the Desert," is one of our most expert writers of western fiction. This story of trust and betrayal is a good example of his ability to handle atmosphere, suspense, and, what is more important, ideas. You'll find "Wine on the Desert" quite different from the conventional western of stereotyped situations and characters.

WINE ON THE DESERT

There was no hurry, except for the thirst, like clotted salt, in the back of his throat, and Durante rode on slowly, rather enjoying the last moments of dryness before he reached the cold water in Tony's house. There was really no hurry at all. He had almost twenty-four hours' head start, for they would not find his dead man until this morning. After that, there would be perhaps several hours of delay before the sheriff gathered a sufficient posse and started on his trail. Or perhaps the sheriff would be fool enough to come alone.

Durante had been able to see the wheel and fan of Tony's windmill for more than an hour, but he could not make out the ten acres of the vineyard until he had topped the last rise, for the vines had been planted in a hollow. The lowness of the ground, Tony used to say, accounted for the water that gathered in the well during the wet season. The rains sank through the desert sand, through the gravels beneath, and gathered in a bowl of clay hardpan far below. In the middle of the rainless season the well ran dry but, long before that, Tony had every drop of the water pumped up into a score of tanks made of cheap corrugated iron. Slender pipelines carried the water from the tanks to the vines and from time to time let them sip enough life to keep them until the winter darkened overhead suddenly, one November day, and the rain came down, and all the earth made a great hushing sound as it drank. Durante had heard that whisper of drinking when he was here before; but he never had seen the place in the middle of the long drought.

The windmill looked like a sacred emblem to Durante, and the twenty stodgy, tar-painted tanks blessed his eyes; but a heavy sweat broke out at once from his body. For the air of the hollow, unstirred by wind, was hot and still as a bowl of soup. A reddish soup. The vines were powdered with thin red dust, also. They were wretched, dying things to look at, for the grapes had been gathered, the new wine had been made, and now the leaves hung in ragged tatters.

Durante rode up to the squat adobe house and right through the entrance into the patio. A flowering vine clothed three sides of the little court. Durante did not know the name of the plant, but it had large white blossoms with golden hearts that poured sweetness on the air. Durante hated the sweetness. It made him more thirsty.

He threw the reins of his mule and strode into the house. The watercooler stood in the hall outside the kitchen. There were two jars made of a porous stone, very ancient things, and the liquid which distilled through the pores kept the contents cool. The jar on the left held water; that on the right contained wine. There was a big tin dipper hanging on a peg beside each jar. Durante tossed off the cover of the vase on the left and plunged it in until the delicious coolness closed well above his wrist.

"Hey, Tony," he called. Out of his dusty throat the cry was a mere groaning. He drank and called again, clearly, "Tony!"

A voice pealed from the distance.

Durante, pouring down the second dipper of water, smelled the alkali dust which had shaken off his own clothes. It seemed to him that heat was radiating like light from his clothes, from his body, and the cool dimness of the house was soaking it up. He heard the wooden leg of Tony bumping on the ground, and Durante grinned; then Tony came in with that hitch and sideswing with which he accommodated the stiffness of his artificial leg. His brown face shone with sweat as though a special ray of light were focused on it.

"Ah, Dick!" he said. "Good old Dick! . . . How long since you came last! . . . Wouldn't Julia be glad! Wouldn't she be glad!"

"Ain't she here?" asked Durante, jerking his head suddenly away from the dripping dipper.

"She's away at Nogalez," said Tony. "It gets so hot. I said, 'You go up to Nogalez, Julia, where the wind don't forget to blow.' She cried, but I made her go."

"Did she cry?" asked Durante.

"Julia . . . that's a good girl," said Tony.

"Yeah. You bet she's good," said Durante. He put the dipper quickly to his lips but did not swallow for a moment; he was grinning too widely. Afterward he said: "You wouldn't throw some water into that mule of mine, would you, Tony?"

Tony went out with his wooden leg clumping loud on the

wooden floor, softly in the patio dust. Durante found the hammock in the corner of the patio. He lay down in it and watched the color of sunset flush the mists of desert dust that rose to the zenith. The water was soaking through his body; hunger began, and then the rattling of pans in the kitchen and the cheerful cry of Tony's voice:

"What you want, Dick? I got some pork. You don't want pork. I'll make you some good Mexican beans. Hot. Ah ha, I know that old Dick. I have plenty of good wine for you, Dick. Tortillas. Even Julia can't make tortillas like me . . . And what about a nice young rabbit?"

"All blowed full of buckshot?" growled Durante.

"No, no. I kill them with the rifle."

"You kill rabbits with a rifle?" repeated Durante, with a quick interest.

"It's the only gun I have," said Tony. "If I catch them in the sights, they are dead. . . . A wooden leg cannot walk very far. . . . I must kill them quick. You see? They come close to the house about sunrise and flop their ears. I shoot through the head."

"Yeah? Yeah?" muttered Durante. "Through the head?" He relaxed, scowling. He passed his hand over his face, over his head.

Then Tony began to bring the food out into the patio and lay it on a small wooden table; a lantern hanging against the wall of the house included the table in a dim half circle of light. They sat there and ate. Tony had scrubbed himself for the meal. His hair was soaked in water and sleeked back over his round skull. A man in the desert might be willing to pay five dollars for as much water as went to the soaking of that hair.

Everything was good. Tony knew how to cook, and he knew how to keep the glasses filled with his wine.

"This is old wine. This is my father's wine. Eleven years old," said Tony. "You look at the light through it. You see that brown in the red? That's the soft that time puts in good wine, my father always said."

"What killed your father?" asked Durante.

Tony lifted his hand as though he were listening or as though he were pointing out a thought.

"The desert killed him. I found his mule. It was dead, too. There was a leak in the canteen. My father was only five miles away when the buzzards showed him to me."

"Five miles? Just an hour. . . . Good Lord!" said Durante. He stared with big eyes. "Just dropped down and died?" he asked.

"No," said Tony. "When you die of thirst, you always die just one way. . . . First you tear off your shirt, then your undershirt. That's to be cooler. . . . And the sun comes and cooks your bare skin. . . . And then you think . . . there is water everywhere, if you dig down far enough. You begin to dig. The dust comes up your nose. You start screaming. You break your nails in the sand. You wear the flesh off the tips of your fingers, to the bone." He took a quick swallow of wine.

"Without you seen a man die of thirst, how d'you know they start to screaming?" asked Durante.

"They got a screaming look when you find them," said Tony. "Take some more wine. The desert never can get to you here. My father showed me the way to keep the desert away from the hollow. We live pretty good here? No?"

"Yeah," said Durante, loosening his shirt collar. "Yeah, pretty good."

Afterward he slept well in the hammock until the report of a rifle waked him and he saw the color of dawn in the sky. It was such a great, round bowl that for a moment he felt as though he were above, looking down into it.

He got up and saw Tony coming in holding a rabbit by the ears, the rifle in his other hand. "You see?" said Tony. "Breakfast came and called on us!" He laughed.

Durante examined the rabbit with care. It was nice and fat and it had been shot through the head. Through the middle of the head. Such a shudder went down the back of Durante that he washed gingerly before breakfast; he felt that his blood was cooled for the entire day.

It was a good breakfast, too, with flapjacks and stewed rabbit with green peppers, and a quart of strong coffee. Before they had finished, the sun struck through the east window and started them sweating. "Gimme a look at that rifle of yours, Tony, will you?" Durante asked.

"You take a look at my rifle, but don't you steal the luck that's in it," laughed Tony. He brought the fifteen-shot Winchester.

"Loaded right to the brim?" asked Durante.

"I always load it full the minute I get back home," said Tony.

"Tony, come outside with me," commanded Durante.

They went out from the house. The sun turned the sweat of Durante to hot water and then dried his skin so that his clothes felt transparent. "Tony, I gotta be damn mean," said Durante. "Stand right there where I can see you. Don't try to get close. . . . Now listen. . . . The sheriff's gunna be along this trail some time today, looking for me. He'll load up himself and all his gang with water out of your tanks. Then he'll follow my sign across the desert. Get me? He'll follow if he finds water on the place. But he's not gunna find water."

"What you done, poor Dick?" said Tony. "Now look. . . . I could hide you in the old wine cellar where nobody . . . "

"The sheriff's not gunna find any water," said Durante. "It's gunna be like this."

He put the rifle to his shoulder, aimed, fired. The shot struck the base of the nearest tank, ranging down through the bottom. A semicircle of darkness began to stain the soil near the edge of the iron wall.

Tony fell on his knees. "No, no, Dick! Good Dick!" he said. "Look! All the vineyard. It will die. It will turn into old, dead wood, Dick . . . "

"Shut your face," said Durante. "Now I've started, I kinda like the job."

Tony fell on his face and put his hands over his ears. Durante drilled a bullet hole through the tanks, one after another. Afterward, he leaned on the rifle.

"Take my canteen and go in and fill it with water out of the cooling jar," he said. "Snap into it, Tony!"

Tony got up. He raised the canteen, and looked around him, not at the tanks from which the water was pouring so that the noise of the earth drinking was audible, but at the rows of his vineyard. Then he went into the house.

Durante mounted his mule. He shifted the rifle to his left hand and drew out the heavy Colt from its holster. Tony came dragging back to him, his head down. Durante watched Tony with a careful revolver but he gave up the canteen without lifting his eyes. "The trouble with you, Tony," said Durante, "is you're yellow. I'd of fought a tribe of wildcats with my bare hands, before I'd let 'em do what I'm doin' to you. But you sit back and take it."

Tony did not seem to hear. He stretched out his hands to the vines.

"Ah, my God," said Tony. "Will you let them all die?"

Durante shrugged his shoulders. He shook the canteen to make sure that it was full. It was so brimming that there was hardly room for the liquid to make a sloshing sound. Then he turned the mule and kicked it into a dogtrot. Half a mile from the house of Tony, he threw the empty rifle to the ground. There was no sense packing that useless weight, and Tony with his peg leg would hardly come this far.

Durante looked back, a mile or so later, and saw the little image of Tony picking up the rifle from the dust, then staring earnestly after his guest. Durante remembered the neat little hole clipped through the head of the rabbit. Wherever he went, his trail never could return again to the vineyard in the desert. But then, commencing to picture to himself the arrival of the sweating sheriff and his posse at the house of Tony, Durante laughed heartily.

The sheriff's posse could get plenty of wine, of course, but without water a man could not hope to make the desert voyage, even with a mule or a horse to help him on the way. Durante patted the full, rounding side of his canteen. He might even now begin with the first sip but it was a luxury to postpone pleasure until desire became greater.

He raised his eyes along the trail. Close by, it was merely dotted with occasional bones, but distance joined the dots into an unbroken chalk line which wavered with a strange leisure across the Apache Desert, pointing toward the cool blue promise of the mountains. The next morning he would be among them.

A coyote whisked out of a gully and ran like a gray puff of dust on the wind. His tongue hung out like a little red rag from the side of his mouth; and suddenly Durante was dry to the marrow. He uncorked and lifted his canteen. It had a slightly sour smell; perhaps the sacking which covered it had grown a trifle old. And then he poured a great mouthful of lukewarm liquid. He had swallowed it before his senses could give him warning.

It was wine!

He looked first of all toward the mountains. They were as calmly blue, as distant as when he had started that morning. Twenty-four hours not on water, but on wine!

"I deserve it," said Durante. "I trusted him to fill the canteen. . . . I deserve it. Curse him!" With a mighty resolution, he quieted the panic in his soul. He would not touch the stuff until noon. Then he would take one discreet sip. He would win through.

Hours went by. He looked at his watch and found it was only ten o'clock. And he had thought that it was on the verge of noon! He uncorked the wine and drank freely and, corking the canteen, felt almost as though he needed a drink of water more than before. He sloshed the contents of the canteen. Already it was horribly light.

Once, he turned the mule and considered the return trip; but he could remember the head of the rabbit too clearly, drilled right through the center. The vineyard, the rows of old twisted, gnarled little trunks with the bark peeling off . . . every vine was to Tony like a human life. And Durante had condemned them all to death!

He faced the blue of the mountains again. His heart raced in his breast with terror. Perhaps it was fear and not the suction of that dry and deadly air that made his tongue cleave to the roof of his mouth.

The day grew old. Nausea began to work in his stomach, nausea alternating with sharp pains. When he looked down, he saw that there was blood on his boots. He had been spurring the mule until the red ran down from its flanks. It went with a curious stagger, like a rocking horse with a broken rocker; and Durante grew aware that he had been keeping the mule at a gallop for a long time. He pulled it to a halt. It stood with wide-braced legs. Its head was down. When he leaned from the saddle, he saw that its mouth was open.

"It's gunna die," said Durante. "It's gunna die . . . what a fool I been . . . "

The mule did not die until after sunset. Durante left everything except his revolver. He packed the weight of that for an hour and discarded it, in turn. His knees were growing weak. When he looked up at the stars they shone white and clear for a moment only, and then whirled into little racing circles and scrawls of red.

He lay down. He kept his eyes closed and waited for the shaking to go out of his body, but it would not stop. And every breath of darkness was like an inhalation of black dust. He got up and went on, staggering. Sometimes he found himself running.

Before you die of thirst, you go mad. He kept remembering that. His tongue had swollen big. Before it choked him, if he lanced it with his knife the blood would help him; he would be able to swallow. Then he remembered that the taste of blood is salty.

Once, in his boyhood, he had ridden through a pass with his father and they had looked down on the sapphire of a mountain lake, a hundred thousand million tons of water as cold as snow. . . .

When he looked up, now, there were no stars; and this frightened him terribly. He never had seen a desert night so dark. His eyes were failing, he was being blinded. When the morning came, he would not be able to see the mountains, and he would walk around and around in a circle until he dropped and died.

No stars, no wind; the air as still as the waters of a stale pool, and he in the dregs at the bottom. . . .

He seized his shirt at the throat and tore it away so that it hung in two rags from his hips.

He could see the earth only well enough to stumble on the rocks. But there were no stars in the heavens. He was blind: he had no more hope than a rat in a well. Ah, but devils know how to put poison in wine that will steal all the senses or any one of them: and Tony had chosen to blind Durante.

He heard a sound like water. It was the swishing of the soft deep sand through which he was treading; sand so soft that a man could dig it away with his bare hands. . . .

Afterward, after many hours, out of the blind face of that sky the rain began to fall. It made first a whispering and then a delicate murmur like voices conversing, but after that, just at the dawn, it roared like the hoofs of ten thousand charging horses. Even through that thundering confusion the big birds with naked heads and red, raw necks found their way down to one place in the Apache Desert.

Understanding the Story _____

Main Idea

1. The expression that best expresses the main idea is: (a) A stitch in time saves nine. (b) A friend in need is a friend indeed. (c) A fool and his money are soon parted. (d) Don't bite the hand that feeds you.

2. Durante rides to Tony's vineyard (a) to pay his old friend a visit (b) to hide there (c) to get water for himself and to prevent the posse from getting any (d) because he likes Tony's wines.

Details

3. Which of the following statements is not true?
   a. Durante is a wanted man.
   b. The vineyards grow in the midst of the desert.
   c. Tony is lonely and very glad to see Durante.
   d. Durante regrets his having to shoot up the tanks.

4. Which of the following is not a blunder committed by Durante?
   a. Making the mule gallop too long
   b. Discarding the rifle too near the vineyard
   c. Not having enough bullets for his revolver
   d. Letting Tony fill the canteen

Inference

5. Durante is relieved when Tony says that his wife Julia is in town because Durante (a) is afraid of her (b) won't have to plan for her too (c) respects her too much (d) doesn't want her to know his plans.

6. Durante tells Tony that he can mistreat Tony because Tony (a) is a coward (b) is an understanding friend (c) is handicapped (d) is alone.

Order of Events

7. Arrange the items in the order in which they occurred. Use letters only.
   A. The buzzards find Durante.
   B. Tony's family moves to the Apache Desert.

   C. The November rains begin.
   D. Durante runs away from the sheriff.
   E. Tony and Durante become friends.

Cause and Effect

8. Tony is no match for him because   (a) Durante is too quick
    on the draw   (b) Tony is caught unprepared   (c) Tony is
    afraid of Durante   (d) Tony pities Durante.

9. Tony will not follow Durante because   (a) Tony is afraid
    (b) Tony wants him to escape   (c) Tony is filled with despair
    (d) Tony forgives Durante.

Outcomes

10. Which of the following is not true?
     a. Durante's fate is similar to that of Tony's father.
     b. Tony recovers his gun and his ability to find food.
     c. The rains probably arrive in time to save the vines.
     d. The sheriff arrives in time to capture Durante as he lay
        dying in the desert.

Words in Context _____

1. The windmill looked like a sacred emblem to Durante, and the
    twenty *stodgy*, tar-painted tanks blessed his eyes.
    Stodgy (399) means   (a) tall   (b) shiny   (c) squat
    (d) sturdy.

2. There were two jars made of *porous* stone, very ancient things,
    and the liquid which distilled through the pores kept the con-
    tents cool.
    Because the jars were *porous* (400)   (a) the water was
    sweeter   (b) the outside of the jars was wet   (c) the water
    stayed fresh   (d) the jars didn't break.

3. He . . . watched *the color of sunset flush the mists of desert dust*
    that rose to the zenith. (401)
    He watched   (a) the clouds roll by   (b) the surrounding air
    turn yellow-red   (c) mists of evening gather   (d) desert
    darkness fall suddenly.

4. Then he turned the mule and kicked it into a *dogtrot.*
    Dogtrot (404) means   (a) path   (b) hollow   (c) fast walk
    (d) closed stall.

5. Suddenly Durante was *dry to the marrow.* (404)
    He was   (a) hungry   (b) thirsty   (c) frightened   (d) not
    sweating.

6. With a mighty *resolution,* he quieted the panic in his soul.
    Resolution (404) means   (a) determination   (b) stroke
    (c) prayer   (d) tug.

7. He would not touch the stuff until noon. Then he would take
    one *discreet* sip.
    Discreet (404) means   (a) small   (b) prudent   (c) steady
    (d) satisfying.

8. He looked at his watch and found it was only ten o'clock. And
    he had thought that it was *on the verge of* noon!
    On the verge of (404) means   (a) past   (b) long before
    (c) just before   (d) the moment of.

9. The vineyard, the rows of old twisted, *gnarled* little trunks . . .
    every vine was to Tony like a human life.
    Gnarled (405) means   (a) smooth   (b) chewed   (c) veined
    (d) knotted.

10. Perhaps it was fear . . . that made his tongue *cleave to* the roof
    of his mouth.
    Cleave to (405) means   (a) separate from   (b) stick to
    (c) rub against   (d) keep away from.

Thinking About the Story _____

1. How does Tony's definition of friendship differ from Durante's?
    Whose is more realistic? How close do their definitions come to
    yours?

2. How does the author turn the Apache Desert into a living
    avenger? How does he help us to imagine the heat and awesome
    power of the desert?

3. Is Tony a coward? Explain your answer. If you refuse to accept
    a challenge are you a coward? If you refuse to fight against im-
    possible odds, or if you refuse to fight on the terms and condi-

tions of another are you to be labeled a coward? In the last analysis, what *is* a coward? What's wrong in being one?

4. At which point in the story did you become aware of the villainy
    of Durante? Does he have any redeeming qualities? Are there
    people in real life who resemble Durante? Can you cite exam-
    ples?

5. The only weakness that Tony reveals in this story is that he can
    be a poor judge of character, in that he trusted Durante. Can
    you explain how he could be fooled by someone like Durante?
    Did you ever put your trust in someone who took unfair advan-
    tage? Were you ever "betrayed" by a so-called friend? How can
    we protect ourselves from being mistreated in this way?

The New Kid

Murray Heyert

♦ Eddie Deakes put his hands to his mouth like
a megaphone. "Attaboy, Marty!" he yelled. "Having you out there is like having another man on
our side!"

In the days before stickball, basketball, and hockey became
the street games of the inner city, punchball reigned supreme.
"The New Kid" opens just as a punchball game is being orga-
nized. It's about a group of boys in a tenement-house block and
the rules according to which they play and fight.

It is a disturbing story because, in one or another of the characters in it, you may see yourself as you were a year or two ago.
If you are the kind of reader who thinks that entertainment means
only the production of laughter or being lulled to drowsiness by
sweet untruths, then you won't enjoy this story. But, if, on the
other hand, you are the kind of person who has respect for truth,
who knows that coming to grips with the harsh realities of life is
part of the process of growing up, then you'll accept this story for
the good you can get out of it. As you read it, keep asking yourself
the question, "Why do these boys behave the way they do?"

THE NEW KID

By the time Marty ran up the stairs, past the dentist's office, where it smelled like the time his father was in the hospital, past the fresh paint smell, where the new kid lived, past the garlic smell from the Italians in 2D; and waited for Mommer to open the door; and threw his schoolbooks on top of the old newspapers that were piled on the sewing machine in the hall; and drank his glass of milk ("How many times must I tell you not to gulp! Are you going to stop gulping like that or must I smack your face!"); and set the empty glass in the sink under the faucet; and changed into his white sneakers; and put trees into his school shoes ("How many times must I talk to you! God in Heaven—when will you learn to take care of your clothes and not make me follow you around like this!"); and ran downstairs again, past the garlic and the paint and the hospital smells; by the time he got into the street and looked breathlessly around him, it was too late. The fellows were all out there, all ready for a game, and just waiting for Eddie Deakes to finish chalking a base against the curb.

Running up the street with all his might, Marty could see that the game would start any minute now. Out in the gutter Paulie Dahler was tossing high ones to Ray-Ray Stickerling, whose father was a bus driver and sometimes gave the fellows transfers so they could ride free. The rest were sitting on the curb, waiting for Eddie to finish making the base and listening to Gelberg, who was a Jew, explain what it meant to be bar-mitzvah'd, like he was going to be next month.

They did not look up as Marty galloped up to them all out of breath. Eddie finished making his base and after looking at it critically a moment, with his head on one side, moved down toward the sewer that was home plate and began drawing a scoreboard alongside it. With his nose running from excitement Marty trotted over to him.

"Just going to play with two bases?" he said, wiping his nose on the sleeve of his lumber jacket, and hoping with all his might that Eddie would think he had been there all the while and was waiting for a game like all the other fellows.

Eddie raised his head and saw that it was Marty. He gave Marty a shove. "Why don't you watch where you're walking?" he said. "Can't you see I'm making a scoreboard!"

He bent over again and with his chalk repaired the lines that Marty had smudged with his sneakers. Marty hopped around alongside him, taking care to keep his feet off the chalked box. "Gimme a game, Eddie?" he said.

"What are you asking me for?" Eddie said, without looking up. "It ain't my game."

"Aw, come on, Eddie. I'll get even on you!" Marty said.

"Ask Gelberg. It's his game," Eddie said, straightening himself and shoving his chalk into his pants pocket. He trotted suddenly into the middle of the street and ran sideways a few feet. "Here go!" he hollered. "All the way!"

From his place up near the corner Paulie Dahler heaved the ball high into the air, higher than the telephone wires. Eddie took a step back, then a step forward, then back again, and got under it.

Marty bent his knees like a catcher, pounded his fist into his palm as though he were wearing a mitt, and held out his hands. "Here go, Eddie!" he hollered. "Here go!"

Holding the ball in his hand, and without answering him, Eddie walked toward the curb, where the rest of the fellows were gathered around Gelberg. Marty straightened his knees, put down his hands, and sniffing his nose, trotted after Eddie.

"All right, I'll choose Gelberg for sides," Eddie said.

Gelberg heaved himself off the curb and put on his punchball glove, which was one of his mother's old kid gloves, with the fingers and thumb cut off short. "Odds, once takes it," he said.

After a couple of preparatory swings of their arms they matched fingers. Gelberg won. He chose Albie Newbauer. Eddie looked around him and took Wally Reinhard. Gelberg took Ray-Ray Stickerling. Eddie took Wally Reinhard's brother, Howey.

Marty hopped around on the edge of the group. "Hey, Gelberg," he hollered, in a high voice. "Gimme a game, will you?"

"I got Arnie," Gelberg said.

Eddie looked around him again. "All right, I got Paulie Dahler."

They counted their men. "Choose you for up first," Gelberg said. Feeling as though he were going to cry, Marty watched them as they swung their arms, stuck out their fingers. This time Eddie won. Gelberg gathered his men around him and they trotted into the street to take up positions on the field. They hollered "Here go!" threw the ball from first to second, then out into the field, and back again to Gelberg in the pitcher's box.

Marty ran over to him. "Gimme a game, will you, Gelberg?"

"We're all choosed up," Gelberg said, heaving a high one to Arnie out in center field.

Marty wiped his nose on his sleeve. "Come on, gimme a game. Didn't I let you lose my Spaulding Hi-Bouncer down the sewer once?"

"Want to give the kid a game?" Gelberg called to Eddie, who was seated on the curb, figuring out his batting order with his men.

"Aw, we got the sides all choosed up!" Eddie said.

Marty stuck out his lower lip and wished that he would not have to cry. "You give Howey Reinhard a game!" he said, pointing at Howey sitting on the curb next to Eddie. "He can't play any better than me!"

"Yeah," Howey yelled, swinging back his arm as though he were going to punch Marty in the jaw. "You couldn't hit the side of the house!"

"Yeah, I can play better than you any day!" Marty hollered.

"You can play left outside!" Howey said, looking around to see how the joke went over.

"Yeah, I'll get even on you!" Marty hollered, hoping that maybe they would get worried and give him a game after all.

With a fierce expression on his face, as if to indicate that he was through joking and now meant serious business, Howey sprang up from the curb and sent him staggering with a shove. Marty tried to duck, but Howey smacked him across the side of the head. Flinging his arms up about his ears Marty scrambled down the street; for no reason at all Paulie Dahler booted him in the pants as he went by.

"I'll get even on you!" Marty yelled, when he was out of reach. With a sudden movement of his legs Howey pretended to rush at him. Almost falling over himself in panic Marty dashed toward the house, but stopped, feeling ashamed, when he saw that Howey had only wanted to make him run.

For a while he stood there on the curb, wary and ready to dive into the house the instant any of the fellows made a move toward him. But presently he saw that the game was beginning, and that none of them was paying any more attention to him. He crept toward them again, and seating himself on the curb a little distance away, watched the game start. For a moment he thought of breaking it up, rushing up to the scoreboard and smudging it with his sneakers before anyone could stop him, and then dashing into the house before they caught him. Or grabbing the ball when it came near him and flinging it down the sewer. But he decided not to; the fellows would catch him in the end, smack him, and make another scoreboard or get another ball, and then he would never get a game.

Every minute feeling more and more like crying, he sat there on the curb, his elbow on his knee, his chin in his palm, and tried to think where he could get another fellow, so that they could give him a game and still have even sides. Then he lifted his chin from his palm and saw that the new kid was sitting out on the stoop in front of the house, chewing something and gazing toward the game; and all at once the feeling that he was going to cry disappeared. He sprang up from the curb.

"Hey, Gelberg!" he hollered. "If I get the new kid for even sides, can I get a game?"

Without waiting for an answer he dashed down the street toward the stoop where the new kid was sitting.

"Hey, fellow!" he shouted. "Want a game? Want a game of punchball?"

He could see now that what the new kid was eating was a slice of rye bread covered with apple sauce. He could see, too, that the new kid was smaller than he was, and had a narrow face and a large nose with a few little freckles across the bridge. He was wearing Boy Scout pants and a brown woolen pullover, and on the back of his head was a skullcap made from the crown of a man's felt hat, the edge turned up and cut into sharp points that were ornamented with brass paper clips.

All out of breath he stopped in front of the new kid. "What do you say?" he hollered. "Want a game?"

The new kid looked at him and took another bite of rye bread. "I don't know," he said, with his mouth full of bread, turning to take another look at the fellows in the street. "I guess I got to go to the store soon."

"You don't have to go to the store right away, do you?" Marty said, in a high voice.

The new kid swallowed his bread and continued looking up toward the game. "I got to stay in front of the house in case my mother calls me."

"Maybe she won't call you for a while," Marty said. He could see that the inning was ending, that they would be starting a new inning in a minute, and his legs twitched with impatience.

"I don't know," the new kid said, still looking up at the game. "Anyway, I got my good shoes on."

"Aw, I bet you can't even play punchball!" cried Marty.

The new kid looked at him with his lower lip stuck out. "Yeah, I can so play! Only I got to go to the store!"

Once more he looked undecidedly up toward the game. Marty could see that the inning was over now. He turned pleadingly to the new kid.

"You can hear her if she calls you, can't you? Can't you play just till she calls you? Come on, can't you?"

Putting the last of his rye bread into his mouth, the new kid got up from the stoop. "Well, when she calls me—" he said, brushing off the seat of his pants with his hand, "when she calls me I got to quit and go to the store."

As fast as he could run Marty dashed up the street with the new kid trailing after him. "Hey, I got another man for even sides!" he yelled. "Gimme a game now? I got another man!"

The fellows looked at the new kid coming up the street behind Marty.

"You new on the block?" Howey Reinhard asked, eying the Boy Scout pants, as Marty and the new kid came up to them.

"You any good?" Gelberg demanded, bouncing the ball at his feet and looking at the skullcap ornamented with brass paper clips. "Can you hit?"

"Come on!" Marty said. He wished that they would just give him a game and not start asking a lot of questions. "I got another man for even sides, didn't I?"

"Aw, we got the game started already!" Ray-Ray Stickerling hollered.

Marty sniffled his nose, which was beginning to run again, and looked at him as fiercely as he was able. "It ain't your game!" he yelled. "It's Gelberg's game! Ain't it your game, Gelberg?"

Gelberg gave him a shove. "No one said you weren't going to get a game!" With a last bounce of his ball he turned to Eddie, who was looking the new kid over carefully.

"All right, Eddie. I'll take the new kid and you can have Marty."

Eddie drew his arm back as though he were going to hit him. "Like fun! Why don't you take Marty, if you're so wise?"

"I won the choose-up!" Gelberg hollered.

"Yeah, that was before! I'm not taking Marty!"

"I won the choose-up, didn't I?"

"Well, you got to choose up again for the new kid!"

Marty watched them as they stood up to each other, each eying the other suspiciously, and swung their arms to choose. Eddie won. "Cheating shows!" he yelled, seizing the new kid by the arm, and pulling him into the group on his side.

Trying to look like the ball players he had seen the time his father had taken him to the Polo Grounds, Marty ran into the outfield and took the position near the curb that Gelberg had selected for him. He tried not to feel bad because Eddie had taken the new kid, that no one knew anything about, how he could hit, or anything; and that he had had to go to the loser of the choose-up. As soon as he was out in the field he leaned forward, with his hands propped on his knees, and hollered: "All right, all right, these guys can't hit!" Then he straightened up and pounded his fist into his palm as though he were wearing a fielder's glove and shouted: "Serve it to them on a silver platter, Gelberg! These guys are just a bunch of fan artists!" He propped his hands on his knees again, like a big-leaguer, but all the while he felt unhappy, not nearly the way he should have felt, now that they had finally given him a game. He hoped that they would hit to him, and he would make one-handed catches over his head, run way out with his back to the ball and spear them blind, or run in with all his might and pick them right off the tops of his shoes.

A little nervous chill ran through his back as he saw Paulie Dahler get up to hit. On Gelberg's second toss Paulie stepped in and sent the ball sailing into the air. A panic seized Marty as he saw it coming at him. He took a step nervously forward, then backward, then forward again, trying as hard as he could to judge the ball. It smacked into his cupped palms, bounced out and dribbled toward the curb. He scrambled after it, hearing them shouting at him, and feeling himself getting more scared every instant. He kicked the ball with his sneaker, got his hand on it, and straightening himself in a fever of fright, heaved it with all his strength at Ray-Ray on first. The moment the ball left his hand he knew he had done the wrong thing. Paulie was already on his way to second; and besides, the throw was wild. Ray-Ray leaped into the air, his arms flung up, but it was way over his head, bouncing beyond him on the sidewalk and almost hitting a woman who was jouncing a baby carriage at the door of the apartment house opposite.

With his heart beating the same way it did whenever anyone chased him, Marty watched Paulie gallop across the plate. He sniffled his nose, which was beginning to run again, and felt like crying.

"Holy Moses!" he heard Gelberg yell. "What do you want, a basket? Can't you hold on to them once in a while?"

"Aw, the sun was in my eyes!" Marty said.

"You wait until you want another game!" Gelberg shouted.

Breathing hard, Ray-Ray got back on first and tossed the ball to Gelberg. "Whose side are you on anyway?" he hollered.

Eddie Deakes put his hands to his mouth like a megaphone. "Attaboy, Marty!" he yelled. "Having you out there is like having another man on our side!"

The other fellows on the curb laughed, and Howey Reinhard made them laugh harder by pretending to catch a fly ball with the sun in his eyes, staggering around the street with his eyes screwed up and his hands cupped like a sissy, so that the wrists touched and the palms were widely separated.

No longer shouting or punching his fist into his palm, Marty took his place out in the field again. He stood there, feeling like crying, and wished that he hadn't dropped that ball, or thrown it over Ray-Ray's head. Then, without knowing why, he looked up to see whether the new kid was laughing at him like all the rest. But the new kid was sitting a little off by himself at one end of the row of fellows on the curb, and with a serious expression on his face gnawed at the skin at the side of his thumbnail. Marty began to wonder if the new kid was any good or not. He saw him sitting there, with the serious look on his face, his ears sticking out, not joking like the other fellows, and from nowhere the thought leaped into Marty's head that maybe the new kid was no good. He looked at the skinny legs, the Boy Scout pants, and the mama's boy shoes and all at once he began to hope that Eddie would send the new kid in to hit, so that he could know right away whether he was any good or not.

But Wally Reinhard was up next. He fouled out on one of Gelberg's twirls, and after him Howey popped up to Albie Newbauer and Eddie was out on first. The fellows ran in to watch Eddie chalk up Paulie's run on the scoreboard alongside the sewer. They were still beefing and hollering at Marty for dropping that ball, but he pretended he did not hear them and sat down on the curb to watch the new kid out in the field.

He was over near the curb, playing in closer than Paulie Dahler. Marty could see that he was not hollering "Here go!" or "All the way!" like the others, but merely stood there with that serious expression on his face and watched them throw the ball around. He held one leg bent at the ankle, so that the side of his shoe rested on the pavement, his belly was stuck out, and he chewed the skin at the side of his thumbnail.

Gelberg got up to bat. Standing in the pitcher's box, Eddie turned around and motioned his men to lay out. The new kid looked around him to see what the other fellows did, took a few steps backward, and then, with his belly stuck out again, went on chewing his thumb.

Marty felt his heart begin to beat hard. He watched Gelberg stand up to the plate and contemptuously fling back the first few pitches.

"Come on, gimme one like I like!" Gelberg hollered.

"What's the matter! You afraid to reach for them?" Eddie yelled.

"Just pitch them to me, that's all!" Gelberg said.

Eddie lobbed one in that bounced shoulder high. With a little sideways skip Gelberg lammed into it.

The ball sailed down toward the new kid. Feeling his heart begin to beat harder, Marty saw him take a hurried step backward, and at the same moment fling his hands before his face and duck his head. The ball landed beyond him and bounded up on the sidewalk. For an instant the new kid hesitated, then he was galloping after it, clattering across the pavement in his polished shoes.

Swinging his arms in mock haste, Gelberg breezed across the plate. "Get a basket!" he hollered over his shoulder. "Get a basket!"

Marty let his nose run without bothering to sniffle. He jumped up from the curb and curved his hands around his mouth like a megaphone. "He's scared of the ball!" he yelled at the top of his lungs. "He's scared of the ball! That's what he is, scared of the ball!"

The new kid tossed the ball back to Eddie. "I wasn't scared!" he said, moistening his lips with his tongue. "I wasn't scared! I just couldn't see it coming!"

With an expression of despair on his face Eddie shook his head. "Holy Moses! If you can't see the ball why do you try to play punchball?" He bounced the ball hard at his feet and motioned Gelberg to send in his next batter. Arnie got up from the curb and wiping his hands on his pants walked toward the plate.

Marty felt his heart pounding in his chest. He hopped up and down with excitement and seizing Gelberg by the arm pointed at the new kid.

"You see him duck?" he yelled. "He's scared of the ball, that's what he is!" He hardly knew where to turn first. He rushed up to Ray-Ray, who was sitting on the curb making marks on the asphalt with the heel of his sneaker. "The new kid's scared to stop a ball! You see him duck!"

The new kid looked toward Marty and wet his lips with his tongue. "Yeah," he yelled, "didn't you muff one that was right in your hands?"

He was looking at Marty with a sore expression on his face, and his lower lip stuck out; and a sinking feeling went through Marty, a sudden sick feeling that maybe he had started something he would be sorry for. Behind him on the curb he could hear the fellows sniggering in that way they did when they picked on him. In the pitcher's box Eddie let out a loud cackling laugh.

"Yeah, the new kid's got your number!"

"The sun was in my eyes!" Marty said. He could feel his face getting red, and in the field the fellows were laughing. A wave of self-pity flowed through him.

"What are you picking on me for!" he yelled, in a high voice. "The sun was so in my eyes. Anyway, I ain't no yellowbelly! I wasn't scared of the ball!"

The instant he said it he was sorry. He sniffled his nose uneasily as he saw Gelberg look at Ray-Ray. For an instant he thought of running into the house before anything happened. But instead he just stood there, sniffling his nose and feeling his heart beating, fast and heavy.

"You hear what he called you?" Paulie Dahler yelled at the new kid.

"You're not going to let him get away with calling you a yellow-belly, are you?" Eddie said, looking at the new kid.

The new kid wet his lips with his tongue and looked at Marty. "I wasn't scared!" he said. He shifted the soles of his new-looking shoes on the pavement. "I wasn't scared! I just couldn't see it coming, that's all!"

Eddie was walking toward the new kid now, bouncing the ball slowly in front of him as he walked. In a sudden panic Marty looked back toward the house where old lady Kipnis lived. She always broke up fights; maybe she would break up this one; maybe she wouldn't even let it get started. But she wasn't out on her porch. He sniffled his nose, and with all his might hoped that the kid's mother would call him to go to the store.

"Any kid that lets himself be called a yellowbelly must be a yellowbelly!" Albie Newbauer said, looking around him for approval.

"Yeah," Gelberg said. "I wouldn't let anyone call me a yellowbelly."

With a sudden shove Eddie sent the new kid scrambling forward toward Marty. He tried to check himself by stiffening his body and twisting to one side, but it was no use. Before he could recover his balance another shove made him stagger forward.

Marty sniffled his nose and looked at the kid's face close in front of him. It seemed as big as the faces he saw in the movies; and he could see that the kid's nose was beginning to run just like his own; and he could see in the corner of his mouth a crumb of the rye bread he had eaten on the stoop. For a moment the kid's eyes looked squarely into Marty's, so that he could see the little dark specks in the colored part around the pupil. Then the glance slipped away to one side; and all at once Marty had a feeling that the new kid was afraid of him.

"You gonna let him get away with calling you a yellowbelly?" he heard Eddie say. From the way it sounded he knew that the fellows were on his side now. He stuck out his jaw and waited for the new kid to answer.

"I got to go to the store!" the new kid said. There was a scared look on his face and he took a step back from Marty.

Paulie Dahler got behind him and shoved him against Marty. Although he tried not to, Marty couldn't help flinging his arms up before his face. But the new kid only backed away and kept his arms at his sides. A fierce excitement went through Marty as he saw how scared the look on the kid's face was. He thrust his chest up against the new kid.

"Yellowbelly!" he hollered, making his voice sound tough. "Scared of the ball!"

The new kid backed nervously away, and there was a look on his face as though he wanted to cry.

"Yeah, he's scared!" Eddie yelled.

"Slam him, Marty!" Wally Reinhard hollered. "The kid's scared of you!"

"Aw, sock the yellowbelly!" Marty heard Gelberg say, and he smacked the kid as hard as he could on the shoulder. The kid screwed up his face to keep from crying, and tried to back through the fellows ringed around him.

"Lemme alone!" he yelled.

Marty looked at him fiercely, with his jaw thrust forward, and felt his heart beating. He smacked the kid again, making him stagger against Arnie in back of him.

"Yeah, yellowbelly!" Marty hollered, feeling how the fellows were on his side, and how scared the new kid was. He began smacking him again and again on the shoulder.

"Three, six, nine, a bottle of wine, I can fight you any old time!" he yelled. With each word he smacked the kid on the shoulder or arm. At the last word he swung with all his strength. He meant to hit the kid on the shoulder, but at the last instant, even while his arm was swinging, something compelled him to change his aim; his fist caught the kid on the mouth with a hard, wet, socking sound. The shock of his knuckles against the kid's mouth, and that sound of it, made Marty want to hit him again and again. He put his head down and began swinging wildly, hitting the new kid without any aim on the head and shoulders and arms.

The new kid buried his head in his arms and began to cry. "Lemme alone!" he yelled. He tried to rush through the fellows crowded around him.

With all his might Marty smacked him on the side of the head. Rushing up behind him Arnie smacked him too. Paulie Dahler shoved the skullcap, with its paper clip ornaments, over the kid's eyes; and as he went by Gelberg booted him in the pants.

Crying and clutching his cap the new kid scampered over to the curb out of reach.

"I'll get even on you!" he cried.

With a fierce expression on his face Marty made a sudden movement of his legs and pretended to rush at him. The kid threw his arms about his head and darted down the street toward the house. When he saw that Marty was not coming after him he sat down on the stoop; and Marty could see him rubbing his knuckles against his mouth.

Howey Reinhard was making fun of the new kid, scampering up and down the pavement with his arms wrapped around his head and hollering, "Lemme alone! Lemme alone!" The fellows laughed, and although he was breathing hard, and his hand hurt from hitting the kid, Marty had to laugh too.

"You see him duck when that ball came at him?" he panted at Paulie Dahler.

Paulie shook his head. "Boy, just wait until we get the yellowbelly in the schoolyard!"

"And on Halloween," Gelberg said. "Wait until we get him on Halloween with our flour stockings!" He gave Marty a little shove and made as though he were whirling an imaginary flour stocking round his head.

Standing there in the middle of the street, Marty suddenly thought of Halloween, of the winter and snowballs, of the schoolyard. He saw himself whirling a flour stocking around his head and rushing at the new kid, who scampered in terror before him hollering, "Lemme alone! Lemme alone!" As clearly as if it were in the movies, he saw himself flinging snowballs and the new kid backed into a corner of the schoolyard, with his hands over his face. Before he knew what he was doing, Marty turned fiercely toward the stoop where the new kid was still sitting, rubbing his mouth and crying.

"Hey, yellowbelly!" Marty hollered; and he pretended he was going to rush at the kid.

Almost falling over himself in fright the new kid scrambled inside the house. Marty stood in the middle of the street and sniffled his nose. He shook his fist at the empty doorway.

"You see him run?" he yelled, so loud that it made his throat hurt. "Boy, you see him run?" He stood there shaking his fist, although the new kid was no longer there to see him. He could hardly wait for the winter, for Halloween, or the very next day in the schoolyard.

Understanding the Story _____

Main Idea

1. The main idea in this story is that   (a) newcomers are poor players   (b) punchball is a game anyone can play well (c) unsupervised free play on city streets has no standards (d) physical ability establishes the pecking order in street games.

Details

2. Marty is   (a) one of the leaders   (b) eager to be one of the crowd   (c) told to go on an errand for one of the boys (d) finer and more sensitive than the other boys.

3. Which of the following statements is not true?
    a. Marty is not selected as one of the first players.
    b. Because he isn't selected, Marty decides never to play with the boys again.
    c. The other boys hit Marty at will.
    d. Marty is allowed to play "left outside."

4. Which of the following statements is not true?
    a. The boys in the story are probably about 13 years old.
    b. The pavement has to be chalked up for the game.
    c. Marty panics when the ball comes to him.
    d. The umpire calls balls and strikes just as in baseball.

5. When Marty's big moment in the game arrives,   (a) he hits a home run   (b) he flies out   (c) he makes an unassisted double play   (d) he drops the ball.

Cause and Effect

6. Marty asks the new kid to play because   (a) the newcomer looks lonely   (b) Marty thinks he looks like a good player (c) Marty wants to become acquainted with him   (d) Marty hopes to get into the game.

Inference

7. When the new kid's opportunity to show his ability arrives, (a) he falls and hurts himself   (b) he does just about what Marty had done   (c) the game is interrupted   (d) his mother calls for him.

8. Marty and the new boy fight because   (a) they dislike each other   (b) the new boy has insulted Marty   (c) they want to see who is the stronger   (d) the other boys force them to.

Order of Events

9. Arrange the items in the order in which they occurred. Use letters only.
   A. Marty bullies the new kid.
   B. Gelberg gives Marty a chance to play.
   C. The new kid moves onto the block.
   D. Howey hits Marty.
   E. Marty is not chosen for the game.

Outcomes

10. One of the important results of the fight is that   (a) Marty runs home crying   (b) someone else has been found to assume the burden of being the "goat"   (c) the new boy's mother comes out to chase the boys away   (d) the new boy is proud of his new friends.

Words in Context

1. By the time Marty . . . put *trees* into his school shoes . . .
   Trees (412) means   (a) inner soles   (b) soothing powder   (c) foot-shaped devices   (d) graffiti decorations.

2. After looking at it *critically* for a moment . . . moved down toward the sewer that was home plate.
   Critically (412)   means   (a) checking   for   faults   (b) carelessly   (c) with approval   (d) with determination.

3. After a couple of *preparatory* swings of their arms they matched fingers.
   Preparatory (413) means   (a) professional   (b) powerful   (c) awkward   (d) practice.

4. On back of his head was a *skullcap* made from the crown of a man's felt hat.
   A *skullcap* (415) is a   (a) hard hat   (b) cap without a brim   (c) baseball cap   (d) derby.

5. "These guys are just a bunch of *fan artists*."
   By *fan artists* (417), the speaker meant   (a) homerun hitters
   (b) portrait painters   (c) poor hitters   (d) boasters.

6. He would make one-handed catches over his head, run way out
   with his back to the ball and *spear them blind*.
   Spear them blind (417) means   (a) catch them as they fall in
   front of him   (b) wait for them to hit the ground   (c) put
   the runner out on first   (d) throw them backhand.

7. It was way over his head . . . almost hitting a woman who was
   jouncing a baby carriage.
   Jouncing (418) means   (a) rocking vigorously   (b) pushing
   quickly   (c) looking into   (d) sitting beside.

8. He watched Gelberg stand up at the plate and *contemptuously*
   fling back the first few pitches.
   Contemptuously (419) means   (a) graciously   (b) cleverly
   (c) scornfully   (d) painstakingly.

9. He curved his hands around his mouth like a *megaphone*. (418)
   He used his hands in this fashion in order to   (a) show his
   scorn   (b) make his voice sound louder   (c) look even
   meaner   (d) show his ability as a catcher.

10. Swinging his arms in mock haste, Gelberg *breezed* across the
    plate.
    Breezed (419) means   (a) ran easily and rapidly   (b) bowed
    briefly and tipped his hat   (c) paused momentarily
    (d) strutted.

Thinking About the Story

1. Why is Marty the butt of the jokes of the boys on the block?
   Why does Marty allow them to mistreat him? Why doesn't
   Marty tell his parents? Will the picking on Marty stop now that
   there is a new boy on the block? Explain.

2. Are these boys "bad"? Are they in danger of becoming criminals? Explain.

3. What is the *theme* of the story? Is it applicable only to boys, or
   is it just as valid for girls? Does this story prove: "Life is filled
   with hard knocks. It is a case of rule or be ruled"? Justify your
   answer. Is the statement a satisfactory rule of life? Explain your
   answer.

4. What is the basis of friendship among these boys? Is it a fair one? Justify your answer. Is the treatment that the new boy receives inevitable? Explain. What do you think is the new kid's opinions of the other boys on the block? How would that compare with your own estimate of the boys in your own neighborhood?

5. "The jungle laws of early adolescence must give way to a spirit of cooperation and a respect for the individuality of others— else democracy becomes a farce." How is this quotation applicable to the story? Is this story true to life or is it exaggerated and melodramatic? Justify your answer.

Raymond's Run

Toni Cade Bambara

♦ "And I've got a roomful of ribbons and medals
and awards. But what has Raymond got to call his
own?"

"Raymond's Run" is not a story of high adventure, ghosts, or
surprise endings. It takes place in an everyday part of Harlem, a
section of New York City. The turf could be part of any community
anywhere in the world. It is told by a young teenager with the
unpleasant nickname of Squeaky. She is anything but a timid
mouse.

Squeaky has learned to fight back hard and furious in the
complex neighborhood in which she is growing up. Everyone
seems ready to pick on her charge, her older brother Raymond
who is not bright enough to take care of himself.

The basic action in the story deals with her success as a runner which leads to her winning Gretchen's friendship, but you get
much more when you read this story. A clue to the greater impact
is in the title. Raymond is the center of the target. Read and at
the end see if you can figure out why the author calls it "Raymond's Run" when the big event is a race that Squeaky wins!

RAYMOND'S RUN

I don't have much work to do around the house like some girls. My mother does that. And I don't have to earn my pocket money by hustling; George runs errands for the big boys and sells Christmas cards. And anything else that's got to get done, my father does. All I have to do in life is mind my brother Raymond, which is enough.

Sometimes I slip and say my little brother Raymond. But as any fool can see he's much bigger and he's older too. But a lot of people call him my little brother cause he needs looking after cause he's not quite right. And a lot of smart mouths got lots to say about that too, especially when George was minding him. But now, if anybody has anything to say to Raymond, anything to say about his big head, they have to come by me. And I don't play the dozens or believe in standing around with somebody in my face doing a lot of talking. I much rather just knock you down and take my chances even if I am a little girl with skinny arms and a squeaky voice, which is how I got the name Squeaky. And if things get too rough, I run. And as anybody can tell you, I'm the fastest thing on two feet.

There is no track meet that I don't win the first place medal. I used to win the twenty-yard dash when I was a little kid in kindergarten. Nowadays, it's the fifty-yard dash. And tomorrow I'm subject to run the quarter-meter relay all by myself and come in first, second, and third. The big kids call me Mercury cause I'm the swiftest thing in the neighborhood. Everybody knows that—except two people who know better, my father and me. He can beat me to Amsterdam Avenue with me having a two fire-hydrant headstart and him running with his hands in his pockets and whistling. But that's private information. Cause can you imagine some thirty-five-year-old man stuffing himself into PAL shorts to race little kids? So as far as everyone's concerned, I'm the fastest and that goes for Gretchen, too, who has put out the tale that she is going to win the first-place medal this year. Ridiculous. In the second place, she's got short legs. In the third place, she's got freckles. In the first place, no one can beat me and that's all there is to it.

I'm standing on the corner admiring the weather and about to take a stroll down Broadway so I can practice my breathing exercises, and I've got Raymond walking on the inside close to the buildings, cause he's subject to fits of fantasy and starts thinking he's a circus performer and that the curb is a tightrope strung high in the air. And sometimes after a rain he likes to step down off his tightrope right into the gutter and slosh around getting his shoes and cuffs wet. Then I get hit when I get home. Or sometimes if you don't watch him he'll dash across traffic to the island in the middle of Broadway and give the pigeons a fit. Then I have to go behind him apologizing to all the old people sitting around trying to get some sun and getting all upset with the pigeons fluttering around them, scattering their newspapers and upsetting the waxpaper lunches in their laps. So I keep Raymond on the inside of me, and he plays like he's driving a stagecoach which is O.K. by me so long as he doesn't run me over or interrupt my breathing exercises, which I have to do on account of I'm serious about my running, and I don't care who knows it.

Now some people like to act like things come easy to them, won't let on that they practice. Not me. I'll high-prance down 34th Street like a rodeo pony to keep my knees strong even if it does get my mother uptight so that she walks ahead like she's not with me, don't know me, is all by herself on a shopping trip, and I am somebody else's crazy child. Now you take Cynthia Procter for instance. She's just the opposite. If there's a test tomorrow, she'll say something like, "Oh, I guess I'll play handball this afternoon and watch television tonight," just to let you know she ain't thinking about the test. Or like last week when she won the spelling bee for the millionth time, "A good thing you got 'receive,' Squeaky, cause I would have got it wrong. I completely forgot about the spelling bee." And she'll clutch the lace on her blouse like it was a narrow escape. Oh, brother. But of course when I pass her house on my early morning trots around the block, she is practicing the scales on the piano over and over and over and over. Then in music class she always lets herself get bumped around so she falls accidently on purpose onto the piano stool and is so surprised to find herself sitting there that she decides just for fun to try out the ole keys. And what do you know—Chopin's waltzes just spring out of her fingertips and she's the most surprised thing in the world. A regular prodigy. I could kill people like that. I stay up all night studying the words for the spelling bee. And you can see me any time of day practicing running. I never walk if I can trot, and shame on Raymond if he can't keep up. But of course he does, cause if he hangs back someone's liable to walk up to him and get smart, or take his allowance from him, or ask him where he got that great big pumpkin head. People are so stupid sometimes.

So I'm strolling down Broadway breathing out and breathing in on counts of seven, which is my lucky number, and here comes Gretchen and her sidekicks: Mary Louise, who used to be a friend of mine when she first moved to Harlem from Baltimore and got beat up by everybody till I took up for her on account of her mother and my mother used to sing in the same choir when they were young girls, but people ain't grateful, so now she hangs out with the new girl Gretchen and talks about me like a dog; and Rosie, who is as fat as I am skinny and has a big mouth where Raymond is concerned and is too stupid to know that there is not a big deal of difference between herself and Raymond and that she can't afford to throw stones. So they are steady coming up Broadway and I see right away that it's going to be one of those Dodge City scenes cause the street ain't that big and they're close to the buildings just as we are. First I think I'll step into the candy store and look over the new comics and let them pass. But that's chicken and I've got a reputation to consider. So then I think I'll just walk straight on through them or even over them if necessary. But as they get to me, they slow down. I'm ready to fight, cause like I said I don't feature a whole lot of chit-chat, I much prefer to just knock you down right from the jump and save everybody a lotta precious time.

"You signing up for the May Day races?" smiles Mary Louise, only it's not a smile at all. A dumb question like that doesn't deserve an answer. Besides, there's just me and Gretchen standing there really, so no use wasting my breath talking to shadows.

"I don't think you're going to win this time," says Rosie, trying to signify with her hands on her hips all salty, completely forgetting that I have whupped her behind many times for less salt than that.

"I always win cause I'm the best," I say straight at Gretchen

who is, as far as I'm concerned, the only one talking in this ventril-
oquist-dummy routine. Gretchen smiles, but it's not a smile, and
I'm thinking that girls never really smile at each other because they
don't know how and don't want to know how and there's probably
no one to teach us how, cause grown-up girls don't know either.
Then they all look at Raymond who has just brought his mule team
to a standstill. And they're about to see what trouble they can get
into through him.

"What grade you in now, Raymond?"

"You got anything to say to my brother, you say it to me, Mary
Louise Williams of Raggedy Town, Baltimore."

"What are you, his mother?" sasses Rosie.

"That's right, Fatso. And the next word out of anybody and I'll
be *their* mother too." So they just stand there and Gretchen shifts
from one leg to the other and so do they. Then Gretchen puts her
hands on her hips and is about to say something with her freckle-
face self but doesn't. Then she walks around me looking me up and
down but keeps walking up Broadway, and her sidekicks follow her.
So me and Raymond smile at each other and he says, "Gidyap" to
his team and I continue with my breathing exercises, strolling down
Broadway toward the ice man on 145th with not a care in the world
cause I am Miss Quicksilver herself.

I take my time getting to the park on May Day because the track
meet is the last thing on the program. The biggest thing on the program is the May Pole dancing, which I can do without, thank you,
even if my mother thinks it's a shame I don't take part and act like
a girl for a change. You'd think my mother'd be grateful not to have
to make me a white organdy dress with a big satin sash and buy me
new white baby-doll shoes that can't be taken out of the box till the
big day. You'd think she'd be glad her daughter ain't out there
prancing around a May Pole getting the new clothes all dirty and
sweaty and trying to act like a fairy or a flower or whatever you're
supposed to be when you should be trying to be yourself, whatever
that is, which is, as far as I am concerned, a poor Black girl who
really can't afford to buy shoes and a new dress you only wear once
a lifetime cause it won't fit next year.

I was once a strawberry in a Hansel and Gretel pageant when
I was in nursery school and didn't have no better sense than to
dance on tiptoe with my arms in a circle over my head doing umbrella steps and being a perfect fool just so my mother and father

could come dressed up and clap. You'd think they'd know better than to encourage that kind of nonsense. I am not a strawberry. I do not dance on my toes. I run. That is what I am all about. So I always come late to the May Day program, just in time to get my number pinned on and lay in the grass till they announce the fifty-yard dash.

I put Raymond in the little swings, which is a tight squeeze this year and will be impossible next year. Then I look around for Mr. Pearson, who pins the numbers on. I'm really looking for Gretchen if you want to know the truth, but she's not around. The park is jam-packed. Parents in hats and corsages and breast-pocket handkerchiefs peeking up. Kids in white dresses and light-blue suits. The parkees unfolding chairs and chasing the rowdy kids from Lenox as if they had no right to be there. The big guys with their caps on backwards, leaning against the fence swirling the basketballs on the tips of their fingers, waiting for all these crazy people to clear out the park so they can play. Most of the kids in my class are carrying bass drums and glockenspiels and flutes. You'd think they'd put in a few bongos or something for real like that.

Then here comes Mr. Pearson with his clipboard and his cards and pencils and whistles and safety pins and fifty million other things he's always dropping all over the place with his clumsy self. He sticks out in a crowd because he's on stilts. We used to call him Jack and the Beanstalk to get him mad. But I'm the only one that can outrun him and get away, and I'm too grown for that silliness now.

"Well, Squeaky," he says, checking my name off the list and handing me number seven and two pins. And I'm thinking he's got no right to call me Squeaky, if I can't call him Beanstalk.

"Hazel Elizabeth Deborah Parker," I correct him and tell him to write it down on his board.

"Well, Hazel Elizabeth Deborah Parker, going to give someone else a break this year?" I squint at him real hard to see if he is seriously thinking I should lose the race on purpose just to give someone else a break. "Only six girls running this time," he continues, shaking his head sadly like it's my fault all of New York didn't turn out in sneakers. "That new girl should give you a run for your money." He looks around the park for Gretchen like a periscope in a submarine movie. "Wouldn't it be a nice gesture if you were . . . to ahhh . . . "

I give him such a look he couldn't finish putting that idea into words. Grownups got a lot of nerve sometimes. I pin number seven to myself and stomp away, I'm so burnt. And I go straight for the track and stretch out on the grass while the band winds up with "Oh, the Monkey Wrapped His Tail Around the Flag Pole," which my teacher calls by some other name. The man on the loudspeaker is calling everyone over to the track and I'm on my back looking at the sky, trying to pretend I'm in the country, but I can't, because even grass in the city feels hard as sidewalk, and there's just no pretending you are anywhere but in a "concrete jungle" as my grandfather says.

The twenty-yard dash takes all of two minutes cause most of the little kids don't know no better than to run off the track or run the wrong way or run smack into the fence and fall down and cry. One little kid, though, has got the good sense to run straight for the white ribbon up ahead so he wins. Then the second-graders line up for the thirty-yard dash and I don't even bother to turn my head to watch cause Raphael Perez always wins. He wins before he even begins by psyching the runners, telling them they're going to trip on their shoelaces and fall on their faces or lose their shorts or something, which he doesn't really have to do since he is very fast, almost as fast as I am. After that is the forty-yard dash which I use to run when I was in first grade. Raymond is hollering from the swings cause he knows I'm about to do my thing cause the man on the loudspeaker has just announced the fifty-yard dash, although he might just as well be giving a recipe for angel food cake cause you can hardly make out what he's sayin for the static. I get up and slip off my sweat pants and then I see Gretchen standing at the starting line, kicking her legs out like a pro. Then as I get into place I see that ole Raymond is on line on the other side of the fence, bending down with his fingers on the ground just like he knew what he was doing. I was going to yell at him but then I didn't. It burns up your energy to holler.

Every time, just before I take off in a race, I always feel like I'm in a dream, the kind of dream you have when you're sick with fever and feel all hot and weightless. I dream I'm flying over a sandy beach in the early morning sun, kissing the leaves of the trees as I fly by. And there's always the smell of apples, just like in the country when I was little and used to think I was a choo-choo train, running through the fields of corn and chugging up the hill to the orchard.

And all the time I'm dreaming this, I get lighter and lighter until I'm flying over the beach again, getting blown through the sky like a feather that weighs nothing at all. But once I spread my fingers in the dirt and crouch over the Get on Your Mark, the dream goes and I am solid again and am telling myself, Squeaky you must win, you must win, you are the fastest thing in the world, you can even beat your father up Amsterdam if you really try. And then I feel my weight coming back just behind my knees then down to my feet then into the earth and the pistol shot explodes in my blood and I am off and weightless again, flying past the other runners, my arms pumping up and down and the whole world is quiet except for the crunch as I zoom over the gravel in the track. I glance to my left and there is no one. To the right, a blurred Gretchen, who's got her chin jutting out as if it would win the race all by itself. And on the other side of the fence is Raymond with his arms down to his side and the palms tucked up behind him, running in his very own style, and it's the first time I ever saw that and I almost stop to watch my brother Raymond on his first run. But the white ribbon is bouncing toward me and I tear past it, racing into the distance till my feet with a mind of their own start digging up footfuls of dirt and brake me short. Then all the kids standing on the side pile on me, banging me on the back and slapping my head with their May Day programs, for I have won again and everybody on 151st Street can walk tall for another year.

"In first place . . . " the man on the loudspeaker is clear as a bell now. But then he pauses and the loudspeaker starts to whine. Then static. And I lean down to catch my breath and here comes Gretchen walking back, for she's overshot the finish line too, huffing and puffing with her hands on her hips taking it slow, breathing in steady time like a real pro and I sort of like her a little for the first time. "In first place . . . " and then three or four voices get all mixed up on the loudspeaker and I dig my sneaker into the grass and stare at Gretchen who's staring back, we both wondering just who did win. I can hear old Beanstalk arguing with the man on the loudspeaker and then a few others running their mouths about what the stopwatches say. Then I hear Raymond yanking at the fence to call me and I wave to shush him, but he keeps rattling the fence like a gorilla in a cage like in them gorilla movies, but then like a dancer or something he starts climbing up nice and easy but very fast. And it occurs to me, watching how smoothly he climbs hand over hand

and remembering how he looked running with his arms down to his side and with the wind pulling his mouth back and his teeth showing and all, it occurred to me that Raymond would make a very fine runner. Doesn't he always keep up with me on my trots? And he surely knows how to breathe in counts of seven cause he's always doing it at the dinner table, which drives my brother George up the wall. And I'm smiling to beat the band cause if I've lost this race, or if me and Gretchen tied, or even if I've won, I can always retire as a runner and begin a whole new career as a coach with Raymond as my champion. After all, with a little more study I can beat Cynthia and her phony self at the spelling bee. And if I bugged my mother, I could get piano lessons and become a star. And I have a big rep as the baddest thing around. And I've got a roomful of ribbons and medals and awards. But what has Raymond got to call his own?

So I stand there with my new plans, laughing out loud by this time as Raymond jumps down from the fence and runs over with his teeth showing and his arms down to the side, which no one before him has quite mastered as a running style. And by the time he comes over I'm jumping up and down so glad to see him—my brother Raymond, a great runner in the family tradition. But of course everyone thinks I'm jumping up and down because the men on the loudspeaker have finally gotten themselves together and compared notes and are announcing "In first place—Miss Hazel Elizabeth Deborah Parker." (Dig that.) "In second place—Miss Gretchen P. Lewis." And I look over at Gretchen wondering what the "P" stands for. And I smile. Cause she's good, no doubt about it. Maybe she'd like to help me coach Raymond; she obviously is serious about running, as any fool can see. And she nods to congratulate me and then she smiles. And I smile. We stand there with this big smile of respect between us. It's about as real a smile as girls can do for each other, considering we don't practice real smiling every day, you know, cause maybe we too busy being flowers or fairies or strawberries instead of something honest and worthy of respect . . . you know . . . like being people.

Understanding the Story _____

Main Idea

1. Which of the following bits of dialogue best expresses the main idea of the story?
   a. "And as anybody can tell you, I'm the fastest thing on two feet."
   b. "All I have to do in life is mind my brother Raymond, which is enough."
   c. "Now some people like to act like things come easy to them, won't let on that they practice."
   d. "That new girl should give you a run for your money."

Details

2. Which of the following is not true?
   a. Squeaky is younger than Raymond.
   b. Raymond has limited intelligence.
   c. Squeaky finds Raymond difficult to control.
   d. Raymond has an odd appearance.

3. The only one who runs faster than Squeaky is   (a) Raymond   (b) Gretchen   (c) the coach   (d) her father.

4. Which of the following statements is not true?
   a. Mary Louise is no longer a friend of Squeaky.
   b. Mary Louise had been protected by Squeaky.
   c. Mary Louise defends Squeaky when others talk against her.
   d. Mary Louise hangs around with Gretchen.

Cause and Effect

5. Squeaky has no friends because   (a) she is a troublemaker   (b) she is scrappy and hard to get along with   (c) she has a thin, high-pitched voice   (d) she doesn't have the time.

6. Squeaky doesn't enter the May Pole ceremony because (a) she would rather be in the race   (b) her last year's dress is too small   (c) her mother doesn't want her to   (d) the costume is expensive.

Inference

7. Squeaky refuses to "let Gretchen win" because   (a) it would be cheating   (b) Squeaky would lose her protective shield

(c) Raymond would object   (d) the judges would disqualify her.

8. Others mistreat Raymond because   (a) he is too aggressive (b) he is indifferent   (c) they can get even with Squeaky through him   (d) he avoids them.

Order of Events

9. Arrange the items in the order in which they occurred. Use letters only.
   A. Squeaky discovers what she can do best—run!
   B. Mary Louise is befriended by Squeaky.
   C. The May Pole is set up for the dance.
   D. Gretchen becomes Squeaky's rival.
   E. Squeaky feels that Raymond can become a star runner.

Outcomes

10. Which of the following is not true?
    a. Squeaky proves her superiority once again.
    b. Gretchen and Squeaky make up.
    c. Raymond's running ability shows that he can be normal some day.
    d. Squeaky hopes that Gretchen and she can make a runner out of Raymond.

Words in Context _____

1. And I don't have to earn my pocket money by *hustling.*
   Hustling (429) means   (a) doing errands   (b) asking my parents   (c) selling newspapers   (d) delivering newspapers.

2. And I don't *play the dozens* or believe in standing around with somebody in my face doing a lot of talking.
   Play the dozens (429) means   (a) have a verbal fight (b) insult others   (c) talk gossip   (d) talk about others behind their backs.

3. A regular *prodigy.* I could kill people like that.
   Prodigy (431) means   (a) scoundrel   (b) show-off (c) highly talented child   (d) wealthy storekeeper.

4. The big kids call me *Mercury* cause I'm the swiftest thing in the neighborhood.

Mercury (429) was originally the name of   (a) an automobile
(b) a candy bar   (c) the local movie house   (d) the messenger of the Roman gods.

5. Can you imagine some thirty-five-year-old man stuffing himself
    into *PAL shorts* to race little kids?
    PAL shorts (429) means   (a) friendly outfit   (b) borrowed
    clothing   (c) club's running uniform   (d) policeman's uniform shorts.

6. I see right away that it's going to be one of those *Dodge City
    scenes.*
    Dodge City scene (431) means   (a) a fight to the finish   (b) a
    duel with sticks and stones   (c) a tragic ending   (d) a dramatic reading.

7. ... with not a care in the world cause I am *Miss Quicksilver*
    herself.
    Miss Quicksilver (432) means   (a) the strongest person
    (b) the fastest runner   (c) the best speller   (d) the best musician.

8. You'd think my mother'd be grateful not to have to make me
    a white *organdy* dress.
    Organdy (432) means   (a) informal   (b) of stiff cloth for
    dress-up clothing   (c) of heavy cloth for denims   (d) of
    highly colored cotton fabric.

9. Most of the kids in my class are carrying bass drums and
    glockenspiels and flutes.
    The *glockenspiel* (433) is a musical instrument that has
    (a) strings   (b) a reed mouthpiece   (c) metal bars   (d) a
    long horn.

10. He wins before he even begins by *psyching* the runners, telling
    them they're going to trip on their shoelaces and fall on their
    faces.
    Psyching (434) means   (a) hypnotizing   (b) putting the hex
    on   (c) defeating   (d) using psychology on.

Thinking About the Story ⸻

1. How well equipped is Squeaky to survive in her neighborhood?
    How well is Raymond equipped to survive in that neighborhood? Would they survive any better in your neighborhood?

2. Why did Squeaky's parents make Raymond her charge? How does this responsibility affect Squeaky? Is it fair to make her her brother's keeper? Explain. How else could they have handled the problem of Raymond?

3. What makes Squeaky so willing to fight? Is she aware of her inner anger? Explain your answer. To what extent is Raymond responsible?

4. Did Squeaky know how to win friends and influence people? Would you choose a person like Squeaky as a friend? Explain your answer. If you were her counselor, what advice would you give her? Will her friendship with Gretchen last? Explain.

5. What is Squeaky's theory of practice? To what extent do you agree with her and her methods? Why is she such a loner?

For Lack of a Friend

ACTIVITIES

Thinking About the Stories

1. Which story has most significance for you?

2. How did Marty's solution of his difficulties differ from Bottles'? from Squeaky's? Which is the best solution?

3. How do the stories in this section prove or disprove the validity of each of the following quotations dealing with friendship?
   (a) "The friends of an unfortunate man are far off."
      —SENECA
   (b) "Of my friends I am the only one I have left."
      —TERENCE
   (c) "The vital air of friendship is composed of confidence. Friendship perishes in proportion as this air diminishes."
      —JOSEPH ROUX
   (d) "The bird a nest, the spider a web, man friendship."
      —WILLIAM BLAKE
   (e) "Friendship requires more time than poor, busy man can usually command."
      —EMERSON
   (f) "Who finds himself without friends is like a body without a soul."
      —ITALIAN PROVERB

4. Draw up a "code of friendship"—one that would lead to an avoidance of the difficulties the characters in these stories encountered.

5. Is true, lasting friendship possible?

Projects

1. Write the plot of a short story telling of a daydream experience that might have been had by one of the following:
   (a) a tone-deaf girl listening to a concert

(b) a puny boy watching the neighborhood hero batting out flies during practice

(c) a slow student listening to the teacher read off the list of scholarship prizes to be awarded to the members of the graduating class

2. Discuss the validity of the following statement: "Daydreams can be safety-valves and therefore may have a beneficial effect; on the other hand they may often be an opiate and cause irreparable damage to the dreamer."

3. Plan to lead a class discussion on one of the following:
   (a) What is the difference between a friend and an acquaintance? How do one's obligations to an acquaintance differ from those to a friend?
   (b) Quarrels between friends: their cause and cure.
   (c) How much should we expect of true friends? Use your own experiences as the basis of your answer.

4. Discuss whether each of the following pairs can form a lasting friendship.
   (a) the brightest boy in the class and a classmate who dislikes school work
   (b) a handicapped boy and the class athlete
   (c) a very pretty, witty girl and a girl who is unattractive and humorless
   (d) one who spends most of his time reading and one whose spare time is spent in sports
   (e) a boy from a well-to-do home and one from a home in a much lower income group
   (f) a pretty but not too bright girl and a plain but clever girl

Additional Readings ————

Short Stories

"Geraldine Moore the Poet" by Toni Cade Bambara

    Geraldine's true-to-life "poem" packs a wallop!

"Louisa, Please Come Home" by Shirley Jackson

    Did Louisa's parents *really* want her to come home?

"The Secret Life of Walter Mitty" by James Thurber

> The meek Mitty follows his wife's orders, but in his dreams— never!

"Champion" by Ring Lardner

> Meet the world champion who needed no friends.

Novels

Lord of the Flies by William Golding

> Disturbing story of children of the nuclear-warfare age marooned on an island.

The Catcher in the Rye by J. D. Salinger

> Holden Caulfield, sixteen-year-old preparatory school student, retells the events of a few days before Christmas.

The Chosen by Chaim Potok

> School days for two boys from different Jewish sects.

I Never Promised You a Rose Garden by Hannah Green

> A sixteen-year-old's harrowing journey from the depths of mental illness to reality and sanity.

A Tree Grows in Brooklyn by Betty Smith

> Francine proves that she can survive and improve herself even though she comes from a poor family.

The Three Musketeers by Alexander Dumas

> Four soldiers in the midst of court intrigue.

Les Miserables by Victor Hugo

> An ex-convict's adventures in search of friendship and understanding.

7 *From One Generation to Another*

The stories in this Unit deal with a universal theme of fiction, the relationship standards between the generations: children's, parents', grandparents'. The first story handles humorously the father who identifies himself too closely with his son, the star center of a championship high school basketball team. In the second, a son almost loses his life in order to prove himself to his father. In the third, a grandson uses righteous anger to teach his father how to behave toward the grandfather. In the fourth story, the love of a grandmother for her grandchild is revealed dramatically.

The nature of the typical American family has been changing. The extended family in which grandparents, parents, and children lived together in close cooperation with each generation having definite roles has been much less in evidence. Many grandparents are moving to retirement villages, and they are much less involved in the lives of their grandchildren. With the rise in the divorce rate and the increase in two working parents in the home, parent-child relationships have been going through reevaluations.

The stories in this Unit bring these changing relationships into focus and offer an opportunity to discuss where the changes are taking us.

THE HERO

Margaret Weymouth Jackson

♦   The Stone City center had driven his elbow into
Marvin's stomach. Marvin was doubled up. Marvin
was down on the floor. A groan went up from the
bleachers.

To a careless reader, "The Hero" appears to be just another
sports story, the sort of story in which you know right away that
the young star will, in spite of all obstacles, lead his team to victory over traditional rivals. But this sports story "formula" is only
secondary in "The Hero." As you read this account of a thrilling
basketball game, we want you to concentrate on Mr. Whalen. Do
you know any other parents like him? Is this merely an interesting
story that is true only for the particular characters in it, or can
you draw from the story a generalization that is applicable to your
observation and experience?

THE HERO

Mr. Whalen came into the kitchen by the back door and closed it softly behind him. He looked anxiously at his wife.

"Is Marv in?" he asked.

"He's resting," she whispered. Mr. Whalen nodded. He tiptoed through the dining room and went into the front hall as quiet as a mouse, and hung his hat and coat away. But he could not resist peeking into the darkened living room. A fire burned on the hearth, and on the couch lay a boy, or young man, who looked, at first glance, as though he were at least seven feet tall. He had a throw pulled up around his neck and his stocking feet stuck out from the cuffs of his corduroy trousers over the end of the sofa.

"Dad?" a husky young voice said.

"Yes. Did I waken you? I'm sorry."

"I wasn't sleeping. I'm just resting."

Mr. Whalen went over to the couch and looked down at the long figure with deep concern.

"How do you feel?" he asked tenderly.

"Swell, dad. I feel fine. I feel as though I'm going to be lucky tonight."

"That's fine! That's wonderful!" said his father fervently.

"What time is it, dad?"

"Quarter to six."

"About time for me to get up and have my supper. Is it ready? I ought to stretch a bit."

"You lie still now, Marv. I'll see about your supper."

Mr. Whalen hurried back into the kitchen.

"He's awake," he informed his wife. "Is his supper ready?"

"In a minute, dear. I'm just making his tea."

Mr. Whalen went back into the living room with his anxious bustling air.

The young man was up from the couch. He had turned on the light in a table lamp. He was putting on his shoes. He looked very young, not more than sixteen. His hair was thick as taffy and about the same color. He was thin, with a nose a little too big, and with clear blue eyes and a pleasant mouth and chin. He was not especially handsome, except to his father, who thought him the finest-looking boy in the whole wide world. The boy looked up a little shyly and smiled, and somehow his father's opinion was justified.

"I couldn't hit a thing in short practice yesterday," Marvin said. "That means I'll be hot tonight. Red-hot!"

"I hope so. I certainly hope so."

"You're going to the game, aren't you, dad? You and mother?"

Wild horses couldn't have kept Mr. Whalen away.

Marvin rose from his chair. He went up and up and up. Six feet four in his stocking feet, a hundred and seventy-six pounds, and sixteen years of age. Marvin flexed his muscles, crouched a little, and made a twisting leap into the air, one arm going up over his head in a swinging circle, his hand brushing the ceiling. He landed lightly as a cat. His father watched him, appearing neither astonished nor amused. There was nothing but the most profound respect and admiration in Mr. Whalen's eyes.

"We've been timing that pivot. Mr. Leach had two guards on me yesterday and they couldn't hold me, but I couldn't hit. Well, dad, let's eat. I ought to be getting up to the gym."

They went into the kitchen, where the supper was laid on a clean cloth at a small round table. There was steak and potatoes and salad and chocolate cake for his parents, toast and tea and coddled eggs for the boy.

"I don't think you ought to put the cake out where Marv can see it, when he can't have any," fussed Mr. Whalen.

Marvin grinned. "It's okay, dad. I don't mind. I'll eat some when I get home."

"Did you take your shower? Dry yourself good?"

"Sure, dad. Of course."

"Was the doctor at school today? This was the day he was to check the team, wasn't it?"

"Yes. He was there. I'm okay. The arch supports Mr. Leach sent for came. You know, my left foot's been getting a little flat. Doc thought I ought to have something while I'm still growing."

"It's a good thing. Have you got them here?"

"Yes. I'll get them."

"No. Just tell me where they are. I'll look at them."

"In my room. In my gym shoes."

Mr. Whalen wasn't eating a bite of supper. It just gave him indigestion to eat on game nights. He got too excited. He couldn't stand it. The boy was eating calmly. He ate four coddled eggs. He ate six pieces of toast. He drank four cups of tea with lemon and sugar. In the boy's room Mr. Whalen checked the things in his bag— the white woolen socks, the clean folded towel, the shoes with their arch supports, and so on. The insets looked all right, his father thought. The fine, heavy satin playing suits would be packed in the box in which they came from the dry cleaner's, to keep them from getting wrinkled before the game.

There, alone in Marvin's room, with Marvin's ties hanging on his dresser, with his windbreaker thrown down in a chair and his high school books on the table, Mr. Whalen felt a little ill. He pressed his hand over his heart. He mustn't show his anxiety, he thought. The boy was calm. He felt lucky. Mustn't break that feeling. Mr. Whalen went back into the kitchen with an air of cheer, a plump middle-aged man with a retreating hairline and kind, anxious brown eyes. Mr. Whalen was a few inches shorter than his wife. But he had never regretted marrying a tall woman. Look at his boy!

Marv was looking at the funnies in the evening paper. Mr. Whalen resisted the temptation to look at the kitchen clock. The boy would know when to go. He took the front part of the paper and sat down and tried to put his mind on the news. Mrs. Whalen quietly washed the supper dishes. Marvin finished the funnies in the local paper and handed it to his father. Mr. Whalen took it and read the news that Hilltown High was to play Sunset High, of Stone City, at the local gym that evening. The Stone City team hadn't lost a game. They were grooming for the state championship. Mr. Whalen felt weak. He hoped Marvin hadn't read this. Indignation grew in the father, as he read on down the column, that the odds were against the local team. How dare Mr. Minton print such nonsense for the boys to read—to discourage them? It was outrageous. Mr. Whalen would certainly give the editor a piece of his mind. Per-

haps Marvin had read it and believed it! Everything was so important—the psychology wasn't good.

Marvin had finished the funnies in the city paper, and he put it
down and rose. He said a little ruefully, "I'm still hungry, but I
can't eat more now."

"I'll have something ready for you when you get home," his
mother said.

Marvin went into his room and came back in his windbreaker,
his hair combed smoothly on his head.

"I'll see you at the gym," he said. "Sit where you always do,
will you, dad?"

"Yes. Yes. We'll be there."

"Okay. I'll be seeing you."

"Don't you want me to take you down in the car?"

"No. Thanks, dad, but no. It'll do me good to run down there.
It won't take me but a minute."

A shrill whistle sounded from the street.

"There's Johnny." Marvin left at once.

Mr. Whalen looked at his watch. "Better hurry, mother. The
first game starts at seven. We won't get our regular seats if we're
late."

"I'm not going to the gym at half past six," said Mrs. Whalen
definitely. "We'll be there in time and no one will take our seats. If
you don't calm down you are going to have a stroke at one of these
games."

"I'm perfectly calm," said Mr. Whalen indignantly; "I'm as calm
as—as calm as a June day. That's how calm I am. You know I'm not
of a nervous temperament. Just because I want to get to the game
on time, you say I am excited. You're as up in the air as I am."

"I am not," said Mrs. Whalen. She sat down at the cleared table
and looked at the advertisements in the paper. Mr. Whalen looked
at his watch again. He fidgeted.

"You can go ahead, if you like," she said. "I'll come alone."

"No, no," he protested, "I'll wait for you. Do you think we had
better take the car? I put it up, but I can get it out again."

"We'll walk," she said. "It will do you good—quiet your nerves."

"I'm not nervous," he almost shouted. Then he subsided again,
muttered a little, pretended to read the paper, checked his watch
against the kitchen clock to see if it had stopped.

"If we're going to walk . . ." he said in a minute.

Mrs. Whalen looked at him with pity. He couldn't help it, she knew. She folded the papers and put them away, took off her white apron, smoothed her hair and went to get her wraps. Mr. Whalen was at the front door, his overcoat on, his hat in his hand. She deliberately pottered, getting the cat off the piano and putting him out-of-doors, locking the kitchen door, turning out lights, hunting for her gloves. Mr. Whalen was almost frantic by the time she joined him on the front porch. They went down the walk together, and when they reached the sidewalk they met neighbors also bound for the gym.

"How's Marv?" asked the man next door. "Is he all right?"

"Marv's fine, just fine. He couldn't be better."

"Boy, oh, boy," said the other enthusiastically, "would I like to see the boys whip Stone City! It would be worth a million dollars— a cool million. Stone City thinks no one can beat them. We'd burn the town down."

"Oh, this game doesn't matter so much," said Mr. Whalen deprecatingly. "The team is working toward the tournaments. Be a shame to show all their stuff tonight."

"Well, we'll see. We'll see."

They went ahead. At the next corner they met other friends.

"How's Marv? How's the big boy?"

"He's fine. He's all right." Mr. Whalen's chest expansion increased. Cars were parked all along the sidewalk before the group of township school buildings—the grade school and the high school, with the fine brick gymnasium between them. The walks were crowded now, for the whole town, except those in wheel chairs or just born, went to the games, and this was an important game with Hilltown's hereditary foe. Mr. Whalen grew very anxious about their seats. If Marvin looked around for them and didn't find them . . . He hurried his wife a little. They went into the outer hall of the gymnasium. The school principal was standing there talking to the coach, Mr. Leach. Mr. Whalen's heart plummeted. Had anything gone wrong? Had something happened to Marvin? He looked at them anxiously, but they spoke in normal tones.

"Good evening, Mrs. Whalen. Good evening, Tom."

Several small boys were running up and down the stairs, and the school principal turned and spoke to them severely. The Whalens had to make room for a young married couple, he carrying a small baby, she holding the hand of a little boy. Then they reached the window where the typing teacher was tearing off ticket stubs. Mr. Whalen paid his half dollar and they went inside the iron bar and up the steps to the gym proper.

The gymnasium wasn't half full. The bleachers which rose on either side of the shining, sacred floor with its cabalistic markings were spotted with people. The Hilltown eighth grade was playing the Sugar Ridge eighth grade. The boys scrambled, fell down, got up and threw the ball, panted and heaved and struggled on the floor. A basketball flew about. A group of smaller children were seated in a tight knot, and two little girls whose only ambition in life was to become high school cheerleaders led a piercing yell:

> *"Hit 'em high,*
> *Hit 'em low;*
> *Come on, eighth grade,*
> *Let's go!"*

The voices of the junior high were almost piping. Mr. Whalen remembered how he had suffered when Marvin was in the eighth grade and they had to go to the games at six o'clock to watch him play. The junior high games were very abbreviated, with six-minute quarters, which was all the state athletic association would let them play. Marvin had been five feet ten at thirteen, but too thin. He had put on a little weight in proportion to his height since then, but his father thought he should be heavier. The present eighth grade team could not compare with Marvin's, Mr. Whalen decided.

But the boys did try hard. They were winning. The gun sounded, the junior high went to pieces with wild cheering, and the teams trotted off the floor, panting, sweating, happy.

Almost at once another group came on in secondhand white wool tops and the old, blue satin trunks from last year. This was the second team. The boys were pretty good. They practiced, throwing the ball from far out, running in under the basket, passing to one another. Mr. and Mrs. Whalen had found their regular seats unoccupied, halfway between the third and fourth uprights which supported the lofty gymnasium ceiling. Mr. Whalen sat down a little weakly and wiped his forehead. Mrs. Whalen began at once to visit with a friend sitting behind her, but Mr. Whalen could not hear what anyone said.

The Stone City reserves came out on the floor to warm up. They looked like first-string men.

Mr. Leach was talking to the timekeeper. He was a good coach—a mighty good coach. They were lucky to keep him here at Hilltown. The luckiest thing that had ever happened to the town was when Mr. Leach had married a Hilltown girl who didn't want to move away. They'd never have been able to hold him otherwise. It meant so much to the boys to have a decent, kindly man to coach them. Some of the high school coaches felt that their teams had to win, no matter how. It would be very bad to have his boy under such an influence, thought Mr. Whalen, who simply could not bear to see the team defeated, and who was always first to yell "Thief!" and "Robber!"

The officials came out in their green shirts, and Mr. Whalen almost had heart failure. There was that tall, thin man who had fouled Marvin every time he had moved in the tournaments last year. He was always against Hilltown. He had been so unfair that Mr. Leach had complained about him to the state association. The only time Mr. Leach had ever done such a thing. Oh, this was awful. Mr. Whalen twisted his hat in his hands. The other official he had seen often. He was fair—very fair. Sugar Ridge had complained about him for favoring Hilltown, but Mr. Whalen thought him an excellent referee.

The gymnasium was filling fast now. All the high school students—two hundred of them—were packed in the cheering section. The junior high was swallowed up, lost. The cheering section looked as though not one more could get into it, and yet youngsters kept climbing up, squeezing in. The rest of the space was filled with townspeople, from toddlers in snow suits to gray-bearded dodderers. On the opposite side of the gymnasium, the visiting fans were filling their seats. Big crowd from Stone City. Businessmen and quarrymen and stone carvers and their wives and children. They must feel confident of winning, Mr. Whalen thought. Their cheerleaders were out on the floor. Where were Hilltown's? Ah, there they were—Beth and Mary. Hilltown's cheerleaders were extremely pretty girls dressed in blue satin slacks with white satin shirts, the word "Yell" in blue letters over their shoulders—a true gilding of the lily. Mary was Marvin's girl. She was the prettiest girl in town. And she had personality, too, and vigor.

Now the two girls leaped into position, spun their hands, spread out their arms, catapulted their bodies into the air in perfect synchronization, and the breathless cheering section came out in a long roll.

> *"Hello, Stone City,*
> *Hello, Stone City.*
> *Hilltown says,*
> *Hello-o-o-o-o!"*

Not to be outdone, the Stone City leaders, in crimson-and-gold uniforms, returned the compliment:

> *"Hello, Hilltown . . ."*

and the sound came nicely across the big gym. Mr. Whalen got a hard knot in his throat, and the bright lights and colors of the gymnasium swam in a mist. He couldn't help it. They were so young. Their voices were so young!

The whistle blew. The reserves were at it.

Mr. Whalen closed his eyes and sat still. It would be so long; the cheering wouldn't really start, the evening wouldn't begin until the team came out. He remembered when Marvin was born. He had been tall then, twenty-two inches. Mr. Whalen prayed, his lips moving a little, that Marvin wouldn't get hurt tonight. Suppose he had a heart attack and fell dead, like that boy at Capital City years ago? Suppose he got knocked against one of the steel uprights and hurt his head—damaged his brain? Suppose he got his knee injured? Mr. Whalen opened his eyes. He must not think of those things. He had promised his wife he would not worry so. He felt her hand, light but firm, on his arm.

"Here are the Lanes," she said.

Mr. Whalen spoke to them. Johnny's parents crowded in behind the Whalens. Johnny's father's hand fell on Mr. Whalen's shoulder.

"How's Marv tonight?"

"Fine, fine. How's Johnny?"

"Couldn't be better. I believe the boys are going to take them."

The two fathers looked at each other and away. Mr. Whalen felt a little better.

"How's business?" asked Johnny's father, and they talked about business a moment or two, but they were not interested.

There was a crisis of some kind on the floor. Several players were down in a pile. Someone was hurt. Mr. Whalen bit the edge of his felt hat. The boy was up now. The Stone City coach was out on the floor, but the boy shook his head. He was all right. The game was resumed.

At last it was over. The reserves had won. Mr. Whalen thought that was a bad omen. The eighth grade had won. The reserves had won. No, it was too much. The big team would lose. If the others had lost, he would have considered that a bad omen too. Every omen was bad to Mr. Whalen at this stage. The floor was empty. The high school band played "Indiana," and "Onward, Hilltown," and everyone stood up and sang.

There was a breathless pause, and then a crashing cheer hit the ceiling of the big gym and bounced back. The Team was out. Out there on the floor in their blue satin suits, with jackets over their white tops, warming up, throwing the ball deftly about. What caused the change? Mr. Whalen never knew, but everything was quick now, almost professional in tone and quality. Self-confidence, authority, had come into the gymnasium. Ten or twelve boys out there warming up. But there was really only one boy on the floor for Mr. Whalen, a tall, thin, fair boy with limber legs still faintly brown from summer swimming. Mr. Whalen did not even attempt to tear his eyes from Marvin.

The Stone City team came out. Mr. Whalen looked away from Marvin for a moment to study them. Two or three of them were as tall as Marvin, maybe taller. He felt indignant. They must be seniors, all of them. Or five-year men. He studied the boys. He liked to see if he could pick out the first-string men from the lot. He could almost always do it—not by their skill or their height, but by their faces. That little fellow with the pug nose—he was a first-string man. And the two big ones—the other tall man Mr. Whalen discarded correctly. And the boy with the thick chest. What it was, he wasn't sure—some carelessness, some ease that marked the first-string men. The others were always a little self-conscious, a little too eager.

The referee blew the whistle. The substitutes left the floor, carrying extra jackets. The boy with the pug nose came forward for

Stone City. So he was captain? Mr. Whalen felt gratified in his judgment. Marvin came forward for his team. He was captain too. There
was a Number 1 in blue on the sleeveless white satin shirt he wore.
The referee talked to them. The boys took their positions, the umpire his along the edge of the floor. The cheering section roared:

> *"We may be rough,*
> *We may be tough,*
> *But we're the team*
> *That's got the stuff!*
> *Fight! Fight! Fight!"*

Mary turned a complete somersault, her lithe young body going
over backward, her heels in the air, then hitting the floor to bounce
her straight up in a spread eagle. Her pretty mouth was open in a
square. The rooting swelled. The substitutes sat down with their
coaches. Marvin stood back out of the center ring until the referee,
ball in hand, waved him in. The ball went into the air as the whistle
blew, and the game was on.

Marvin got the tip-off straight to Johnny. Marv ran down into
the corner, where he circled to confuse his guard. Johnny brought
the ball down over the line, faked a pass and drew out Marvin's
guard, bounced the ball to Perk, who carried it almost to the foul
line and passed to Marvin, who threw the ball into the basket. Stone
City leaped outside, threw the ball in, a long pass. Perk leaped for
it, but missed. The tall Stone City forward dribbled, dodging skillfully. The guards were smothering him, but he pivoted, flung the
ball over his head and into the basket. A basket each in the first
minute of play!

Mr. Whalen had stopped breathing. He was in a state of suspended animation. The game was very fast—too fast. Stone City
scored a second and a third time. Marvin called time out. Someone
threw a wet towel from the bench, and it slid along the floor. The
boys wiped their faces with it, threw it back. They whispered together. The referee blew the whistle. Yes, they were going to try the
new trick play they had been practicing. It worked. Marvin's pivot
was wonderful. The score was four to six.

Marvin played with a happy romping abandon. He was skillful,
deft, acute. But he was also joyful. The youngsters screamed his

name. Mr. Whalen saw Mary's rapt, adoring look. Marvin romped down the floor like a young colt.

At the end of the quarter, the score was fourteen to ten in Stone City's favor. At the end of the half, it was still in Stone City's favor, but only fourteen to thirteen. Stone City didn't score in the second quarter.

Mr. Whalen felt a deep disquietude. He had been watching the tall center on the other team, the pivot man. He had thick black curly hair and black eyes. Mr. Whalen thought he looked tough. He had fouled Marvin twice in the first half. That is, he had been called for two fouls, but he had fouled him oftener. Mr. Whalen was sure he had tripped Marvin that time Marvin fell on the floor and cracked his elbow. Marvin had jumped up again at once. The Stone City center was a dirty player and ought to be taken off the floor. The school band was playing, but Mr. Whalen couldn't hear it. He was very upset. If the referees were going to let Stone City foul Hilltown and get away with it . . . He felt hot under the collar. He felt desperate.

"Why don't you go out and smoke?" his wife asked. Mr. Whalen folded his overcoat to mark his place and went out of the gym. He smoked two cigarettes as fast as he could. He would stay out here. The stars were cool and calm above his head. The night air was fresh. He couldn't stand it in the gymnasium. He would wait here until the game was over. If Marvin was hurt, he wouldn't see it. He resolved this firmly. But when the whistle blew and he heard the burst of cheering, he rushed back into the gymnasium like a man going to a fire.

The second half had begun. Again the big center fouled Marvin. A personal foul this time. Marvin got two free throws and made both good.

Fifteen to fourteen now! The crowd went wild. The game got very fast again. Mr. Whalen watched Marvin and his opponent like a hawk. There! It happened.

Mr. Whalen was on his feet, yelling, "Watch him! Watch him!"

The Stone City center had driven his elbow into Marvin's stomach. Marvin was doubled up. Marvin was down on the floor. A groan went up from the bleachers. Mr. Whalen started out on the floor. Something held him. He looked around blindly. His wife had a firm grip on his coattails. She gave a smart yank and pulled him unexpectedly down on the bench beside her.

"He doesn't want you on the floor," she said fiercely.

Mr. Whalen was very angry, but he controlled himself. He sat still. Marvin was up again. Mary led a cheer for him. Marvin was all right. He got two more free throws. Now Hilltown was three points ahead. Marvin was fouled again, got two more free throws and missed them both. He was hurt! He never missed free throws—well, hardly ever. What was the matter with the referee? Was he crazy? Was he bribed? Mr. Whalen groaned.

Stone City took time out, and in the last minute of the third quarter they made three quick baskets. It put them ahead again, three points. A foul was called on Marvin—for pushing.

"Why, he never did at all!" yelled Mr. Whalen. "He couldn't stop fast enough—that's not a foul! Just give them the ball, boys! Don't try to touch it!"

"Will you hush?" demanded his wife.

The Stone City forward made one of the two throws allowed. It was the quarter.

The game was tied three times in the last quarter. With five minutes to play, the big center fouled Marvin again. His fourth personal. He was out of the game. The Hilltown crowd booed him. None so loud as Mr. Whalen, who often talked long and seriously to Marvin about sportsmanship.

Then Marvin got hot. He couldn't miss. Everyone on the team fed him the ball, and he could throw it from anywhere and it went, plop, right into the basket. Marvin pivoted. His height, his spring, carried him away from his guards. Marvin pranced. His long legs carried him where he would. He threw the ball over his head and from impossible angles. Once he was knocked down on the floor, and he threw from there and made the basket. His joy, his perfection, his luck, caused the crowd to burst into continuous wild cheering. Stone City took time out. They ran in substitutes, but they couldn't stop Marvin. Perk would recover the ball; he and Johnny fed it skillfully to Marvin, and Marvin laid it in. The gun went off with Hilltown twelve points ahead.

Mr. Whalen was a wreck. He could hardly stand up. Mrs. Whalen took his arm and half supported him toward the stairs that led down to the school grounds. The Stone City fans were angry. A big broad-shouldered man with fierce black eyes complained in a loud, quarrelsome voice:

"That skinny kid—that Whalen boy—he foul my boy! Who

cares? But when my boy protect himself, what happens? They put him off the floor. They put my Guido out, so Hilltown wins. I get my hands on that tall monkey and I'll fix him."

"Be careful. That's my son you're talking about." The strength had returned to Mr. Whalen. He was strong as a lion. Mrs. Whalen pulled at his arm, but he jerked away. He turned in the crowded stairs. "Before you do anything to Marvin," he said, his voice loud and high, "you'd better do something to me. Your son fouled repeatedly."

"That's a lie!" yelled the other, and Mr. Whalen hit him. He hit him right in the stomach as hard as he could punch him. Instantly there was a melee. Guido's father was punching somebody, and for a moment the crowd heaved and milled on the stairs. Someone screamed. Something like a bolt of lightning hit Mr. Whalen in the eye, and he struck back.

Friends were pulling him away. The town marshal shouldered good-naturedly between the combatants. The big man was in the grip of others from Stone City, who dragged him back up the stairs. Mr. Whalen struggled with his captors, fellow townsmen, who sympathized with him but had no intention of letting him fight. Johnny's mother and Marvin's mother hustled their men out into the cold night air.

"Really!" the high school principal was saying anxiously. "Really, we mustn't have any trouble. The boys don't fight. If we could just keep the fathers away from the games! Really, Mrs. Whalen, this won't do."

"I've got a good notion to take a poke at him too," said Mr. Whalen, who was clear above himself.

In the kitchen, Mr. Whalen looked in a small mirror at his reflection. He felt wonderful. He felt marvelous. He was going to have a black eye. He grabbed his wife and kissed her soundly.

"They beat them!" he said. "They beat Stone City!"

"You old fool!" cried Mrs. Whalen. "I declare I'd be ashamed of Marvin if he acted like that. You and Johnny's father—fighting like hoodlums."

"I don't care!" said Mr. Whalen. "I'm glad I hit him. Teach him a lesson. I feel great. I'm hungry. Make some coffee, mother."

Marvin wouldn't be in for an hour. He would have a date with Mary at the soda parlor, to which the whole high school would repair. They heard the siren blowing; they looked out of the window and saw the reflection of the bonfire on the courthouse lawn. They heard the fire engine. The team was having a ride on the fire engine. Mr. Whalen stood on his front porch and cheered. The town was wild with joy. Not a citizen that wasn't up in the air tonight.

At last Marvin came in. He was cheerful, practical.

"Did you really have a fight, dad? Someone told me you popped Guido's father . . . Boy, are you going to have a shiner!" Marvin was greatly amused. He examined his father's eye, recommended an ice pack.

"I want it to get black," said Mr. Whalen stubbornly.

"We sure fixed Guido," said Marvin, and laughed.

"Did you have a fight?" asked his father eagerly.

"Heck, no! I'm going to get him a date with Betty. He noticed her. He's coming up next Sunday. Their team went downtown for sodas because Guido wanted to meet Betty. I wasn't sore at him. I only mean he was easy to handle. I saw right away that I could make him foul me, give me extra shots, get him off the floor. It's very easy to do with a big clumsy guy like that."

Mr. Whalen fingered his swelling eye and watched Marvin eat two hot ham sandwiches and a big slab of chocolate cake and drink a quart of milk. Marvin had already had a soda.

"You must sleep late in the morning," Mr. Whalen said. "Maybe you got too tired tonight. Now, don't eat too much cake."

Mr. Whalen's eye hurt. Mrs. Whalen got him to bed and put a cold compress on it.

"Old ninny," she murmured, and stooped and kissed him. Mr. Whalen sighed. He was exhausted. He was getting too old to play basketball, he thought confusedly.

Understanding the Story

Main Idea

1. Which of the following best expresses the main idea of the story?
   a. All is fair in love and war, but not in basketball where you can't get away with it.
   b. Small towns take their high school basketball too seriously.
   c. Some fathers seek a second chance through their sons.
   d. Mothers are less levelheaded than fathers when sons are involved.

Details

2. Which one of the following statements is true?
   a. Mrs. Whalen hurries so that they can arrive early at the game.
   b. Mr. Whalen enjoys seeing both the eighth grade and the reserve teams win.
   c. Mr. Whalen does not like the way the coach handles Marv.
   d. Mr. Whalen is afraid that Marv may get hurt.

Cause and Effect

3. Marv expects to play well because   (a) his father will be present   (b) he is well trained   (c) he has done poorly in practice   (d) he is well rested.

4. Marv scores points by   (a) outracing his opponent   (b) causing the other center to foul him   (c) pushing   (d) running along the sidelines.

Inference

5. In the fight, the neighbors   (a) side with Guido's father   (b) join Mr. Whalen in the fight   (c) complain to the police   (d) just want the fight to stop.

Order of Events

6. Arrange the items in the order in which they occurred. Use letters only.
   A. Guido dates a Hilltown girl.
   B. The doctor examines Marv.

C. Guido's father accuses Marv of fouling Guido.
D. Guido is taken out of the game.
E. Mr. Whalen discovers that he is hungry.

Outcomes

7. The game ends   (a) in an overtime tie   (b) with Marvin's team losing   (c) with the game being called   (d) in a lop-sided win for Marv's team.

8. Immediately after the game   (a) Mr. Whalen meets Guido's father   (b) Mr. Whalen takes Marv home   (c) Mr. Whalen has to rest   (d) Marv is carried off on his teammates' shoulders.

9. Mr. Whalen's reward is   (a) congratulations from the principal   (b) a black eye   (c) winning the bet   (d) a new car.

10. Which of the following statements is not true?
    a. Marv and Guido go on a double date.
    b. Mr. Whalen is completely exhausted by the game.
    c. Mr. Whalen sees Marv as both a victim and a victor.
    d. Mrs. Whalen is angered by Mr. Whalen's behavior after the game.

Words in Context ━━━━━━━━━━━━━━━

1. "That's fine! That's wonderful!" said his father *fervently*.
    Fervently (447) means   (a) very earnestly   (b) rather slowly   (c) suddenly   (d) quietly.

2. Marvin *flexed* his muscles, crouched a little, and made a twisting leap into the air . . .
    Flexed (448) means   (a) pulled   (b) felt   (c) bent   (d) relaxed.

3. "I don't think you ought to put the cake out where Marv can see it, when he can't have any," *fussed* Mr. Whalen.
    Fussed (448) means   (a) shouted   (b) agreed   (c) ordered   (d) complained.

4. *Indignation* grew in the father, as he read on down the column, that the odds were against the local team.

Indignation (449) means (a) deep anxiety (b) confidence (c) righteous anger (d) triumphant joy.

5. He said a little *ruefully*, "I'm still hungry, but I can't eat more now."
   Ruefully (450) means (a) proudly (b) sadly (c) confidently (d) sternly.

6. "I'm not nervous," he almost shouted. Then he *subsided* again, muttered a little, pretended to read the paper, checked his watch against the kitchen clock to see if it had stopped.
   Subsided (450) means (a) grew even more tense (b) lost his dignity (c) realized his error (d) calmed down.

7. Now the two girls leaped into position, spun their hands, spread out their arms, *catapulted their bodies into the air in perfect synchronization . . .*
   Catapulted their bodies into the air in perfect synchronization (454) means (a) jumped as one (b) did cartwheels (c) did a handstand (d) pirouetted.

8. The Team was out . . . warming up, throwing the ball *deftly* about.
   Deftly (455) means (a) slowly (b) speedily (c) often (d) skillfully.

9. Mr. Whalen had stopped breathing. He was *in a state of suspended animation*. The game was very fast—too fast.
   In a state of suspended animation (456) means Mr. Whalen
   a. had fainted.
   b. was in a state of shock.
   c. was unaware of himself.
   d. was not worrying about Marv.

10. Guido's father was punching somebody, and for a moment the crowd *heaved and milled* on the stairs.
    Heaved and milled (459) means (a) became ill (b) surged back and forth (c) shouted and yelled (d) stood motionless.

Thinking About the Story ⸻

1. How does Mr. Whalen's attitude toward Marvin and his basketball activities differ from that of Mrs. Whalen? What is Marv's attitude toward his father?

2. In what instances does Mr. Whalen's prejudice in favor of his son give him the wrong slant on situations? What is the meaning of the last sentence?

3. Is Marv justified in making Guido foul him? Explain. How does Marv's sense of sportsmanship compare with his father's? With yours?

4. Is there really a "Hero" in this story? If so, who would it be?

5. What is gained by telling the story from Mr. Whalen's point of view? Is he a caricature? Justify your answer. Could this story be just as plausible if Marv were a college star? . . . a professional star? Could this story be turned into a TV play? Explain.

The Erne From the Coast

T. O. Beachcroft

♦   "Next time it will be a real beating," his father shouted after him. "Bring the eagle back, and then I'll believe you."

Humiliation is a cruel taskmaster. Goaded on by his father's refusal to accept him as other than a helpless child, Harry Thorburn is forced into a battle which many a brave grown man would shun. His opponent is a murderous sea eagle, with a wing span of seven and a half feet. Harry has only two weapons: one, an iron-tipped stick—to beat off the attacks of the flesh-tearing talons and the curved beak capable of piercing his skull—and the other, his pride—which compels him to risk horrible mutilation, and perhaps death, to prove himself to his father.

Not all readers agree that Harry behaved sensibly. Some feel that Harry did the only thing possible under the circumstances, and that their own behavior in a like situation would be very much the same; others maintain that what he actually gained as a result of the risk he assumed was not worth having. What do you think?

THE ERNE FROM THE COAST

WHERE'S Harry?'' Mr. Thorburn came out of the back of the farmhouse. He stood in the middle of the well-kept farmyard. "Here, Harry!" he shouted. "Hi, Harry!"

He stood leaning on a stick and holding a letter in his hand, as he looked round the farmyard.

Mr. Thorburn was a red-faced, powerful man; he wore knee breeches and black leather gaiters. His face and well-fleshed body told you at a glance that Thorburn's Farm had not done too badly during the twenty years of his married life.

Harry, a fair-haired boy, came running across the yard.

"Harry," said the farmer to his son, "here's a letter come for old Michael. It will be about this visit he's to pay to his sick brother. Nice time of year for this to happen, I must say. You'd better take the letter to him at once."

"Where to?" said Harry.

"He's up on the hill, of course," said the farmer. "In his hut, or with the sheep somewhere. Your own brains could have told you that. Can't you ever use them? Go on, now."

"Right," said Harry. He turned to go.

"Don't take all day," said his father.

Mr. Thorburn stood looking after his son. He leaned heavily on the thorn stick which he always carried. Harry went through the gate in the low gray wall which ran round one side of the yard, where there were no buildings. Directly he left the farmyard, he began to climb. Thorburn's Farm was at the end of a valley. Green fields lay in front of it, and a wide road sloped gently down to the village a mile away; behind, the hill soared up, and high on the ridge of the hill was Michael's hut, three miles off, and climbing all the way.

Harry was thirteen, very yellow-haired and blue-eyed. He was a slip of a boy. It seemed unlikely that he could ever grow into such a stolid, heavy man as his father. Mr. Thorburn was every pound of fourteen stone, as the men on the farm could have told you the day he broke his leg and they had to carry him back to the farmhouse on a hurdle.

Harry started off far too fast, taking the lower slopes almost at a run. His body was loose in its movements, and coltish, and by the time the real work began he was already tiring. However, the April day was fresh and rainy, and the cold of it kept him going. Gray gusts and showers swept over the hillside, and between them, with changing light, came faint gleams of sunshine, so that the shadows of the clouds raced along the hill beside him. Presently he cleared the gorse and heather, and came out on to the open hillside, which was bare except for short, tussocky grass. His home began to look far off beneath him. He could see his mother walking down toward the village with one of the dogs, and the baker's cart coming up from the village toward her. The fields were brown and green round the farmhouse, and the buildings were gray, with low stone walls.

He stopped several times to look back on the small distant farm. It took him well over an hour to reach the small hut where Michael lived by day and slept during most nights throughout the lambing season. He was not in his hut, but after a few minutes' search Harry found him. Michael was sitting without movement, watching the sheep and talking to his gray and white dog. He had a sack across his shoulders, which made him look rather like a rock with gray lichen on it. He looked up at Harry without moving.

"It's a hildy wildy day," he said, "but there'll be a glent of sunsheen yet."

Harry handed Michael the letter. Michael looked at it, opened it very slowly, and spread the crackling paper out on his knee with brown hands. Harry watched him for some minutes as he studied the letter in silence.

"Letter'll be aboot my brother," said Michael at length. "I'm to goa and see him." He handed the letter to Harry. "Read it, Harry," he said. Harry read the letter to him twice.

"Tell thy dad," said Michael. "I'll be doon at farm i' the morn. Happen I'll be away three days. And tell him new lamb was born last neet, but it's sickly."

They looked at the small white bundle that lay on the grass beside its mother, hardly moving.

"'T'll pick up," said Michael. He slowly stood and looked round at the distance.

Michael had rather long hair; it was between gray and white in color, and it blew in the wind. It was about the hue of an old sheep's skull that has lain out on the bare mountain. Michael's clothes and face and hair made Harry feel that he had slowly faded out on the hillside. He was all the color of rain on the stones and last year's bracken.

"It'll make a change," said Michael, "going off and sleeping in a bed."

"Good-bye," said Harry. "You'll be down at the farm tomorrow, then?"

"Aw reet," said Michael.

"Aw reet," said Harry.

Harry went slowly back to the farm. The rain had cleared off, and the evening was sunny, with a watery light, by the time he was home. Michael had been right. Harry gave his father the message, and told him about the lamb.

"It's a funny thing," said Harry, "that old Michael can't even read."

"Don't you be so smart," said Mr. Thorburn. "Michael knows a thing or two you don't. You don't want to go making fun of an old fellow like Michael—best shepherd I've ever known."

Harry went away feeling somewhat abashed. Lately it seemed his father was always down on him, telling him he showed no sign of sense; telling him he ought to grow up a bit; telling him he was more like seven than thirteen.

He went to the kitchen. This was a big stone-floored room with a huge plain table, where the whole household and several of the farm hands could sit down to dinner or tea at the same time. His mother and his aunt from the village were still lingering over their teacups, but there was no one else in the room except a small tortoise-shell cat, which was pacing round them asking for milk in a loud voice. The yellow evening light filled the room. His mother gave him tea and ham and bread and butter, and he ate it in silence, playing with the cat as he did so.

Next morning at nine o'clock there was a loud rap with a stick at the kitchen door, and there by the pump, with the hens running round his legs, stood Michael.

"Good morning, Mrs. Thorburn," he said. "Is Measter about?"

"Come on in with you," said Mrs. Thorburn, "and have a good hot cup o' tea. Have you eaten this morning?"

Michael clanked into the kitchen, his hobnails striking the flags, and he sat down at one end of the table.

"Aye," he said, "I've eaten, Missus. I had a good muffin when I rose up, but a cup of tea would be welcome."

As he drank the tea, Mr. Thorburn came in, bringing Harry with him. Michael, thought Harry, always looked rather strange when he was down in the village or in the farmhouse; rather as a pile of bracken or an armful of leaves would look if it were emptied out onto the parlor floor.

Michael talked to Mr. Thorburn about the sheep; about the new lamb; about young Bob, his nephew, who was coming over from another farm to look after the sheep while he was away.

"Tell en to watch new lamb," said Michael; "it's sickly. I've put en in my little hut, and owd sheep is looking roun' t' doorway."

After his cup of tea Michael shook hands all round. Then he set off down to the village, where he was going to fall in with a lift.

Soon after he had gone, Bob arrived at the farm. He was a tall young man with a freckled face, and red hair, big-boned and very gentle in his voice and movements. He listened to all Mr. Thorburn's instructions and then set out for the shepherd's hut.

However, it seemed that Mr. Thorburn's luck with his shepherds was dead out. For the next evening, just as it was turning dark, Bob walked into the farmhouse kitchen. His face was tense with pain, and he was nursing his left arm with his right hand. Harry saw the ugly distorted shape and swelling at the wrist. Bob had fallen and broken the wrist earlier in the day, and by evening the pain had driven him back.

"I'm sorry, Mr. Thorburn," he kept on saying. "I'm a big fool."

The sheep had to be left for that night. Next morning it was again a cold, windy day, and clouds the color of gunmetal raced over the hill. The sun broke through fitfully, filling the valley with a steel-blue light in which the green grass looked vivid. Mr. Thorburn decided to send Harry out to the shepherd's hut for the day and night.

"Happen old Michael will be back some time tomorrow," he said. "You can look to the sheep, Harry, and see to that sick lamb for us. It's a good chance to make yourself useful."

Harry nodded.

"You can feed the lamb. Bob said it didn't seem to suck enough, and you can let me know if anything else happens. And you can keep an eye on the other lambs and see they don't get over the edges. There's no need to fold them at night; just let the dog round them up and see the flock is near the hut."

"There's blankets and everything in the hut, Harry," said Mrs. Thorburn, "and a spirit lamp to make tea. You can't come to harm."

Harry set off up the hill and began to climb. Out on the hilltop it was very lonely, and the wind was loud and gusty, with sudden snatches of rain. The sheep kept near the wooden hut most of the time; it was built in the lee of the ridge, and the best shelter was to be found near it. Harry looked after the sick lamb and brewed himself tea. He had Tassie, the gray and white sheepdog, for company. Time did not hang heavy. When evening came he rounded up the sheep and counted them, and, true to advice that Michael had given him, he slept in his boots as a true shepherd does, warmly wrapped up in the rugs.

He was awakened as soon as it was light by the dog barking. He went out in the gray dawn light, and found a rustle and agitation among the sheep. Tassie ran to him and back toward the sheep. The sheep were starting up alert, and showed a tendency to scatter. Harry looked round, wondering what the trouble was. Then he saw. A bird was hovering over the flock, and it was this that had attracted the sheep's attention. But what bird was it? It hovered like a hawk, soaring on outstretched wings; yet it was much too big for a hawk. As the bird came nearer Harry was astonished at its size. Once or twice it approached and then went soaring and floating away again. It was larger than any bird he had ever seen before— brownish in color, with a gray head and a hawk's beak.

Suddenly the bird began to drop as a hawk drops. A knot of sheep dashed apart. Tassie rushed toward the bird, his head down and his tail streaming out behind him. Harry followed. This must be an eagle, he thought. He saw it, looking larger still now it was on the ground, standing with outstretched wings over a lamb.

Tassie attacked, snarling in rage. The eagle rose at him. It struck at him with its feet and a flurry of beating wings. The dog was thrown back. He retreated slowly, snarling savagely as he went, his tail between his legs. He was frightened now, and uncertain what to do.

The eagle turned back to the lamb, took it in its talons again, and began to rise. It could not move quickly near the ground, and Harry came up with it. At once the eagle put the lamb on a rock and turned on him. He saw its talons driving toward his face, claws and spurs of steel—a stroke could tear your eyes out. He put up his arms in fear, and he felt the rush of wings round his face. With his arm above his head he sank on one knee.

When he looked up again, the eagle was back on the lamb. It began to fly with long slow wingbeats. At first it scarcely rose, and flew with the lamb almost on the ground.

Harry ran, throwing a stone. He shouted. Tassie gave chase, snapping at the eagle as it went. But the eagle was working toward a chasm, a sheer drop in the hillside where no one could follow it. In another moment it was floating in the air, clear and away. Then it rose higher, and headed toward the coast, which was a few miles away over the hill.

Harry stood and watched it till it was out of sight. When it was gone, he turned and walked slowly back to the hut. There was not a sound to be heard now except the sudden rushes of wind. The hillside was bare and coverless except for the scattered black rocks. Tassie walked beside him. The dog was very subdued and hardly glanced to right or left.

It took some time to round the sheep up, or to find, at least, where the various parts of the flock had scattered themselves. The sick lamb and its mother had been enclosed all this time in a small fold near the hut. The ewe was still terrified.

An hour later Harry set off down the mountainside to the farm. Tassie looked after him doubtfully. He ran several times after him, but Harry sent him back to the hut.

It was the middle of the morning when Harry came back to the farmyard again. His father was standing in the middle of the yard, leaning on his stick, and giving advice to one of his cowmen. He broke off when he saw Harry come in through the gate, and walk toward him across the farmyard.

"Well," he said, "anything wrong, Harry? I thought you were going to stay till Michael came back."

"We've lost a lamb," said Harry, breathlessly. "It's been carried off by an eagle. It must have been an eagle."

"An eagle?" said Mr. Thorburn. He gave a laugh which mocked Harry. "Why didn't you stop it?"

"I tried," said Harry. "But I. . . ."

Mr. Thorburn was in a bad mood. He had sold some heifers the day before at a disappointing price. He had had that morning a letter from the builders about repairs to some of the farm buildings, and there was work to be done which he could hardly afford. He was worried about Michael's absence. He felt as if the world were bearing down on him, and he had too many burdens to support.

He suddenly shouted at Harry, and his red face turned darker red.

"That's a lie!" he said. "There's been no eagle here in my lifetime. What's happened? Go on—tell me."

Harry stood before him. He looked at his father, but said nothing.

"You've lost that lamb," said Thorburn. "Let it fall down a hole or something. Any child from the village could have watched those sheep for a day. Then you're frightened, and come back here and lie to me."

Harry still said nothing.

"Come here," said Thorburn suddenly. He caught him by the arm and turned him round. "I'll teach you not to lie to me," he said. He raised his stick and hit Harry as hard as he could; then again and again.

"It's true," began Harry, and then cried out with pain at the blows.

At the third or fourth blow he wrenched himself away. Thorburn let him go. Harry walked away as fast as he could, through the gate and out of the yard without looking round.

"Next time it will be a real beating," his father shouted after him. "Bring the eagle back, and then I'll believe you."

As soon as Harry was through the gate, he turned behind one

of the barns where he was out of sight from the yard. He stood trembling and clenching his fists. He found there were tears on his face, and he forced himself not to cry. The blows hurt, yet they did not hurt very seriously. He would never have cried for that. But it had been done in front of another man. The other man had looked on, and he and his father had been laughing as he had almost run away. Harry clenched his fists; even now they were still talking about him.

He began to walk and then run up the hillside toward the hut. When he reached it, he was exhausted. He flung himself on the mattress and punched it again and again and clenched his teeth.

The day passed and nobody came from the farm. He began to feel better, and presently a new idea struck him, and with it a new hope. He prayed now that old Michael would not return today; that he would be able to spend another night alone in the hut; and that the eagle would come back next morning and attack the sheep again, and give him one more chance.

Harry went out and scanned the gray sky, and then knelt down on the grass and prayed for the eagle to come. Tassie, the gray and white sheepdog, looked at him questioningly. Soon it was getting dark, and he walked about the hill and rounded up the sheep. He counted the flock, and all was well. Then he looked round for a weapon. There was no gun in the hut, but he found a thick stave tipped with metal, part of some broken tool that had been thrown aside. He poised the stave in his hand and swung it; it was just a good weight to hit with. He would have to go straight at the eagle without hesitation and break its skull. After thinking about this for some time, he made himself tea, and ate some bread and butter and cold meat.

Down at the farm Mr. Thorburn in the evening told his wife what had happened. He was quite sure there had been no eagle. Mrs. Thorburn did not say much, but she said it was an extraordinary thing for Harry to have said. She told her husband that he ought not to have beaten the boy, but should have found out what the trouble really was.

"But I dare say there is no great harm done," she ended, philosophically.

Harry spent a restless night. He slept and lay awake by turns, but, sleeping or waking, he was tortured by the same images. He saw all the events of the day before. He saw how the eagle had first appeared above him; how it had attacked; how it had driven off Tassie and then him. He remembered his fear, and he planned again just how he could attack the eagle when it came back. Then he thought of himself going down toward the farm and he saw again the scene with his father.

All night long he saw these pictures and other scenes from his life. In every one of them he had made some mistake; he had made himself look ridiculous, and grown men had laughed at him. He had failed in strength or in common sense; he was always disappointing himself and his father. He was too young for his age. He was still a baby.

So the night passed. Early in the morning he heard Tassie barking.

He jumped up, fully clothed, and ran outside the hut. The cold air made him shiver; but he saw at once that his prayer had been answered. There was the eagle, above him, and already dropping down toward the sheep. It floated, poised on huge wings. The flock stood nervously huddled. Suddenly, as before, the attacker plunged toward them. They scattered, running in every direction. The eagle followed, and swooped on one weakly running lamb. At once it tried to rise again, but its heavy wing-beats took it along the earth. Near the ground it seemed cumbersome and awkward. Tassie was after it like a flash; Harry seized his weapon, the stave tipped with iron, and followed. When Tassie caught up with the eagle it turned and faced him, standing over the lamb.

Harry, as he ran, could see blood staining the white wool of the lamb's body; the eagle's wings were half spread out over it, and moving slowly. The huge bird was grayish-brown, with a white head and tail. The beak was yellow, and the legs yellow and scaly.

It lowered its head, and with a fierce movement threatened Tassie; then, as the dog approached, it began to rock and stamp from foot to foot in a menacing dance; then it opened its beak and gave its fierce, yelping cry. Tassie hung back, his ears flattened against his head, snarling, creeping by inches toward the eagle; he was frightened, but he was brave. Then he ran in to attack.

The eagle left the lamb. With a lunging spring it aimed heavily at Tassie. It just cleared the ground and beat about Tassie with its wings, hovering over him. Tassie flattened out his body to the earth and turned his head upward with snapping jaws. But the eagle was over him and on him, its talons plunged into his side, and a piercing scream rang out. The eagle struck deliberately at the dog's skull three times; the beak's point hammered on his head, striking downward and sideways. Tassie lay limp on the ground, and, where his head had been, a red mixture of blood and brains flowed on the grass. When Harry took his eyes away from the blood, the eagle was standing on the lamb again.

Harry approached the eagle slowly, step by step. He gripped his stick firmly as he came. The eagle put its head down. It rocked on its feet as if preparing to leap. Behind the terrific beak, sharp as metal, was a shallow head, flat and broad as a snake's, glaring with light yellow un-animal eyes. The head and neck made weaving movements toward him.

At a pace or two from the eagle Harry stood still. In a second he would make a rush. He could break the eagle's skull, he told himself, with one good blow; then he could avenge Tassie and stand up to his father.

But he waited too long. The eagle tried to rise, and with its heavy sweeping beats was beginning to gain speed along the ground. Harry ran, stumbling over the uneven ground, among boulders and outcroppings of rock, trying to strike at the eagle as he went. But as soon as the eagle was in the air it was no longer heavy and clumsy. There was a sudden rush of wings and buffeting about his head as the eagle turned to drive him off. For a second he saw the talons sharp as metal, backed by the metal strength of the legs, striking at his face. He put up his arm. At once it was seared with a red-hot pain, and he could see the blood rush out.

He stepped back, and back again. The eagle, after this one fierce swoop at him, went round in a wide, low circle, and returned to the lamb. Harry saw that his coat sleeve was in ribbons, and that blood was running off the ends of his fingers and falling to the ground.

He stood panting; the wind blew across the empty high ground. The sheep had vanished from sight. Tassie lay dead nearby, and he was utterly alone on the hills. There was nobody to watch what he did. The eagle might hurt him, but it could not jeer at him. He attacked it again, but already the eagle with its heavy wingbeats had cleared the ground; this time it took the lamb with it. Harry saw that it meant to fly, as it had flown yesterday, to an edge; and then out into the free air over the chasm, and over the valley far below.

Harry gave chase, stumbling over the broken ground and between the boulders—striking at the eagle as he went, trying to beat it down before it could escape. The eagle was hampered by his attack; and suddenly it swooped onto a projection of rock and turned again to drive him off. Harry was now in a bad position. The eagle stood on a rock at the height of his own shoulders, with the lamb beside it. It struck at his chest with its talons, beating its wings as it did so. Harry felt clothes and flesh being torn; buffeting blows began about his head; but he kept close to the eagle and struck at it again. He did not want simply to frighten it away, but to kill it. The eagle fought at first simply to drive Harry off; then, as he continued to attack, it became ferocious.

Harry saw his only chance was to keep close to the eagle and beat it down; but already it was at the height of his face. It struck at him from above, driving its steel claws at him, beating its wings about him. He was dazed by the buffeting which went on and on all round him; then with an agonizing stab he felt the claws seize and pierce his shoulder and neck. He struck upward desperately and blindly. As the eagle drove its beak at his head, his stick just turned the blow aside. The beak struck a glancing blow off the stick, and tore away his eyebrow.

Harry found that something was blinding him, and he felt a new sickening fear that already one of his eyes was gone. The outspread beating wings and weight of the eagle dragged him about, and he nearly lost his footing. He had forgotten, now, that he was proving anything to his father; he was fighting for his eyes. Three times he fended off the hammer stroke of the beak, and at these close quarters the blows of his club found their mark. He caught the eagle's head each time, and the bird was half stunned.

Harry, reeling and staggering, felt the grip of the claws gradually loosen, and almost unbelievably the body of his enemy sagged, half fluttering to the ground. With a sudden spurt of new strength, Harry attacked, and rained blows on the bird's skull. The eagle struggled, and he followed, beating it down among the rocks. At last the eagle's movements stopped. He saw its skull was broken, and that it lay dead.

He stood for many minutes panting and unmoving, filled with a tremendous excitement; then he sat on a boulder. The fight had taken him near a steep edge a long way from the body of Tassie.

His wounds began to ache and burn. The sky and the horizon spun round him, but he forced himself to be firm and collected.

After a while he stooped down and hoisted the eagle onto his shoulder. The wings dropped loosely down in front and behind. He set off toward the farm.

When he reached his home, the low gray walls, the plowed fields, and the green pasture fields were swimming before his eyes in a dizzy pattern. It was still the early part of the morning, but there was plenty of life in the farmyard, as usual. Some cows were being driven out. One of the carthorses was standing harnessed to a heavy wagon. Harry's father was talking to the carter and looking at the horse's leg.

When they saw Harry come toward them they waited, unmoving. They could hardly see at first who or what it was. Harry came up and dropped the bird at his father's feet. His coat was gone. His shirt hung in bloodstained rags about him; one arm was caked in blood; his right eyebrow hung in a loose flap, with the blood still oozing stickily down his cheek.

"Good God!" said Thorburn, catching him by the arm as he reeled.

He led the boy into the kitchen. There they gave him a glass of brandy and sponged him with warm water. There was a deep long wound in his left forearm. His chest was crisscrossed with cuts. The flesh was torn away from his neck where the talons had sunk in.

Presently the doctor came. Harry's wounds began to hurt like fire, but he talked excitedly. He was happier than he had ever been in his life. Everybody on the farm came in to see him and to see the eagle's body.

All day his father hung about him, looking into the kitchen every half hour. He said very little, but asked Harry several times how he felt. "Are you aw reet?" he kept saying. Once he took a cup of tea from his wife and carried it across the kitchen in order to give it to Harry with his own hands.

Later in the day old Michael came back, and Harry told him the whole story. Michael turned the bird over. He said it was an erne, a white-tailed sea eagle from the coast. He measured the wing span, and it was seven and a half feet. Michael had seen two or three when he was a boy—always near the coast—but this one, he said, was easily the largest.

Three days later Mr. Thorburn took Harry, still stiff and bandaged, down to the village inn. There he set him before a blazing fire all the evening, and in the presence of men from every cottage and farm Thorburn praised his son. He bought him a glass of beer and made Harry tell the story of his fight to everyone.

As he told it, Thorburn sat by him, hearing the story himself each time, making certain that Harry missed nothing about his struggle. Afterward every man drank Harry's health, and clapped Thorburn on the back and told him he ought to be proud of his son.

Later, in the silent darkness, they walked back to the farm again, and neither of them could find anything to say. Harry wondered if his father might not refer to the beating and apologize. Thorburn moved round the house, raking out fires and locking up. Then he picked up the lamp and, holding it above his head, led the way upstairs.

"Good night, Harry," said his father at last, as he took him to his bedroom door. "Are you aw reet?"

His father held the lamp up and looked into Harry's face. As the lamplight fell on it, he nodded. He said nothing more.

"Aye," said Harry, as he turned into his bedroom door, "I'm aw reet."

Understanding the Story _____

Main Idea

1. Harry risks his life   (a) to save the lamb   (b) to prove his father wrong   (c) to show how brave he is   (d) to show how wrong the farmhand is.

Details

2. Which of the following statements is not true?
   a. Harry is thirteen years old.
   b. Mr. Thorburn is a successful farmer.
   c. The erne is a familiar sight inland.
   d. Michael is a trusted helper.

3. Which one of the following statements is not true? When the erne appears the first time:
   a. The eagle terrifies the dog.
   b. Harry is unsuccessful in his first attempt to drive off the eagle.
   c. Mr. Thorburn does not believe Harry's story of the attack by the erne.
   d. One of the farmhands returns with Harry to protect the sheep.

4. On its second appearance, the erne   (a) is chased away by the dog   (b) kills the dog   (c) flies off with another sheep   (d) is frightened away by a shot from Harry's gun.

Cause and Effect

5. Harry had been given the job of caring for the sheep because (a) the shepherd quit   (b) the shepherd's nephew had an accident   (c) his father wanted to give him more responsibility   (d) he loved sheep.

6. After Harry tells the story of the first raid, he feels humiliated because (a) his father doesn't even answer him   (b) his mother chides him   (c) his father strikes him in the presence of the farmhand   (d) the farmhands all say that the story is highly improbable.

Inference

7. When Harry is fighting the eagle, he soon realizes that   (a) he is going to win   (b) the eagle is afraid   (c) the eagle could kill him   (d) his father would be proud of him.

Order of Events

8. Arrange the items in the order in which they occurred. Use letters only.
    A. Harry returns for help.
    B. Michael's nephew injures his wrist.
    C. Harry proves himself.
    D. Mrs. Thorburn chides her husband.
    E. Harry takes a letter to Michael.

Outcomes

9. In   the   end,   Mr.   Thorburn   (a) never   apologizes (b) apologizes openly   (c) apologizes indirectly   (d) refuses to apologize.

10. Mr. Thorburn's real reason for taking Harry to the inn is (a) to show his neighbors Harry's wounds   (b) to buy him a glass of beer   (c) to show Harry that he now accepts him as a grown-up   (d) to prove that money isn't everything.

Words in Context

1. Mr. Thorburn was a red-faced, powerful man; he wore knee breeches and black leather *gaiters.*
    Gaiters (466) means   (a) shoes   (b) leg coverings   (c) shirt (d) belt.

2. He was a slip of a boy. It seemed unlikely that he could ever grow into such a *stolid,* heavy man as his father.
    Stolid   (467)   means   (a) strong   (b) unemotional (c) commanding   (d) stern.

3. Presently he cleared the *gorse and heather,* and came out on to the open hillside . . .
    Gorse and heather (467) are   (a) low shrubs   (b) tall trees (c) hedgerows   (d) swamplands.

4. Michael had rather long hair; it was between gray and white

in color . . . It was about the *hue* of an old sheep's skull that has lain out on the bare mountain.
Hue (468) means   (a) tint   (b) shape   (c) strength (d) dryness.

5. He was all the color of rain on the stones and *last year's bracken*.
    Last year's bracken (468) means   (a) large fern turned brown (b) raw wool not dyed   (c) rusty metal shears (d) shepherd's crook.

6. Harry went away feeling somewhat *abashed*. Lately it seemed his father was always down on him.
    Abashed (468) means   (a) annoyed   (b) excited (c) encouraged   (d) put down.

7. Next morning it was again a cold, windy day, and clouds the color of *gunmetal* raced over the hill.
    Gunmetal (469) means   (a) red-orange   (b) fleecy white (c) bluish-gray   (d) gray-black.

8. There was no gun in the hut, but he found a thick *stave* tipped with metal, part of some broken tool that had been thrown aside.
    Stave (473) means   (a) chunk of iron   (b) barrel lid (c) wooden stick   (d) steel bar.

9. He put up his arm. At once it was *seared* with a red-hot pain.
    Seared (475) means   (a) wounded   (b) scorched (c) numbed   (d) tingling.

10. Harry felt clothes and flesh being torn; *buffeting* blows began about his head; but he kept close to the eagle and struck at it again.
    Buffeting (476) means   (a) fatal   (b) battering (c) swirling   (d) penetrating.

Thinking About the Story

1. There are, generally, two ways for an author to tell you what a character is like. One way is for him to *tell* you *directly* what kind of person the character is; the other way (which may be called the *indirect* method) is to have the character say and do things that will *illustrate* the kind of person he is. Which one of these methods is used by Beachcroft in describing Mr. Thor-

burn at the beginning of the story? Prove your point. How does Mr. Thorburn compare with the adults in your own life?

2. What is the significance of the following sentences (on page 477)? *Harry's wounds began to hurt like fire, but he talked excitedly. He was happier than he had ever been in his life.*

3. Why doesn't Harry attempt to kill the erne when it first appears? How does the author convince us of the murderous ferocity of the erne? Why does Harry overcome his fear of the erne? Is the fight with the erne inevitable? Explain.

4. Why doesn't Mr. Thorburn apologize openly for the beating? Is Harry still resentful at the end of the story? What is his attitude now toward his father? How is this attitude indicated by the last line in the story? Did Mr. Thorburn learn a lesson? Will he change? Explain.

5. Some readers feel that it would not be natural for anyone in Harry's place to forget the cruelty his father had shown toward him up until the time he returned home with the dead erne over his bleeding shoulders. They put it this way: "It's true that Mr. Thorburn now respects Harry. But Harry must realize that he has won his father's respect only by risking his life and returning home with the evidence of his battle, evidence to prove something Mr. Thorburn should have believed in the first place. Since this is so, can Harry respect his father? Shouldn't a father worthy of respect have a natural respect for his son, a feeling that does not depend on evidence or accident? Mr. Thorburn had said, *'Bring the eagle back, and then I'll believe you.'* Suppose Harry had been unsuccessful in his second attempt?" What do you think?

The Blanket

Floyd Dell

♦ It was like Granddad to be saying that. He was trying to make it easier. He'd pretended all along it was he that was wanting to go away to the great brick building—the government place, where he'd be with so many other old fellows having the best of everything.

CHARACTERS: An eleven-year-old boy; his widowed father about to remarry; the woman, his prospective stepmother; his grandfather, who is moving out of the house to please the woman.

PROPS: A fiddle, a blanket, a pair of scissors.

SETTING: Anywhere.

TIME: Anytime.

We'd like to warn you about Floyd Dell's "The Blanket." This short short story has fewer than 1200 words and not a single one of them is difficult. But the story is not so simple as it appears to be on the surface. Or, perhaps, like the hiding place of the purloined letter in Poe's story, the meaning of "The Blanket" is so obvious that it escapes the notice of people who are looking for complexity. Some readers carelessly read meanings into the story that it doesn't have. Permit us to tell you what the story does *not* say. The story does *not* say that it is foolish for a widower to remarry. It does *not* say that stepmothers are an undesirable breed of humanity. It does *not* say that old people are full of tricks and usually get their way in the long run. If you understand what the blanket signifies to each of the four characters involved, then you'll have no trouble in deciding what the story means.

THE BLANKET

Petey hadn't really believed that Dad would be doing it—sending Granddad away. "Away" was what they were calling it. Not until now could he believe it of Dad.

But here was the blanket that Dad had that day bought for him, and in the morning he'd be going away. And this was the last evening they'd be having together. Dad was off seeing that girl he was to marry. He'd not be back till late, and they could sit up and talk.

It was a fine September night, with a silver moon riding high over the gully. When they'd washed up the supper dishes they went out on the shanty porch, the old man and the bit of a boy, taking their chairs. "I'll get me fiddle," said the old man, "and play ye some of the old tunes." But instead of the fiddle he brought out the blanket. It was a big, double blanket, red, with black cross stripes.

"Now, isn't that a fine blanket!" said the old man, smoothing it over his knees. "And isn't your father a kind man to be giving the old fellow a blanket like that to go away with? It cost something, it did—look at the wool of it! And warm it will be these cold winter nights to come. There'll be few blankets there the equal of this one!"

It was like Granddad to be saying that. He was trying to make it easier. He'd pretended all along it was he that was wanting to go away to the great brick building—the government place, where he'd be with so many other old fellows having the best of everything . . . But Petey hadn't believed Dad would really do it, until this night when he brought home the blanket.

"Oh, yes, it's a fine blanket," said Petey, and got up and went into the shanty. He wasn't the kind to cry, and, besides, he was too old for that, being eleven. He'd just come in to fetch Granddad's fiddle.

The blanket slid to the floor as the old man took the fiddle and stood up. It was the last night they'd be having together. There wasn't any need to say, "Play all the old tunes." Granddad tuned up for a minute, and then said, "This is one you'll like to remember."

The silver moon was high overhead, and there was a gentle breeze playing down the gully. He'd never be hearing Granddad play like this again. It was as well Dad was moving into that new house, away from here. He'd not want, Petey wouldn't, to sit here on the old porch of fine evenings, with Granddad gone.

The tune changed. "Here's something gayer." Petey sat and stared out over the gully. Dad would marry that girl. Yes, that girl who'd kissed him and slobbered over him, saying she'd try to be a good mother to him, and all . . . His chair creaked as he involuntarily gave his body a painful twist.

The tune stopped suddenly, and Granddad said: "It's a poor tune, except to be dancing to." And then: "It's a fine girl your father's going to marry. He'll be feeling young again, with a pretty wife like that. And what would an old fellow like me be doing around their house, getting in the way, an old nuisance, what with my talk of aches and pains! And then there'll be babies coming, and I'd not want to be there to hear them crying at all hours. It's best that I take myself off, like I'm doing. One more tune or two, and then we'll be going to bed to get some sleep against the morning, when I'll pack up my fine blanket and take my leave. Listen to this, will you? It's a bit sad, but a fine tune for a night like this."

They didn't hear the two people coming down the gully path, Dad and the pretty girl with the hard, bright face like a china doll's. But they heard her laugh, right by the porch, and the tune stopped on a wrong, high, startled note. Dad didn't say anything, but the girl came forward and spoke to Granddad prettily: "I'll not be seeing you leave in the morning, so I came over to say good-bye."

"It's kind of you," said Granddad, with his eyes cast down; and then, seeing the blanket at his feet, he stooped to pick it up. "And will you look at this," he said in embarrassment, "the fine blanket my son has given me to go away with!"

"Yes," she said, "it's a fine blanket." She felt of the wool, and repeated in surprise, "A fine blanket—I'll say it is!" She turned to Dad, and said to him coldly, "It cost something, that."

He cleared his throat, and said defensively. "I wanted him to have the best. . . . "

The girl stood there, still intent on the blanket. "It's double, too," she said reproachfully to Dad.

"Yes," said Granddad, "it's double—a fine blanket for an old fellow to be going away with."

The boy went abruptly into the shanty. He was looking for something. He could hear that girl reproaching Dad, and Dad becoming angry in his slow way. And now she was suddenly going away in a huff . . . As Petey came out, she turned and called back, "All the same, he doesn't need a double blanket!" And she ran up the gully path.

Dad was looking after her uncertainly.

"Oh, she's right," said the boy coldly. "Here, Dad"—and he held out a pair of scissors. "Cut the blanket in two."

Both of them stared at the boy, startled. "Cut it in two, I tell you, Dad!" he cried out. "And keep the other half!"

"That's not a bad idea," said Granddad gently. "I don't need so much of a blanket."

"Yes," said the boy harshly, "a single blanket's enough for an old man when he's sent away. We'll save the other half, Dad; it will come in handy later."

"Now, what do you mean by that?" asked Dad.

"I mean," said the boy slowly, "that I'll give it to you, Dad— when you're old and I'm sending you—away."

There was a silence, and then Dad went over to Granddad and stood before him, not speaking. But Granddad understood, for he put out a hand and laid it on Dad's shoulder. Petey was watching them. And he heard Granddad whisper, "It's all right, son—I knew you didn't mean it. . . ." And then Petey cried.

But it didn't matter—because they were all three crying together.

Understanding the Story _____

Main Idea

1. The blanket becomes a symbol of (a) Petey's dislike for the woman (b) the woman's dislike for Granddad (c) the father's love for the woman (d) justice for grandparents.

Details

2. Petey spends his last evening with Granddad (a) crying (b) admiring the blanket (c) listening to Granddad tell stories (d) listening to Granddad play his violin.

3. We are told (a) the setting—time and place—of the story (b) the names of the tunes Granddad recalled (c) the name of only one of the characters (d) the price of the blanket.

4. The woman becomes angry because (a) Granddad has not left (b) Petey is with Granddad (c) the father sides with Granddad (d) the gift is too expensive.

Inference

5. Which of the following statements is not true?
   a. Petey is eleven years old.
   b. The family has a limited income.
   c. The woman is unsympathetic toward Granddad.
   d. Granddad is looking forward eagerly to life in the retirement home.

6. Which of the following could not be the reason for the woman's leaving?
   a. The house is too shabby.
   b. She has argued too many times about Granddad.
   c. She wants to be free and not marry father.
   d. She is jealous of the relationship between Petey and Granddad.

Order of Events

7. Arrange the items in the order in which they occurred. Use letters only.
   A. Petey makes an important announcement.
   B. Father buys a present.
   C. Father decides to remarry.

D. Granddad accepts a rough decision.

E. Father's fiancée leaves in anger.

Cause and Effect

8. Petey wants to cut the blanket　(a) to save money　(b) to save part of it for Dad　(c) to give part to the woman　(d) to have part of it for his own use.

Outcomes

9. Petey makes his father　(a) give up the marriage　(b) return the blanket　(c) reconsider his solution　(d) send Granddad away.

10. At the end of the story, the blanket is　(a) cut in half　(b) disregarded　(c) thrown away　(d) given to the woman.

Words in Context

1. He'd just come in to *fetch* Granddad's fiddle.
   Fetch (484) means　(a) tune　(b) admire　(c) get　(d) pack.

2. There was a gentle breeze *playing down the gully.* (485)
   The breeze was　(a) bending branches　(b) almost at a standstill　(c) moving leaves here and there　(d) whistling through the trees.

3. His chair creaked as he *involuntarily* gave his body a painful twist.
   Involuntarily (485) means　(a) suddenly　(b) unconsciously　(c) violently　(d) carelessly.

4. Granddad said: "It's a poor tune, except to be dancing to." (485)
   Granddad meant that the song he played was　(a) too loud　(b) rather slow　(c) too fast　(d) very rhythmical.

5. "It's best I *take myself off*, like I'm doing."
   Take myself off (485) means　(a) go away　(b) control my anger　(c) accept my fate　(d) show my disappointment.

6. . . . the pretty girl with a hard, bright face like a china doll's. (485)
   The girl's face　(a) was full of fun　(b) was full of joy　(c) had heavy make-up　(d) had a cunning look.

7. "It's kind of you," said Granddad, *with his eyes cast down*. Granddad kept his *eyes cast down* (485)   (a) to hide his feelings   (b) to show his anger   (c) to avoid falling   (d) to show his pleasure.

8. She turned to Dad, and said to him *coldly*, "It cost something, that."
   She spoke *coldly* (485) because   (a) she disliked Dad   (b) she liked Granddad   (c) she thought Dad had been cheated   (d) she was displeased.

9. "It's double, too," she said *reproachfully* to Dad.
   Reproachfully (486) means   (a) with pride   (b) with satisfaction   (c) with disapproval   (d) with scorn.

10. And now she was suddenly going away *in a huff*.
    In a huff (486) means   (a) noisily   (b) angrily   (c) silently   (d) reluctantly.

Thinking About the Story

1. What seems to be special about the relationship between Petey and his grandfather? How does this compare with the relationships in your family? In the families in your neighborhood?

2. How does Granddad really feel about going away? Why does the woman want him sent to a retirement home? Although the author obviously sympathizes with Granddad and Petey, can you see any justification for the woman's point of view? What experience has your family or your neighbors' had with such institutions? What is your opinion of this solution?

3. What does the blanket symbolize for each of the four characters? What solution does the author offer to the problems the four characters face? Do you agree with him? Explain.

4. Why doesn't the author tell us the names of the characters, other than that of the little boy? Should he have told us more about them? Explain. Does this story contain a universal truth? Explain.

5. Is the author guilty of distorting reality in making Petey "wise beyond his years" or do children sometimes exhibit this kind of insight into the heart of things? Base your answer on your own experience with children you have known or heard about.

A Worn Path

Eudora Welty

♦ Old Phoenix would have been lost if she had
not distrusted her eyesight and depended on her
feet to know where to take her.

The traditional favorite Christmas story in America is O. Henry's "Gift of the Magi" in which the exchange of gifts creates the magical O. Henry touch. "A Worn Path" also takes place at Christmastime, and it also centers around gifts, but that is where the resemblance ends.

"A Worn Path" is told from the point of view of an elderly back-country woman, Phoenix Jackson. She has left her simple cabin deep in the mountains and is walking through the winter woods to Natchez to get the medicine needed by her ailing grandson. The deep pine and oak forest is inhabited by a fascinating variety of creatures that Phoenix either encounters or imagines she encounters.

Phoenix reaches the city filled with Christmastime spirit and decorations. She gets the medicine and decides to buy a gift for the grandchild. There is no mystery or high adventure in this tale.

Be patient with the story. Let the author weave her magic, and your reward will be the same emotional impact and enjoyment you should be finding in stories with more definite plots. Read it to understand not only the action, but more important, the people in it.

The key to the story is in its title. What is the Worn Path? Is it Phoenix's continuing quiet acceptance of life and its hardships? Is it the recurring Christmas season? Is it the gift-giving from one generation to another? Is it . . . , but read and find out for yourself. This is a Christmas story, but different!

490

A WORN PATH

It was December—a bright frozen day in the early morning. Far out in the country there was an old black woman with her head tied in a red rag, coming along a path through the pinewoods. Her name was Phoenix Jackson. She was very old and small and she walked slowly in the dark pine shadows, moving a little from side to side in her steps, with the balanced heaviness and lightness of a pendulum in a grandfather clock. She carried a thin, small cane made from an umbrella, and with this she kept tapping the frozen earth in front of her. This made a grave and persistent noise in the still air, that seemed meditative, like the chirping of a solitary little bird.

She wore a dark striped dress reaching down to her shoetops, and an equally long apron of bleached sugar sacks, with a full pocket; all neat and tidy, but every time she took a step she might have fallen over her shoelaces, which dragged from her unlaced shoes. She looked straight ahead. Her eyes were blue with age. Her skin had a pattern all its own of numberless branching wrinkles and as though a whole little tree stood in the middle of her forehead, but a golden color ran underneath, and the two knobs of her cheeks were illuminated by a yellow burning under the dark. Under the red rag her hair came down on her neck in the frailest of ringlets, still black, and with an odor like copper.

Now and then there was a quivering in the thicket. Old Phoenix said, "Out of my way, all you foxes, owls, beetles, jack rabbits, coons, and wild animals! . . . Keep out from under these feet, little bobwhites . . . Keep the big wild hogs out of my path. Don't let none of those come running my direction. I got a long way." Under her small black-freckled hand her cane, limber as a buggy whip, would switch at the brush as if to rouse up any hiding things.

On she went. The woods were deep and still. The sun made the pine needles almost too bright to look at, up where the wind rocked. The cones dropped as light as feathers. Down in the hollow was the mourning dove—it was not too late for him.

The path ran up a hill. "Seem like there is chains about my feet, time I get this far," she said, in the voice of argument old people keep to use with themselves. "Something always take a hold on this hill—pleads I should stay."

After she got to the top she turned and gave a full, severe look behind her where she had come. "Up through pines," she said at length. "Now down through oaks."

Her eyes opened their widest and she started down gently. But before she got to the bottom of the hill a bush caught her dress.

Her fingers were busy and intent, but her skirts were full and long, so that before she could pull them free in one place they were caught in another. It was not possible to allow the dress to tear. "I in the thorny bush," she said. "Thorns, you doing your appointed work. Never want to let folks pass—no sir. Old eyes thought you was a pretty little *green* bush."

Finally, trembling all over, she stood free, and after a moment dared to stoop for her cane.

"Sun so high!" she cried, leaning back and looking, while the thick tears went over her eyes. "The time getting all gone here."

At the foot of this hill was a place where a log was laid across the creek.

"Now comes the trial," said Phoenix.

Putting her right foot out, she mounted the log and shut her eyes. Lifting her skirt, leveling her cane fiercely before her, like a festival figure in some parade, she began to march across. Then she opened her eyes and she was safe on the other side.

"I wasn't as old as I thought," she said.

But she sat down to rest. She spread her skirts on the bank around her and folded her hands over her knees. Up above her was a tree in a pearly cloud of mistletoe. She did not dare to close her eyes, and when a little boy brought her a little plate with a slice of marble cake on it she spoke to him. "That would be acceptable," she said. But when she went to take it there was just her own hand in the air.

So she left that tree, and had to go through a barbed wire fence. There she had to creep and crawl, spreading her knees and stretching her fingers like a baby trying to climb the steps. But she talked loudly to herself: she could not let her dress be torn now, so late in the day, and she could not pay for having her arm or her leg sawed off if she got caught fast where she was.

At last she was safe through the fence and risen up out in the clearing. Big dead trees, like black men with one arm, were standing in the purple stalks of the withered cotton field. There sat a buzzard.

"Who you watching?"

In the furrow she made her way along.

"Glad this not the season for bulls," she said, looking sideways, "and the good Lord made his snakes to curl up and sleep in the winter. A pleasure I don't see no two-headed snake coming around that tree, where it come once. It took a while to get by him, back in the summer."

She passed through the old cotton and went into a field of dead corn. It whispered and shook, and was taller than her head. "Through the maze now," she said, for there was no path.

Then there was something tall, black, and skinny there, moving before her.

At first she took it for a man. It could have been a man dancing in the field. But she stood still and listened, and it did not make a sound. It was as silent as a ghost.

"Ghost," she said sharply, "who be you the ghost of? For I have heard of nary death close by."

But there was no answer, only the ragged dancing in the wind.

She shut her eyes, reached out her hand, and touched a sleeve. She found a coat and inside that an emptiness, cold as ice.

"You scarecrow," she said. Her face lighted. "I ought to be shut up for good," she said with laughter. "My senses is gone. I too old. I the oldest people I ever know. Dance, old scarecrow," she said, "while I dancing with you."

She kicked her foot over the furrow, and with mouth drawn down shook her head once or twice in a little strutting way. Some husks blew down and whirled in streamers about her skirts.

Then she went on, parting her way from side to side with the cane, through the whispering field. At last she came to the end, to a wagon track, where the silver grass blew between the red ruts. The quail were walking around like pullets, seeming all dainty and unseen.

"Walk pretty," she said. "This the easy place. This the easy going."

She followed the track, swaying through the quiet bare fields, through the little strings of trees silver in their dead leaves, past cabins silver from weather, with the doors and windows boarded shut, all like old women under a spell sitting there. "I walking in their sleep," she said, nodding her head vigorously.

In a ravine she went where a spring was silently flowing through a hollow log. Old Phoenix bent and drank. "Sweetgum makes the water sweet," she said, and drank more. "Nobody knows who made this well, for it was here when I was born."

The track crossed a swampy part where the moss hung as white as lace from every limb. "Sleep on, alligators, and blow your bubbles." Then the track went into the road.

Deep, deep the road went down between the high green-colored banks. Overhead the live oaks met, and it was as dark as a cave.

A black dog with a lolling tongue came up out of the weeds by the ditch. She was meditating, and not ready, and when he came at her she only hit him a little with her cane. Over she went in the ditch, like a little puff of milkweed.

Down there, her senses drifted away. A dream visited her, and she reached her hand up, but nothing reached down and gave her a pull. So she lay there and presently went to talking. "Old woman," she said to herself, "that black dog came up out of the weeds to stall you off, and now there he sitting on his fine tail, smiling at you."

A white man finally came along and found her—a hunter, a young man, with his dog on a chain.

"Well, Granny!" he laughed. "What are you doing there?"

"Lying on my back like a june bug waiting to be turned over, mister," she said, reaching up her hand.

He lifted her up, gave her a swing in the air, and set her down, "Anything broken, Granny?"

"No sir, them old dead weeds is springy enough," said Phoenix, when she had got her breath. "I thank you for your trouble."

"Where do you live, Granny?" he asked, while the two dogs were growling at each other.

"Away back yonder, sir, behind the ridge. You can't even see it from here."

"On your way home?"

"No, sir, I going to town."

"Why, that's too far! That's as far as I walk when I come out myself, and I get something for my trouble." He patted the stuffed bag he carried, and there hung down a little closed claw. It was one of the bobwhites, with its beak hooked bitterly to show it was dead. "Now you go on home, Granny!"

"I bound to go to town, mister," said Phoenix. "The time come around."

He gave another laugh, filling the whole landscape. "I know you black people! Wouldn't miss going to town to see Santa Claus!"

But something held Old Phoenix very still. The deep lines in her face went into a fierce and different radiation. Without warning she had seen with her own eyes a flashing quarter fall out of the man's pocket on to the ground.

"How old are you, Granny?" he was saying.

"There is no telling, mister," she said, "no telling."

Then she gave a little cry and clapped her hands, and said, "Git on away from here, dog! Look! Look at that dog!" She laughed as if in admiration. "He ain't scared of nobody. He a big black dog." She whispered, "Sick him!"

"Watch me get rid of that cur," said the man. "Sick him, Pete! Sick him!"

Phoenix heard the dogs fighting and heard the man running and throwing sticks. She even heard a gunshot. But she was slowly bending forward by that time, further and further forward, the lids stretched down over her eyes, as if she were doing this in her sleep. Her chin was lowered almost to her knees. The yellow palm of her hand came out from the fold of her apron. Her fingers slid down and along the ground under the piece of money with the grace and care they would have in lifting an egg from under a sitting hen. Then she slowly straightened up, she stood erect, and the quarter was in her apron pocket. A bird flew by. Her lips moved. "God watching me the whole time. I come to stealing."

The man came back, and his own dog panted about them. "Well, I scared him off that time," he said, and then he laughed and lifted his gun and pointed it at Phoenix.

She stood straight and faced him.

"Doesn't the gun scare you?" he said, still pointing it.

"No, sir, I seen plenty go off closer by, in my day, and for less than what I done," she said, holding utterly still.

He smiled, and shouldered the gun. "Well, Granny," he said, "you must be a hundred years old, and scared of nothing. I'd give you a coin if I had any money with me. But you take my advice and stay home, and nothing will happen to you."

"I bound to go on my way, mister," said Phoenix. She inclined her head in the red rag. Then they went in different directions, but she could hear the gun shooting again and again over the hill.

She walked on. The shadows hung from the oak trees to the road like curtains. Then she smelled wood smoke, and smelled the river, and she saw a steeple and the cabins on their steep steps. Dozens of little black children whirled around her. There ahead was Natchez shining. Bells were ringing. She walked on.

In the paved city it was Christmas time. There were red and green electric lights strung and crisscrossed everywhere, and all turned on in the daytime. Old Phoenix would have been lost if she had not distrusted her eyesight and depended on her feet to know where to take her.

She paused quietly on the sidewalk, where people were passing by. A lady came along in the crowd, carrying an armful of red-, green-, and silver-wrapped presents; she gave off perfume like the red roses in hot summer, and Phoenix stopped her.

"Please, missy, will you lace up my shoe?" She held up her foot.

"What do you want, Grandma?"

"See my shoe," said Phoenix. "Do all right for out in the country, but wouldn't look right to go in a big building."

"Stand still then, Grandma," said the lady. She put her packages down carefully on the sidewalk beside her and laced and tied both shoes tightly.

"Can't lace 'em with a cane," said Phoenix. "Thank you, missy. I doesn't mind asking a nice lady to tie up my shoe when I gets out on the street."

Moving slowly and from side to side, she went into the stone building and into a tower of steps, where she walked up and around and around until her feet knew to stop.

She entered a door, and there she saw nailed up on the wall the document that had been stamped with the gold seal and framed in the gold frame which matched the dream that was hung up in her head.

"Here I be," she said. There was a fixed and ceremonial stiffness over her body.

"A charity case, I suppose," said an attendant who sat at the desk before her.

But Phoenix only looked above her head. There was sweat on her face; the wrinkles shone like a bright net.

"Speak up, Grandma," the woman said. "What's your name? We must have your history, you know. Have you been here before? What seems to be the trouble with you?"

Old Phoenix only gave a twitch to her face as if a fly were bothering her.

"Are you deaf?" cried the attendant.

But then the nurse came in.

"Oh, that's just old Aunt Phoenix," she said. "She doesn't come for herself—she has a little grandson. She makes these trips just as regular as clockwork. She lives away back off the Old Natchez Trace." She bent down. "Well, Aunt Phoenix, why don't you just take a seat? We won't keep you standing after your long trip." She pointed.

The old woman sat down, bolt upright in the chair.

"Now, how is the boy?" asked the nurse.

Old Phoenix did not speak.

"I said, how is the boy?"

But Phoenix only waited and stared straight ahead, her face very solemn and withdrawn into rigidity.

"Is his throat any better?" asked the nurse. "Aunt Phoenix, don't you hear me? Is your grandson's throat any better since the last time you came for medicine?"

With her hand on her knees, the old woman waited, silent, erect and motionless, just as if she were in armor.

"You mustn't take up our time this way, Aunt Phoenix," the nurse said. "Tell us quickly about your grandson, and get it over. He isn't dead, is he?"

At last there came a flicker and then a flame of comprehension across her face, and she spoke.

"My grandson. It was my memory had left me. There I sat and forgot why I made my long trip."

"Forgot?" The nurse frowned. "After you came so far?"

Then Phoenix was like an old woman begging a dignified forgiveness for waking up frightened in the night. "I never did go to school—I was too old at the Surrender," she said in a soft voice. "I'm an old woman without an education. It was my memory fail me. My little grandson, he is just the same, and I forgot it in the coming."

"Throat never heals, does it?" said the nurse, speaking in a loud, sure voice to Old Phoenix. By now she had a card with something written on it, a little list. "Yes. Swallowed lye. When was it—January—two—three years ago—"

Phoenix spoke unasked now. "No, missy, he not dead, he just the same. Every little while his throat begin to close up again, and he not able to swallow. He not get his breath. He not able to help himself. So the time come around, and I go on another trip for the soothing medicine."

"All right. The doctor said as long as you came to get it you could have it," said the nurse. "But it's an obstinate case."

"My little grandson, he sit up there in the house all wrapped up, waiting by himself," Phoenix went on. "We is the only two left in the world. He suffer and it don't seem to put him back at all. He got a sweet look. He going to last. He wear a little patch quilt and peep out, holding his mouth open like a little bird. I remembers so plain now. I not going to forget him again, no, the whole enduring time. I could tell him from all the others in creation."

"All right." The nurse was trying to hush her now. She brought her a bottle of medicine. "Charity," she said, making a check mark in a book.

Old Phoenix held the bottle close to her eyes and then carefully put it into her pocket.

"I thank you," she said.

"It's Christmas time, Grandma," said the attendant. "Could I give you a few coins out of my purse?"

"Five nickels is a quarter," said Phoenix stiffly.

"Here's a quarter," said the attendant.

Phoenix rose carefully and held out her hand. She received the quarter and then fished the other quarter out of her pocket and laid it beside the new one. She stared at her palm closely, with her head on one side.

Then she gave a tap with her cane on the floor.

"This is what come to me to do," she said. "I going to the store and buy my child a little windmill they sells, made out of paper. He going to find it hard to believe there such a thing in the world. I'll march myself back where he waiting, holding it straight up in this hand."

She lifted her free hand, gave a little nod, turning round, and walked out of the doctor's office. Then her slow step began on the stairs, going down.

Understanding the Story ————————

Main Idea

1. The characters in this story reveal   (a) a distrust of other people   (b) a feeling of superiority over others   (c) a disregard of the Christmas spirit   (d) different aspects of giving and sharing.

Details

2. Which one of the following is not true of Phoenix?
    a. She lives alone with her grandson.
    b. She is afraid to be alone in the woods.
    c. Her mind plays tricks on her.
    d. She is unaware of her odd appearance.

3. The black dog   (a) wants to be petted   (b) rushes at her   (c) wants to be friendly   (d) is hungry.

4. Which one of the following statements is not true?
    a. The hunter arrives in time to save Phoenix from being hurt.
    b. The hunter gives Phoenix a coin as a present.
    c. The hunter and his dog chase the black dog.
    d. The hunter may have shot at the black dog.

5. The little boy who brings her a plate with a slice of marble cake in the woods is   (a) her grandchild   (b) imaginary   (c) related to the hunter   (d) the farmer's son.

Cause and Effect

6. To get to Natchez, Phoenix trespasses on private land because (a) she missed the bus   (b) the owners give her permission (c) she enjoys doing so   (d) she has always done so.

7. Phoenix buys the windmill   (a) to enjoy it herself   (b) as a Christmas present   (c) to please the storekeeper (d) because the nurse suggests that she do so.

Inference

8. The attendant gives Phoenix the quarter   (a) to pay for the medicine   (b) to give to her grandchild   (c) as a holiday gift (d) to buy some food.

Order of Events

9. Arrange the items in the order in which they occurred. Use letters only.
   A. The grandchild is having difficulty swallowing.
   B. Phoenix is frightened by the scarecrow.
   C. Phoenix buys a Christmas present.
   D. Up through the pines. Now down through the oaks.
   E. Phoenix sees Christmas decorations.

Outcomes

10. At the end of the story, we know that   (a) the grandchild recovers   (b) Phoenix goes to church   (c) Phoenix is too weak to travel   (d) Phoenix will reach home safely.

Words in Context

1. She walked slowly . . . moving a little from side to side in her steps, with the balanced heaviness and lightness of a pendulum in a grandfather clock. (491)
   Her walk was like that of   (a) a stalking cat   (b) a person with a stiff knee   (c) an angry child   (d) a trained athlete.

2. This made a grave and persistent noise in the still air, that seemed meditative, like the chirping of a solitary little bird. (491)
   The sound of the cane tapping on the frozen earth was (a) lost among the other sounds of the forest   (b) loud and alarming   (c) like that of a sparrow   (d) distinct from the usual forest sounds.

3. Now and then there was a quivering in the thicket. (491)
   The quivering was caused by   (a) an animal in hiding (b) Phoenix's cane   (c) the breeze   (d) Phoenix's skirt.

4. Under her small black-freckled hand her cane, limber as a buggy whip, would switch at the brush as if to rouse up any hiding things. (491)
   Her cane was   (a) as rigid as a sword   (b) heavy and dependable   (c) very flexible   (d) an attraction that brought animals near.

5. The sun made the pine needles almost too bright to look at, up where the wind rocked. (491–492)

The pine needles in the top branches   (a) fell softly around her   (b) shimmered in the light   (c) created long shadows (d) rustled in the wind.

6. Putting her right foot out, she mounted the log and shut her eyes. Lifting her skirt, leveling her cane fiercely before her, like a festival figure in some parade, she began to march across. (492)
    To cross the creek, Phoenix closed her eyes and   (a) inched forward sideways and slowly   (b) walked heavy-footed and waved her cane for balance   (c) prayed for help with each step   (d) took a deep breath and ran across as rapidly as she could.

7. She shut her eyes, reached out her hand, and touched a sleeve. She found a coat and inside that an emptiness, cold as ice. (493)
    The cold emptiness was   (a) the air   (b) the body   (c) the lining   (d) wisps of straw.

8. Then she went on, parting her way from side to side with the cane, through the whispering field. (493)
    The whispering was   (a) Phoenix talking to herself   (b) the dried leaves and cornstalks rubbing against each other (c) the sound of the wind in the trees   (d) the busy night insects at work.

9. Overhead the live oaks met, and it was dark as a cave. (494)
    The area was dark because   (a) she was in a hollow   (b) the branches and leaves cut out the sunlight   (c) night was falling   (d) the day had become cloudy and rain would fall.

10. But Phoenix only waited and stared straight ahead, her face very solemn and withdrawn into rigidity. (497)
    Phoenix was   (a) examining the people in the office (b) waiting impatiently for attention   (c) unaware of why she was there   (d) deciding whom to speak to.

Thinking About the Story ───────────

1. Which details did the author add to emphasize Phoenix's age? her poverty? her acceptance of life? her love for her grandchild? Why did she emphasize these aspects?

2. Throughout her journey, not once did Phoenix complain. What are some happenings she could have railed against? What

makes her a memorable character? Is her attitude typical of most people? Explain. Is it typical of most elderly people? of poor people? of the people you know?

3. How does the author convey to us Phoenix's attitude toward nature as she walks through the woods? How does her attitude toward "wild nature" compare with yours?

4. How does the attitude of the nurse differ from that of the attendant when Phoenix enters the doctor's office? Why is there this sharp difference? How do most young people react to elderly people whom they meet for the first time? to elderly people whom they have grown up with? Why is there such a difference? Do we react differently toward people our own age and those 10 years older, 20 years older, 40 years older, 60 years older? Explain your answers.

5. What aspects of Christmas are present in this story? Why is there no snow mentioned? How will Phoenix be celebrating Christmas? To what extent does she reveal her sense of Christmas spirit?

From One Generation to Another

ACTIVITIES

Thinking About the Stories

1. Which of the adults in the four stories in this Unit has the best attitude toward teenagers? Justify your choice.

2. Suppose that you are in charge of casting for a producer who is going to make a TV movie out of each of the four stories in this Unit. What actors and actresses would you select to play each of the following roles?

Mr. Whalen	Mr. Thorburn	Dad	Phoenix Jackson
Mrs. Whalen	Mrs. Thorburn	the woman	
Marvin	Harry	Petey	
		Granddad	

3. Compare Mrs. Whalen, Mrs. Thorburn, the woman in "The Blanket" and Phoenix Jackson in respect to their attitudes toward young people and toward life.

4. Which character in these four stories has the best sense of fair play?

5. In the light of the four stories in this Unit, are the following quotations true? Justify your answers.

   a. "He that has his parent for judge goes safe to the trial."

   b. "One parent is more than a hundred schoolmasters."

   c. "The commonest axiom of history is that every generation revolts against its parents and makes friends with its grandparents."

   d. "The fundamental defect of parents is that they want their children to be a credit to them."

   e. "What harsh judges parents are to all young folks."

Projects

1. Describe the last quarter of a basketball game as seen by one of the following:
   (a) The star center who, because he has been injured, must watch the game from the sidelines.
   (b) An anxious mother of one of the players, a woman who doesn't understand the game too well.
   (c) An old grad who has returned by chance on the night of the big game.
   (d) The coach who is facing his big test in this game.

2. Write the plot of a story in which a typical parent attempts to settle an argument—in his or her typical way—between two of the children of the family.

3. Select a news item containing the story of an animal attacking a human being. Retell the story from the viewpoint of one of the close relatives of the person so attacked.

4. Write the plot of a story which contrasts the excitement inherent in an incident and the mood of the narrator. Here are some suggestions:
   (a) The "wallflower" watching the belle of the evening do a solo.
   (b) A youngster listening to his or her older brother speak to a girlfriend over the phone.
   (c) A wife listening to her husband tell one of his favorite stories.
   (d) An only child listening to two brothers or two sisters quarreling.

5. Plan a panel discussion for class presentation of the following topic: *How to educate parents of high school students.*

Additional Readings ⸺⸺⸺⸺⸺⸺

Short Stories

"One Throw" by W. C. Heinz

> Will Pete throw the whole game with one throw?

"Too Soon a Woman" by Dorothy M. Johnson

> Hardly 20 years old, she had no fear of risk and danger.

"Mother Knows Best" by Edna Ferber

> Should a mother make many important decisions for her daughter?

"My Old Man" by Ernest Hemingway

> A chance remark disillusions a son about his father.

"The Oratory Contest" by James T. Farrell

> Should he have been ashamed of his hard-working father?

Novels

The Prime of Miss Jean Brodie by Muriel Spark

> How an unusual teacher influences her students.

To Kill a Mockingbird by Harper Lee

> Three youngsters save an innocent man's life.

So Big by Edna Ferber

> A mother and son on a farm in the Midwest.

Sorrell and Son by Warwick Deeping

> A tender story of a father's sacrifices for his son.

Memoirs

Life With Father by Clarence Day

> Family life in New York many years ago. Father was tyrannical but lovable.

A Genius in the Family by Hiram Percy Maxim

> The trials of being the son of an absent-minded inventor.

Boy on Horseback by Lincoln Steffens

> The best way to handle this boy was to give him what he wanted.

The Diary of a Young Girl by Anne Frank

> A young Dutch Jewish girl tells of hiding from the Gestapo.

GLOSSARY

The best way to build a vocabulary is to meet new words in helpful contexts. A word's context is the setting it appears in, all the other words that surround it. The following list contains a great many new words that are worth adding to your word store.

All the words in the list appear in the stories you have read. Here you will find helpful definitions. In addition, you will meet the words in new contexts, sentences designed to suggest the meaning of the listed words. These sentences, together with the contexts in which the words originally appeared, will help you add the words to your use vocabulary.

A

abashed   embarrassed; humiliated; disconcerted
> He was *abashed* by his own inability to recall the names of the visitors.

abate   lessen; diminish
> We could not leave the house until the fury of the storm had *abated*.

aboriginal   native; earliest; first
> Because Columbus thought he had reached Asia, the *aboriginal* tribes of America were called Indians.

accentuated   accented; emphasized
> The tenant's appearance of frailty was *accentuated* by a limp that seemed to tax all her strength.

accosted   stopped and spoke to; hailed; addressed
> The stranger *accosted* a passerby and asked directions to the Metropolitan Museum of Art.

acrid   irritating; harsh in taste or odor
> The *acrid* smoke from the fire made her breathing painful.

adept   skilled; expert; proficient
> We were amazed at how quickly the *adept* craftsmen repaired the damage to the antique chair.

admonish   scold; rebuke; warn
> The guard *admonished* the children who had not waited until the traffic signal had changed fully.

adverse   unfavorable; hostile
> Don't become discouraged by their *adverse* criticism.

all-pervading   spread everywhere
The *all-pervading* smoke from the factories gave the houses, the lawns, and the people the same gray look.

allusion   implied reference
The works of John Milton have many *allusions* to Greek and Roman mythology.

amiable   agreeable; sociable; genial
Helen's *amiable* demeanor masks an intensely competitive nature.

anguish   torment; suffering
We waited in *anguish* for the list of survivors of the plane crash.

anguished   sorrowful; agonizing; anxious
When Romeo saw the supposedly dead body of Juliet, he gave an *anguished* cry and resolved to kill himself.

animation   liveliness; spirit
A state of suspended *animation* is close to unconsciousness, a temporary suspension of vital functions as in a near drowning.

animus   hatred; hostility; dislike
The dean achieved his reputation for fairness when it was obvious that he penalized offenders without *animus*.

apathetic   without interest; spiritless; unconcerned; unmoved
The play was a failure; its message never reached the *apathetic* audience.

apathetically   showing no interest; unemotionally
Boredom caused Nan to study *apathetically*.

aperture   open space; opening
The castle wall was solid except for a small *aperture* near one of the top turrets.

apoplectic   enraged; angry; infuriated
When Mr. Perkins saw the dent his son had put in the family car, he was *apoplectic*.

appalled   dismayed; shocked; stunned
We were *appalled* by the misery of the victims of the flood.

apparelled   clothed; dressed; adorned
Queen Elizabeth I was always *apparelled* in rich and elaborate gowns.

apprehensive   uneasy; anxious; fearful
I am so *apprehensive* because I just don't trust her judgment.

approbation   approval
This worthy project has received the *approbation* of our highest officials.

arch   mischievous; playful
   Belinda's *arch* manner is sometimes too cute, too self-consciously playful.
ardor   enthusiasm; eagerness; gusto
   Clym fell in love almost immediately and began to woo Eustacia with *ardor*.
aromatic   fragrant
   I love to walk through a northern forest and smell the *aromatic* breath of spruce and pine.
asinine   stupid; silly; unintelligent
   At first, Carla's suggestion seemed almost *asinine*, but the more we thought about it, the better it sounded.
aspiring   rising; hopeful; desiring
   Aspiring to become an actress, Susanna spent endless hours studying all TV movies.
asseverated   affirmed; declared positively
   The prisoner steadfastly *asseverated* his innocence even when confronted with clearcut evidence of his guilt.
attribute   to blame on; charge to; credit
   The fatal accident was *attributed* to pilot error.
audacious   bold; daring; fearless
   The *audacious* feats of the high-wire circus performers kept us breathless.
au revoir   until we meet again; good-bye
   Don't say "Good-bye!" Just *"Au revoir!"*
averse   unfavorably inclined; opposed
   I'm not *averse* to hard work as long as it isn't boring.
awed   filled with respectful fear or wonder
   Who wouldn't be *awed* by the sight of an approaching interplanetary flying saucer!
azaleas   flowering shrubs
   The *azaleas* in bloom welcome spring across the land.

B

baleful   evil; harmful
   The defendant cast many *baleful* looks at the witness whose testimony would convict him.
bar mitzvah   Jewish religious ceremony celebrating admission to religious responsibility of a 13-year-old boy.
   At his *bar mitzvah*, a boy receives presents from relatives and friends in recognition of his new status.
basked   took pleasure

After a long winter, the inhabitants *basked* in the sun of the first beautiful day and enjoyed its warmth.

bay   reddish brown; a horse of that color
The big *bay* is the strongest and gentlest horse in the corral.

belabor   bother; assail; harp upon
The hikers began to *belabor* the guide with senseless and repetitive questions.

beseech   beg earnestly; implore
Joseph's brothers came to Egypt to *beseech* the pharaoh for help.

beseechingly   imploringly; in a begging manner
The actor *beseechingly* asked his agent to find him a part in a new television series.

bezabor   fellow; guy
Bezabor is a dated slang term that was once popular among the men working along the Erie Canal.

blanched   become ashen or pale
She *blanched* at the sight, and all the blood drained from her face.

blandly   calmly; mildly; dully; soothingly
Though obviously upset, Sheila answered her questioners *blandly*.

bleak   bare; dreary; dismal; piercing
How *bleak* a sunless wintry day can seem when the TV is in need of repair!

bodice   upper part of a woman's dress
If you ever expect to fit comfortably into this *bodice*, you will have to lose weight.

bolster   support; cushion; pillow
I placed the *bolster* under my head and stretched out for a nap.

bountiful   abundant; plentiful; generous
For thy *bountiful* gifts, O Mother Nature, we thank thee.

bracken   a large fern
Pastured animals avoid eating *bracken* since it can cause illness if ingested.

breeching   part of the harness around the back legs of a horse, enabling horse to hold vehicle back
The hill was so steep that only the *breeching* saved the horse from being run over by the wagon behind it.

bridled   took offense; resented
The driver *bridled* at the charge he had been careless and began to defend himself strongly.

broached   suggested; introduced; opened
When the idea of women's suffrage was *broached* for the first time, most people were amused but opposed.

buffeting   beating; battering
The winds were *buffeting* him mercilessly as he climbed the mast.

bullock   ox
A pair of *bullocks* slowly pulled the cart through the mountain village.

C

cabalistic   having mystical meaning; mysterious
The magician made certain *cabalistic* passes with his hands over the covered box, and suddenly four pigeons flew out of it.

caldron   large kettle
In *Macbeth*, the witches' *caldron* contained many disgusting objects supposed to effect the charm.

calico   multicolored; spotted animal
Calico texts on the wall contained memorable quotations.

canter   lope; type of gallop
The tough ponies were able to *canter* for hours as they crossed the plains.

caricature   exaggerated representation
Instead of a lifelike, realistic sketch of his subject, the painter drew a *caricature*.

carouse   frolic noisily; drink excessively
In Shakespeare's *Twelfth Night*, Sir Toby Belch loved to *carouse* through the night, making merry with drunken companions.

casual   accidental; halfhearted; vague; informal
I am not a devoted fan; I have only a *casual* interest in TV football.

catapult   to shoot into the air; hurl; propel
Huge rocks were *catapulted* miles away when the volcano erupted.

catspaw   dupe; tool; person used by another
A crooked investor may use an innocent victim as a *catspaw* to get bank loans or establish credit.

cavorted   romped; pranced; frisked
In the pasture, the young colts kicked their heels and *cavorted* in sheer delight.

chaff   tease; poke good-natured fun at
The two brothers always *chaffed* each other about any possible romantic attachments.

cited mentioned especially
Alice *cited* three examples to support her point of view.

cleave to stick to; split
Sincere people always *cleave* to their principles.

coddled cooked in hot water; spoiled; pampered
My least favorite meal is *coddled* eggs on toast.

cogitation deep thought; meditation
Marian was deep in *cogitation* and did not notice the newcomer who had taken a seat near her.

colic stomach pain
The *colic* kept the ailing child fretful, and us awake all night.

commodious large; roomy; spacious
On the sailing vessel the captain's quarters were comfortable and *commodious*, but the sailors' bunks were cramped.

complacency self-satisfaction; smugness
Tona's *complacency* remained untouched, though all the other candidates were worried and uneasy.

comprehension understanding
Comprehension comes when you are fully aware of the meaning of the words being used.

computation calculation; act of computing
By my *computation*, I will have several hundred dollars saved by the end of the summer.

condole sympathize; mourn with; share grief
On the death of President Kennedy, the entire nation *condoled* with his wife and small children.

connesewer (connoisseur) expert
Only a *connoisseur* would be able to tell the difference between this and the original.

constitute to form; make up; establish
What are the elements that *constitute* a balanced diet?

contrives manages; plans; arranges
Though Mr. McManus lives solely on his social security payments, he somehow *contrives* to be comfortable and happy.

converge come together; approach
The Hudson and the Sacandaga *converge* at Lake Luzerne.

corrugated wrinkled; furrowed
The ridges in the *corrugated* roof ran at right angles to the slope.

corrugated iron metal sheet with regular ridges and hollows
Iron sheets are *corrugated* to make them sturdier.

countenance face; look; feature; approval; to tolerate
She has the *countenance* of an angel, and the will of a mule!

covertly   secretly
He slipped the key *covertly* into his napkin when Ellen's attention was elsewhere.

creachy   infirm; ailing
Creachy is a term common in rural England but not in the United States.

crinkly   wrinkled
Tom took the directions and thoughtlessly stuffed them into his pocket. When he took the paper out, it was all *crinkly*.

cross-grained   difficult to deal with
I just cannot manage this *cross-grained* brute of a horse!

crucial   decisive; important; significant
At this *crucial* moment in our nation's affairs, you must remain aware of the basic issues.

D

daft   insane; mad; crazy
You would have to be *daft* to believe the tall tales spun by our friend Timmy.

debacle   disaster; complete failure; fiasco
The *debacle* at the company was brought on by the complete incompetence of the new president.

deem   think; believe; consider
Unfortunately, they *deemed* that his silence was an admission of guilt.

defray   reimburse; pay
The award will *defray* all the winner's expenses, but a husband or wife will have to pay full fare.

deft   skillful; expert; handy
With a few *deft* motions of the needle, the tailor repaired the torn buttonhole.

demeanor   conduct; behavior; bearing; manner
His is not the *demeanor* of someone willing to submit to unfair pressure.

depleted   empty; exhausted; barren
There were so many demands for funds, the club's treasury was *depleted*.

deprecatingly   intended to belittle; in mild disapproval
"You needn't have bothered; I could have handled it myself," she said *deprecatingly*.

derange   disturb; upset; make insane
Even a small setback can sometimes *derange* our basketball coach.

derelict   abandoned ship; vagrant; hobo; negligent
Every large city has a South Street where *derelicts* gather for handouts and companionship.

derision   scorn; ridicule
When attacked for his absenteeism in voting, the Congressman replied to his critics with *derision.*

desolation   ruined condition
How can one book picture all the *desolation* resulting from a worldwide war?

devoid   lacking; without
How can a person *devoid* of humor appreciate the finer things in life?

dilated   opened wide; expanded
In dim light the iris of the eye is *dilated*, to catch as much light as possible.

diminutive   small; tiny
Roger, at five feet seven, was a *diminutive* figure out on the basketball court with the six-feet-six giants.

dire   extremely bad; horrible; disastrous; dreadful
She warned us of *dire* punishments if we failed to meet our obligations.

discern   to see clearly; detect
Someday I hope that you will *discern* a difference between respect and admiration.

discomfiture   uneasiness; frustration; embarrassment
Because of his shyness, the winning contestant showed great *discomfiture* when called upon to speak.

discreet   wisely cautious; tactful
The entourage followed at a *discreet* distance behind the royal couple.

discrepancies   differences; disagreements; inconsistencies
There are several *discrepancies* between the two accounts of the events in South Africa.

dispatching   sending; killing; completing
Cyrano de Bergerac had a habit of *dispatching* any unfortunate duelist who commented about his famous nose.

dispel   drive away; scatter; banish
A Laurel and Hardy comedy is guaranteed to *dispel* the gloom.

disperse   to scatter
To prevent a recurrence of violence, the police *dispersed* the gathering groups.

dissembled   disguised; feigned; pretended
When the jury considered the question of the defendant's guilt

or innocence, it was clear that at least one of the witnesses had *dissembled*.

disposed   inclined to
They are not *disposed* to hold another meeting at this time.

disquietude   uneasiness
Her initial feeling of *disquietude* turned to fear as defeat became a certainty.

dissipated   destroyed; scattered; squandered
The hot sun soon *dissipated* the heavy mists of morning.

dissolute   corrupt; immoral; wicked
Many of the Roman emperors were *dissolute* dictators, excelling in evil without restraint.

distended   expanded; stretched; swollen
After the snake had swallowed the rat, its body looked abnormally *distended*.

distension   swelling; expansion; stretching
The sharp pains and *distension* of his abdomen made us make a beeline for the emergency room

docility   gentleness; meekness; mildness
The agreeable *docility* of one brother contrasted with the aggressive competitiveness of the other.

Dodge City scene   bloody shoot-out in the old-time western movie style
The coming of the Federal marshals ended the duels and shootings in *Dodge City* and other frontier towns.

dogged   persistent; stubborn; obstinate
With *dogged* determination, she learned to type well, but only after countless hours of practice.

dogtrot   slow, easy run
A well-trained marathon runner can keep up a *dogtrot* for many hours.

drayman   wagon driver
Truck drivers have long replaced the *draymen*.

dun   dull-brown color
The oncoming *dun*-colored cloud warned us of the approaching storm.

dwindling   decreasing; lessening; fading
Our *dwindling* hopes turned to despair as the hours passed without a sign of a rescue effort.

E

edifice   building; structure
A forty-story *edifice* will be built on this site.

eerie scary; weird; mysterious
An *eerie* wail from the canyon below the cabin frightened the visitors.

eerily frighteningly; mysteriously; weirdly
The wind sounds whipping *eerily* through the cracks in the window frame made us feel uneasy.

effigies copies; painted or sculptured representations; likenesses
The *effigies* of knights on medieval tombs are often lifelike and eerie.

egotistically boastfully; conceitedly; arrogantly; proudly
"I can solve any of these problems," he confided *egotistically*.

eked out supplemented; strained to fill out
Miles *eked out* his meager salary by taking a second job at night.

elicited drew forth; evoked
The lawyer's probing questions *elicited* no coherent response from the nervous witness.

engender to cause to develop
His cheerful optimism *engendered* hope in the hearts of millions.

enigmatic puzzling; elusive; mysterious
The enigmatic smile of Mona Lisa has puzzled many generations.

ensnarer one who traps
Don Juan was famous as the *ensnarer* of women's hearts.

ensued followed; happened; resulted
The Montagues and the Capulets met on the street and a free-for-all *ensued*.

ensuing following; resulting
The rock concert got out of hand, and in the *ensuing* turmoil, several people were injured.

erne a long-winged, white-tailed sea eagle
The *erne* is one of the largest birds of prey.

errant straying; wandering; roving
Many brilliant theories have started with unexpected, *errant* thoughts.

espied caught sight of; saw
With our binoculars we *espied* three hikers on Catellated Ridge, on their way to the summit of Mt. Jefferson.

essayed tried; attempted; put to a test
Have climbers *essayed* the north face of Mt. Everest?

exasperation annoyance; irritation; testiness
Though Ron was annoyed at the speaker's reply, he concealed his *exasperation*.

execrated detested; denounced; cursed
 The memory of Adolph Hitler is *execrated* by all those who have a reverence for human life.

exhaustive thorough; complete
 An *exhaustive* analysis of the accident showed that the driver of the sedan had been careless in making a left turn.

exodus departure; movement away
 The *exodus* of the middle classes from the cities has reversed, and now many of the same people are moving back.

expend to use up; exhaust
 Don't *expend* so much energy on insignificant details.

exultant very joyful; elated; in high spirits
 Exultant because of the unexpected victory, the spectators gave the home team a standing ovation.

F

fauna and flora animals and plants
 The *fauna and flora* of the Galapagos Islands have been extensively studied by biologists ever since the time of Charles Darwin.

facetiousness inappropriate wittiness; playful flippancy
 The comic's *facetiousness* came sometimes close to ill-mannered foolishness.

feigned pretended
 When Monty heard his mother coming to the bedroom, he put out the light and *feigned* sleep.

feint move to trick or deceive; to make such a move
 He *feinted* with his left and then drove in with a right cross to the chin.

ferret to search out; pry; weasel-like animal
 I am not one given to *ferreting* into people's pasts for scandal and gossip.

fervently intensely; earnestly
 The lawyer pleaded *fervently* for clemency for his client.

fey marked by a feeling of disaster
 The quiet before the storm gave a *fey* warning.

fitful unsteady; changeable; uneven
 I stayed by her bedside to be there whenever she awoke from her *fitful* sleep.

flex to bend repeatedly; to contract a muscle
 The next day my muscles were so stiff from the workout that I could barely *flex* my arm.

flue   pipe carrying smoke from stove
We cheerily burned the old letters in the stove and watched our past go up the *flue*.

flush   to blush; turn red
Just before sunset, the last rays *flush* the gathering clouds and fill the air with a rosy glow.

flushed   rosy; roused
After an hour of sit-ups, he slumped on the ground, his face *flushed* and sweaty.

foible   minor fault; weakness; defect
Is vanity a serious shortcoming or just a *foible*?

fold   pen for sheep
The sheep were led into the *fold* at nightfall to protect them from the coyotes.

foundered   broke down or went lame; became disabled
The horse *foundered* when we were three miles from the fort.

frowsy   untidy; having an uncared-for appearance
Her *frowsy* appearance made her appear much older than her years.

furtive   shifty; stealthy
The thief's *furtive* manner tipped off the police, who were ready for him.

fussed   complained
The children *fussed* about the toys that the young relatives had misused.

G

gaiters   leg coverings
General Pershing of World War I fame wore leather *gaiters* as a basic part of his uniform.

galluses   suspenders
The older farmers always wore both a belt and *galluses* for support.

geared   set; prepared; adjusted
After we had scored the first two touchdowns, we were *geared* for a ferocious counterattack, which never came.

ghastly   extremely unpleasant; dreadful; terrifying
The radiation leak at Chernobyl in Russia was a *ghastly* experience for those who lived near the nuclear power plant.

gibbous   hunchbacked
Why does a *gibbous* moon occur twice in each cycle?

gild   cover with gold leaf or paint
A lily is so beautiful that it is unnecessary to *gild* it.

gill net   fishing net that entangles the gills of the fish as they try to swim through
The swift current drew the salmon into the upright *gill net*, making their capture a certainty.

gingerly   with great caution
He *gingerly* put down the cage containing the two rattlesnakes.

glockenspiel   a portable musical instrument consisting of a series of metal bars played with two hammers
As a youngster, I was fascinated by the tinkling of the *glockenspiel* that softens the blaring sounds of the trumpets and cornets.

gnarled   full of knots; wrinkled; twisted
That *gnarled* olive tree is many hundreds of years old.

gorse   European shrub
Spiny, yellow-flowered *gorse* filled the lower reaches of the mountain.

gout   mass; glob; blob
He turned the valve and a great *gout* of oil shot out of the pipe.

grave   dignified; serious
The judge in measured, *grave* tones explained the sentence he had just handed down to the guilty couple.

gravity   seriousness; earnestness
The *gravity* of the situation in Vietnam in the early 1970s caused a rethinking of American strategy.

grizzled   gray-haired
He tried in vain to retain a youthful appearance by dyeing his *grizzled* hair.

grotesque   fantastic; freakish; strange
The members considered Anne's suggestion too *grotesque* for serious consideration.

grueling   exhausting; hard; brutal
Very few of the starting contestants ever finished this *grueling* cross-country race.

guise   dress; appearance; disguise
She came to the masquerade in the *guise* of a good-natured wicked witch.

gunmetal   dark gray
The *gunmetal* cloth was neutral in color and harmonized well with the surrounding tones.

gunyah   crude native hut in Australia
The native Australians used to live in *gunyahs* the year round.

H

haggard gaunt; drawn; weary
After a sleepless night, spent worrying about bankruptcy, the treasurer appeared *haggard* and careworn.

hardpan bedrock; clayey layer of soil impenetrable by roots
Let's get down to the *hardpan* of this question.

harry to bother; pester; plunder
I was so *harried* by doubts of my ability that I was unable to do any of the work.

haughtily proudly; scornfully; contemptuously
Filled with a sense of self-importance, she *haughtily* waved us off and told us that she was too busy with her makeup to see us.

heather low evergreen of northern and Alpine regions
The valley was filled with the tiny purplish-pink flowers of the *heather*.

hectoring bullying; intimidating; dominating
In *Romeo and Juliet*, Tybalt is a *hectoring* bully, ever ready for a fight.

heliograph signal sent by flashing reflections of the sun's rays in a mirror.
It is simple to *heliograph* messages from one height to another over long distances.

heliotrope a shade of purple; flower
Which jacket harmonizes with the *heliotrope* in your favorite tie?

heyday best years
In his *heyday* he was the World's Champion Figure Skater.

higher pragmatism a belief is true because of its results
We can learn the *higher pragmatism* only through resulting events.

hobnob be friendly with
His greatest joy is to *hobnob* with chess players.

hock ankle area of an animal
The horse went lame when its *hock* was injured by the falling rock.

horde big crowd; throng
Every evening, during the summer months, the *hordes* of mosquitoes drove us indoors at dusk.

hue color
The tie splattered with all the *hues* of the rainbow clashed with his tweed jacket.

hulking clumsy and bulky; massive
The gorilla is a huge, *hulking* animal that does poorly when confined in crowded quarters.

hunkered down squatted
The visitors *hunkered down* around the campfire and demanded food.

hustling working for money; moving rapidly
By *hustling* for our neighbors, I earned enough to buy a basketball.

I

ill-defined vague; fuzzy; indistinct
The point of the debater's arguments was *ill-defined*, and the audience soon became impatient.

illusive unreal; deceptive
Joy can be all too brief when it is filled with *illusive* hopes.

imminent threatening; impending
There were many signs to show that a major eruption of Mt. St. Helens was *imminent*.

impending menacing; threatening; about to occur
The *impending* takeover of the company by a corporate giant will throw many employees out of work.

imperceptible undetectable; unnoticeable
I can hardly tell them apart; the difference in color is almost *imperceptible*.

imperturbably serenely; coolly; tranquilly
The speaker answered the heckler *imperturbably*, even though he was seething inside.

impious unholy; lacking reverence or respect; profane
Vandalism on houses of worship is a senseless, *impious* action.

importunate annoyingly insistent
Their need is so great; how can I refuse to honor their *importunate* requests for assistance.

impromptu unrehearsed; improvised; unplanned
Megan's *impromptu* comments were more meaningful than the obviously rehearsed comments of her opponent.

improvised without extensive preparation; spur of the moment
When Pat sprained her ankle while camping, she *improvised* a crutch from a tree branch.

imprudent unwise; incautious; lacking discretion
Miller's *imprudent* remarks embarrassed his friends and infuriated his enemies.

imprudently   rashly; indiscreetly; thoughtlessly
He *imprudently* drove at high speeds on balding tires.

impudence   rudeness; disrespect; insolence
The child's *impudence* may have seemed cute to her parents, but the visitors were antagonized.

incarceration   imprisonment; confinement
The *incarceration* of the Count of Monte Cristo made him bitter toward his enemies outside the prison.

incoherently   unclearly; in a jumbled manner
When little Teddy gets excited, he tends to talk rapidly and *incoherently*.

indifference   not caring; unconcern; lack of feeling
I would have much preferred an outburst of anger to the complete *indifference* with which they treated us.

indifferent   not caring; unconcerned; mediocre
She always does what she wants; she is completely *indifferent* to our criticism.

indignantly   angrily; with displeasure
He replied *indignantly*, "I never said that!"

indignity   insult; injury to dignity
As a prisoner of war he had suffered many *indignities* at the hands of the guards.

indiscernible   invisible
With time, I hope, the scar will become *indiscernible*.

indubitably   unquestionably; certainly
The only conclusion that I can come to is that Albert is *indubitably* the one who took the book.

indulge   humor; yield to whims of oneself or another
Though Marcia is pretty strict in her dieting, she occasionally does *indulge* her craving for chocolate.

ineffectual   useless; unsatisfactory
His unwillingness to make decisions made him an *ineffectual* manager.

ineradicable   can't be rooted out, eliminated, or erased
The frontiers of science were advanced as formerly *ineradicable* diseases came under control with the discovery of antibiotics.

inexplicable   unexplainable; not able to be accounted for
Though the appearance of some UFOs is still *inexplicable*, most reputable scientists disbelieve their existence.

infirmities   weaknesses; disabilities
Many of the *infirmities* of old age can be lessened or avoided by proper exercise and diet during the earlier years.

insatiable   limitless; unable to be satisfied
>Even after retirement, he spends endless hours in the library, his desire for knowledge still *insatiable*.

insubstantial   flimsy; frail
>The eight-year-old's delicate, *insubstantial* ankles were encased in heavy iron rings chained together.

insurgence   rebellion; revolt
>The dictator used tanks and bombs to wipe out those who led the *insurgence* against his government.

intangible   vague; untouchable
>An *intangible* feeling of trouble ahead made me uneasy all morning.

interminably   endlessly
>The lecturer spoke on and on *interminably*, putting most of his listeners to sleep.

introspective   self-questioning
>You will have to be most gentle with this quiet, *introspective* child.

invariably   without change; unfailingly
>Follow Harold's advice since he is *invariably* correct.

inveigle   to trick; entice; mislead
>They *inveigled* me into joining them before I fully realized what I was letting myself in for.

invincible   unconquerable; unbeatable
>Only time could defeat this *invincible* athlete.

irresistible   attractive; overwhelming; tempting
>When they made an offer high enough to be *irresistible*, we sold the property.

J

jamb   frame, or vertical post of a frame, around the sides of a door or window
>The thieves smashed the *jamb* to bypass the lock and break into the house.

jounce   to bump; jolt; move up and down violently
>The truck *jounced* over the unpaved road, and a package almost fell out.

L

laconic   brief in speech
>He used a *laconic* "Yep!" to answer practically all requests for assistance.

lament mourn; express grief for; regret deeply
Alfred Tennyson *lamented* the death of his friend Arthur Hallam and wrote a poem in his memory.

lapse cease; decline; vanish
If you let your driving license *lapse*, you'll be inconvenienced in getting another.

larrikin noisy, disorderly person; rowdy; hoodlum
We changed our direction abruptly to avoid meeting the young *larrikins* gathered on the street corner.

laurels honors; glory; fame
She won her *laurels* in the 100-yard dash.

lee with the wind; protected
The wind ceased battering us the moment we reached the *lee* of the ridge.

leghorn type of chicken
The silence in the yard was broken by the clucking of the *leghorns*.

lithe flexible; limber; supple
To learn the twists and turns a gymnast must, first of all, be *lithe*.

lithograph type of reproduced picture
I often go to the museum galleries to look at old *lithographs*.

loath unwilling; reluctant
We are very *loath* to accept the recommendations of the new sales manager.

loathing extreme dislike; disgust
After learning of his father's murder, Hamlet looked upon the villainous King with *loathing*.

lob to throw in a high arc
They *lobbed* hand grenades over the rocks onto the enemy encampment on the other side.

lock tender caretaker of the canal lock
The *lock tender* closed the gates to let water in to raise the boat to the next level of the canal.

loftily in a superior manner; haughtily
After his sudden rise to stardom, the star spoke coolly and *loftily* to his former friends.

lowering scowling; looking dark and threatening
The *lowering* glare that greeted me was enough to make me realize that my mistake had been fatal!

lusty vigorous; sturdy
The youths raised their *lusty* voices in a song of praise for their beloved high school.

M

magnitude   size; hugeness; brightness
How can we offset the *magnitude* of the effects of poverty on growing minds?

maim   disable; injure; mutilate; disfigure
The explosion *maimed* three of the workers so badly that they are lucky to be alive.

malevolent   spiteful; malicious
The *malevolent* sneer froze on the face of the villain when the hero beat him at his game.

maw   animal's throat; mouth; jaws or stomach
The farmer crammed grain down the *maw* of the geese destined for the holiday table.

maze   network of paths; puzzle
It is easy to get lost in the *maze* of tunnels surrounding a major subway station.

melee   scuffle; brawl; free-for-all; confused fight
The police had to bring back order when a *melee* broke out between the fans of the rival teams.

Mercury   Roman god; messenger of the gods
With his winged shoes, *Mercury* would outrace the clouds and the sun.

mesmerism   hypnotism
Mesmerism, another word for *hypnotism*, was named after Franz Anton Mesmer, an Austrian physician.

milling   swarming; wandering; moving aimlessly
At five o'clock I was sitting in the bus station, watching the homegoing crowds *milling* around.

mincing   grossly exaggerated; excessively prim
The *mincing* steps of the Chinese ladies of centuries ago was partly traceable to their bound feet.

misgives   frightens; arouses suspicion or concern
The report of my finances *misgives* me, making me wonder why I didn't budget better.

Miss Quicksilver   a girl who is speedy; swift-footed
Quicksilver is another name for the metal mercury. *Miss Quicksilver* then must be as swift as the mythical god Mercury after which the metal was named.

mite   very small creature or object; small coin or amount
I would appreciate a *mite* of food, sir, since I have not eaten all day.

moleskin   strong cotton cloth with thick, velvety nap
His casual dress jacket was of the *moleskin* that resembled velvet.

monolog speech; oration; lecture
We taped her hilarious *monolog* on "How I always get a seat on the rush-hour bus."

morose gloomy; sad; depressed; grumpy; sullen
The unintended slight left him *morose* and silent, a scowling outsider in the midst of noisy party-goers.

mortal deadly; severe
A scratch if carelessly handled can be just as *mortal* as a bullet wound.

mote speck of dust; small bit
Lucy used the tip of her kerchief to remove the *mote* that caused my eye to smart.

multiple many; having more than one part
In her fall from the horse, Charlotte suffered *multiple* fractures of the right arm.

munificent generous; bountiful; charitable
The new library is just one of their *munificent* gifts to the university.

murk darkness; gloom
In the heavy *murk* that overlay the harbor, the shapes of other boats could be seen only dimly.

murky dark; gloomy; unclear
We groped our way far into the *murky* cave where sunlight never appears.

N

navvy unskilled laborer on construction work
Without any formal education and with a strong back, he worked for years as a *navvy* in a road-repair crew.

nemesis undoing; downfall; punishment
Cake and cookies have been my *nemesis* every time I have tried to diet.

nettled annoyed; irritated; provoked
The debater's clear thinking and direct attack *nettled* his weaker opponent.

nocturnal occurring or active at night
Though raccoons are considered *nocturnal* animals, they can often be seen strolling about in full daylight.

nomenclature name designation; process of naming
George Stewart, a student of *nomenclature*, has written several books on names.

nonchalantly coolly; casually; indifferently; unconcernedly
Meg seemed to be studying her lines *nonchalantly*, but when the play was rehearsed, she was prepared.

notoriety ill fame; bad reputation
>Despite the *notoriety* attendant upon their convictions, many Watergate criminals told their story and gained financially from the experience.

notorious outstanding and well-known in an unfavorable sense
>The *notorious* Jesse James gang was finally destroyed on the death of the leader in 1882.

nuzzle rub with nose; snuggle
>The horse bent his head to *nuzzle* the newly fallen snow.

O

obscurely vaguely; unclearly
>What their plans were was only *obscurely* hinted at; they never revealed them to me.

obstinate stubborn; difficult to cure
>Don't be *obstinate* and assume that there is only one way to approach the problem!

onslaught attack; assault
>Our planes and artillery successfully beat back the first *onslaught* of the enemy.

opaque unclear; hard to understand; not able to be seen through
>Alcohol is transparent; paint is *opaque*.

organdy very stiff, transparent cotton fabric
>Graduation dresses traditionally were made with an *organdy* shell.

outcropping of rock exposed portion of bedrock
>The winds blew away the topsoil and exposed more of the *outcroppings of rock* beneath the surface.

overprepossessing overly attractive or striking
>Dressed in a drab-green coverall and dark glasses, she did not look at all *overprepossessing*.

override to reverse a decision; overrule
>Congress has the power to *override* the President's veto.

overwrought overexcited; agitated; overdone
>How can you tell *overwrought* parents to control their anxieties and handle the crisis calmly!

P

paddock enclosed grassy area for horses
>I stood on the fence of the *paddock* and watched the young colts grow accustomed to each other.

PAL Police Athletic League
The *PAL* instructors taught me to swim when I joined the local group.

palisade fence of stakes; line of cliffs
The lighthouse was atop the *palisades* and overlooked the beach far below.

pallor paleness
Too many days cooped up inside his tiny office had given Brad's face an unhealthy *pallor*.

palpitation rapid beating; throbbing
The *palpitation* in his stomach reminded him of how hungry he was.

pandemonium wild confusion; bedlam; chaos
Pandemonium broke out in the stadium when the umpire reversed his decision.

pang ache; pain; twinge
I felt a *pang* of regret at leaving them on their own, but I so wanted them to grow up.

parable story with a moral
What is the lesson to be learned from the *parable*, "The Prodigal Son"?

paraphernalia equipment; personal belongings
When you go scuba diving, be sure you have all your *paraphernalia* with you.

pariah outcast
Because he put up an ugly-looking fence, Mr. Murray became a *pariah* in his own neighborhood.

parquet patterned wooden floor
Dancing a waltz on a polished *parquet* floor is almost like flying.

parsimonious thrifty; frugal; stingy
Fearful of financial want, the old couple became very *parsimonious*, spending little even on necessities.

pathos sadness; ability to arouse sympathy
The story of his downfall has so much *pathos* in it that I was weepy for hours after reading it.

Paul Bunyan mythical giant lumberman
Paul Bunyan was taller, tougher, stronger than Samson, Hercules, and Joe Louis combined.

peal to ring; resound; blare; roar
The *peal* of thunder shook the house and blasted our ears.

peavey lumberjack's long pole with hook on one end
From the shore, the lumberjack used his *peavey* to push the logs away from the jutting rock.

perceptibly   noticeably; obviously
We were *perceptibly* distressed by her behavior, and we did not try to hide our displeasure.

perception   awareness; recognition
He has no *perception* of how much he had embarrassed us with his crude comments.

perforce   of necessity
On the hike we *perforce* had to follow his lead at all times since he alone had the experience.

perfunctory   unenthusiastic; done routinely without interest
Many greetings are *perfunctory*, matters of custom rather than actual interest.

perpetrated   committed; performed
It was discovered that the convicted criminal had *perpetrated* even more crimes than those for which he was charged.

perpetual   continuing; incessant; constant
Mr. Eller's face wore a *perpetual* frown which even laughter around him could not erase.

perturbation   anxiety; agitation; distress
Frequent interruptions increased the speaker's *perturbation*, which was shown by his nervous mannerisms.

pessimist   one who expects everything to turn out badly
The *pessimist* was fearful that if he won the million-dollar prize, someone would cheat him out of it.

petulantly   crossly; crankily; irritably
When Jeb's wishes were not followed out, he always reacted *petulantly* and peevishly.

pinafore   protective covering like an apron
The *pinafore* as an outer covering over a dress has lost its popularity.

pirouette   whirling on toes
The ballerina *pirouetted* across the stage to the applause of the enthusiastic audience.

placid   calm; quiet
Someone with a peculiar sense of humor named this treacherous body of water Lake *Placid*!

play the dozens   (street slang) to have a verbal duel
A favorite pastime was *playing the dozens* with my friends to see who could create the best insults.

plummet   to fall headlong; plunge
The meteor *plummeted* toward earth and buried itself into a mountainside.

ponderous awkward; massive
Although the package was not heavy, it was so *ponderous* that three of us had to carry it.

porous soaks up liquids; penetrable
Ground water seeped into our basement through the *porous* foundation.

potently powerfully; capably; authoritatively
Enforcement of the new law *potently* restrained drug smuggling.

potion brew; liquid mixture
No *potion* has ever turned Jane Plain into a glamorous TV star.

pottered wasted time
While she *pottered* over trifles, I had to make the important decisions.

pragmatism belief that truth depends on outcome
Pragmatism counts outcomes only, but I believe that truth must be tested by consequences.

precipitated caused; provoked; stimulated
Rapidly rising oil prices *precipitated* a crisis in the American economy.

precipitous steep; sheer; impulsive
There are places along the rim of Grand Canyon where cliffs are *precipitous* and the drops sheer.

preen to primp; dress with care
Edna resisted the temptation to *preen* herself as she walked through the Hall of Mirrors.

pricey expensive; costly
The trip to Egypt will be too *pricey*; we'll go instead to Spain.

prodigal wasteful; extravagant; lavish
Because of his *prodigal* ways, he soon had nothing left of the prize money.

prodigy a highly talented child
Too few *prodigies* at four are labeled geniuses at twenty.

profusely abundantly; plentifully; extravagantly
The mother of the nearly drowned child thanked the rescuer *profusely*.

prospective likely; expected
Even before the wedding, Mr. Esposito trained his *prospective* son-in-law to become a part of the firm's management.

protuberance swelling; bulge
The famous nose of Cyrano de Bergerac was no mere nose but a huge *protuberance* about which Cyrano was most sensitive.

Providence   divine assistance
I am certain that *Providence* played a major role when the speeding sports car just missed me.

provocation   incitement; something that arouses or stimulates
The Western Allies overlooked many of Adolph Hitler's *provocations* before trying to stop him by force.

psyche   to use psychology to defeat
The canny coach spent hours thinking of strategies that his team could use to *psyche* the opponents.

psychical   mentally sensitive to supernatural forces; having extraordinary understanding or sensitivity
Psychical timidity means state of fearfulness brought on by imagining the consequences.

pugilist   fighter; professional boxer
The beatings a *pugilist* takes wear away mental and physical power at too fast a pace.

pungency   sharp; stinging; biting quality
Who can forget the *pungency* of burning oak leaves in the crisp autumn air!

pylon   towerlike structure
The planes in the race flew past the last *pylon*, turning close to the tower as they sought to gain time.

Q

quarry   prey; victim
The cheetah stalked its *quarry* silently and then broke into a furious run.

R

radiantly   brightly; brilliantly; dazzlingly
These artificial gems glitter as *radiantly* as do genuine diamonds and rubies.

rapt   absorbed; spellbound
The children gave *rapt* attention to the snake-feeding exhibition.

raveling   untangling
The *raveling* sleeve of that sweater should be fixed before the entire sleeve has been lost.

rebuffs   snubs; repulses; setbacks
The young salesperson was used to *rebuffs* while selling, but he always persisted and refused to give up.

rebuke   scolding; disapproval
The batter expected praise, not a *rebuke*, when he got a base hit on a bunt signal.

reconciliation   renewal of association; settlement of a dispute
The Montagues and Capulets waited until their children had died before effecting a *reconciliation*.

recrudescences   reappearances; returns
Many of the current hairstyles are *recrudescences* of those from earlier times.

rectory   minister's residence
The minister is living at a parishioner's house while the *rectory* is being repainted.

recumbent   lying down; resting
The *recumbent* figure on the lawn proved to be Eileen, who rose to greet us as we approached.

reek   disagreeable odor
During the strike, the *reek* of rotting garbage filled the city's streets.

reiterated   repeated; restated
The candidate *reiterated* several times his contention that his opponent's voting record was very poor.

reproach   to blame; criticize; to condemn; shame
His older brother *reproached* him for his rude behavior and compelled him to apologize.

reprobate   scoundrel; ruffian; villain
The convicted criminal, an old *reprobate* with a long record, showed no sign of emotion when the verdict was rendered.

reserved   undemonstrative; formal; distant; booked
His quiet *reserved* manner took the enthusiasm out of our greeting.

resolute   determined; persevering; unbending
Though many persons tried to change her mind about selling the house, Ms. Walker was *resolute*.

resolution   proposal; promise; persistence; solution
Why do so many people make New Year's *resolutions* that they are never going to keep?

restive   uneasy; fidgety
The crowd became *restive* when the main speaker was late in approaching the platform.

retaliate   to get revenge; repay
The parent threatened to *retaliate* by cutting off the son's allowance.

reverie daydream; fantasy
When the teacher called on him unexpectedly, Todd was jolted from his *reverie*.

rigidity stiffness
The *rigidity* of his body showed how much pain he was in.

ritual observance; rites; ceremonial forms
Jack's breakfast is a daily *ritual*, with each step followed carefully in order each morning.

rivulet small stream
Before he finished chopping the wood in the summer heat, *rivulets* of sweat were running down his face.

roguish playfully mischievous
Natty gave Ross a *roguish* look as she told him of her other admirer.

rough-hewn crudely made
The *rough-hewn* hut was made of logs and mud hastily put together for warmth and not comfort.

ruefully sadly; regretfully
"When I make a mistake, it certainly isn't a little one!" Phil said *ruefully*.

rugged sturdy; rough; coarse; difficult
This *rugged* stress test will reveal the limits of your endurance.

ruminating pondering; mulling over
I spent hours *ruminating* about what could have happened and should have happened if . . .

S

salver serving tray
The miniature sandwiches were carefully placed on the silver *salver* before they were offered to the guests.

sal volatile smelling salts
For years people have used *sal volatile* as a cure or preventive for fainting.

sanguine hopeful; confident; optimistic
Though Chris had lost to Martina at the two previous meetings, she was *sanguine* that she could win the tournament.

sapphire precious stone; deep blue
The tones of color of the tropical ocean ranged from a light yellow to a gaudy *sapphire*.

satiated fully satisfied
When the lions were *satiated* with their feeding, they left their kill to the hyenas.

saturated   drenched; soaked thoroughly; filled
The all-night downpour had *saturated* the playing field, and the games were called off.

saucily   mischievously; flippantly; impudently
In *The Taming of the Shrew*, Katharina at first speaks *saucily* and angrily to Petruchio, but she later becomes respectful.

score   make a line with
The jet planes *scored* the cloudless sky with their vapor trails.

scrawl   hasty, careless writing
From these few *scrawls* on the notepaper I was supposed to gather that you wanted to see me!

scrutiny   close examination; inspection; study
Close *scrutiny* of the ancient map revealed a few lines showing the outline of the Cape of Good Hope.

scuttle   to hurry; speed; sink; destroy
When snorkeling, I watched the giant crabs *scuttle* across the ocean floor.

seared   withered; burned; scorched
His arm bears a scar where it was *seared* by the soldering iron.

sector   section; part; division
After the war, the victorious Allies divided Berlin into four sectors. Each *sector* was administered by one of the Allies.

sedentary   inactive; settled
Some exercise is especially important for those who otherwise live a *sedentary* life.

self-assertion   sticking up for one's rights; advancement of one's views
What Ron loses by a lack of *self-assertion*, he wins by his natural charm and pleasant disposition.

self-possessed   confident; poised
Though only eight years old, the young violinist was completely *self-possessed* during his performance.

severally   singly; separately; one at a time
The detectives spoke to the gang members *severally*, hoping to trip them up into revealing inconsistencies.

sheen   brightness; luster; shine
What cloth can match the *sheen* of satin in bright light!

sheik   an Arab chief; glamor boy
What is the current term that has replaced *sheik* to describe the well-dressed young man on a date?

shrouding   covering; wrapping; screening; hiding
A dense fog had rolled into the seaside town, *shrouding* the church steeple in mist.

simultaneous   occurring at the same time; coincident
The general planned *simultaneous* bombardments by land, sea, and air.

singular   unusual; peculiar; odd
The lawyer had a *singular* way of using his hands, a habit that constantly called attention to itself.

siren   temptress; enchantress; charmer; signal
Has the *siren* disappeared as a character in modern TV productions?

slitherings   slidings
On the smooth laboratory floor, the *slitherings* of the snakes were almost noiseless.

sloth   laziness; sluggishness; idleness
The summer sun in its full noonday splendor is most *sloth*-provoking.

smitten   hit hard; have a crush on; infatuated
Smitten by pangs of conscience, Alice returned the borrowed book—months later.

sodden   soaked through; drenched; soggy; dull
The football field, made *sodden* by the storm, was a sea of mud.

solicitous   concerned; worried
When unemployment rises, I become very *solicitous* about our future.

soot   carbon particles
The *soot* from the smoky fire smudged our faces.

spare   lean; thin; meager
Though he had a *spare* frame, Doug had unusual power in his arms.

sparring   boxing
The skilled boxer was *sparring* for an opening that would allow him to snake his right through to his opponent's jaw.

spectral   ghostly; insubstantial
The prisoners released from Dachau had a *spectral* appearance, reflecting their long period of starvation.

spirit lamp   a lamp in which alcohol is burned
We heated the water for coffee over a *spirit lamp*.

stamina   endurance; vigor
At his advanced age, he no longer has the *stamina* for long walks through city streets.

stark   utter; complete; bare
The room was as *stark* as an unfurnished vacated apartment.

stave   side of a barrel; stick; staff; pole
They used two *staves* and my jacket to make the stretcher on which they could carry the injured away from the road.

stealthily   slyly; secretly; cautiously
The cat *stealthily* approached the bird, but a sudden motion frightened its prey away.

stodgy   dull; heavy; thick; slow; inflexible; boring; drab
Suburbs with their endless rows of *stodgy*, unvaried houses stretched out around the city.

stolid   hard to excite; unemotional; sluggish
He is a *stolid* citizen, one who takes everything in stride and never loses his cool.

stone   official British weight unit equal to 14 pounds
A man of fourteen *stone* weighs close to 200 pounds.

straggly   arranged irregularly or without planned order
I had hoped that as I grew older my *straggly* beard would become full and luxuriant.

strident   harsh; grating; shrill
The *strident* voice of the drill sergeant drowned out all other sounds.

subdued   overcome; conquered; curbed; checked; lowered in spirit
The sight of such unnecessary violence put us in a *subdued* mood for hours.

subterranean   hidden; secret; under the surface of the earth
I can just imagine the depth of fear in the *subterranean* recesses of her mind.

supple   limber; flexible
She did the two handsprings with the *supple* abandon of a twelve-year-old.

surmised   realized; inferred; guessed
When Joel did not arrive on time, we all *surmised* he had missed the ferry.

surmises   guesses; beliefs; opinions
We must get more facts; *surmises* are not enough.

susceptible   sensitive; yielding; unresistant
Though Donna is *susceptible* to colds, they are usually not severe.

swallowtails   fashionable men in formal clothing; formal jacket
I had to hire a fully formal outfit down to *swallowtails* to act as one of the ushers at their wedding.

synchronization   act of making things occur at the same time or in order

His major responsibility was the *synchronization* of artillery fire and troop movements during the attack on the enemy stronghold.

T

tantalize to bother; tease
The smell of fresh-baked bread *tantalized* the hungry workers returning home at dinnertime.

tawdry gaudy; showy; flashy; vulgar
Jewelry that seems elegant, novel, and impressive to some is often dismissed as *tawdry* by others.

terminating ending; ceasing; finishing
The flight from St. Louis will be *terminating* at La Guardia Airport, New York City.

tersely briefly; crisply; pointedly
When questioned about the accident, Mark replied *tersely*, but his facial expression spoke volumes.

thewed muscled
Who does not admire the strong-*thewed* members of varsity football teams!

tinder material that burns easily
To start the fire, we gathered small twigs to be used as *tinder* to ignite the logs.

tocsin warning bell or signal
The alert guard sounded the *tocsin* when he detected the nearness of the enemy scouts.

toff a person of the upper social classes (British, informal)
The seldom used term *top hat* is the American equivalent of the British *toff*.

toils nets; traps
While being brought to jail, the criminal escaped from the *toils* of the law and disappeared into the city.

toque woman's brimless hat
Toques in the sixteenth century sported a large plume.

torpid slow-moving; sluggish
The heat and high humidity in the room made all of us *torpid*.

tortoise-shell mottled brown and yellow coloring; a cat
Our friendly *tortoise-shell* cat is a frequent stroller down our village streets.

transgressors sinners; criminals
Within a week of the adoption of the new law, dozens of *transgressors* had been caught.

treading walking; stepping
You are *treading* on dangerous ground when you accuse her of being concerned with only herself.

trivial commonplace; unimportant; slight
Sometimes a *trivial* event triggers a serious result.

trotter type of horse
The racing rig was pulled by a champion *trotter.*

tuberoses flowers that resemble small lilies
She was wearing a corsage of *tuberoses.*

tussock a compact tuft of grass
The *tussocky* grass was uneven and hard underfoot.

twirpish insignificant; contemptible
Don't underestimate the newcomer's abilities just because he looks small and *twirpish*!

U

unaccountably unexplainably; strangely; lacking explanation
We could not replace the key which had *unaccountably* disappeared from the drawer.

unique incomparable; one of a kind
You have a *unique* opportunity and should take advantage of it.

unkempt uncombed; mussed up; untidy
I am positive that a bird could build a nest, unnoticed, in his massive *unkempt* beard.

unquenchable not able to be satisfied, discouraged, or crushed
My faith in the superiority of the democratic process is *unquenchable.*

untenanted unpopulated; empty of people
The old buildings, now deserted and *untenanted,* stood like sentinels in the inner city.

untoward unfavorable; unruly; improper; unlucky
The *untoward* turn of events plunged us into the depths of gloom.

unutterable unable to be spoken; too profound for expression
The survivors of the Mexican earthquake spoke of their *unutterable* terror as tall buildings around them began to topple.

unwavering steady; sure
Aaron Copland had one *unwavering* goal in life—to become a great composer and interpret the American scene in music.

utterly completely; thoroughly; totally
We found the play *utterly* delightful and recommended it to all our friends.

V

vagrant   homeless person; hobo; vagabond
>During the cold months, the city supplies bed and breakfast to the *vagrants* of Skid Row.

vehemently   heatedly; energetically; furiously
>The defendant *vehemently* denied that his car had crossed the center divider before the crash.

veranda   long porch
>During the warm summers, we sat in rockers on the *veranda*, enjoying the occasional breezes that came off the ocean.

verge   to edge; border on; near; approach
>He'll never succeed; his present course of action *verges* on stupidity.

verges   edges; rims; margins; borders
>The *verges* of the stream were covered with wildflowers.

vernacularism   slang; regional expression
>*Vernacularisms* belonging to a specific period or place are mystifying to outsiders.

vigil   watch; watchfulness; period of wakefulness
>The guard dog keeps his lonely *vigil* inside the chain-link fence.

vile   evil; depraved; wretched
>Hitler's *vile* treatment of the Jews was foreshadowed in his book *Mein Kampf*.

W

wane   to diminish; lessen; decline
>Advertising on radio *waned* with the coming of commercial television.

wary   alert; cautious; guarded
>We grew even more *wary* when the salesman lengthened his sales talk and began to make unrequested promises.

weals   lumps; bumps; welts
>His fall from the bicycle raised many *weals* on Chet's arms and legs.

welter   confusion; turmoil
>We could not hear the church bells over the *welter* of traffic sounds at the busy intersection.

wheeze   whistling sound in breathing
>When he began to *wheeze* as he walked up the steep hill, we stopped to rest.

whither   to what place
>"*Whither* thou goest, I will go."

(The Book of Ruth)

winsome   winning; charming; engaging
    Marie had a *winsome* smile that won her many friends and admirers.

wisp   small amount; a small handful
    Wisps of smoke rose from the embers of the dying fire.

wistful   longing; melancholy; forlorn
    Helen always has a *wistful* look when she sees any child playing with a doll.

withers   ridge between the shoulder bones of a horse
    He vaulted over the horse's *withers* to ride bareback to the nearest town.

writhed   distorted; twisted; wrenched
    Laocoön *writhed* in pain as the serpents attacked him and his sons.

writhing   twisting
    To our horror, Alan fell to the floor, *writhing* in pain and calling for help.

wroth   angry
    According to the old myth, Washington's father was *wroth* with George over the cherry-tree incident, but he forgave George after George had told the truth.

Z

zenith   climax; summit; highest point; point in sky directly overhead
    At the *zenith* of her career, she was the acknowledged leader in her field.

Acknowledgments

Grateful acknowledgment is made to the following sources for permission to reprint copyrighted stories.

"The Invisible Man," page 4. Reprinted by permission of Dodd, Mead & Company, Inc. from THE INNOCENCE OF FATHER BROWN by G. K. Chesterton. Copyright 1911 by Dodd, Mead & Company, Inc. Copyright renewed 1938 by Frances B. Chesterton.

"The Tragedy at Marsdon Manor," page 56. Reprinted by permission of Harold Ober Associates Incorporated. Copyright © 1925 by Agatha Christie Limited. Copyright renewed 1953 by Agatha Christie Limited. Canadian rights by Aitken & Stone Limited.

"The Fever Tree," page 122. From THE FEVER TREE AND OTHER STORIES OF SUSPENSE, by Ruth Rendell. Copyright © 1982 by Ruth Rendell. Reprinted by permission of Pantheon Books, a division of Random House, Inc. Canadian rights by Century Hutchinson Publishing Group Limited.

"The Open Window," page 144. From the COMPLETE SHORT STORIES OF SAKI (H. H. Munro). Copyright 1930, renewed © 1958 by The Viking Press, Inc. Reprinted by permission of Viking Penguin, Inc.

"The Lottery," page 171. From THE LOTTERY by Shirley Jackson. Copyright 1948, 1949 by Shirley Jackson. Copyright renewed © 1976, 1977 by Laurence Hyman, Barry Hyman, Mrs. Sarah Webster and Mrs. Joanne Schnurer. Reprinted by permission of Farrar, Straus and Giroux.

"The Fog Horn," page 223. Reprinted by permission of Don Congdon Associates, Inc. Copyright © 1951 by The Curtis Publishing Co.; Renewed 1979 by Ray Bradbury.

"The Secret," page 235. Copyright © 1963 by Arthur C. Clarke. Reprinted from his volume THE WIND FROM THE SUN by permission of Harcourt Brace Jovanovich.

"The Fun They Had," page 245. Reprinted by permission of the author, Isaac Asimov.

"The Higher Pragmatism," page 258. By O. Henry. Copyright 1909 by Doubleday & Company, Inc. from OPTIONS. Used by permission of the publisher.

"Her First Ball," page 269. Copyright 1922 by Alfred A. Knopf, Inc. and renewed 1950 by John Middleton Murry. Reprinted from THE SHORT STORIES OF KATHERINE MANSFIELD, by permission of the publisher.

"The Party," page 280. By Herman Wouk, from THE CITY BOY. Copyright 1948 by Herman Wouk. Copyright renewed in 1976 by the author. Reprinted by permission of Doubleday & Company, Inc.

"The Chaser," page 296. Copyright 1940, 1967 by John Collier. Reprinted by permission of Harold Matson Company, Inc.

"Fire in the Bush," page 330. By James Warwick. From Story, September 1934; copyright 1934 by Story Magazine. Reprinted by permission of Scholastic Inc.

"Death of Red Peril," page 350. Reprinted by permission of Harold Ober Associates Incorporated. Copyright © 1928 by Walter D. Edmonds. Copyright renewed 1956 by Walter D. Edmonds.

"Sixty Acres," page 365. Reprinted by permission of the author, Raymond Carver.

"That's What Happened to Me," page 386. Copyright 1935, renewed 1963 by Michael Fessier. Reprinted by permission of Harold Matson Company, Inc.

"Wine on the Desert," page 398. Reprinted by permission of Dodd, Mead & Company, Inc. from WINE ON THE DESERT AND OTHER STORIES by Max Brand. Copyright 1936 by Frederick Faust. Copyright renewed 1964 by Jane F. Easton, Judith Faust and John Frederick Faust.

"The New Kid," page 411. By Murray Heyert. Reprinted by permission of Barthold Fles, literary agent; copyright 1944 by Harper and Row, Publishers, Inc.

"Raymond's Run," page 428. Copyright © 1970 by Toni Cade Bambara. Reprinted from GORILLA, MY LOVE, by Toni Cade Bambara, by permission of Random House, Inc.

"The Hero," page 446. Reprinted by permission of Harold Ober Associates Incorporated. Copyright © 1939 by The Curtis Publishing Co. Copyright renewed 1966 by Margaret Weymouth Jackson.

"The Erne from the Coast," page 465. From THE PARENTS LEFT ALONE, by T. O. Beachcroft. Reprinted by permission of the author. Canadian rights by The Bodley Head.

"A Worn Path," page 503. Copyright 1941, 1969 by Eudora Welty. Reprinted from her volume A CURTAIN OF GREEN AND OTHER STORIES by permission of Harcourt Brace Jovanovich, Inc.